SYMBOLS

RELIEF

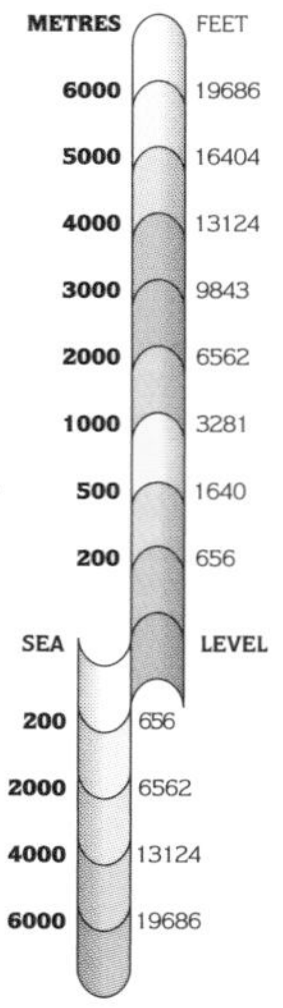

METRES	FEET
6000	19686
5000	16404
4000	13124
3000	9843
2000	6562
1000	3281
500	1640
200	656
SEA	LEVEL
200	656
2000	6562
4000	13124
6000	19686

Additional bathymetric contour layers are shown at scales greater than 1:2 million. These are labelled on an individual basis.

213 △ Summit *height in metres*

BOUNDARIES

- International
- International disputed
- Ceasefire line
- Main administrative (U.K.)
- Main administrative
- Main administrative through water

COMMUNICATIONS

- Motorway
- Motorway tunnel

Motorways are classified separately at scales greater than 1:5 million. At smaller scales motorways are classified with main roads.

- Main road
- Main road under construction
- Main road tunnel
- Other road
- Other road under construction
- Other road tunnel
- Track
- Main railway
- Main railway under construction
- Main railway tunnel
- Other railway
- Other railway under construction
- Other railway tunnel
- ⊕ Main airport
- ✈ Other airport

PHYSICAL FEATURES

- Freshwater lake
- Seasonal freshwater lake
- Saltwater lake *or* Lagoon
- Seasonal saltwater lake
- Dry salt lake *or* Salt pan
- Marsh
- River
- Waterfall
- Dam *or* Barrage
- Seasonal river *or* Wadi
- Canal
- Flood dyke
- Reef
- ▲ Volcano
- Lava field
- Sandy desert
- Rocky desert
- ˘ Oasis
- Escarpment
- ⊃⊂ 923 Mountain pass *height in metres*
- Ice cap *or* Glacier

STYLES OF LETTERING

Country name	**FRANCE**	Island	*Gran Canaria*
	BARBADOS	Lake	*LAKE ERIE*
Main administrative name	HESSEN	Mountain	*ANDES*
Area name	*ARTOIS*	River	*Zambeze*

OTHER FEATURES

- National park
- Reserve
- Ancient wall
- ∴ Historic or Tourist site

SETTLEMENTS

POPULATION	NATIONAL CAPITAL	ADMINISTRATIVE CAPITAL	CITY OR TOWN
Over 5 million	⊡ **Beijing**	⊙ **Tianjin**	⊙ **New York**
1 to 5 million	⊡ **Seoul**	⊙ **Lagos**	⊙ **Barranquilla**
500000 to 1 million	⊡ **Bangui**	⊙ **Douala**	⊙ **Memphis**
100000 to 500000	⊡ Wellington	○ Mansa	○ Mara
50000 to 100000	⊡ Port of Spain	○ Lubango	○ Tuzla
10000 to 50000	▫ Malabo	○ Chinhoyi	○ El Tigre
Less than 10000	▫ Roseau	○ Ati	○ Soledad
Urban area			

READER'S DIGEST
Bartholomew

ILLUSTRATED

ATLAS OF THE

WORLD

FIFTH REVISED EDITION

Reader's
Digest

The Reader's Digest Association, Inc.
Pleasantville, NY/Montreal

ATLAS OF THE
WORLD

A READER'S DIGEST BOOK

This edition published by The Reader's Digest Association
by arrangement with HarperCollins*Publishers* Ltd

Fifth Revised Edition 2004
First published by Bartholomew 1987

Copyright © HarperCollins*Publishers* Ltd 2004
Maps © Collins Bartholomew Ltd 2004

Collins
An Imprint of HarperCollins*Publishers*
77-85 Fulham Palace Road
London W6 8JB

For Reader's Digest
Executive Editor, Trade Publishing: Dolores York
Senior Designer: George McKeon
Associate Publisher, Trade Publishing: Christopher T. Reggio
Vice President & Publisher, Trade Publishing: Harold Clarke

Library of Congress Cataloging-in-Publication Data

Reader's Digest Association.
  Illustrated atlas of the world / Reader's Digest Association, Inc.– 5th rev. ed.
    p. cm.
  "Copyright 2004 HarperCollins Publishers Ltd."
  Includes indexes.
  ISBN 0-7621-0510-0
  1. Atlases. 2. Physical geography–Maps. 3. Political geography–Maps. 4. Economic
geography–Maps. I. Title: Reader's Digest Bartholomew illustrated atlas of the world. II.
Title: Atlas of the world. III. HarperCollins (Firm) IV. Title.

G1021.R534 2004
912–dc22
                                                            2003055022

Photo credits:
Antarctica image: NRSC Ltd/Science Photo Library
Page 17 New York: Corbis UK Ltd
Other photos on pages 16-19: Getty Images
All other photos: ImageState

For more Reader's Digest products and information,
visit our website:
www.rd.com (in the United States)
www.readersdigest.ca (in Canada)

Printed in Singapore

RF11683

1 3 5 7 9 10 8 6 4 2

CONTENTS

THE WORLD

NORTH AMERICA

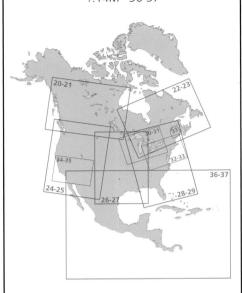

SOUTH AMERICA

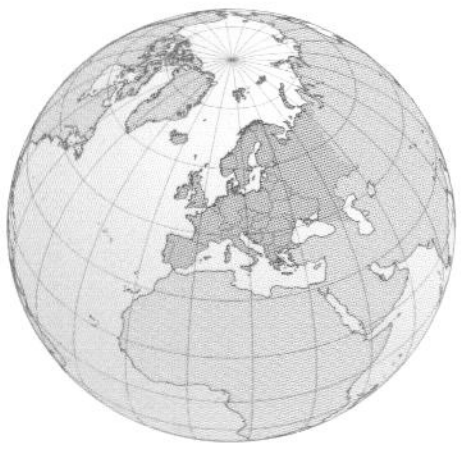
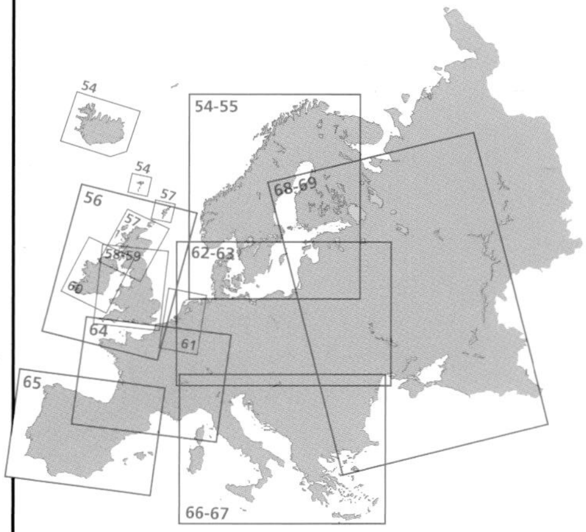
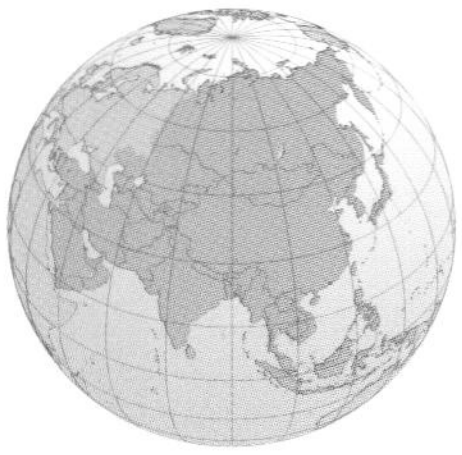
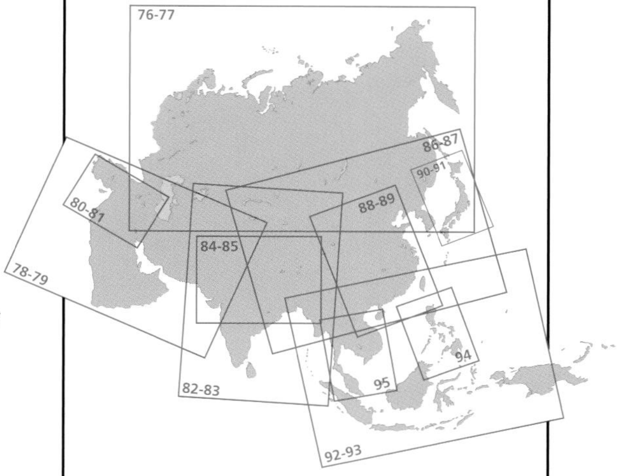
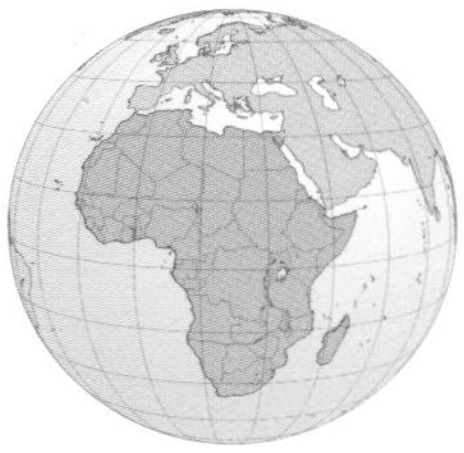
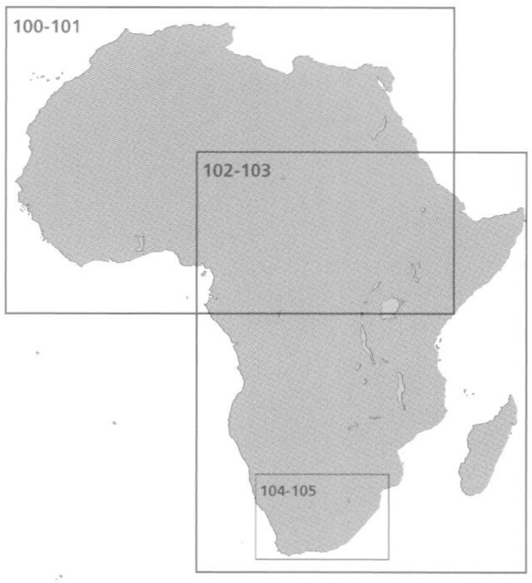
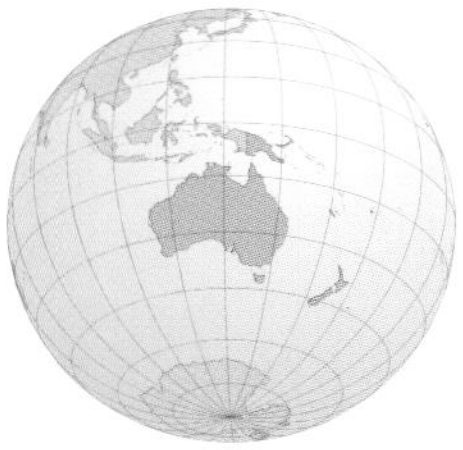
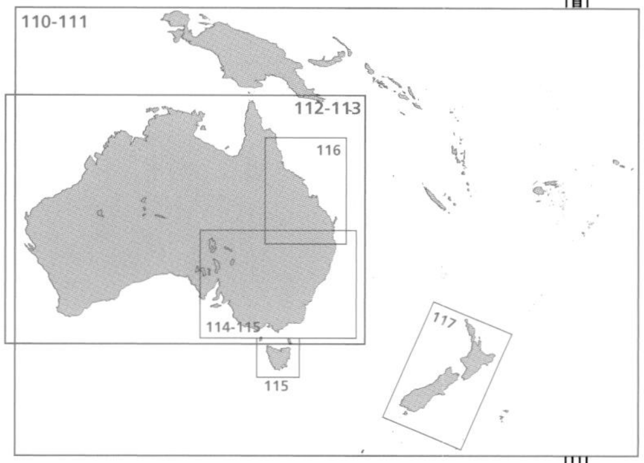

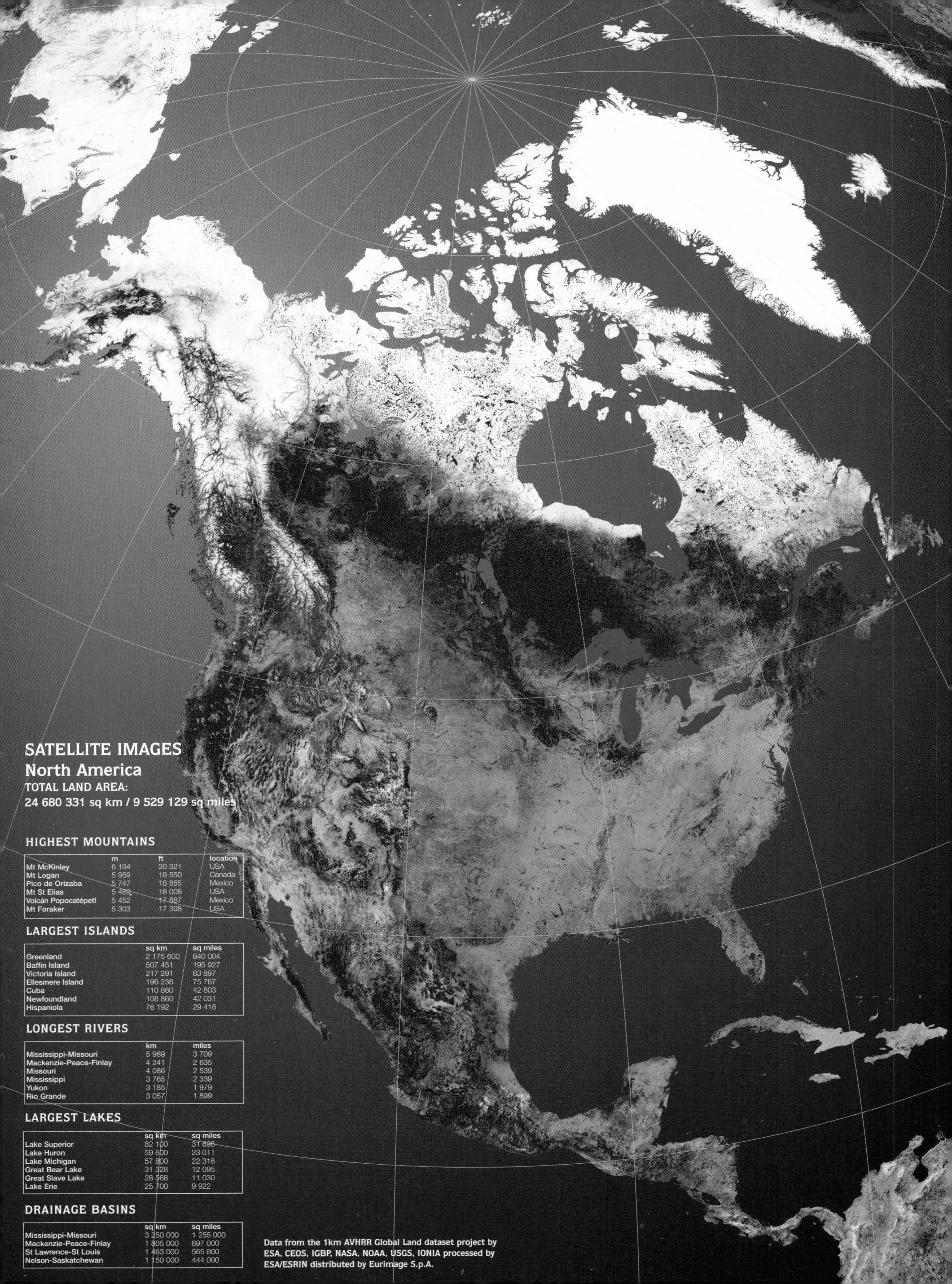

SATELLITE IMAGES
North America
TOTAL LAND AREA:
24 680 331 sq km / 9 529 129 sq miles

HIGHEST MOUNTAINS

	m	ft	location
Mt McKinley	6 194	20 321	USA
Mt Logan	5 959	19 550	Canada
Pico de Orizaba	5 747	18 855	Mexico
Mt St Elias	5 489	18 008	USA
Volcán Popocatépetl	5 452	17 887	Mexico
Mt Foraker	5 303	17 398	USA

LARGEST ISLANDS

	sq km	sq miles
Greenland	2 175 600	840 004
Baffin Island	507 451	195 927
Victoria Island	217 291	83 897
Ellesmere Island	196 236	75 767
Cuba	110 860	42 803
Newfoundland	108 860	42 031
Hispaniola	76 192	29 418

LONGEST RIVERS

	km	miles
Mississippi-Missouri	5 969	3 709
Mackenzie-Peace-Finlay	4 241	2 635
Missouri	4 086	2 539
Mississippi	3 765	2 339
Yukon	3 185	1 979
Rio Grande	3 057	1 899

LARGEST LAKES

	sq km	sq miles
Lake Superior	82 100	31 698
Lake Huron	59 600	23 011
Lake Michigan	57 800	22 316
Great Bear Lake	31 328	12 095
Great Slave Lake	28 568	11 030
Lake Erie	25 700	9 922

DRAINAGE BASINS

	sq km	sq miles
Mississippi-Missouri	3 250 000	1 255 000
Mackenzie-Peace-Finlay	1 805 000	697 000
St Lawrence-St Louis	1 463 000	565 600
Nelson-Saskatchewan	1 150 000	444 000

Data from the 1km AVHRR Global Land dataset project by
ESA, CEOS, IGBP, NASA, NOAA, USGS, IONIA processed by
ESA/ESRIN distributed by Eurimage S.p.A.

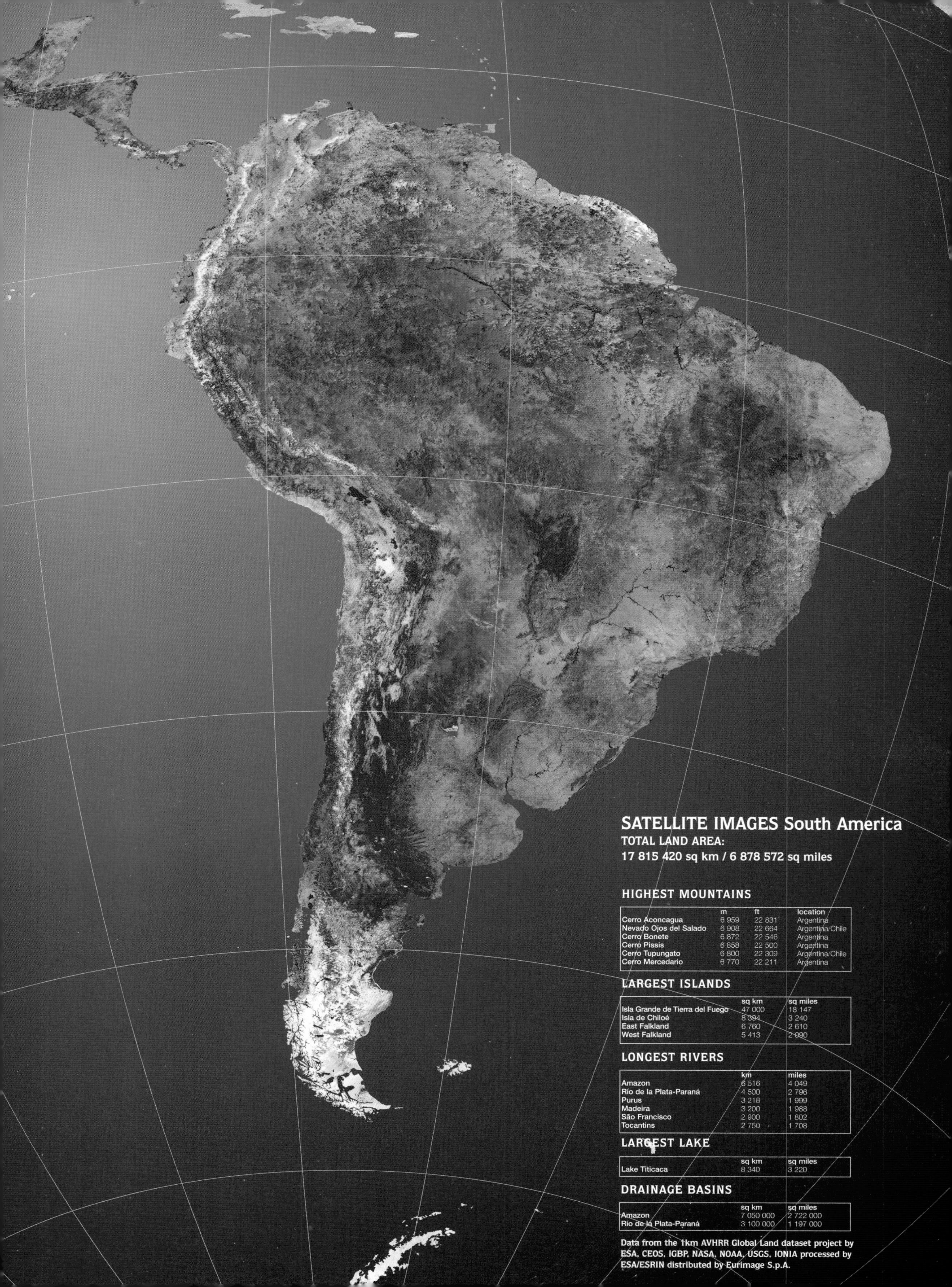

SATELLITE IMAGES South America
TOTAL LAND AREA:
17 815 420 sq km / 6 878 572 sq miles

HIGHEST MOUNTAINS

	m	ft	location
Cerro Aconcagua	6 959	22 831	Argentina
Nevado Ojos del Salado	6 908	22 664	Argentina/Chile
Cerro Bonete	6 872	22 546	Argentina
Cerro Pissis	6 858	22 500	Argentina
Cerro Tupungato	6 800	22 309	Argentina/Chile
Cerro Mercedario	6 770	22 211	Argentina

LARGEST ISLANDS

	sq km	sq miles
Isla Grande de Tierra del Fuego	47 000	18 147
Isla de Chiloé	8 394	3 240
East Falkland	6 760	2 610
West Falkland	5 413	2 090

LONGEST RIVERS

	km	miles
Amazon	6 516	4 049
Río de la Plata-Paraná	4 500	2 796
Purus	3 218	1 999
Madeira	3 200	1 988
São Francisco	2 900	1 802
Tocantins	2 750	1 708

LARGEST LAKE

	sq km	sq miles
Lake Titicaca	8 340	3 220

DRAINAGE BASINS

	sq km	sq miles
Amazon	7 050 000	2 722 000
Río de la Plata-Paraná	3 100 000	1 197 000

Data from the 1km AVHRR Global Land dataset project by
ESA, CEOS, IGBP, NASA, NOAA, USGS, IONIA processed by
ESA/ESRIN distributed by Eurimage S.p.A.

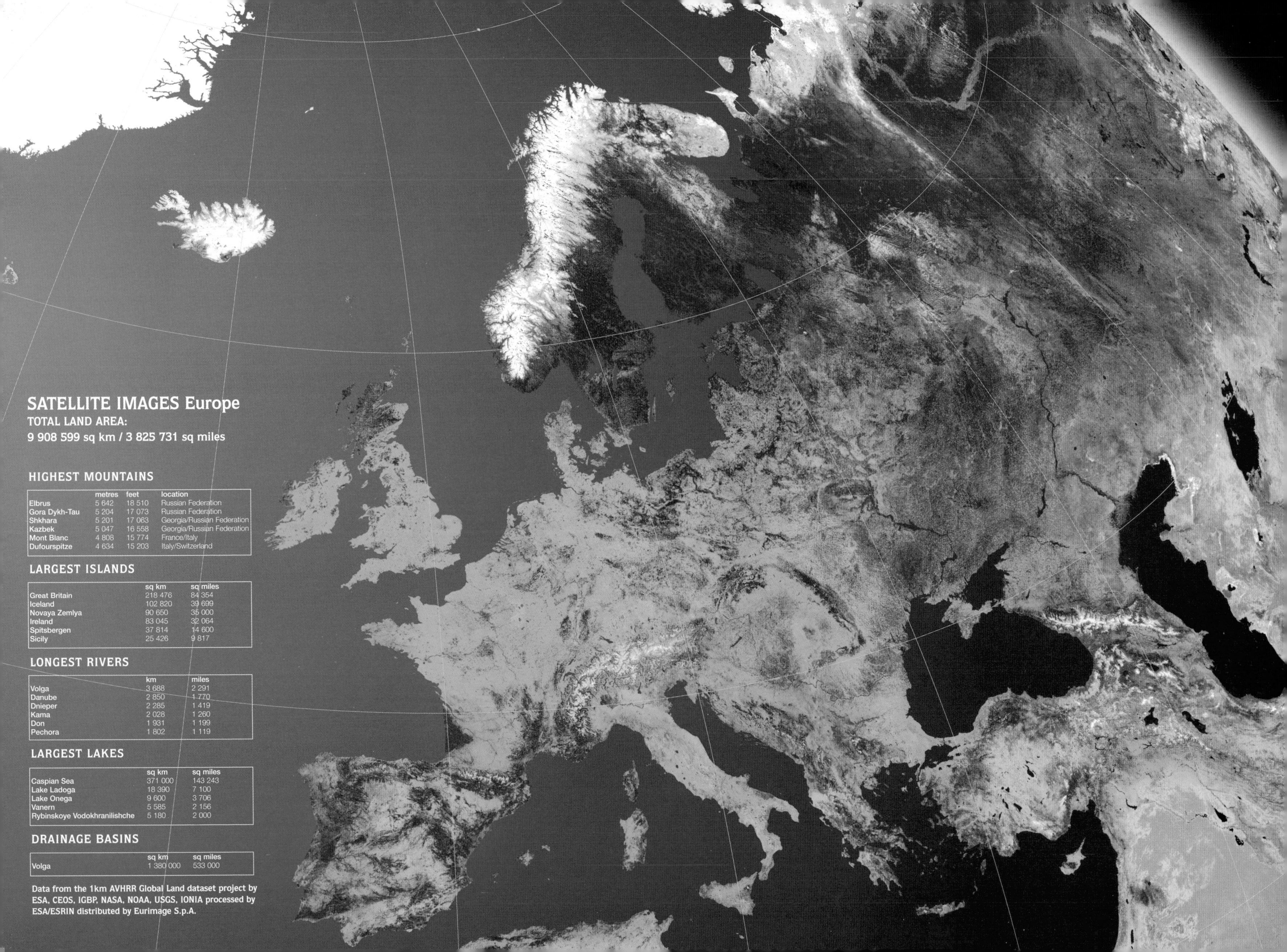

SATELLITE IMAGES Europe

TOTAL LAND AREA:
9 908 599 sq km / 3 825 731 sq miles

HIGHEST MOUNTAINS

	metres	feet	location
Elbrus	5 642	18 510	Russian Federation
Gora Dykh-Tau	5 204	17 073	Russian Federation
Shkhara	5 201	17 063	Georgia/Russian Federation
Kazbek	5 047	16 558	Georgia/Russian Federation
Mont Blanc	4 808	15 774	France/Italy
Dufourspitze	4 634	15 203	Italy/Switzerland

LARGEST ISLANDS

	sq km	sq miles
Great Britain	218 476	84 354
Iceland	102 820	39 699
Novaya Zemlya	90 650	35 000
Ireland	83 045	32 064
Spitsbergen	37 814	14 600
Sicily	25 426	9 817

LONGEST RIVERS

	km	miles
Volga	3 688	2 291
Danube	2 850	1 770
Dnieper	2 285	1 419
Kama	2 028	1 260
Don	1 931	1 199
Pechora	1 802	1 119

LARGEST LAKES

	sq km	sq miles
Caspian Sea	371 000	143 243
Lake Ladoga	18 390	7 100
Lake Onega	9 600	3 706
Vänern	5 585	2 156
Rybinskoye Vodokhranilishche	5 180	2 000

DRAINAGE BASINS

	sq km	sq miles
Volga	1 380 000	533 000

Data from the 1km AVHRR Global Land dataset project by ESA, CEOS, IGBP, NASA, NOAA, USGS, IONIA processed by ESA/ESRIN distributed by Eurimage S.p.A.

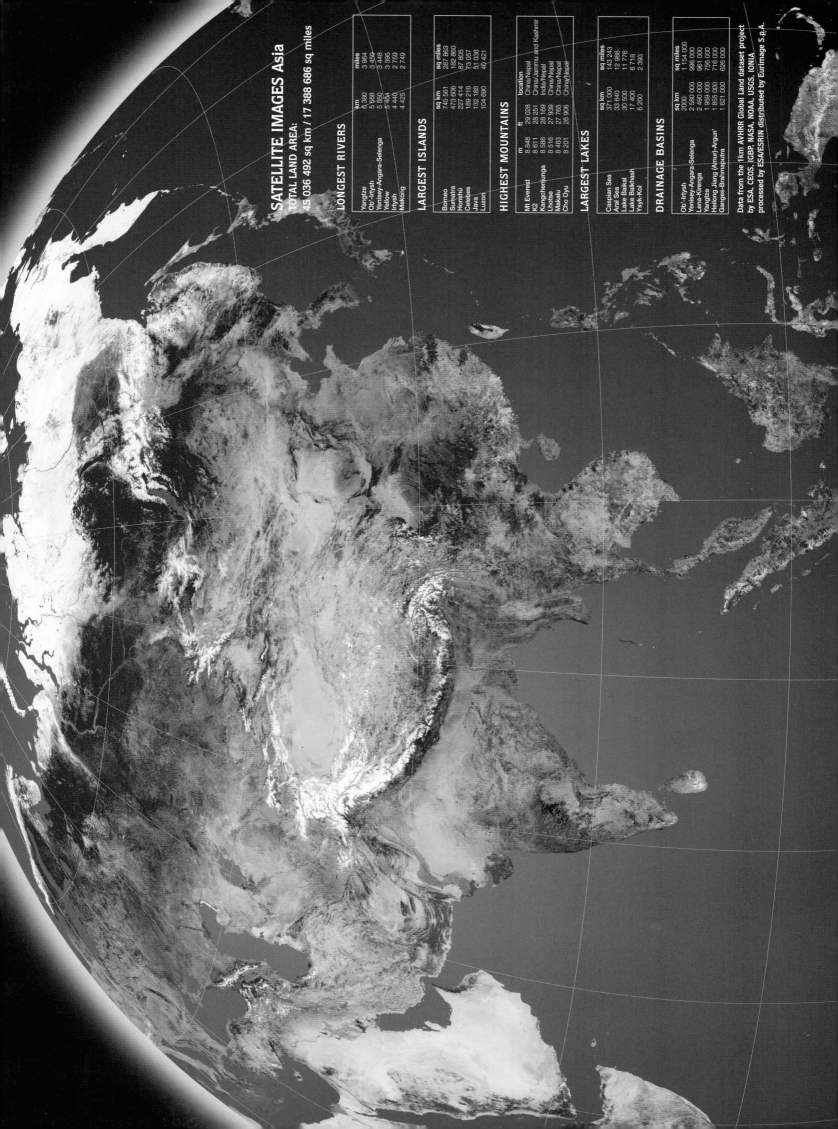

SATELLITE IMAGES Asia

TOTAL LAND AREA:
45 036 492 sq km / 17 388 686 sq miles

LONGEST RIVERS

	km	miles
Yangtze	6 380	3 964
Ob'-Irtysh	5 568	3 459
Yenisey-Angara-Selenga	5 550	3 448
Yellow	5 464	3 395
Irtysh	4 440	2 759
Mekong	4 425	2 749

LARGEST ISLANDS

	sq km	sq miles
Borneo	745 561	287 863
Sumatra	473 606	182 860
Honshū	227 414	87 805
Celebes	189 216	73 057
Java	132 188	51 038
Luzon	104 690	40 421

HIGHEST MOUNTAINS

	m	ft	location
Mt Everest	8 848	29 028	China/Nepal
K2	8 611	28 251	China/Jammu and Kashmir
Kangchenjunga	8 586	28 169	India/Nepal
Lhotse	8 516	27 939	China/Nepal
Makalu	8 463	27 765	China/Nepal
Cho Oyu	8 201	26 906	China/Nepal

LARGEST LAKES

	sq km	sq miles
Caspian Sea	371 000	143 243
Aral Sea	33 640	12 988
Lake Baikal	30 500	11 776
Lake Balkhash	17 400	6 718
Ysyk-Köl	6 200	2 393

DRAINAGE BASINS

	sq km	sq miles
Ob'-Irtysh	2 990 000	1 154 000
Yenisey-Angara-Selenga	2 580 000	996 000
Lena-Kirenga	2 490 000	961 000
Yangtze	1 959 000	756 000
Heilong Jiang (Amur)-Argun'	1 855 000	716 000
Ganges-Brahmaputra	1 621 000	626 000

Data from the 1km AVHRR Global Land dataset project
by ESA, CEOS, IGBP, NASA, NOAA, USGS, IONIA
processed by ESA/ESRIN distributed by Eurimage S.p.A.

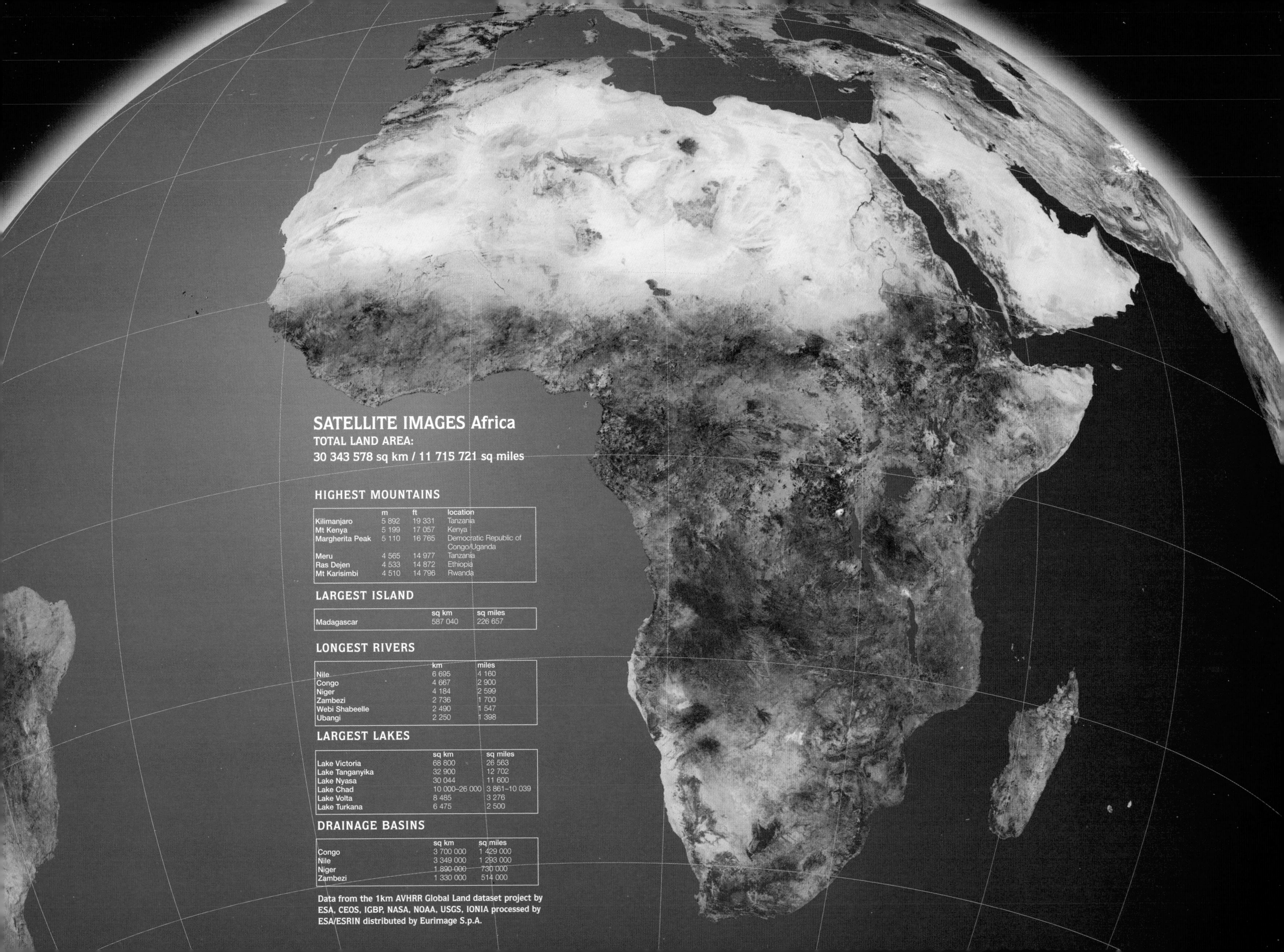

SATELLITE IMAGES Africa

TOTAL LAND AREA:
30 343 578 sq km / 11 715 721 sq miles

HIGHEST MOUNTAINS

	m	ft	location
Kilimanjaro	5 892	19 331	Tanzania
Mt Kenya	5 199	17 057	Kenya
Margherita Peak	5 110	16 765	Democratic Republic of Congo/Uganda
Meru	4 565	14 977	Tanzania
Ras Dejen	4 533	14 872	Ethiopia
Mt Karisimbi	4 510	14 796	Rwanda

LARGEST ISLAND

	sq km	sq miles
Madagascar	587 040	226 657

LONGEST RIVERS

	km	miles
Nile	6 695	4 160
Congo	4 667	2 900
Niger	4 184	2 599
Zambezi	2 736	1 700
Webi Shabeelle	2 490	1 547
Ubangi	2 250	1 398

LARGEST LAKES

	sq km	sq miles
Lake Victoria	68 800	26 563
Lake Tanganyika	32 900	12 702
Lake Nyasa	30 044	11 600
Lake Chad	10 000–26 000	3 861–10 039
Lake Volta	8 485	3 276
Lake Turkana	6 475	2 500

DRAINAGE BASINS

	sq km	sq miles
Congo	3 700 000	1 429 000
Nile	3 349 000	1 293 000
Niger	1 890 000	730 000
Zambezi	1 330 000	514 000

Data from the 1km AVHRR Global Land dataset project by
ESA, CEOS, IGBP, NASA, NOAA, USGS, IONIA processed by
ESA/ESRIN distributed by Eurimage S.p.A.

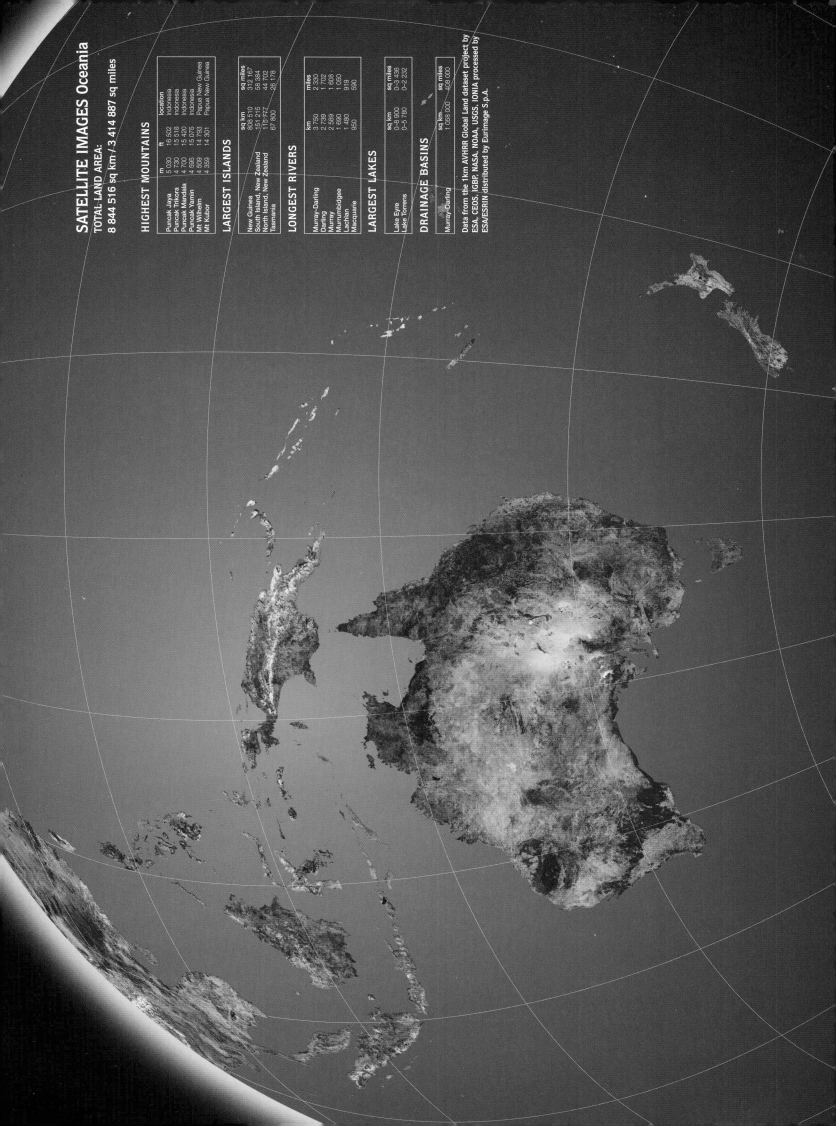

SATELLITE IMAGES Oceania

TOTAL LAND AREA:
8 844 516 sq km / 3 414 887 sq miles

HIGHEST MOUNTAINS

	m	ft	location
Puncak Jaya	5 030	16 502	Indonesia
Puncak Trikora	4 730	15 518	Indonesia
Puncak Mandala	4 700	15 420	Indonesia
Puncak Yamin	4 595	15 075	Indonesia
Mt Wilhelm	4 509	14 793	Papua New Guinea
Mt Kubor	4 359	14 301	Papua New Guinea

LARGEST ISLANDS

	sq km	sq miles
New Guinea	808 510	312 167
South Island, New Zealand	151 215	58 384
North Island, New Zealand	115 777	44 702
Tasmania	67 800	26 178

LONGEST RIVERS

	km	miles
Murray-Darling	3 750	2 330
Darling	2 739	1 702
Murray	2 589	1 608
Murrumbidgee	1 690	1 050
Lachlan	1 480	919
Macquarie	950	590

LARGEST LAKES

	sq km	sq miles
Lake Eyre	0-8 900	0-3 436
Lake Torrens	0-5 780	0-2 232

DRAINAGE BASINS

	sq km	sq miles
Murray-Darling	1 058 000	408 000

Data from the 1km AVHRR Global Land dataset project by
ESA, CEOS, IGBP, NASA, NOAA, USGS, IONIA processed by
ESA/ESRIN distributed by Eurimage S.p.A.

SATELLITE IMAGES
Antarctica

TOTAL LAND AREA:
12 093 000 sq km /
4 669 133 sq miles
(excluding ice shelves)

AREA

	sq km	sq miles
Total land area (excluding ice shelves)	12 093 000	4 669 133
Ice shelves	1 559 000	601 933
Exposed rock	49 000	18 919

HIGHEST MOUNTAINS

	m	ft
Vinson Massif	4 897	16 066
Mt Tyree	4 852	15 918
Mt Kirkpatrick	4 528	14 855
Mt Markham	4 351	14 275
Mt Jackson	4 190	13 747
Mt Sidley	4 181	13 717

HEIGHTS

	m	ft
Lowest bedrock elevation (Bentley Subglacial Trench)	-2 496	-8 189
Maximum ice thickness (Astrolabe Subglacial Basin)	4 776	15 669
Mean ice thickness (including ice shelves)	1 859	6 099

VOLUME

	cubic km	cubic miles
Ice sheet (including ice shelves)	25 400 000	10 160 000

Data from the 1km AVHRR Global Land dataset project by ESA, CEOS, IGBP, NASA, NOAA, USGS. IONIA processed by ESA/ESRIN distributed by Eurimage S.p.A.

TIME ZONES

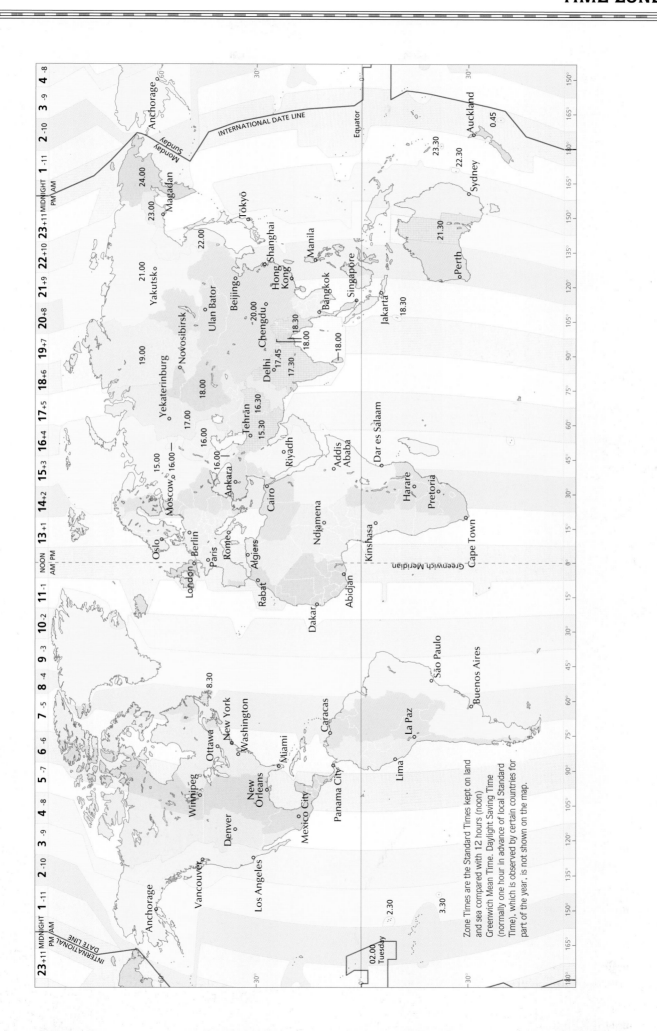

Zone Times are the Standard Times kept on land and sea compared with 12 hours (noon) Greenwich Mean Time. Daylight Saving Time (normally one hour in advance of local Standard Time), which is observed by certain countries for part of the year, is not shown on the map.

4

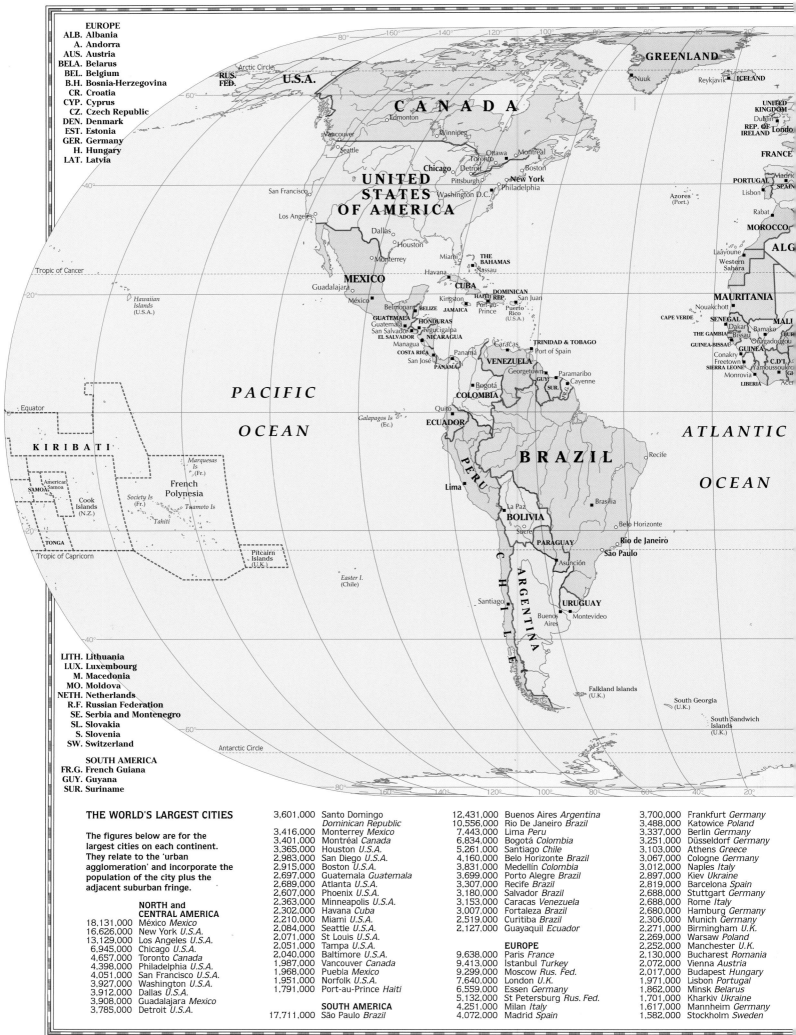

EUROPE
ALB. Albania
A. Andorra
AUS. Austria
BELA. Belarus
BEL. Belgium
B.H. Bosnia-Herzegovina
CR. Croatia
CYP. Cyprus
CZ. Czech Republic
DEN. Denmark
EST. Estonia
GER. Germany
H. Hungary
LAT. Latvia

LITH. Lithuania
LUX. Luxembourg
M. Macedonia
MO. Moldova
NETH. Netherlands
R.F. Russian Federation
SE. Serbia and Montenegro
SL. Slovakia
S. Slovenia
SW. Switzerland

SOUTH AMERICA
FR.G. French Guiana
GUY. Guyana
SUR. Suriname

THE WORLD'S LARGEST CITIES

The figures below are for the
largest cities on each continent.
They relate to the 'urban
agglomeration' and incorporate the
population of the city plus the
adjacent suburban fringe.

**NORTH and
CENTRAL AMERICA**
18,131,000	México *Mexico*
16,626,000	New York *U.S.A.*
13,129,000	Los Angeles *U.S.A.*
6,945,000	Chicago *U.S.A.*
4,657,000	Toronto *Canada*
4,398,000	Philadelphia *U.S.A.*
4,051,000	San Francisco *U.S.A.*
3,927,000	Washington *U.S.A.*
3,912,000	Dallas *U.S.A.*
3,908,000	Guadalajara *Mexico*
3,785,000	Detroit *U.S.A.*

3,601,000	Santo Domingo *Dominican Republic*
3,416,000	Monterrey *Mexico*
3,401,000	Montréal *Canada*
3,365,000	Houston *U.S.A.*
2,983,000	San Diego *U.S.A.*
2,915,000	Boston *U.S.A.*
2,697,000	Guatemala *Guatemala*
2,689,000	Atlanta *U.S.A.*
2,607,000	Phoenix *U.S.A.*
2,363,000	Minneapolis *U.S.A.*
2,302,000	Havana *Cuba*
2,210,000	Miami *U.S.A.*
2,084,000	Seattle *U.S.A.*
2,071,000	St Louis *U.S.A.*
2,051,000	Tampa *U.S.A.*
2,040,000	Baltimore *U.S.A.*
1,987,000	Vancouver *Canada*
1,968,000	Puebla *Mexico*
1,951,000	Norfolk *U.S.A.*
1,791,000	Port-au-Prince *Haiti*

SOUTH AMERICA
17,711,000	São Paulo *Brazil*

12,431,000	Buenos Aires *Argentina*
10,556,000	Rio De Janeiro *Brazil*
7,443,000	Lima *Peru*
6,834,000	Bogotá *Colombia*
5,261,000	Santiago *Chile*
4,160,000	Belo Horizonte *Brazil*
3,831,000	Medellín *Colombia*
3,699,000	Porto Alegre *Brazil*
3,307,000	Recife *Brazil*
3,180,000	Salvador *Brazil*
3,153,000	Caracas *Venezuela*
3,007,000	Fortaleza *Brazil*
2,519,000	Curitiba *Brazil*
2,127,000	Guayaquil *Ecuador*

EUROPE
9,638,000	Paris *France*
9,413,000	İstanbul *Turkey*
9,299,000	Moscow *Rus. Fed.*
7,640,000	London *U.K.*
6,559,000	Essen *Germany*
5,132,000	St Petersburg *Rus. Fed.*
4,251,000	Milan *Italy*
4,072,000	Madrid *Spain*

3,700,000	Frankfurt *Germany*
3,488,000	Katowice *Poland*
3,337,000	Berlin *Germany*
3,251,000	Düsseldorf *Germany*
3,103,000	Athens *Greece*
3,067,000	Cologne *Germany*
3,012,000	Naples *Italy*
2,897,000	Kiev *Ukraine*
2,819,000	Barcelona *Spain*
2,688,000	Stuttgart *Germany*
2,688,000	Rome *Italy*
2,680,000	Hamburg *Germany*
2,306,000	Munich *Germany*
2,271,000	Birmingham *U.K.*
2,269,000	Warsaw *Poland*
2,252,000	Manchester *U.K.*
2,130,000	Bucharest *Romania*
2,072,000	Vienna *Austria*
2,017,000	Budapest *Hungary*
1,971,000	Lisbon *Portugal*
1,862,000	Minsk *Belarus*
1,701,000	Kharkiv *Ukraine*
1,617,000	Mannheim *Germany*
1,582,000	Stockholm *Sweden*

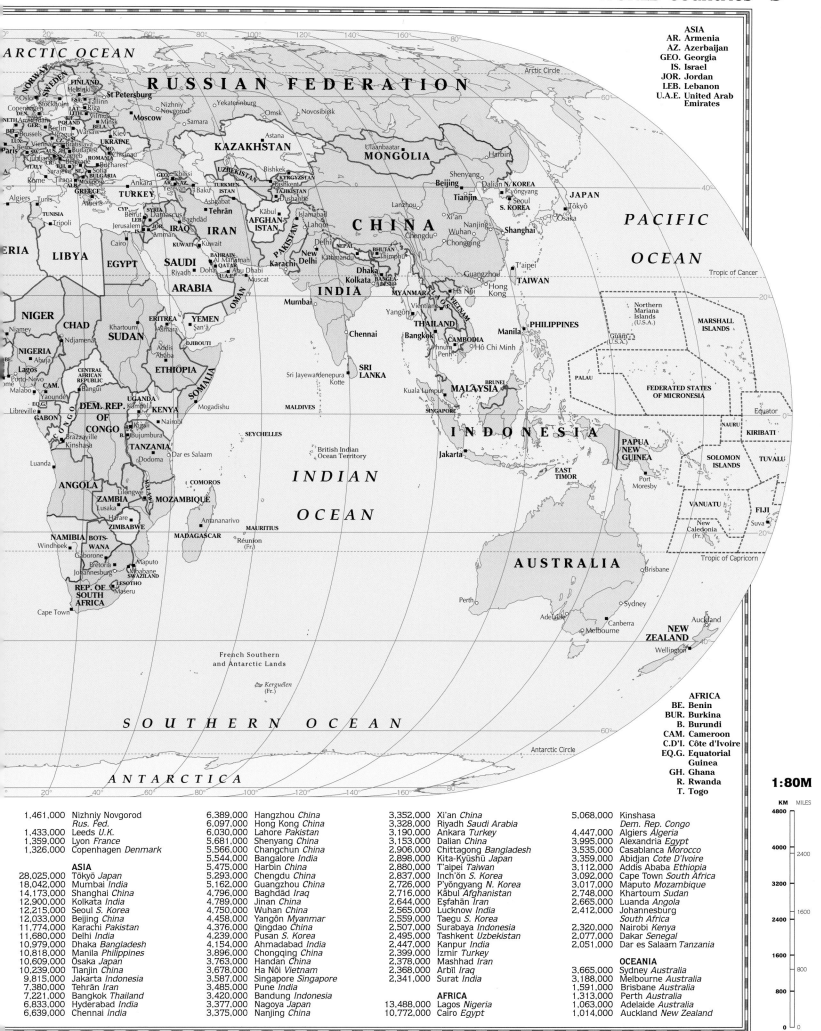

ASIA
AR. Armenia
AZ. Azerbaijan
GEO. Georgia
IS. Israel
JOR. Jordan
LEB. Lebanon
U.A.E. United Arab
Emirates

AFRICA
BE. Benin
BUR. Burkina
B. Burundi
CAM. Cameroon
C.D'I. Côte d'Ivoire
EQ.G. Equatorial
Guinea
GH. Ghana
R. Rwanda
T. Togo

1:80M

KM   MILES
4800

4000   2400

3200   1600

2400   800

1600

800

0

1,461,000	Nizhniy Novgorod *Rus. Fed.*	
1,433,000	Leeds *U.K.*	
1,359,000	Lyon *France*	
1,326,000	Copenhagen *Denmark*	

ASIA

28,025,000	Tōkyō *Japan*
18,042,000	Mumbai *India*
14,173,000	Shanghai *China*
12,900,000	Kolkata *India*
12,215,000	Seoul *S. Korea*
12,033,000	Beijing *China*
11,774,000	Karachi *Pakistan*
11,680,000	Delhi *India*
10,979,000	Dhaka *Bangladesh*
10,818,000	Manila *Philippines*
10,609,000	Ōsaka *Japan*
10,239,000	Tianjin *China*
9,815,000	Jakarta *Indonesia*
7,380,000	Tehrān *Iran*
7,221,000	Bangkok *Thailand*
6,833,000	Hyderabad *India*
6,639,000	Chennai *India*

6,389,000	Hangzhou *China*
6,097,000	Hong Kong *China*
6,030,000	Lahore *Pakistan*
5,681,000	Shenyang *China*
5,566,000	Changchun *China*
5,544,000	Bangalore *India*
5,475,000	Harbin *China*
5,293,000	Chengdu *China*
5,162,000	Guangzhou *China*
4,796,000	Baghdād *Iraq*
4,789,000	Jinan *China*
4,750,000	Wuhan *China*
4,458,000	Yangôn *Myanmar*
4,376,000	Qingdao *China*
4,239,000	Pusan *S. Korea*
4,154,000	Ahmadabad *India*
3,896,000	Chongqing *China*
3,763,000	Handan *China*
3,678,000	Ha Nôi *Vietnam*
3,587,000	Singapore *Singapore*
3,485,000	Pune *India*
3,420,000	Bandung *Indonesia*
3,377,000	Nagoya *Japan*
3,375,000	Nanjing *China*

3,352,000	Xi'an *China*
3,328,000	Riyadh *Saudi Arabia*
3,190,000	Ankara *Turkey*
3,153,000	Dalian *China*
2,906,000	Chittagong *Bangladesh*
2,898,000	Kita-Kyūshū *Japan*
2,880,000	T'aipei *Taiwan*
2,837,000	Inch'ŏn *S. Korea*
2,726,000	P'yŏngyang *N. Korea*
2,716,000	Kābul *Afghanistan*
2,644,000	Eşfahān *Iran*
2,565,000	Lucknow *India*
2,559,000	Taegu *S. Korea*
2,507,000	Surabaya *Indonesia*
2,495,000	Tashkent *Uzbekistan*
2,447,000	Kanpur *India*
2,399,000	İzmir *Turkey*
2,378,000	Mashhad *Iran*
2,368,000	Arbīl *Iraq*
2,341,000	Surat *India*

AFRICA

13,488,000	Lagos *Nigeria*
10,772,000	Cairo *Egypt*

5,068,000	Kinshasa *Dem. Rep. Congo*
4,447,000	Algiers *Algeria*
3,995,000	Alexandria *Egypt*
3,535,000	Casablanca *Morocco*
3,359,000	Abidjan *Cote D'Ivoire*
3,112,000	Addis Ababa *Ethiopia*
3,092,000	Cape Town *South Africa*
3,017,000	Maputo *Mozambique*
2,748,000	Khartoum *Sudan*
2,665,000	Luanda *Angola*
2,412,000	Johannesburg *South Africa*
2,320,000	Nairobi *Kenya*
2,077,000	Dakar *Senegal*
2,051,000	Dar es Salaam *Tanzania*

OCEANIA

3,665,000	Sydney *Australia*
3,188,000	Melbourne *Australia*
1,591,000	Brisbane *Australia*
1,313,000	Perth *Australia*
1,063,000	Adelaide *Australia*
1,014,000	Auckland *New Zealand*

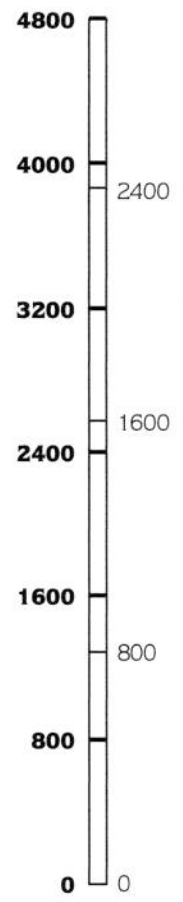

6

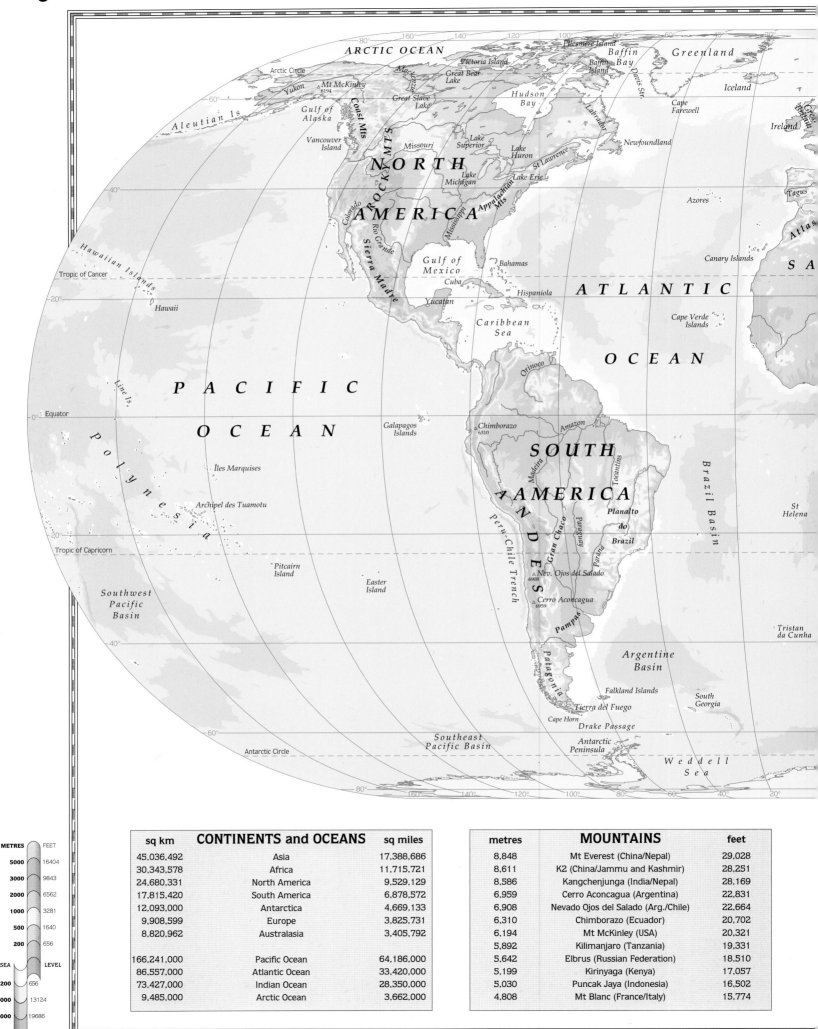

METRES	FEET
5000	16404
3000	9843
2000	6562
1000	3281
500	1640
200	656
SEA	LEVEL
200	656
4000	13124
6000	19686

Eckert IV Projection

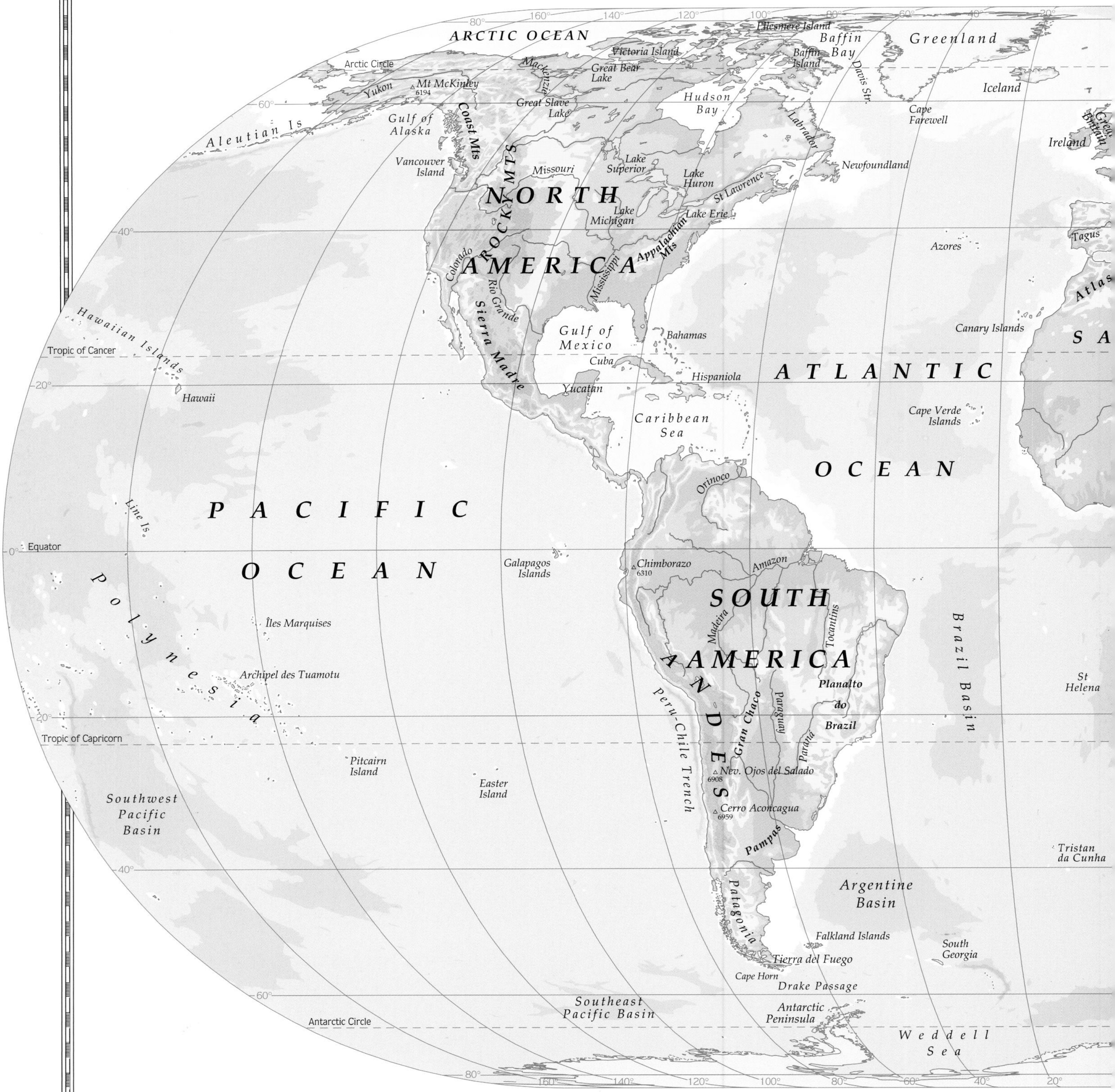

sq km	CONTINENTS and OCEANS	sq miles
45,036,492	Asia	17,388,686
30,343,578	Africa	11,715,721
24,680,331	North America	9,529,129
17,815,420	South America	6,878,572
12,093,000	Antarctica	4,669,133
9,908,599	Europe	3,825,731
8,820,962	Australasia	3,405,792
166,241,000	Pacific Ocean	64,186,000
86,557,000	Atlantic Ocean	33,420,000
73,427,000	Indian Ocean	28,350,000
9,485,000	Arctic Ocean	3,662,000

metres	MOUNTAINS	feet
8,848	Mt Everest (China/Nepal)	29,028
8,611	K2 (China/Jammu and Kashmir)	28,251
8,586	Kangchenjunga (India/Nepal)	28,169
6,959	Cerro Aconcagua (Argentina)	22,831
6,908	Nevado Ojos del Salado (Arg./Chile)	22,664
6,310	Chimborazo (Ecuador)	20,702
6,194	Mt McKinley (USA)	20,321
5,892	Kilimanjaro (Tanzania)	19,331
5,642	Elbrus (Russian Federation)	18,510
5,199	Kirinyaga (Kenya)	17,057
5,030	Puncak Jaya (Indonesia)	16,502
4,808	Mt Blanc (France/Italy)	15,774

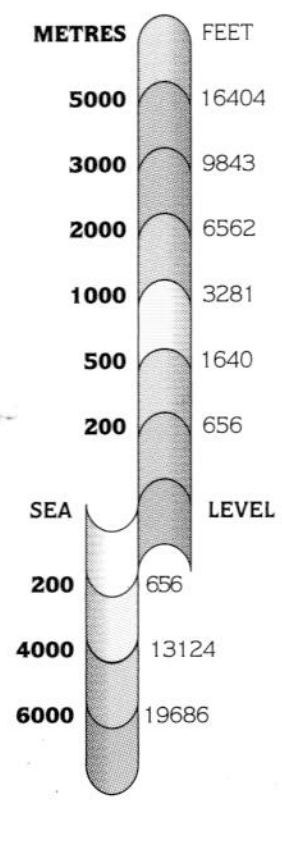

Norwegian Sea
Scandinavia
North Sea
Baltic Sea
ARCTIC   OCEAN
Barents Sea
Ural Mts
Ob'
West Siberian Plain
Yenisey
Central Siberian Plateau
Lena
Arctic Circle
Kamchatka Pen.
Sea of Okhotsk
Kuril Trench
E U R O P E
Rhine
ALPS
4808 Mt Blanc
Apennines
Carpathian Mts
Dnieper
Volga
Lake Ladoga
Elbrus 5642
Black Sea
Caucasus
Caspian Sea
Kara Bogaz Gol
Aral Sea
Irtysh
Ozero Balkhash
Altai Mts
A S I A
GOBI
Amur
Vityaz Depth 10542
Sea of Japan
Mediterranean Sea
Taurus Mts
Kalha-ye Zagros
Suez Canal
Tigris
Euphrates
Amudar'ya
Tien Shan
Hindu Kush
K2 8611
Kunlun Shan
Tibetan Plateau
HIMALAYA
Huang He
Yangtze (Chang Jiang)
Yellow Sea
Honshū
East China Sea
Japan Trench
Ramapo Deep 10374
SAHARA
Hoggar
Tibesti
Nile
Red Sea
The Gulf
Indus
Thar Desert
Mt Everest 8848
Kangchenjunga 8586
Ganges
Bay of Bengal
Taiwan
Tropic of Cancer
P A C I F I C
AFRICA
Benue
Gulf of Guinea
Congo
Blue Nile
White Nile
Lake Turkana
Kirinyaga 5199
Lake Victoria
Great Rift Valley
Kilimanjaro 5892
Lake Tanganyika
Arabian Sea
Western Ghats
Laccadive Is
Maldives
Sri Lanka
Seychelles
Chagos Archipelago
I N D I A N
Mekong
Peninsular Malaysia
South China Sea
Philippines
Philippine Trench 10497
Cape Johnson Depth
Challenger Deep 10920
Mariana Trench
Caroline Is
Marshall Is
O C E A N
Lake Nyasa
Comoro Islands
Lake
Zambezi
Mozambique Channel
Madagascar
Mauritius
Réunion
O C E A N
Sumatera
Java
Celebes Sea
Sulawesi
Borneo
Banda Sea
Puncak Jaya 5030
New Guinea
Solomon Is
O C E A N I A
Angola Basin
Kalahari Desert
Orange
Drakensberg
West Australian Basin
Great Sandy Desert
A u s t r a l i a
Great Victoria Desert
Great Dividing Range
Darling
Coral Sea
Gt Barrier Reef
Fiji
New Caledonia
Tropic of Capricorn
Cape of Good Hope
Great Australian Bight
Murray
Tasman Sea
Tasmania
North Island
New Zealand
South Island
Prince Edward Is
Crozet Is
Kerguélen
S O U T H E R N   O C E A N
Antarctic Circle
A N T A R C T I C A
1:80M

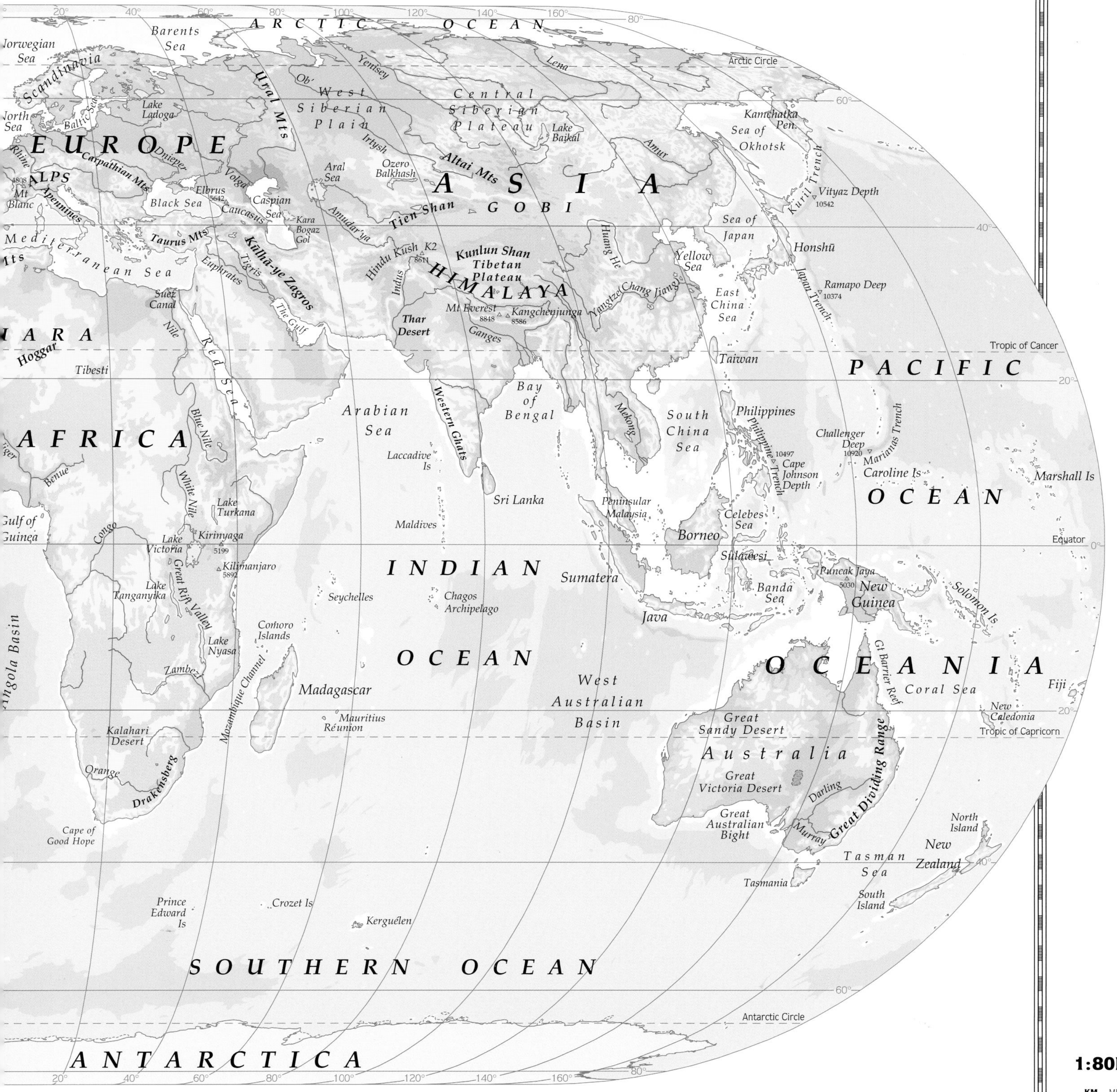

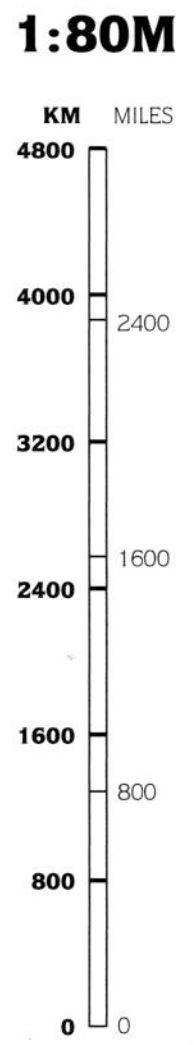

sq km	LAKES	sq miles
371,000	Caspian Sea (Asia)	143,243
82,100	Lake Superior (N. America)	31,698
68,800	Lake Victoria (Africa)	26,563
59,600	Lake Huron (N. America)	23,011
57,800	Lake Michigan (N. America)	22,316
33,640	Aral Sea (Asia)	12,988
32,900	Lake Tanganyika (Africa)	12,702
31,328	Great Bear Lake (N. America)	12,095
30,500	Lake Baikal (Asia)	11,776
28,568	Great Slave Lake (N. America)	11,030
25,700	Lake Erie (N. America)	9,922
30,044	Lake Nyasa (Africa)	11,600

kilometres	RIVERS	miles
6,695	Nile (Africa)	4,160
6,516	Amazon (S. America)	4,049
6,380	Yangtze (Chang Jiang) (Asia)	3,964
5,969	Mississippi-Missouri (N. America)	3,709
5,568	Ob'-Irtysh (Asia)	3,459
5,464	Huang He (Asia)	3,395
4,667	Congo (Africa)	2,900
4,425	Mekong (Asia)	2,749
4,416	Amur (Asia)	2,744
4,400	Lena (Asia)	2,734
4,241	Mackenzie (N. America)	2,635
4,090	Yenisey (Asia)	2,541

KM   MILES
4800
4000   2400
3200
2400   1600
1600   800
800
0   0

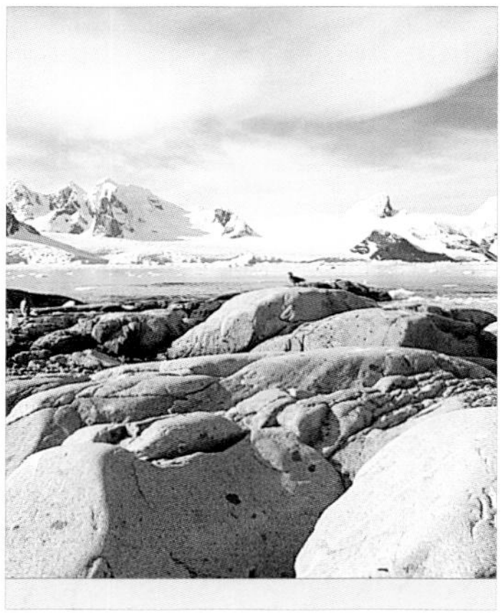

ICE CAP
Areas of permanent ice cap around the north and south poles. The intense cold, dry weather and the ice cover render these regions almost lifeless. In Antarctica, tiny patches of land free of ice have a cover of mosses and lichens which provide shelter for some insects and mites.

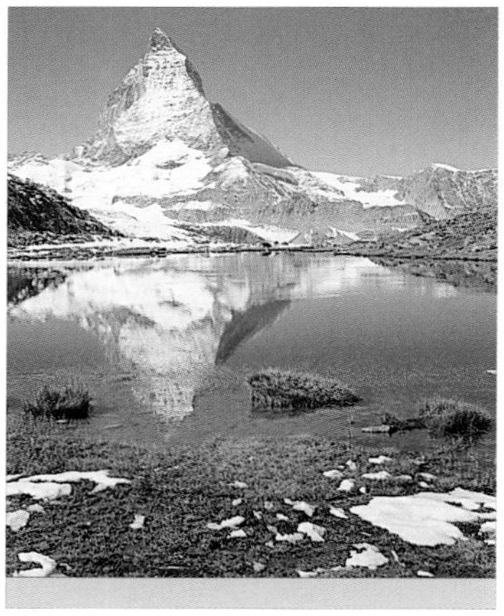

TUNDRA and MOUNTAIN
Sub-arctic areas or mountain tops which are usually frozen. Tundra vegetation is characterized by mosses, lichens, rushes, grasses and flowering herbs; animals include the arctic fox and reindeer. Mountain vegetation is also characterized by mosses and lichens, and by low growing birch and willow.

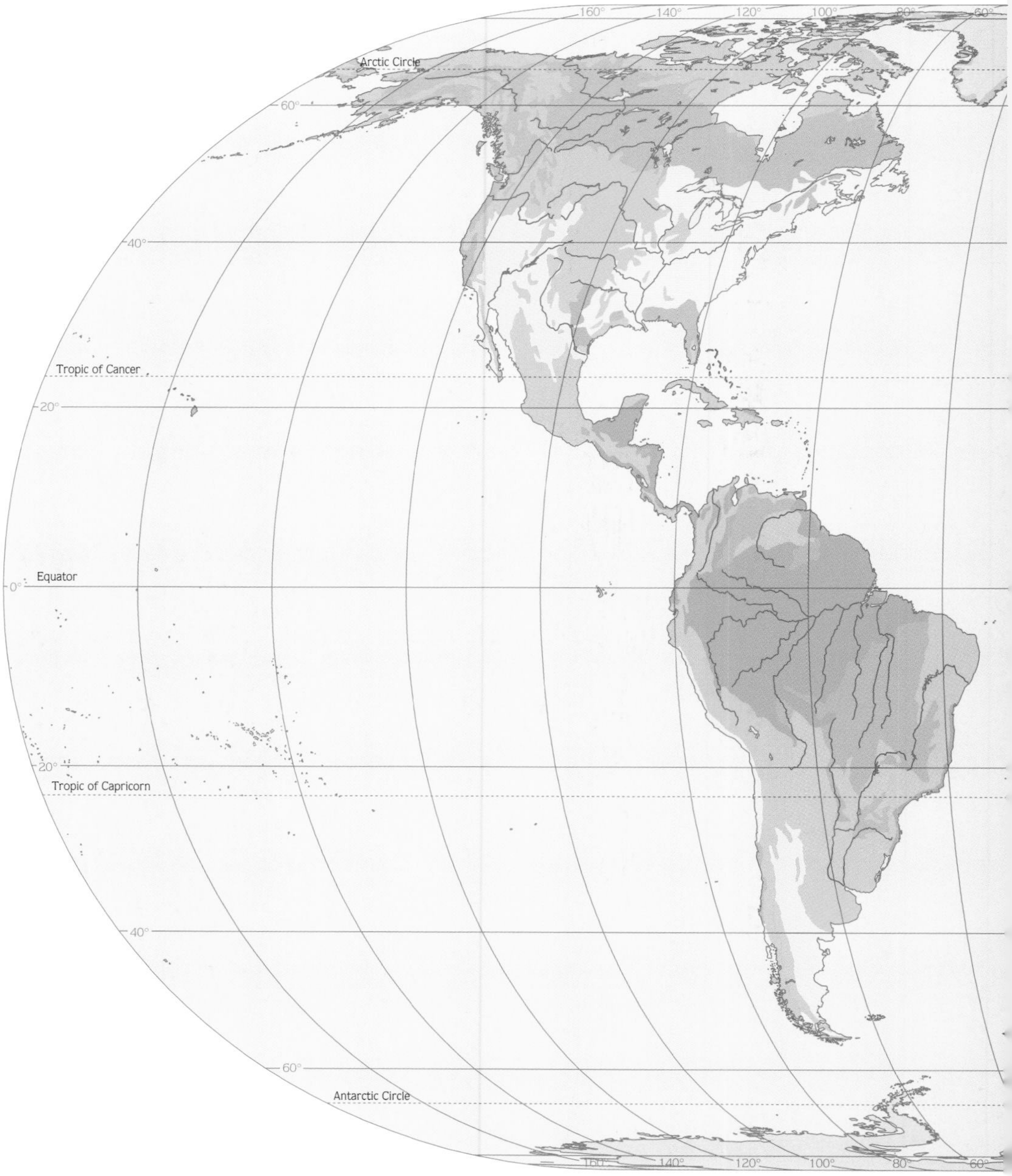

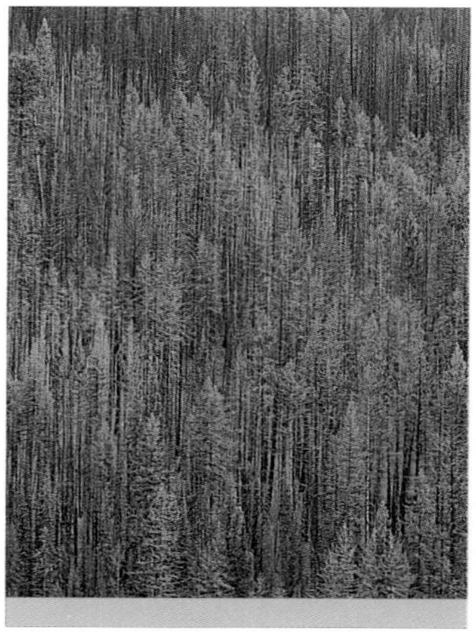

TAIGA (NORTHERN FOREST)
Found only in the high latitudes of the northern hemisphere where winters are long and very cold, and summers are short. The characteristic vegetation is coniferous trees, including spruce and fir; animals include beavers, squirrels and deer.

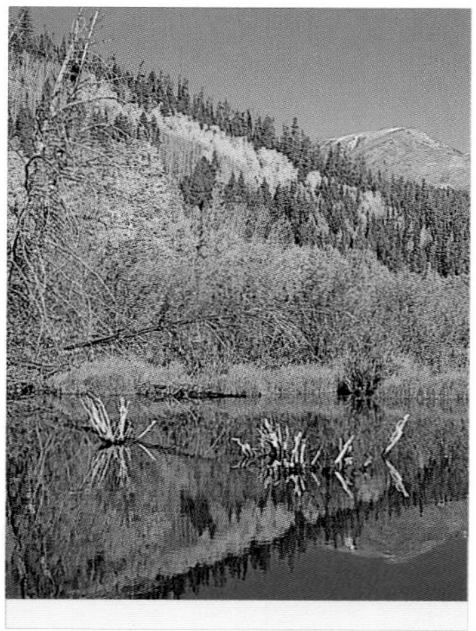

MIXED and DECIDUOUS FOREST
Typical of both temperate mid-latitude regions and of eastern subtropical regions. The vegetation is a mixture of broadleaf and coniferous trees, including oak, beech and maple. Humankind has had a major impact on these regions, and in many areas little natural vegetation remains.

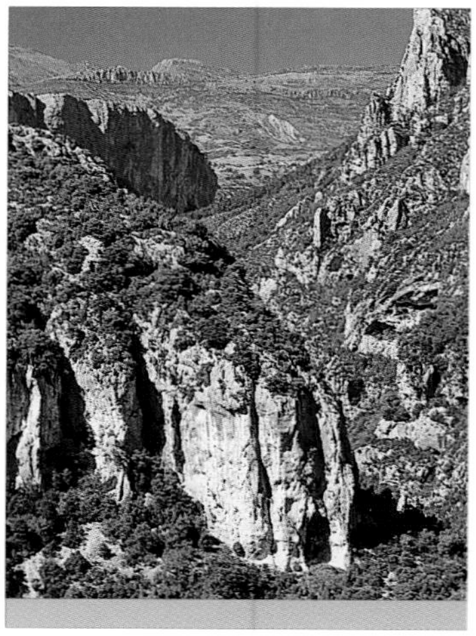

MEDITERRANEAN SCRUB
Long, hot, dry summers and short, warm, wet winters characterize these areas. A variety of herbaceous plants grow beneath shrub thickets with pine, oak and gorse.

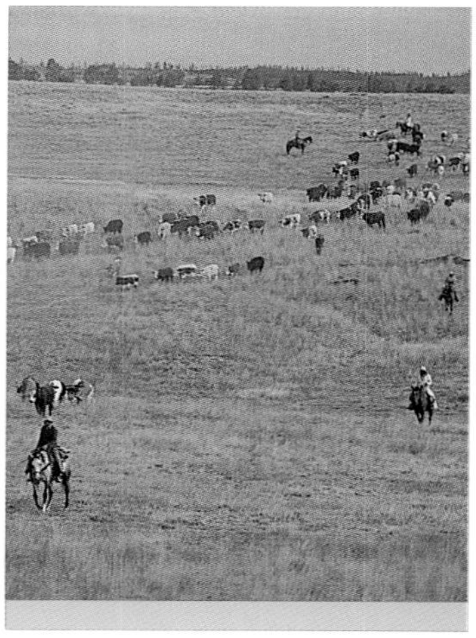

GRASSLAND
Areas of long grasslands (prairies) and short grasslands (steppe) in both the northern and southern hemispheres. These grasslands have hot summers, cold winters and moderate rainfall.

Arctic Circle
60°
40°
Tropic of Cancer
20°
Equator 0°
20°
Tropic of Capricorn
40°
60°
Antarctic Circle

160° 140° 120° 100°
160° 140° 120° 100° 80° 60°

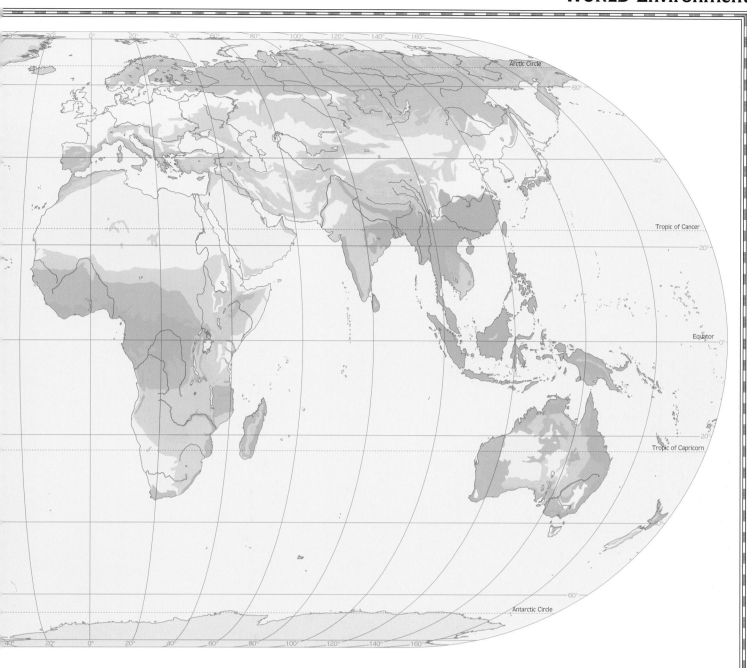

SAVANNA
Tropical grasslands with a short rainy season; areas of grassland are interspersed with thorn bushes and deciduous trees such as acacia and eucalyptus.

RAINFOREST
Dense evergreen forests found in areas of high rainfall and continuous high temperatures. Up to three tree layers grow above a variable shrub layer: high trees, the tree canopy and the open canopy.

DRY TROPICAL FOREST and SCRUB
Low to medium size semi-deciduous trees and thorny scrub with thick bark and long roots characterize the forest areas; in the scrub areas the trees are replaced by shrubs, bushes and succulents.

DESERT
Little vegetation grows in the very hot, dry climate of desert areas. The few shrubs, grasses and cacti have adapted by storing water when it is available.

1:100M

KM MILES
6000

5000
3000

4000
2000

3000

2000
1000

1000

0

CLIMATE TYPES and OCEAN CURRENTS

POLAR
- Ice Cap
- Tundra

COOLER HUMID
- Subarctic
- Continental cool summer
- Continental warm summer

WARMER HUMID
- Temperate
- Humid subtropical
- Mediterranean

DRY
- Steppe
- Desert

TROPICAL HUMID
- Savanna
- Rain forest

- Warm Currents
- Cold Currents

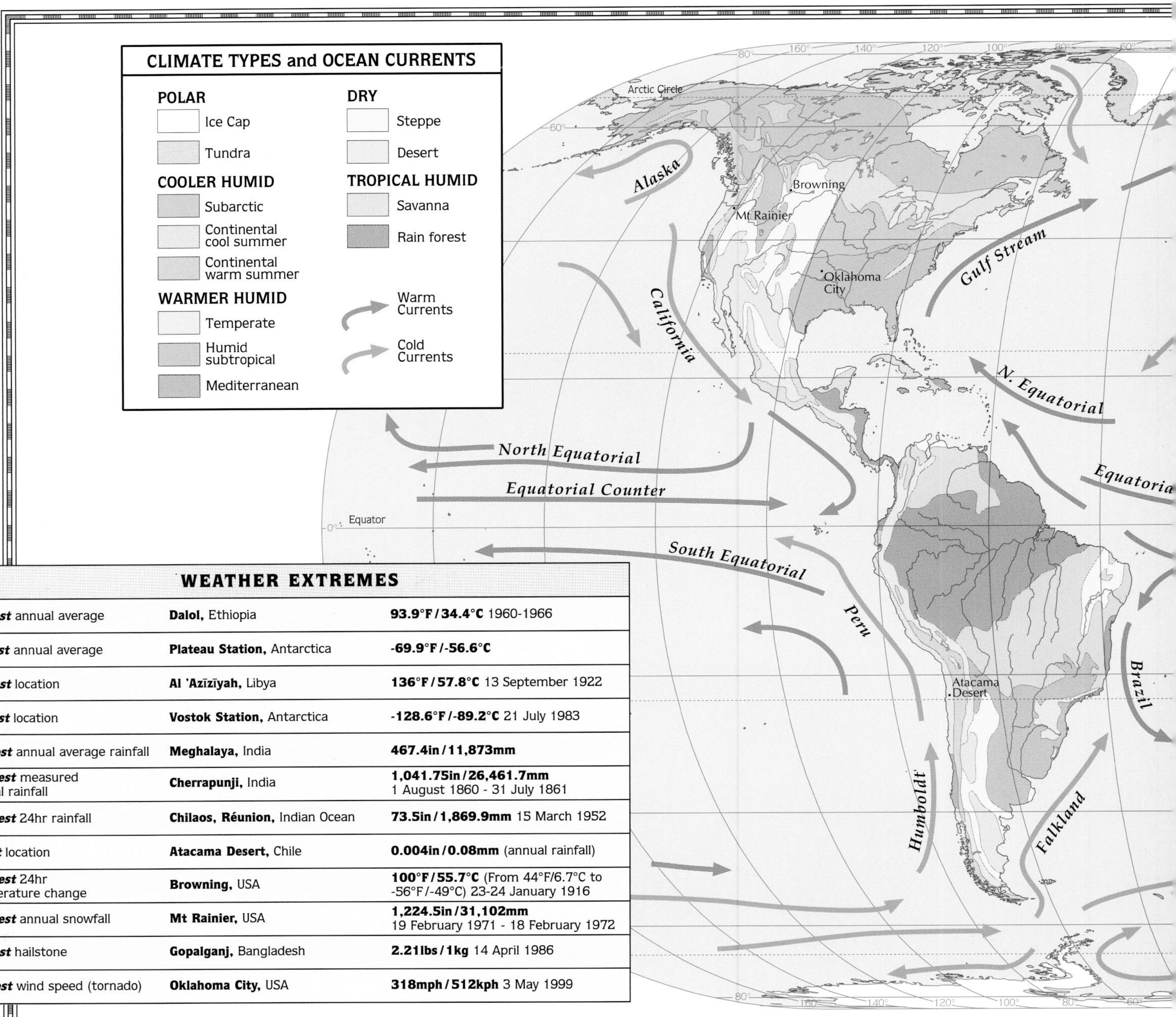

WEATHER EXTREMES

Hottest annual average	**Dalol,** Ethiopia	**93.9°F/34.4°C** 1960-1966
Coldest annual average	**Plateau Station,** Antarctica	**-69.9°F/-56.6°C**
Hottest location	**Al 'Azīzīyah,** Libya	**136°F/57.8°C** 13 September 1922
Coldest location	**Vostok Station,** Antarctica	**-128.6°F/-89.2°C** 21 July 1983
Highest annual average rainfall	**Meghalaya,** India	**467.4in/11,873mm**
Greatest measured annual rainfall	**Cherrapunji,** India	**1,041.75in/26,461.7mm** 1 August 1860 - 31 July 1861
Greatest 24hr rainfall	**Chilaos, Réunion,** Indian Ocean	**73.5in/1,869.9mm** 15 March 1952
Driest location	**Atacama Desert,** Chile	**0.004in/0.08mm** (annual rainfall)
Greatest 24hr temperature change	**Browning,** USA	**100°F/55.7°C** (From 44°F/6.7°C to -56°F/-49°C) 23-24 January 1916
Greatest annual snowfall	**Mt Rainier,** USA	**1,224.5in/31,102mm** 19 February 1971 - 18 February 1972
Largest hailstone	**Gopalganj,** Bangladesh	**2.21lbs/1kg** 14 April 1986
Highest wind speed (tornado)	**Oklahoma City,** USA	**318mph/512kph** 3 May 1999

RAINFALL
Mean Annual Precipitation
0 200 500 1000 2000 3000 mm
0 7.9 19.7 39.4 78.7 118.1 in

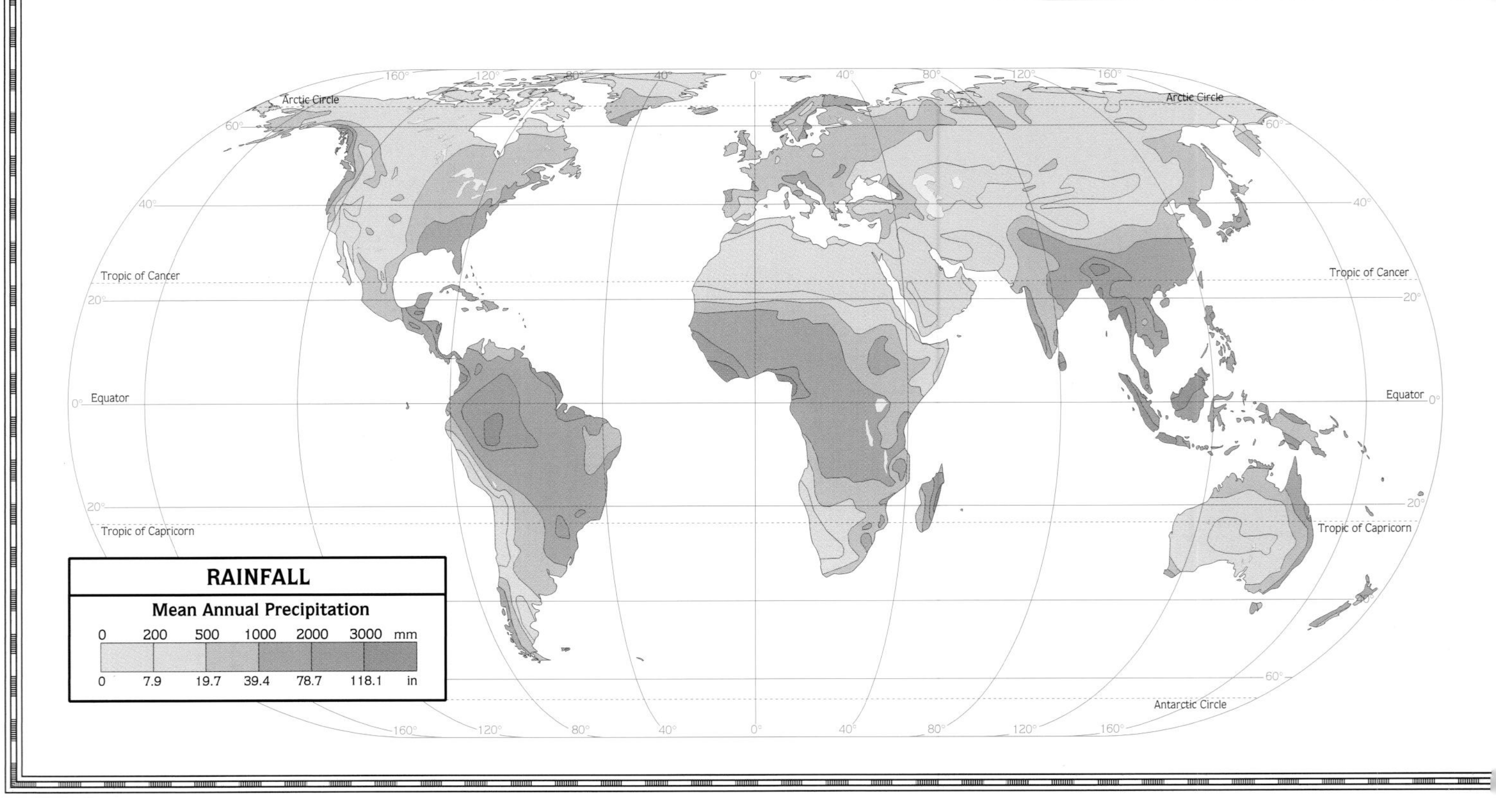

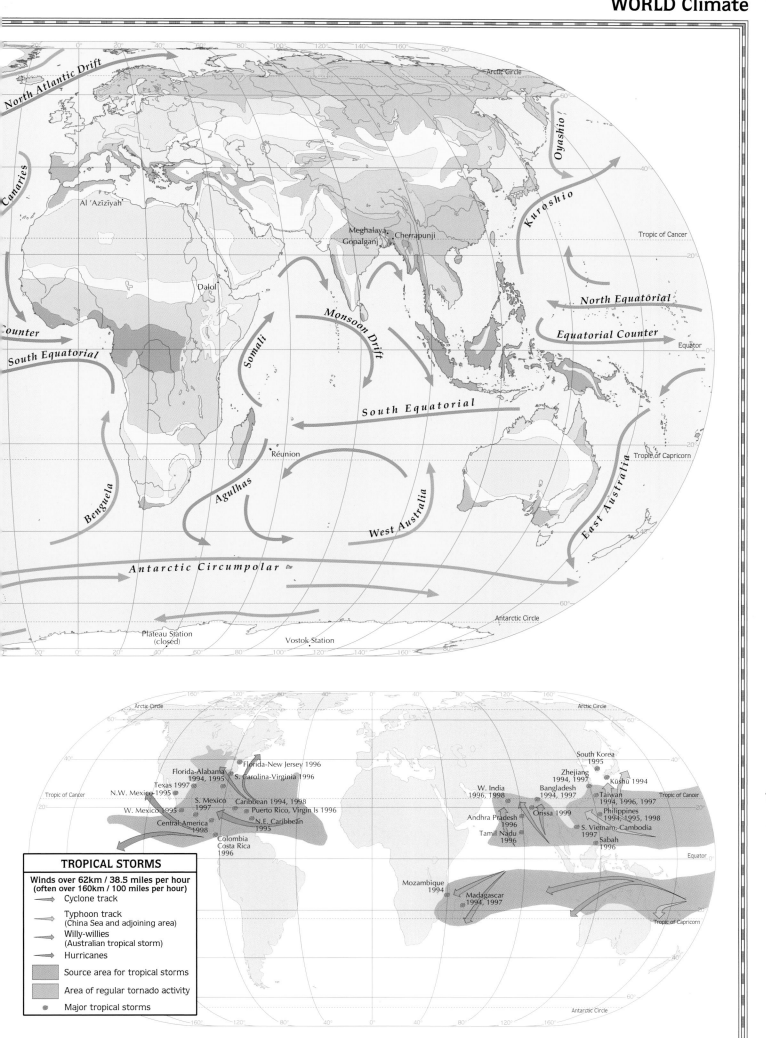

North Atlantic Drift

Canaries

Al 'Azīzīyah

Meghalaya
Gopalganj • Cherrapunji

Dalol

Counter

South Equatorial

Somali

Monsoon Drift

South Equatorial

Réunion

Benguela

Agulhas

West Australia

Antarctic Circumpolar

Plateau Station
(closed)

Vostok Station

Oyashio !

Kuroshio

Tropic of Cancer

North Equatorial

Equatorial Counter

Equator

Tropic of Capricorn

East Australia

Arctic Circle

Antarctic Circle

Arctic Circle

Tropic of Cancer

Florida-New Jersey 1996

Florida-Alabama
1994, 1995

S. Carolina-Virginia 1996

Texas 1997

N.W. Mexico 1995

W. Mexico 1995

S. Mexico
1997

Caribbean 1994, 1998

Puerto Rico, Virgin Is 1996

N.E. Caribbean
1995

Central America
1998

Colombia
Costa Rica
1996

South Korea
1995

Zhejiang
1994, 1997

Kūshū 1994

W. India
1996, 1998

Bangladesh
1994, 1997

Taiwan
1994, 1996, 1997

Andhra Pradesh
1996

Orissa 1999

Philippines
1994, 1995, 1998

Tamil Nadu
1996

S. Vietnam, Cambodia
1997

Sabah
1996

Mozambique
1994

Madagascar
1994, 1997

Equator

Tropic of Capricorn

Antarctic Circle

TROPICAL STORMS

Winds over 62km / 38.5 miles per hour
(often over 160km / 100 miles per hour)

→ Cyclone track

→ Typhoon track
(China Sea and adjoining area)

→ Willy-willies
(Australian tropical storm)

→ Hurricanes

◼ Source area for tropical storms

◼ Area of regular tornado activity

• Major tropical storms

1 : 100M

KM	MILES
6000	
5000	3000
4000	2000
3000	
2000	1000
1000	
0	

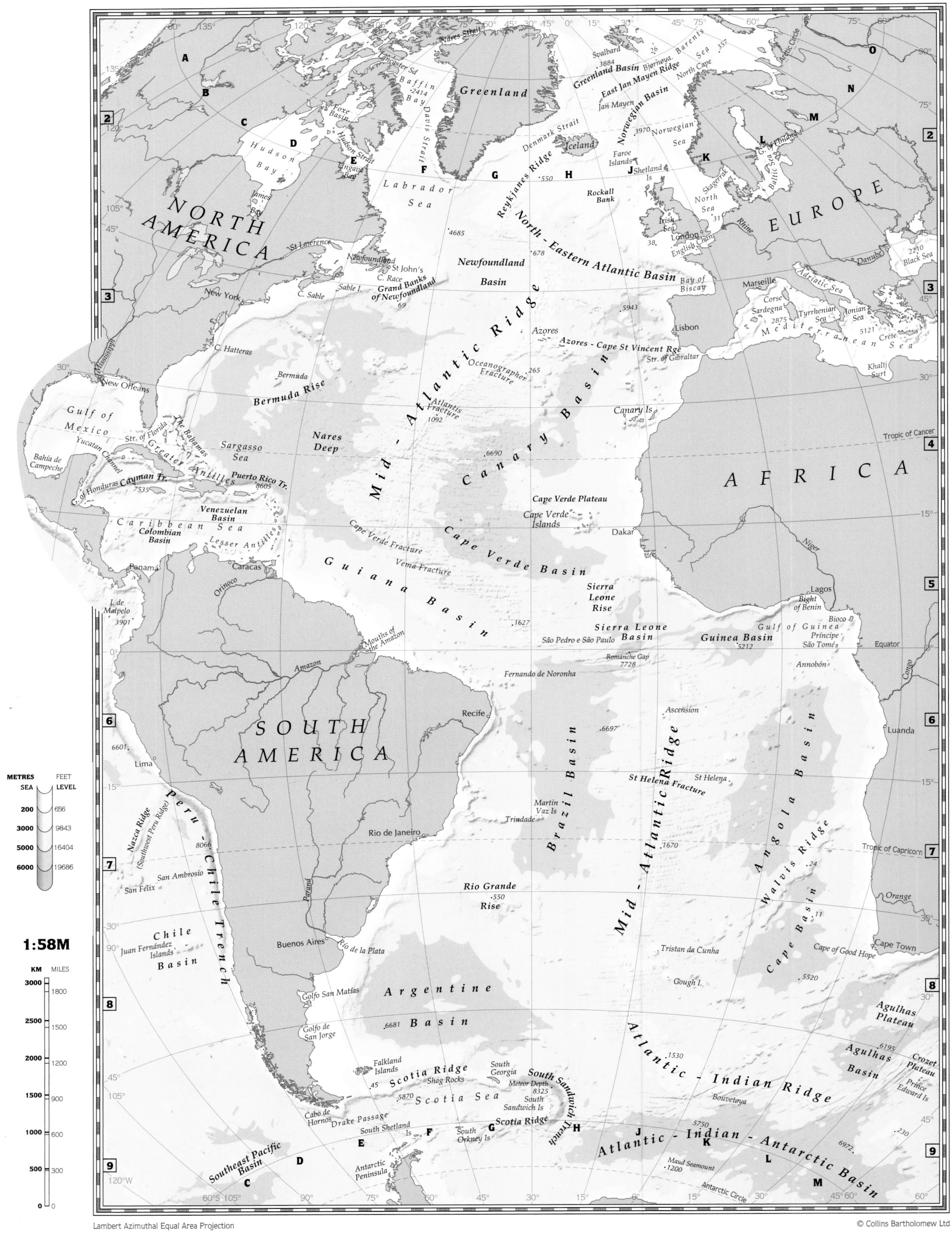

NORTH AMERICA

SOUTH AMERICA

EUROPE

AFRICA

Greenland

Iceland

Greenland Basin
East Jan Mayen Ridge
Norwegian Basin
Norwegian Sea
Jan Mayen
Spalbard
Bjørnøya
Barents Sea
North Cape

Reykjanes Ridge
Denmark Strait
Faroe Islands
Shetland Is

Labrador Sea
Davis Strait
Baffin Bay
Foxe Basin
Hudson Strait
Ungava Bay
Lancaster Sd
Nares Strait

Hudson Bay
James Bay

Rockall Bank
North-Eastern Atlantic Basin

North Sea
Skagerrak
Kattegat
Baltic Sea
G. of Finland
Irish Sea
London
English Channel
Rhine
Danube
Black Sea

Newfoundland Basin
Grand Banks of Newfoundland
Newfoundland
St John's
C. Race
C. Sable
Sable I.
St Lawrence
New York
C. Hatteras

Bay of Biscay
Lisbon
Marseille
Corse
Sardegna
Tyrrhenian Sea
Ionian Sea
Adriatic Sea
Crète
Mediterranean Sea
Str. of Gibraltar

Azores
Azores-Cape St Vincent Rge
Oceanographer Fracture
Atlantis Fracture
Canary Is
Tropic of Cancer

Bermuda
Bermuda Rise
Sargasso Sea
Nares Deep

Mid-Atlantic Ridge

Canary Basin

Khalij Surt

Gulf of Mexico
New Orleans
Bahía de Campeche
Yucatan Channel
Str. of Florida
The Bahamas
Greater Antilles
Cayman Tr.
G. of Honduras
Puerto Rico Tr.
Venezuelan Basin
Colombian Basin
Caribbean Sea
Lesser Antilles
Panama
Caracas
Orinoco

Cape Verde Plateau
Cape Verde Islands
Dakar

AFRICA

Cape Verde Fracture
Vema Fracture
Cape Verde Basin

Guiana Basin

Sierra Leone Rise
Sierra Leone Basin
São Pedro e São Paulo
Romanche Gap 7728

Guinea Basin
Gulf of Guinea
Bioco
Príncipe
São Tomé
Annobón
Lagos
Bight of Benin
Niger
Congo
Equator

Mouths of the Amazon
Amazon
Fernando de Noronha
Recife

SOUTH AMERICA

L. de Malpelo 3901
Lima
Nazca Ridge
Peru-Chile Trench
(Southwest Peru Ridge)
San Félix
San Ambrosio
Juan Fernández Islands
Chile Basin

Rio de Janeiro
Rio de la Plata
Paraná
Buenos Aires
Golfo San Matías
Golfo de San Jorge

Brazil Basin
St Helena Fracture
St Helena
Ascension
Martin Vaz Is
Trindade

Luanda
Angola Basin
Mid-Atlantic Ridge
Walvis Ridge
Cape Basin
Cape Town
Cape of Good Hope
Orange
Tropic of Capricorn

Rio Grande Rise

Argentine Basin
Falkland Islands
Scotia Ridge
Shag Rocks
South Georgia
Scotia Sea
South Sandwich Trench
South Sandwich Is
Meteor Depth 8325
Cabo de Hornos
Drake Passage
South Shetland Is
South Orkney Is
Scotia Ridge
Antarctic Peninsula

Tristan da Cunha
Gough I.

Atlantic-Indian Ridge

Agulhas Plateau
Agulhas Basin
Crozet Plateau
Prince Edward Is
Bouvetøya

Atlantic-Indian-Antarctic Basin
Maud Seamount 1200
Antarctic Circle

Southeast Pacific Basin

METRES SEA **FEET** LEVEL
200 — 656
3000 — 9843
5000 — 16404
6000 — 19686

1:58M

KM MILES
3000 — 1800
2500 — 1500
2000 — 1200
1500 — 900
1000 — 600
500 — 300
0 — 0

Lambert Azimuthal Equal Area Projection

© Collins Bartholomew Ltd

ASIA
AFRICA
AUSTRALIA
ANTARCTICA
SOUTHERN OCEAN
Black Sea
Caspian Sea
Aral Sea
Mediterranean Sea
Red Sea
The Gulf
Gulf of Oman
Gulf of Aden
Arabian Sea
Arabian Basin
Bay of Bengal
Andaman Basin
South China Sea
East China Sea
Yellow Sea
Sea of Japan
Java Sea
Flores Sea
Banda Sea
Timor Sea
Arafura Sea
Celebes Sea
Sulu Sea
Somali Basin
Mascarene Basin
Mid - Indian Basin
West Australian Basin
Madagascar Basin
Crozet Basin
Natal Basin
Agulhas Basin
Agulhas Plateau
Crozet Plateau
Kerguelen Plateau
Carlsberg Ridge
Chagos - Laccadive Ridge
Mascarene Ridge
Ninetyeast Ridge
Mid Indian Ridge
Southwest Indian Ridge
Madagascar Ridge
Mozambique Ridge
W. Australian Ridge
Java Ridge
Java Trench (Sunda Trench)
Indian - Antarctic Basin
Indian - Antarctic Ridge
Atlantic - Indian - Antarctic Basin
Pacific - Antarctic Ridge
South Australian Basin
Great Australian Bight
Exmouth Plateau
Naturaliste Plateau
Tasman Basin
Tasman Plateau
Weddell Sea
Scotia Sea
Ross Sea
Davis Sea
Tropic of Cancer
Tropic of Capricorn
Equator
Antarctic Circle
South Pole
Lambert Azimuthal Equal Area Projection
© Collins Bartholomew Ltd
METRES SEA LEVEL FEET
200 656
3000 9843
5000 16404
6000 19686
1:58M
KM MILES
3000 1800
2500 1500
2000 1200
1500 900
1000 600
500 300
0 0

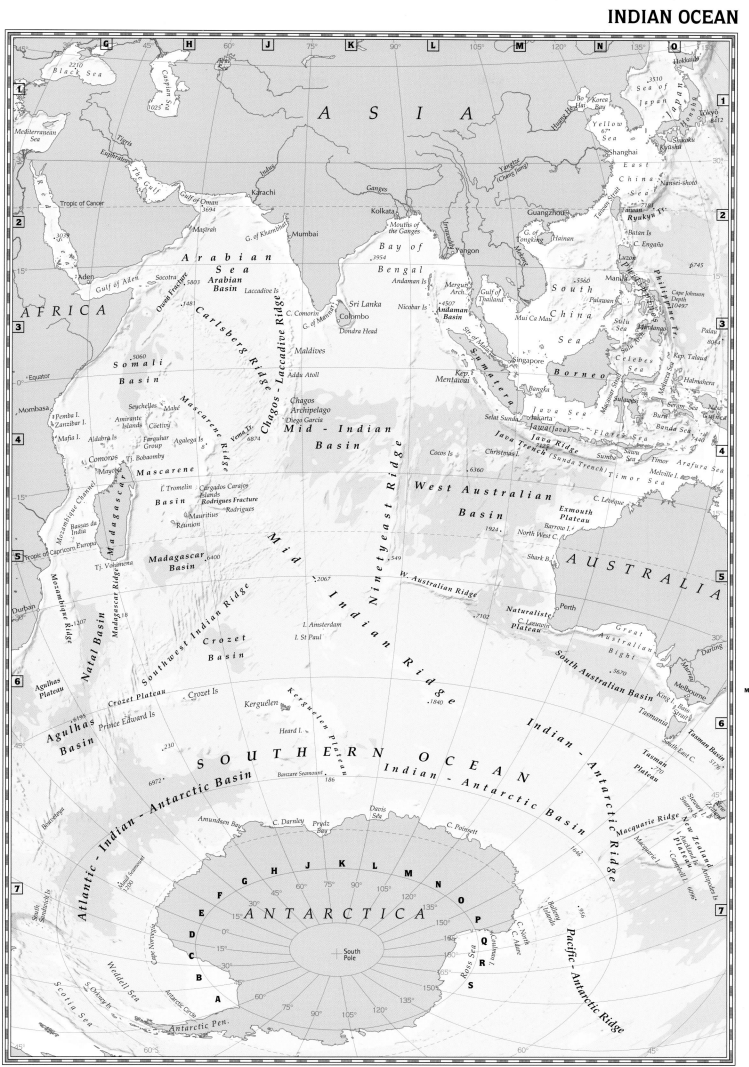

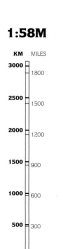

14

O. Vrangelya
Chukchi Sea
Arctic Circle
Anadyrskiy Zaliv
St Lawrence I.
Zaliv Shelikhova
St Matthew I.
Bering Strait
Nunivak I.
Pribilof Is
Sea of Okhotsk
Bering Sea
Attu I. Aleutian Islands
Andreanof Is. Unalask
7822
Aleutian Trench
Emperor Seamount-Chain
Aleutian Trench
Ostrov Sakhalin
3916
Hokkaido
Kuril'skiye Ostrova
Kuril Trench
6671
1240
7900
Sea of Japan
Honshu
Vityaz Depth 10542
183 73
Tōkyō
6412
Hachijō-jima
Ramapo Deep 10374
18
Kyūshū
Ogasawara-shotō
6345
Kure Atoll Hawaiian Is
104 Midway Is
Necker I.
Laysan I. Gardner Pinnacles
Hawaiian R.

ASIA
Tropic of Cancer
Ganges
Argun
3
B
C
D
E
F
G
H

Huang He Bo Korea Hai Bay
Yangtze (Chang Jiang)
Yellow Sea
67
Shanghai
Shikoku
3510

45°
90°
105°
60°
120°
135°
150°
165°
180°
165°

30°

4

East China Sea
Nansei-shotō
Daito-jima
Kazan-rettō 9156
Mariana Ridge
Magellan Seamounts
Mid - Pacific Mountains
1823
Johnston Atoll
Wake I.
Guangzhou
Bay of Bengal 3954
Mouth of the Ganges
Irrawaddy
G. of Tongking
Hainan
Taiwan
Taiwan Strait Tr.
Ryukyu Tr.
South Honshu Ridge
Kyushu - Palau Ridge
Japan Tr.

15°

Andaman Is Mergui Arch.
Andaman Basin 4507
Nicobar Is
Sri Lanka
Gulf of Thailand
Mekong
5560
Manila
Luzon Strait
C. Engaño
Luzon
Batan Is
6745
Challenger Deep 10920
Mariana Trench
1564
Saipan
Rota
Guam
31
Taongi
MICRONESIA
6530
POLYNESIA
Palmyra Atoll
6957
Terain

5

Sumatra
Str. of Malacca
Kep. Mentawai
Singapore
South China Sea
Palawan
Cape Johnson Depth 10497
Philippine Trench
Sulu Sea Mindanao
Sulu Arch.
Kep. Talaud
Celebes Sea
Yap 8597
Palau 8054
Yap Tr.
Palau Tr.
Eauripik Rise
W. Caroline Basin
E. Caroline Basin
Gaferut Pikelot
Hall Is Chuuk
Pohnpei
Enewetak Bikini Rongelap
Kwajalein Wotje
Ailinglapalap Majuro
Ebon
Butaritari
Kosrae
Nomoi Is
Kapingamarangi Rise
Caroline Islands
Kapingamarangi
7208
Marshall Islands
Abaiang
Nauru
Banaba
Tabiteuea
Onotoa
Kiribati
Nonouti
Howland I.
Baker I.
Kanton I.
Phoenix Islands
McKean I.
Nikumaroro
Manra
Orona

Equator 0

Borneo
Sulawesi
T'k Tomini
Buru
Seram Sea
Halmahera
Molucca Sea
Banda Sea
Admiralty Is
Bismarck Sea
New Ireland
New Britain
Planet Deep 9140
New Guinea
Solomon Islands
Solomon Sea
D'Entrecasteaux Is
8487
Santa Cruz Is
Rotuma
Nanumea Tuvalu
Vaitupu
Nukufetau Funafuti
Nukulaelae
Atafu
Samoan Islands
Tokelau
Savaii
Manihiki
Danger Is
Nassau
MELANESIA

Java Sea
Jakarta
7440
Kep. Aru
Flores Sea
Kep. Tanimbar
Bangka
Bangka
Selat Sunda
Jawa (Java)
Flores
Sawu Sea
Sumba
Timor
G. of Papua
Port Moresby
Arafura Sea
Torres Strait
C. York
Louisiade Arch.
Rennell
Coral Sea Basin
Espiritu Santo
Vanua Levu
Upolu
Tutuila
Manua Is
Suvorov
Îles Wallis
13
Îles de Hoorn

Mid - Indian Basin
Java Trench (Sunda Trench) 7125
Java Ridge
Melville I.
C. Arnhem
66
Gulf of Carpentaria
Timor Sea
Coral Sea
Banks Is
Vanua Levu
Vitt Levu
Fiji
Vava'u Group
Tofua
Niue
Coo Island

6

Christmas I.
Cocos Is
6360
C. Lévêque
Timor Sea
Great Barrier Reef
Coral Sea
Vanuatu
Tanna
Erromango
Îles Loyauté
New Caledonia
7633
Hunter I.
Tonga
Tongatapu Group
Tonga Tr.
Horizon Depth 10882
Palmerston I.

15°

Ninetyeast Ridge
West Australian Basin
Exmouth Plateau
Barrow I.
North West C.
1924
Brisbane
AUSTRALIA
Île des Pins
Lord Howe Ridge
New Caledonia Island Ridge
Norfolk Island Ridge
South Fiji Basin
Norfolk I.
Raoul
Kermadec Tr.
10047
Sou
Pacif

Shark B.
Darling
Lord Howe I.
Tasman Sea
Auckland
North Island
East C.

7

W. Australian Ridge
Naturaliste Plateau 7102
C. Leeuwin
Great Australian Bight
Spencer G.
Murray
Melbourne
King I.
Bass Strait
Tasmania
South East C.
5670
South Australian Basin
Sydney
New Zealand
Lord Howe Rise
Tasman Sea
Tasman Basin 5176
South Island
Wellington
Chatham Rise
Chatham Is

Tropic of Capricorn
549
Tasman Plateau 770
Stewart I.
Bounty Is
Campbell Plateau
Auckland Is
Campbell I.
Antipodes Is
6096

Mid - Indian Ridge
9067
Indian - Antarctic Ridge
Indian - Antarctic Basin
1646
Balleny Islands
Fisher Bay
C. North
C. Adare
Coulman I.
Ross Sea
C. Poinsett
956

8

30°
45°S
90°E
60°
105°
120°
135°
150°
165°
180°

G H
F
E
D
C
B

METRES SEA | FEET LEVEL
200 | 656
3000 | 9843
5000 | 16404
6000 | 19686

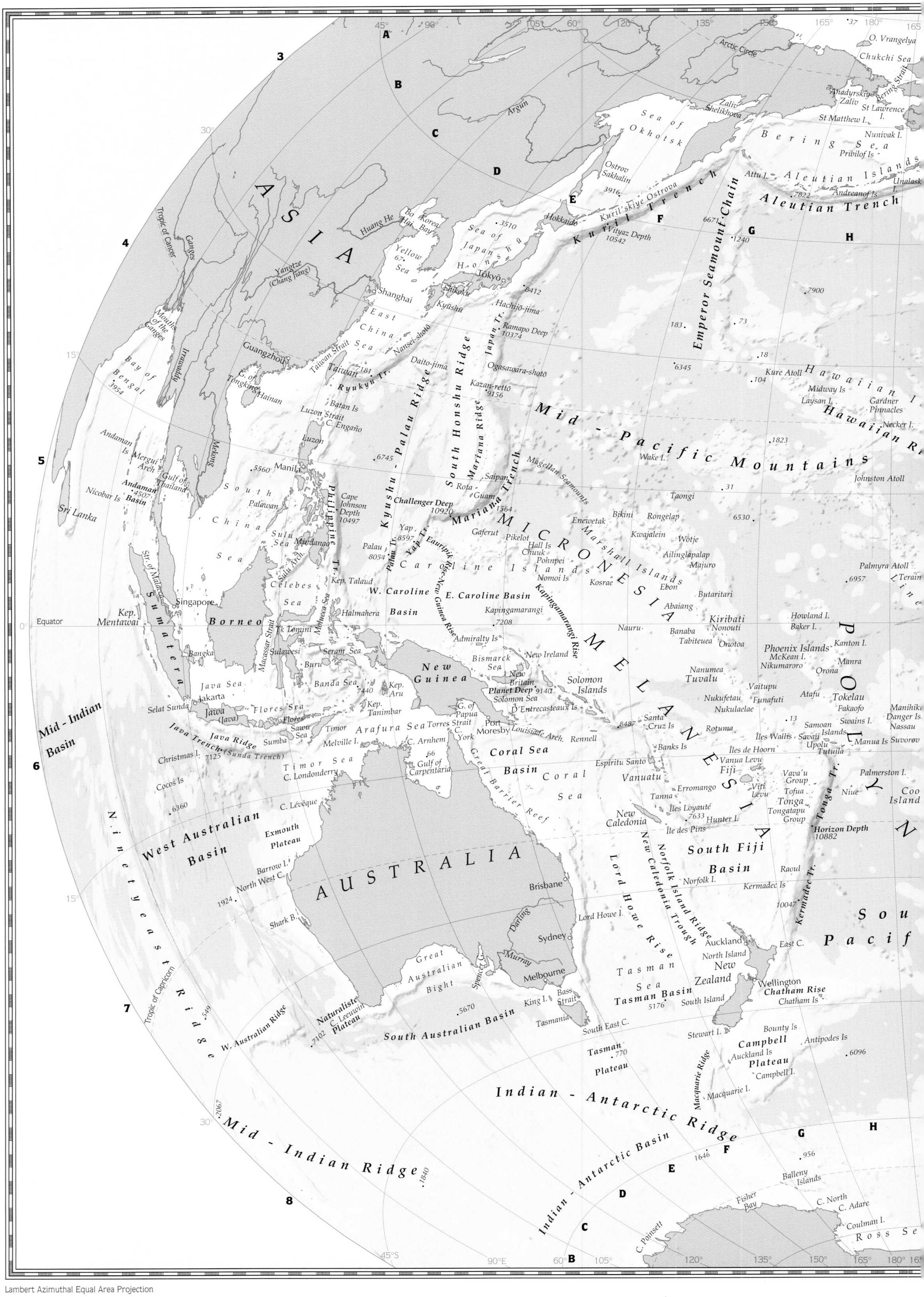

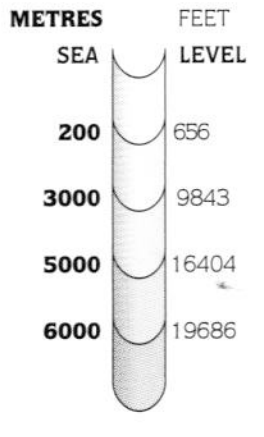

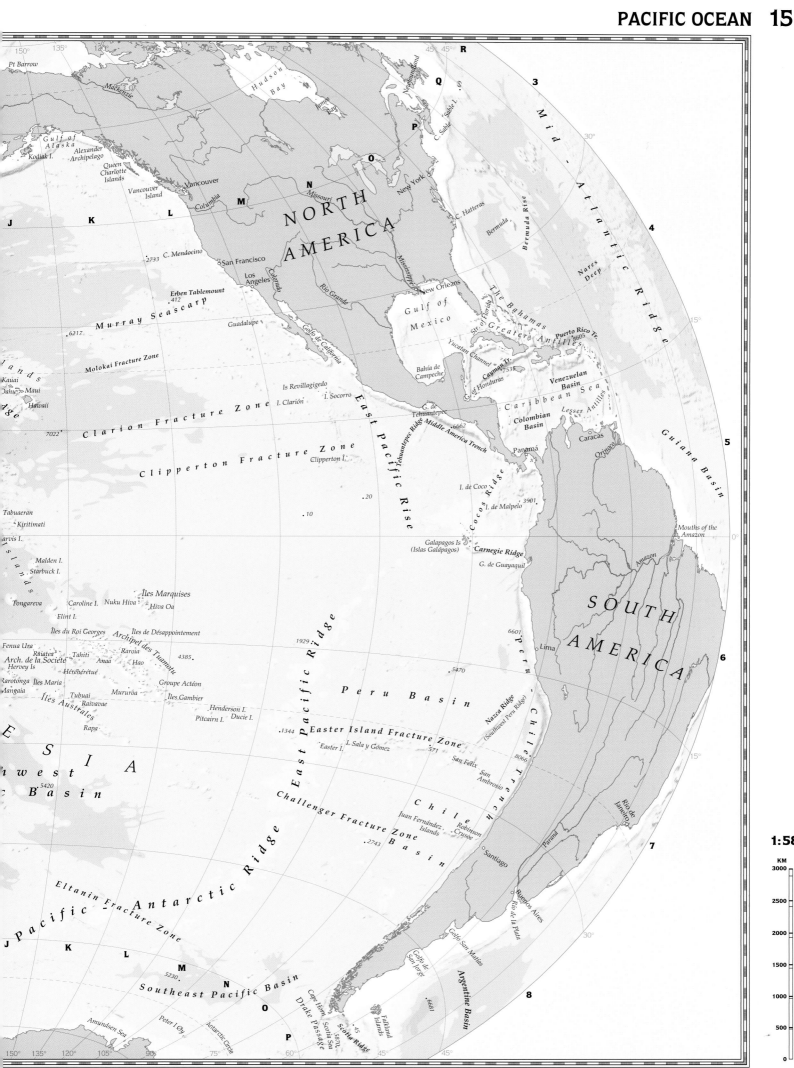

Pt Barrow

Mackenzie

Gulf of
Alaska
Kodiak I.
Queen
Charlotte
Islands
Alexander
Archipelago
Vancouver
Island
Vancouver

Hudson
Bay

Newfoundland

R
Q
69°
P
C. Sable
O
New York
C. Hatteras

Bermuda Rise

3

Mid - Atlantic Ridge

30°

Nares
Deep

4

J
K
L
M
N
Columbia
Missouri

NORTH

AMERICA

.2733 C. Mendocino
San Francisco
Los
Angeles
Colorado
Rio Grande

Erben Tablemount
.412

Murray Seascarp

.6217
Guadalupe
Golfo de California

New Orleans
Gulf of
Mexico
The Bahamas
Str. of Florida
Greater Antilles
Puerto Rico Tr.
8605
Bermuda

15°

Molokai Fracture Zone

lands
Kauai
Oahu Maui
Hawaii
dge

Is Revillagigedo
I. Clarión
I. Socorro

Clarion Fracture Zone

7022.

Clipperton Fracture Zone
Clipperton I.

East Pacific Rise
Tehuantepec Ridge Middle America Trench

G. de
Tehuantepec
.6662

Bahía de
Campeche
Yucatan Channel
G. of Honduras
Cayman Tr.
7535

Venezuelan
Basin
Colombian
Basin

Caribbean Sea
Lesser Antilles
Caracas
Orinoco

Guiana Basin

5

Tabuaeran
Kiritimati

arvis I.
slands

.20

.10

I. de Coco
Cocos Ridge
I. de Malpelo
3901.

Mouths of the
Amazon

0°

Galapagos Is
(Islas Galápagos)
Carnegie Ridge
G. de Guayaquil

Amazon

Malden I.
Starbuck I.

Îles Marquises
Nuku Hiva
Caroline I. Hiva Oa

SOUTH

Tongareva
Flint I.
Îles du Roi Georges
Archipel des Tuamotu
Îles de Désappointement

East Pacific Ridge

1929.

6601
Lima
Peru-Chile Trench

AMERICA

6

Fenua Ura
Raiatea Tahiti
Arch. de la Société
Hervey Is
Rarotonga Îles Maria
Mangaia
Anaa
Hao
Raroia
4385.
Héréhérétué
Groupe Actéon
Mururoa
Îles Gambier
Tubuai Raivavae
Îles Australes
Rapa

Henderson I.
Pitcairn I. Ducie I.

Peru Basin

.5470

Nazca Ridge
(Southwest Peru Ridge)

Easter Island Fracture Zone
.1344
Easter I. I. Sala y Gómez
571
San Félix
San
Ambrosio

8066

15°

ESIA

hwest
.5420
Basin

Challenger Fracture Zone
Basin

Chile Basin
Juan Fernández
Islands
Robinson
Crusoe

Rio de
Janeiro

Paraná

7

.2743

Santiago

1:58M

Pacific - Antarctic Ridge
Eltanin Fracture Zone

J
K
L
M
5230.
N
O

Southeast Pacific Basin
Amundsen Sea
Peter I Øy
Antarctic Circle
Cape Horn
Drake Passage
Scotia Ridge
Scotia Sea
5872
Falkland
Islands
6601

Buenos Aires
Río de la Plata
Golfo San Matías
Golfo de
San Jorge
Argentine Basin

30°

8

P

45°

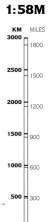

KM MILES
3000 — 1800
2500 — 1500
2000 — 1200
1500 — 900
1000 — 600
500 — 300
0 — 0

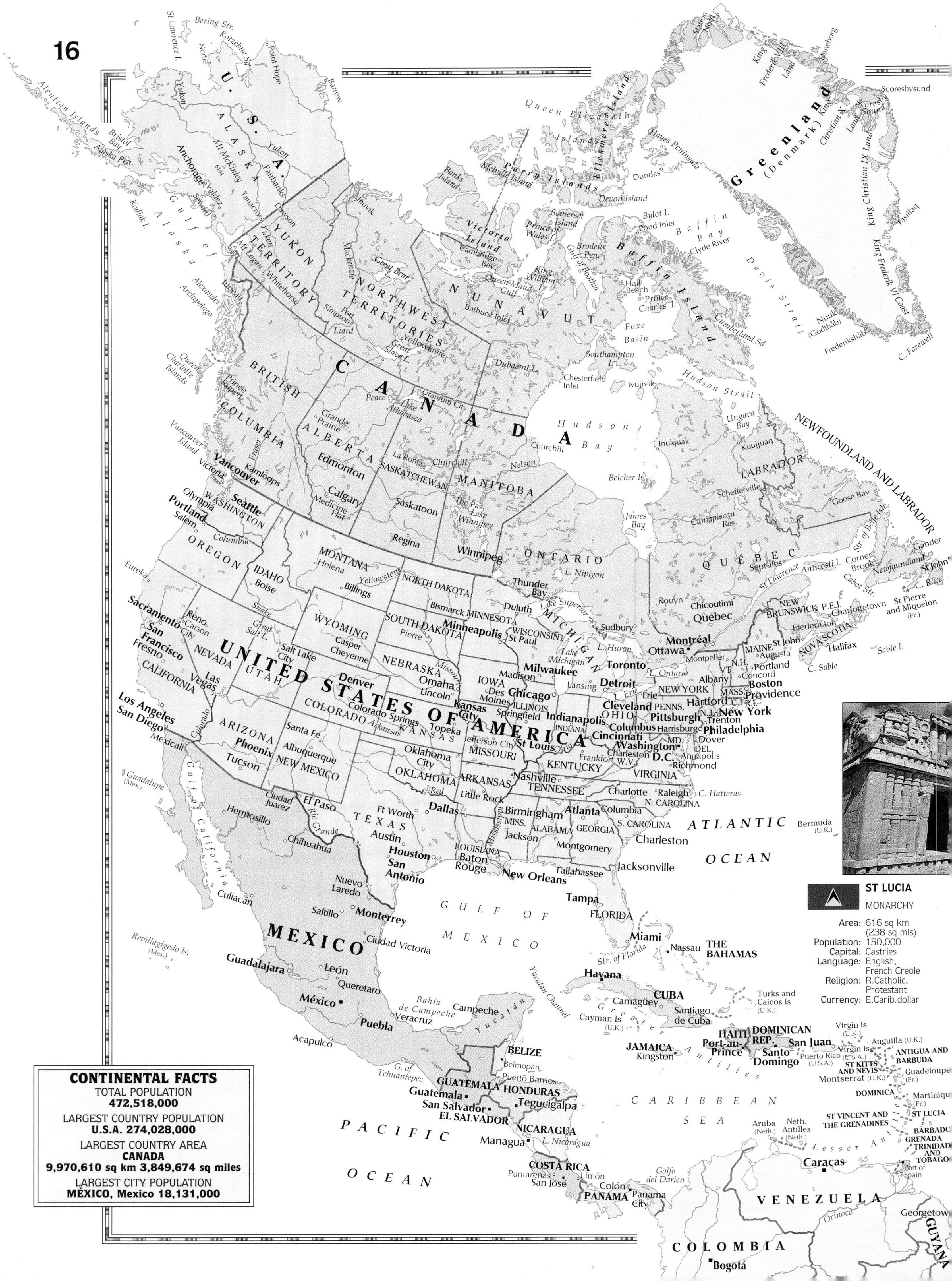

Bering Str.
St Lawrence I.
Kotzebue Sd
Nome
Point Hope
Barrow

Aleutian Islands
Bristol Bay
Alaska Pen.
Kodiak I.
Gulf of Alaska
Alexander Archipelago
Queen Charlotte Islands

U. S. A.

A L A S K A
Mt McKinley
Anchorage
Valdez
Seward
Fairbanks
Tanacross
Yukon

Yukon
Dawson
Mayo
Whitehorse
Watson

**Y U K O N
T E R R I T O R Y**

**N O R T H W E S T
T E R R I T O R I E S**

Mackenzie
Fort Simpson
Liard
Yellowknife
Great Slave L.
Uranium City
Great Bear L.
Peace

**B R I T I S H
C O L U M B I A**
Prince Rupert
Vancouver Island
Kamloops
Fraser
Vancouver
Victoria

C A N A D A

Inuvik

N U N A V U T

Banks Island
Victoria Island
Prince of Wales I.
King William I.
Queen Maud Gulf
Cambridge Bay
Gulf of Boothia
Somerset Island
Prince of Wales I.
Bathurst Inlet

Parry Islands
Melville Island
Devon Island
Bylot I.
Pond Inlet

Queen Elizabeth Islands
Ellesmere Island

King Frederik VIII Land
Christian X Land
Peary Land
Danneborg
Scoresbysund

**G r e e n l a n d
(Denmark)**
King Christian IX Land
King Frederik VI Coast
Scoresby Sound
Scoresbysund

Hayes Peninsula
Dundas
Nuuk (Godthåb)
Frederikshåb
C. Farewell

Baffin Bay
Clyde River
Brodeur Pen.
Baffin Island
Hall Beach
Foxe Basin
Southampton I.
Chesterfield Inlet
Dubawnt L.
Ivujivik

Davis Strait
Cumberland Sd

Hudson Strait
Ungava Bay
Inukjuak
Kuujjuaq

**H u d s o n
B a y**
Churchill
Belcher Is
James Bay
Caniapiscau Res.
Schefferville

N E W F O U N D L A N D   A N D   L A B R A D O R
L A B R A D O R
Goose Bay

Q U É B E C
Rouyn
Chicoutimi
Sept-Iles
St Lawrence
Anticosti I.
Corner Brook
Gander
Newfoundland
St John's
C. Race
Str. of Belle Isle
Cabot Str.

Point Lake
La Ronge
Lake Athabasca
Fort Liard

A L B E R T A
Grande Prairie
Edmonton
Calgary
Medicine Hat

S A S K A T C H E W A N
La Ronge
Saskatoon
Regina
Churchill

M A N I T O B A
the Pas
Lake Winnipeg
Nelson
Winnipeg

O N T A R I O
Thunder Bay
L. Nipigon
Sudbury
Ottawa
Montréal
Toronto
Québec

Duluth
Lake Superior

M I C H I G A N
L. Huron
L. Michigan
Lansing
Detroit
Milwaukee
Madison

W I S C O N S I N
St Paul
Minneapolis

Montpelier
N.H.
MAINE
St John
Portland
Augusta
Concord
Fredericton
NEW BRUNSWICK P.E.I.
Charlottetown
St Pierre and Miquelon
(Fr.)
NOVA SCOTIA
Halifax
Sable I.
C. Sable

WASHINGTON
Seattle
Olympia
Portland
Salem
Columbia

OREGON
Eureka

IDAHO
Boise

MONTANA
Helena
Billings
Yellowstone

NORTH DAKOTA
Bismarck

SOUTH DAKOTA
Pierre

MINNESOTA

Sacramento
Reno
Carson City
San Francisco
Fresno

NEVADA
Las Vegas

CALIFORNIA
Los Angeles
San Diego

Salt Lake City
Great Salt L.

UTAH

WYOMING
Casper
Cheyenne

Snake
Colorado

NEBRASKA
Lincoln
Omaha

IOWA
Des Moines

ILLINOIS
Springfield

Madison

Chicago

Lake Michigan

UNITED STATES OF AMERICA

Denver
Colorado Springs

COLORADO

Topeka
Kansas City

KANSAS

Missouri

St Louis

MISSOURI
Jefferson City

INDIANA
Indianapolis

Cincinnati

OHIO
Columbus

KENTUCKY
Frankfort

Erie
L. Erie
Cleveland
Pittsburgh

PENNS.
Harrisburg

NEW YORK
Albany
L. Ontario

Toronto

MASS.
Boston
Providence
Hartford
C.T.R.I.

Trenton
N.J.
New York
Philadelphia

DEL.
Dover
MD.
Annapolis
Washington
D.C.
Richmond
W.V.
Charleston

VIRGINIA

Nashville

TENNESSEE
Charlotte
Raleigh
N. CAROLINA
C. Hatteras

ARIZONA
Phoenix
Tucson

Santa Fe
Albuquerque

NEW MEXICO

Oklahoma City

OKLAHOMA
Red

ARKANSAS
Little Rock

MISS.
Birmingham
Jackson

ALABAMA
Montgomery

GEORGIA
Atlanta

S. CAROLINA
Columbia
Charleston

Mexicali
Guadalupe (Mex.)

Hermosillo

Ciudad Juárez
El Paso
Rio Grande

TEXAS
Ft Worth
Dallas
Austin
San Antonio
Houston

LOUISIANA
Baton Rouge
New Orleans

Chihuahua

Nuevo Laredo

Tallahassee
Jacksonville

FLORIDA
Tampa
Miami

Gulf of California

Culiacán
Saltillo
Monterrey
Ciudad Victoria

MEXICO

Guadalajara
León
Querétaro
México
Puebla
Veracruz
Campeche
Bahía de Campeche

Acapulco

Revillagigedo Is. (Mex.)

**G U L F   O F
M E X I C O**

Nassau
THE BAHAMAS
Str. of Florida

Havana
CUBA
Camagüey
Santiago de Cuba

Cayman Is (U.K.)

Turks and Caicos Is (U.K.)

**ATLANTIC
OCEAN**
Bermuda (U.K.)

HAITI
Port-au-Prince
DOMINICAN REP.
Santo Domingo
San Juan
Puerto Rico (U.S.A.)
Virgin Is (U.K.)
Virgin Is (U.S.A.)
Anguilla (U.K.)
ANTIGUA AND BARBUDA
ST KITTS AND NEVIS
Montserrat (U.K.)
Guadeloupe (Fr.)

JAMAICA
Kingston

Lesser Antilles
Greater Antilles

**C A R I B B E A N
S E A**
Aruba (Neth.)
Neth. Antilles (Neth.)

DOMINICA
Martinique (Fr.)
ST LUCIA
ST VINCENT AND THE GRENADINES
BARBADOS
GRENADA
TRINIDAD AND TOBAGO
Port of Spain

Yucatán
Yucatán Channel

BELIZE
Belmopan
Puerto Barrios
GUATEMALA
Guatemala
HONDURAS
Tegucigalpa
San Salvador
EL SALVADOR
NICARAGUA
Managua
L. Nicaragua

G. of Tehuantepec

**PACIFIC
OCEAN**

Puntarenas
COSTA RICA
San José
Limón
Colón
PANAMA
Panama City
Golfo del Darién

Caracas
VENEZUELA
Orinoco

COLOMBIA
Bogotá

Georgetown
GUYANA

CONTINENTAL FACTS
TOTAL POPULATION
472,518,000
LARGEST COUNTRY POPULATION
U.S.A. 274,028,000
LARGEST COUNTRY AREA
CANADA
9,970,610 sq km 3,849,674 sq miles
LARGEST CITY POPULATION
MÉXICO, Mexico 18,131,000

New York. Covering an area of 777 sq km, the city is made up of five boroughs, of which only one, the Bronx, is on the mainland.

CANADA
FEDERATION

Area: 9,970,610 sq km
(3,849,674 sq mls)
Population: 30,563,000
Capital: Ottawa
Language: English, French,
Amerindian
Languages,
Inuktitut
Religion: R.Catholic,
Protestant,
Greek Orthodox
Currency: Canadian dollar

UNITED STATES OF AMERICA (USA)
REPUBLIC

Area: 9,809,378 sq km
(3,787,422 sq mls)
Population: 274,028,000
Capital: Washington
Language: English, Spanish,
Amerindian
Languages
Religion: Protestant,
R.Catholic,
Muslim, Jewish
Currency: US dollar

MEXICO
REPUBLIC

Area: 1,972,545 sq km
(761,604 sq mls)
Population: 95,831,000
Capital: México (Mexico City)
Language: Spanish, Amerindian
Languages
Religion: R.Catholic,
Protestant
Currency: Mexican peso

THE BAHAMAS
MONARCHY

Area: 13,939 sq km
(5,382 sq mls)
Population: 296,000
Capital: Nassau
Language: English, Creole,
French Creole
Religion: Protestant,
R.Catholic
Currency: Bahamian dollar

CUBA
REPUBLIC

Area: 110,860 sq km
(42,803 sq mls)
Population: 11,116,000
Capital: Havana (La Habana)
Language: Spanish
Religion: R.Catholic,
Protestant
Currency: Cuban peso

JAMAICA
MONARCHY

Area: 10,991 sq km
(4,244 sq mls)
Population: 2,538,000
Capital: Kingston
Language: English, Creole
Religion: Protestant,
R.Catholic,
Rastafarian
Currency: Jamaican dollar

GUATEMALA
REPUBLIC

Area: 108,890 sq km
(42,043 sq mls)
Population: 10,801,000
Capital: Guatemala
(Guatemala City)
Language: Spanish
Mayan Languages
Religion: R.Catholic,
Protestant
Currency: Quetzal, US dollar

BELIZE
MONARCHY

Area: 22,965 sq km
(8,867 sq mls)
Population: 230,000
Capital: Belmopan
Language: English, Creole,
Spanish, Mayan
Religion: R.Catholic,
Protestant, Hindu
Currency: Belize dollar

EL SALVADOR
REPUBLIC

Area: 21,041 sq km
(8,124 sq mls)
Population: 6,032,000
Capital: San Salvador
Language: Spanish
Religion: R.Catholic, Protestant
Currency: El Salvador colón,
US dollar

DOMINICAN REPUBLIC
REPUBLIC

Area: 48,442 sq km
(18,704 sq mls)
Population: 8,232,000
Capital: Santo Domingo
Language: Spanish,
French Creole
Religion: R.Catholic,
Protestant
Currency: Dominican peso

HAITI
REPUBLIC

Area: 27,750 sq km
(10,714 sq mls)
Population: 7,952,000
Capital: Port-au-Prince
Language: French,
French Creole
Religion: R.Catholic,
Protestant, Voodoo
Currency: Gourde

HONDURAS
REPUBLIC

Area: 112,088 sq km
(43,277 sq mls)
Population: 6,147,000
Capital: Tegucigalpa
Language: Spanish,
Amerindian
Languages
Religion: R.Catholic,
Protestant
Currency: Lempira

NICARAGUA
REPUBLIC

Area: 130,000 sq km
(50,193 sq mls)
Population: 4,807,000
Capital: Managua
Language: Spanish, Amerindian
Languages
Religion: R.Catholic,
Protestant
Currency: Córdoba

COSTA RICA
REPUBLIC

Area: 51,100 sq km
(19,730 sq mls)
Population: 3,841,000
Capital: San José
Language: Spanish
Religion: R.Catholic,
Protestant
Currency: Costa Rican colón

PANAMA
REPUBLIC

Area: 77,082 sq km
(29,762 sq mls)
Population: 2,767,000
Capital: Panamá (Panama
City)
Language: Spanish, English
Creole, Amerindian
Languages
Religion: R.Catholic,
Protestant, Sunni
Muslim, Baha'i
Currency: Balboa

ANTIGUA AND BARBUDA
MONARCHY

Area: 442 sq km
(171 sq mls)
Population: 67,000
Capital: St John's
Language: English, Creole
Religion: Protestant,
R.Catholic
Currency: E.Carib.dollar

BARBADOS
MONARCHY

Area: 430 sq km
(166 sq mls)
Population: 268,000
Capital: Bridgetown
Language: English, Creole
(Bajan)
Religion: Protestant,
R.Catholic
Currency: Barbados dollar

Sayil, Yucatan, Mexico. Mayan palace of about 85 rooms built between 6thC and 9thC AD.

DOMINICA
REPUBLIC

Area: 750 sq km
(290 sq mls)
Population: 71,000
Capital: Roseau
Language: English, French Creole
Religion: R.Catholic, Protestant
Currency: E.Carib.dollar

ST KITTS AND NEVIS
MONARCHY

Area: 261 sq km
(101 sq mls)
Population: 39,000
Capital: Basseterre
Language: English, Creole
Religion: Protestant,
R.Catholic
Currency: E.Carib.dollar

ST VINCENT AND THE GRENADINES
MONARCHY

Area: 389 sq km
(150 sq mls)
Population: 112,000
Capital: Kingstown
Language: English, Creole
Religion: Protestant,
R.Catholic
Currency: E.Carib.dollar

TRINIDAD AND TOBAGO
REPUBLIC

Area: 5,130 sq km
(1,981 sq mls)
Population: 1,283,000
Capital: Port of Spain
Language: English, Creole,Hindi
Religion: R.Catholic, Hindu,
Protestant, Muslim
Currency: Trinidad and
Tobago dollar

GRENADA
MONARCHY

Area: 378 sq km
(146 sq mls)
Population: 93,000
Capital: St George's
Language: English, Creole
Religion: R.Catholic,
Protestant
Currency: E.Carib.dollar

POPULATION

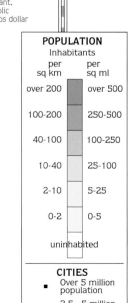

POPULATION
Inhabitants

per sq km	per sq ml
over 200	over 500
100-200	250-500
40-100	100-250
10-40	25-100
2-10	5-25
0-2	0-5
uninhabited	

CITIES
■ Over 5 million population
● 2.5 - 5 million population

Paramaribo

Cayenne

SURINAME French Guiana

18

St Lawrence I. Nunivak I. Nunivak L. Seward Pen. Norton Sound **Brooks Range** Pt Barrow

Beaufort Sea

Queen Elizabeth Islands
Ellef Ringnes I. Axel Heiberg Island
Prince Patrick Island Borden I.
Meighen I. Parry Islands Devon I.

King Frederik VIII Land
Shannon I. King Oscar Fj. Scoresby Sound
Christian X Land King Christian IX Land
King Frederik VI Coast

Greenland

Aleutian Is. Alaska Pen. **Mt McKinley**
Kodiak I. **Alaska Range** Mt Logan
Yukon Porcupine

Banks I.
Melville I.

Victoria Island
Prince of Wales I. Somerset Boothia Pen.
Bylot I. *Baffin Bay*
Qeqertarsuaq (Disko)

Alexander Archipelago
Dixon Entrance
Queen Charlotte Islands
Vancouver Island

Coast Mountains Stikine Mts Mackenzie **Mackenzie Mts** Liard Great Bear
Great Slave Caribou Mts Peace
Lake Athabasca Wollaston L. Reindeer L. Southern Indian L. Churchill
Dubawnt L.
G. of Boothia
King William I.
Melville Peninsula Prince Charles I.
Foxe Basin Nettilling L. **Baffin Island** Cumberland Pen. Cumberland Sd
Home B. Frobisher B.
Davis Strait C. Farewell

Gulf of Alaska

Cassiar Mts

C. Blanco
Columbia **ROCKY MOUNTAINS** F.D. Roosevelt L. Fort Peck Res.
Snake Yellowstone L. Sakakawea L. Oahe
Cascade Range Bitterroot Ra.
Sierra Nevada Great Basin Great Salt L.
Colorado Plateau Grand Canyon Colorado
Missouri Arkansas
Nelson Severn
L. Winnipegosis Lake Winnipeg Lake of the Woods L. Nipigon

Southampton I.
Coats I. Mansel I.
Hudson Bay
Belcher Is James Bay
Ungava Bay
Labrador L. Bienville Caniapiscau Res. Smallwood Res. La Grande Res.

C. Chidley Hudson Strait
Labrador Sea

Newfoundland
St Lawrence Anticosti I. Str. of Belle Isle
Gulf of St Lawrence Cabot Str. St Pierre and Miquelon C. Race
Cape Breton I. Sable I.
B. of Fundy
Massachusetts Bay C. Sable
C. Cod
Long I.
Chesapeake B.

Lake Superior
L. Michigan L. Huron L. Ontario L. Erie
Ohio
Allegheny Mts
Appalachian Mts
Ozark Plateau
Llano Estacado Red Mississippi
Rio Grande **Edwards Plateau**
C. Hatteras
C. Fear

Bermuda

Baja California *Gulf of California*
Sierra Madre Occidental
I. Socorro

Sierra Madre Oriental
Bahía de Campeche
Yucatán
Sa Madre del Sur

ATLANTIC OCEAN

C. Canaveral
Gd Bahama
Gt Abaco
Str. of Florida Andros
Acklins I.
Gt Inagua Turks and Caicos Is
Cuba
Cayman Is
Yucatán Channel
Greater Antilles
Hispaniola Puerto Rico Anguilla
Virgin Is
Jamaica *Lesser Antilles* Guadeloupe
Dominica Martinique
St Lucia

GULF OF MEXICO

PACIFIC OCEAN

G. of Honduras
L. Nicarâgua
Pen. de Nicoya
Golfo del Darién
Orinoco

CARIBBEAN SEA
Aruba Neth. Antilles
Trinidad

<table>
<tr><td colspan="2">**CONTINENTAL FACTS**</td></tr>
<tr><td colspan="2">TOTAL AREA</td></tr>
<tr><td>24,680,331 sq km</td><td>9,529,129 sq miles</td></tr>
<tr><td colspan="2">HIGHEST PEAK, MT McKINLEY</td></tr>
<tr><td>6,194 m</td><td>20,321 ft</td></tr>
<tr><td colspan="2">LARGEST LAKE, SUPERIOR</td></tr>
<tr><td>82,100 sq km</td><td>31,698 sq miles</td></tr>
<tr><td colspan="2">LONGEST RIVER, MISSISSIPPI-MISSOURI</td></tr>
<tr><td>5,969 km</td><td>3,709 miles</td></tr>
</table>

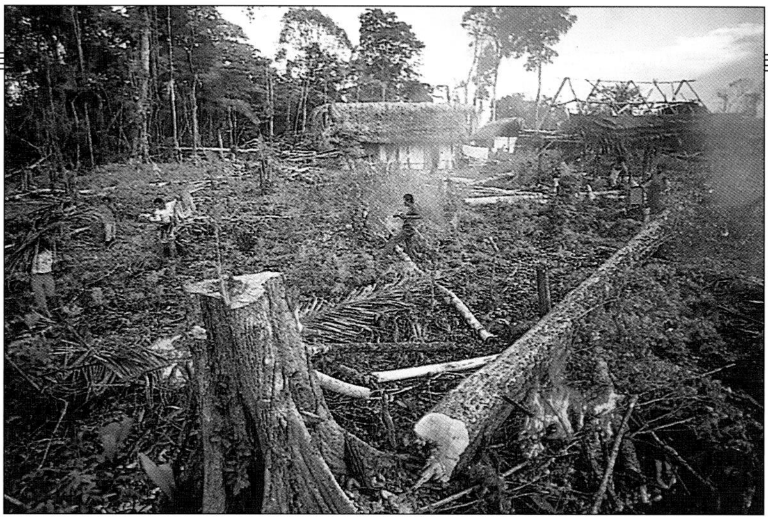

Guatemala. Deforestation as a result of pressure for land to sustain families and their crops.

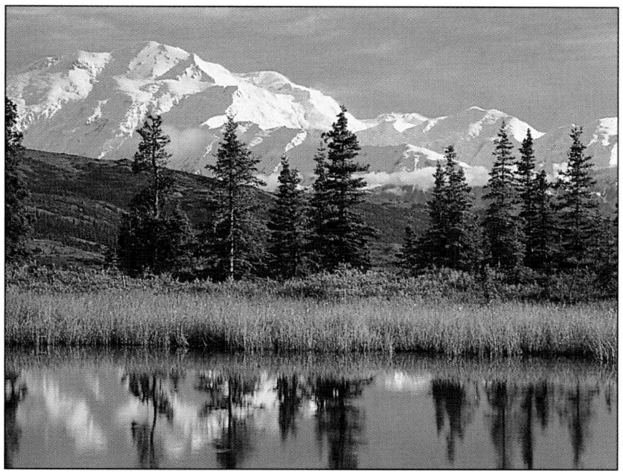

Mt McKinley, Alaska. The highest peak in North America can generate its own weather system due to its comparative height and isolation.

CLIMATE

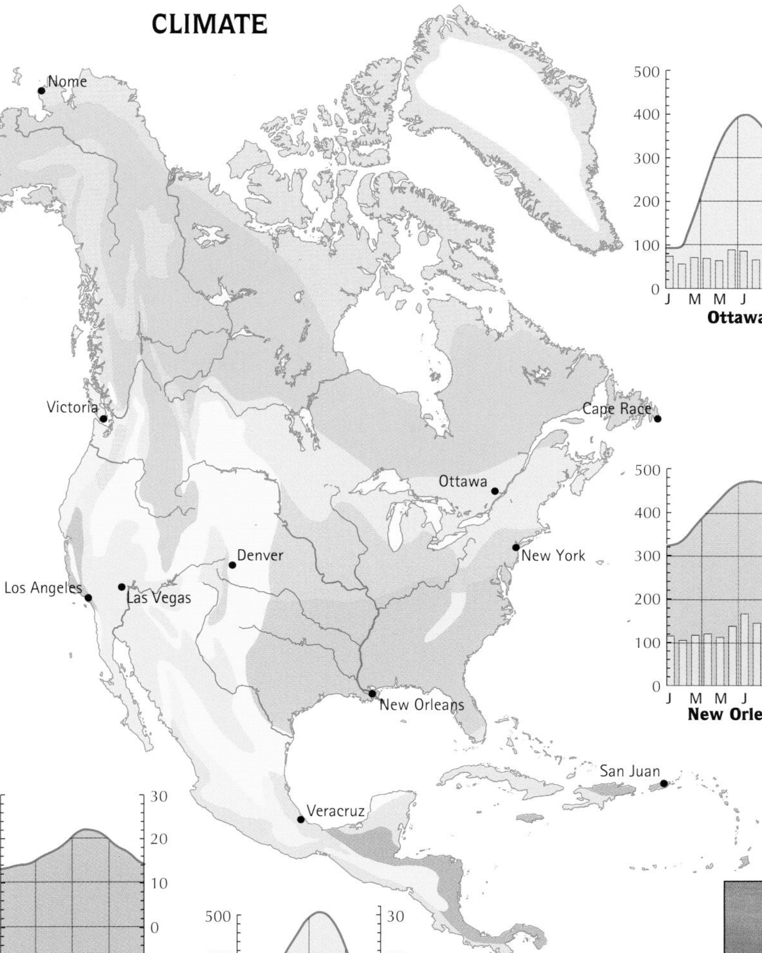

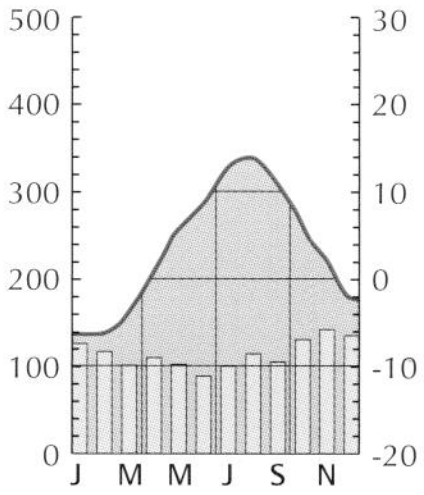

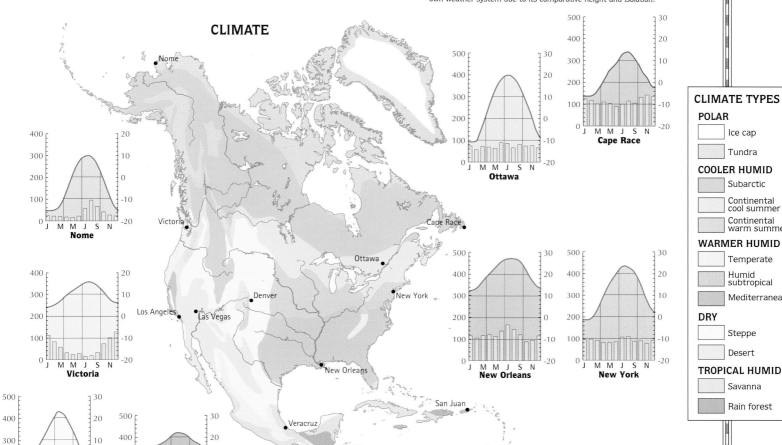

Nome

Cape Race

Ottawa

Victoria

New York

New Orleans

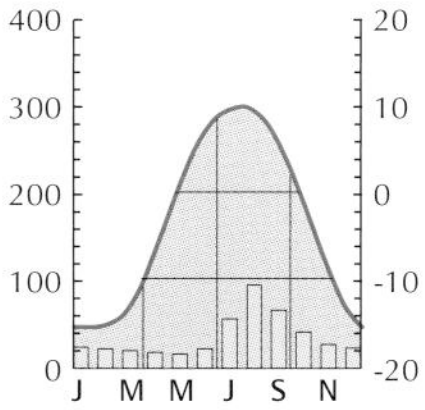

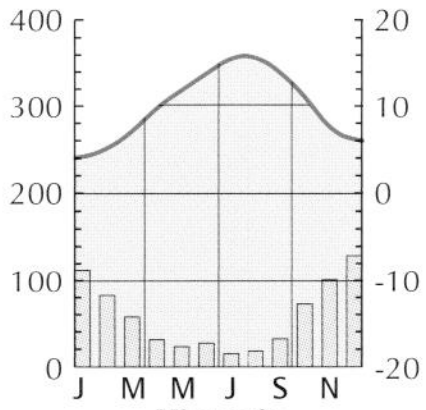

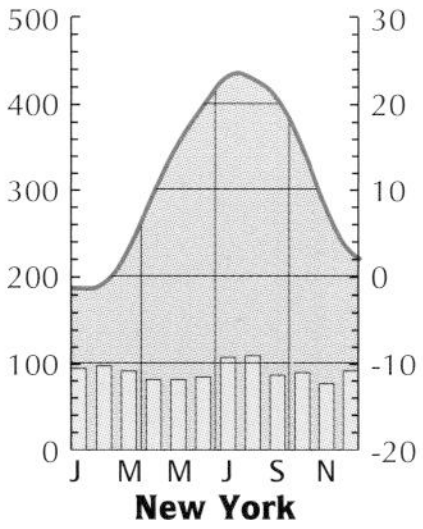

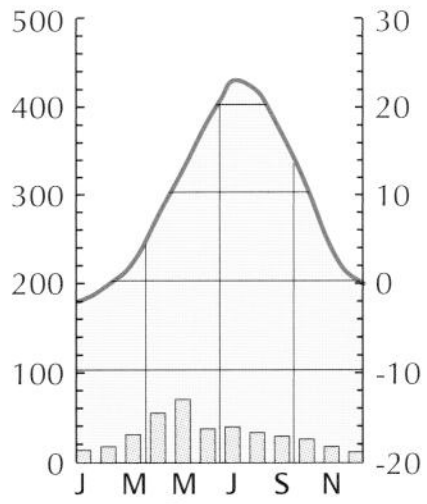

Denver

Los Angeles

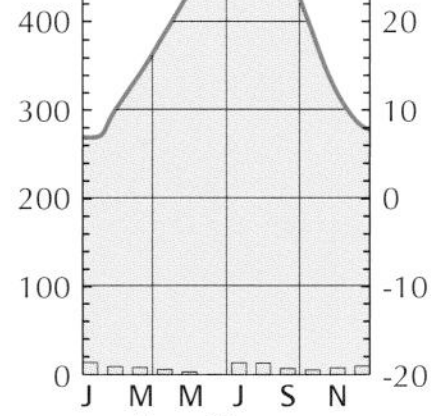

Las Vegas

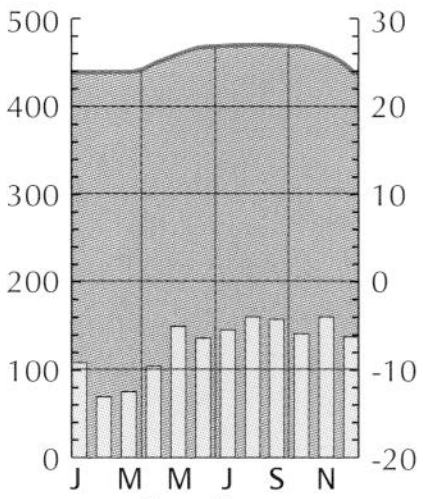

San Juan

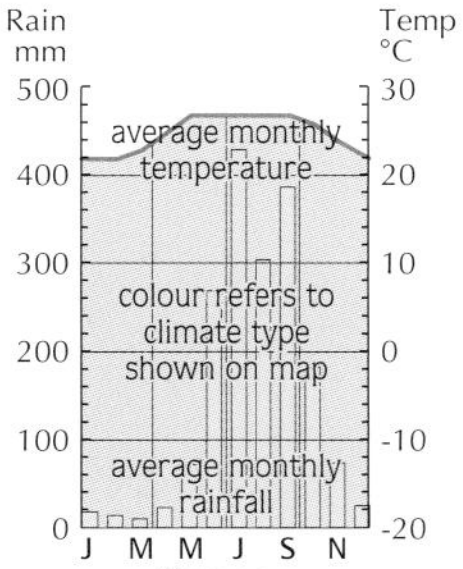

Rain mm

Temp °C

average monthly temperature

colour refers to climate type shown on map

average monthly rainfall

Veracruz

CLIMATE TYPES

POLAR
- Ice cap
- Tundra

COOLER HUMID
- Subarctic
- Continental cool summer
- Continental warm summer

WARMER HUMID
- Temperate
- Humid subtropical
- Mediterranean

DRY
- Steppe
- Desert

TROPICAL HUMID
- Savanna
- Rain forest

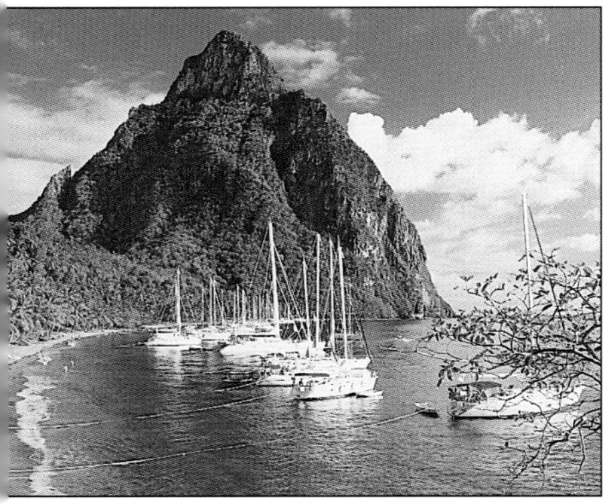

St Lucia. Stunning scenery and a tropical climate have helped make the Caribbean a popular holiday destination.

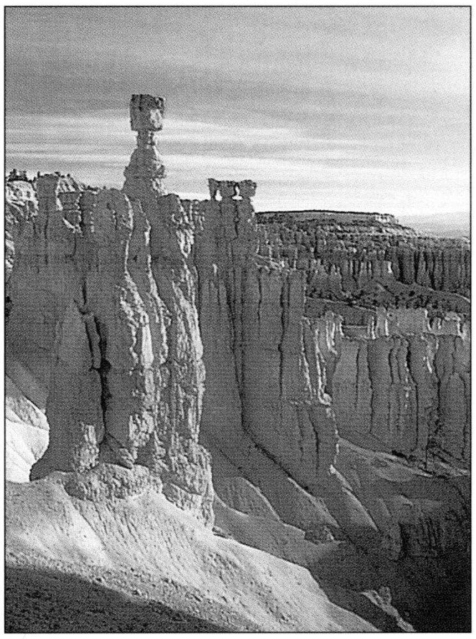

Bryce Canyon, Utah. Weathered sandstone formations in canyons up to 300m deep.

© Collins Bartholomew Ltd

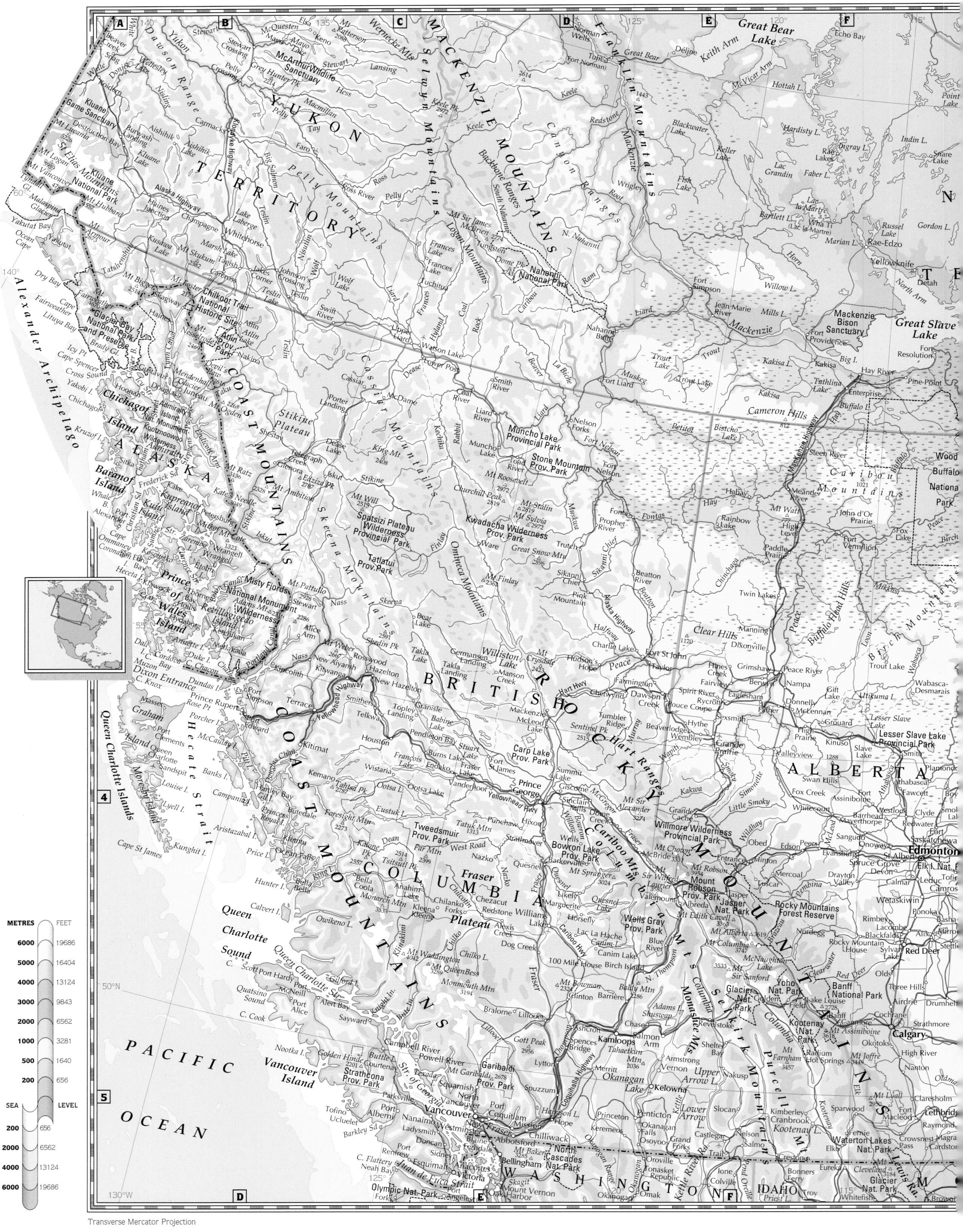
YUKON
TERRITORY
MACKENZIE MOUNTAINS
Selwyn Mountains
Franklin Mountains
Great Bear Lake
Great Slave Lake
BRITISH COLUMBIA
ROCKY MOUNTAINS
COAST MOUNTAINS
ALBERTA
ALASKA
WASHINGTON
IDAHO
PACIFIC OCEAN
Alexander Archipelago
Queen Charlotte Islands
Queen Charlotte Sound
Hecate Strait
Dixon Entrance
Vancouver Island
Fraser Plateau
Stikine Plateau
Cassiar Mountains
Skeena Mountains
Omineca Mountains
Cariboo Mountains
Monashee Mts
Selkirk Mountains
Purcell Mountains
Caribou Mountains
Whitehorse
Dawson Creek
Prince George
Prince Rupert
Kamloops
Kelowna
Vancouver
Victoria
Edmonton
Calgary
Red Deer
Lethbridge
Yellowknife
Hay River
Fort Nelson
Fort St John
Grande Prairie
Juneau
Ketchikan
Sitka
Kluane National Park
Jasper Nat. Park
Banff National Park
Yoho Nat. Park
Glacier Nat. Park
Kootenay Nat. Park
Wood Buffalo National Park
Nahanni National Park
Glacier Bay National Park and Preserve
Misty Fjords National Monument Wilderness
Alaska Highway
Yellowhead Highway
METRES
FEET
6000
19686
5000
16404
4000
13124
3000
9843
2000
6562
1000
3281
500
1640
200
656
SEA
LEVEL
200
656
2000
6562
4000
13124
6000
19686

Transverse Mercator Projection

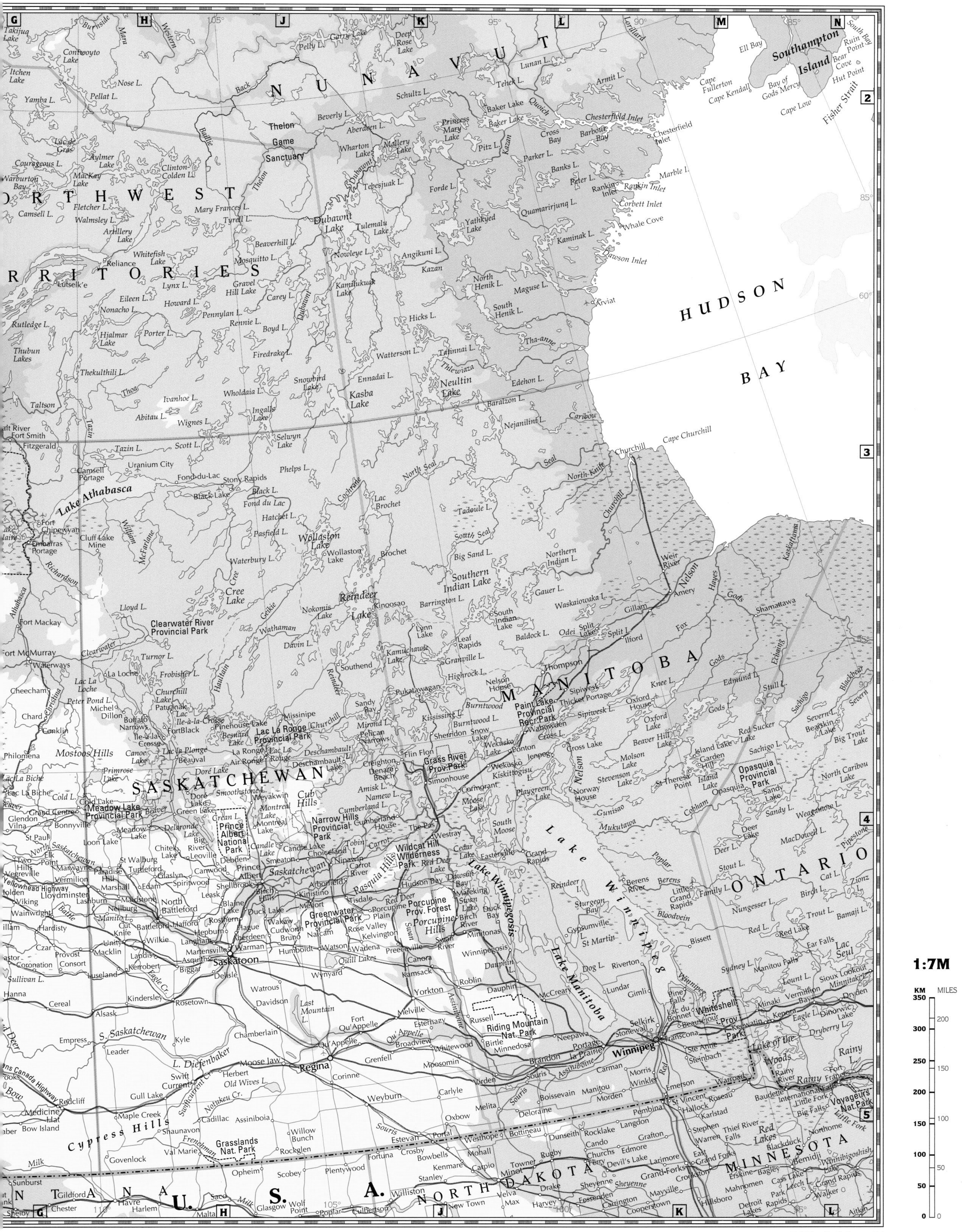

1:7M

KM	MILES
350	
300	200
250	150
200	
150	100
100	50
50	
0	0

A
B
C
D
E
90°
85°
80°
75°
2
3
4
5
HUDSON
BAY
JAMES
BAY
MANITOBA
ONTARIO
QU
PÉNINS
D'UNG
LAKE SUPERIOR
LAKE MICHIGAN
LAKE HURON
LAKE ONTARIO
LAKE ERIE
WISCONSIN
MICHIGAN
NEW YORK
U. S. A.
Seal
North Knife
Churchill
Cape Churchill
Northern Indian L.
Weir River
Nelson
Gillam
Hayes
Fox
Gods
Shamattawa
Kaskattama
Oxford House
Knee L.
Oxford L.
Beaver Hill Lake
Gods L.
Edmund L.
Echoing
Stull L.
Island Lake
Garden Hill
St Theresa Point
Red Sucker L.
Sachigo L.
Sachigo
Opasquia Provincial Park
Opasquia
Bearskin Lake
Severn L.
Blackbear
Severn
Big Trout Lake
Big Trout Lake
Sandy Lake
Sandy L.
Deer Lake
Deer L.
North Caribou Lake
Weagamow L.
Kasabonika
Kasabonika L.
Wapikopa L.
Webequie
Winisk River Provincial Park
Summer Beaver
Pipestone
MacDowell L.
Nungesser L.
Cat L.
Birch L.
Trout L.
Zionz L.
Pickle Lake
Otoskwin
Attawapiskat L.
Missisa L.
Eabamet L.
Albany
Bamaji L.
Manitou Falls
Ear Falls
Lac Seul
Lac St Joseph
Wabakimi L.
Whitewater L.
Sioux Lookout
Savant Lake
Sturgeon L.
Ogoki
Ogoki Res.
Smoothrock L.
Armstrong
Little Current
Dryden
Minnitaki L.
Dinorwic Lake
Seseganaga L.
Ignace
Lake Nipigon
Nakina
Kenogami
Longlac
Pagwa River
Marmion L.
Upsala
Lac des Mille Lacs
Seine
Atikokan
Raith
Beardmore
Long L.
Nipigon
Red Rock
Dog L.
Kakabeka Falls
Northern Light L.
Thunder Bay
Schreiber
Terrace Bay
St Ignace I.
Marathon
Hornepayne
Kabinakagami L.
White River
Oba
Kapuskasing
Hearst
Fort Severn
Beaver
Severn
Fawn
Winisk
Winisk
Wabuk Pt
Peawanuck
Cape Lookout
Sutton
Opinnagau
Polar Bear Provincial Park
Sutton L.
Ekwan
Ekwan Pt
Attawapiskat
Akimiski Island
Kapiskau
Kashechewan
Fort Albany
Cape Henrietta Maria
Lake River
Moosonee
Moose River
Moose
Moose Factory
Hannah Bay
Missinaibi
N. French
Kesagami L.
Otter Rapids
Smoky Falls
Fraserdale
Harricanaw
Baie Korak
Pte Cusson
Pte Dufrost
Puvurnituq
Ottawa Islands
Gilmour Island
Pte aux Écueils
Baie de Kogaluc
Kogaluc
Cape Dufferin
Hopewell Islands
Inukjuak (Port Harrison)
Farmer I.
Marcopeet Is
Sleeper Is
King George Islands
North Belcher Islands
Bakers Dozen Islands
Belcher Islands
Sanikiluaq
Flaherty Island
Churchill Sd
Tukarak I.
Nastapoka Islands
Nastapoca
Umiujaq
Lac Guillaume-Delisle
Petite Rivière de la Baleine
Poste-de-la-Baleine (Kuujjuarapik)
Whapmagoostui
Long I.
Pte Louis-XIV
Bear I.
Fort George
Chisasibi
La Grande
Radisson
North Twin I.
South Twin I.
Wemindji (Nouveau-Comptoir)
Cape Duncan
Charlton I.
Eastmain
Rupert Bay
Waskaganish
Fort Rupert
Rupert
Broadback
Nottaway
Lac Klotz
Lac Bécard
Lac Couture
Lac Payne
Lac Anuc
Lac Tasiat
La Potherie
Lac Le Roy
Lac Rocheforf
Lac Dune
Lac Chavigny
Lac Bacqueville
Lac Minto
Lac Nedlouc
Lacs des Loups-Marins
Lac à l'Eau Claire
Lac D'Iberville
Gde Rivière de la Baleine
Lac Bienville
Lac Burton
Roggan
Kanaaupscow
Rés. La Grande 2
Rés. La Grande 4
Sakami
Rés. La Grande 3
Lac Sakami
Rés. Opinaca
Lac Low
Opinaca
Eastmain
Mesgouez L.
L. Evans
L. Mistassini
L. Comencho
L. Poncheville
Opataca L.
Mistissini (Baie du Poste)
L. Matagami
Matagami
L. Maicasagi
L. au Goéland
Chibougamau
L. Waswanipi
Miquelon
L. Doda
Parc de Chibougamau
Lebel-sur-Quévillon
Beattyville
Val-Paradis
La Sarre
Taschereau
Amos
Senneterre
L. Parent
Réservoir Gouin
Noranda
Rouyn
Malartic
Val-d'Or
Smooth Rock Falls
Cochrane
L. Abitibi
Abitibi
Groundhog
Mattagami
Kapuskasing
Timmins
Ansonville
S. Porcupine
Matheson
Nighthawk L.
Kirkland Lake
Foleyet
Missinaibi L.
Wabatongushi L.
Pukaskwa Nat. Park
Dog L.
Wawa
Manitowik L.
Michipicoten River
Michipicoten I.
Chapleau
Matachewan
Gogama
Englehart
New Liskeard
Haileybury
Lac Témiscamingue
L. Simard
Lac Decelles
Rés. Dozois
Réserve Faunique de la Vérendrye
Rés. Cabonga
L. Dumoine
L. Kipawa
Temiscaming
Rés. Baskatong
Mont-Laurier
Maniwaki
Gatineau
Lièvre
L. Kempt
La Tuque
St Maurice
Shawinigan
Labelle
Mt Tremblant
Joliette
St-Jovité
St-Jérôme
Lachute
Laval
Montreal
Longueuil
Gatineau
Hull
Vanier
Ottawa
Nepean
Winchester
Beauharnois
Valleyfield
Cornwall
Carleton Place
Smiths Falls
Perth
Rideau Lakes
Brockville
Massena
Ogdensburg
Malone
Potsdam
Plattsburgh
Champlain
Saranac Lakes
Canton
Gananoque
Kingston
Clayton
Tupper Lake
Adirondack Mountains
Watertown
Carthage
Lowville
Cranberry L.
Pulaski
Boonville
Oswego
Fulton
Rome
Utica
Syracuse
Amsterdam
Schenectady
Albany
Saratoga Springs
Glens Falls
Cohoes
Auburn
Cortland
Rochester
Greece
Brockport
Lockport
Niagara Falls
Buffalo
Lackawanna
Hamburg
Dunkirk
Fredonia
Jamestown
Geneseo
Dansville
Hornell
Geneva
Finger Lakes
Ithaca
Cobleskill
Gowanda
Salamanca
Westfield
St Catharines
Welland
Grimsby
Hamilton
Mississauga
Brampton
Toronto
Scarborough
Oshawa
Whitby
Cobourg
Belleville
Trenton
Rice L.
Napanee
Peterborough
Lindsay
Kawartha Lakes
Lakefield
Bancroft
Renfrew
Arnprior
Pembroke
Deep River
Fort-Coulonge
Algonquin Prov. Park
Lake Traverse
Barrys Bay
Madawaska
Huntsville
Lake of Bays
Bracebridge
Gravenhurst
L. Muskoka
Orillia
Barrie
L. Simcoe
Orangeville
Collingwood
Midland
Owen Sound
Wiarton
Southampton
Port Elgin
Kincardine
Walkerton
Hanover
Goderich
Fergus
Guelph
Kitchener
Cambridge
Stratford
Woodstock
Brantford
Ingersoll
London
St Thomas
West Lorne
Chatham
Windsor
Sarnia
Port Huron
Forest
Georgian Bay
Bruce Pen.
Tobermory
Main Channel
C. Hurd
Parry Sound
Rosseau L.
Burk's Falls
Callander
North Bay
L. Nipissing
Key Harbour
Sturgeon Falls
Mattawa
Sudbury
Coniston
Copper Cliff
Webbwood
Espanola
Massey
Blind River
Thessalon
Echo Bay
Wanapitei L.
L. Temagami
Onaping L.
Rocky I. L.
Biscotasi L.
Spanish
Manitoulin I.
North Channel
South Baymouth
St Joseph I.
Drummond I.
Sault Ste Marie
Rudyard
Batchawana Mtn
Whitefish Pt
Coppermine Pt
Montreal River
Mackinaw City
Cheboygan
Bois Blanc I.
Rogers City
Alpena
Gaylord
Harrisville
Grayling
Traverse City
Charlevoix
Petoskey
Beaver I.
Manistique
Gladstone
Escanaba
Seney
Munising
Marquette
Ishpeming
Crystal Falls
Iron Mountain
Iron River
Kingsford
Niagara
Rapid River
Garden Pen.
Green Bay
Gills Rock
Sturgeon Bay
Door Pen.
Manitou Is.
Manistee
Cadillac
West Branch
Au Sable
Tawas City
Saginaw Bay
Bay City
Midland
Saginaw
Mount Pleasant
Clare
Big Rapids
Reed City
Ludington
Shelby
Muskegon
Grand Haven
Holland
Grand Rapids
Wyoming
Kentwood
Ithaca
Owosso
Flint
Lapeer
Lansing
St Johns
Charlotte
Battle Creek
Kalamazoo
South Haven
Benton Harbor
Three Rivers
Coldwater
Sturgis
Jackson
Ann Arbor
Livonia
Pontiac
Sterling Heights
Warren
Detroit
Dearborn
Taylor
Wyandotte
Monroe
Adrian
Hillsdale
Angola
Elkhart
South Bend
Michigan City
Niles
Portage
Hammond
Gary
Chicago
Evanston
Des Plaines
Arlington Heights
Waukegan
Kenosha
Racine
Milwaukee
West Allis
Waukesha
Brookfield
Menomonee Falls
West Bend
Sheboygan
Manitowoc
Two Rivers
Kewaunee
Green Bay
Appleton
Menasha
Neenah
Oshkosh
Fond du Lac
L. Winnebago
Waupun
Beaver Dam
Watertown
Madison
Janesville
Beloit
Monroe
Rockford
Belvidere
Elgin
De Kalb
Aurora
Joliet
Oak Lawn
Park Forest
Streator
Kewanee
Princeton
Ottawa
La Salle
Dixon
Sterling
Rock Falls
Freeport
Galena
Clinton
Savanna
Platteville
Dodgeville
Richland Center
Baraboo
Sun Prairie
Portage
Wisconsin Rapids
Stevens Point
Wausau
Antigo
Marshfield
Mauston
Tomah
Sparta
Black River Falls
Viroqua
Westby
Shawano
New London
Waupaca
Merrill
Tomahawk
Rhinelander
Crandon
Stephenson
Menominee
Marinette
Wolf
Medford
Abbotsford
Ladysmith
Prentice
Park Falls
Phillips
Hayward
L. Chippewa
Chippewa
Glidden
Mellen
Hurley
Ironwood
Wakefield
Bruce Crossing
Watersmeet
Three Lakes
Rockland
Watton
Ontonagon
Houghton
Hancock
Keweenaw Pen.
Keweenaw Bay
Copper Harbor
Chequamegon Bay
Ashland
Bayfield
Apostle Is
Two Harbors
Silver Bay
Grand Marais
Isle Royale Nat. Park
Isle Royale
Ely
Birch L.
Pie I.
Fox

METRES
FEET
6000
19686
5000
16404
4000
13124
3000
9843
2000
6562
1000
3281
500
1640
200
656
SEA
LEVEL
200
656
2000
6562
4000
13124
6000
19686

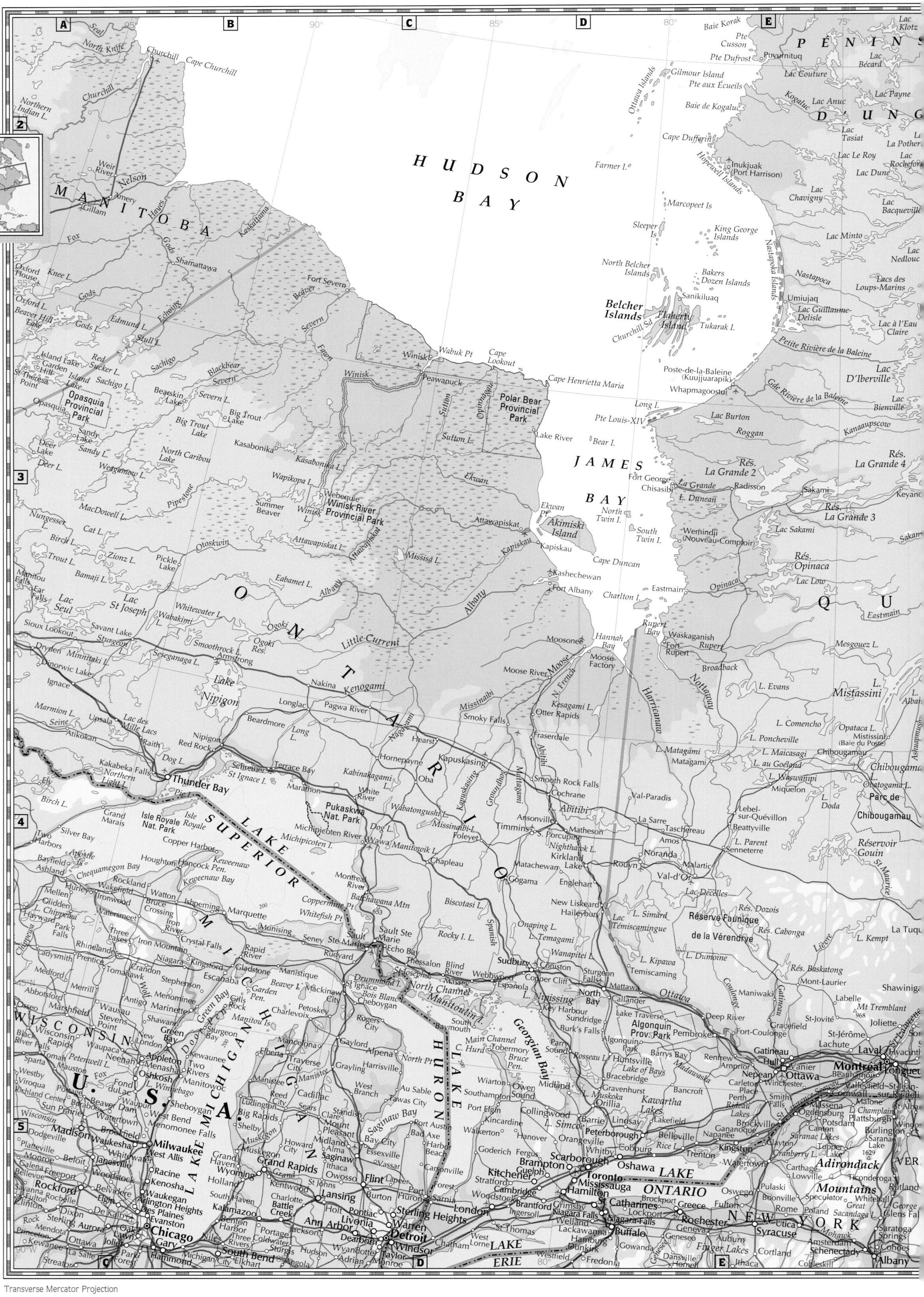

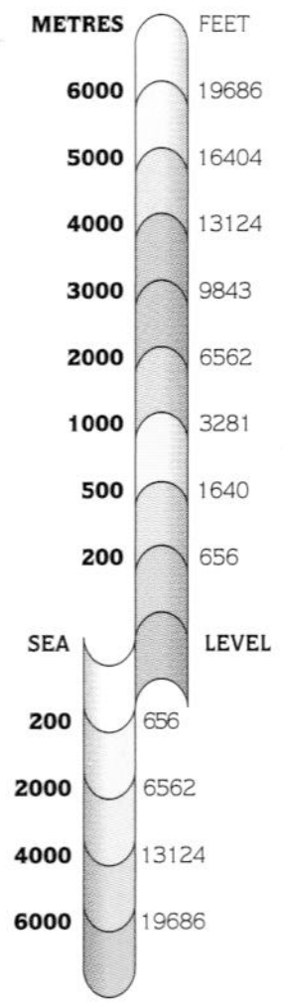

Transverse Mercator Projection

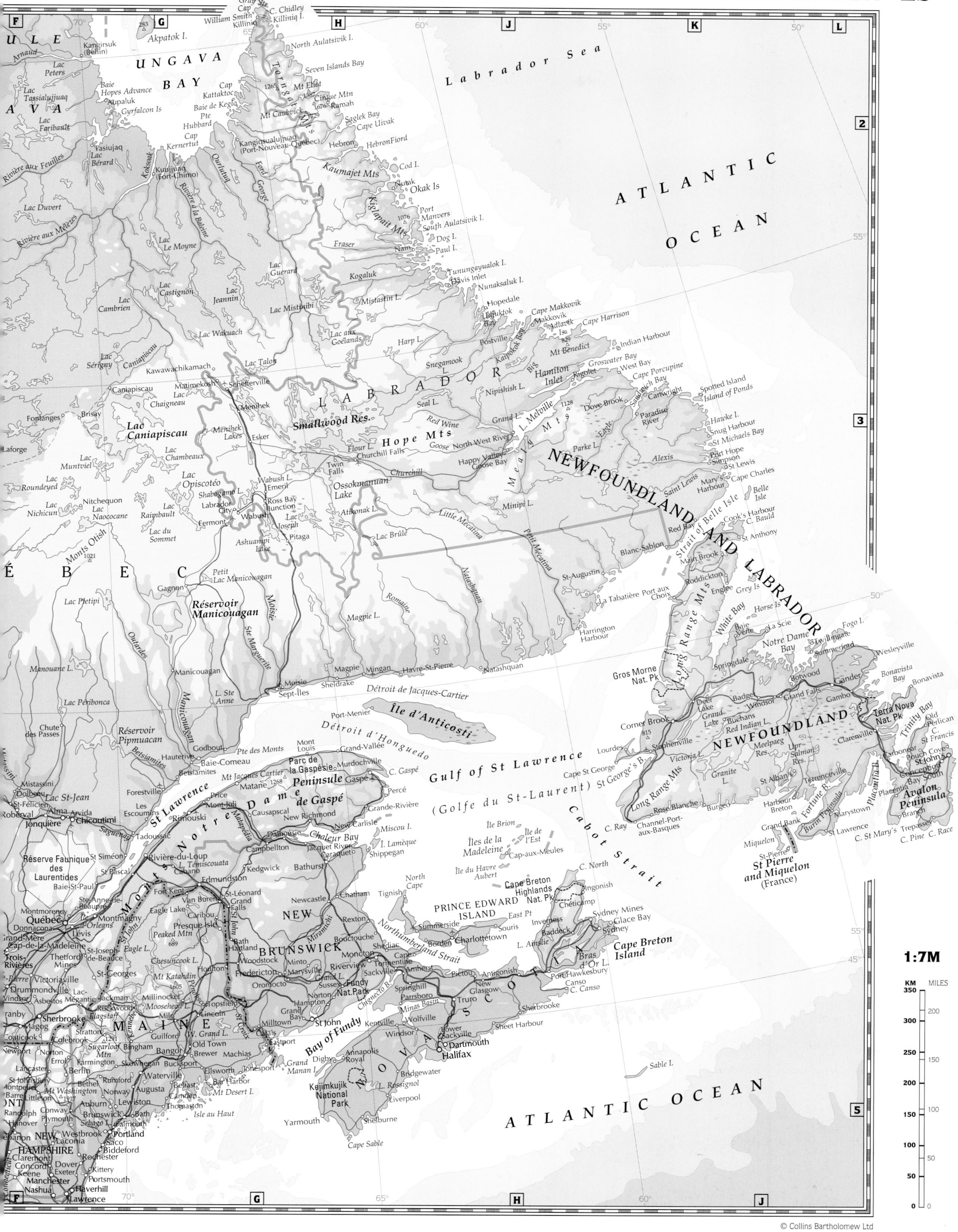

ATLANTIC OCEAN

Labrador Sea

UNGAVA BAY

LABRADOR

NEWFOUNDLAND AND LABRADOR

NEWFOUNDLAND

QUÉBEC

Gulf of St Lawrence
(Golfe du St-Laurent)

Île d'Anticosti

Cabot Strait

St Pierre and Miquelon (France)

NEW BRUNSWICK

PRINCE EDWARD ISLAND

NOVA SCOTIA

Cape Breton Island

MAINE

NEW HAMPSHIRE

Bay of Fundy

ATLANTIC OCEAN

1:7M

KM	MILES
350	
300	200
250	150
200	
150	100
100	
50	50
0	0

© Collins Bartholomew Ltd

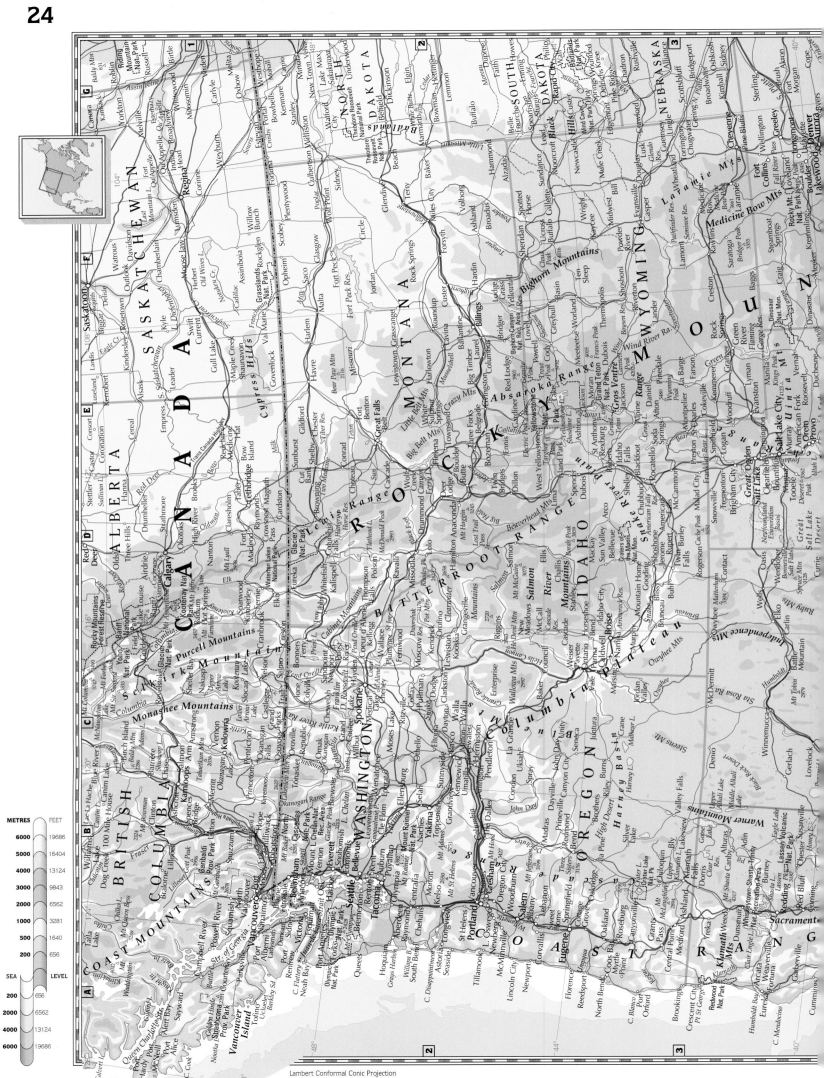
BRITISH COLUMBIA
ALBERTA
SASKATCHEWAN
CANADA
WASHINGTON
OREGON
IDAHO
MONTANA
WYOMING
NORTH DAKOTA
SOUTH DAKOTA
NEBRASKA
ROCKY MOUNTAINS
COAST MOUNTAINS
COAST RANGES
BITTERROOT RANGE
Columbia Plateau
Snake River Plain
METRES
FEET
6000
19686
5000
16404
4000
13124
3000
9843
2000
6562
1000
3281
500
1640
200
656
SEA
LEVEL

Lambert Conformal Conic Projection

1:7M

KM MILES
350
        200
300
250   150
200
150   100
100
        50
50
0   0

C A N A D A
O N T A R I O
MANITOBA
SASKATCHEWAN
NORTH DAKOTA
SOUTH DAKOTA
MINNESOTA
WISCONSIN
MICHIGAN
IOWA
NEBRASKA
KANSAS
MISSOURI
ILLINOIS
INDIANA
MONTANA
WYOMING
COLORADO
LAKE SUPERIOR
LAKE MICHIGAN
ROCKY MOUNTAINS
Black Hills
Bighorn Mts
Laramie Mts
Medicine Bow Mts
Sawatch Mts
Smoky Hills
Badlands
Badlands Nat. Park
Theodore Roosevelt National Park
Theodore Roosevelt Nat. Park
Wind Cave Nat. Park
Voyageurs Nat. Park
Isle Royale Nat. Park
Pukaskwa Nat. Park
Grasslands Nat. Park
Rocky Mt. Nat. Park
Whiteshell Prov. Park
Bighorn Canyon Nat. Recreation Area
Curecanti Nat. Recreation Area
Cypress Hills
Lake of the Woods
Red Lakes
Lake Sakakawea
Lake Oahe
Fort Peck Res.
Lake Nipigon
Green Bay
Missouri
Mississippi
Winnipeg
Thunder Bay
Duluth
Minneapolis
St Paul
Fargo
Bismarck
Pierre
Sioux Falls
Sioux City
Omaha
Lincoln
Des Moines
Kansas City
Topeka
St Louis
Springfield
Peoria
Chicago
Milwaukee
Madison
Green Bay
Grand Rapids
Lansing
South Bend
Fort Wayne
Indianapolis
Louisville
Evansville
Denver
Aurora
Colorado Springs
Pueblo
Cheyenne
Casper
Billings
Rapid City
Sault Ste Marie

Lambert Conformal Conic Projection

METRES
FEET
6000
19686
5000
16404
4000
13124
3000
9843
2000
6562
1000
3281
500
1640
200
656
SEA
LEVEL
200
656
2000
6562
4000
13124
6000
19686

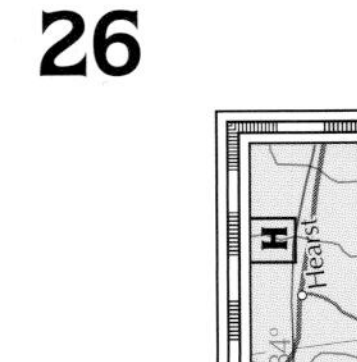

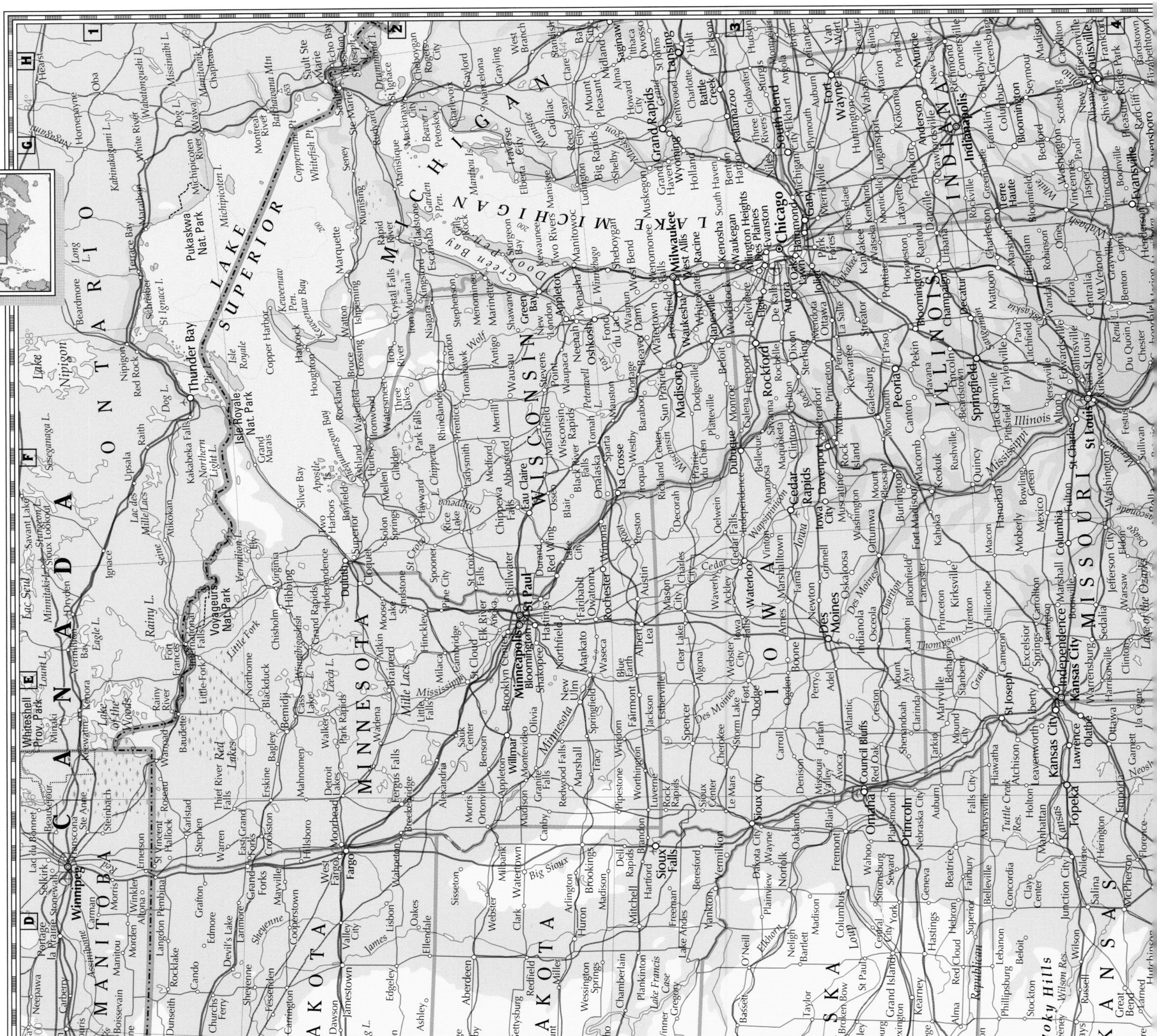

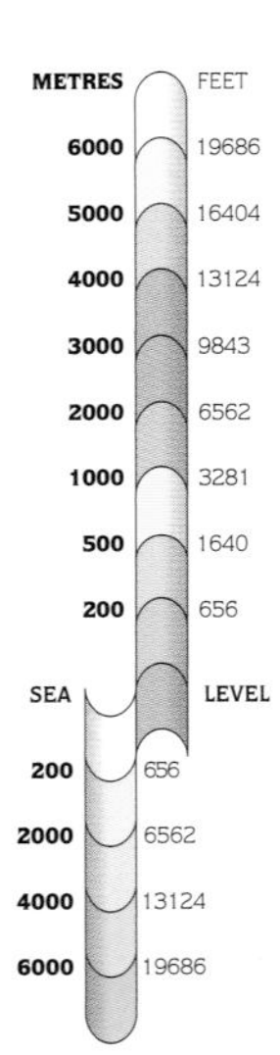

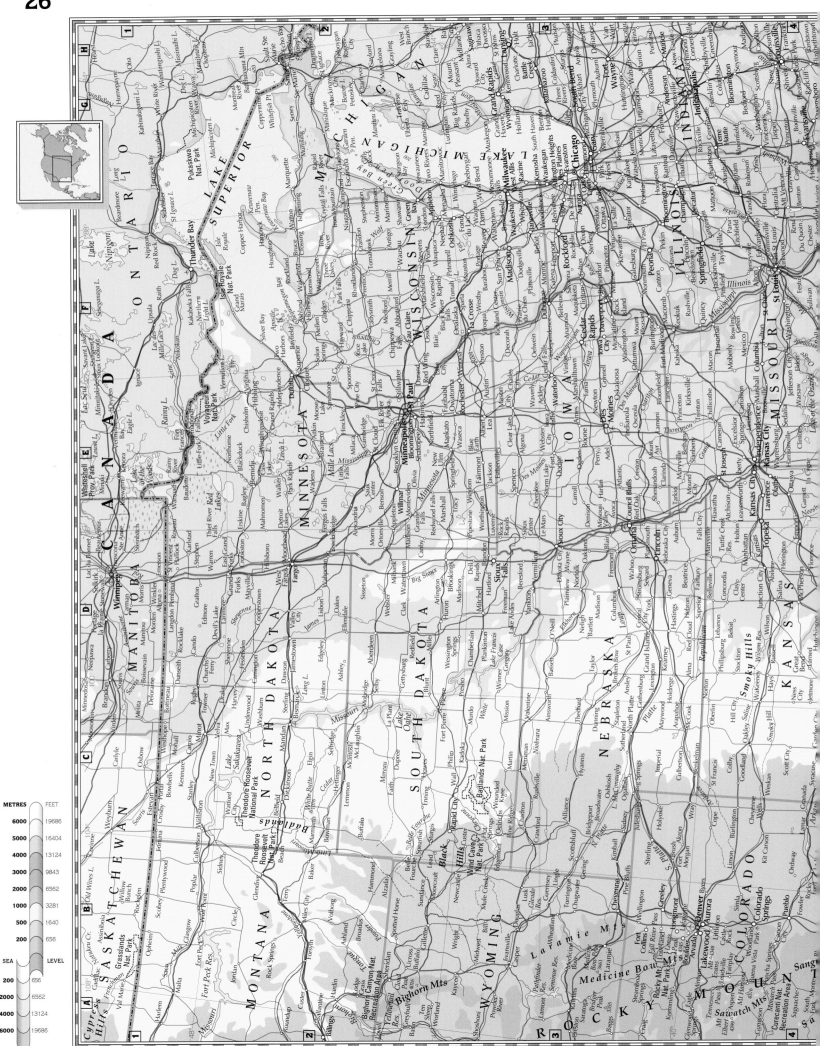

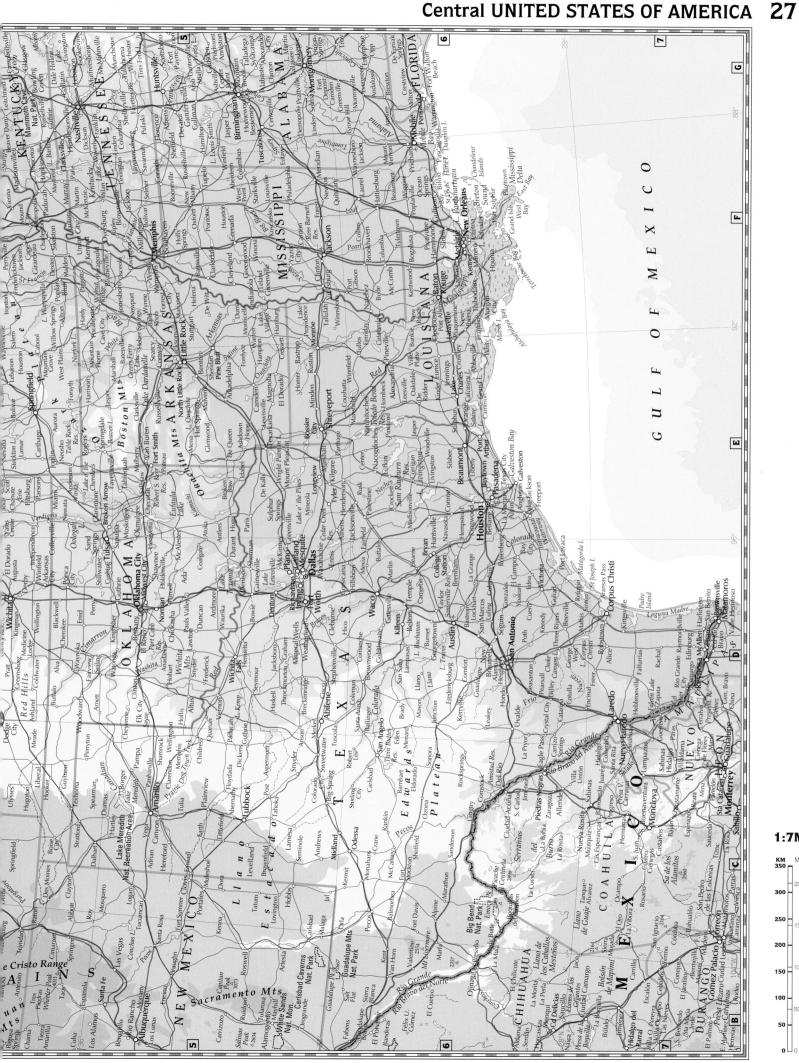

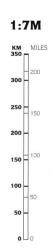

1:7M

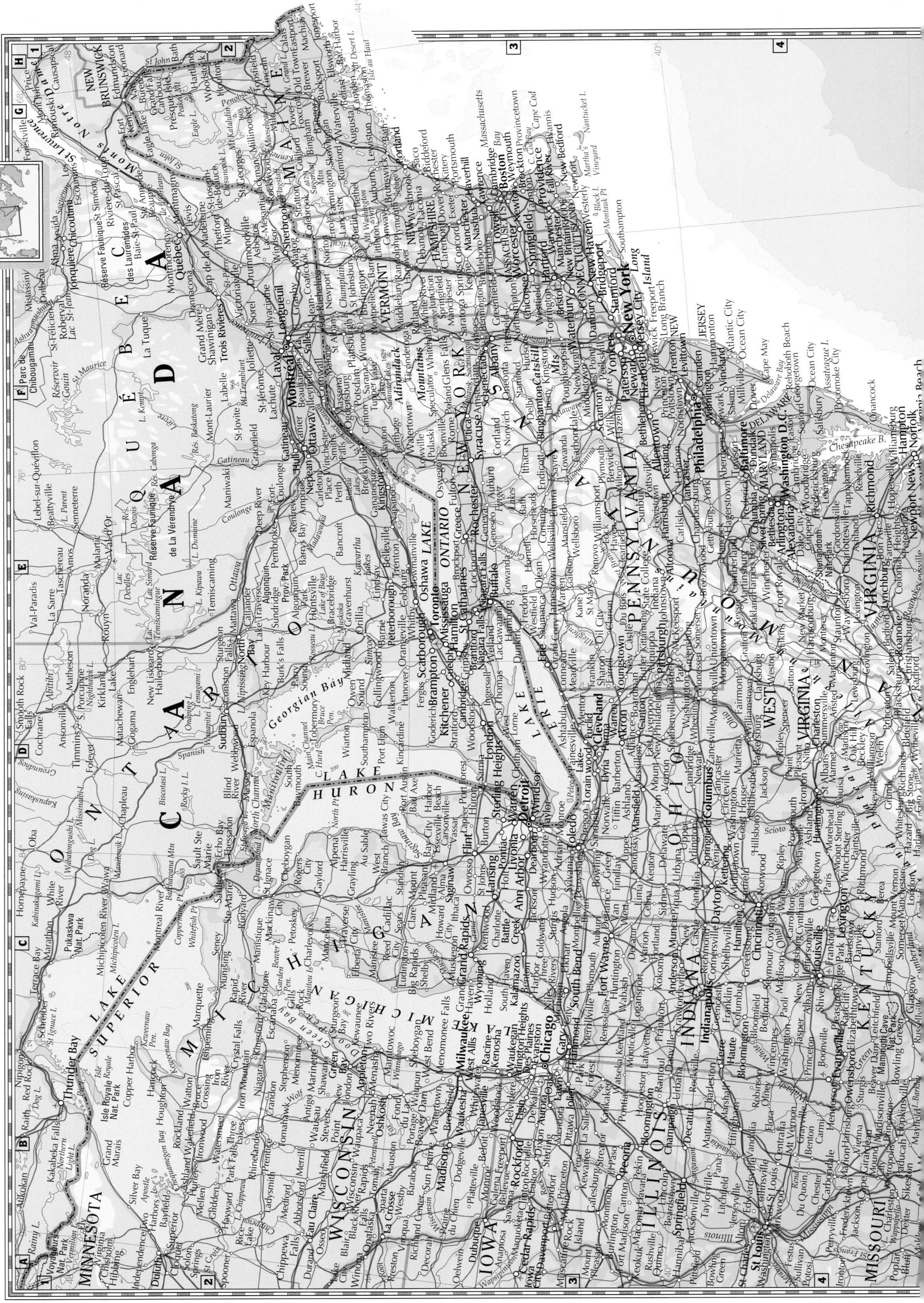
CANADA
ONTARIO
QUÉBEC
NEW BRUNSWICK
MAINE
VERMONT
NEW HAMPSHIRE
MASSACHUSETTS
CONNECTICUT
NEW YORK
PENNSYLVANIA
NEW JERSEY
DELAWARE
MARYLAND
WEST VIRGINIA
VIRGINIA
OHIO
INDIANA
ILLINOIS
MICHIGAN
WISCONSIN
MINNESOTA
IOWA
MISSOURI
KENTUCKY
LAKE SUPERIOR
LAKE MICHIGAN
LAKE HURON
LAKE ERIE
LAKE ONTARIO
Georgian Bay
Long Island
Chesapeake B.
Lambert Conformal Conic Projection

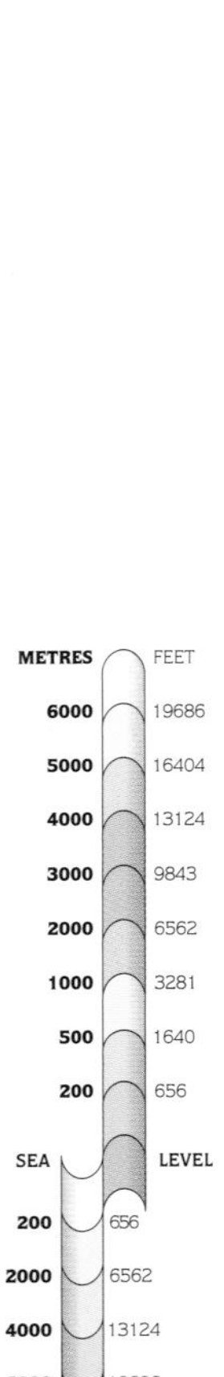
METRES
FEET
6000
19686
5000
16404
4000
13124
3000
9843
2000
6562
1000
3281
500
1640
200
656
SEA
LEVEL
200
656
2000
6562
4000
13124
6000
19686

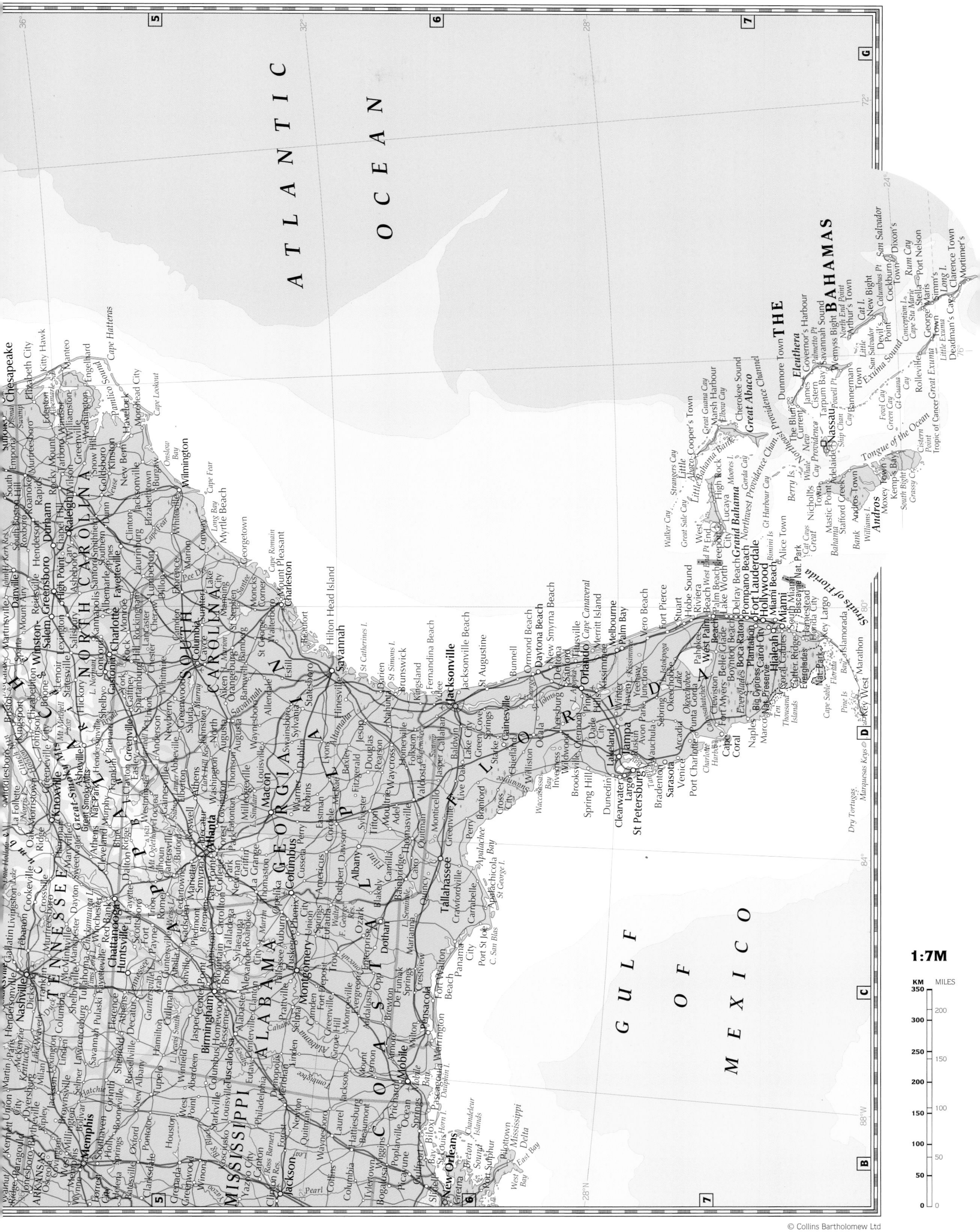

ATLANTIC

OCEAN

THE BAHAMAS

GULF

OF

MEXICO

1:7M

KM   MILES
350
300   200
250   150
200
150   100
100
50
50
0   0

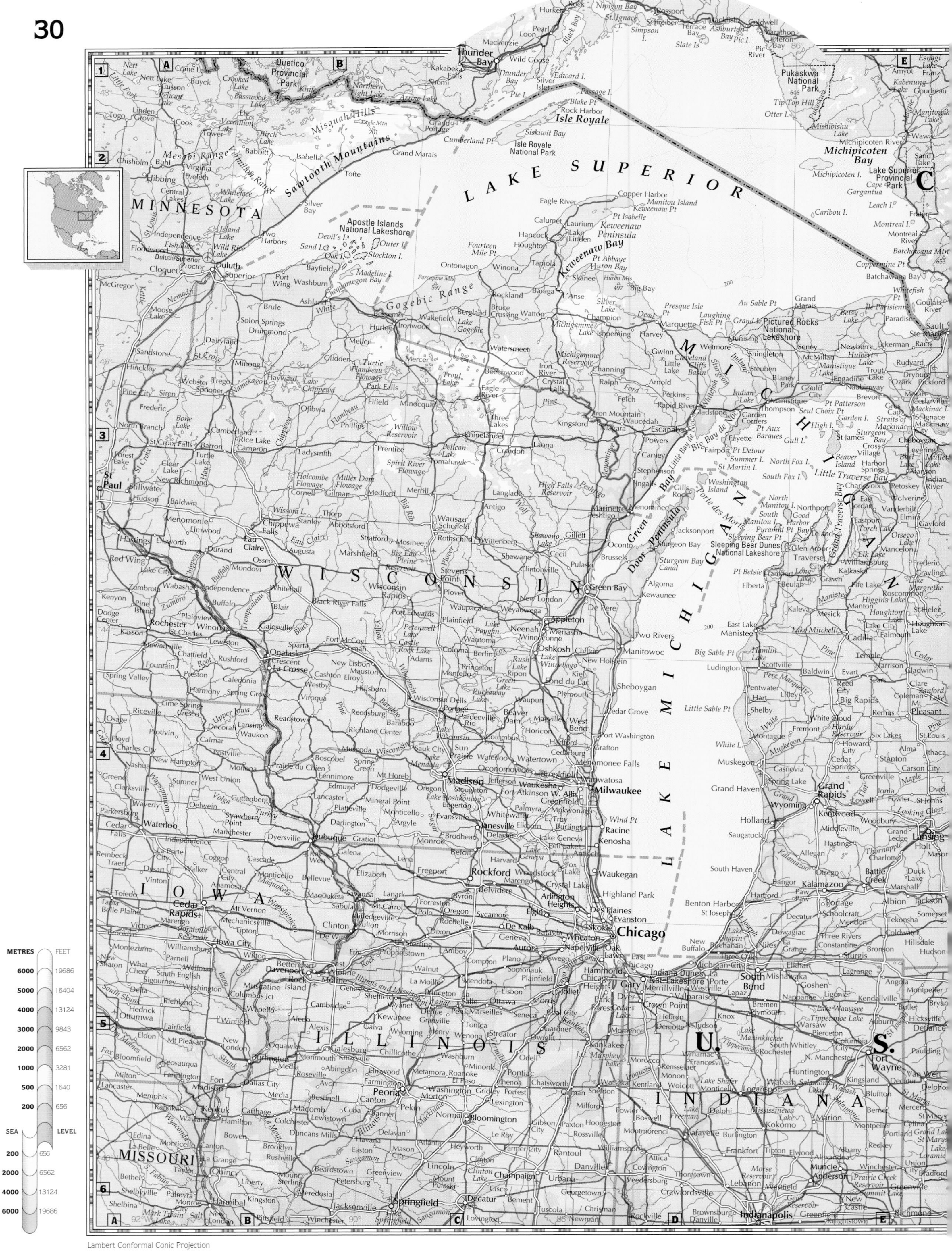
MINNESOTA
WISCONSIN
IOWA
ILLINOIS
MISSOURI
INDIANA
MICHIGAN
U. S.
C
LAKE SUPERIOR
LAKE MICHIGAN
Isle Royale
Isle Royale National Park
Apostle Islands National Lakeshore
Pictured Rocks National Lakeshore
Sleeping Bear Dunes National Lakeshore
Indiana Dunes Nat. Lakeshore
Pukaskwa National Park
Lake Superior Provincial Park
Quetico Provincial Park
Thunder Bay
Duluth
St Paul
Milwaukee
Madison
Chicago
Green Bay
Grand Rapids
Lansing
Fort Wayne
South Bend
Peoria
Springfield
Indianapolis
Rockford
Cedar Rapids
Keweenaw Peninsula
Keweenaw Bay
Green Bay
Door Peninsula
Grand Traverse Bay
Michipicoten Bay
Sawtooth Mountains
Gogebic Range
Mesabi Range
METRES
FEET
6000
19686
5000
16404
4000
13124
3000
9843
2000
6562
1000
3281
500
1640
200
656
SEA
LEVEL
200
656
2000
6562
4000
13124
6000
19686

Lambert Conformal Conic Projection

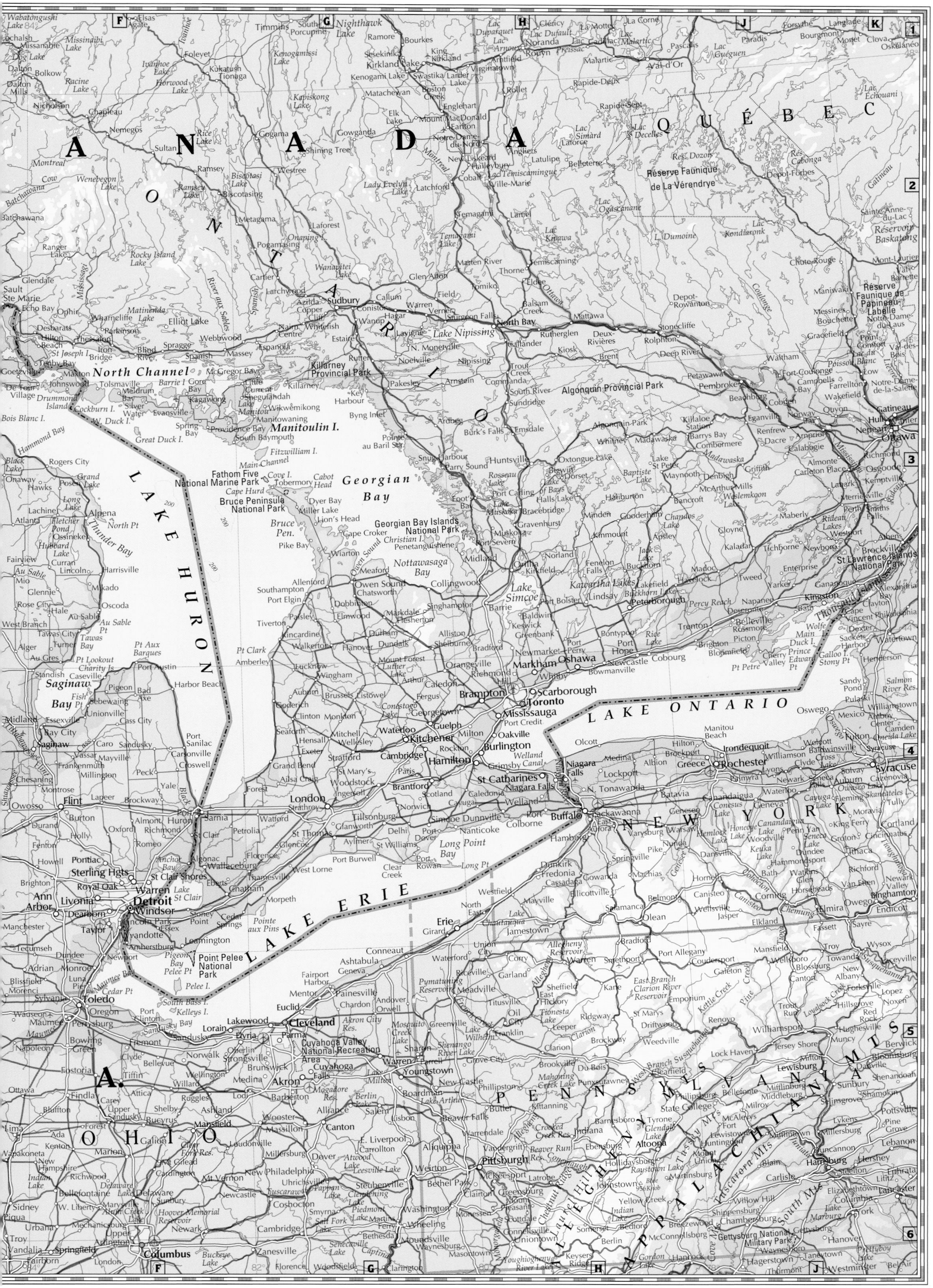

1:3.5M

© Collins Bartholomew Ltd

C A N A D A
O N T A R I O
Q U É B E C
U. S. A.
N E W Y O R K
P E N N S Y L V A N I A
O H I O
LAKE HURON
LAKE ERIE
LAKE ONTARIO
Georgian Bay
Saginaw Bay
North Channel
Manitoulin I.
Lake Nipissing
Algonquin Provincial Park
Réserve Faunique de La Vérendrye
Toronto
Ottawa
Detroit
Cleveland
Buffalo
Pittsburgh
Rochester
Syracuse
Hamilton
London
Toledo
Columbus
Sudbury
North Bay
APPALACHIAN MTS
ALLEGHENY MTS
KM 175 150 125 100 75 50 25 0
MILES 100 75 50 25 0

A
B
C
D
E
2
3
4
5
6
LAKE HURON
Georgian Bay
C A N A D A
O N T A R I O
LAKE ONTARIO
LAKE ERIE
M I C H I G A N
Saginaw Bay
O H I O
P E N N S Y L V A N I A
W E S T V I R G I N I A
V I R G I N I A
K E N T U C K Y
T E N N E S S E E
NEW
A L L E G H E N Y M O U N T A I N S
A P P A L A C H I A N M O U N T A I N S
B L U E R I D G E
Bruce Peninsula National Park
Georgian Bay Islands National Park
Algonquin Prov Park
Point Pelee National Park
Cuyahoga Valley National Recreation Area
Shenandoah National Park
Gettysburg National Military Park
Mt Rogers National Recreation Area
Toronto
Detroit
Windsor
Cleveland
Columbus
Pittsburgh
Buffalo
Rochester
Toledo
Cincinnati
Lansing
Flint
London
Hamilton
Kitchener
Mississauga
Harrisburg
Baltimore
Washington D.C.
Richmond
Roanoke
Charleston
Huntington
Dayton
Akron
Erie
Lynchburg

METRES
FEET
6000
19686
5000
16404
4000
13124
3000
9843
2000
6562
1000
3281
500
1640
200
656
SEA
LEVEL
200
656
2000
6562
4000
13124
6000
19686

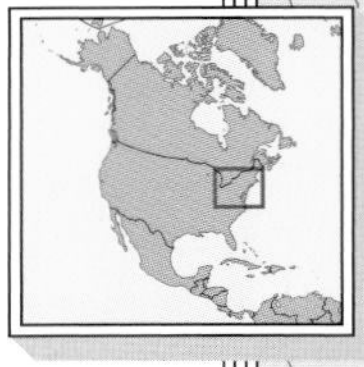

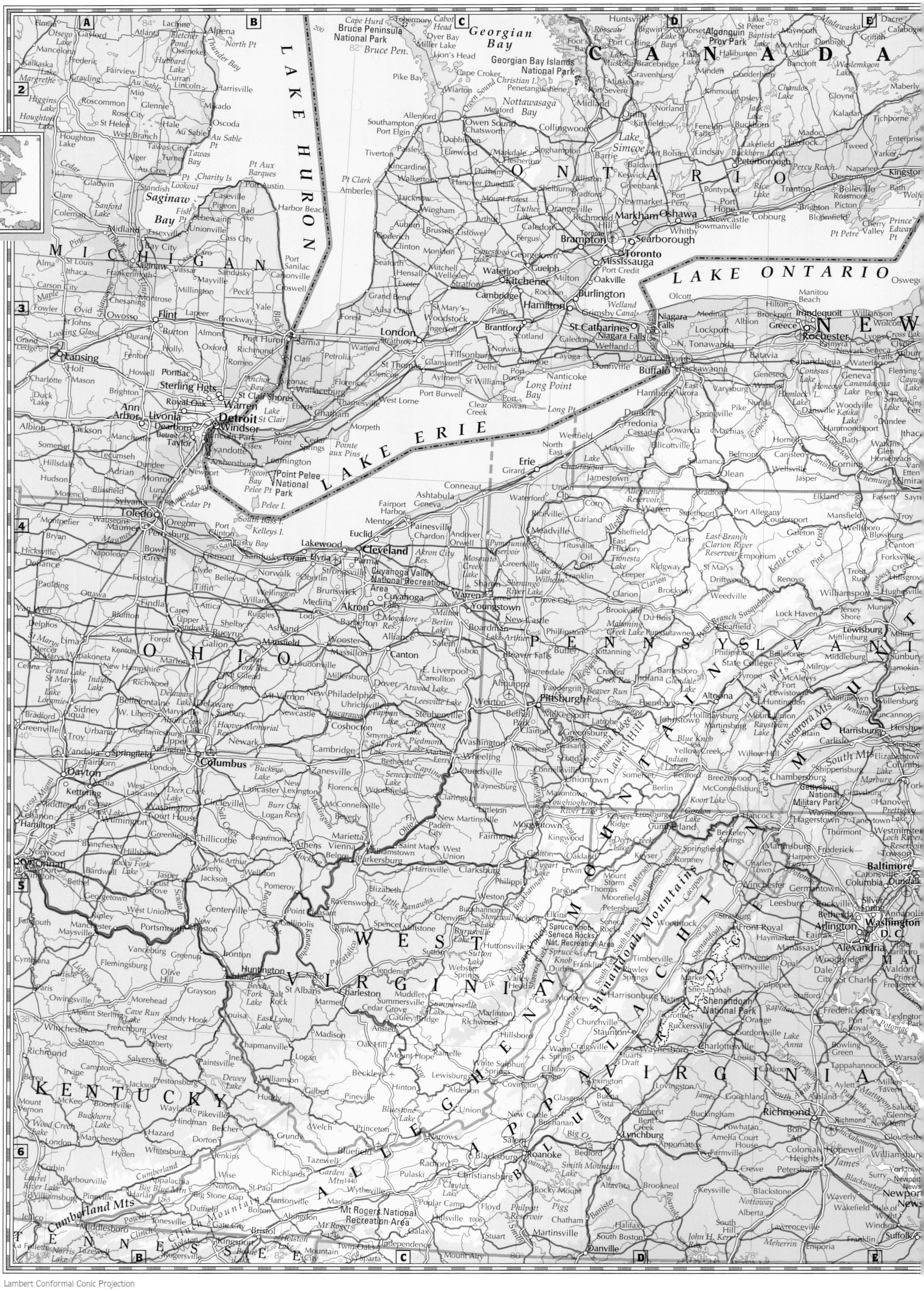

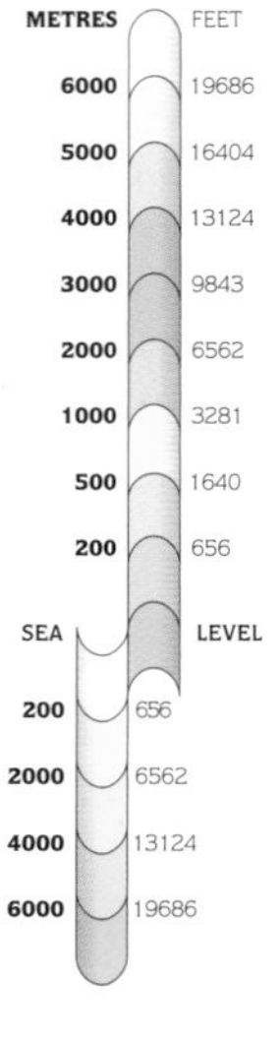

Lambert Conformal Conic Projection

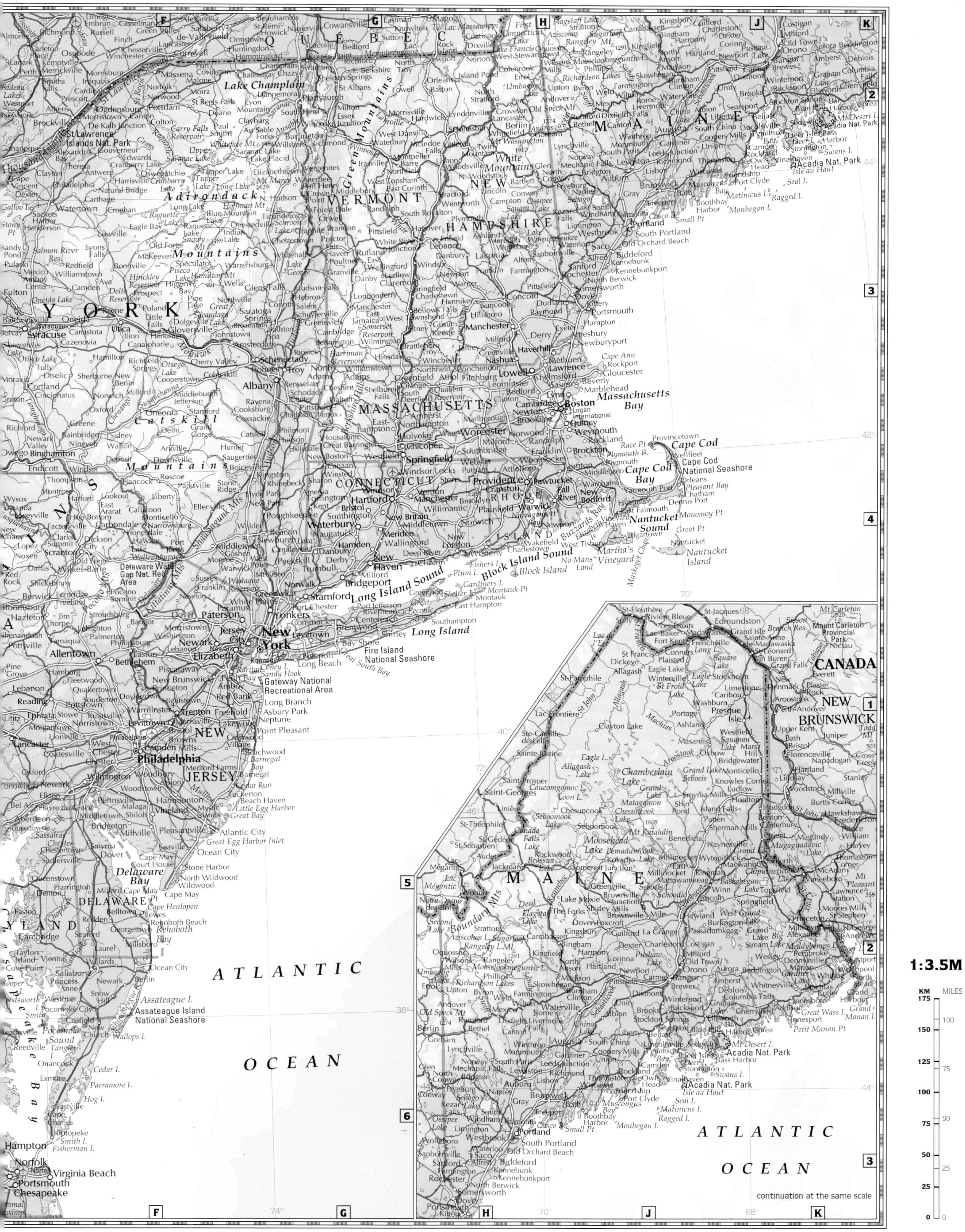
QUÉBEC
YORK
VERMONT
NEW HAMPSHIRE
MAINE
MASSACHUSETTS
CONNECTICUT
RHODE ISLAND
NEW JERSEY
DELAWARE
CANADA
NEW BRUNSWICK
Adirondack Mountains
Catskill Mountains
Green Mountains
White Mountains
Lake Champlain
Massachusetts Bay
Cape Cod Bay
Cape Cod
Cape Cod National Seashore
Nantucket Sound
Nantucket Island
Martha's Vineyard
Block Island Sound
Long Island Sound
Long Island
Fire Island National Seashore
Gateway National Recreational Area
Delaware Water Gap Nat. Rec. Area
Delaware Bay
Chesapeake Bay
Assateague Island National Seashore
Acadia Nat. Park
ATLANTIC OCEAN
New York
Boston
Philadelphia
Providence
Hartford
Albany
Springfield
Worcester
Portland
Manchester
Concord
Augusta
Trenton
Newark
Bridgeport
New Haven
Syracuse
Binghamton
Allentown
Norfolk
Virginia Beach
Portsmouth
Chesapeake
F G H J K
1 2 3 4 5 6
1:3.5M
KM MILES
175 150 125 100 75 50 25 0
100 75 50 25 0
continuation at the same scale

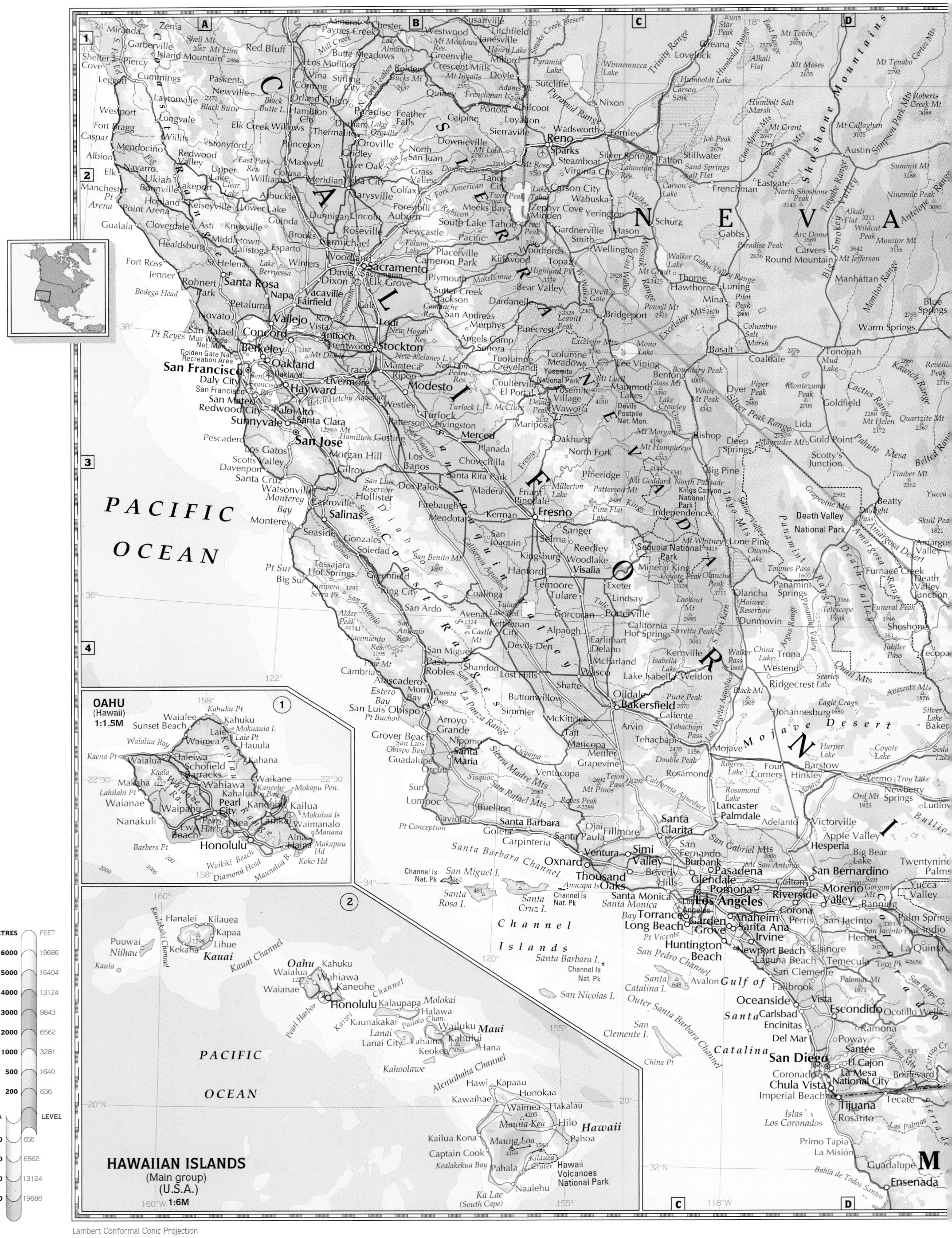
PACIFIC OCEAN
CALIFORNIA
NEVADA
SIERRA NEVADA
Coast Ranges
Diablo Range
San Joaquin Valley
Mojave Desert
Death Valley National Park
Sequoia National Park
Kings Canyon National Park
Yosemite National Park
Channel Islands
Channel Is Nat. Pk
Santa Barbara Channel
Gulf of Santa Catalina
Sacramento
San Francisco
Oakland
Berkeley
San Jose
Stockton
Modesto
Fresno
Bakersfield
Los Angeles
Long Beach
Santa Ana
Anaheim
Riverside
San Bernardino
San Diego
Tijuana
Ensenada
Reno
Sparks
Carson City
Santa Rosa
Salinas
Monterey
Santa Barbara
Oxnard
Ventura
Visalia
Merced
Chico
Redding
Eureka
Lake Tahoe
Mono Lake
Bishop
Tonopah
Lone Pine
Owens Lake
Ridgecrest
Lancaster
Palmdale
Pasadena
Glendale
Burbank
Pomona
Torrance
Huntington Beach
Irvine
Oceanside
Escondido
Chula Vista
Salinas
Hollister
Gilroy
Santa Cruz
Palo Alto
Hayward
Vallejo
Napa
Concord
Antioch
Lodi
Davis
Woodland
Yuba City
Marysville
Oroville
Auburn
Placerville
Sonora
Mariposa
Madera
Hanford
Porterville
Delano
Tehachapi
Mojave
Barstow
Victorville
Hesperia
Paso Robles
San Luis Obispo
Santa Maria
Lompoc
San Nicolas I.
Santa Catalina I.
San Clemente I.
Santa Cruz I.
Santa Rosa I.
San Miguel I.
Point Conception
Pt Reyes
Walker Lake
Pyramid Lake
Humboldt Range
Shoshone Mountains
Toiyabe Range
Inyo Mts
Panamint Range
OAHU (Hawaii) 1:1.5M
Honolulu
Pearl City
Kailua
Kaneohe
Waianae
Wahiawa
HAWAIIAN ISLANDS (Main group) (U.S.A.) 1:6M
Kauai
Niihau
Oahu
Molokai
Lanai
Maui
Kahoolawe
Hawaii
Hilo
Kailua Kona
Mauna Kea 4205
Mauna Loa 4169
Hawaii Volcanoes National Park
Ka Lae (South Cape)
METRES FEET
6000 19686
5000 16404
4000 13124
3000 9843
2000 6562
1000 3281
500 1640
200 656
SEA LEVEL
200 656
2000 6562
4000 13124
6000 19686

Lambert Conformal Conic Projection

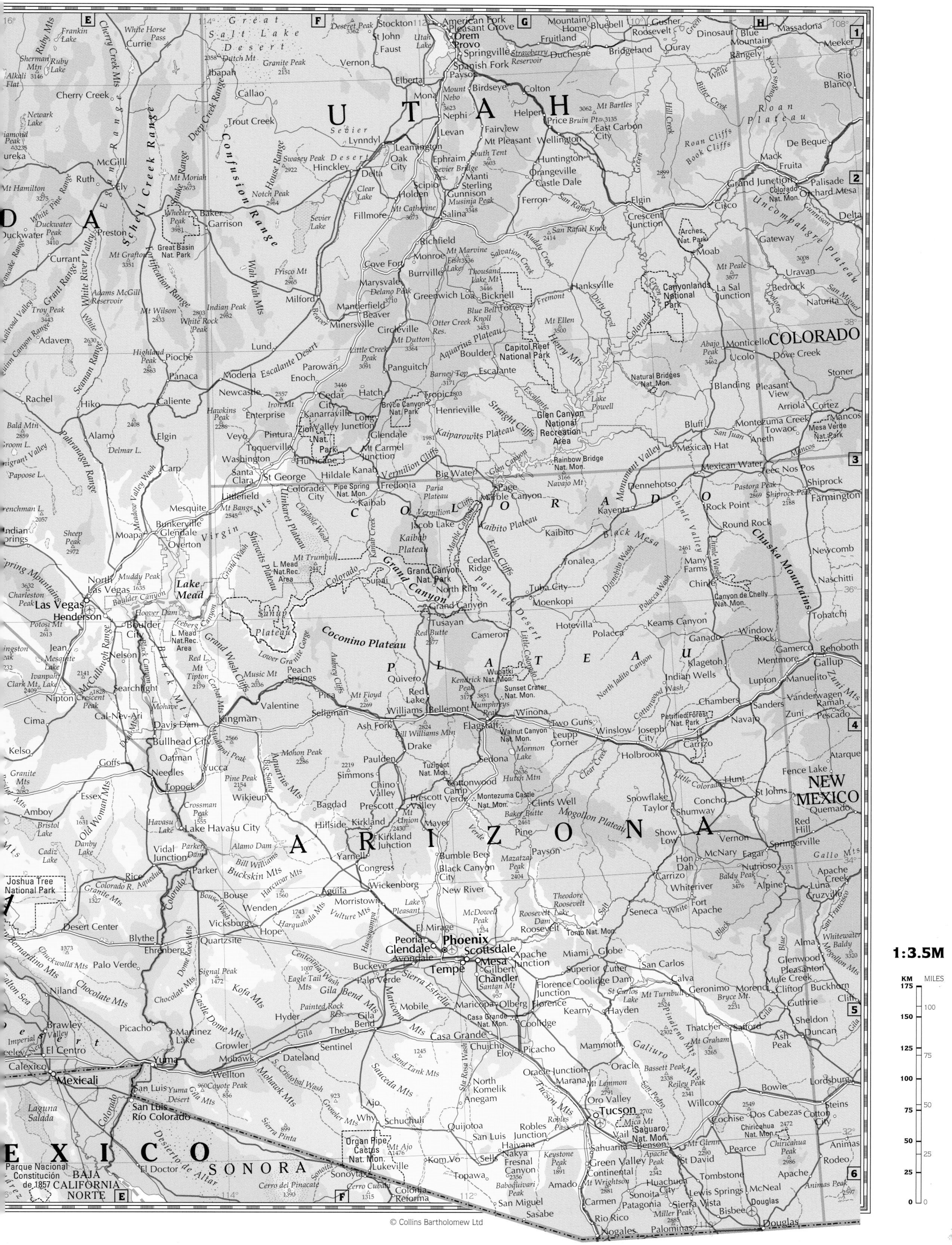
UTAH
ARIZONA
COLORADO
NEW MEXICO
MEXICO
SONORA
BAJA CALIFORNIA NORTE
Great Salt Lake Desert
Sevier Desert
Escalante Desert
COLORADO PLATEAU
Coconino Plateau
Kaibab Plateau
Kaiparowits Plateau
Aquarius Plateau
Roan Plateau
Uncompahgre Plateau
Mogollon Plateau
Painted Desert
Grand Canyon
Grand Canyon Nat. Park
Lake Mead
Lake Powell
Glen Canyon National Recreation Area
Capitol Reef National Park
Canyonlands National Park
Arches Nat. Park
Bryce Canyon Nat. Park
Zion Nat. Park
Great Basin Nat. Park
Mesa Verde Nat. Park
Petrified Forest Nat. Park
Joshua Tree National Park
Saguaro Nat. Mon.
Organ Pipe Cactus Nat. Mon.
Canyon de Chelly Nat. Mon.
Natural Bridges Nat. Mon.
Rainbow Bridge Nat. Mon.
Wupatki Nat. Mon.
Sunset Crater Nat. Mon.
Walnut Canyon Nat. Mon.
Montezuma Castle Nat. Mon.
Tuzigoot Nat. Mon.
Casa Grande Nat. Mon.
Chiricahua Nat. Mon.
Tonto Nat. Mon.
Pipe Spring Nat. Mon.
Colorado Nat. Mon.
Provo
Orem
Spanish Fork
Nephi
Price
Delta
Richfield
Cedar City
St George
Moab
Grand Junction
Montrose
Cortez
Durango
Farmington
Gallup
Las Vegas
Henderson
Boulder City
Kingman
Lake Havasu City
Bullhead City
Flagstaff
Sedona
Prescott
Winslow
Holbrook
Show Low
Phoenix
Glendale
Scottsdale
Tempe
Mesa
Chandler
Casa Grande
Tucson
Yuma
El Centro
Calexico
Mexicali
Nogales
Douglas
Bisbee
Sierra Vista
Tombstone
1:3.5M
KM
MILES
175
150
125
100
75
50
25
0
100
75
50
25
0
E
F
G
H
1
2
3
4
5
6

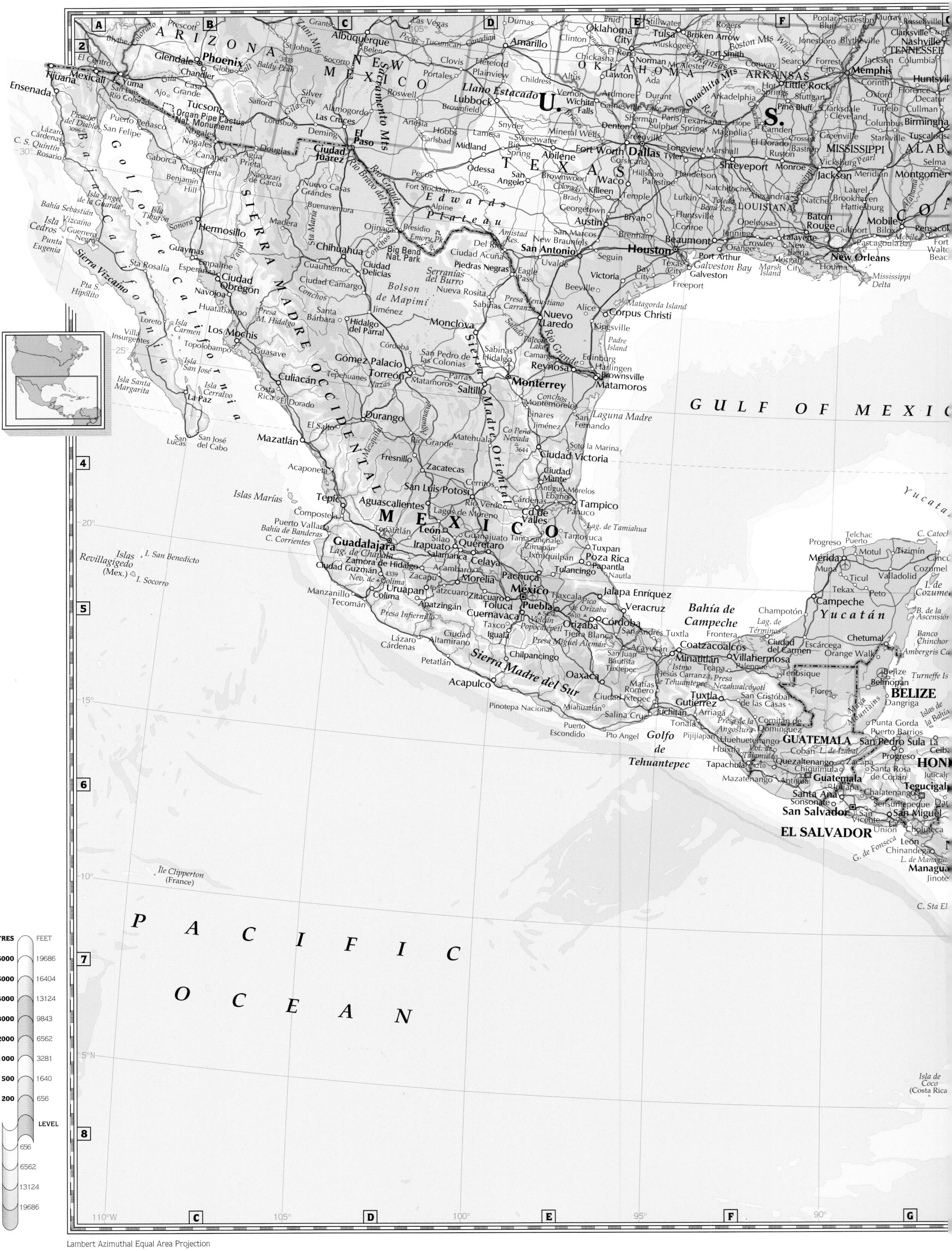

Lambert Azimuthal Equal Area Projection

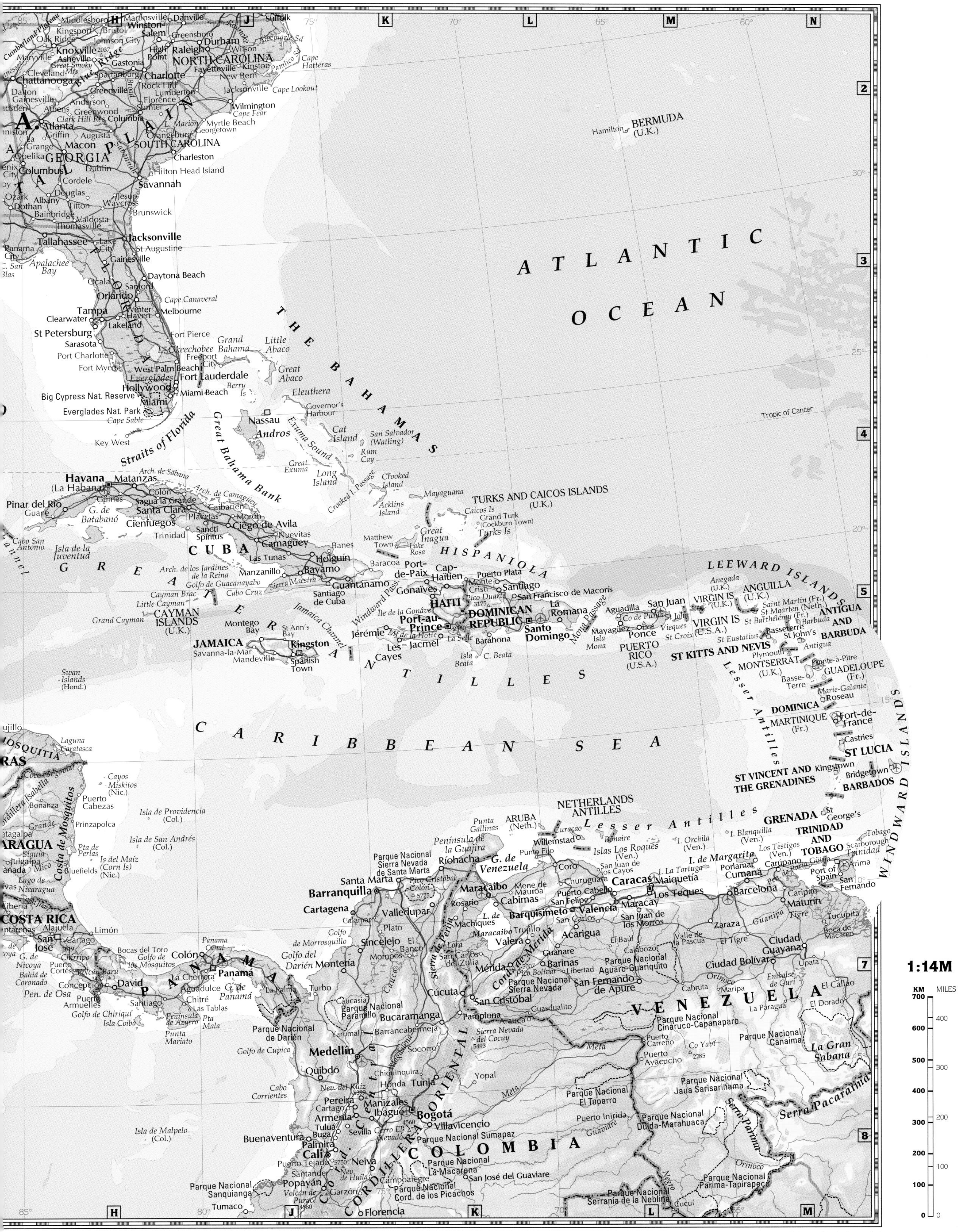

ATLANTIC OCEAN

CARIBBEAN SEA

BERMUDA (U.K.)
Hamilton

Tropic of Cancer

THE BAHAMAS

NORTH CAROLINA
Winston-Salem
Durham
Raleigh
Greensboro
High Point
Charlotte
Gastonia
Rock Hill
Fayetteville
New Bern
Wilmington
Cape Fear
Myrtle Beach
Georgetown

SOUTH CAROLINA
Columbia
Charleston
Hilton Head Island

GEORGIA
Atlanta
Macon
Augusta
Savannah
Columbus
Albany

Tallahassee
Jacksonville
St Augustine
Gainesville
Daytona Beach
Orlando
Tampa
Melbourne
Clearwater
Lakeland
St Petersburg
Sarasota
Fort Pierce
Port Charlotte
West Palm Beach
Fort Myers
Fort Lauderdale
Hollywood
Miami Beach
Big Cypress Nat. Reserve
Miami
Everglades Nat. Park
Cape Sable
Key West

Grand Bahama
Freeport
Little Abaco
Great Abaco
Berry Is
Eleuthera
Governor's Harbour
Nassau
Andros
Cat Island
San Salvador (Watling)
Exuma Sound
Great Exuma
Rum Cay
Long Island
Crooked Island
Acklins Island
Mayaguana
Great Inagua
Matthew Town
Lake Rosa

TURKS AND CAICOS ISLANDS (U.K.)
Caicos Is
Grand Turk (Cockburn Town)
Turks Is

CUBA
Havana (La Habana)
Matanzas
Pinar del Río
Colón
Güines
Sagua la Grande
Santa Clara
G. de Batabanó
Cienfuegos
Placetas
Caibarién
Morón
Ciego de Ávila
Sancti Spíritus
Trinidad
Nuevitas
Camagüey
Las Tunas
Banes
Holguín
Bayamo
Manzanillo
Guantánamo
Santiago de Cuba
Isla de la Juventud
Cabo San Antonio

HISPANIOLA
Baracoa
Port-de-Paix
Cap-Haïtien
Monte Cristi
Puerto Plata
Santiago
San Francisco de Macorís
Pico Duarte 3175
Gonaïves
HAITI
Île de la Gonâve
Port-au-Prince
Jérémie
DOMINICAN REPUBLIC
La Romana
Santo Domingo
Jacmel
Les Cayes
Barahona
La Selle
Isla Beata
C. Beata

Aguadilla
San Juan
Mayagüez
Ponce
PUERTO RICO (U.S.A.)
Isla Mona
Vieques
St Croix
St Thomas
St John

VIRGIN IS (U.K.)
VIRGIN IS (U.S.A.)
Anegada (U.K.)

LEEWARD ISLANDS
ANGUILLA (U.K.)
Saint Martin (Fr.)
St Maarten (Neth.)
St Barthélemy (Fr.)
Barbuda
ANTIGUA AND BARBUDA
Antigua
ST KITTS AND NEVIS
Basseterre
St John's
Plymouth
MONTSERRAT (U.K.)
Basse-Terre
Pointe-à-Pitre
GUADELOUPE (Fr.)
Marie-Galante
Roseau
DOMINICA
Fort-de-France
MARTINIQUE (Fr.)
Castries
ST LUCIA
Kingstown
Bridgetown
ST VINCENT AND THE GRENADINES
BARBADOS
GRENADA
St George's
TRINIDAD AND TOBAGO
Scarborough
Tobago
Port of Spain
Arima
San Fernando

Lesser Antilles
Windward Islands

JAMAICA
Montego Bay
St Ann's Bay
Savanna-la-Mar
Mandeville
Kingston
Spanish Town

CAYMAN ISLANDS (U.K.)
Cayman Brac
Little Cayman
Grand Cayman

GREATER ANTILLES

Swan Islands (Hond.)

MOSQUITIA
Laguna Caratasca
Cayos Miskitos (Nic.)
Puerto Cabezas
Prinzapolca
Isla de Providencia (Col.)
Isla de San Andrés (Col.)
Is del Maíz (Corn Is) (Nic.)
Bluefields
Lago de Nicaragua

NICARAGUA
Matagalpa
Juigalpa
Granada
Liberia

COSTA RICA
San José
Alajuela
Cartago
Limón
Puntarenas
Chirripó 3819
G. de Nicoya
Pen. de Osa

PANAMA
Colón
Panama Canal
Panamá
David
Santiago
Aguadulce
Chitré
Las Tablas
Golfo de Chiriquí
Isla Coiba
Punta Mariato
Pta Mala

NETHERLANDS ANTILLES
ARUBA (Neth.)
Curaçao
Willemstad
Bonaire
Punta Gallinas
Punta Fijo
I. Orchila (Ven.)
Islas Los Roques (Ven.)
I. La Tortuga (Ven.)
Los Testigos (Ven.)
I. Blanquilla (Ven.)
I. de Margarita (Ven.)
Porlamar
Carúpano
Cumaná

Punta Gallinas
Península de la Guajira
Riohacha
G. de Venezuela
Maracaibo
Coro
Churuguara
San Felipe
Barquisimeto
Caracas
Maiquetía
Los Teques
Barcelona
Maturín
Tucupita
Boca de Macareo

Santa Marta
Parque Nacional Sierra Nevada de Santa Marta
Pico Cristóbal Colón 5775
Barranquilla
Cartagena
Valledupar
Cabimas
Mene de Mauroa
Puerto Cabello
Valencia
Maracay
San Juan de los Morros
Zaraza
Guanipa
El Tigre

Sincelejo
El Banco
Mompós
Plato
Calamar
Golfo de Morrosquillo
Montería
Turbo
Caucasia
Yarumal
Maracaibo
L. de Maracaibo
Machiques
Trujillo
Mérida
Pico Bolívar 5007
Barinas
San Carlos del Zulia
Guanare
Acarigua
San Carlos
El Baúl
Calabozo
Valle de la Pascua
Ciudad Bolívar
Ciudad Guayana
Upata

Golfo del Darién
Parque Nacional Paramillo
Bucaramanga
Barrancabermeja
Cúcuta
Pamplona
San Cristóbal
Arauca
Guasdualito
San Fernando de Apure
Cabruta
El Callao
El Dorado
Maripa
Puerto Carreño
Cravo Yaví 2285

Parque Nacional de Darién
Golfo de Cupica
Cabo Corrientes
Medellín
Quibdó
Socorro
Tunja
Yopal
Parque Nacional El Cocuy 5493
Parque Nacional Sierra Nevada
San Fernando
Meta
Puerto Ayacucho
Parque Nacional Cinaruco-Capanaparo

VENEZUELA
Parque Nacional Canaima
La Gran Sabana
Serra Pacaraima

Pereira
Manizales
Nev. del Ruiz
Honda
Armenia
Cartago
Ibagué
Cerro El Nevado 4560
Bogotá
Villavicencio
Tuluá
Buga
Sevilla
Parque Nacional Sumapaz
Puerto Inírida
Parque Nacional Duida-Marahuaca
Serranía Parima

Buenaventura
Cali
Palmira
Puerto Tejada
Neiva
La Plata
San José del Guaviare
Parque Nacional Serranía de la Neblina
Cucuí

Popayán
Volcán Puracé 4750
Santander
Garzón
Campoalegre
La Macarena
COLOMBIA
Parque Nacional Tinigua
Parque Nacional Sierra de la Macarena
Parque Nacional Cord. de los Picachos
Florencia
Orinoco
Parque Nacional Jaua Sarisariñama
Parque Nacional El Tuparro

Tumaco
Sanquianga
Parque Nacional Sanquianga

CORDILLERA OCCIDENTAL
CORDILLERA CENTRAL
CORDILLERA ORIENTAL

Cauca
Magdalena
Meta

1:14M

KM	MILES
700	
600	400
500	300
400	
300	200
200	100
100	
0	0

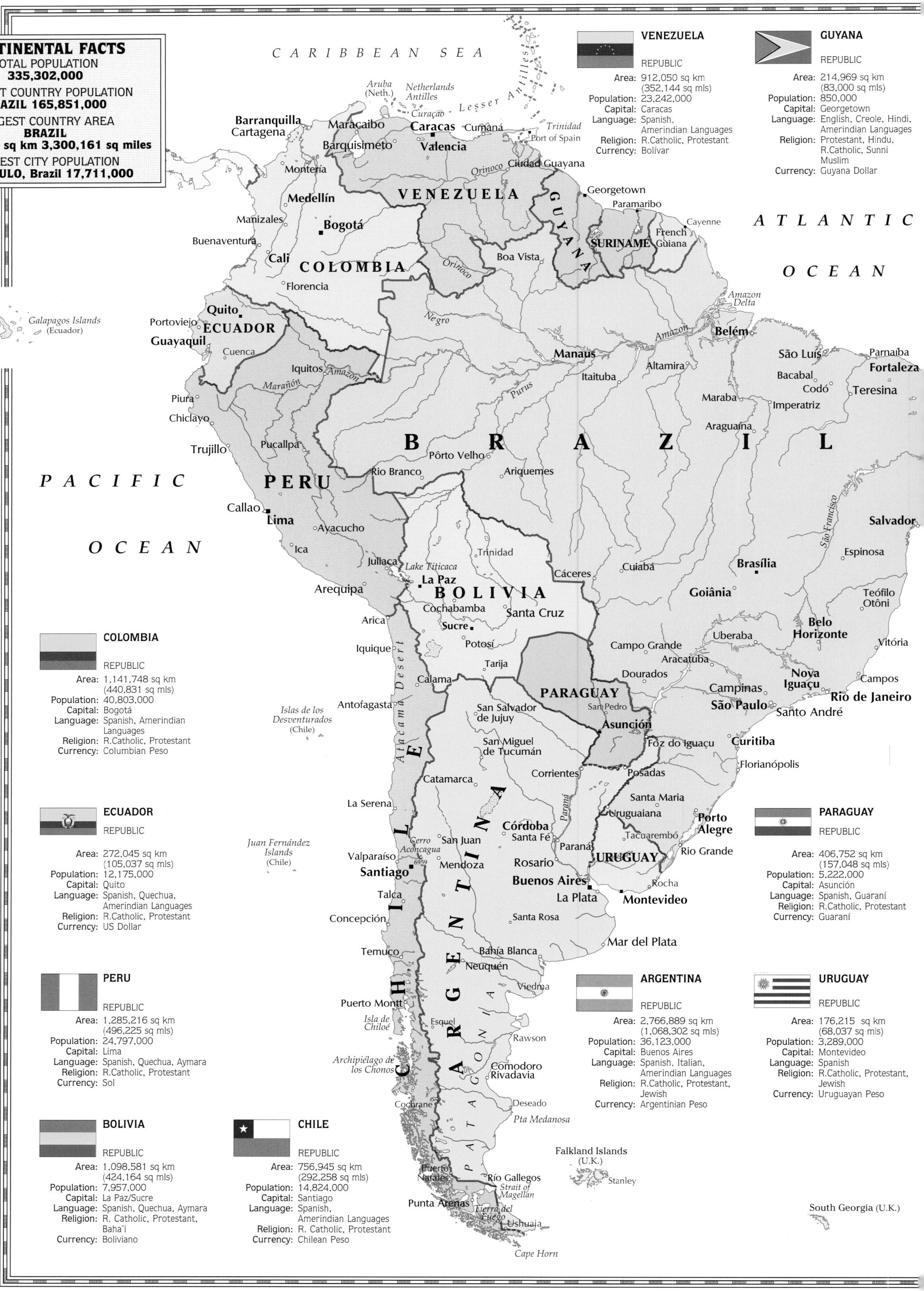

CONTINENTAL FACTS
TOTAL POPULATION
335,302,000
LARGEST COUNTRY POPULATION
BRAZIL 165,851,000
LARGEST COUNTRY AREA
BRAZIL
8,547,379 sq km 3,300,161 sq miles
LARGEST CITY POPULATION
SÃO PAULO, Brazil 17,711,000

CARIBBEAN SEA

VENEZUELA
REPUBLIC
Area: 912,050 sq km
(352,144 sq mls)
Population: 23,242,000
Capital: Caracas
Language: Spanish,
Amerindian Languages
Religion: R.Catholic, Protestant
Currency: Bolívar

GUYANA
REPUBLIC
Area: 214,969 sq km
(83,000 sq mls)
Population: 850,000
Capital: Georgetown
Language: English, Creole, Hindi,
Amerindian Languages
Religion: Protestant, Hindu,
R.Catholic, Sunni
Muslim
Currency: Guyana Dollar

Aruba
(Neth.)
Netherlands
Antilles
Curaçao
Lesser Antilles
Trinidad
Port of Spain

ATLANTIC

OCEAN

Barranquilla
Cartagena
Maracaibo
Barquisiméto
Caracas
Valencia
Cumaná

Montería
Orinoco
Ciudad Guayana

Medellín
VENEZUELA
GUYANA
Georgetown
Paramaribo

Manizales
Bogotá
Boa Vista
SURINAME
Cayenne
French
Guiana

Buenaventura
Cali
COLOMBIA
Orinoco

Florencia

Galapagos Islands
(Ecuador)

Portoviejo
Quito
ECUADOR
Negro
Amazon
Delta

Guayaquil
Cuenca
Belém

Iquitos
Amazon
Manaus
Altamira
São Luís
Parnaíba
Fortaleza

Piura
Marañón
Itaituba
Bacabal
Codó
Teresina

Chiclayo
Purus
Maraba
Imperatriz

Trujillo
Pucallpa
B   R   A   Z   I   L

Pôrto Velho
Araguaína

PACIFIC
PERU
Rio Branco
Ariquemes

Callao
Lima
Ayacucho
Salvador

OCEAN
Ica
Espinosa

Juliaca
Lake Titicaca
Trinidad
Cáceres
Cuiabá
Brasília
Teófilo
Otôni

La Paz
São Francisco

Arequipa
BOLIVIA
Goiânia
Belo
Horizonte
Vitória

Arica
Cochabamba
Santa Cruz

Sucre
Uberaba
Nova
Iguaçu
Campos

Iquique
Potosí
Campo Grande
Aracatúba

Tarija
Dourados
Campinas
São Paulo
Rio de Janeiro

Calama
PARAGUAY
Santo André

Antofagasta
Islas de los
Desventurados
(Chile)
San Salvador
de Jujuy
San Pedro
Asunción
Foz do Iguaçu
Curitiba

San Miguel
de Tucumán
Florianópolis

Atacama Desert
Posadas

Catamarca
Corrientes
Santa Maria

La Serena
Paraná
Uruguaiana
Tacuarembó
Porto
Alegre

Juan Fernández
Islands
(Chile)
Córdoba
Santa Fé
Rio Grande

Cerro
Aconcagua
6959
San Juan
Paraná
URUGUAY

Valparaíso
Rosario

Santiago
Mendoza
Buenos Aires
Rocha

Talca
La Plata
Montevideo

Concepción
Santa Rosa
Mar del Plata

Temuco
Bahía Blanca

Neuquén

Viedma

Puerto Montt
ARGENTINA

Isla de
Chiloé
Esquel
Rawson

Archipiélago de
los Chonos
PATAGONIA
Comodoro
Rivadavia

Deseado

Cochrane
Pta Medanosa

Falkland Islands
(U.K.)
Stanley

Puerto
Natales
CHILE
Río Gallegos
Strait of
Magellan

Punta Arenas
Tierra del
Fuego
Ushuaia

South Georgia (U.K.)

Cape Horn

COLOMBIA
REPUBLIC
Area: 1,141,748 sq km
(440,831 sq mls)
Population: 40,803,000
Capital: Bogotá
Language: Spanish, Amerindian
Languages
Religion: R.Catholic, Protestant
Currency: Columbian Peso

ECUADOR
REPUBLIC
Area: 272,045 sq km
(105,037 sq mls)
Population: 12,175,000
Capital: Quito
Language: Spanish, Quechua,
Amerindian Languages
Religion: R.Catholic, Protestant
Currency: US Dollar

PERU
REPUBLIC
Area: 1,285,216 sq km
(496,225 sq mls)
Population: 24,797,000
Capital: Lima
Language: Spanish, Quechua, Aymara
Religion: R.Catholic, Protestant
Currency: Sol

BOLIVIA
REPUBLIC
Area: 1,098,581 sq km
(424,164 sq mls)
Population: 7,957,000
Capital: La Paz/Sucre
Language: Spanish, Quechua, Aymara
Religion: R. Catholic, Protestant,
Baha'i
Currency: Boliviano

CHILE
REPUBLIC
Area: 756,945 sq km
(292,258 sq mls)
Population: 14,824,000
Capital: Santiago
Language: Spanish,
Amerindian Languages
Religion: R. Catholic, Protestant
Currency: Chilean Peso

PARAGUAY
REPUBLIC
Area: 406,752 sq km
(157,048 sq mls)
Population: 5,222,000
Capital: Asunción
Language: Spanish, Guaraní
Religion: R.Catholic, Protestant
Currency: Guaraní

ARGENTINA
REPUBLIC
Area: 2,766,889 sq km
(1,068,302 sq mls)
Population: 36,123,000
Capital: Buenos Aires
Language: Spanish, Italian,
Amerindian Languages
Religion: R.Catholic, Protestant,
Jewish
Currency: Argentinian Peso

URUGUAY
REPUBLIC
Area: 176,215 sq km
(68,037 sq mls)
Population: 3,289,000
Capital: Montevideo
Language: Spanish
Religion: R.Catholic, Protestant,
Jewish
Currency: Uruguayan Peso

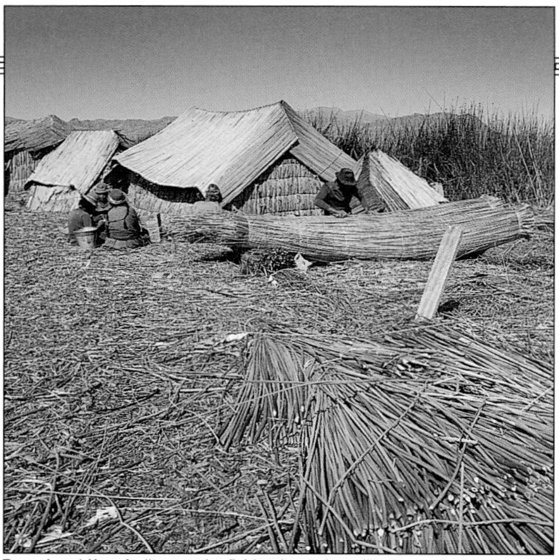

Peru. Local Uros Indians make fishing boats by collecting and tying together the reeds found around Lake Titicaca.

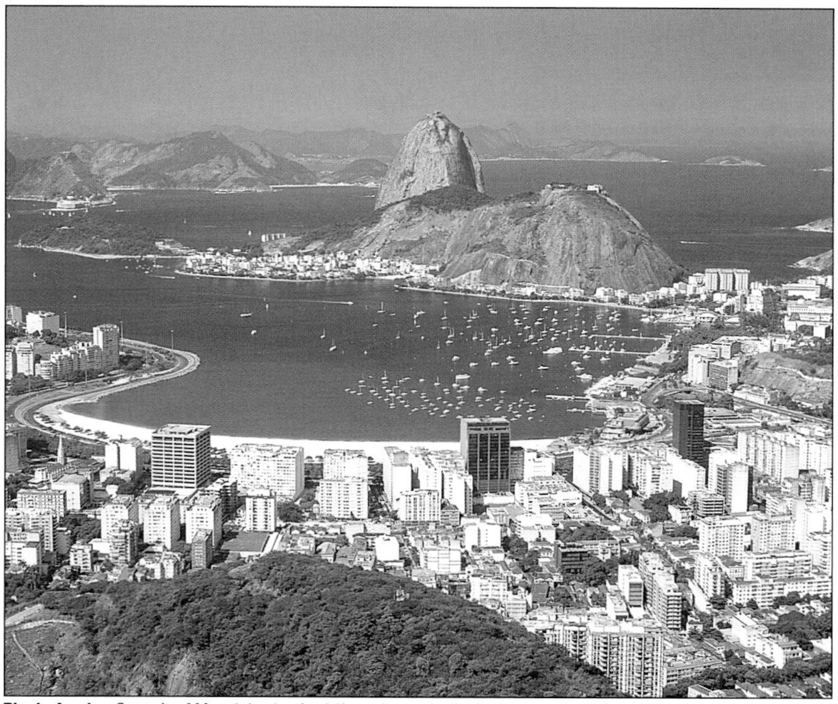

Rio de Janeiro. Sugar Loaf Mountain stands at the entrance to the harbour in one of Brazil's major ports.

Natal
João Pessoa
Recife
Maceió
racaju

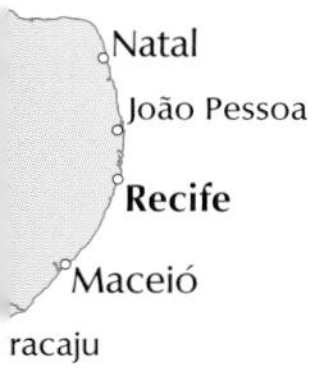

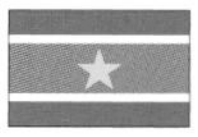

SURINAME

REPUBLIC
Area: 163,820 sq km
(63,251 sq mls)
Population: 414,000
Capital: Paramaribo
Language: Dutch, Surinamese,
English, Hindi, Javanese
Religion: Hindu, R.Catholic,
Protestant, Sunni
Muslim
Currency: Suriname Guilder

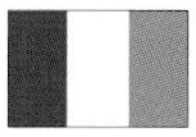

FRENCH GUIANA

FRENCH TERRITORY
Area: 90,000 sq km
(34,749 sq mls)
Population: 167,000
Capital: Cayenne
Language: French, French Creole
Religion: R.Catholic, Protestant
Currency: Euro

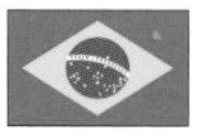

BRAZIL

REPUBLIC
Area: 8,547,379 sq km
(3,300,161 sq mls)
Population: 165,851,000
Capital: Brasília
Language: Portuguese, German,
Japanese, Italian,
Amerindian Languages
Religion: R. Catholic, Spiritist,
Protestant
Currency: Real

POPULATION

Caracas
Medellín
Bogotá
Fortaleza
Recife
Lima
Salvador
Belo Horizonte
Rio de Janeiro
São Paulo
Curitiba
Pôrto Alegre
Santiago
Buenos Aires

POPULATION
Inhabitants

per sq km	per sq ml
over 200	over 500
100-200	250-500
40-100	100-250
10-40	25-100
2-10	5-25
0-2	0-5
uninhabited	

CITIES
- Over 5 million population
- 2.5 - 5 million population

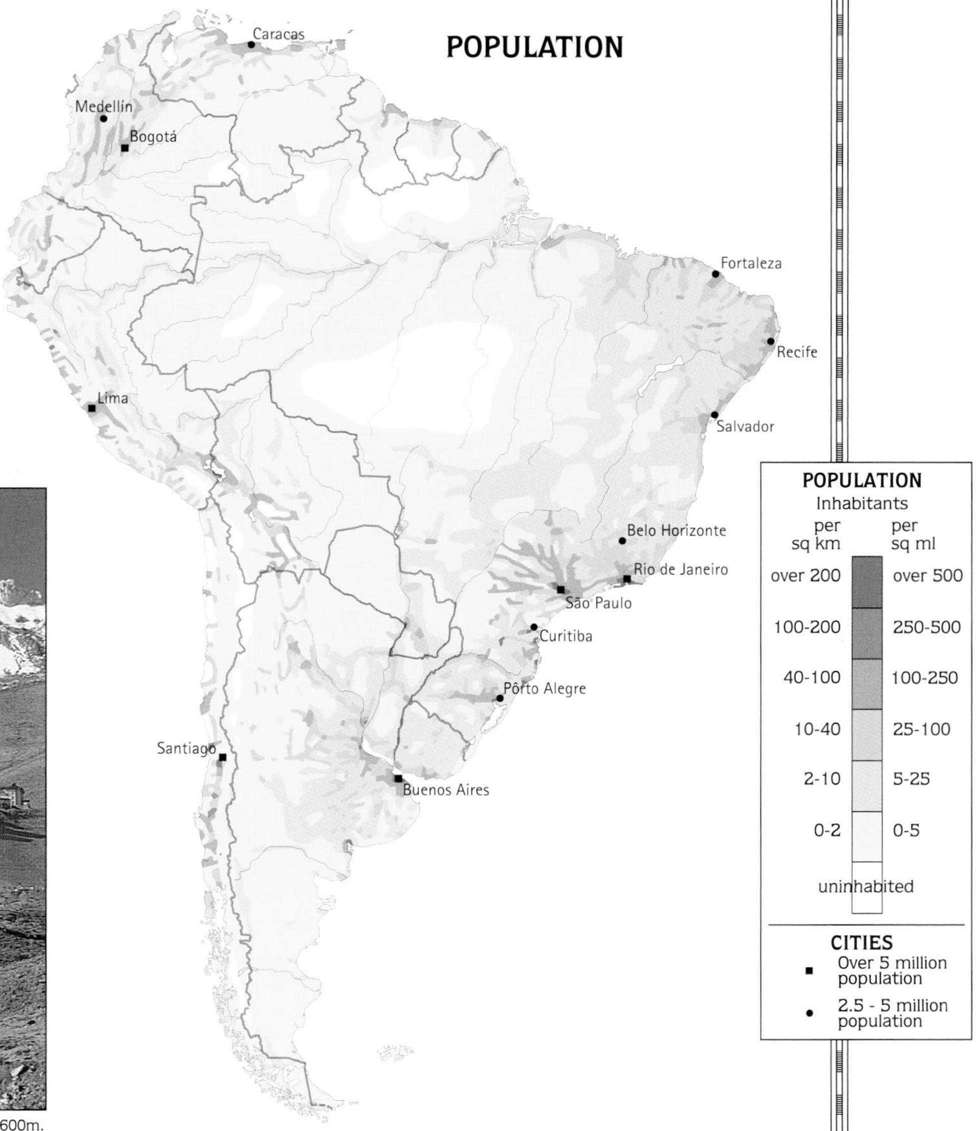

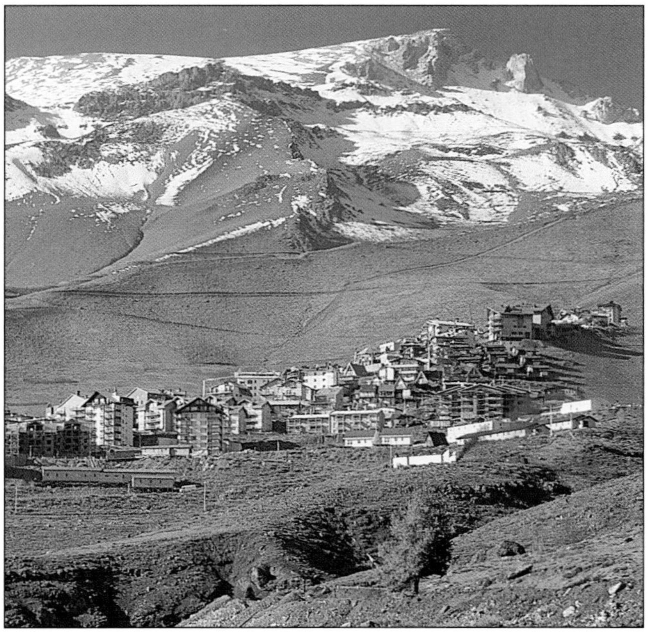

La Parva, Chile. A resort in the Andes near Santiago where skiing is possible to over 3600m.

CARIBBEAN SEA

ATLANTIC OCEAN

L. Nicaragua

Gallinas Pt.
Aruba
Netherlands
Antilles
Curaçao
Lesser Antilles
Margarita
Trinidad

G. of Darien
L. Maracaibo
Orinoco
Orinoco Delta
Waini Point

Pointe Isère

Cabo Orange

Cotopaxi
5897
Chimborazo
6310
Caquetá
Putumayo
Japurá
Amazon
Ucayali
Juruá

Meta
Guaviare
Branco
Negro
Balbina Resr.
Amazon
Amazon Delta
I. de Marajó

Huascarán
6768

Selvas

Purus
Madeira
Iriri
Xingu
Tapajós
Tocantins
Tucuruí Resr.
Parnaíba

Beni
Guaporé
Jiparaná
Juruena
Arinos
Teles Pires
Araguaia
Tocantins

Lago de San Luis
San Miguel

Planalto do Mato Grosso

Planalto do Brasil

Lake Titicaca
Yungas
Izozog Marshes

L. Poopó

Altiplano

Cordillera Oriental
Cordillera Occidental
Cordillera Central

Paraguaibá
Grande
Velhas
São Francisco

Gran Chaco

Paraná
Paranapanema

Cabo de São Tomé
Cabo Frio

PACIFIC OCEAN

Pta Tetas

Islas de los Desventurados
(Chile)

Pta Ballena
Pta Morro

Atacama Desert

Pilcomayo
Teuco

Iguaçu Falls

ATLANTIC OCEAN

Salado
Desaguadero
Salinas Grandes
Sierras de Córdoba

Uruguay
Paraná

Juan Fernández Islands
(Chile)

Cerro Aconcagua
6959

Pampas

Lagoa dos Patos
Lagoa Mirim

Río de la Plata

ANDES

Colorado

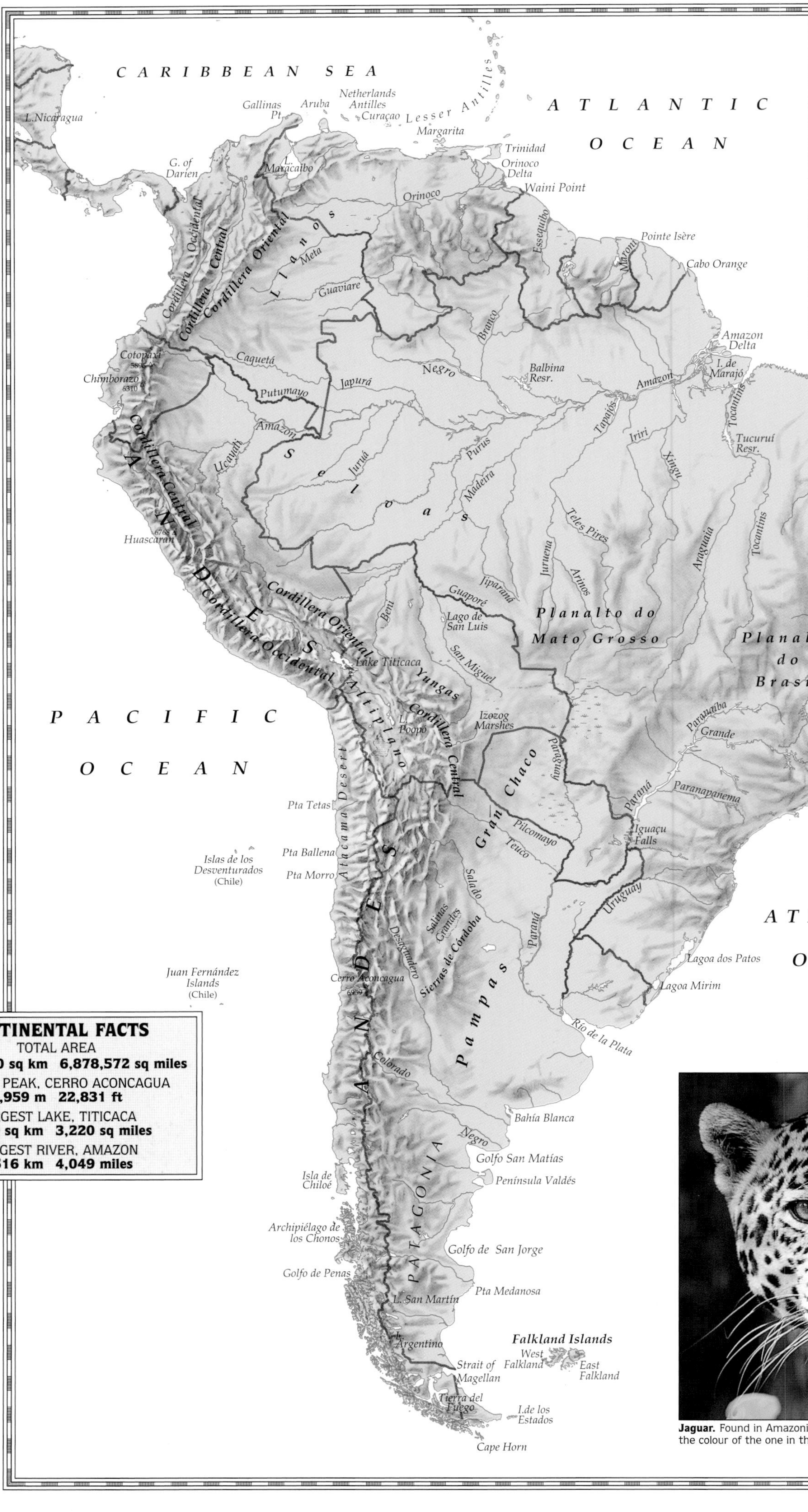

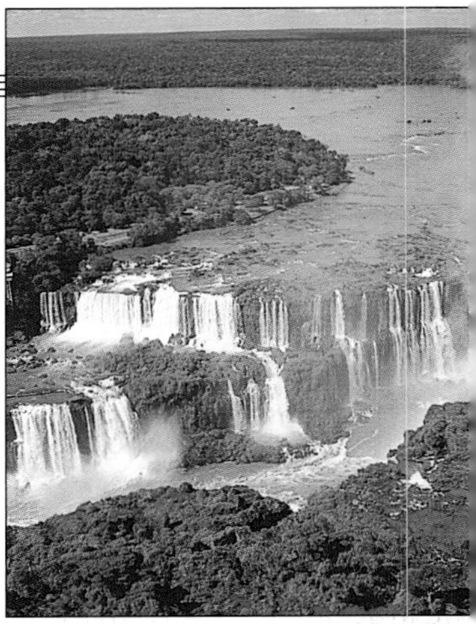

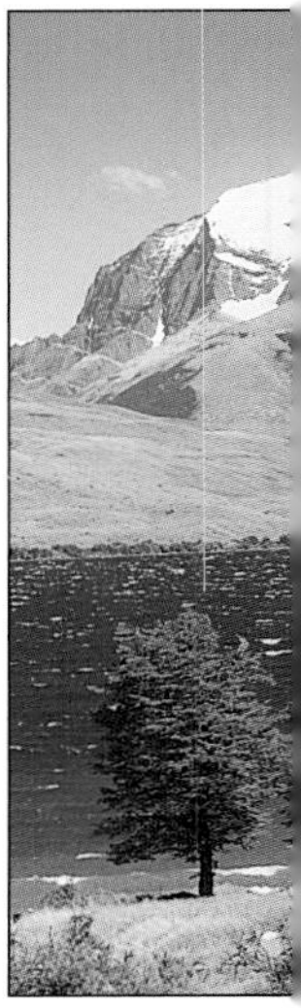

CONTINENTAL FACTS
TOTAL AREA
17,815,420 sq km   6,878,572 sq miles
HIGHEST PEAK, CERRO ACONCAGUA
6,959 m   22,831 ft
LARGEST LAKE, TITICACA
8,340 sq km   3,220 sq miles
LONGEST RIVER, AMAZON
6,516 km   4,049 miles

Negro
Bahía Blanca

Golfo San Matías
Península Valdés

Isla de Chiloé

Archipiélago de los Chonos

Golfo de San Jorge

Golfo de Penas

Pta Medanosa

PATAGONIA

L. San Martín

L. Argentino

Falkland Islands
West Falkland
East Falkland

Strait of Magellan
Tierra del Fuego
I. de los Estados

Cape Horn

Iguaçu Falls. These spectacular waterfalls on the border of Brazil and Argentina plunge between 60 and 80 m.

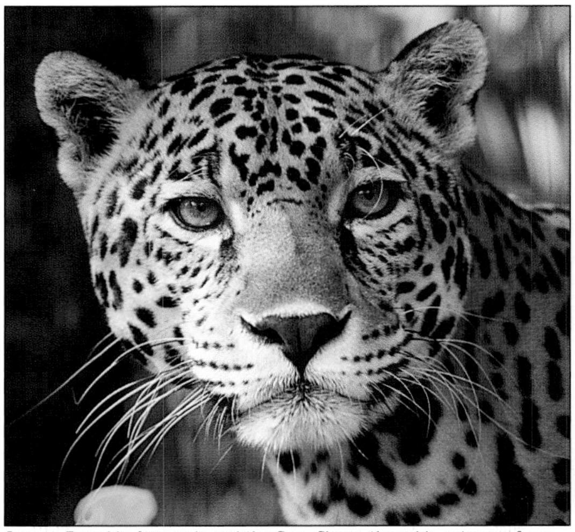

Jaguar. Found in Amazonia and the Gran Chaco, these big cats vary from the colour of the one in the photograph to plain black or white coats.

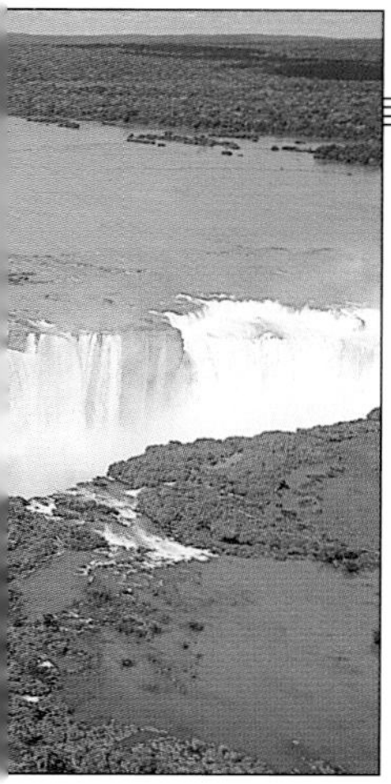

CLIMATE

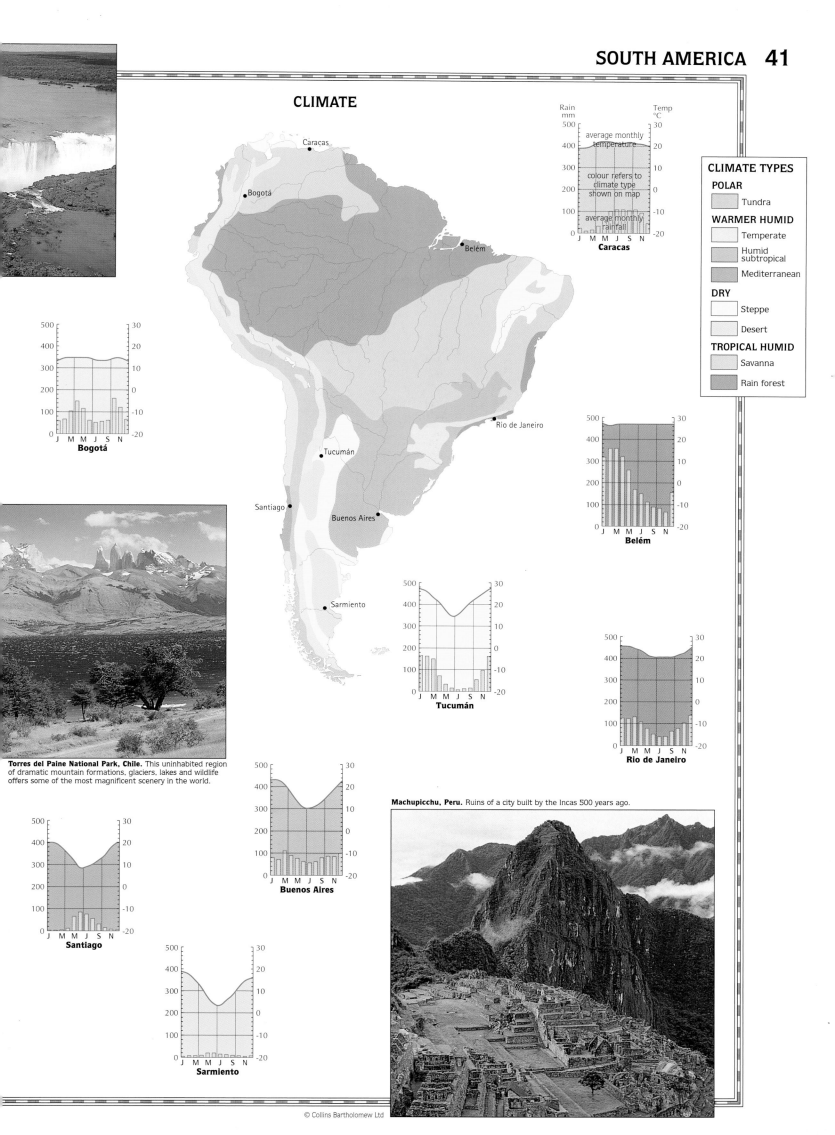

Caracas

average monthly temperature

colour refers to climate type shown on map

average monthly rainfall

Bogotá

Belém

Tucumán

Rio de Janeiro

Buenos Aires

Santiago

Sarmiento

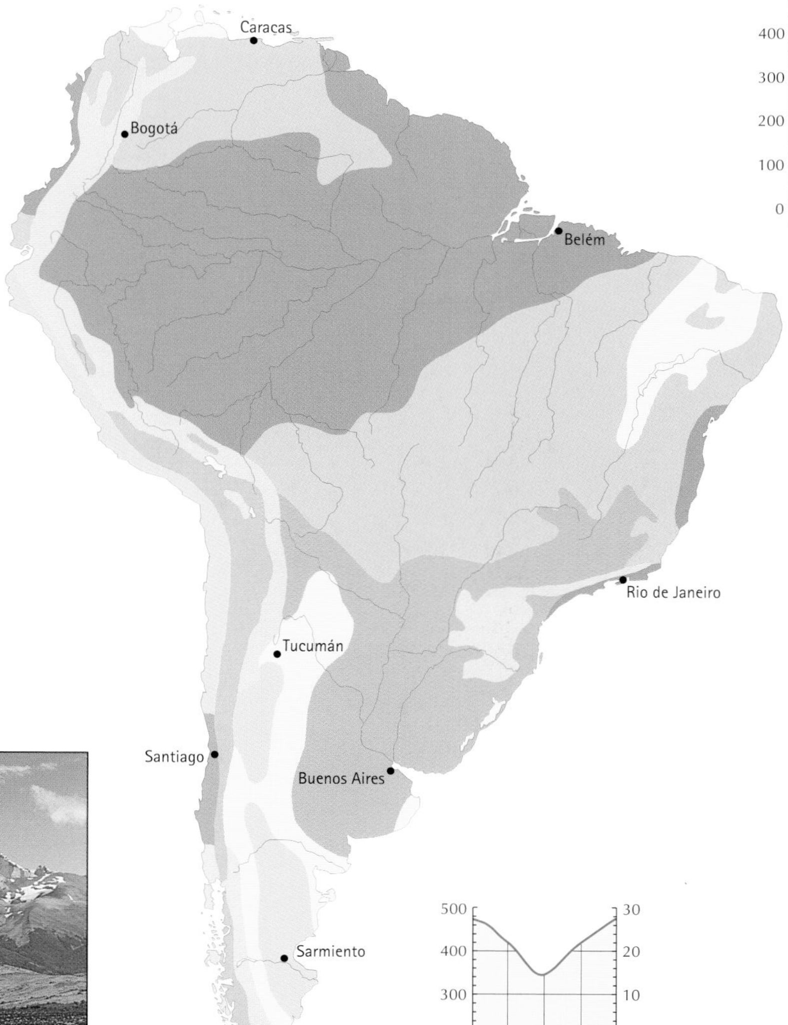

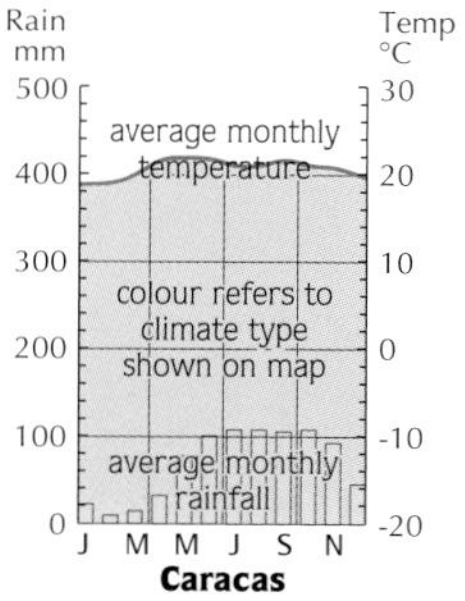

CLIMATE TYPES

POLAR

Tundra

WARMER HUMID

Temperate

Humid subtropical

Mediterranean

DRY

Steppe

Desert

TROPICAL HUMID

Savanna

Rain forest

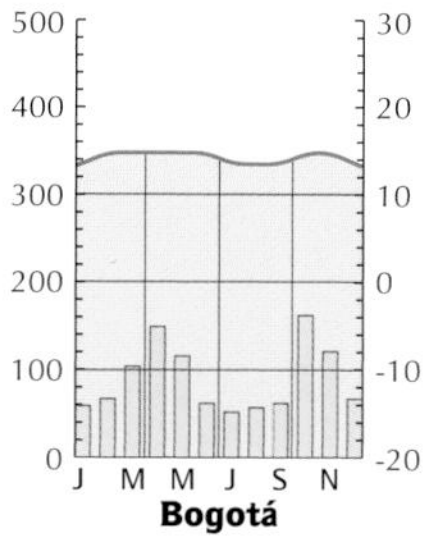

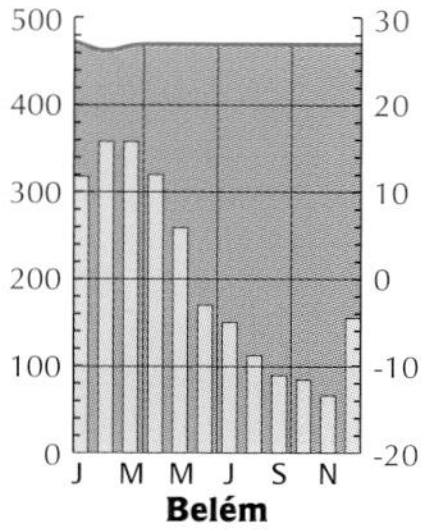

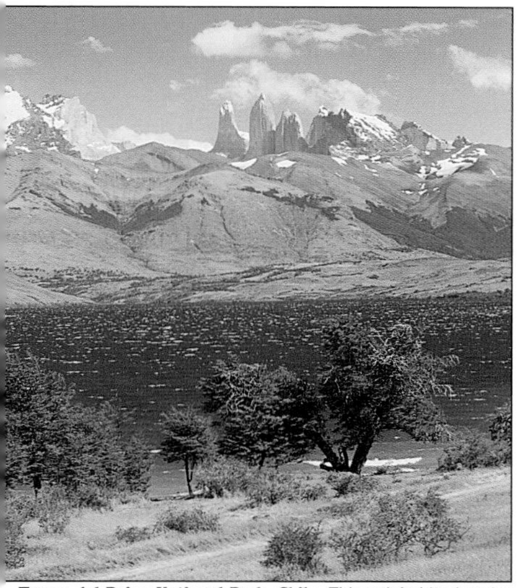

Torres del Paine National Park, Chile. This uninhabited region of dramatic mountain formations, glaciers, lakes and wildlife offers some of the most magnificent scenery in the world.

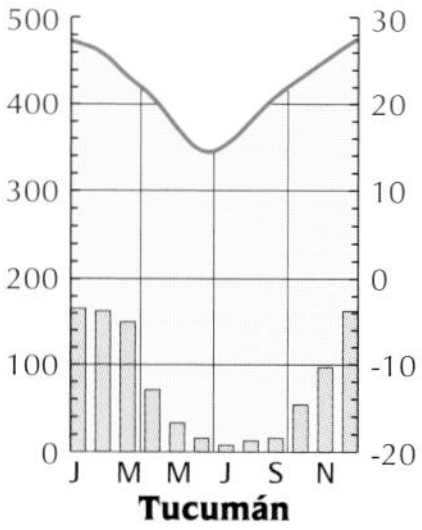

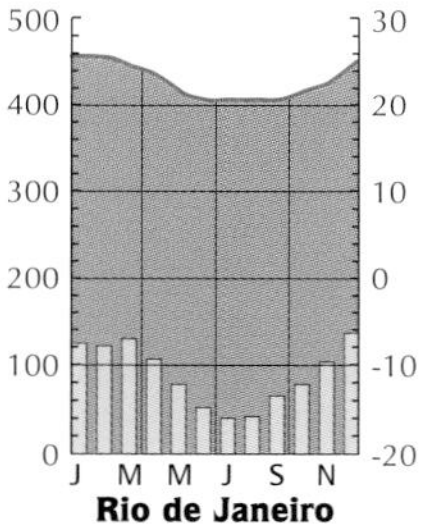

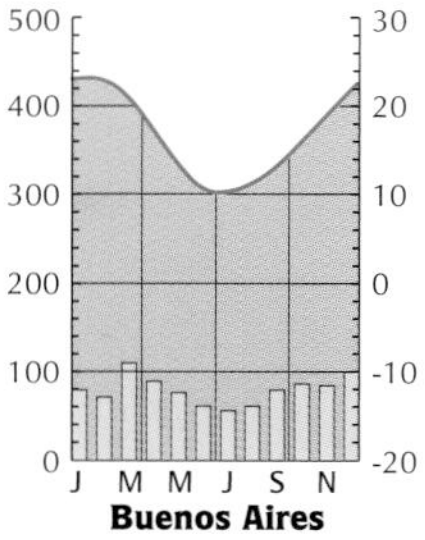

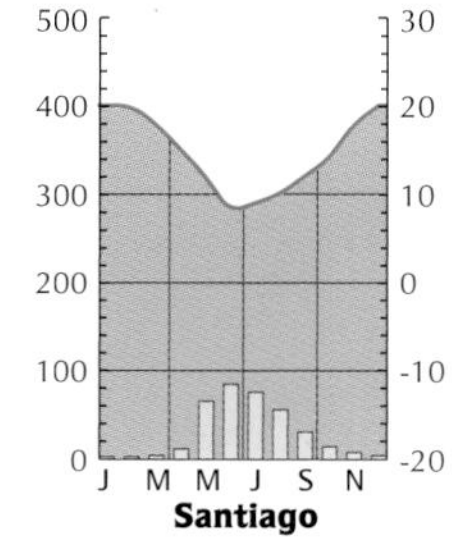

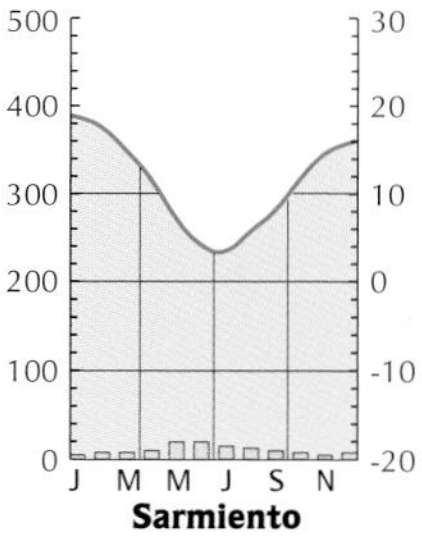

Machupicchu, Peru. Ruins of a city built by the Incas 500 years ago.

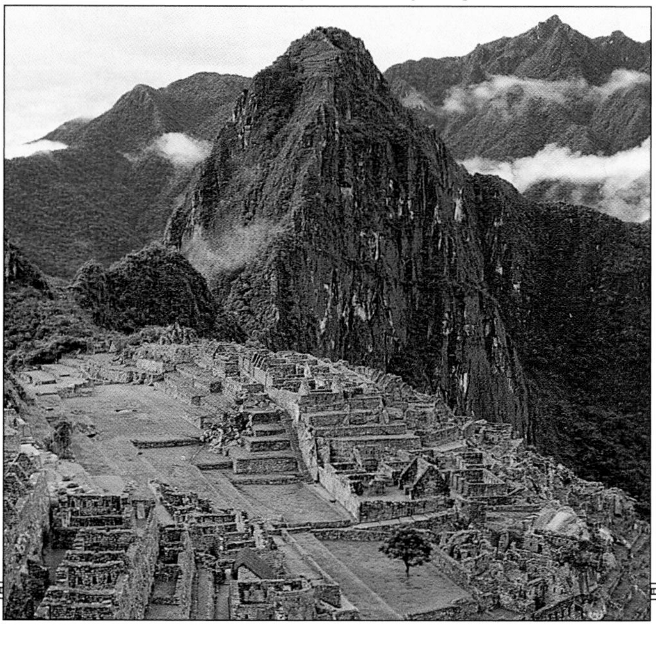

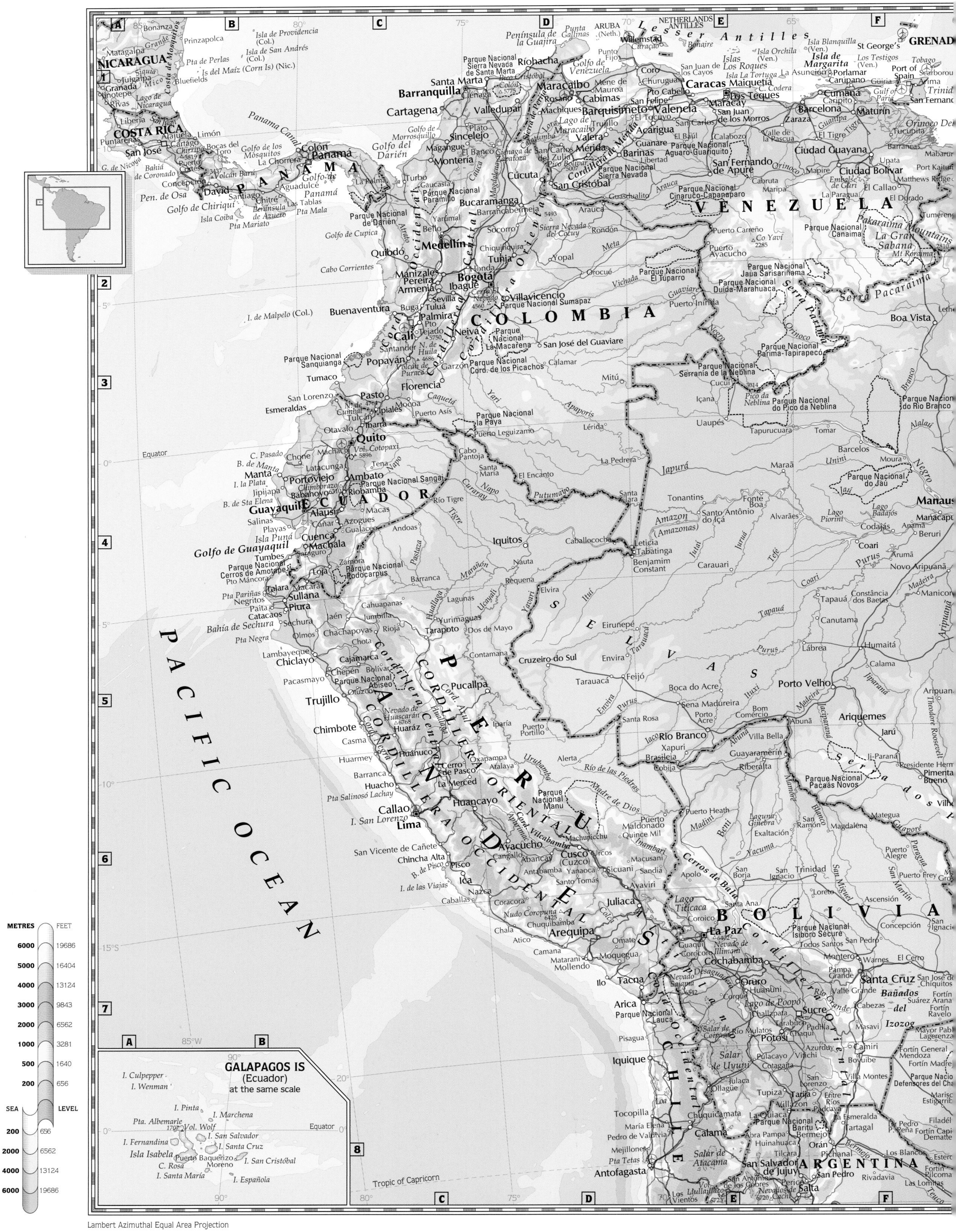
NICARAGUA
COSTA RICA
PANAMÁ
COLOMBIA
VENEZUELA
ECUADOR
PERU
BOLIVIA
CHILE
ARGENTINA
PACIFIC OCEAN
Lesser Antilles
NETHERLANDS ANTILLES
ARUBA (Neth.)
SELVAS
ANDES
CORDILLERA OCCIDENTAL
CORDILLERA CENTRAL
CORDILLERA ORIENTAL
Cordillera Real
Cordillera Occidental
Cordillera Oriental
Golfo de Panamá
Golfo de Guayaquil
Golfo de Venezuela
Golfo del Darién
Lago de Maracaibo
Lago Titicaca
Amazon (Amazonas)
Orinoco
Equator
Tropic of Capricorn
Bogotá
Caracas
Quito
Lima
La Paz
Medellín
Cali
Barranquilla
Cartagena
Maracaibo
Valencia
Guayaquil
Cuenca
Iquitos
Manaus
Arequipa
Cusco (Cuzco)
Cochabamba
Santa Cruz
Sucre
Potosí
Oruro
Arica
Iquique
Antofagasta
Trujillo
Chiclayo
Piura
Callao
Panamá
Colón
David
San José
Limón
Ciudad Guayana
Ciudad Bolívar
Barquisimeto
Cúcuta
Bucaramanga
Porto Velho
Rio Branco
GALAPAGOS IS
(Ecuador)
at the same scale
Isla Isabela
I. Fernandina
I. San Cristóbal
I. Santa Cruz
I. Española
METRES
FEET
6000
19686
5000
16404
4000
13124
3000
9843
2000
6562
1000
3281
500
1640
200
656
SEA
LEVEL

Lambert Azimuthal Equal Area Projection

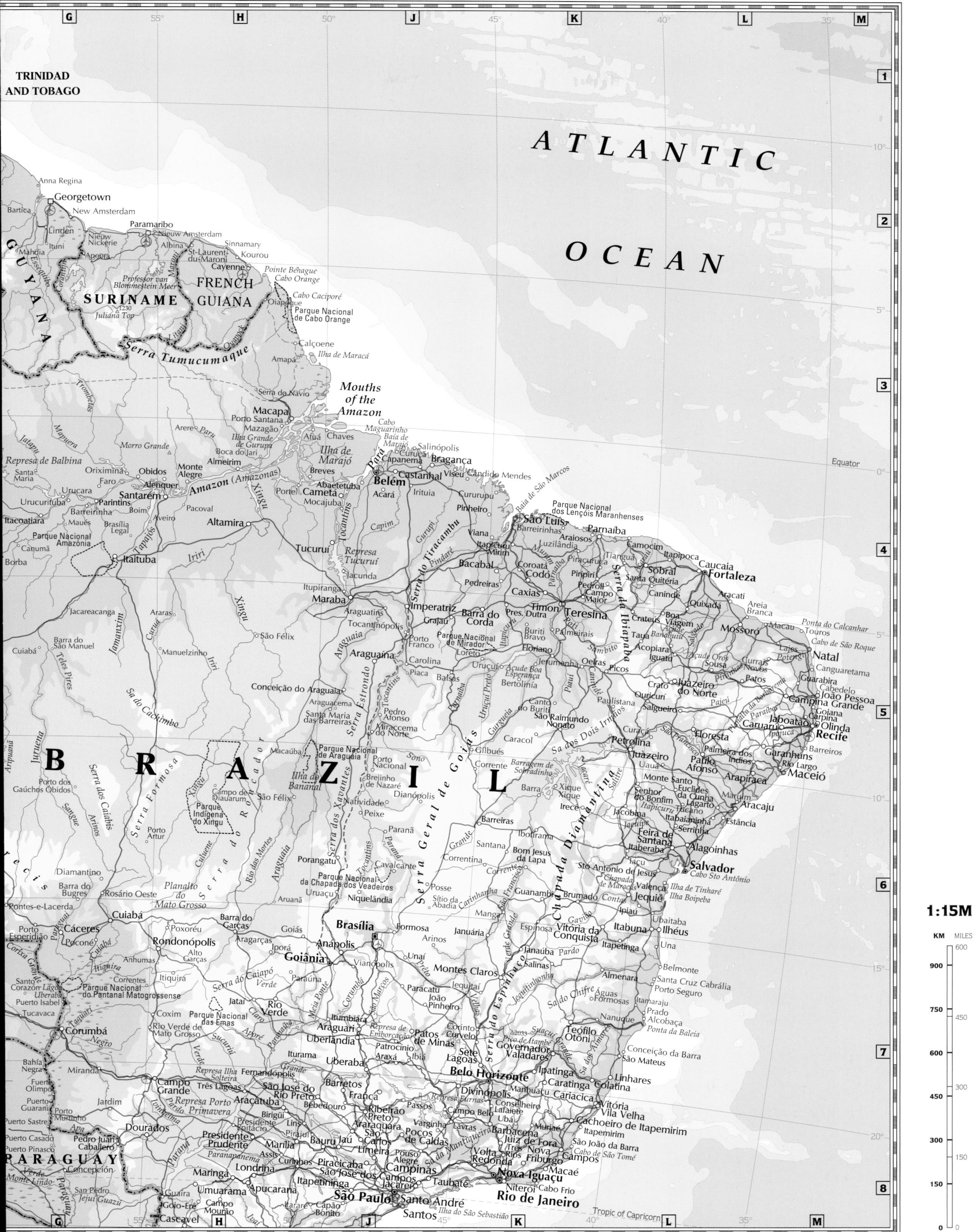

ATLANTIC

OCEAN

TRINIDAD
AND TOBAGO

Equator

Mouths
of the
Amazon

1:15M

KM   MILES
           600

900
           450

750

600   300

450

           150

300

150

© Collins Bartholomew Ltd

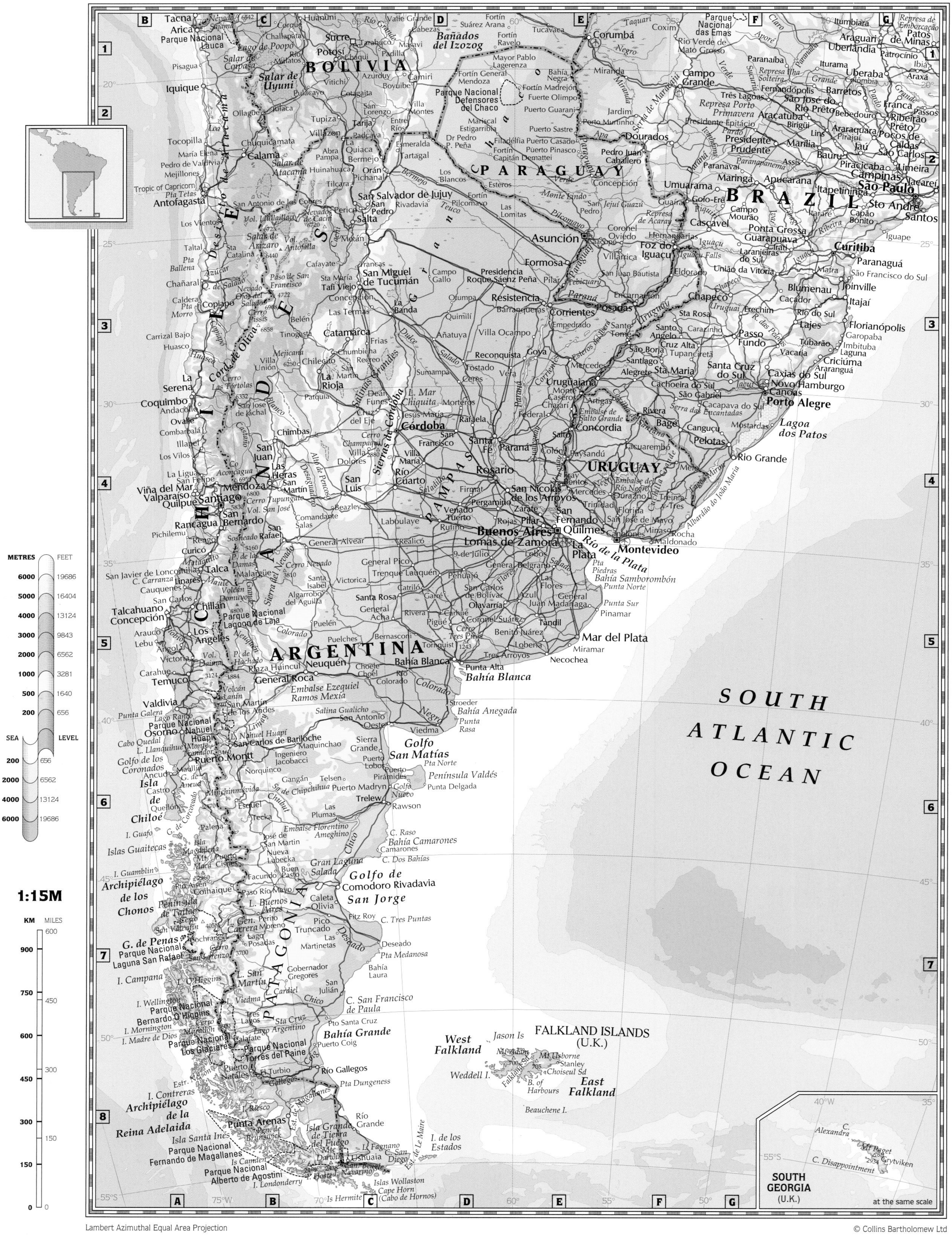

METRES | FEET
6000 | 19686
5000 | 16404
4000 | 13124
3000 | 9843
2000 | 6562
1000 | 3281
500 | 1640
200 | 656
SEA | LEVEL
200 | 656
2000 | 6562
4000 | 13124
6000 | 19686

1:15M

KM | MILES
900 | 600
750 | 450
600 | 300
450 |
300 | 150
150 |
0 | 0

SOUTH ATLANTIC OCEAN

FALKLAND ISLANDS (U.K.)
West Falkland
East Falkland

SOUTH GEORGIA (U.K.)
at the same scale

Lambert Azimuthal Equal Area Projection

© Collins Bartholomew Ltd

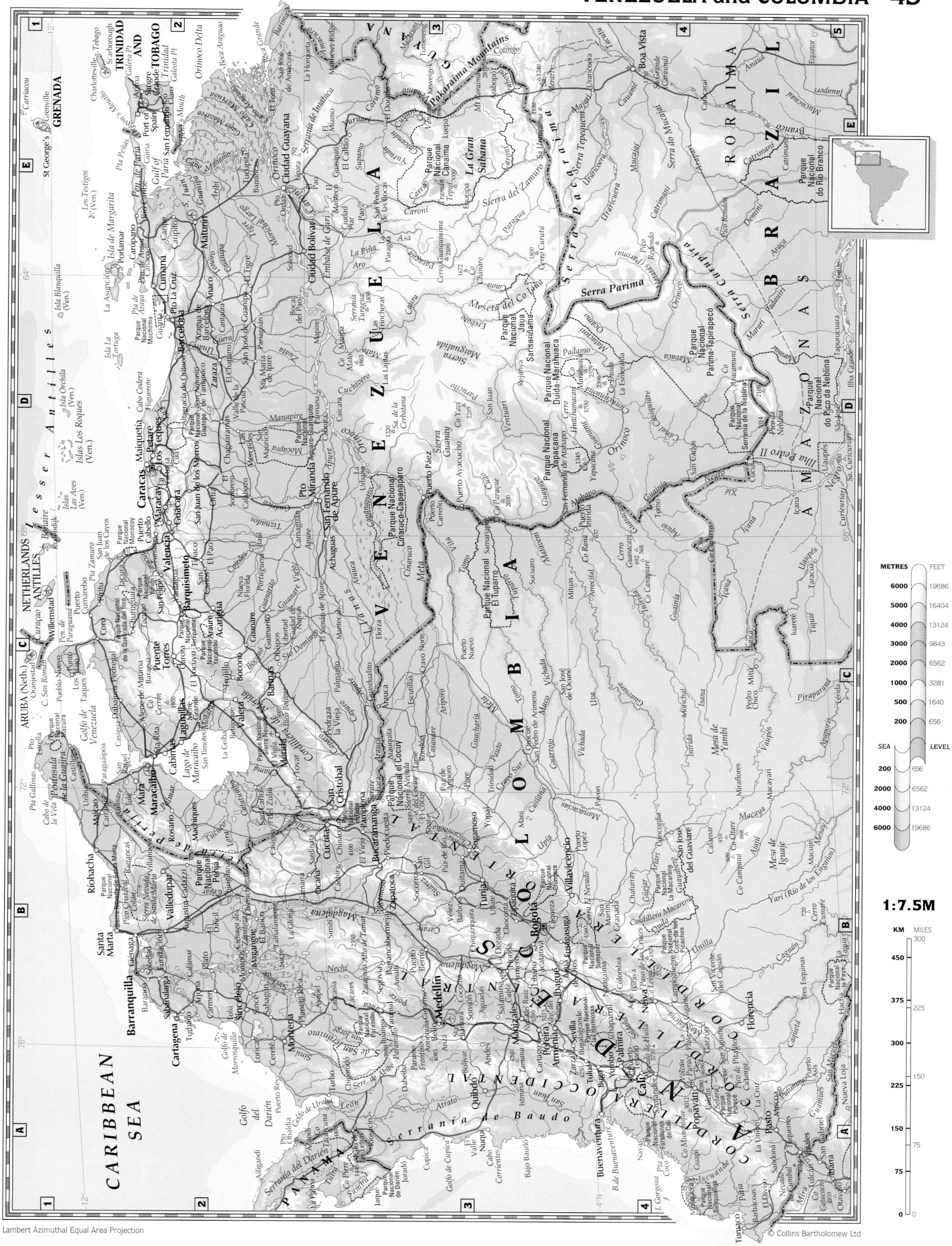
VENEZUELA
COLOMBIA
BRAZIL
CARIBBEAN SEA
NETHERLANDS ANTILLES
TRINIDAD AND TOBAGO
GRENADA
PANAMA
Lesser Antilles
Caracas
Bogotá
METRES
FEET
6000
19686
5000
16404
4000
13124
3000
9843
2000
6562
1000
3281
500
1640
200
656
SEA
LEVEL
200
656
2000
6562
4000
13124
6000
19686
1:7.5M
KM
MILES
450
375
300
225
150
75
0
300
225
150
75
0

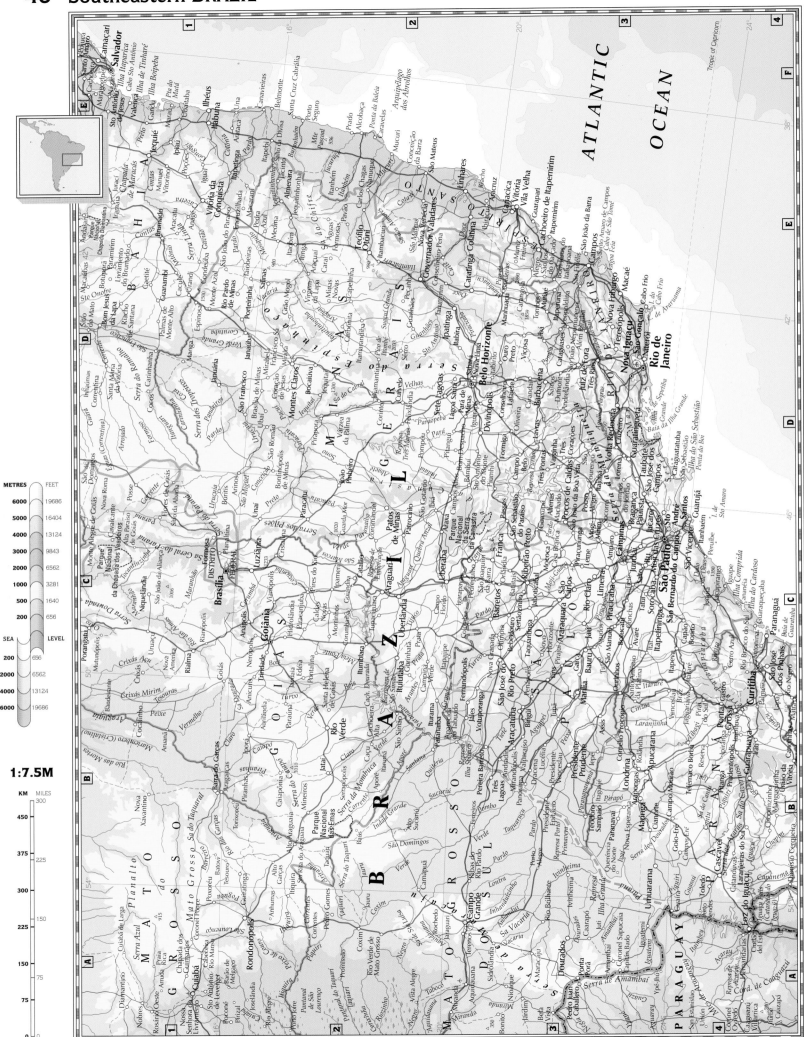

1:7.5M

Lambert Azimuthal Equal Area Projection

© Collins Bartholomew Ltd

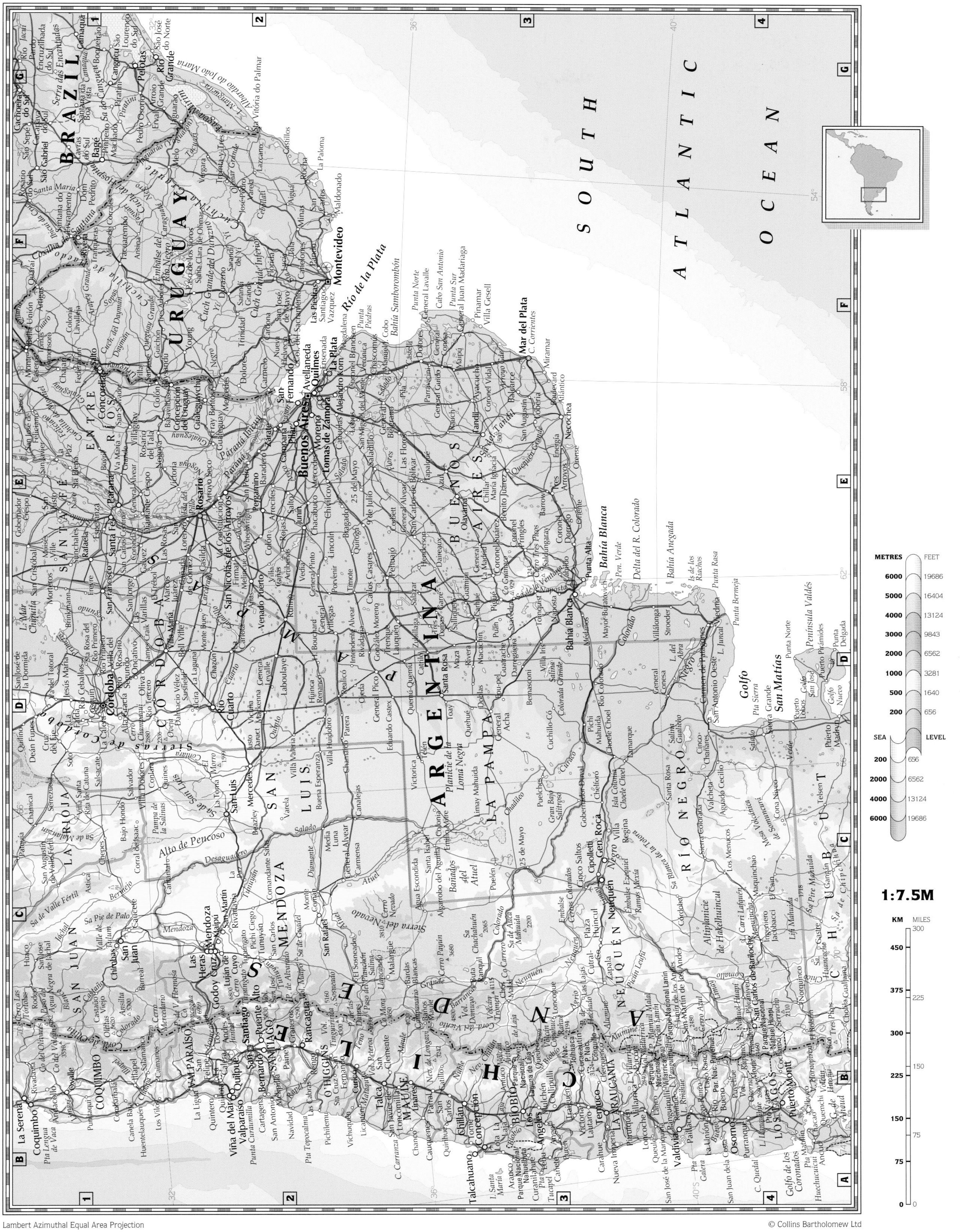

Lambert Azimuthal Equal Area Projection

© Collins Bartholomew Ltd

ICELAND

REPUBLIC

Area: 102,820 sq km
(39,699 sq mls)
Population: 276,000
Capital: Reykjavik
Language: Icelandic
Religion: Protestant,
R.Catholic
Currency: Icelandic krôna

SWEDEN

MONARCHY

Area: 449,964 sq km
(173,732 sq mls)
Population: 8,875,000
Capital: Stockholm
Language: Swedish
Religion: Protestant,
R.Catholic
Currency: Swedish krona

NORWAY

MONARCHY

Area: 323 878 sq km
(125,050 sq mls)
Population: 4,419,000
Capital: Oslo
Language: Norwegian
Religion: Protestant,
R.Catholic
Currency: Norwegian krone

FINLAND

REPUBLIC

Area: 338,145 sq km
(130,559 sq mls)
Population: 5,154,000
Capital: Helsinki (Helsingfors)
Language: Finnish, Swedish
Religion: Protestant,
R.Catholic
Currency: Euro

CONTINENTAL FACTS

TOTAL POPULATION
687,852,000

LARGEST COUNTRY POPULATION
**RUSSIAN FEDERATION in EUROPE
106,152,000**

LARGEST COUNTRY AREA
**RUSSIAN FEDERATION in EUROPE
3,955,800 sq km 1,527,343 sq miles**

LARGEST CITY POPULATION
PARIS, France 9,638,000

REPUBLIC OF IRELAND
REPUBLIC

Area: 70,282 sq km
(27,136 sq mls)
Population: 3,681,000
Capital: Dublin (Baile Átha
Cliath)
Language: English, Irish
Religion: R.Catholic,
Protestant
Currency: Euro

PORTUGAL

REPUBLIC

Area: 88,940 sq km
(34,340 sq mls)
Population: 9,869,000
Capital: Lisbon (Lisboa)
Language: Portuguese
Religion: R.Catholic,
Protestant
Currency: Euro

SPAIN

MONARCHY

Area: 504,782 sq km
(194,897 sq mls)
Population: 39,628,000
Capital: Madrid
Language: Spanish, Catalan,
Galician, Basque
Religion: R.Catholic
Currency: Euro

ANDORRA

PRINCIPALITY

Area: 465 sq km
(180 sq mls)
Population: 72,000
Capital: Andorra la Vella
Language: Catalan, Spanish,
French
Religion: R.Catholic
Currency: Euro

UNITED KINGDOM
MONARCHY

Area: 244,082 sq km
(94,241 sq mls)
Population: 58,649,000
Capital: London
Language: English, South Indian
Languages, Chinese,
Welsh, Gaelic
Religion: Protestant, R.Catholic,
Muslim, Sikh, Hindu,
Jewish
Currency: Pound sterling

MONACO

MONARCHY

Area: 2 sq km
(1 sq ml)
Population: 33,000
Capital: Monaco-Ville
Language: French,
Monegasque,
Italian
Religion: R.Catholic
Currency: Euro

LUXEMBOURG

MONARCHY

Area: 2,586 sq km
(998 sq mls)
Population: 422,000
Capital: Luxembourg
Language: Letzeburgish,
German, French,
Portuguese
Religion: R.Catholic, Protestant
Currency: Euro

BELGIUM

MONARCHY

Area: 30,520 sq km
(11,784 sq mls)
Population: 10,141,000
Capital: Brussels (Bruxelles)
Language: Dutch (Flemish),
French, Walloon,
German, Italian
Religion: R.Catholic, Protestant
Currency: Euro

NETHERLANDS

MONARCHY

Area: 41,526 sq km
(16,033 sq mls)
Population: 15,678,000
Capital: Amsterdam/The Hague
('s-Gravenhage)
Language: Dutch, Frisian,
Turkish
Religion: R.Catholic, Protestant,
Sunni Muslim
Currency: Euro

BARENTS SEA

North Cape

Ostrov Kolguyev

Murmansk

Kola Peninsula

Mezen

Pechora

White Sea

LAPLAND

Luleå Kemi

Gulf of Bothnia

North Dvina

FINLAND

RUSSIAN

Turku Helsinki

Åland

Gulf of Finland

Tallinn

ESTONIA

Lake Onega

Petrozavodsk

Lake Ladoga

St Petersburg

FEDERATION

Vologda

Vyatka

Perm'

Izhevsk

Ufa

Lake Peipus

Gulf of Riga

LATVIA

Riga

Yaroslavl'

Nizhniy Novgorod

Kazan'

LITHUANIA

Vitsyebsk

Smolensk

Moscow

Ul'yanovsk

Orenburg

RUS. FED.

Vilnius

Kaliningrad

Minsk

Tula

Penza

Samara

Białystok

BELARUS

Homyel'

Voronezh

Saratov

Volga

Warsaw

Brest

Belgorod

Don

AND

Łódź

Kiev

Volgograd

Astrakhan'

Wisła

UKRAINE

Kharkiv

VAKIA

L'viv

Kirovohrad

Dnipropetrovs'k

Donets'k

Volga

Chernivtsi

MOLDOVA

Rostov-na-Donu

RY

Iaşi

Chişinău

Mykolayiv

Sea of Azov

Stavropol'

ROMANIA

Odesa

Krasnodar

Grozny

Brasov

Crimea

Simferopol'

Elbrus 5642

SERBIA

Belgrade

Bucharest

Morava

Craiova

Constanţa

Black Sea

AND MONT

BULGARIA

Varna

Sofia

Skopje

Plovdiv

Istanbul

MACEDONIA

Tirana

TURKEY

ALBANIA

Thessaloniki

ASIA

GREECE

Aegean Sea

Athens

Dodecanese

Rhodes

Crete

A N S E A

MEDITERRANEAN SEA

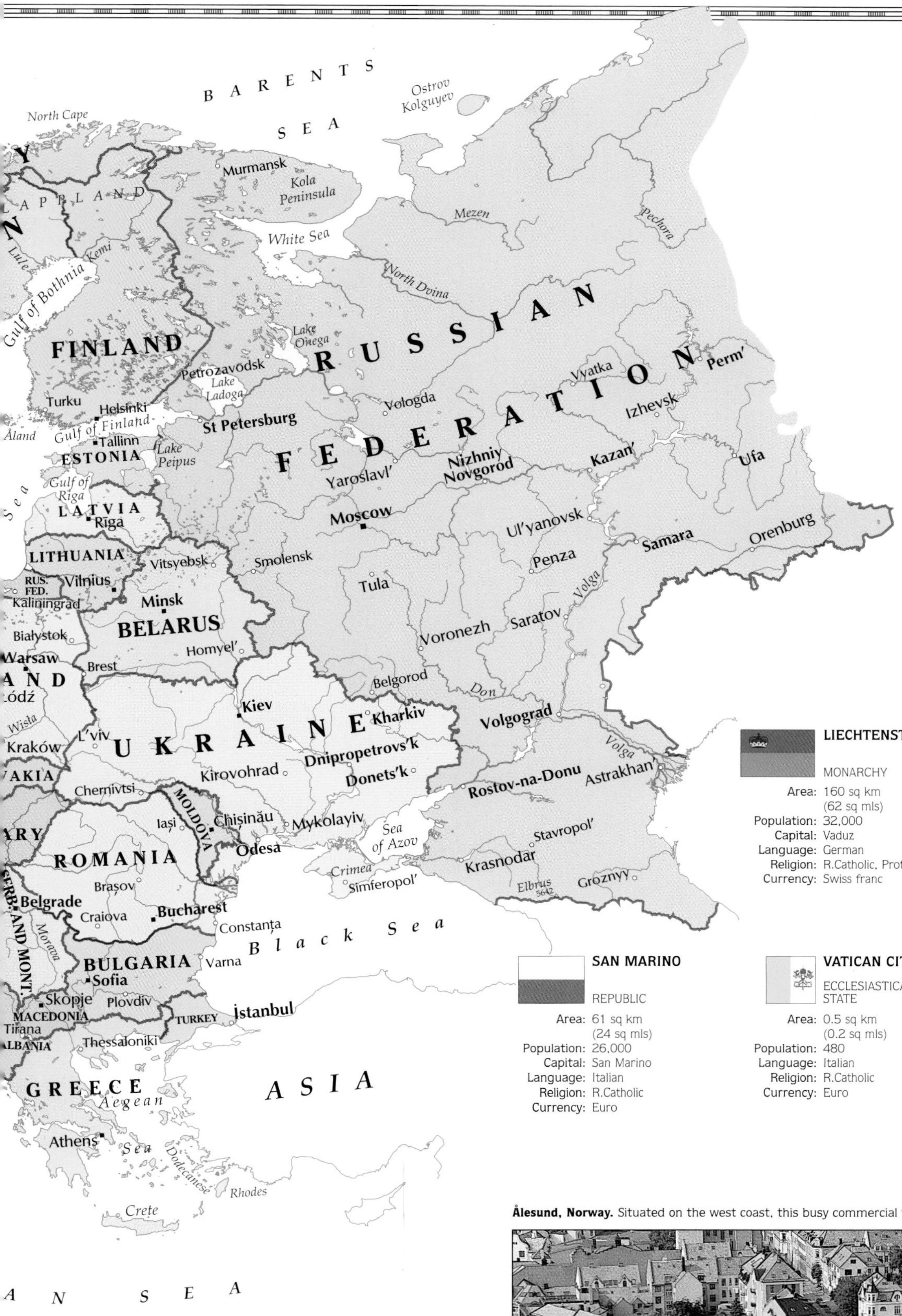

DENMARK
MONARCHY
- Area: 43,075 sq km (16,631 sq mls)
- Population: 5,270,000
- Capital: Copenhagen (København)
- Language: Danish
- Religion: Protestant, R.Catholic
- Currency: Danish krone

GERMANY
REPUBLIC
- Area: 357,028 sq km (137,849 sq mls)
- Population: 82,133,000
- Capital: Berlin
- Language: German, Turkish
- Religion: Protestant, R.Catholic, Sunni Muslim
- Currency: Euro

SWITZERLAND
FEDERATION
- Area: 41,293 sq km (15,943 sq mls)
- Population: 7,299,000
- Capital: Bern (Berne)
- Language: German, French, Italian, Romansch
- Religion: R.Catholic, Protestant
- Currency: Swiss franc

LIECHTENSTEIN
MONARCHY
- Area: 160 sq km (62 sq mls)
- Population: 32,000
- Capital: Vaduz
- Language: German
- Religion: R.Catholic, Protestant
- Currency: Swiss franc

ITALY
REPUBLIC
- Area: 301,245 sq km (116,311 sq mls)
- Population: 57,369,000
- Capital: Rome (Roma)
- Language: Italian, Italian dialects
- Religion: R.Catholic
- Currency: Euro

SAN MARINO
REPUBLIC
- Area: 61 sq km (24 sq mls)
- Population: 26,000
- Capital: San Marino
- Language: Italian
- Religion: R.Catholic
- Currency: Euro

VATICAN CITY
ECCLESIASTICAL STATE
- Area: 0.5 sq km (0.2 sq mls)
- Population: 480
- Language: Italian
- Religion: R.Catholic
- Currency: Euro

MALTA
REPUBLIC
- Area: 316 sq km (122 sq mls)
- Population: 384,000
- Capital: Valletta
- Language: Maltese, English
- Religion: R.Catholic
- Currency: Maltese lira

FRANCE
REPUBLIC
- Area: 543,965 sq km (210,026 sq mls)
- Population: 58,683,000
- Capital: Paris
- Language: French, French dialects, Arabic, German (Alsatian), Breton
- Religion: R.Catholic, Protestant, Sunni Muslim
- Currency: Euro

AUSTRIA
REPUBLIC
- Area: 83,855 sq km (32,377 sq mls)
- Population: 8,140,000
- Capital: Vienna (Wien)
- Language: German, Croatian, Turkish
- Religion: R.Catholic, Protestant
- Currency: Euro

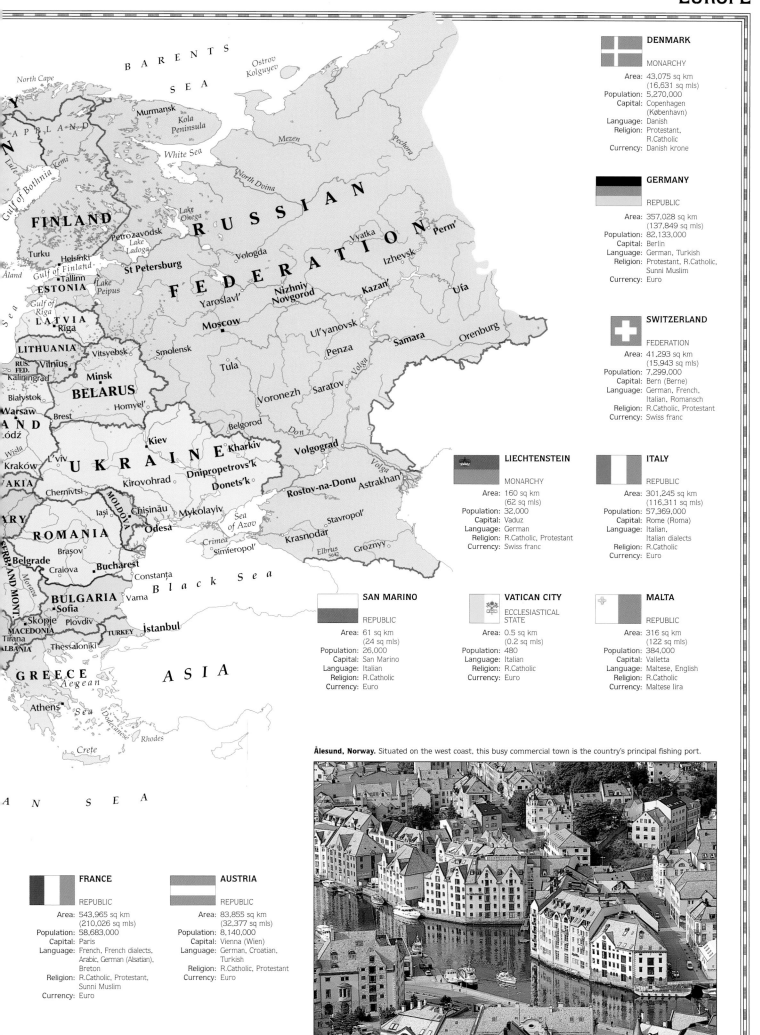

Ålesund, Norway. Situated on the west coast, this busy commercial town is the country's principal fishing port.

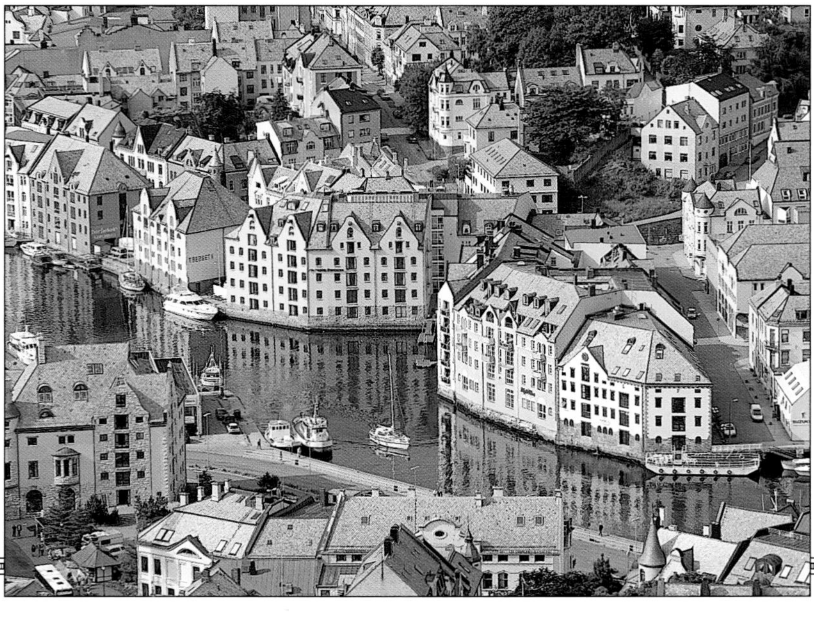

50

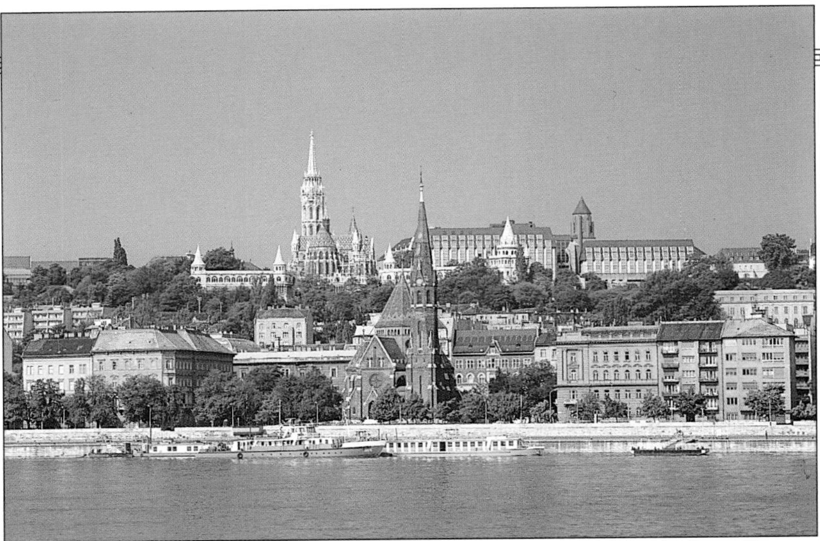

Budapest, Hungary. The picturesque old part of the city (Buda) shown in the photograph is separated from the administrative and commercial centre (Pest) by the River Danube.

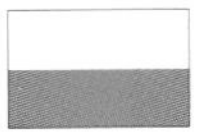

 POLAND
REPUBLIC
Area: 312,683 sq km
(120,728 sq mls)
Population: 38,718,000
Capital: Warsaw (Warszawa)
Language: Polish, German
Religion: R.Catholic,
Polish Orthodox
Currency: Złoty

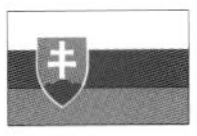

SLOVAKIA
REPUBLIC
Area: 49,035 sq km
(18,933 sq mls)
Population: 5,377,000
Capital: Bratislava
Language: Slovak, Hungarian,
Czech
Religion: R.Catholic, Protestant,
Orthodox
Currency: Slovakian koruna

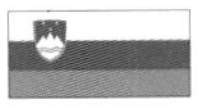

 SLOVENIA
REPUBLIC
Area: 20,251 sq km
(7,819 sq mls)
Population: 1,993,000
Capital: Ljubljana
Language: Slovene, Serbian,
Croatian
Religion: R.Catholic, Protestant
Currency: Tólar

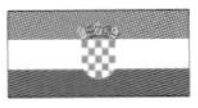

 CROATIA
REPUBLIC
Area: 56,538 sq km
(21,829 sq mls)
Population: 4,481,000
Capital: Zagreb
Language: Croatian, Serbian
Religion: R.Catholic, Orthodox,
Sunni Muslim
Currency: Kuna

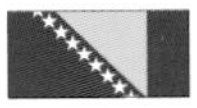

 BOSNIA-HERZEGOVINA
REPUBLIC
Area: 51,130 sq km
(19,741 sq mls)
Population: 3,675,000
Capital: Sarajevo
Language: Bosnian, Serbian,
Croatian
Religion: Sunni Muslim,
Serbian Orthodox,
R.Catholic, Protestant
Currency: Marka

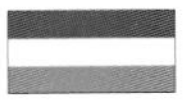

 SERBIA AND MONTENEGRO
REPUBLIC
Area: 102,173 sq km
(39,449 sq mls)
Population: 10,635,000
Capital: Belgrade (Beograd)
Language: Serbian, Albanian
Religion: Serbian Orthodox,
Montenegrin Orthodox,
Sunni Muslim
Currency: Dinar, Euro

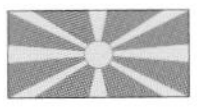

 MACEDONIA (F.Y.R.O.M.)
REPUBLIC
Area: 25,713 sq km
(9,928 sq mls)
Population: 1,999,000
Capital: Skopje
Language: Macedonian, Albanian,
Croatian, Serbian,
Turkish, Romany
Religion: Macedonian Orthodox,
Sunni Muslim,
R.Catholic
Currency: Macedonian denar

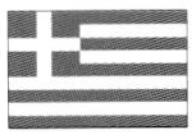

GREECE
REPUBLIC
Area: 131,957 sq km
(50,949 sq mls)
Population: 10,600,000
Capital: Athens (Athína)
Language: Greek, Macedonian
Religion: Greek Orthodox,
Sunni Muslim
Currency: Euro

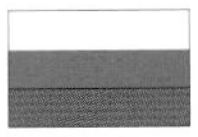

 BULGARIA
REPUBLIC
Area: 110,994 sq km
(42,855 sq mls)
Population: 8,336,000
Capital: Sofia (Sofiya)
Language: Bulgarian, Turkish,
Romany, Macedonian
Religion: Bulgarian Orthodox,
Sunni Muslim
Currency: Lev

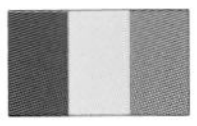

 ROMANIA
REPUBLIC
Area: 237,500 sq km
(91,699 sq mls)
Population: 22,474,000
Capital: Bucharest (Bucureşti)
Language: Romanian,
Hungarian
Religion: Romanian Orthodox,
R.Catholic, Protestant
Currency: Romanian leu

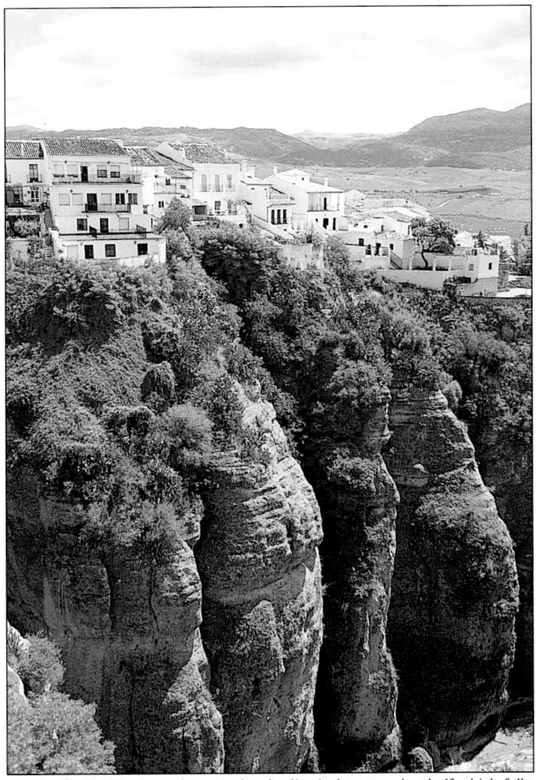

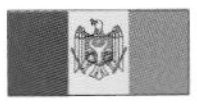

 MOLDOVA
REPUBLIC
Area: 33,700 sq km
(13,012 sq mls)
Population: 4,378,000
Capital: Chişinău (Kishinev)
Language: Romanian, Russian,
Ukrainian, Gagauz
Religion: Moldovan Orthodox,
Russian Orthodox
Currency: Moldavian leu

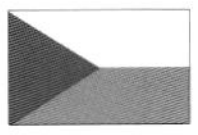

 CZECH REPUBLIC
REPUBLIC
Area: 78,864 sq km
(30,450 sq mls)
Population: 10,282,000
Capital: Prague (Praha)
Language: Czech, Moravian,
Slovak
Religion: R.Catholic, Protestant
Currency: Czech koruna

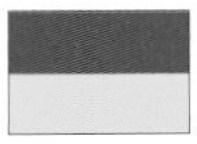

 UKRAINE
REPUBLIC
Area: 603,700 sq km
(233,090 sq mls)
Population: 50,861,000
Capital: Kiev (Kyiv)
Language: Ukrainian, Russian,
Regional Languages
Religion: Ukrainian Orthodox,
R.Catholic
Currency: Hryvnia

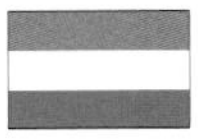

 HUNGARY
REPUBLIC
Area: 93,030 sq km
(35,919 sq mls)
Population: 10,116,000
Capital: Budapest
Language: Hungarian, Romany,
German, Slovak
Religion: R.Catholic, Protestant
Currency: Forint

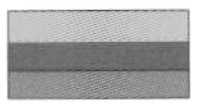

 LITHUANIA
REPUBLIC
Area: 65,200 sq km
(25,174 sq mls)
Population: 3,694,000
Capital: Vilnius
Language: Lithuanian, Russian,
Polish
Religion: R.Catholic, Protestant,
Russian Orthodox
Currency: Litas

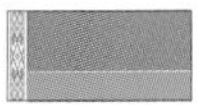

BELARUS
REPUBLIC
Area: 207,600 sq km
(80,155 sq mls)
Population: 10,315,000
Capital: Minsk
Language: Belorussian,
Russian, Ukrainian
Religion: Belorussian Orthodox,
R.Catholic
Currency: Belarus rouble

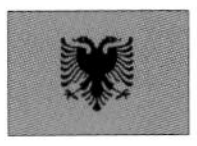

 ALBANIA
REPUBLIC
Area: 28,748 sq km
(11,100 sq mls)
Population: 3,119,000
Capital: Tirana (Tiranë)
Language: Albanian (Gheg, Tosk
dialects), Greek
Religion: Sunni Muslim, Greek
Orthodox, R.Catholic
Currency: Lek

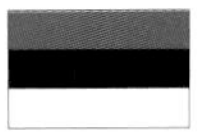

 ESTONIA
REPUBLIC
Area: 45,200 sq km
(17,452 sq mls)
Population: 1,429,000
Capital: Tallinn
Language: Estonian, Russian
Religion: Protestant,
Russian Orthodox
Currency: Kroon

Ronda, Spain. The town is precariously situated on a rocky shelf which falls on three sides to a depth of 120m.

POPULATION

St Petersburg

Moscow

Hamburg

Berlin

London

Essen-Dortmund

Dusseldorf

Cologne

Frankfurt
am Main

Katowice

Kiev

Paris

Stuttgart

Madrid

Barcelona

Rome

Naples

Istanbul

Athens

POPULATION
Inhabitants

per sq km	per sq ml
over 200	over 500
100-200	250-500
50-100	130-250
10-50	25-130
1-10	2.5-25
0-1	0-2.5
uninhabited	

CITIES
■ Over 5 million population

● 2.5 - 5 million population

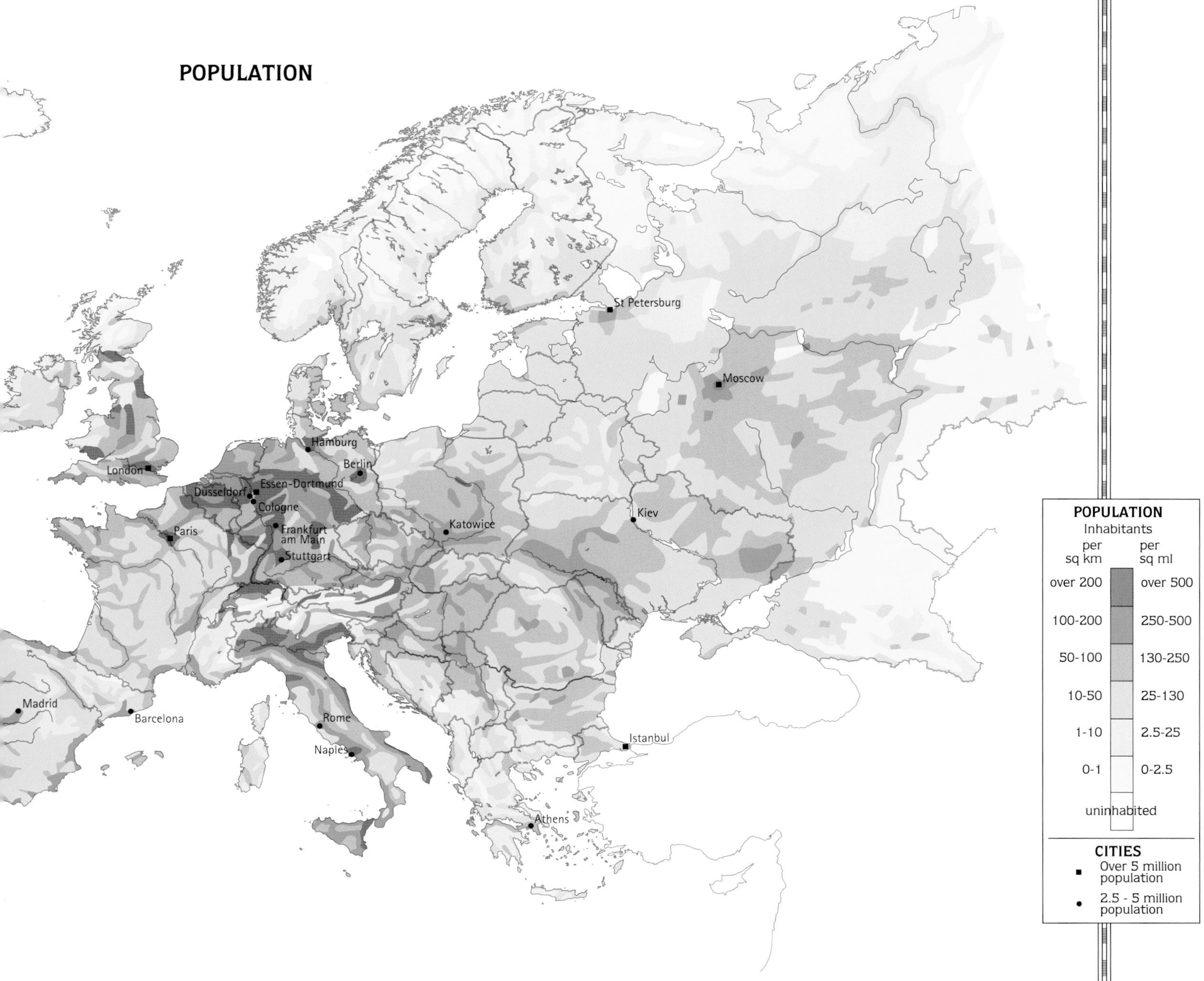

Grindelwald, Switzerland. A resort popular with skiers and climbers, as it is spread across an expanse of Alpine meadows and is near many majestic peaks and glaciers.

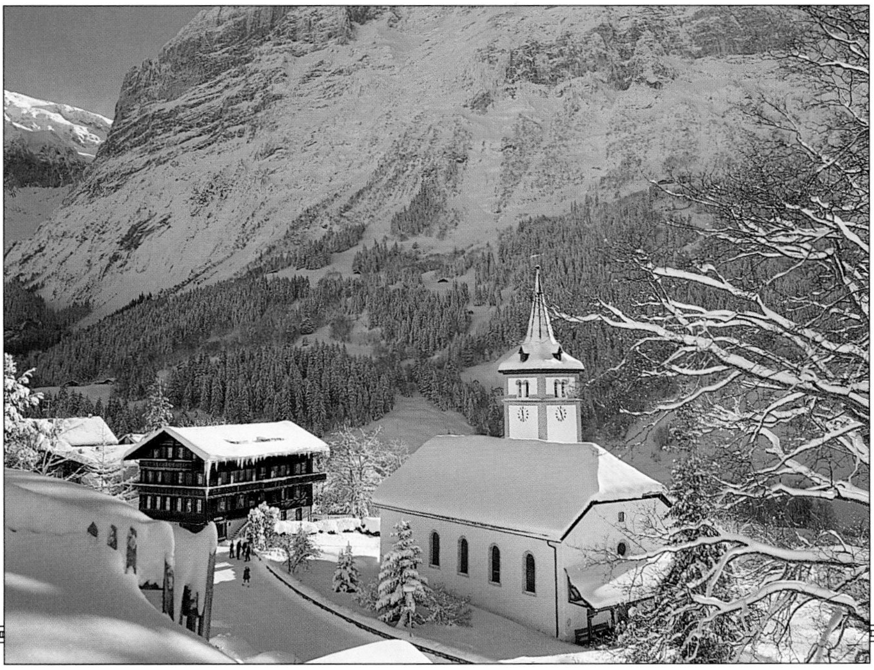

LATVIA
REPUBLIC

Area: 63,700 sq km
(24,595 sq mls)
Population: 2,424,000
Capital: Riga
Language: Latvian, Russian
Religion: Protestant, R.Catholic,
Russian Orthodox
Currency: Lats

RUSSIAN FEDERATION
REPUBLIC   in Europe
Area: 17,075,400 sq km   3,955,800 sq km
(6,592,849 sq mls)   (1,527,343 sq mls)
Population: 147,434,000   106,152,000
Capital: Moscow (Moskva)
Language: Russian, Tatar,
Ukrainian, Local
Languages
Religion: Russian Orthodox,
Sunni Muslim,
Other Christian, Jewish
Currency: Russian rouble

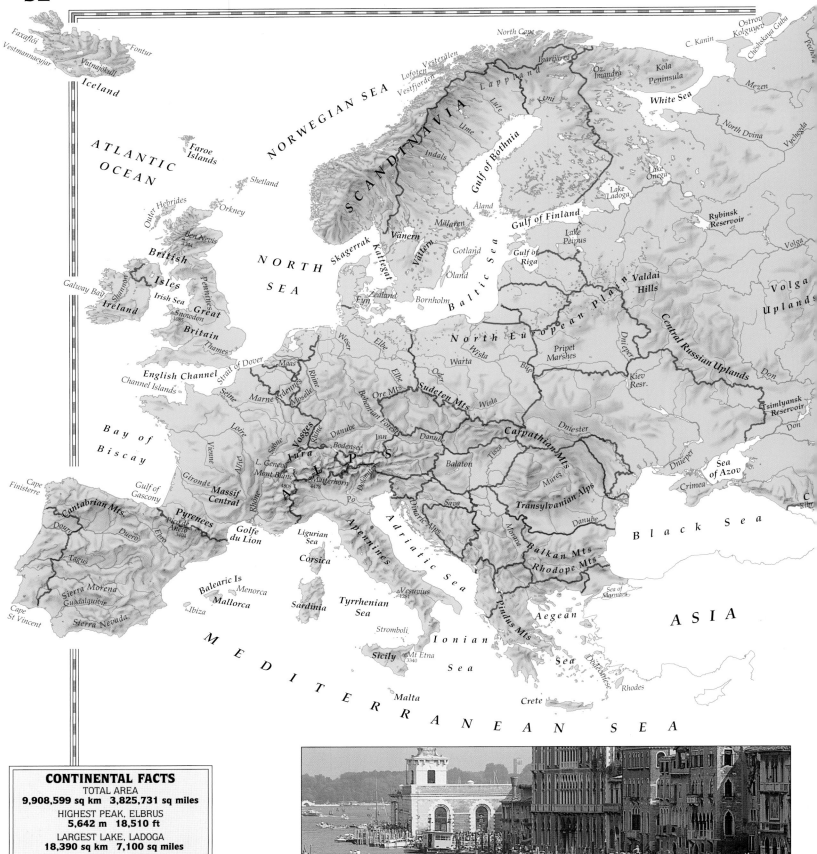

Venice, Italy. Boats are the primary mode of transport as the town is built on 118 islands and traversed by over 100 canals.

CONTINENTAL FACTS
TOTAL AREA
9,908,599 sq km 3,825,731 sq miles

HIGHEST PEAK, ELBRUS
5,642 m 18,510 ft

LARGEST LAKE, LADOGA
18,390 sq km 7,100 sq miles

LONGEST RIVER, VOLGA
3,688 km 2,291 miles

Strokkur Geyser, Iceland. This hot spring erupts every 3 minutes, throwing steam clouds up to 20m high.

CLIMATE

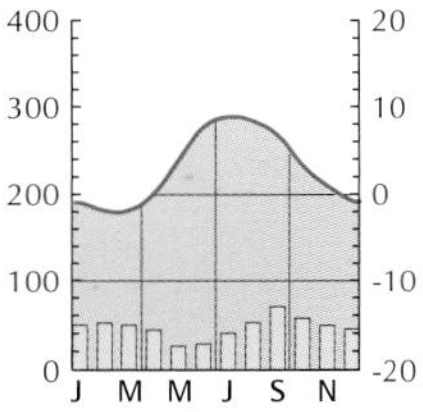

Grímsey

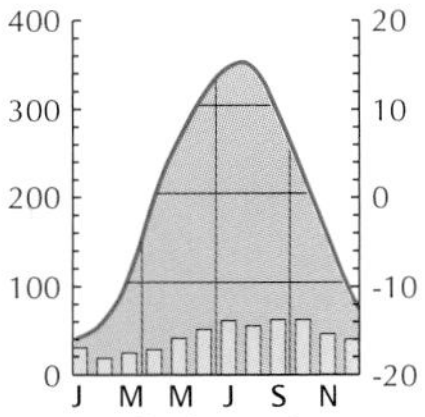

Archangel

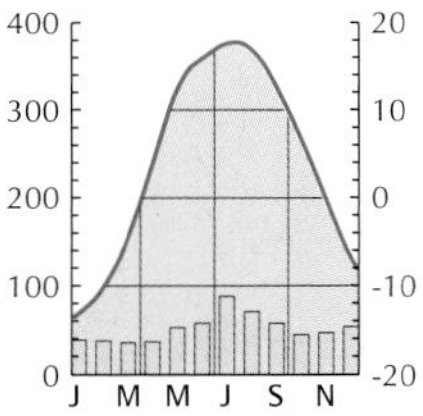

Moscow

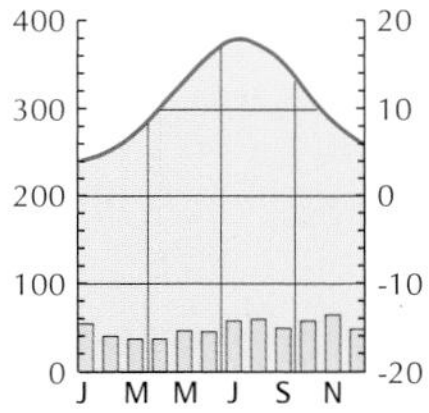

London

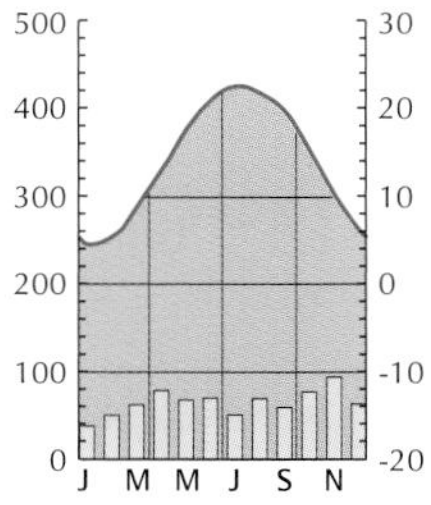

Venice

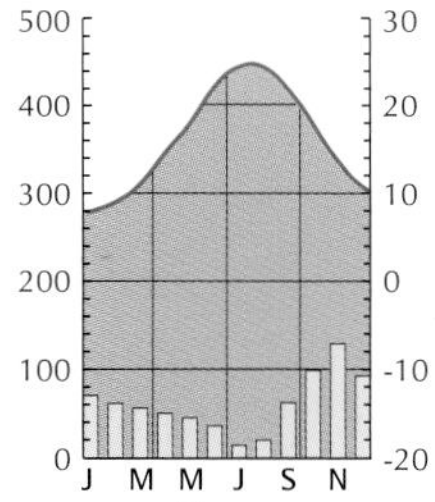

Rome

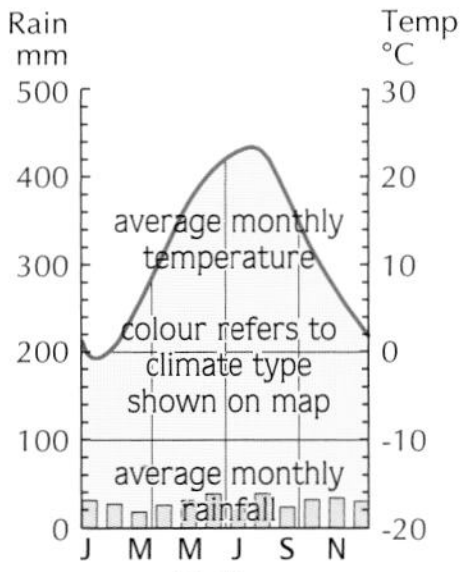

Rain mm
Temp °C
average monthly temperature
colour refers to climate type shown on map
average monthly rainfall
Sulina

CLIMATE TYPES

POLAR
Tundra

COOLER HUMID
Subarctic

Continental cool summer

WARMER HUMID
Temperate

Humid subtropical

Mediterranean

DRY
Steppe

Desert

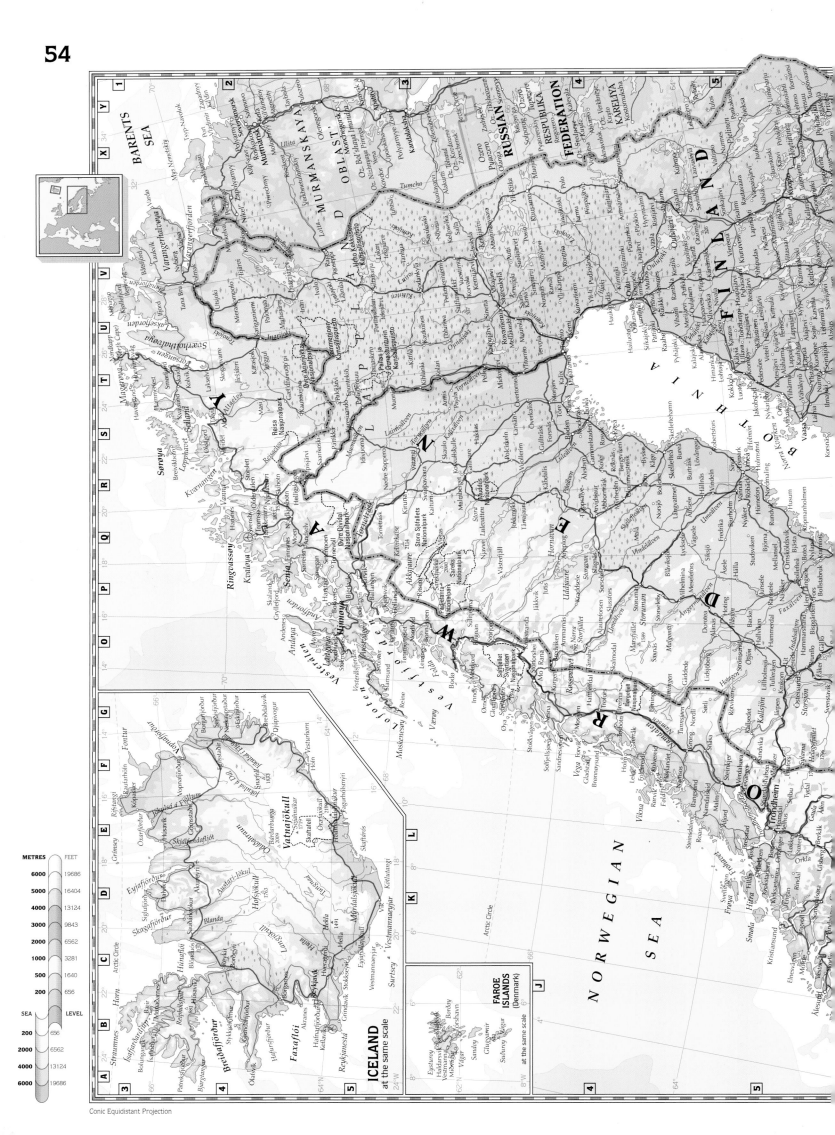
BARENTS SEA
NORWEGIAN SEA
GULF OF BOTHNIA
RUSSIAN FEDERATION
RESPUBLIKA KARELIYA
MURMANSKAYA OBLAST'
FINLAND
SWEDEN
NORWAY
LAPLAND
Lofoten
Vestfjorden
Vesterålen
Arctic Circle
Tromsø
Kiruna
Bodø
Trondheim
Oulu
Vaasa
Murmansk
Kandalaksha
Rovaniemi
Luleå
Umeå
Narvik
Hammerfest
Kemi
Tornio
Haparanda
Östersund
ICELAND
at the same scale
Reykjavík
Akureyri
Vatnajökull
Hofsjökull
Langjökull
Mýrdalsjökull
Faxaflói
Breiðafjörður
FAROE ISLANDS
(Denmark)
at the same scale
Tórshavn
METRES
FEET
6000
19686
5000
16404
4000
13124
3000
9843
2000
6562
1000
3281
500
1640
200
656
SEA
LEVEL
200
656
2000
6562
4000
13124
6000
19686

Conic Equidistant Projection

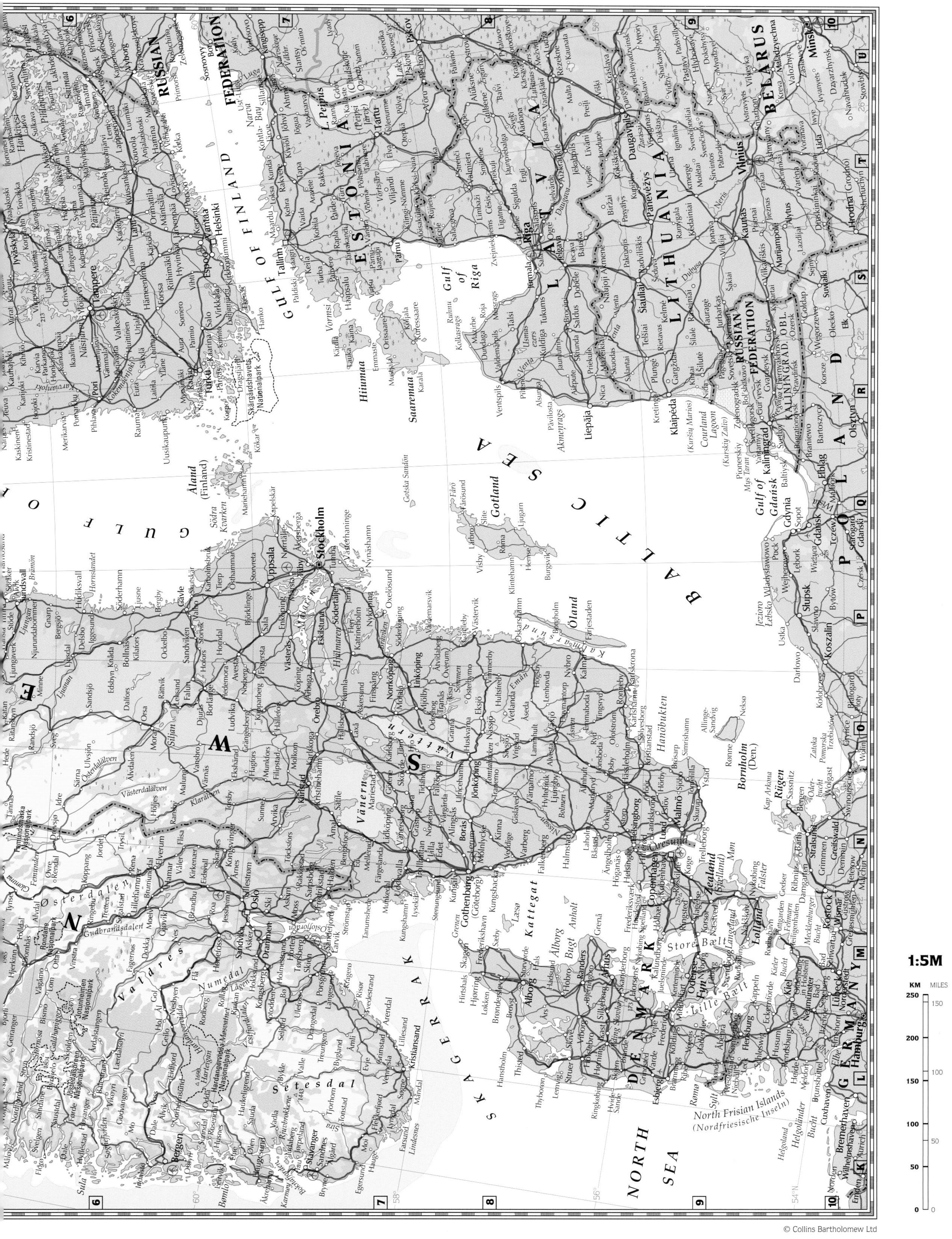
1:5M
KM MILES
250 150
200 100
150 50
100
50
0 0
BALTIC SEA
GULF OF FINLAND
Gulf of Riga
SKAGERRAK
Kattegat
NORTH SEA
ESTONIA
LATVIA
LITHUANIA
BELARUS
RUSSIAN FEDERATION
POLAND
GERMANY
DENMARK
Stockholm
Helsinki
Tallinn
Riga
Vilnius
Minsk
Oslo
Copenhagen
Gothenburg (Göteborg)
Gotland
Öland
Bornholm (Den.)
Åland (Finland)

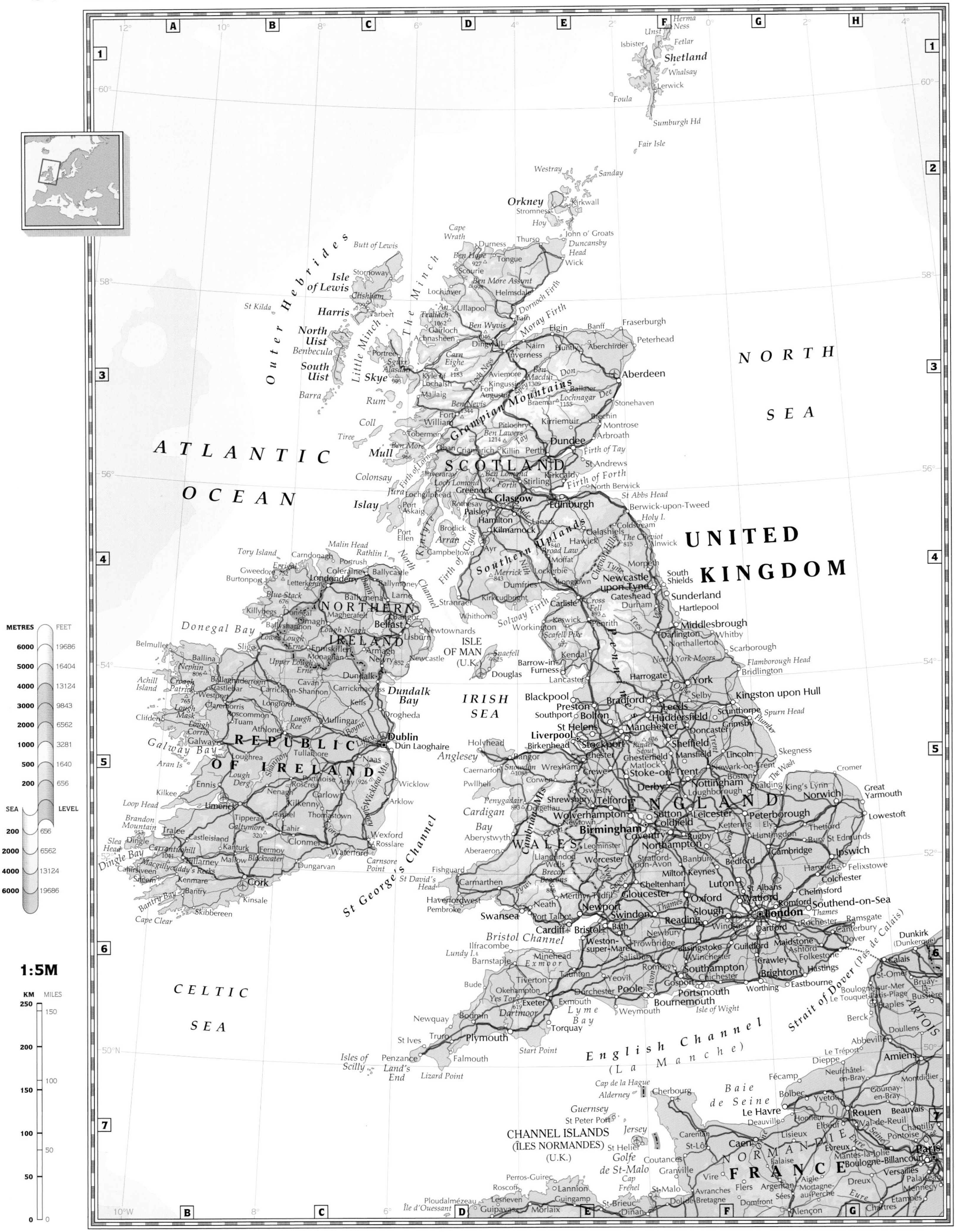

Conic Equidistant Projection

© Collins Bartholomew Ltd

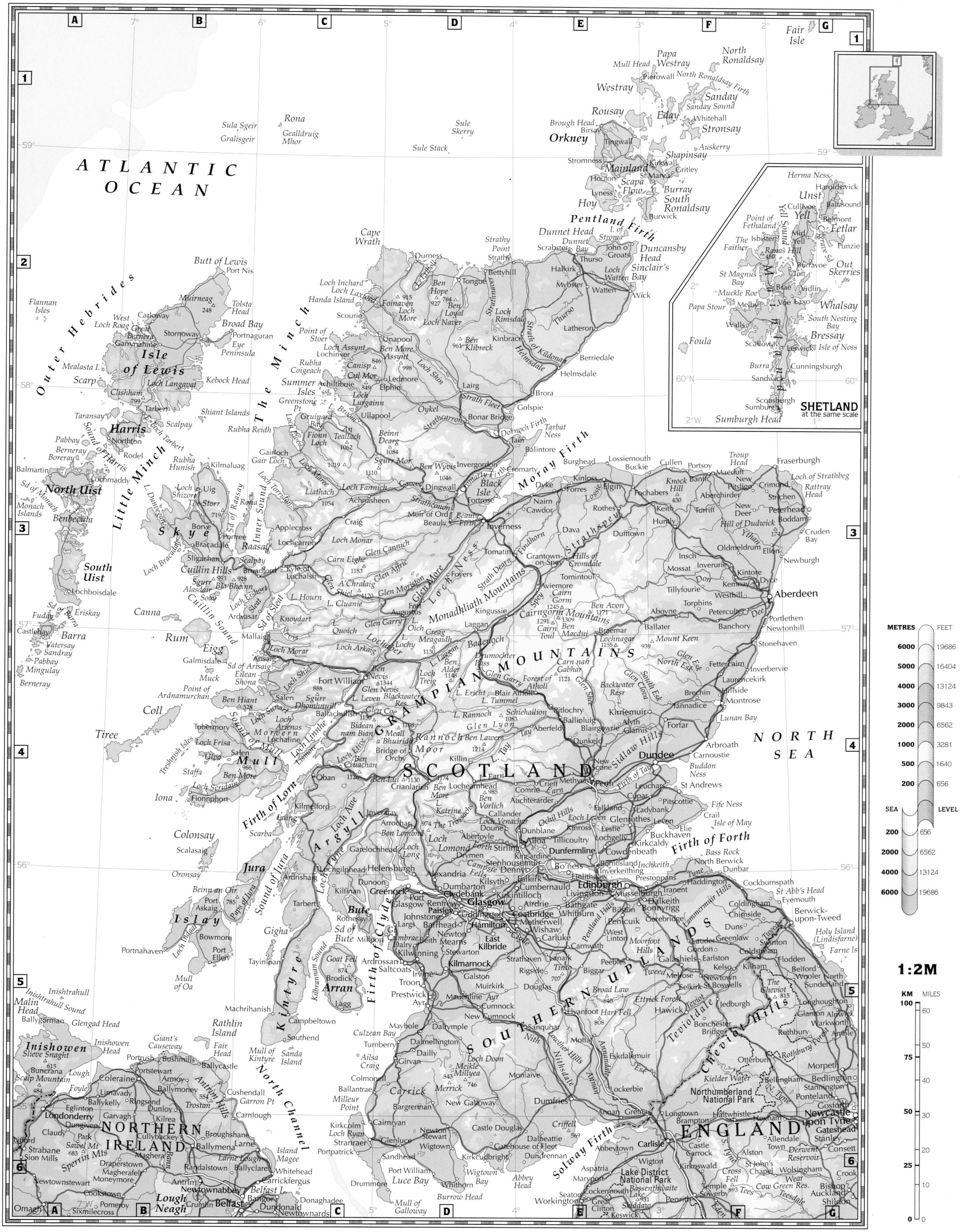
ATLANTIC OCEAN
NORTH SEA
SCOTLAND
ENGLAND
NORTHERN IRELAND
Outer Hebrides
The Minch
Little Minch
Inner Sound
Sea of the Hebrides
GRAMPIAN MOUNTAINS
SOUTHERN UPLANDS
Monadhliath Mountains
Cairngorm Mountains
Cheviot Hills
Lammermuir Hills
Pentland Hills
Moorfoot Hills
Sidlaw Hills
Ochil Hills
Campsie Fells
Lowther Hills
North Channel
Firth of Clyde
Firth of Lorn
Firth of Forth
Firth of Tay
Moray Firth
Dornoch Firth
Pentland Firth
Solway Firth
Sound of Jura
Sound of Mull
Sound of Sleat
Cuillin Sound
Sound of Harris
Sound of Barra
Kilbrannan Sound
Orkney
Mainland
Hoy
Westray
Papa Westray
North Ronaldsay
Sanday
Eday
Stronsay
Rousay
Shapinsay
South Ronaldsay
Scapa Flow
Kirkwall
Stromness
Fair Isle
Sule Skerry
Sule Stack
Rona
Sula Sgeir
Flannan Isles
Butt of Lewis
Isle of Lewis
Stornoway
Harris
North Uist
Benbecula
South Uist
Barra
Mingulay
Berneray
Skye
Raasay
Cuillin Hills
Canna
Rum
Eigg
Muck
Coll
Tiree
Mull
Iona
Staffa
Colonsay
Jura
Islay
Gigha
Kintyre
Arran
Bute
Cape Wrath
Dunnet Head
Duncansby Head
John o' Groats
Thurso
Wick
Helmsdale
Brora
Golspie
Tain
Dingwall
Invergordon
Inverness
Nairn
Forres
Elgin
Lossiemouth
Buckie
Banff
Fraserburgh
Peterhead
Ellon
Aberdeen
Stonehaven
Montrose
Arbroath
Forfar
Dundee
Perth
St Andrews
Kirkcaldy
Dunfermline
Stirling
Falkirk
Edinburgh
Glasgow
Paisley
Greenock
Hamilton
Motherwell
Kilmarnock
Ayr
Troon
Girvan
Stranraer
Dumfries
Galashiels
Hawick
Jedburgh
Kelso
Berwick-upon-Tweed
Dunbar
North Berwick
Oban
Fort William
Ben Nevis 1344
Ben Macdui 1309
Ben Lawers 1214
Loch Ness
Loch Lomond
Loch Tay
Loch Rannoch
Loch Awe
Loch Fyne
Loch Linnhe
Loch Shin
Loch Maree
Campbeltown
Mull of Kintyre
Mull of Galloway
Newcastle upon Tyne
Carlisle
Lake District National Park
Northumberland National Park
Londonderry
Coleraine
Ballymena
Belfast
Lough Neagh
SHETLAND at the same scale
Unst
Yell
Fetlar
Mainland
Whalsay
Lerwick
Bressay
Foula
Sumburgh Head
Fair Isle
1:2M
METRES FEET
6000 19686
5000 16404
4000 13124
3000 9843
2000 6562
1000 3281
500 1640
200 656
SEA LEVEL
200 656
2000 6562
4000 13124
6000 19686
KM MILES
100 60
75 50
50 30
25 20
0 10 0

NORTH SEA
IRISH SEA
SCOTLAND
GRAMPIAN MOUNTAINS
SOUTHERN UPLANDS
PENNINES
NORTHERN IRELAND
ISLE OF MAN (U.K.)
North Channel
Firth of Forth
Firth of Clyde
Solway Firth
Firth of Lorn
Sound of Jura
Kintyre
Arran
Bute
Islay
Jura
Mull
Coll
Rum
Eigg
Edinburgh
Glasgow
Dundee
Perth
Stirling
Newcastle upon Tyne
Sunderland
Middlesbrough
Carlisle
York
Leeds
Bradford
Kingston upon Hull
Belfast
Douglas
Blackpool
Preston
Lake District National Park
Yorkshire Dales National Park
North York Moors National Park
Northumberland National Park
Cheviot Hills
Teviotdale
Annandale
Nithsdale
Vale of York
Yorkshire Wolds
Lough Neagh
Dundalk Bay
REPUBLIC

METRES
FEET
6000
19686
5000
16404
4000
13124
3000
9843
2000
6562
1000
3281
500
1640
200
656
SEA
LEVEL
200
656
2000
6562
4000
13124
6000
19686

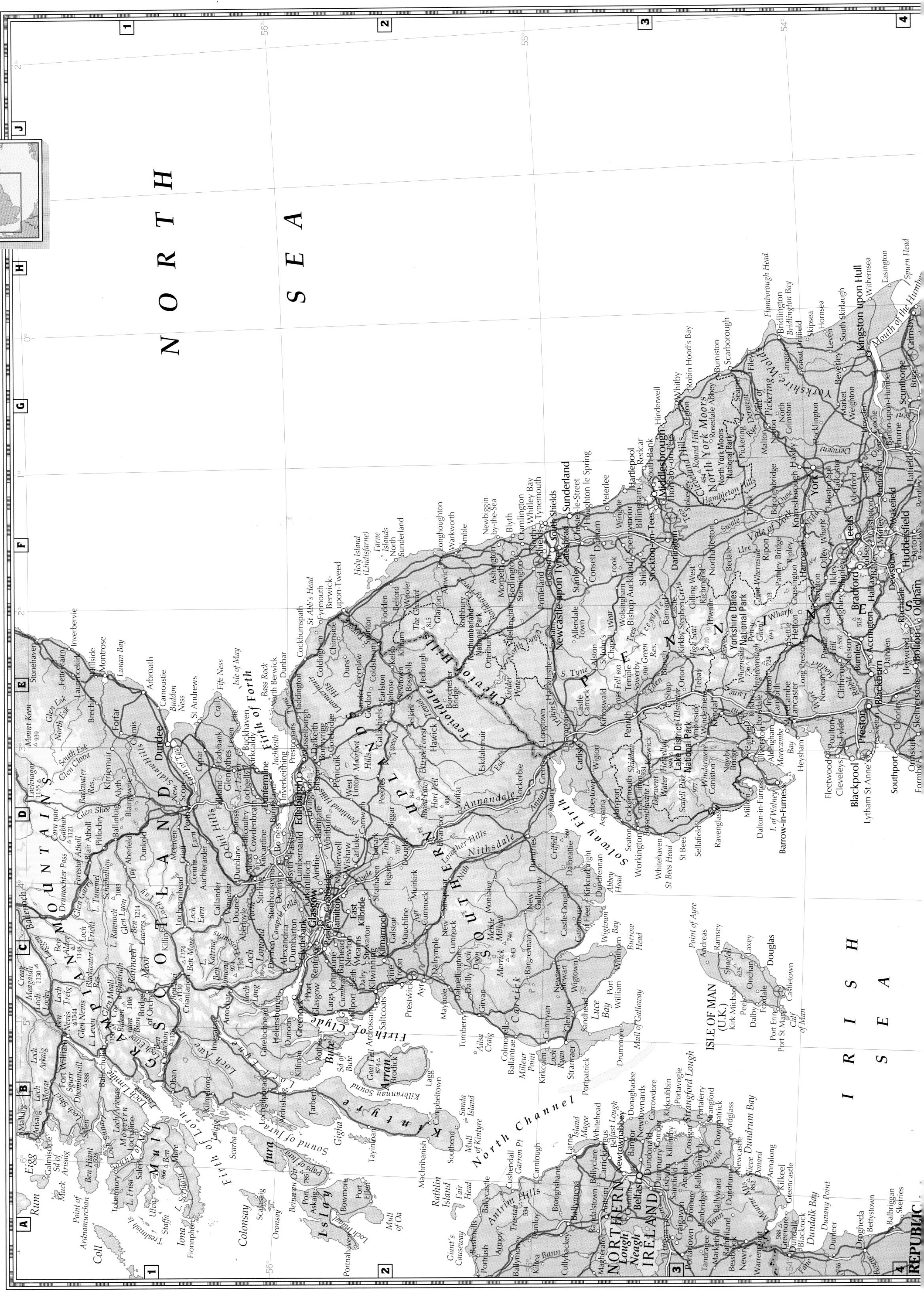

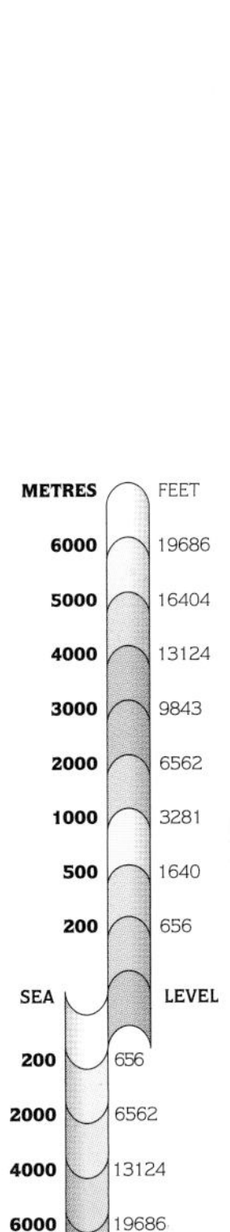

Conic Equidistant Projection

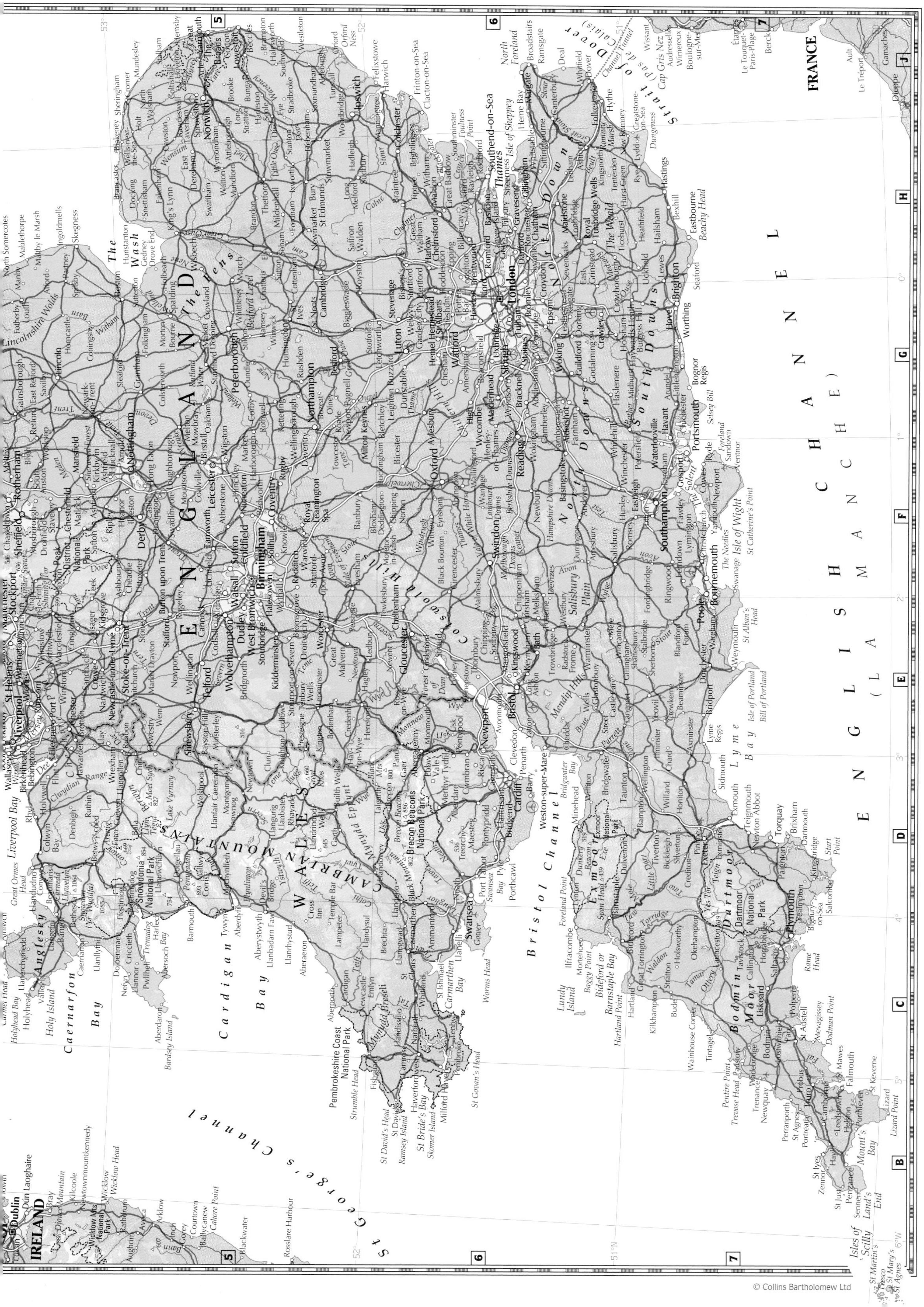

1:2M

KM   MILES

© Collins Bartholomew Ltd

ENGLAND
WALES
FRANCE
IRELAND
ENGLISH CHANNEL
(LA MANCHE)
Bristol Channel
Cardigan Bay
St George's Channel
Caernarfon Bay
Liverpool Bay
The Wash
Strait of Dover (Pas de Calais)
Lyme Bay
London
Birmingham
Manchester
Liverpool
Sheffield
Nottingham
Leicester
Coventry
Northampton
Peterborough
Cambridge
Norwich
Ipswich
Colchester
Chelmsford
Oxford
Reading
Swindon
Gloucester
Cheltenham
Worcester
Wolverhampton
Stoke-on-Trent
Derby
Bristol
Bath
Cardiff
Newport
Swansea
Exeter
Plymouth
Southampton
Portsmouth
Bournemouth
Brighton
Canterbury
Dover
Dublin
Isle of Wight
Isles of Scilly
Anglesey
Dartmoor
Exmoor
Snowdonia National Park
Brecon Beacons National Park
Pembrokeshire Coast National Park
CAMBRIAN MOUNTAINS
Cotswold Hills
Chiltern Hills
North Downs
South Downs
Salisbury Plain
Lincolnshire Wolds
The Fens
Land's End
Lizard Point
100 60
50
75
40
50 30
20
25
10
0 0

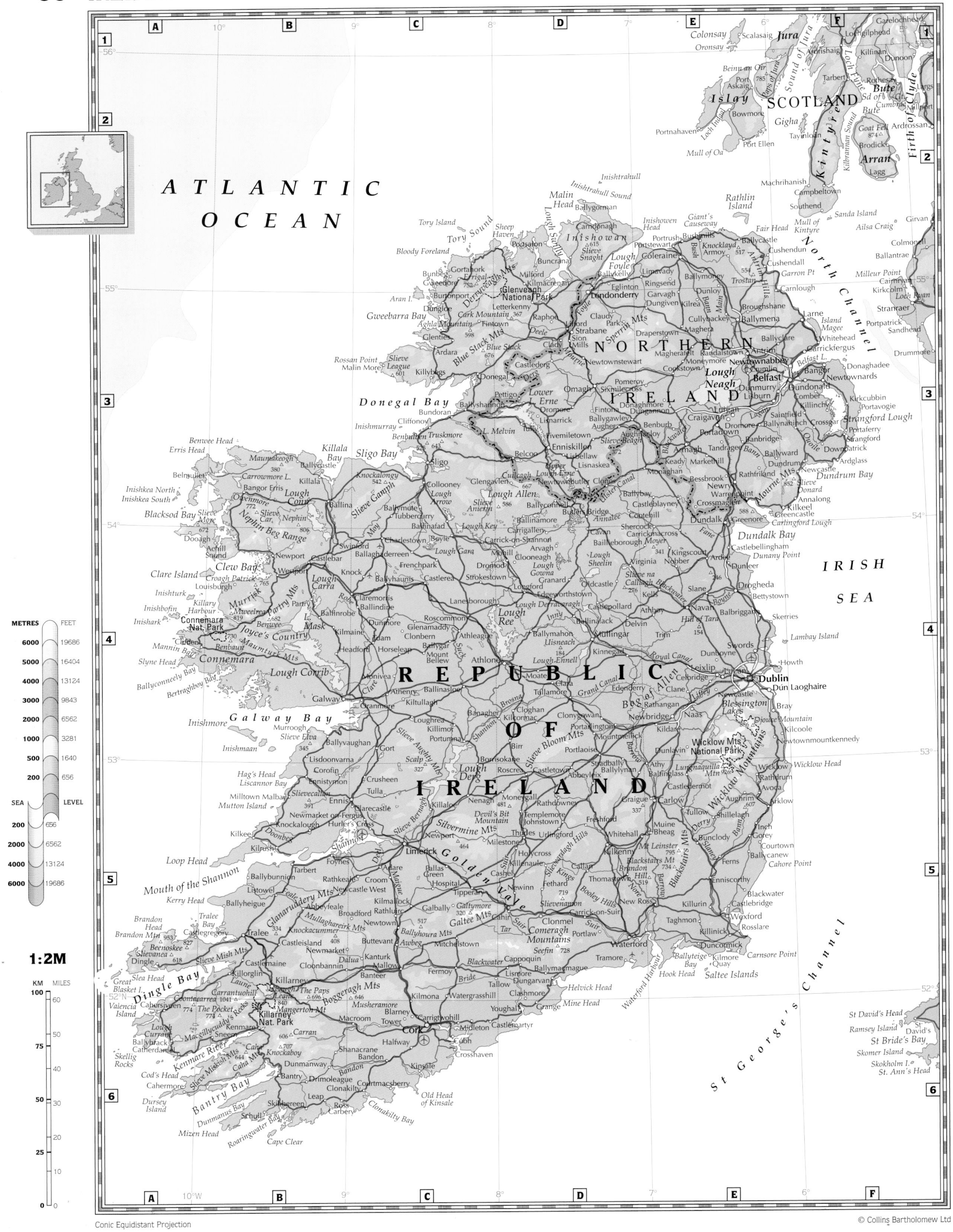

ATLANTIC
OCEAN

IRISH
SEA

NORTHERN
IRELAND

REPUBLIC
OF
IRELAND

SCOTLAND

St George's Channel

METRES	FEET
6000	19686
5000	16404
4000	13124
3000	9843
2000	6562
1000	3281
500	1640
200	656
SEA	LEVEL
200	656
2000	6562
4000	13124
6000	19686

1:2M

KM	MILES
100	60
75	50
	40
50	30
25	20
	10
0	0

Conic Equidistant Projection

© Collins Bartholomew Ltd

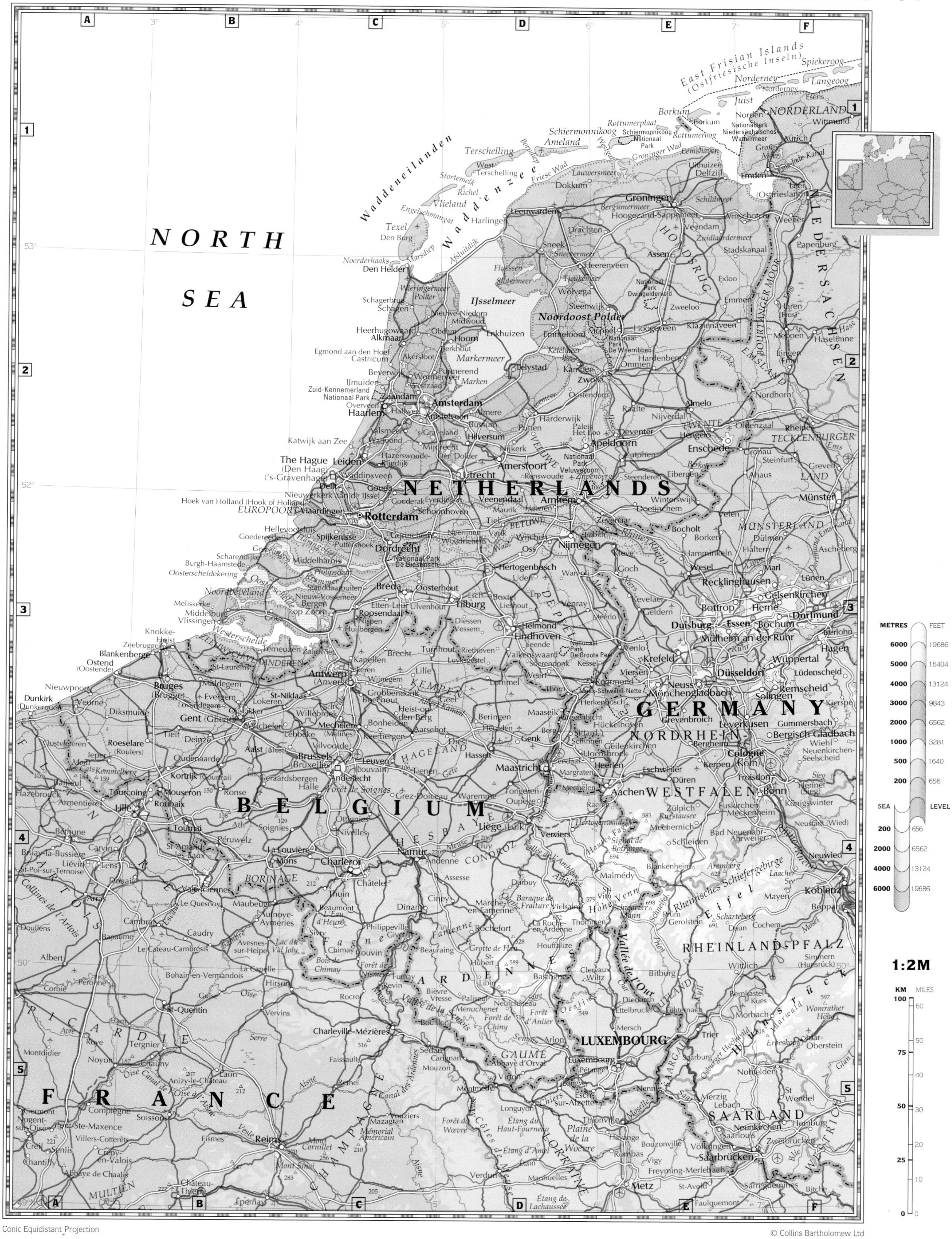

NORTH
SEA

NETHERLANDS

BELGIUM

GERMANY

NORDRHEIN-

WESTFALEN

RHEINLAND-PFALZ

LUXEMBOURG

FRANCE

SAARLAND

East Frisian Islands
(Ostfriesische Inseln)

NORDERLAND

MÜNSTERLAND

METRES FEET
6000 19686
5000 16404
4000 13124
3000 9843
2000 6562
1000 3281
500 1640
200 656
SEA LEVEL
200 656
2000 6562
4000 13124
6000 19686

1:2M

KM MILES
100 60
75
50 30
25
0

Conic Equidistant Projection

© Collins Bartholomew Ltd

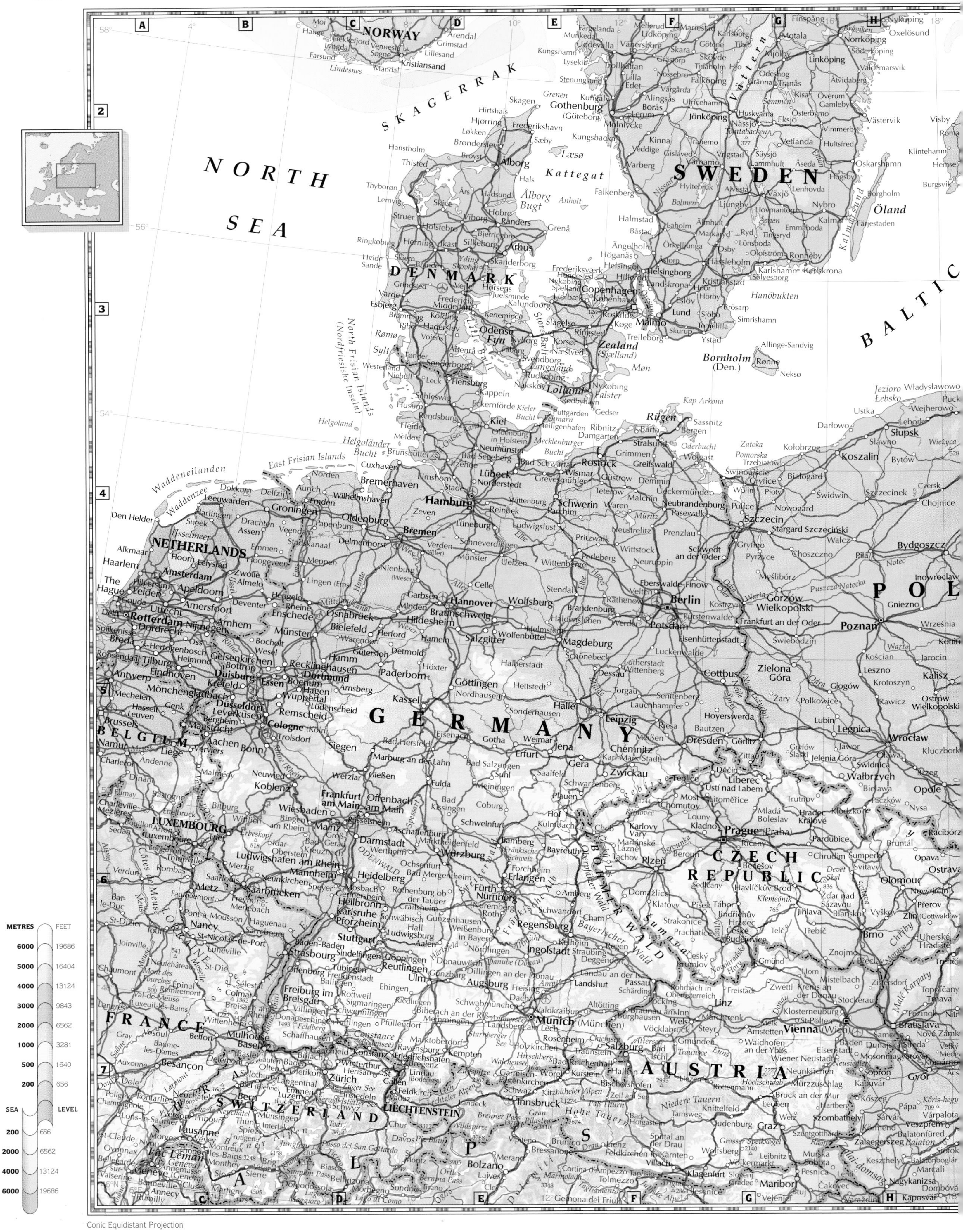

METRES | FEET
6000 | 19686
5000 | 16404
4000 | 13124
3000 | 9843
2000 | 6562
1000 | 3281
500 | 1640
200 | 656
SEA | LEVEL
200 | 656
2000 | 6562
4000 | 13124
6000 | 19686

Conic Equidistant Projection

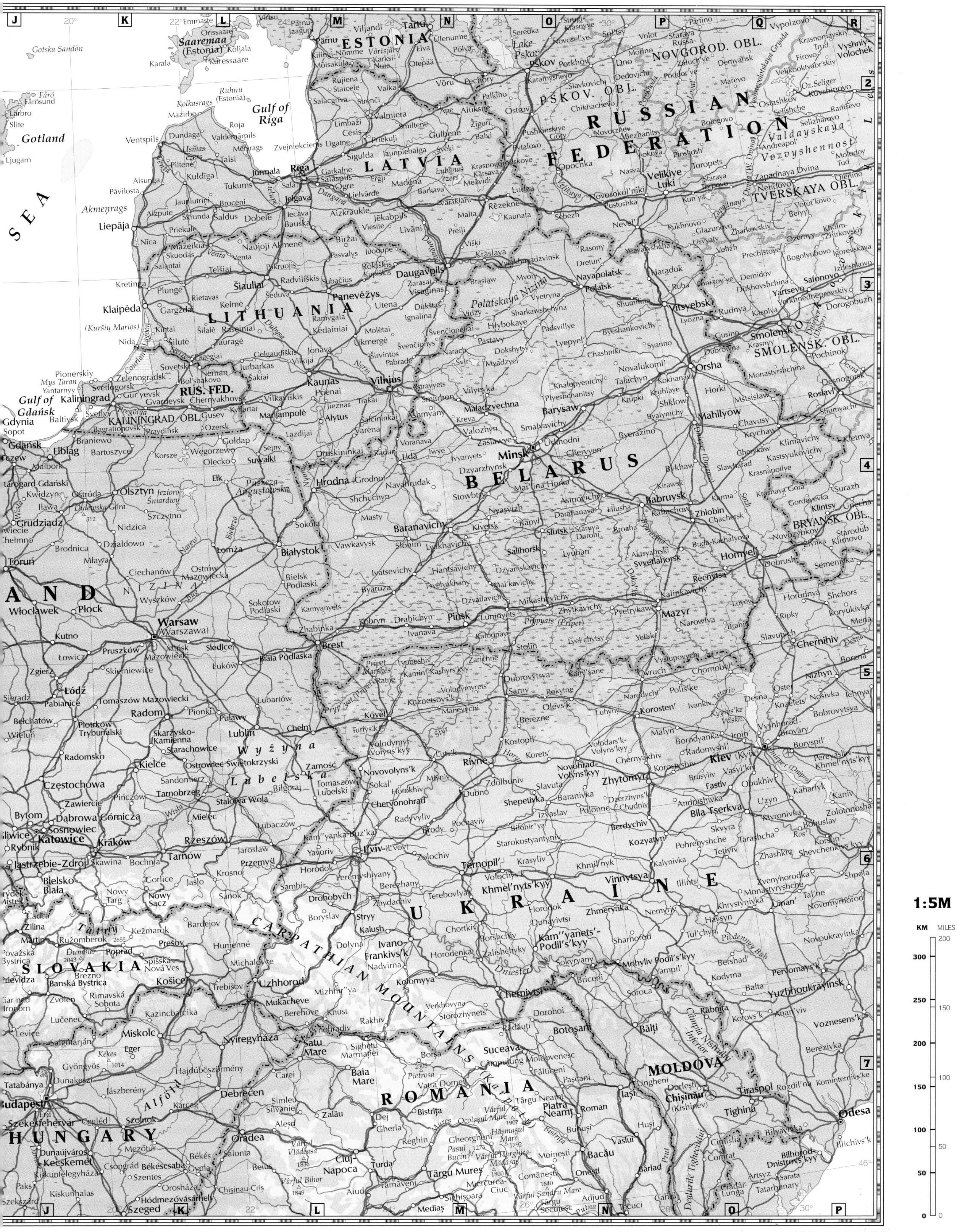

1:5M

KM	MILES
	200
300	
	150
250	
200	100
150	
	50
100	
50	
0	0

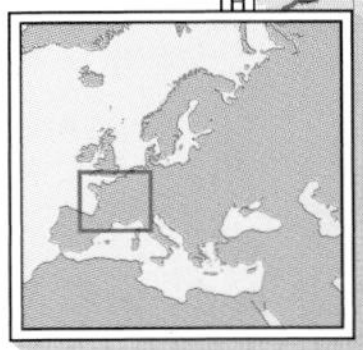

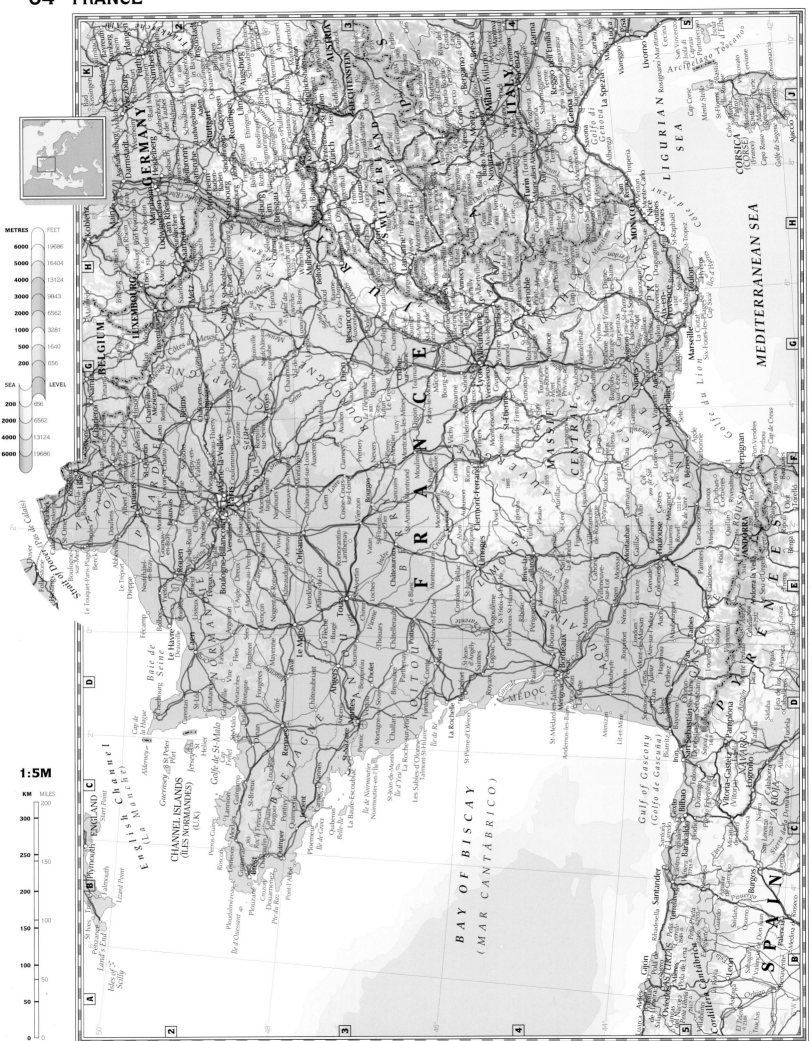

1:5M

Conic Equidistant Projection

© Collins Bartholomew Ltd

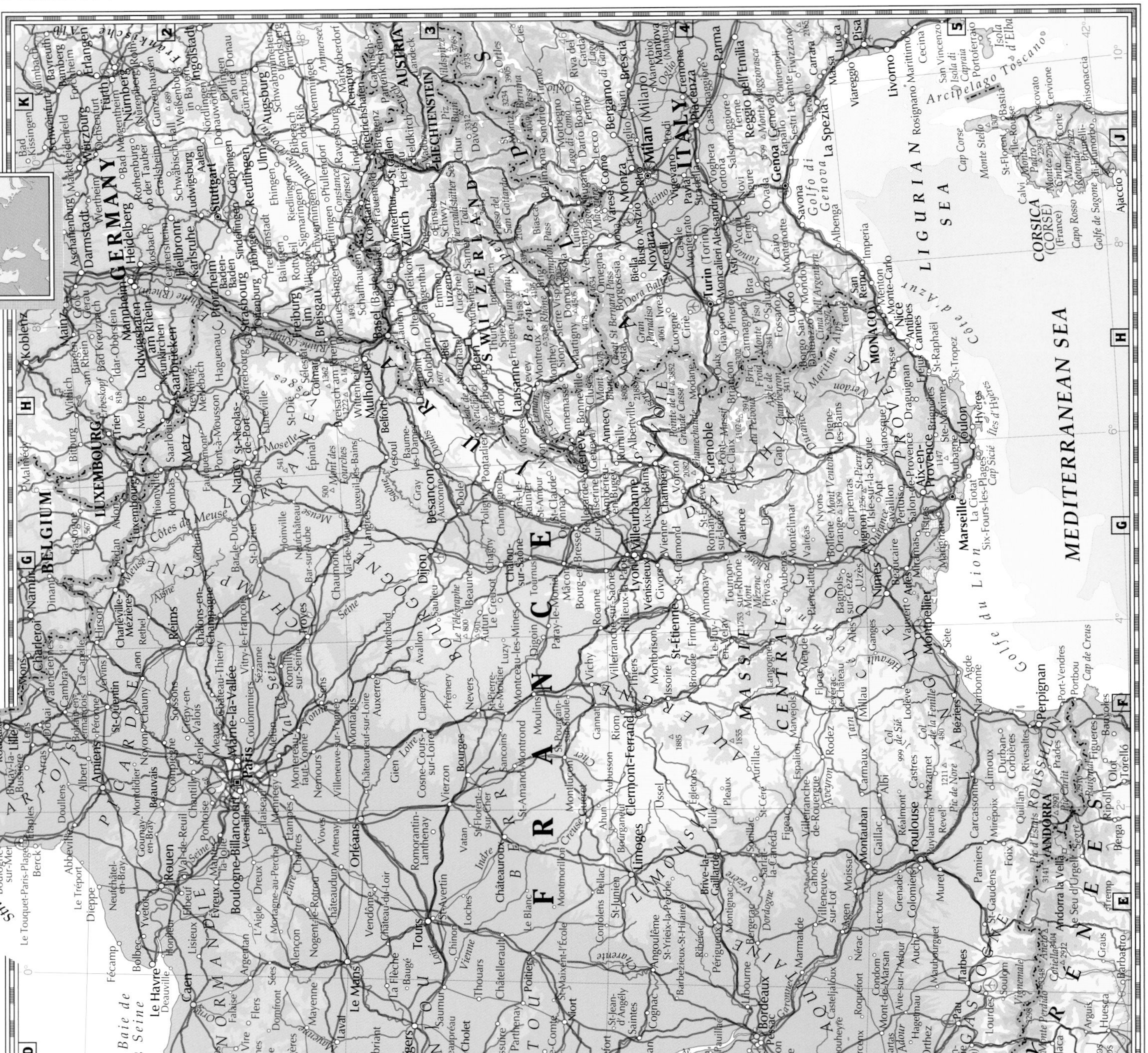

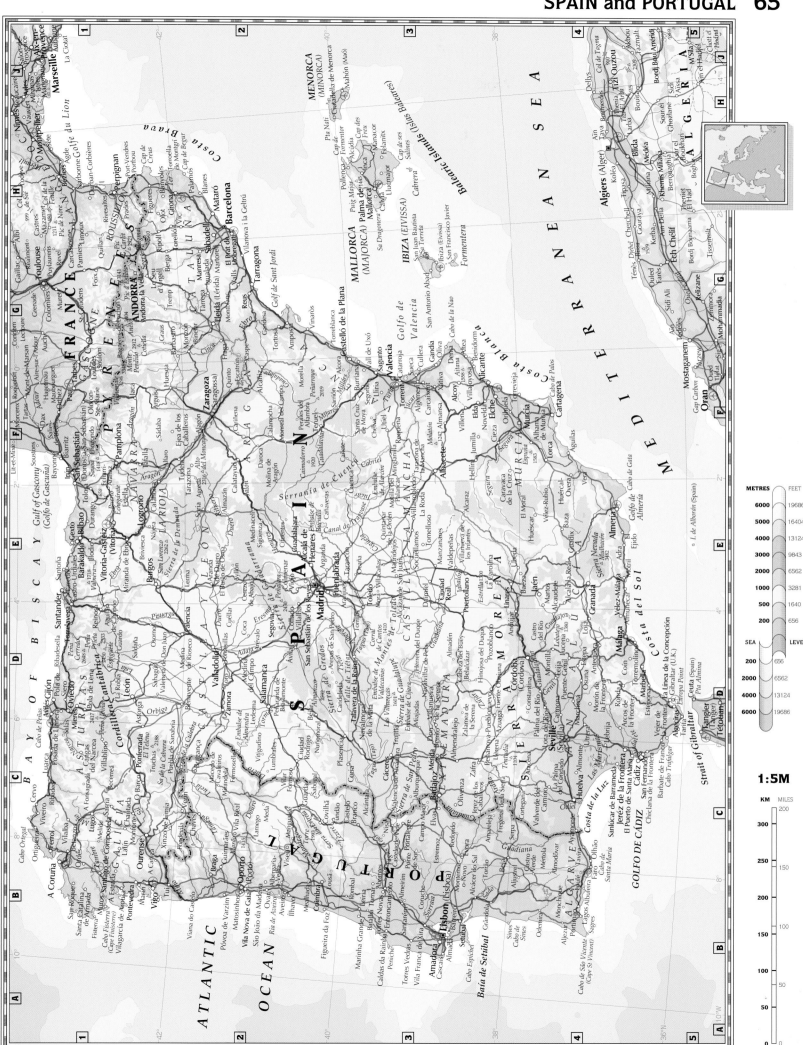
SPAIN
PORTUGAL
FRANCE
ALGERIA
ANDORRA
ATLANTIC OCEAN
BAY OF BISCAY
MEDITERRANEAN SEA
Gulf of Gascony (Golfe de Gascuña)
Golfe du Lion
Golfo de Valencia
GOLFO DE CÁDIZ
Strait of Gibraltar
Balearic Islands (Islas Baleares)
MALLORCA (MAJORCA)
MENORCA (MINORCA)
IBIZA (EIVISSA)
Formentera
Cabrera
PYRENEES
CASTILLA Y LEÓN
CASTILLA-LA MANCHA
EXTREMADURA
ANDALUCÍA
ARAGÓN
CATALUÑA
GALICIA
ASTURIAS
NAVARRA
LA RIOJA
MURCIA
ALGARVE
Madrid
Lisboa (Lisbon)
Barcelona
Valencia
Seville (Sevilla)
Zaragoza
Bilbao
Porto
Oporto
Málaga
Granada
Córdoba (Cordova)
Murcia
Alicante
Palma de Mallorca
Toulouse
Marseille
Montpellier
Perpignan
Algiers (Alger)
Oran
Tangier (Tanger)
Gibraltar (U.K.)
Ceuta (Spain)
Costa Brava
Costa Blanca
Costa del Sol
Costa de la Luz
Sierra Nevada
Sierra Morena
Cordillera Cantábrica
Sierra de Gredos
Serranía de Cuenca
Montes de Toledo
METRES FEET
6000 19686
5000 16404
4000 13124
3000 9843
2000 6562
1000 3281
500 1640
200 656
SEA LEVEL
200 656
2000 6562
4000 13124
6000 19686
1:5M
KM MILES
300 200
250 150
200
150 100
100
50 50
0 0

Conic Equidistant Projection

FRANCE
SWITZERLAND
LIECHTENSTEIN
AUSTRIA
SLOVENIA
CROATIA
ITALY
SAN MARINO
MONACO
CORSICA (CORSE) (France)
SARDINIA (SARDEGNA) (Italy)
SICILY (SICILIA)
MALTA
TUNISIA
ALGERIA
Ligurian Sea
Golfo di Genova
TYRRHENIAN SEA
ADRIATIC SEA
Gulf of Venice
Strait of Bonifacio
Sicilian Channel
Malta Channel
MEDITERRANEAN
IONIAN
Golfo di Taranto
Isole Lipari
Rome (Roma)
Milan (Milano)
Naples (Napoli)
Turin (Torino)
Genoa (Genova)
Venice (Venezia)
Florence (Firenze)
Bologna
Palermo
Cagliari
Bari
Ljubljana
Zagreb
Tunis
Valletta
Messina
Catania
Reggio di Calabria
Ajaccio
Bastia
Sassari
Trieste
Ancona
Pescara
Taranto
Bizerte
Sfax
Annaba
Sousse
Kairouan
Bolzano
Trento
Verona
Padua (Padova)
Pisa
Livorno
Perugia
Salerno
Foggia
Cosenza
Catanzaro
Syracuse (Siracusa)
Trapani
Marsala
Agrigento
Klagenfurt
Graz
Innsbruck
Lausanne
Bern
Genève
Nice
Cannes
Rijeka
Split
Zadar

METRES
FEET
6000
19686
5000
16404
4000
13124
3000
9843
2000
6562
1000
3281
500
1640
200
656
SEA
LEVEL
200
656
2000
6562
4000
13124
6000
19686

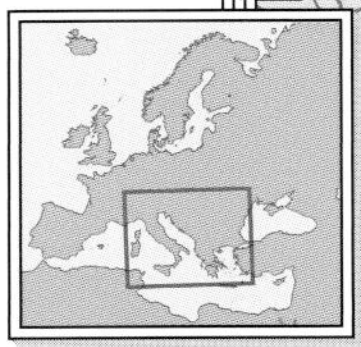

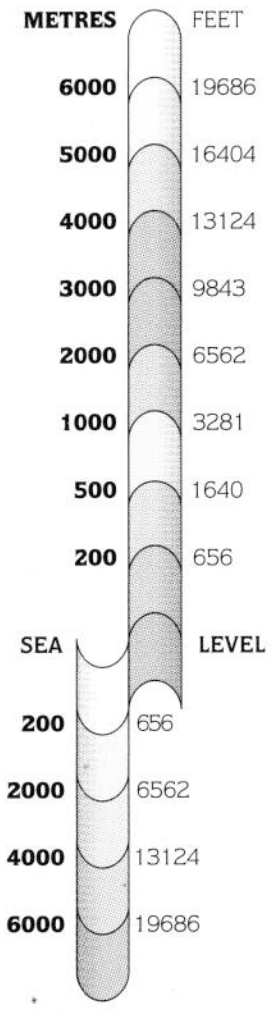

Conic Equidistant Projection

HUNGARY
ROMANIA
MOLDOVA
UKRAINE
SERBIA AND MONTENEGRO
SERBIA (SRBIJA)
MONTENEGRO (CRNA GORA)
KOSOVO
VOJVODINA
BULGARIA
MACEDONIA (F.Y.R.O.M.)
ALBANIA
GREECE
TURKEY
BLACK SEA
AEGEAN SEA
Sea of Marmara (Marmara Denizi)
Ionian Islands (Ionioi Nisoi)
Strait of Otranto
CARPATHIAN MTS
Transylvanian Alps (Carpații Meridionali)
BALKAN MTS (STARA PLANINA)
Rhodope Mountains
Thrakiko Pelagos
Thermaikos Kolpos
Mirtoö Pelagos
Krytiko Pelagos
Cyclades (Kyklades)
Dodecanese (Dodekanisos)
CRETE (KRITI)
EVVOIA (EUBOEA)
Budapest
Szeged
Cluj-Napoca
Bucharest (București)
Constanța
Odesa
Chișinău
Belgrade (Beograd)
Novi Sad
Sarajevo
Podgorica
Priština
Sofia (Sofiya)
Plovdiv
Varna
Burgas
Skopje
Tirana (Tiranë)
Thessaloniki
Athens (Athina)
Peiraias (Piraeus)
Patra
Larisa
Istanbul
Edirne
Bursa
Izmir
Lesbos (Lesvos)
Chios
Samos
Rhodes (Rodos)
Naxos
Kythira
Corfu (Kerkyra)
Kefallonia (Cephalonia)
Zakynthos
Lecce
1:5M
KM
MILES
250
200
150
100
50
0
150
100
50
0

METRES
FEET
6000
19686
5000
16404
4000
13124
3000
9843
2000
6562
1000
3281
500
1640
200
656
SEA
LEVEL
200
656
2000
6562
4000
13124
6000
19686
RUSSIAN FEDERATION
FINLAND
ESTONIA
LATVIA
LITHUANIA
BELARUS
SWEDEN
RESPUBLIKA KOMI
ARKHANGEL'SKAYA OBLAST'
RESPUBLIKA KARELIYA
LENINGRAD OBLAST'
VOLOGOD. OBLAST'
KIROVSKAYA
KOSTROM. OBLAST'
TVERSKAYA OBLAST'
SMOLENSK OBLAST'
Gulf of Bothnia
Gulf of Finland
Gulf of Riga
BALTIC SEA
Lake Ladoga
Lake Onega
Onezhskaya Guba
Moscow
St Petersburg
Helsinki
Stockholm
Tallinn
Riga
Vilnius
Minsk
Warsaw
Archangel
Nizhniy Novgorod
Kazan'
Yaroslavl
Smolensk
Kaliningrad
Saaremaa
Hiiumaa
Gotland (Sweden)
Aland (Finland)
Timanskiy
Nyandomskiy Vozvyshennost'
Galichskaya Vozvyshennost'
Danilovskaya Vozvyshennost'

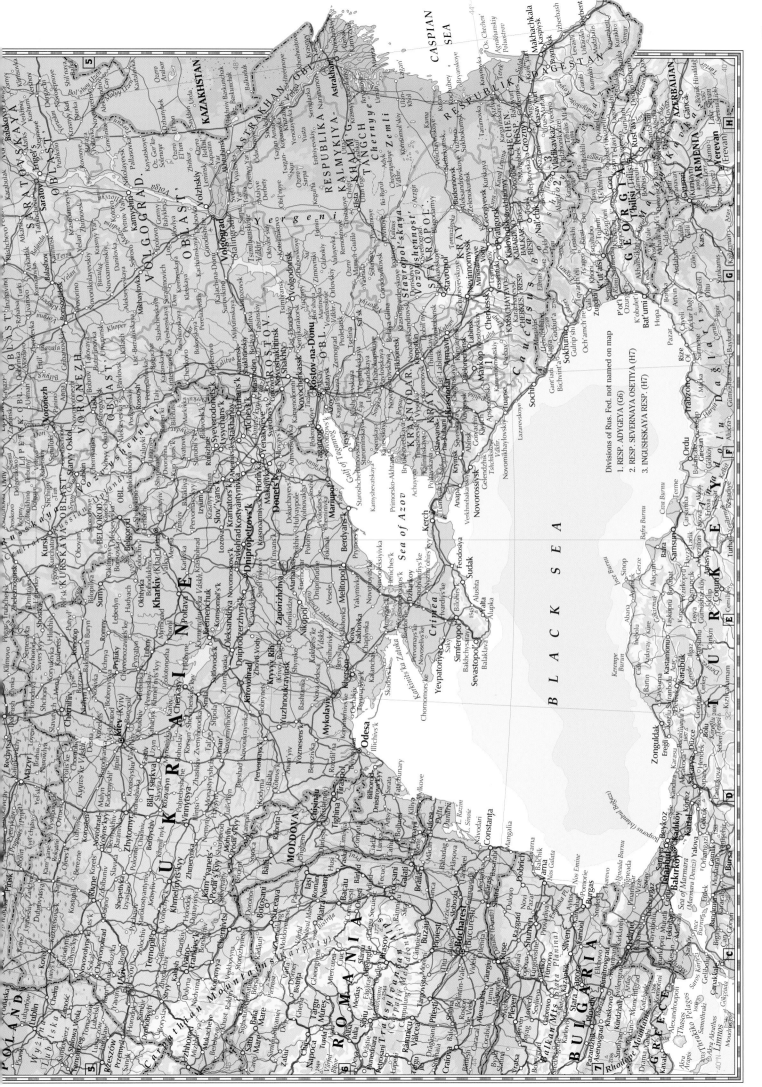

1:7M

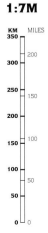

Divisions of Rus. Fed. not named on map
1. RESP. ADYGEYA (G6)
2. RESP. SEVERNAYA OSETIYA (H7)
3. INGUSHSKAYA RESP. (H7)

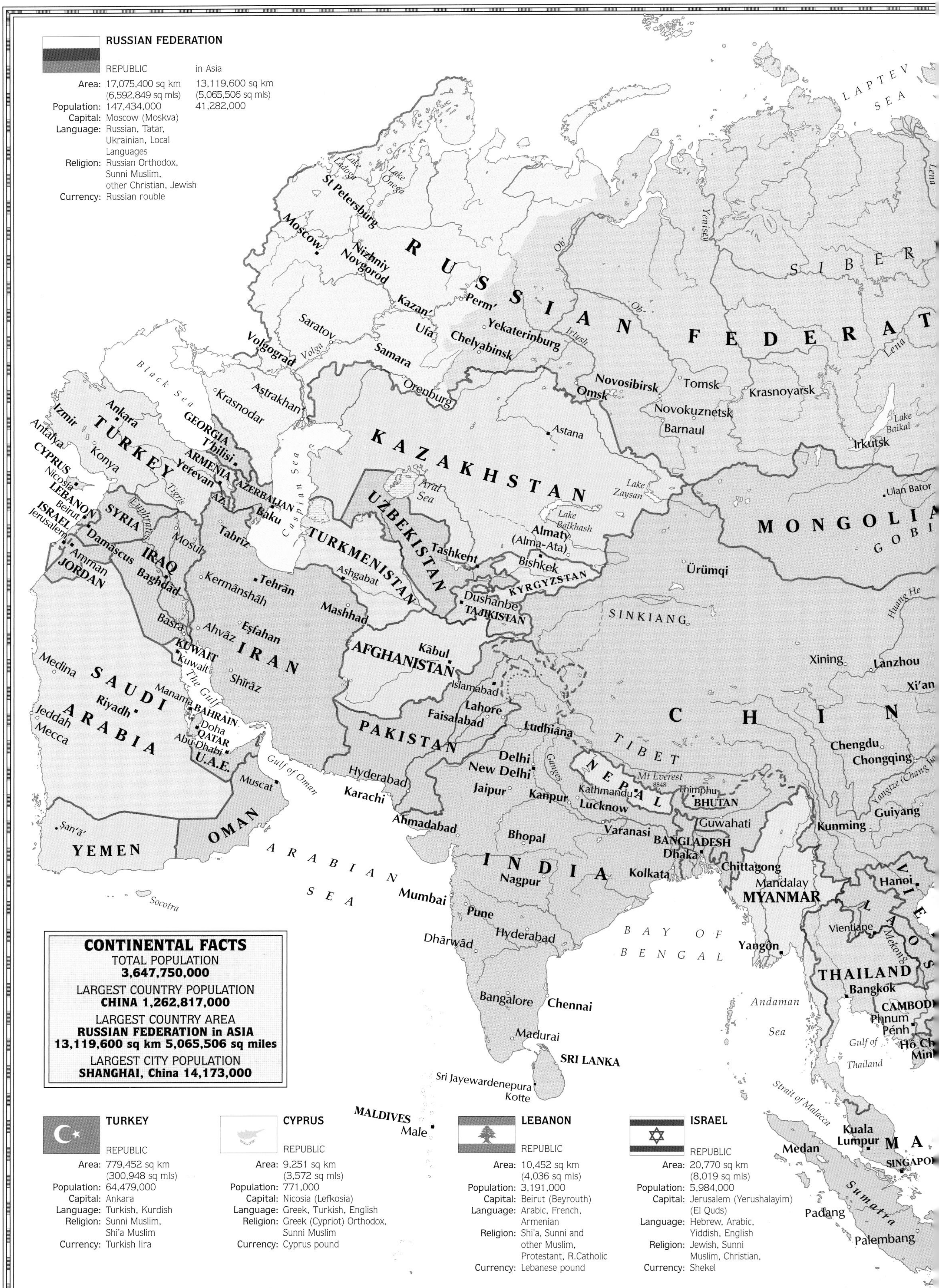

RUSSIAN FEDERATION

REPUBLIC

		in Asia
Area:	17,075,400 sq km (6,592,849 sq mls)	13,119,600 sq km (5,065,506 sq mls)
Population:	147,434,000	41,282,000
Capital:	Moscow (Moskva)	
Language:	Russian, Tatar, Ukrainian, Local Languages	
Religion:	Russian Orthodox, Sunni Muslim, other Christian, Jewish	
Currency:	Russian rouble	

CONTINENTAL FACTS

TOTAL POPULATION
3,647,750,000

LARGEST COUNTRY POPULATION
CHINA 1,262,817,000

LARGEST COUNTRY AREA
RUSSIAN FEDERATION in ASIA
13,119,600 sq km 5,065,506 sq miles

LARGEST CITY POPULATION
SHANGHAI, China 14,173,000

TURKEY

REPUBLIC

Area:	779,452 sq km (300,948 sq mls)
Population:	64,479,000
Capital:	Ankara
Language:	Turkish, Kurdish
Religion:	Sunni Muslim, Shi'a Muslim
Currency:	Turkish lira

CYPRUS

REPUBLIC

Area:	9,251 sq km (3,572 sq mls)
Population:	771,000
Capital:	Nicosia (Lefkosia)
Language:	Greek, Turkish, English
Religion:	Greek (Cypriot) Orthodox, Sunni Muslim
Currency:	Cyprus pound

LEBANON

REPUBLIC

Area:	10,452 sq km (4,036 sq mls)
Population:	3,191,000
Capital:	Beirut (Beyrouth)
Language:	Arabic, French, Armenian
Religion:	Shi'a, Sunni and other Muslim, Protestant, R.Catholic
Currency:	Lebanese pound

ISRAEL

REPUBLIC

Area:	20,770 sq km (8,019 sq mls)
Population:	5,984,000
Capital:	Jerusalem (Yerushalayim) (El Quds)
Language:	Hebrew, Arabic, Yiddish, English
Religion:	Jewish, Sunni Muslim, Christian,
Currency:	Shekel

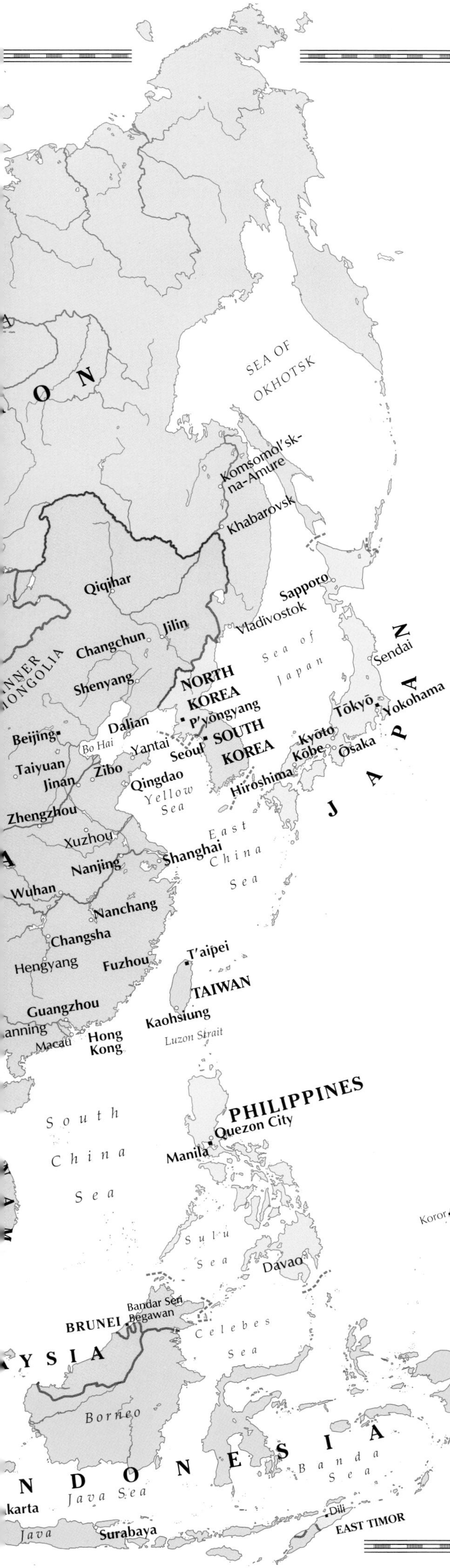

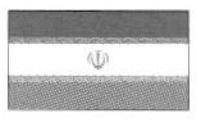

IRAN
REPUBLIC
Area: 1,648,000 sq km
(636,296 sq mls)
Population: 65,758,000
Capital: Tehrān
Language: Farsi, Azeri, Kurdish,
Regional Languages
Religion: Shi'a Muslim,
Sunni Muslim, Baha'i,
Christian, Zoroastrian
Currency: Iranian rial

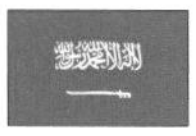

SAUDI ARABIA
MONARCHY
Area: 2,200,000 sq km
(849,425 sq mls)
Population: 20,181,000
Capital: Riyadh (Ar Riyāḍ)
Language: Arabic
Religion: Sunni Muslim,
Shi'a Muslim
Currency: Saudi Arabian riyal

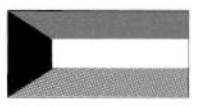

KUWAIT
MONARCHY
Area: 17,818 sq km
(6,880 sq mls)
Population: 1,811,000
Capital: Kuwait (Al Kuwayt)
Language: Arabic
Religion: Sunni, Shi'a and
other Muslim,
Christian, Hindu
Currency: Kuwaiti dinar

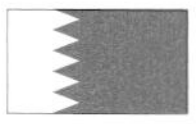

BAHRAIN
MONARCHY
Area: 691 sq km
(267 sq mls)
Population: 595,000
Capital: Manama (Al Manāmah)
Language: Arabic, English
Religion: Shi'a Muslim,
Sunni Muslim,
Christian
Currency: Bahraini dinar

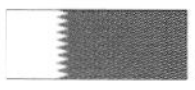

QATAR
MONARCHY
Area: 11,437 sq km
(4,416 sq mls)
Population: 579,000
Capital: Doha (Ad Dawḩah)
Language: Arabic, Indian
Languages
Religion: Sunni Muslim,
Christian, Hindu
Currency: Qatari riyal

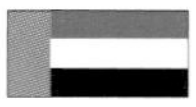

UNITED ARAB EMIRATES
FEDERATION
Area: 83,600 sq km
(32,278 sq mls)
Population: 2,377,000
Capital: Abu Dhabi (Abū Ẓabī)
Language: Arabic,
English, Hindi,
Urdu, Farsi
Religion: Sunni Muslim,
Shi'a Muslim,
Christian
Currency: UAE dirham

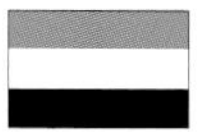

YEMEN
REPUBLIC
Area: 527,968 sq km
(203,850 sq mls)
Population: 16,887,000
Capital: Ṣan'ā'
Language: Arabic
Religion: Sunni Muslim,
Shi'a Muslim
Currency: Yemeni rial

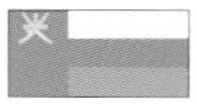

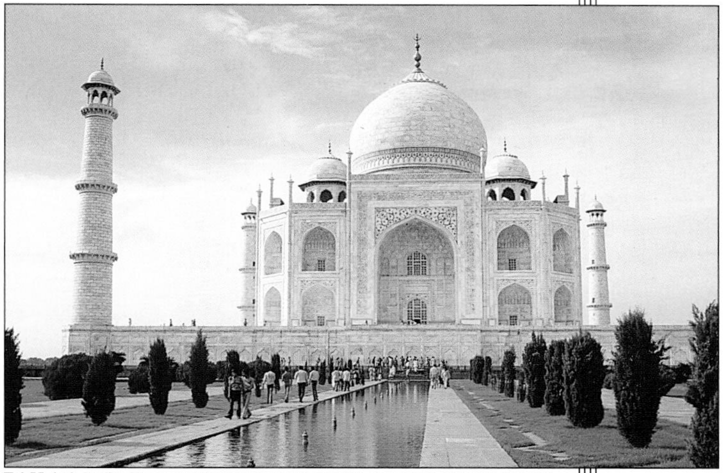

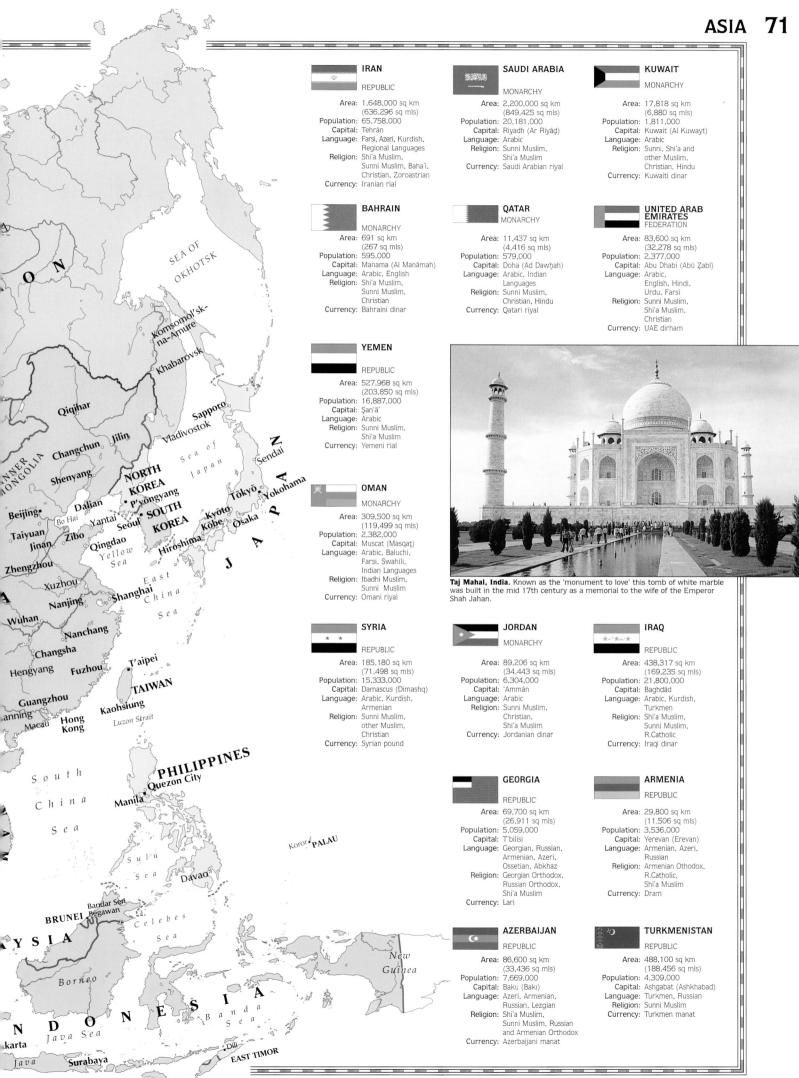

Taj Mahal, India. Known as the 'monument to love' this tomb of white marble was built in the mid 17th century as a memorial to the wife of the Emperor Shah Jahan.

OMAN
MONARCHY
Area: 309,500 sq km
(119,499 sq mls)
Population: 2,382,000
Capital: Muscat (Masqaṭ)
Language: Arabic, Baluchi,
Farsi, Swahili,
Indian Languages
Religion: Ibadhi Muslim,
Sunni Muslim
Currency: Omani riyal

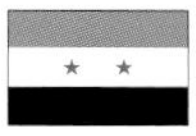

SYRIA
REPUBLIC
Area: 185,180 sq km
(71,498 sq mls)
Population: 15,333,000
Capital: Damascus (Dimashq)
Language: Arabic, Kurdish,
Armenian
Religion: Sunni Muslim,
other Muslim,
Christian
Currency: Syrian pound

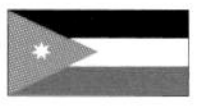

JORDAN
MONARCHY
Area: 89,206 sq km
(34,443 sq mls)
Population: 6,304,000
Capital: 'Ammān
Language: Arabic
Religion: Sunni Muslim,
Christian,
Shi'a Muslim
Currency: Jordanian dinar

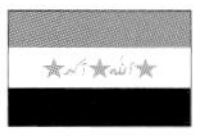

IRAQ
REPUBLIC
Area: 438,317 sq km
(169,235 sq mls)
Population: 21,800,000
Capital: Baghdād
Language: Arabic, Kurdish,
Turkmen
Religion: Shi'a Muslim,
Sunni Muslim,
R.Catholic
Currency: Iraqi dinar

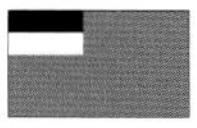

GEORGIA
REPUBLIC
Area: 69,700 sq km
(26,911 sq mls)
Population: 5,059,000
Capital: T'bilisi
Language: Georgian, Russian,
Armenian, Azeri,
Ossetian, Abkhaz
Religion: Georgian Orthodox,
Russian Orthodox,
Shi'a Muslim
Currency: Lari

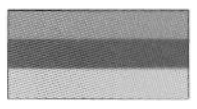

ARMENIA
REPUBLIC
Area: 29,800 sq km
(11,506 sq mls)
Population: 3,536,000
Capital: Yerevan (Erevan)
Language: Armenian, Azeri,
Russian
Religion: Armenian Othodox,
R.Catholic,
Shi'a Muslim
Currency: Dram

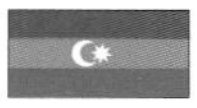

AZERBAIJAN
REPUBLIC
Area: 86,600 sq km
(33,436 sq mls)
Population: 7,669,000
Capital: Baku (Bakı)
Language: Azeri, Armenian,
Russian, Lezgian
Religion: Shi'a Muslim,
Sunni Muslim, Russian
and Armenian Orthodox
Currency: Azerbaijani manat

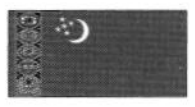

TURKMENISTAN
REPUBLIC
Area: 488,100 sq km
(188,456 sq mls)
Population: 4,309,000
Capital: Ashgabat (Ashkhabad)
Language: Turkmen, Russian
Religion: Sunni Muslim
Currency: Turkmen manat

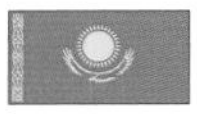

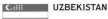

KAZAKHSTAN
REPUBLIC

Area: 2,717,300 sq km
(1,049,155 sq mls)
Population: 16,319,000
Capital: Astana (Akmola)
Language: Kazakh, Russian,
German, Ukrainian,
Uzbek, Tatar
Religion: Sunni Muslim, Russian
Orthodox, Protestant
Currency: Tenge

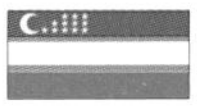

UZBEKISTAN
REPUBLIC

Area: 447,400 sq km
(172,742 sq mls)
Population: 23,574,000
Capital: Tashkent
Language: Uzbek, Russian,
Tajik, Kazakh
Religion: Sunni Muslim
Russian Orthodox
Currency: Uzbek som

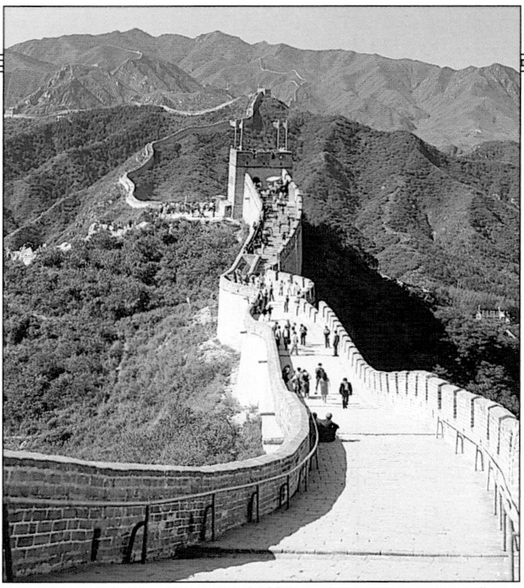

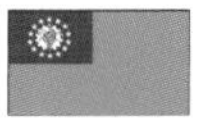

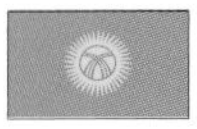

KYRGYZSTAN
REPUBLIC

Area: 198,500 sq km
(76,641 sq mls)
Population: 4,643,000
Capital: Bishkek (Frunze)
Language: Kirghiz, Russian,
Uzbek
Religion: Sunni Muslim,
Russian Orthodox
Currency: Kyrgyz som

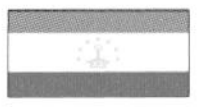

TAJIKISTAN
REPUBLIC

Area: 143,100 sq km
(55,251 sq mls)
Population: 6,015,000
Capital: Dushanbe
Language: Tajik, Uzbek,
Russian
Religion: Sunni Muslim
Currency: Somoni

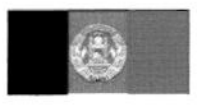

AFGHANISTAN
REPUBLIC

Area: 652,225 sq km
(251,825 sq mls)
Population: 21,354,000
Capital: Kābul
Language: Dari, Pushtu,
Uzbek, Turkmen
Religion: Sunni Muslim,
Shi'a Muslim
Currency: Afghani

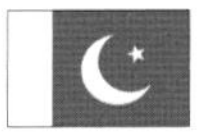

PAKISTAN
REPUBLIC

Area: 803,940 sq km
(310,403 sq mls)
Population: 148,166,000
Capital: Islamabad
Language: Urdu (official),
Punjabi, Sindhi,
Pushtu, English
Religion: Sunni Muslim,
Shi'a Muslim,
Christian, Hindu
Currency: Pakistani rupee

Great Wall of China. Stretching 3460 km, this is the longest wall in the world and dates from the 3rdC BC.

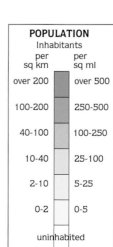

MYANMAR
REPUBLIC

Area: 676,577 sq km
(261,228 sq mls)
Population: 44,497,000
Capital: Yangôn (Rangoon)
Language: Burmese, Shan,
Karen, Local Languages
Religion: Buddhist, Sunni Muslim,
Protestant, R.Catholic
Currency: Kyat

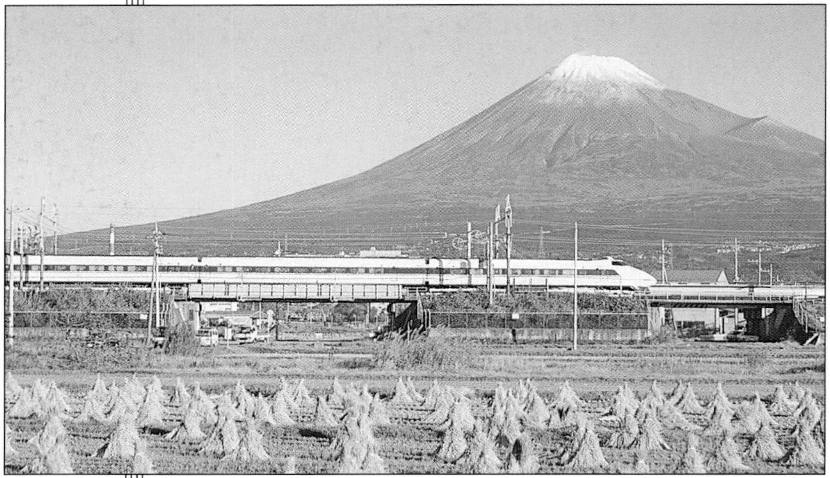

Japan. The speedy 'Bullet train' travels past Mount Fuji, a volcano which last erupted in 1707.

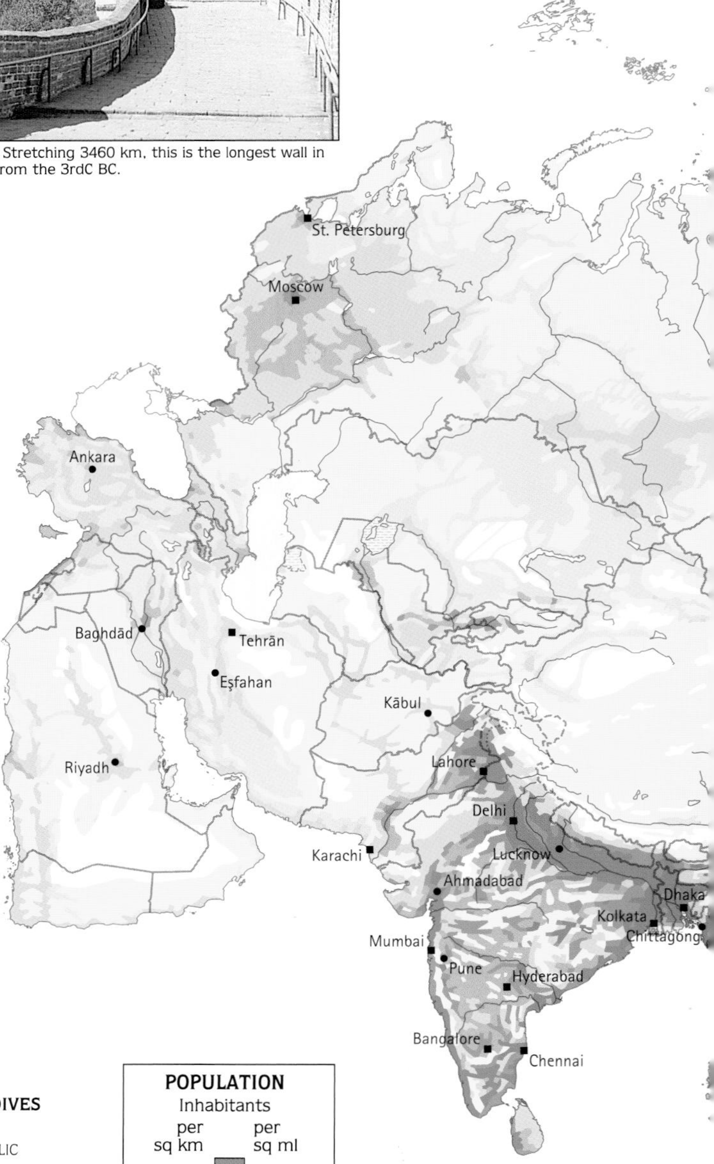

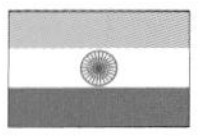

INDIA
REPUBLIC

Area: 3,065,027 sq km
(1,183,414 sq mls)
Population: 982,223,000
Capital: New Delhi
Language: Hindi, English (official),
Many Regional Languages
Religion: Hindu, Sunni Muslim,
Sikh, Christian,
Buddhist, Jain
Currency: Indian rupee

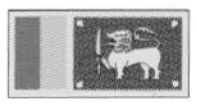

SRI LANKA
REPUBLIC

Area: 65,610 sq km
(25,332 sq mls)
Population: 18,455,000
Capital: Sri Jayewardenepura
Kotte
Language: Sinhalese, Tamil,
English
Religion: Buddhist, Hindu,
Sunni Muslim,
R. Catholic
Currency: Sri Lankan rupee

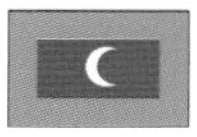

MALDIVES
REPUBLIC

Area: 298 sq km
(115 sq mls)
Population: 271,000
Capital: Male
Language: Divehi (Maldivian)
Religion: Sunni Muslim
Currency: Rufiyaa

NEPAL
MONARCHY

Area: 147,181 sq km
(56,827 sq mls)
Population: 22,847,000
Capital: Kathmandu
Language: Nepali, Maithili,
Bhojpuri, English,
Many Local Languages
Religion: Hindu, Buddhist,
Sunni Muslim
Currency: Nepalese rupee

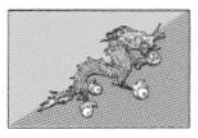

BHUTAN
MONARCHY

Area: 46,620 sq km
(18,000 sq mls)
Population: 2,004,000
Capital: Thimphu
Language: Dzongkha, Nepali
Assamese, English
Religion: Buddhist, Hindu
Currency: Ngultrum,
Indian rupee

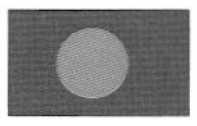

BANGLADESH
REPUBLIC

Area: 143,998 sq km
(55,598 sq mls)
Population: 124,774,000
Capital: Dhaka (Dacca)
Language: Bengali, Bihari,
Hindi, English,
Local Languages
Religion: Sunni Muslim, Hindu,
Buddhist, Christian
Currency: Taka

POPULATION
Inhabitants

per sq km	per sq ml
over 200	over 500
100-200	250-500
40-100	100-250
10-40	25-100
2-10	5-25
0-2	0-5
uninhabited	

CITIES
■ Over 5 million population
● 2.5 - 5 million population

THAILAND
MONARCHY
Area: 513,115 sq km
(198,115 sq mls)
Population: 60,300,000
Capital: Bangkok (Krung Thep)
Language: Thai, Lao, Chinese,
Malay,
Mon-Khmer Languages
Religion: Buddhist,
Sunni Muslim
Currency: Baht

LAOS
REPUBLIC
Area: 236,800 sq km
(91,429 sq mls)
Population: 5,163,000
Capital: Vientiane (Viangchan)
Language: Lao, Local Languages
Religion: Buddhist,
Trad. Beliefs,
R.Catholic,
Sunni Muslim
Currency: Kip

CAMBODIA
MONARCHY
Area: 181,000 sq km
(69,884 sq mls)
Population: 10,716,000
Capital: Phnum Pénh
(Phnom Penh)
Language: Khmer,
Vietnamese
Religion: Buddhist, R.Catholic,
Sunni Muslim
Currency: Riel

VIETNAM
REPUBLIC
Area: 329,565 sq km
(127,246 sq mls)
Population: 77,562,000
Capital: Ha Nôi (Hanoi)
Language: Vietnamese, Thai,
Khmer, Chinese, Many
Local Languages
Religion: Buddhist, Taoist,
R.Catholic, Cao Dai
Currency: Dong

CHINA
REPUBLIC
Area: 9,584,492 sq km
(3,700,593 sq mls)
Population: 1,262,817,000
Capital: Beijing (Peking)
Language: Chinese (Mandarin
official), Many
Regional Languages
Religion: Confucian, Taoist, Buddhist,
Sunni Muslim, R.Catholic
Currency: Yuan, HK dollar,
Macau pataca

MONGOLIA
REPUBLIC
Area: 1,565,000 sq km
(604,250 sq mls)
Population: 2,579,000
Capital: Ulaanbaatar
(Ulan Bator)
Language: Khalka (Mongolian),
Kazakh, Local Languages
Religion: Buddhist, Sunni Muslim,
Trad. Beliefs
Currency: Tugrik (Tögrög)

NORTH KOREA
REPUBLIC
Area: 120,538 sq km
(46,540 sq mls)
Population: 23,348,000
Capital: P'yŏngyang
Language: Korean
Religion: Trad. Beliefs,
Chondoist, Buddhist,
Confucian, Taoist
Currency: North Korea won

SOUTH KOREA
REPUBLIC
Area: 99,274 sq km
(38,330 sq mls)
Population: 46,109,000
Capital: Seoul (Sŏul)
Language: Korean
Religion: Buddhist, Protestant,
R.Catholic, Confucian,
Trad. Beliefs
Currency: South Korea won

POPULATION

JAPAN
MONARCHY
Area: 377,727 sq km
(145,841 sq mls)
Population: 126,281,000
Capital: Tōkyō
Language: Japanese
Religion: Shintoist, Buddhist,
Christian
Currency: Yen

TAIWAN
REPUBLIC
Area: 36,179 sq km
(13,969 sq mls)
Population: 21,908,000
Capital: T'aipei
Language: Chinese (Mandarin
official, Fukien,
Hakka), Local Languages
Religion: Buddhist, Taoist,
Confucian, Christian
Currency: Taiwan dollar

Hong Kong. A traditional Chinese sailing ship, known as a junk, sails in the spectacular harbour.

BRUNEI
MONARCHY
Area: 5,765 sq km
(2,226 sq mls)
Population: 315,000
Capital: Bandar Seri Begawan
Language: Malay, English,
Chinese
Religion: Sunni Muslim,
Buddhist, Christian
Currency: Brunei dollar

PHILIPPINES
REPUBLIC
Area: 300,000 sq km
(115,831 sq mls)
Population: 72,944,000
Capital: Manila
Language: English, Filipino
(Tagalog), Cebuano
Religion: R.Catholic, Aglipayan,
Sunni Muslim,
Protestant
Currency: Philippine peso

PALAU
REPUBLIC
Area: 497 sq km
(192 sq mls)
Population: 19,000
Capital: Koror
Language: Palauan, English
Religion: R.Catholic, Protestant,
Trad. Beliefs
Currency: US dollar

MALAYSIA
FEDERATION
Area: 332,965 sq km
(128,559 sq mls)
Population: 21,410,000
Capital: Kuala Lumpur
Language: Malay, English,
Chinese, Tamil,
Local Languages
Religion: Sunni Muslim,
Buddhist, Hindu,
Christian, Trad. Beliefs
Currency: Ringgit

SINGAPORE
REPUBLIC
Area: 639 sq km
(247 sq mls)
Population: 3,476,000
Capital: Singapore
Language: Chinese, English,
Malay, Tamil
Religion: Buddhist, Taoist,
Sunni Muslim,
Christian, Hindu
Currency: Singapore dollar

INDONESIA
REPUBLIC
Area: 1,919,445 sq km
(741,102 sq mls)
Population: 206,338,000
Capital: Jakarta
Language: Indonesian (official),
Many Local Languages
Religion: Sunni Muslim, Protestant,
R.Catholic, Hindu,
Buddhist
Currency: Rupiah

Map labels: Harbin, Changchun, Shenyang, Beijing, Tianjin, Dalian, Inch'ŏn, Pyŏngyang, Seoul, Taegu, Nagoya, Tōkyō, Handan, Jinan, Pusan, Osaka, Kita-Kyūshū, Qingdao, Xi'an, Nanjing, Shanghai, Chengdu, Wuhan, Hangzhou, Chongqing, T'aipei, Guangzhou, Hong Kong, Ha Nôi, Yangon, Bangkok, Manila, Singapore, Jakarta, Surabaya, Bandung

74

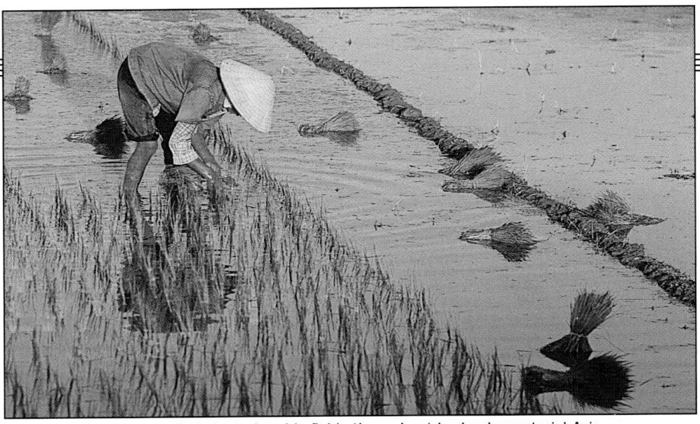

Vietnam. Rice is grown in irrigated paddy fields throughout lowland equatorial Asia.

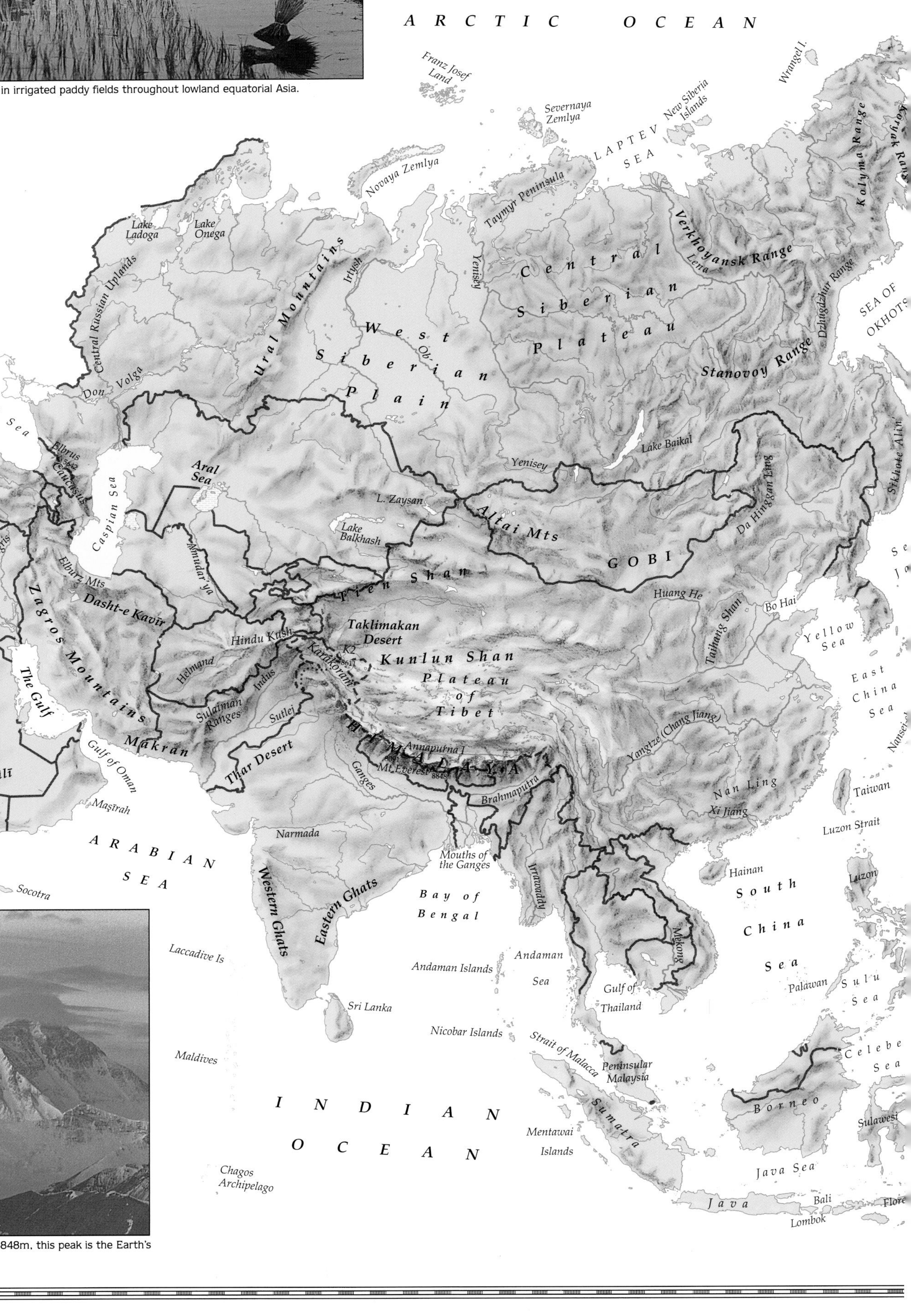

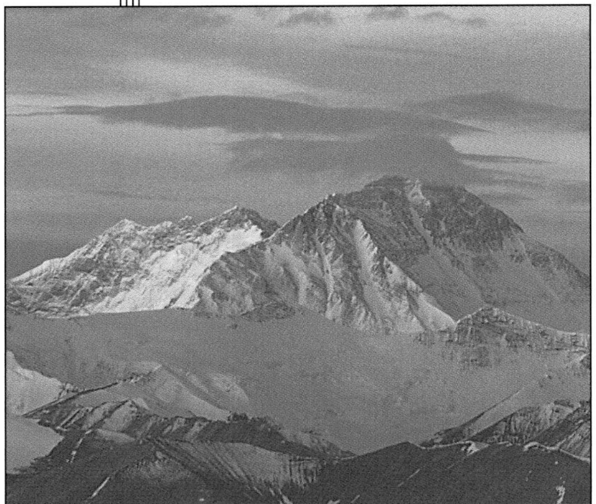

Mt Everest. Rising to 8848m, this peak is the Earth's highest point.

CLIMATE

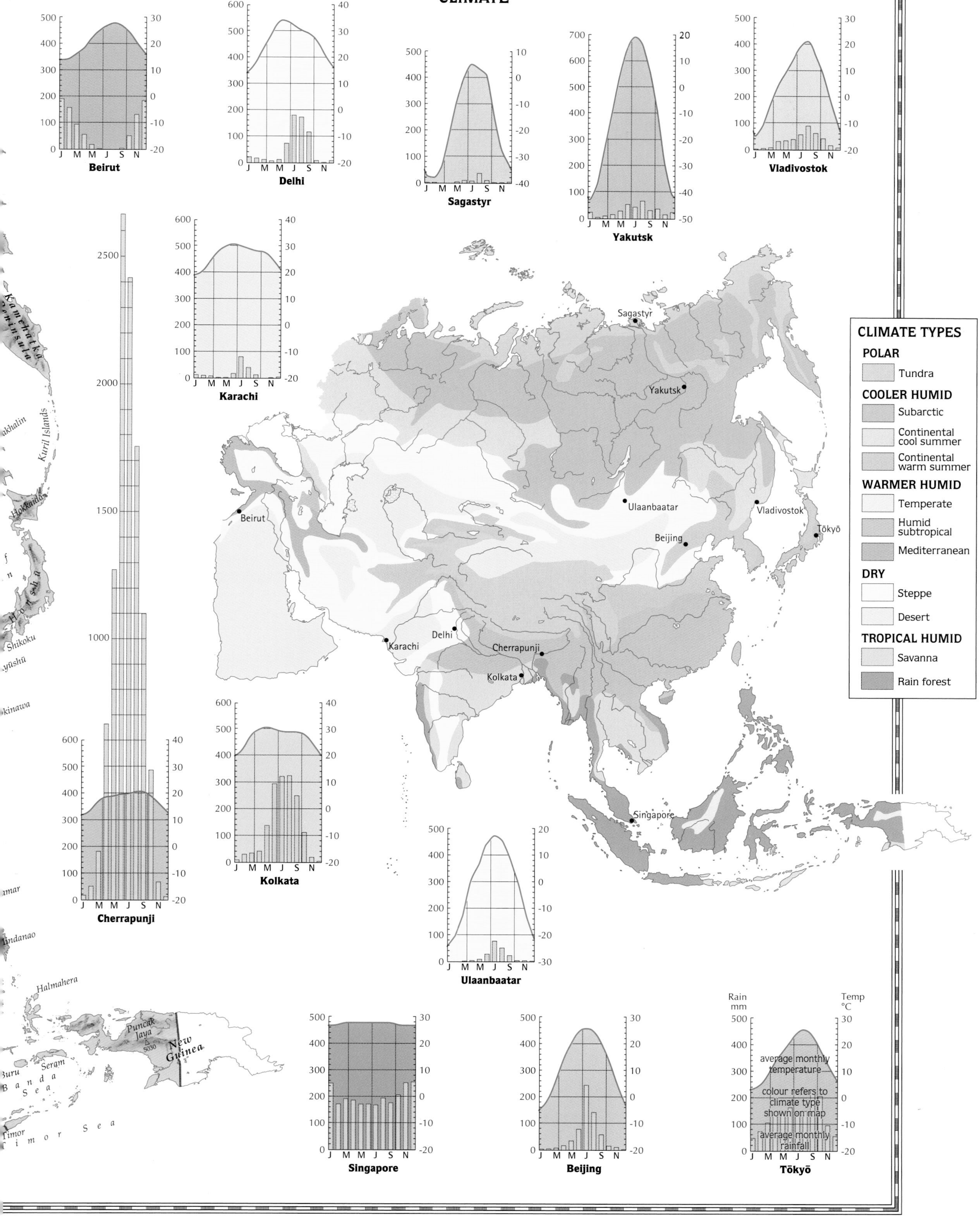

Beirut

Delhi

Sagastyr

Yakutsk

Vladivostok

Karachi

Cherrapunji

Kolkata

Ulaanbaatar

Singapore

Beijing

Tōkyō

Rain
mm

Temp
°C

average monthly
temperature

colour refers to
climate type
shown on map

average monthly
rainfall

CLIMATE TYPES

POLAR
Tundra

COOLER HUMID
Subarctic
Continental
cool summer
Continental
warm summer

WARMER HUMID
Temperate
Humid
subtropical
Mediterranean

DRY
Steppe
Desert

TROPICAL HUMID
Savanna
Rain forest

© Collins Bartholomew Ltd

NORWAY
SWEDEN
FINLAND
ESTONIA
LATVIA
LITHUANIA
POLAND
BELARUS
UKRAINE
GEORGIA
ARMENIA
AZERBAIJAN
TURKEY
IRAN
TURKMENISTAN
UZBEKISTAN
KAZAKHSTAN
KYRGYZSTAN
TAJIKISTAN
AFGHANISTAN
RUSSIAN F
UNITED KINGDOM
FAROE ISLANDS (FAEROES) (Denmark)
SVALBARD (Norway)
Norwegian Sea
BARENTS SEA
ARCTIC
Kara Sea (Karskoye More)
White Sea (Beloye More)
Gulf of Bothnia
Baltic Sea
Sea of Azov
Caspian Sea
Aral Sea
Ozero Balkhash
Novaya Zemlya
Franz Josef Land (Zemlya Frantsa-Iosifa)
Zapadno Sibirskaya Ravnina (West Siberian Plain)
Kazakhskiy Melkosopochnik
Karakum Desert
Kyzylkum Desert
TIEN SHAN
Tarim Pendi
Hindu Kush
Ural'skiy Khrebet
Stockholm
Oslo
Helsinki
Tallinn
Riga
Vilnius
Minsk
Warsaw
Kiev
Moscow
St. Petersburg
Murmansk
Archangel
Nizhniy Novgorod
Kazan'
Samara
Saratov
Volgograd
Rostov-na-Donu
Kharkiv
Dnipropetrovs'k
Donets'k
Tbilisi
Yerevan
Baku
Tehrān
Mashhad
Ashgabat
Tashkent
Bishkek
Almaty (Alma-Ata)
Dushanbe
Astana (Akmola)
Karaganda
Yekaterinburg (Sverdlovsk)
Chelyabinsk
Perm'
Ufa
Omsk
Novosibirsk
Barnaul
Krasnoyarsk
Tomsk
Ürümqi (Urumchi)
Vorkuta
Noril'sk

METRES
FEET
6000
19686
5000
16404
4000
13124
3000
9843
2000
6562
1000
3281
500
1640
200
656
SEA
LEVEL
200
656
2000
6562
4000
13124
6000
19686

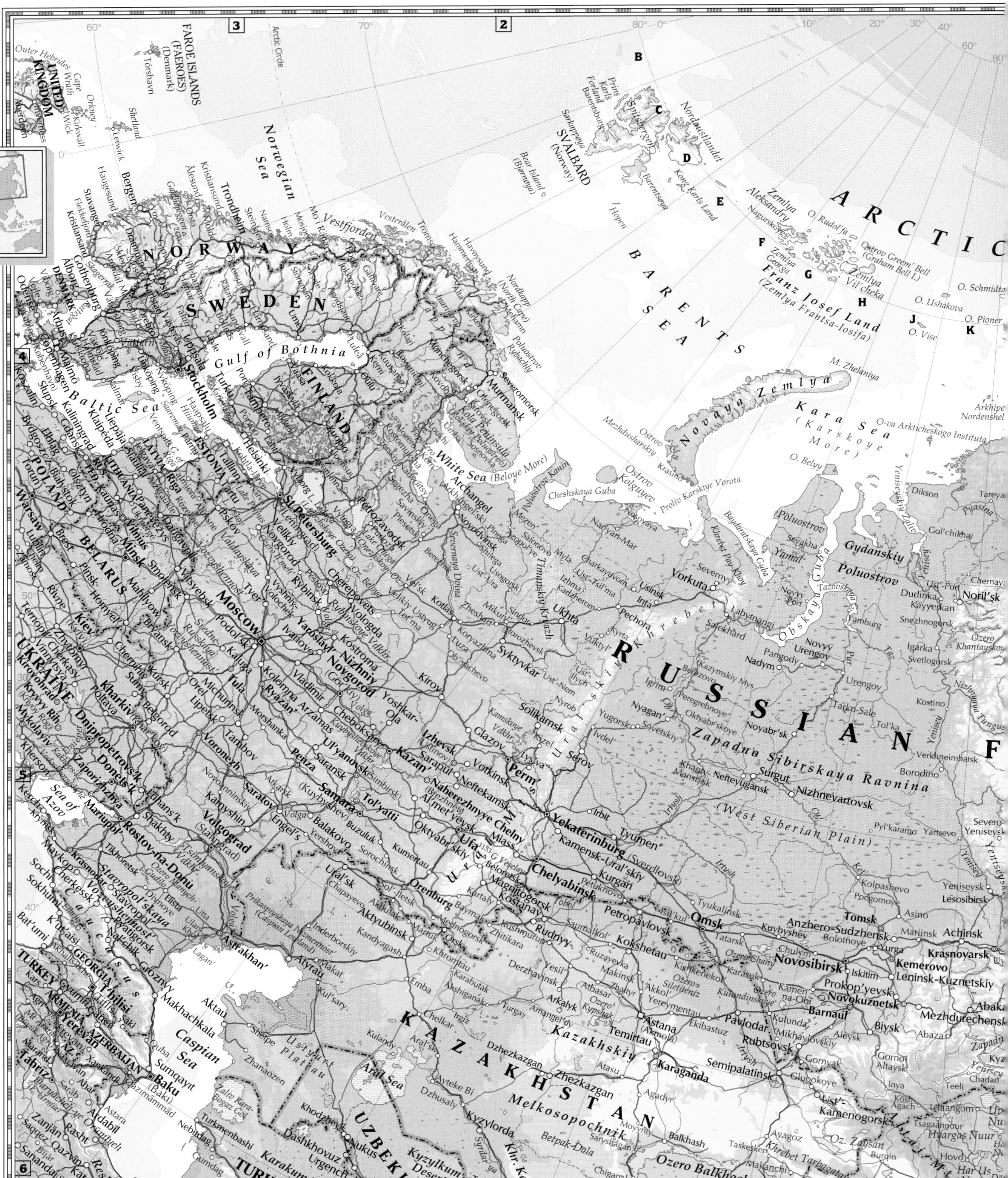

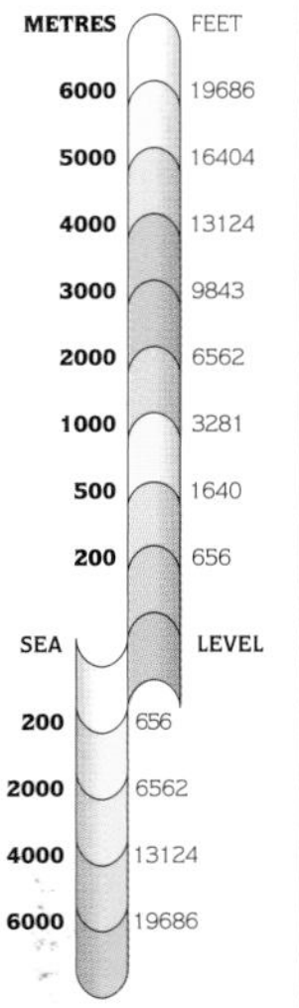

Conic Equidistant Projection

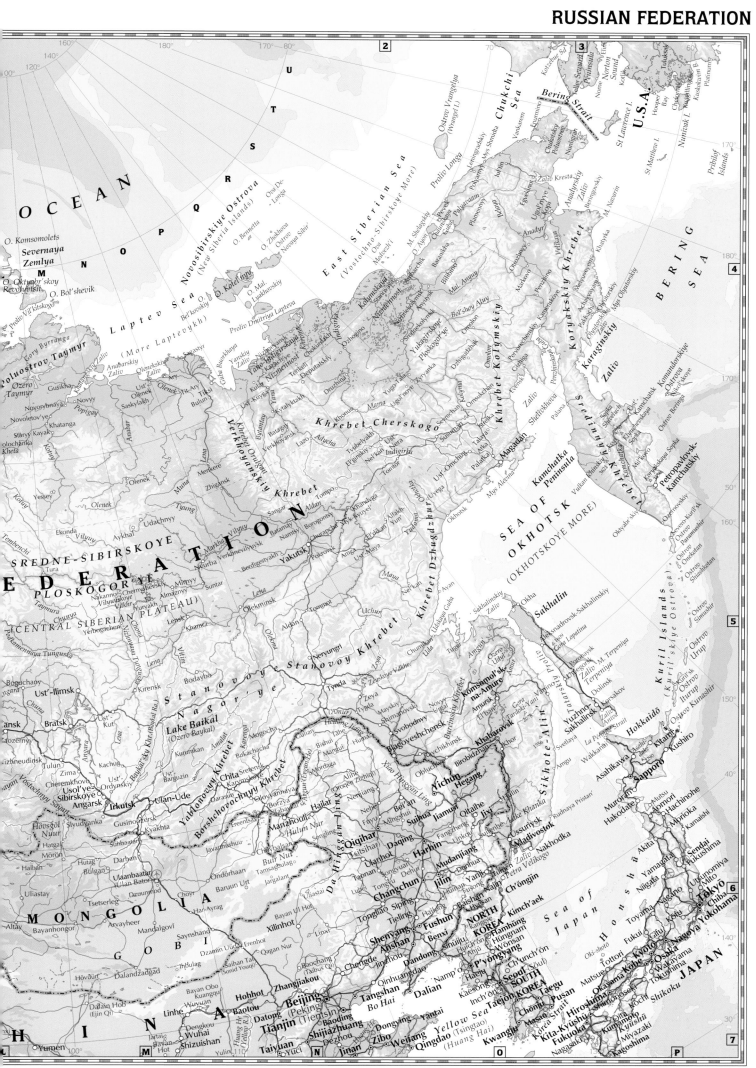

1:21M

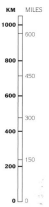

© Collins Bartholomew Ltd

OCEAN
Severnaya Zemlya
O. Komsomolets
O. Oktyabr'skoy Revolyutsii
O. Bol'shevik
Laptev Sea
(More Laptevykh)
Novosibirskiye Ostrova
(New Siberia Islands)
East Siberian Sea
(Vostochno-Sibirskoye More)
Ostrov Vrangelya
(Wrangel I.)
Chukchi Sea
Bering Strait
U.S.A.
St Lawrence I.
BERING SEA
Poluostrov Taymyr
Khrebet Cherskogo
Verkhoyanskiy Khrebet
Khrebet Kolymskiy
Koryakskiy Khrebet
Sredinnyy Khrebet
Kamchatka Peninsula
Petropavlovsk-Kamchatskiy
Magadan
SEA OF OKHOTSK
(OKHOTSKOYE MORE)
Sakhalin
Kuril Islands
(Kuril'skiye Ostrova)
SREDNE-SIBIRSKOYE PLOSKOGOR'YE
(CENTRAL SIBERIAN PLATEAU)
FEDERATION
Yakutsk
Stanovoy Khrebet
Stanovoye Nagor'ye
Lake Baikal
(Ozero Baykal)
Irkutsk
Ulan-Ude
Chita
Bratsk
Angarsk
Komsomol'sk-na-Amure
Khabarovsk
Vladivostok
Nakhodka
Blagoveshchensk
Yuzhno-Sakhalinsk
Sikhote-Alin'
Hokkaidō
Sapporo
Honshū
Tōkyō
Yokohama
Sendai
Nagoya
Ōsaka
Kōbe
Kyōto
Hiroshima
Kita-Kyūshū
Fukuoka
Kyūshū
Shikoku
Kagoshima
JAPAN
Sea of Japan
NORTH KOREA
P'yŏngyang
SOUTH KOREA
Seoul
Taegu
Pusan
Kwangju
Taejŏn
Korea Strait
Yellow Sea
(Huang Hai)
Bo Hai
MONGOLIA
Ulaanbaatar
(Ulan Bator)
GOBI
CHINA
Beijing
(Peking)
Tianjin
(Tientsin)
Harbin
Changchun
Shenyang
Dalian
Qiqihar
Jilin
Qingdao
Hohhot
Baotou
Taiyuan
Jinan
Da Hinggan Ling
Xiao Hinggan Ling
KM
MILES
1000
800
600
400
200
0
600
450
300
150
0

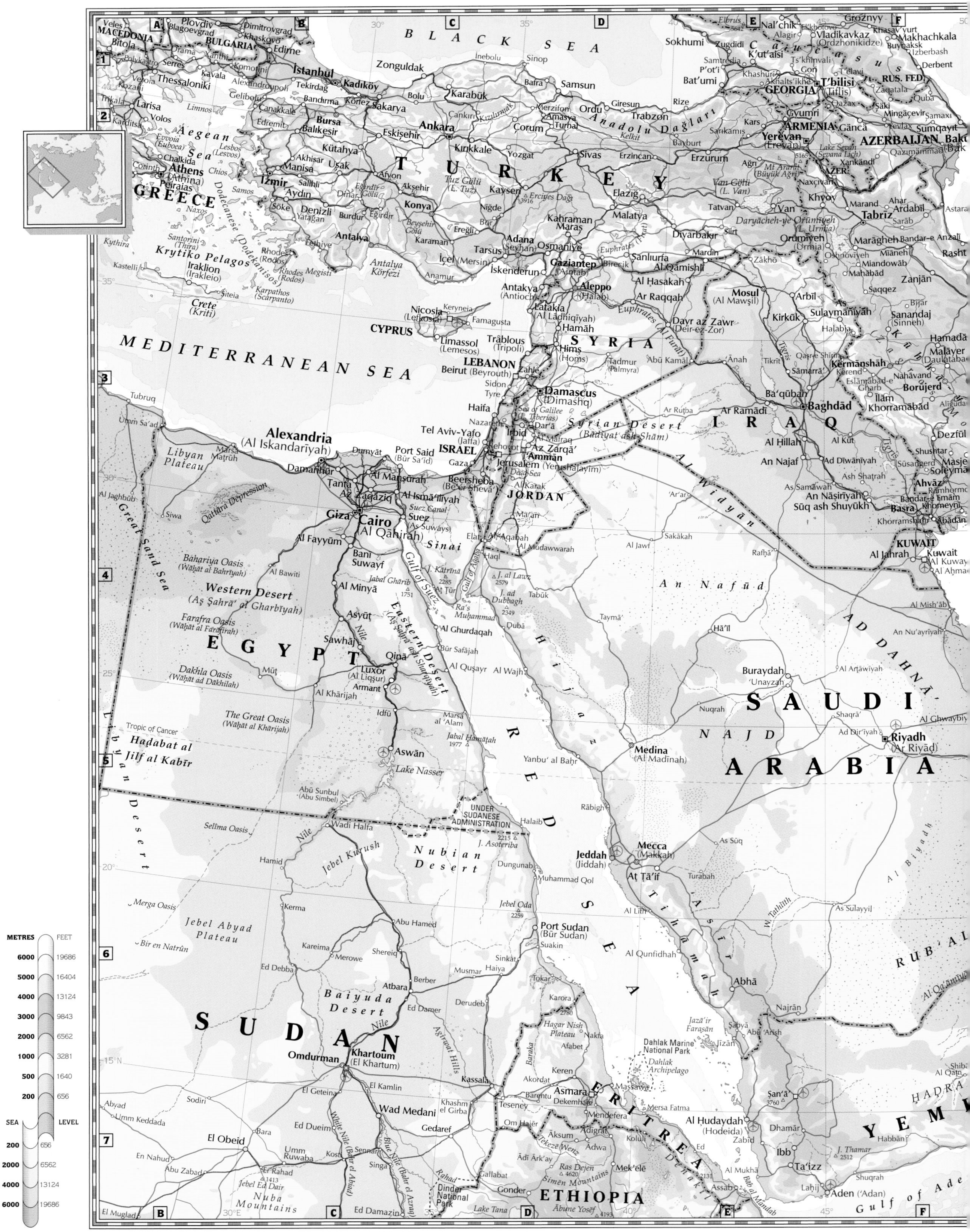

Albers Equal Area Conic Projection

BLACK SEA
MEDITERRANEAN SEA
RED SEA
Aegean Sea
TURKEY
GREECE
CYPRUS
SYRIA
LEBANON
ISRAEL
JORDAN
IRAQ
EGYPT
SUDAN
ERITREA
ETHIOPIA
SAUDI ARABIA
KUWAIT
GEORGIA
ARMENIA
AZERBAIJAN
RUS. FED.
MACEDONIA
BULGARIA
YEMEN
İstanbul
Ankara
İzmir
Bursa
Konya
Adana
Antalya
Samsun
Trabzon
Erzurum
Sivas
Kayseri
Malatya
Diyarbakır
Gaziantep
Athens (Athina)
Thessaloniki
Nicosia (Lefkoşa)
Beirut (Beyrouth)
Damascus (Dimashq)
Aleppo (Halab)
Ḥamāh
Ḥimṣ (Homs)
Tel Aviv-Yafo (Jaffa)
Jerusalem (Yerushalayim)
'Ammān
Baghdād
Mosul (Al Mawṣil)
Kirkūk
Al Baṣrah
Kuwait
Riyadh (Ar Riyāḍ)
Mecca (Makkah)
Medina (Al Madīnah)
Jeddah (Jiddah)
Aṭ Ṭā'if
Alexandria (Al Iskandarīyah)
Cairo (Al Qāhirah)
Giza
Port Said (Būr Sa'īd)
Suez (As Suways)
Asyūṭ
Luxor (Al Uqṣur)
Aswān
Lake Nasser
Khartoum (El Khartum)
Omdurman
Port Sudan (Būr Sudan)
Kassala
Wad Medani
El Obeid
Asmara
Ṣan'ā'
Aden ('Adan)
Al Ḥudaydah (Hodeida)
Tbilisi (Tiflis)
Yerevan (Erevan)
Tabrīz
Sinai
Gulf of Suez
Gulf of Aqaba
Western Desert
Eastern Desert
Libyan Desert
Nubian Desert
Syrian Desert
An Nafūd
NAJD
Ad Dahnā'
Tropic of Cancer
UNDER SUDANESE ADMINISTRATION
Dahlak Marine National Park
METRES
FEET
6000
19686
5000
16404
4000
13124
3000
9843
2000
6562
1000
3281
500
1640
200
656
SEA
LEVEL

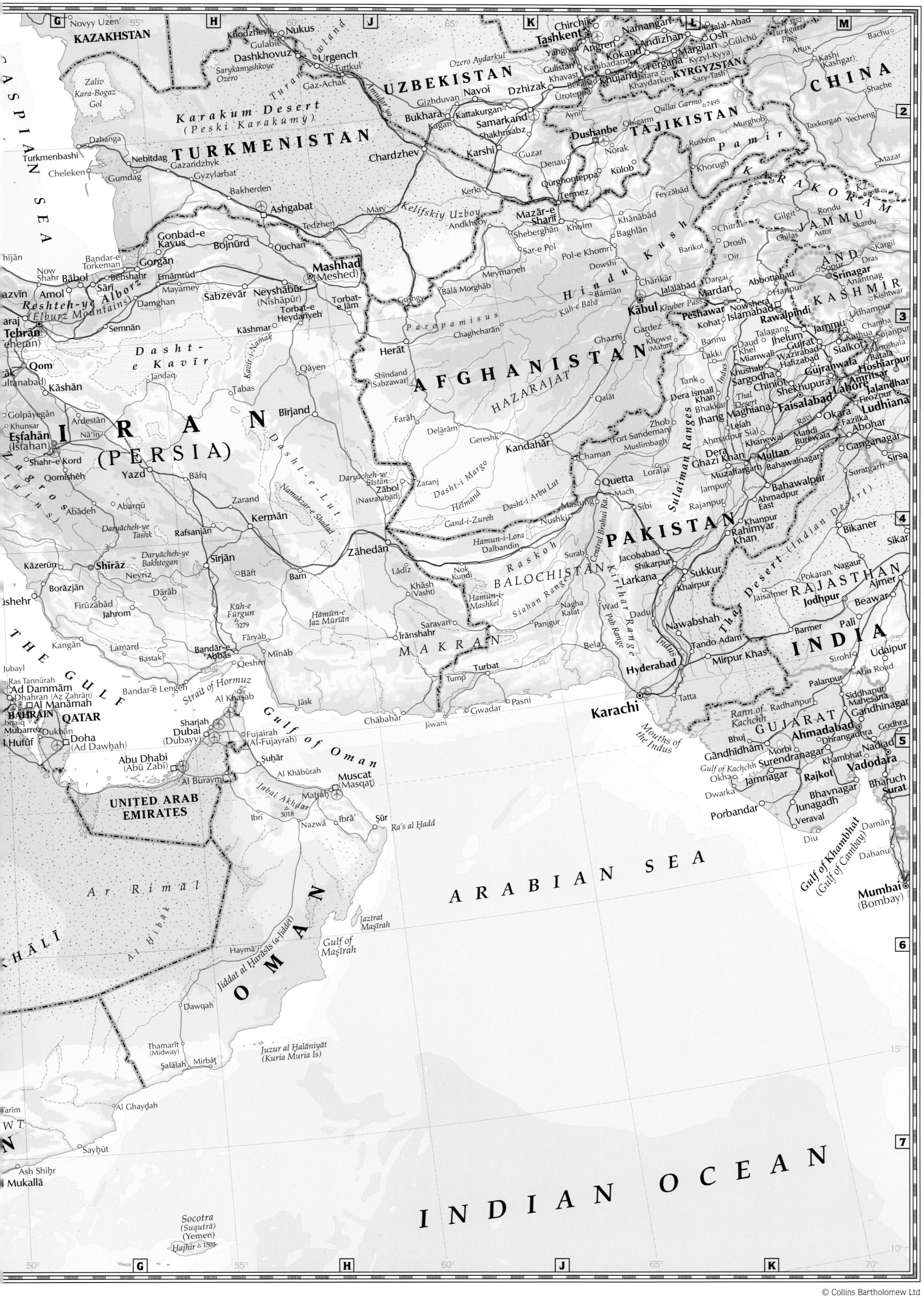

KAZAKHSTAN

Novyy Uzen'

UZBEKISTAN

CHINA

Tashkent

Namangan

Andizhan

Osh

Gülchö

KYRGYZSTAN

Kashi (Kashgar)

Shache

Nukus

Khodzheyli

Urgench

Dashkhovuz

Turtkul'

Gulabie

Gaz-Achak

Navoi

Dzhizak

Gulistan

Kokand

Margilan

Fergana

Sary-Tash

Yecheng

Sarykamyshkoye Ozero

Zaliv Kara-Bogaz Gol

Karakum Desert (Peski Karakumy)

Bukhara

Kagan

Kattakurgan

Samarkand

Shakhrisabz

Khujand

Ayni

TAJIKISTAN

Murghob

Taxkorgan

Rushon

Axtu

K2

CASPIAN SEA

Dzhanga

Turkmenbashi

Cheleken

Nebitdag

Gazandzhyk

TURKMENISTAN

Chardzhev

Karshi

Guzar

Denau

Dushanbe

Norak

Kŭlob

Khorugh

Pamir

Rondu

Skardu

Mazar

Gumdag

Gyzylarbat

Bakherden

Mary

Tedzhen

Kerki

Termez

Qŭrghonteppa

Feyzābād

Kelifskiy Uzboy

Andkhvoy

Mazār-e Sharīf

Khānābād

Baghlān

Barikot

Chitrāl

Drosh

Dir

Gilgit

Astor

Chilas

KARAKORAM

JAMMU

AND

Kargil

Dras

Ashgabat

Gonbad-e Kāvus

Bojnūrd

Quchan

Gushgy

Bālā Morghāb

Meymaneh

Sheberghān

Kholm

Sar-e Pol

Pol-e Khomrī

Dowshī

Chārīkār

Bāmīān

Hindu Kush

Dargai

Mardan

Abbottābād

Mānsehra

Srinagar

Anantnag

KASHMIR

Kishtwar

hījān

Now Shahr

Bandar-e Torkeman

Gorgān

Bandar-e Torkeman

Sarī

Reshteh-ye Alborz

Emāmrūd

Mayamey

Sabzevār

Neyshābūr (Nīshāpūr)

Torbat-e Jām

Torbat-e Heydārīyeh

Kāshmar

Mashhad (Meshed)

Qāyen

Paropamisus

Chaghcharān

Herāt

Kabul

Khyber Pass

Peshawar

Kohat

Islamabad

Rawalpindi

Talagang

Udhampur

Jammu

Kathua

Dharmshala

azvīn

Amol

Bābol

Benshahr

Damghan

Semnān

Tehrān (Teheran)

Elburz Mountains

Dasht-e Kavīr

Shindand (Sabzawar)

Farāh

AFGHANISTAN

HAZARAJAT

Ghaznī

Gardez

Khowst (Matun)

Bannu

Daud Khel

Jhelum

Gujrat

Sialkot

Wazirabad

Hafizabad

Gujrānwāla

Hoshiarpur

Chamba

Qom

ltanabad

Kāshān

Khunsar

Golpāyegān

Na'īn

Ardestān

Dasht-e Namak

Kavir-i Namak

Jandaq

Tabas

Delārām

Gereshk

Qalāt

Tank

Dera Ismail Khan

Lakki

Khushab

Sargodha

Mianwali

Chiniot

Sheikhupura

Lahore

Jalandhar

Faisalabad

Firozpur

Ludhiana

Abohar

Esfahān (Isfahan)

Shahr-e Kord

Qomisheh

Yazd

Bāfq

IRAN

(PERSIA)

Bīrjand

Dasht-i Margo

Kandahār

Chaman (Fort Sandeman)

Zhob

Muslimbagh

Loralai

Sulaiman Ranges

Jhang Maghiana

Khanewal

Mandi Burewala

Okara

Fazilka

Sirsa

Multan

Ganganagar

Zarand

Rafsanjān

Kermān

Zāranj

Gand-i-Zureh

Helmand

Dasht-i Arbu Lut

Quetta

Mach

Mastūng

Kālat

Dera Ghazi Khan

Muzaffargarh

Bahawalnagar

Bahawalpur

Ahmadpur Sial

Suratgarh

Zāgros

Daryācheh-ye Tashk

Shīrāz

Sīrjān

Bāft

Bam

Zāhedān

Lādīz

Khāsh (Vasht)

Hamun-i-Lora

Dalbandin

Nushki

Nok Kundi

BALOCHISTAN

Raskoh

Surab

Central Brahui Ra.

Sibi

PAKISTAN

Jacobabad

Shikarpur

Larkana

Sukkur

Khairpur

Jampur

Rajanpur

Khanpur

Rahimyar Khan

Bikaner

Sikar

Pokaran

Nagaur

RAJASTHAN

Ajmer

Jodhpur

Beawar

Pali

Kāzerūn

Borāzjān

Neyrīz

Dārāb

Jahrom

Firūzābād

Kūh-e Fŭrgun 3279

Hamūn-e Jaz Mūrīān

Saravan

Siahan Range

Nagha

Panjgur

Wad

Pab Range

Dadu

Nawabshah

Thar Desert (Indian Desert)

Barmer

INDIA

Jaisalmer

Sirohi

Abu Road

Udaipur

ishehr

THE GULF

Kangān

Lamard

Bastak

Bandar-e Lengeh

Strait of Hormuz

Qeshm

Bandar-e Abbās

Mīnāb

Jāsk

Tump

Turbat

Chābahār

Jiwani

Gwadar

Pasni

MAKRAN

Bela

Kirthar Range

Tando Adam

Indus

Mirpur Khas

Siroh

Radhanpur

Palanpur

Siddhpur

Mahesana

Gandhinagar

Jubayl

Ras Tannūrah

Ad Dammām

Dhahran (Az Zahrān)

Al Manāmah

bqaiq

Mubarrez

BAHRAIN

QATAR

Dukhān

Doha (Ad Dawḥah)

Hufūf

Sharjah

Dubai (Dubayy)

Fujairah (Al-Fujayrah)

Abu Dhabi (Abū Ẓabī)

Al Buraymi

Ibrī

Ṣuḥār

Al Khābūrah

Matrah

Muscat (Masqaṭ)

Jabal Akhdar 3018

Nazwā

Ibrā

Ṣūr

Ra's al Ḥadd

Hyderabad

Tatta

Karachi

Mouths of the Indus

Bhuj

Gāndhīdhām

Rann of Kachchh

GUJARAT

Ahmadabad

Godhra

Dhrangadhra

Morbi

Surendranagar

Nadiad

Khambhat

Vadodara

Bharuch

Surat

Daman

Dahanu

UNITED ARAB EMIRATES

Ar Rimāl

Al Ḥibak

ARABIAN SEA

Jazīrat Maṣīrah

OMAN

Haymā'

Jiddat al Ḥarāsīs (al-Jiddah)

Dawqah

Gulf of Maṣīrah

Okha

Dwarka

Porbandar

Veraval

Junagadh

Jamnagar

Rajkot

Bhavnagar

Bharuch

Gulf of Kachchh

Gulf of Khambhat (Gulf of Cambay)

Mumbai (Bombay)

Diu

KHĀLĪ

Thamarīt (Midway)

Ṣalālah

Mirbāṭ

Juzur al Halānīyāt (Kuria Muria Is)

ārīm

Al Ghaydah

N

WT

Sayḥūt

Ash Shiḥr

Mukallā

Socotra (Suquṭrā) (Yemen)

Ḥajhīr 1503

INDIAN OCEAN

1:12.5M

KM	MILES
750	450
600	300
450	150
300	
150	
0	

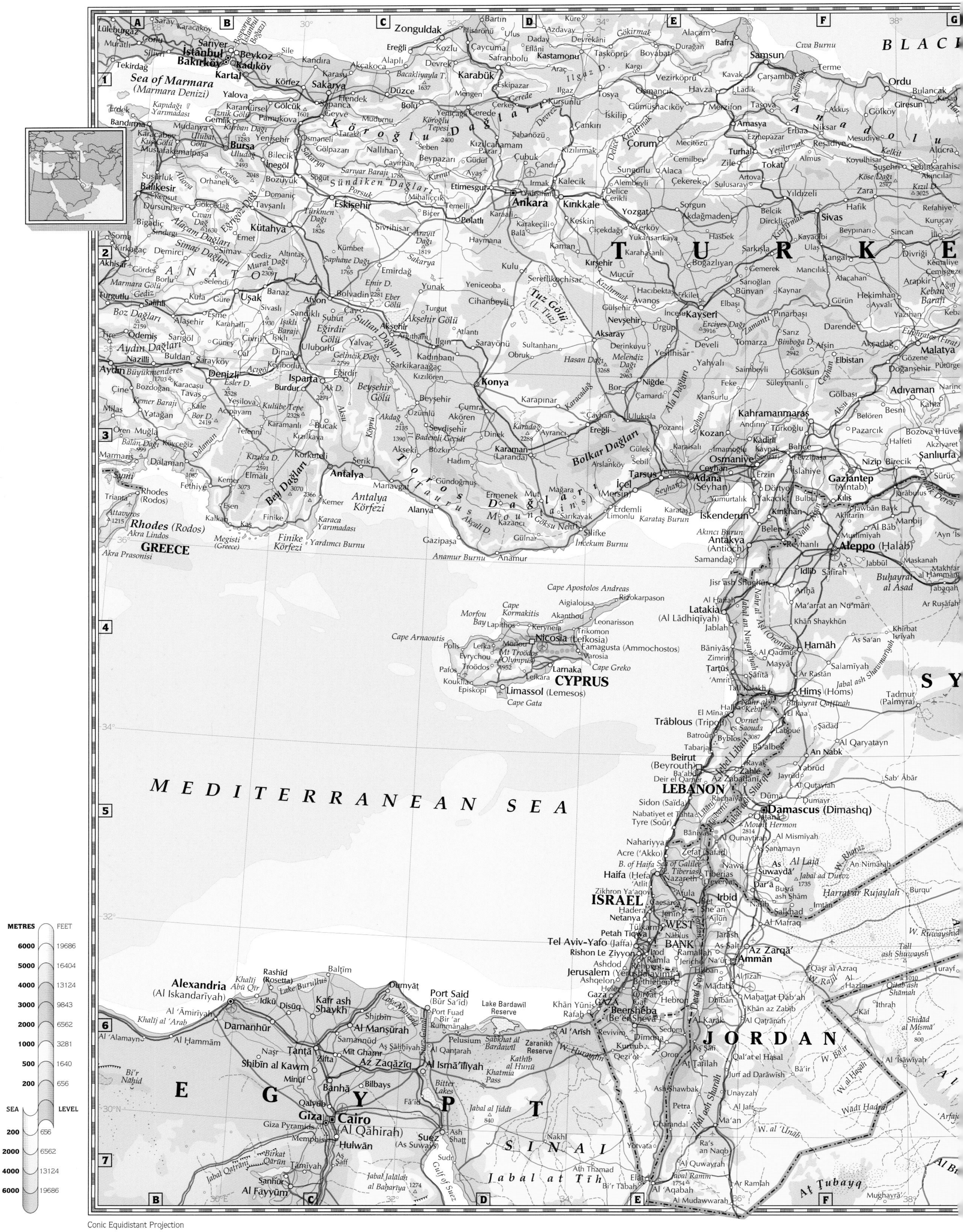

80

BLACK

Sea of Marmara
(Marmara Denizi)

ANATOLIA

TURKEY

GREECE

MEDITERRANEAN SEA

CYPRUS

Rhodes (Rodos)

SYRIA

Aleppo (Halab)

Latakia
(Al Lādhiqīyah)

Hamāh

Himş (Homs)

Trâblous (Tripoli)

Beirut
(Beyrouth)

LEBANON

Damascus (Dimashq)

ISRAEL

WEST
BANK

Amman

Jerusalem (Yerushalayim)

JORDAN

Alexandria
(Al Iskandarīyah)

EGYPT

SINAI

Cairo
(Al Qāhirah)

Jabal at Tīh

METRES	FEET
6000	19686
5000	16404
4000	13124
3000	9843
2000	6562
1000	3281
500	1640
200	656
SEA	LEVEL
200	656
2000	6562
4000	13124
6000	19686

Conic Equidistant Projection

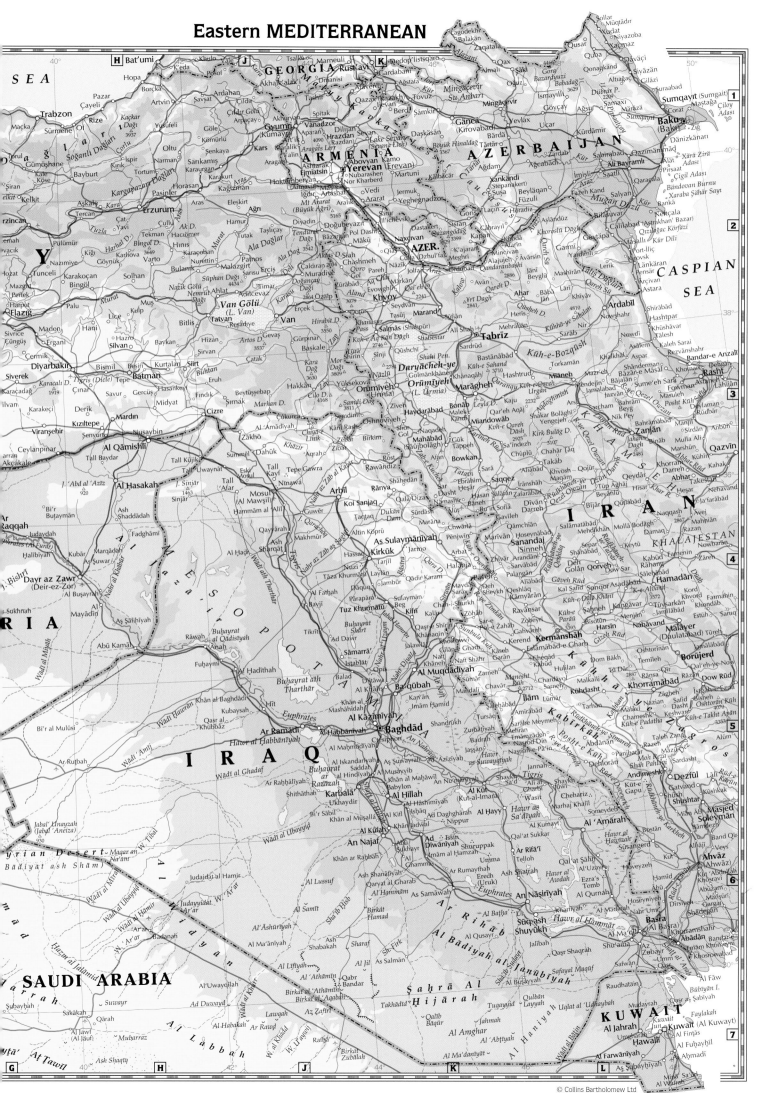

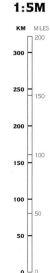

1:5M

© Collins Bartholomew Ltd

GEORGIA
ARMENIA
AZERBAIJAN
AZER.
IRAN
IRAQ
KUWAIT
SAUDI ARABIA
CASPIAN SEA
SEA
Bat'umi
Trabzon
Rize
Erzurum
Kars
Gyumri
Yerevan
Tbilisi
Rust'avi
Gäncä
Baku
Sumqayıt
Naxçıvan
Tabrīz
Ardabīl
Rasht
Bandar-e Anzali
Zanjān
Qazvīn
Hamadān
Kermanshāh
Sanandaj
Urūmīyeh
Daryācheh-ye Orūmīyeh
Van Gölü
Van
Diyarbakır
Batman
Mardin
Nusaybin
Al Qāmishlī
Al Ḩasakah
Mosul
Arbīl
Kirkūk
As Sulaymānīyah
Dayr az Zawr
Ar Raqqah
Tikrīt
Sāmarrā'
Ba'qūbah
Baghdād
Ar Ramādī
Al Fallūjah
Karbalā'
Al Ḩillah
An Najaf
Ad Dīwānīyah
Al Kūt
Al 'Amārah
An Nāşirīyah
Al Başrah
Abādān
Khorramshahr
Ahvāz
Dezfūl
Khorramābād
Borūjerd
Ilām
Kuwait
Al Jahrah
Euphrates
Tigris
MESOPOTAMIA
Al Jazīrah
Al Widyān
Syrian Desert
Al Ḩijārah
Kūh-e Bozqūsh
Zagros
2
3
4
6
7
G
J
K
40°
42°
44°
46°
48°
50°
36°
38°
40°
KM	MILES
300	200
250	150
200	
150	100
100	50
50	
0	0

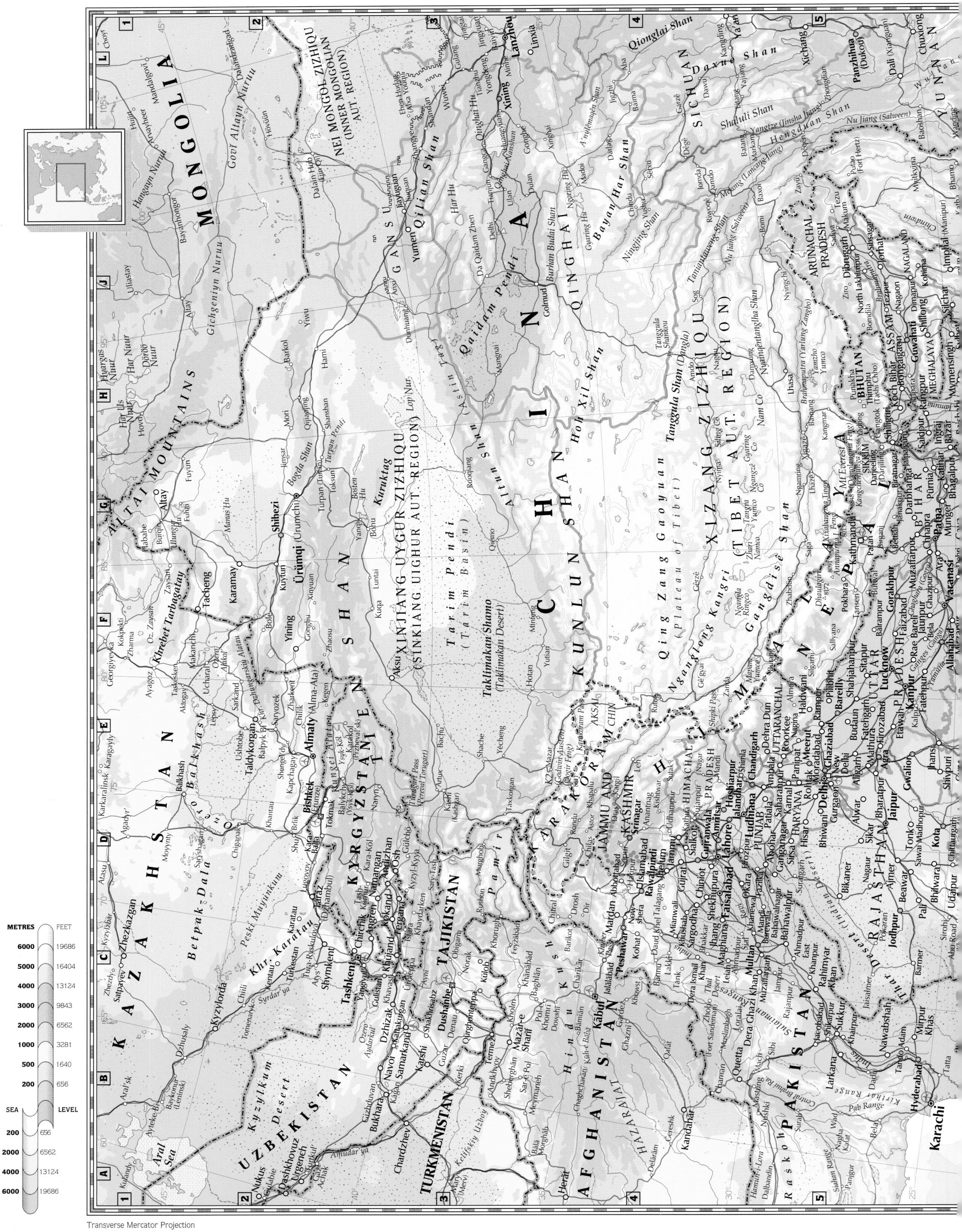
KAZAKHSTAN
UZBEKISTAN
TURKMENISTAN
TAJIKISTAN
KYRGYZSTAN
AFGHANISTAN
PAKISTAN
MONGOLIA
CHINA
NEI MONGOL ZIZHIQU (INNER MONGOLIA AUT. REGION)
XINJIANG UYGUR ZIZHIQU (SINKIANG UIGHUR AUT. REGION)
XIZANG ZIZHIQU (TIBET AUT. REGION)
QINGHAI
GANSU
SICHUAN
YUNNAN
JAMMU AND KASHMIR
NEPAL
BHUTAN
ALTAI MOUNTAINS
TIEN SHAN
KUNLUN SHAN
KARAKORAM
HIMALAYA
Hindu Kush
Pamir
Taklimakan Shamo (Taklimakan Desert)
Tarim Pendi (Tarim Basin)
Qaidam Pendi
Qing Zang Gaoyuan (Plateau of Tibet)
Kyzylkum Desert
Aral Sea
Ozero Balkhash
Thar Desert
Ürümqi
Almaty (Alma-Ata)
Bishkek
Tashkent
Dushanbe
Kabul
Islamabad
Lahore
Karachi
Delhi
Lhasa
Kathmandu
Lanzhou
Xining
METRES
FEET
6000
19686
5000
16404
4000
13124
3000
9843
2000
6562
1000
3281
500
1640
200
656
SEA
LEVEL
200
656
2000
6562
4000
13124
6000
19686

Transverse Mercator Projection

1:14M

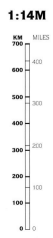

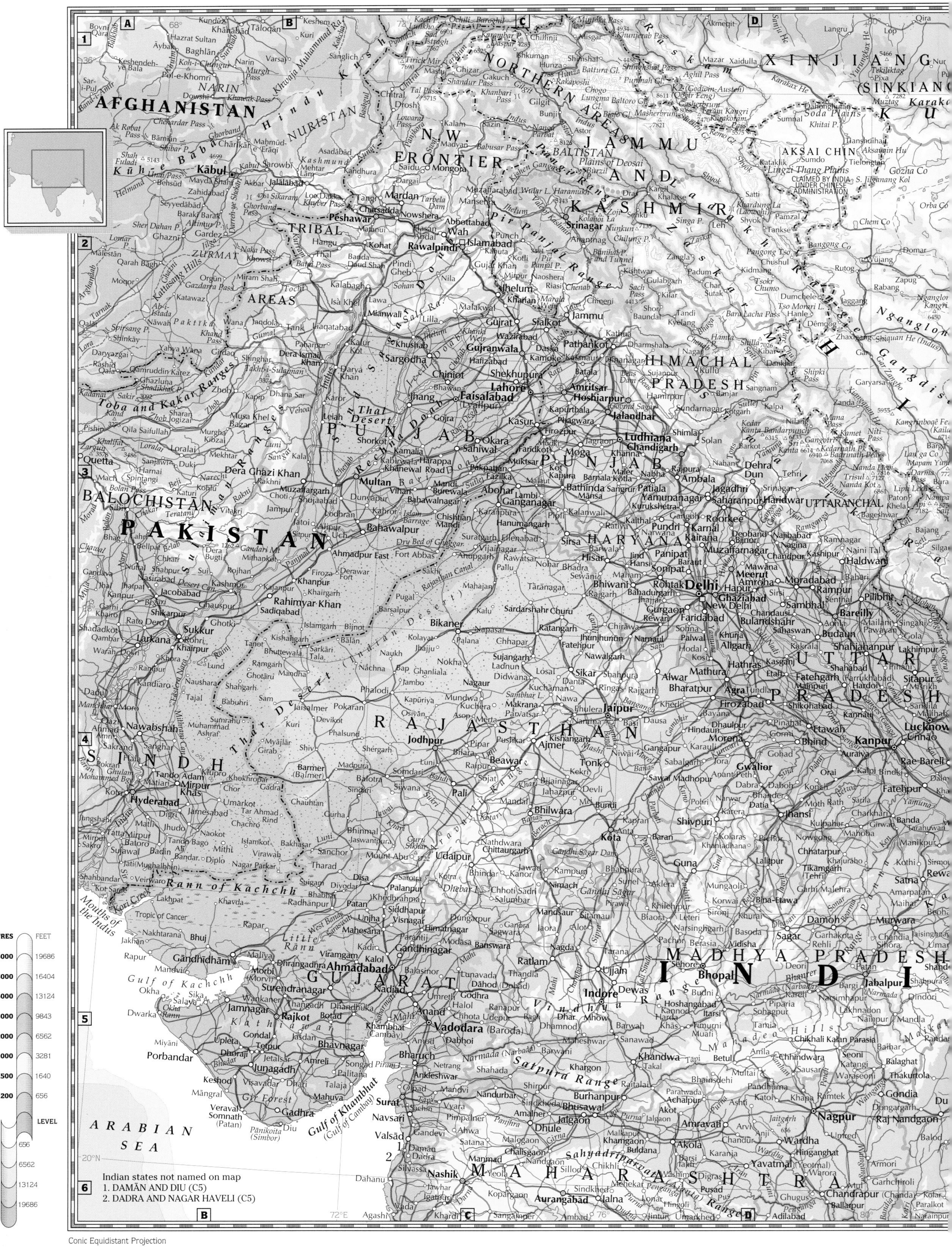

METRES | FEET
6000 | 19686
5000 | 16404
4000 | 13124
3000 | 9843
2000 | 6562
1000 | 3281
500 | 1640
200 | 656
SEA | LEVEL
200 | 656
2000 | 6562
4000 | 13124
6000 | 19686

Indian states not named on map
1. DAMĀN AND DIU (C5)
2. DADRA AND NAGAR HAVELI (C5)

Conic Equidistant Projection

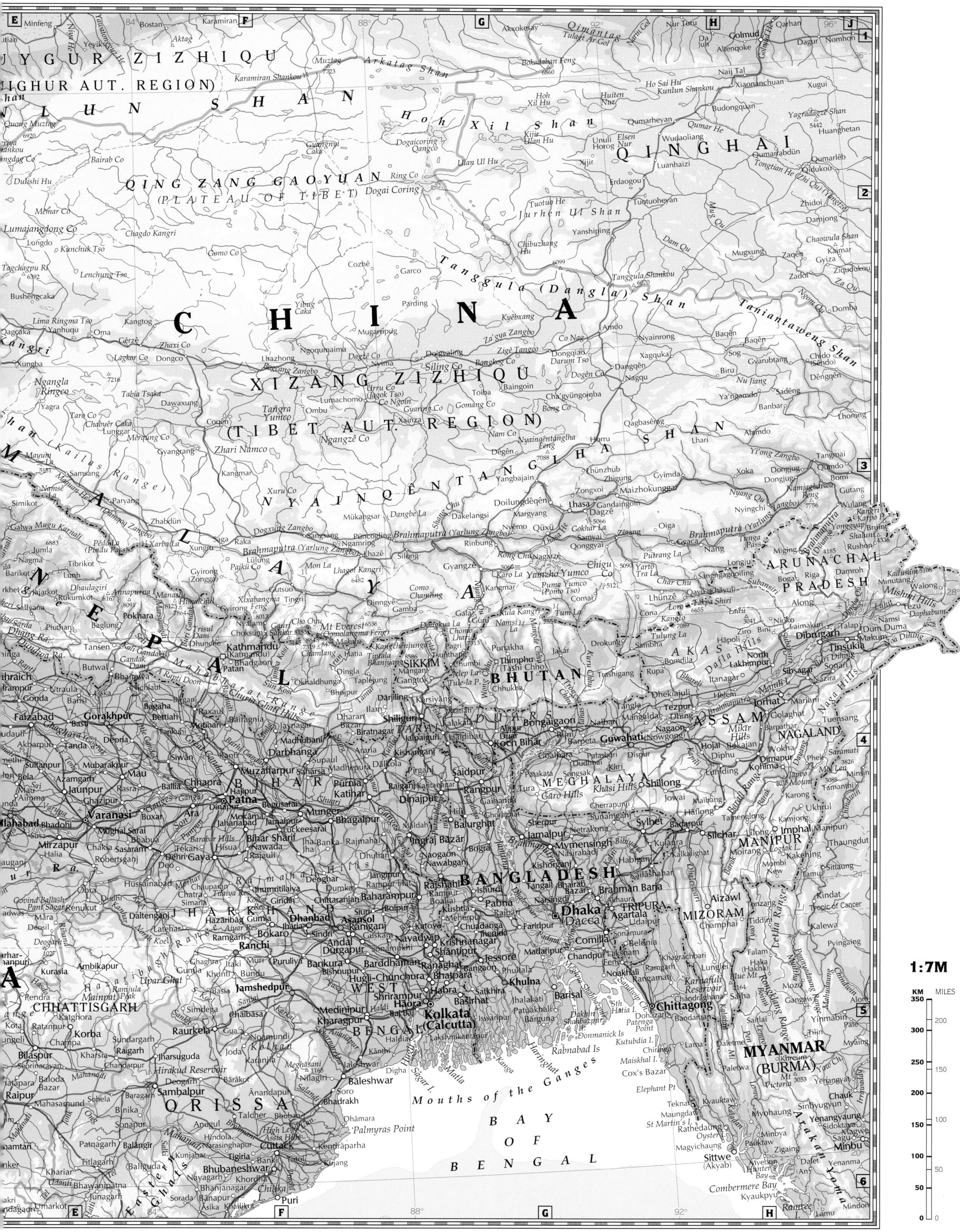

1:7M

KM   MILES
350
       200
300
250
       150
200
       100
150
100
       50
50
       0

© Collins Bartholomew Ltd

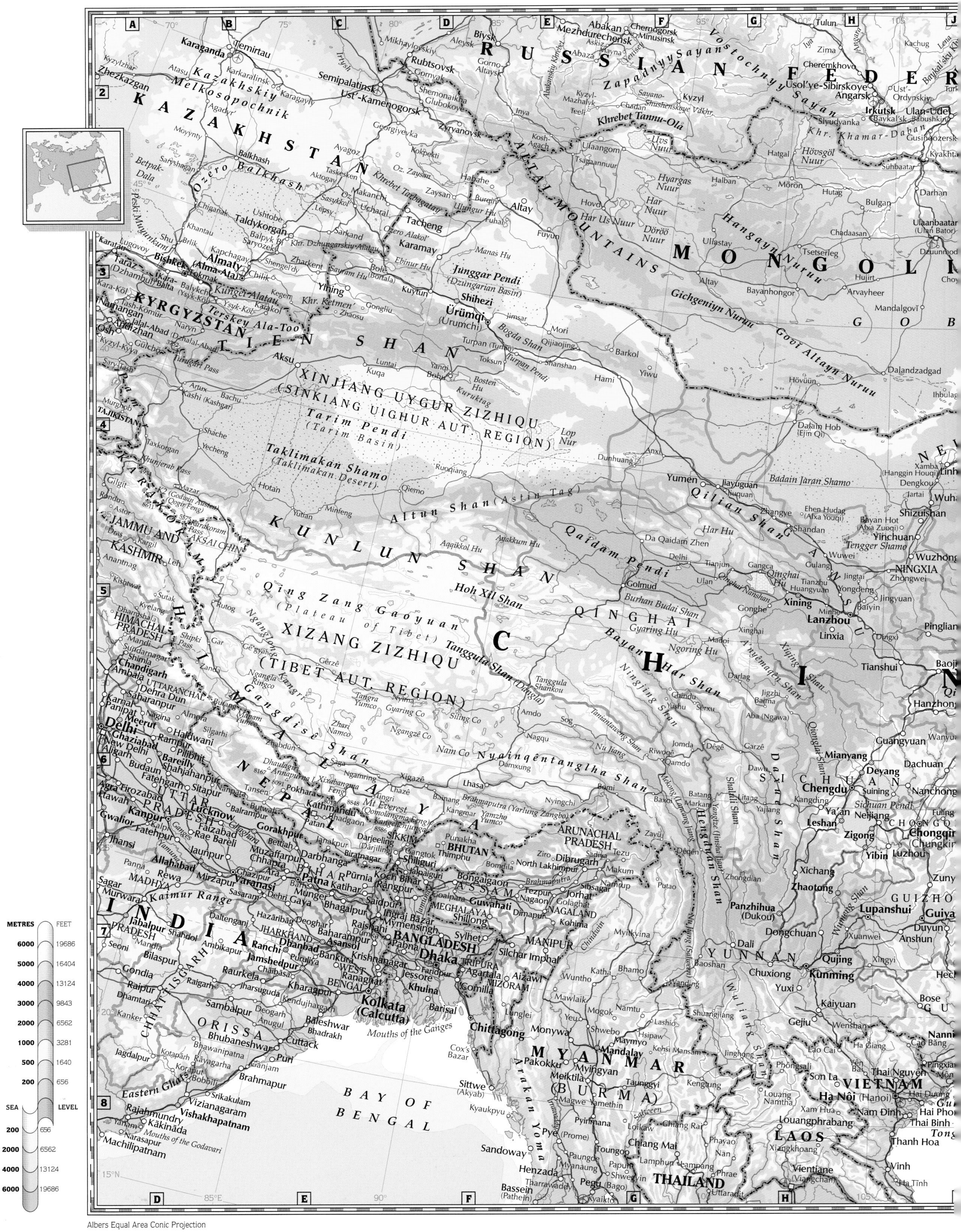

METRES		FEET
6000		19686
5000		16404
4000		13124
3000		9843
2000		6562
1000		3281
500		1640
200		656
SEA		LEVEL
200		656
2000		6562
4000		13124
6000		19686

Albers Equal Area Conic Projection

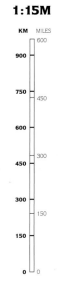

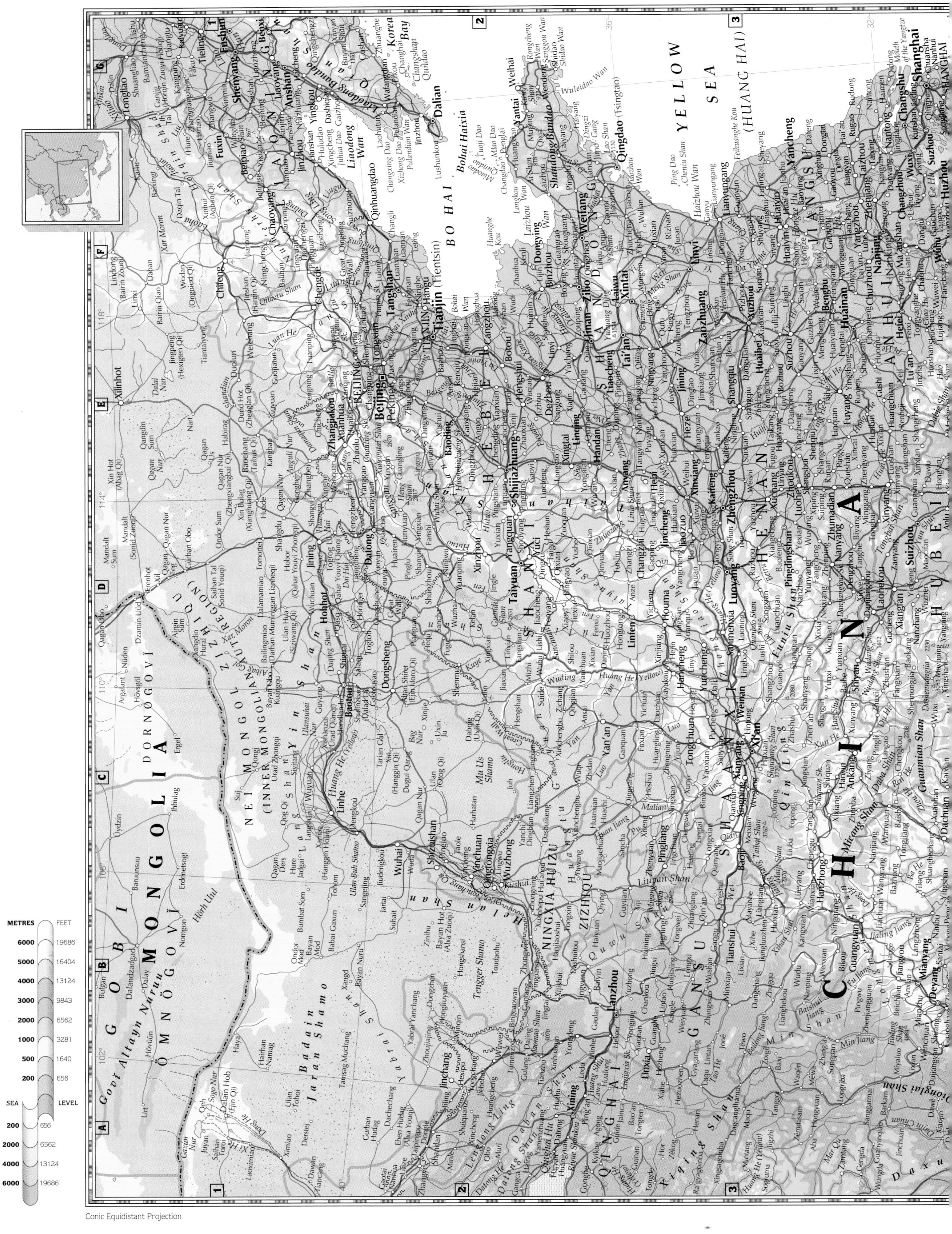
METRES
FEET
6000 19686
5000 16404
4000 13124
3000 9843
2000 6562
1000 3281
500 1640
200 656
SEA LEVEL
200 656
2000 6562
4000 13124
6000 19686
MONGOLIA
GOBI
DORNOGOVĬ
ÖMNÖGOVĬ
NEI MONGOL ZIZHIQU
(INNER MONGOLIAN AUTONOMOUS REGION)
NINGXIA HUIZU ZIZHIQU
QINGHAI
GANSU
SHAANXI
SHANXI
HEBEI
HENAN
SHANDONG
JIANGSU
ANHUI
HUBEI
LIAONING
CHINA
YELLOW SEA
(HUANG HAI)
BO HAI
Bohai Haixia
Liaodong Wan
Korea Bay
Liaodong Bandao
Shandong Bandao
Beijing
Tianjin
Shijiazhuang
Taiyuan
Zhengzhou
Xi'an
Lanzhou
Xining
Yinchuan
Hohhot
Baotou
Jinan
Qingdao
Dalian
Shenyang
Shanghai
Nanjing
Hefei
Huang He
Badain Jaran Shamo
Tengger Shamo
Mu Us Shamo
Qin Ling
Yin Shan
Conic Equidistant Projection

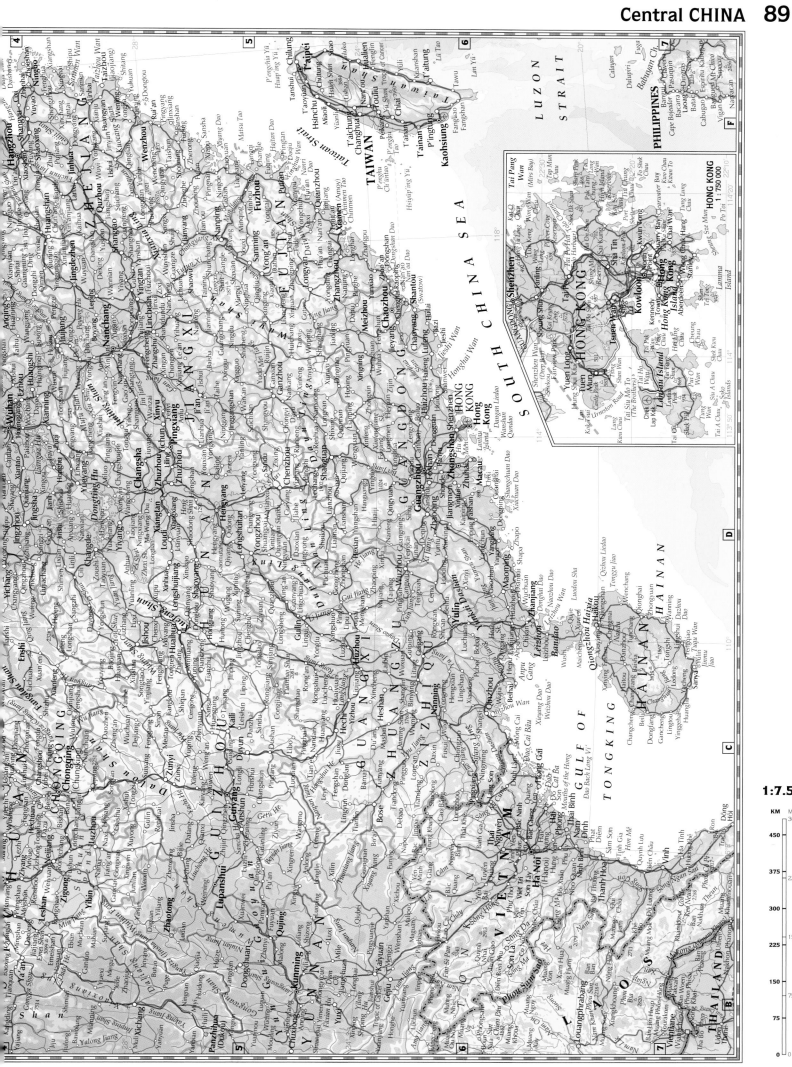

1:7.5M

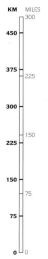

KM MILES
450 — 300
— 225
375 —
300 — 150
225 —
— 75
150 —
75 —
0 — 0

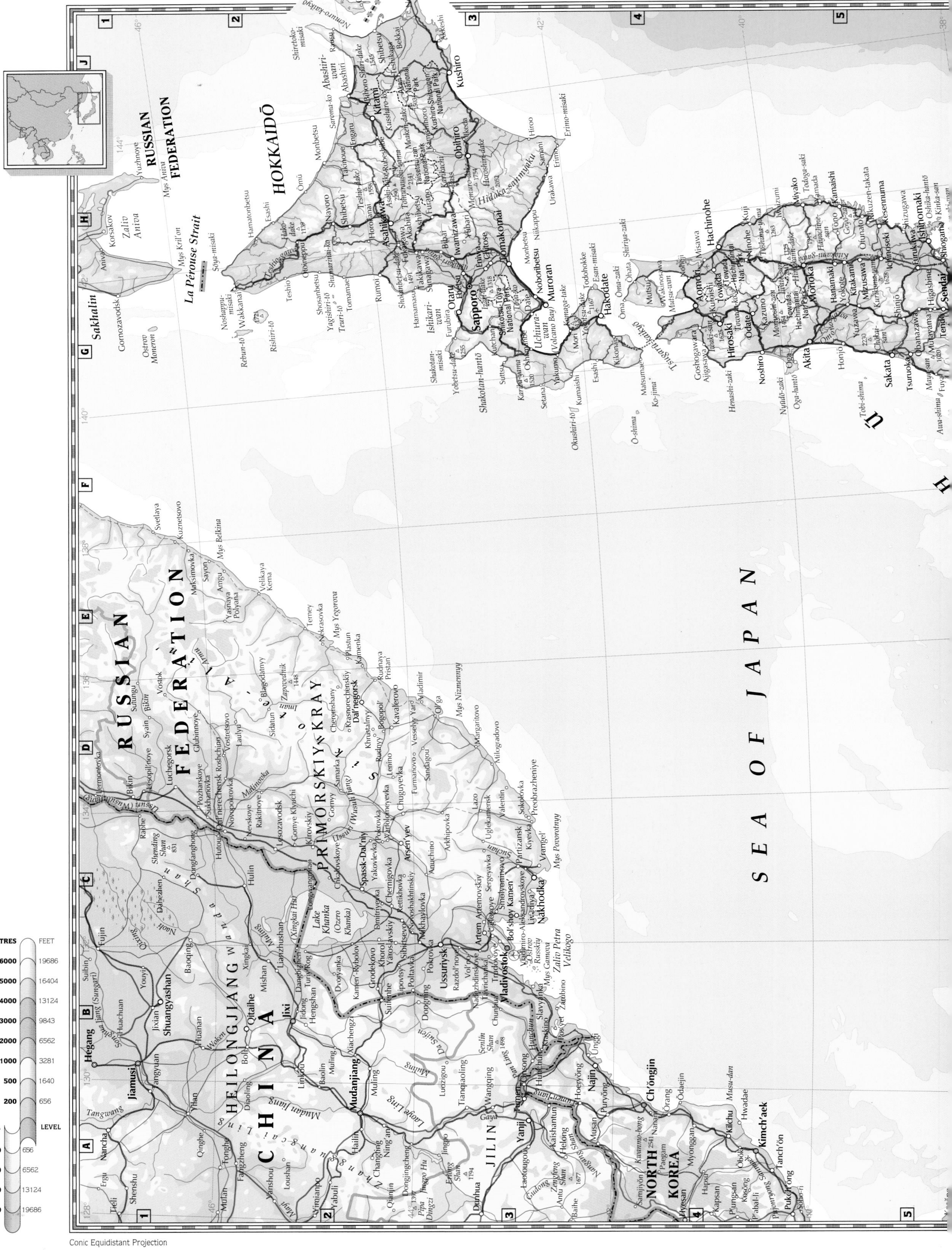

SEA OF JAPAN
RUSSIAN FEDERATION
PRIMORSKIY KRAY
CHINA
HEILONGJIANG
JILIN
NORTH KOREA
HOKKAIDŌ
Sakhalin
La Pérouse Strait
Zaliv Aniva
Tsugaru-kaikyō
Uchiura-wan (Volcano Bay)
Ishikari-wan
Lake Khanka (Ozero Khanka)
Zaliv Petra Velikogo
Vladivostok
Ussuriysk
Nakhodka
Artem
Spassk-Dal'niy
Dal'negorsk
Lesozavodsk
Dal'nerechensk
Luchegorsk
Bikin
Sapporo
Asahikawa
Hakodate
Muroran
Otaru
Kushiro
Obihiro
Kitami
Wakkanai
Tomakomai
Aomori
Hirosaki
Hachinohe
Akita
Morioka
Sendai
Sakata
Jiamusi
Hegang
Shuangyashan
Qitaihe
Jixi
Mudanjiang
Yanji
Hunchun
Ch'ŏngjin
Kimch'aek
Korsakov
Yuzhnoye
Gornozavodsk
METRES
FEET
6000
19686
5000
16404
4000
13124
3000
9843
2000
6562
1000
3281
500
1640
200
656
SEA
LEVEL

Conic Equidistant Projection

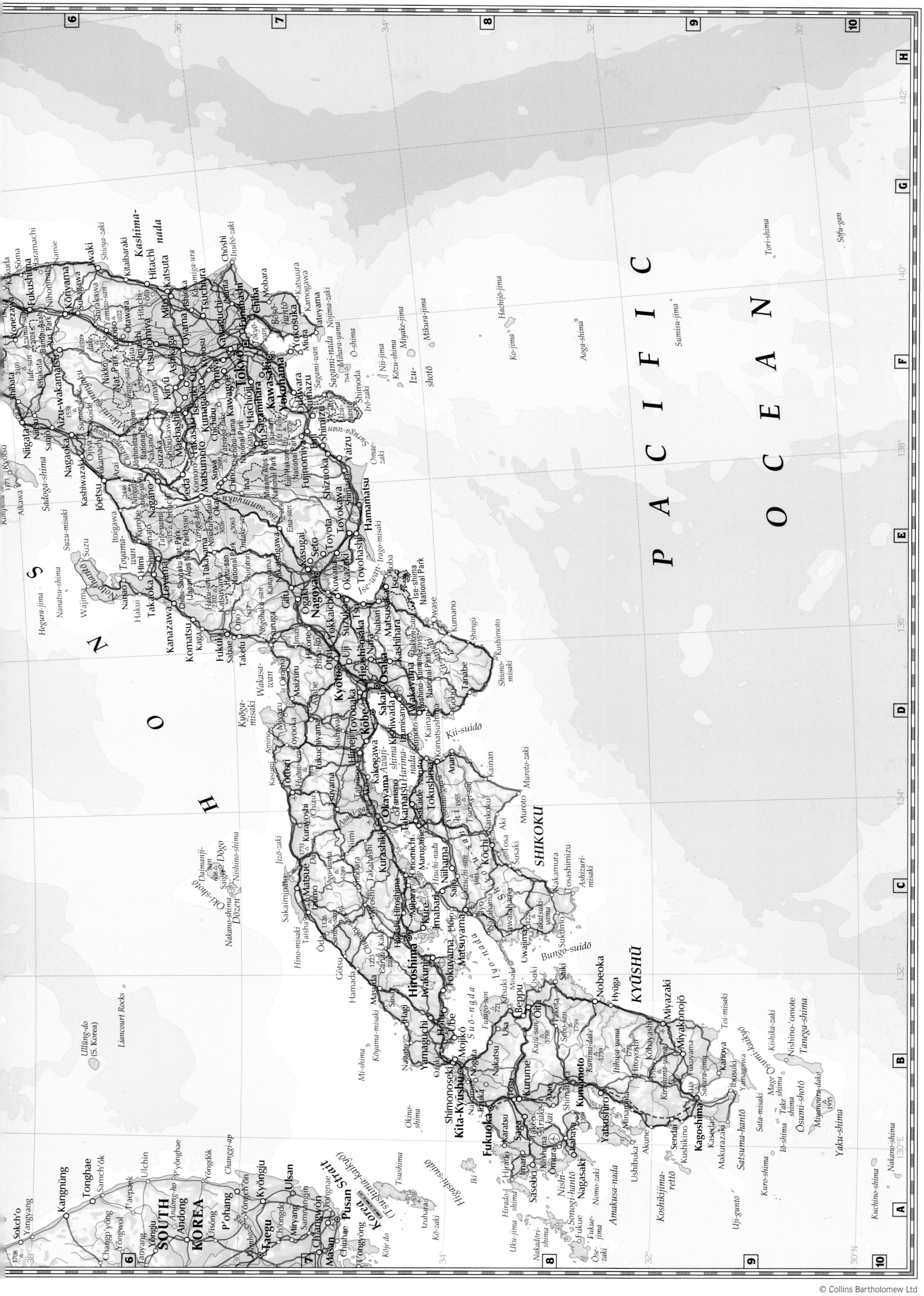
PACIFIC OCEAN
SOUTH KOREA
Korea Strait
(Tsushima-kaikyō)
SHIKOKU
KYŪSHŪ
Tōkyō
Yokohama
Kawasaki
Chiba
Nagoya
Kyōto
Ōsaka
Kōbe
Hiroshima
Fukuoka
Kita-Kyūshū
Kumamoto
Kagoshima
Miyazaki
Niigata
Kanazawa
Okayama
Matsuyama
Kōchi
Pusan
Ulsan
Taegu
Izu-shotō
Ōsumi-shotō
Tsushima
Liancourt Rocks
Ullŭng-do (S. Korea)

1:5M

KM MILES

300 250 200 150 100 50 0

200 150 100 50 0

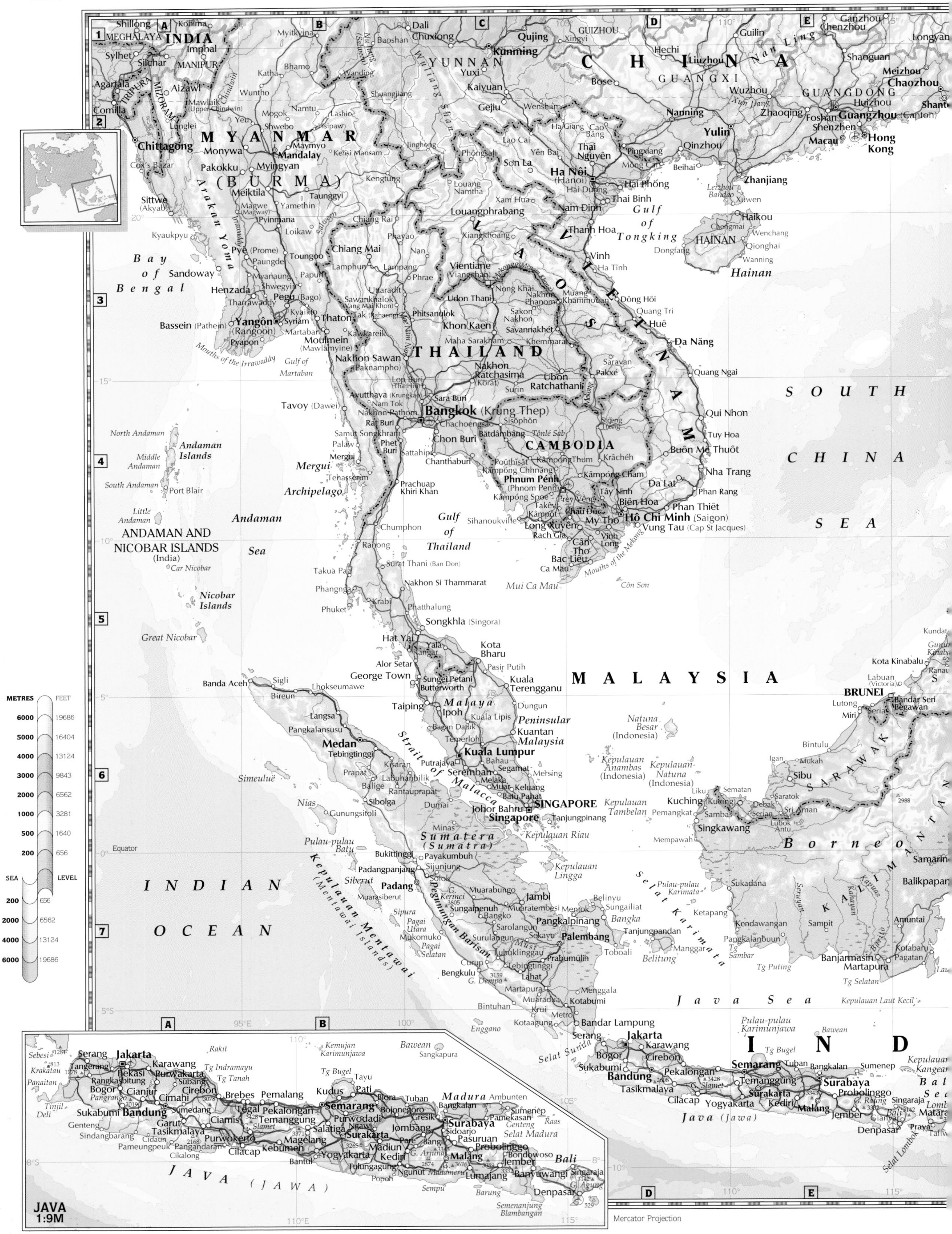

1

Shillong A Kohima B Dali Chuxiong C Qujing Xingyi GUIZHOU D Guilin Ganzhou Chenzhou E
MEGHALAYA INDIA Imphal Myitkyina Baoshan Kunming Liuzhou Nan Ling Longyan
Sylhet Silchar MANIPUR Katha Bhamo YUNNAN Yuxi Kaiyuan Wenshan Nanning Hechi Shaoguan
Agartala Aizawl Wuntho Mogok Namtu Lashio Jinghong Gejiu Lao Cai Ha Giang Cao Pingxiang Qinzhou Wuzhou GUANGDONG Meizhou Chaozhou

2

Comilla TRIPURA MIZORAM (Upper Chindwin) Yen Sipaw Kehsi Mansam Son La Thai Nguyen Beihai Zhaoqing Foshan Guangzhou (Canton) Shantou
MYANMAR Chittagong Monywa Mandalay Myingyan Louang Namtha Ha Noi (Hanoi) Mong Cai Shenzhen Macau Hong Kong
Cox's Bazar Pakokku Meiktila Maymyo Taunggyi Phongsali Yen Bai Hai Phong Leizhou Xuwen Yulin
(BURMA) Magwe (Magway) Yamethin Pyinmana Chiang Rai LAO KHOANG Nam Dinh Thai Binh Bando Zhanjiang
Sittwe (Akyab) Pye (Prome) Loikaw Chiang Mai Vientiane (Viangchan) Nong Khai Vinh Gulf Haikou Chengmai Wenchang

3

Kyaukpyu Henzada Toungoo Paungde Lamphun Lampang Nan Phrae Udon Thani Nong Khai Ha Tinh of HAINAN Qionghai Wanning
Bay Sandoway Pegu (Bago) Shwegyin Papun Uttaradit Savan Sakon Nakhon Savannakhét Dong Hoi Tongking Dongfang Hainan
of Yangôn Thaton Tak (Raheng) Phitsanulok Khon Kaen Maha Sarakham Khammouan Quang Tri
Bengal Thaton Kawkareik Mawlamyine Nakhon Sawan THAILAND Hué Da Nang
Bassein (Pathein) Moulmein Maha Sarakham Khammouan

4

North Andaman Tavoy (Dawei) Nakhon Ratchasima Ubon Ratchathani Pakxé Quang Ngai SOUTH
Middle Andaman Andaman Islands Ayutthaya (Krungkao) Sara Buri Surin Qui Nhon CHINA
South Andaman Port Blair Mergui Tenasserim Prachuap Khiri Khan Chon Buri Bátdâmbâng Tônlé Sap Buôn Me Thuôt Tuy Hoa
Little Andaman ANDAMAN AND NICOBAR ISLANDS (India) Chanthaburi Kâmpóng Thum Krâchéh Da Lat Nha Trang SEA
Car Nicobar Andaman Sea Chumphon Poûthisat Kâmpóng Cham Phan Rang
Phnum Pénh (Phnom Penh) Biên Hoa Phan Thiêt

5

Nicobar Islands Ranong Gulf of Thailand Prey Vêng Hô Chi Minh (Saigon)
Great Nicobar Surat Thani (Ban Don) Sihanoukville Kâmpóng Spoe Kâmpôt Châu Dôc My Tho Vung Tau (Cap St Jacques)
Takua Pa Nakhon Si Thammarat Long Xuyên Vinh Long Cân Tho
Phangnga Rach Gia Bac Liêu Côn Son
Krabi Phatthalung Mui Ca Mau Ca Mau Mouths of the Mekong
Phuket Songkhla (Singora)

6

Hat Yai Yala Kota Bharu MALAYSIA Kota Kinabalu
Alor Setar Narathiwat Pasir Putih Labuan (Victoria) Kundat Gunun Kinabalu
George Town Sungei Petani Kuala Terengganu Natuna Besar (Indonesia) BRUNEI
Banda Aceh Sigli Butterworth Dungun Lutong Bandar Seri Begawan
Bireun Taiping Ipoh Malaya Miri Serian
Langsa Kuala Lipis Peninsular Bintulu SARAWAK
Pangkalansusu Bagan Datuk Kuantan Malaysia Natuna Igan Mukah Saratok

7

Medan Temerloh Kepulauan Anambas (Indonesia) Sibu Sri Antu
Tebingtinggi Putrajaya Bahau Segamat Mersing Liku Sematan Kuching (Kucing) Pemangkat Sambas Singkawang KALIMANTAN
Prapat Kisaran Labuhanbilik Seremban Melaka Kepulauan Tambelan Mempawah BORNEO Samarin
Balige Rantauprapat Muar Keluang Batu Pahat SINGAPORE Balikpapan
Nias Sibolga Dumai Johor Bahru Singapore Tanjungpinang Kepulauan Riau Sukadana Kapuas
Gunungsitoli Minas Sumatera (Sumatra) Kendawangan Sampit Banjarmasin Martapura Kotabaru Pagatan

Pulau-pulau Batu Bukittinggi Kepulauan Lingga Selat Karimata Pangkalanbuun Amuntai
Padangpanjang Sijunjung Tanjungpandan Ketapang Pangkalpinang Bangka
Siberut Padang Solok Muarabungo Jambi Belinyu Sungailiat Tanjungpandan Tg Puting Tg Sambar
Muarasiberut G. Kerinci Sungaipenuh Muaratembesi Mentok Sungai Pangkalpinang Belitung
Sipura 3805 Bangko Sarolangun Sekayu Palembang Toboali
Pagai Utara Mukomuko Sungaisalungun Prabumulih Tg Selatan
Pagai Selatan Curup Tebingtinggi Tukulinggau Martapura

INDIAN OCEAN Bengkulu 3159 G. Dempo Lahat Menggala Java Sea Kepulauan Laut Kecil
Bintuhan Muaradua Kotabumi Pulau-pulau Karimunjawa Bawean
Kotaagung Krui Metro Selat Sunda Bandar Lampung Jakarta Karawang Kepulauan Kangean
Enggano Bogor Cirebon Tuban Bangkalan Sumenep IND
Bandung Pekalongan Semarang Tegal Temanggung Surabaya
Selat Sukabumi Tasikmalaya Slamet Surakarta Java (Jawa) Bali Sea
Cilacap Yogyakarta Kediri Malang Jember Singaraja Praya Selat Lombok Matar

METRES FEET
6000 19686
5000 16404
4000 13124
3000 9843
2000 6562
1000 3281
500 1640
200 656
SEA LEVEL
200 656
2000 6562
4000 13124
6000 19686

Equator

INDONESIA

A 95°E **B** 100° **C** 105° **D** 110° **E** 115°

A Sebesi 128° Serang Jakarta Karawang Rakit Kemujan Karimunjawa Bawean 110°
Krakatau 813 Tangerang Purwakarta Tg Indramayu Tg Tanah Tayu Sangkapura
1578 Rangkasbitung Bekasi Cianjur Subang Cirebon Tg Bugel Kudus Pati Tuban
Panaitan Bogor Cimahi Sumedang Brebes Pemalang Semarang Blora Bojonegoro Gresik Madura Ambunten
Tinjil Sukabumi Bandung Garut Ciamis Tegal Pekalongan Purwodadi Salatiga Jombang Pamekasan Sumenep
Deli Genteng Sindangbarang Tasikmalaya 3078 Slamet Temanggung Sawi Surakarta Madiun Pare Bangil Pasuruan Genteng Raas
Pangrango Purwokerto Cidaun Pangandaran Cilacap Kebumen Magelang 2165 Surakarta Madiun Kediri Malang Selat Madura
Pameungpeuk Cikalong Bantul Yogyakarta G. Merapi 3676 Bondowoso Jember B Bali
JAVA (JAWA) Popoh Tulungagung Ngunut Madiun Lumajang Banyuwangi Singaraja G. Agung
110°E 115° Sempu Barung Denpasar 3142 Semenanjung Blambangan 529 Selat Lombok

Mercator Projection

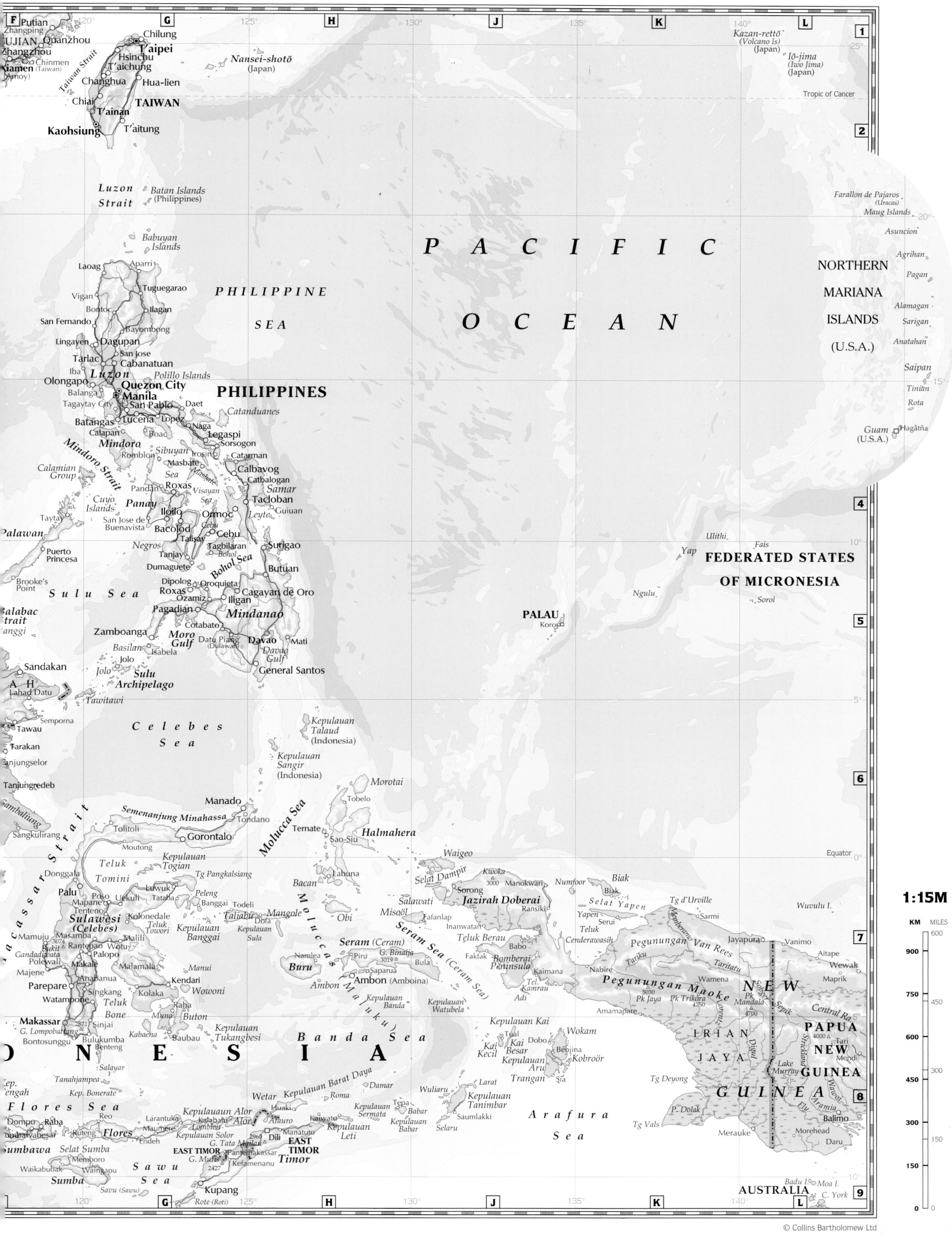

F · · G · · H · · J · · K · · L · · 1

PACIFIC

OCEAN

Tropic of Cancer

Kazan-rettō
(Volcano Is)
(Japan)

Iō-jima
(Iwo Jima)
(Japan)

Putian
Zhangping
Quanzhou
UJIAN
Zhangzhou
Xiamen
(Amoy)
Chinmen
(Taiwan)

Chilung
T'aipei
Hsinchu
T'aichung
Changhua
Hua-lien
Chiai
T'ainan
TAIWAN
Kaohsiung
T'aitung

Nansei-shotō
(Japan)

Farallon de Pajaros
(Uracas)
Maug Islands

Asuncion

Agrihan

Pagan

NORTHERN

MARIANA

ISLANDS

(U.S.A.)

Alamagan

Sarigan

Anatahan

Saipan

Tinian

Rota

Guam
(U.S.A.)

*Luzon
Strait*

Batan Islands
(Philippines)

PHILIPPINE

SEA

*Babuyan
Islands*

Laoag
Aparri
Vigan
Tuguegarao
Bontoc
Ilagan
San Fernando
Bayombong
Lingayen
Dagupan
Tarlac
San Jose
Iba
Cabanatuan
Olongapo
Luzon
Quezon City
Balanga
Manila
Tagaytay City
San Pablo
Batangas
Tucena
Lopez
Calapan
Boac
Naga
Mindoro
Legaspi
Romblon
Sorsogon
Sibuyan
Irosin
Mindoro Strait
Pandan
Sea
Catarman
*Calamian
Group*
Masbate
Calbayog
*Cuyo
Islands*
Roxas
Catbalogan
Taytay
Panay
San Jose de
Buenavista
Iloilo
Ormoc
Samar
Tacloban
Leyte
Guiuan
Bacolod
Cebu
Talisay
Tagbilaran
Surigao
Negros
Tanjay
Dumaguete
Bohol Sea
Butuan
Dipolog
Oroquieta
Cagayan de Oro
Roxas
Ozamiz
Iligan
Pagadian
Mindanao
Zamboanga
*Moro
Gulf*
Datu Piang
(Dulawan)
Davao
Mati
Basilan
Isabela
Jolo
*Davao
Gulf*
General Santos

Polillo Islands

PHILIPPINES

Catanduanes

Daet

*Visayan
Sea*

Masbate

Pandan

Sulu Sea

Cotabato

Sandakan

Lahad Datu

Semporna

Tawau

Tarakan

Tanjungselor

Tanjungredeb

A H

*Balabac
Strait*

langgi

Palawan

Puerto
Princesa

Brooke's
Point

*Celebes
Sea*

*Kepulauan
Talaud
(Indonesia)*

Tawitawi

*Sulu
Archipelago*

Jolo

*Kepulauan
Sangir
(Indonesia)*

Morotai

Tobelo

Manado

Semenanjung Minahassa

Tondano

Tolitoli

Gorontalo

Moutong

Molucca Sea

Ternate

Sao-Siu

Halmahera

Waigeo

Selat Dampir

Sorong

Kwoka

Manokwari

Biak

*Teluk
Tomini*

Donggala

*Kepulauan
Togian*

Tg Pangkalsiang

Luwuk

Peleng

Bacan

Salawati

Jazirah Doberai

Ransiki

Numfoor

Palu
Mapane
Poso
Uekuli
Tataba
Banggai
Todeli

Obi

Misoöl

Inanwatan

Yapen

Yapen
Teluk
Cenderawasih

Tenteno
Kolonedale
*Kepulauan
Banggai*
Mangole
*Kepulauan
Sula*
Fafanlap

Semenanjung Minahassa

*Sulawesi
(Celebes)*

Mamuju
Masamba
Malili
Rantepao
Palopo
Makale
Anabanua
Parepare
Watampone
Pinrang
Polewali
Majene
*Teluk
Bone*

*Macassar
Strait*

Taliabu

Mangole

Molucca

Todeli

Seram (Ceram)

G. Binatja

Piru

Bula

Namlea

Buru

Ambon (Amboina)

Saparua

Seram Sea (Ceram Sea)

Faktak

Teluk Berau

Babo

*Bomberai
Peninsula*

Kaimana

Tel.
Kamrau

Adi

Amamapate

Nabire

Wamena

Serui

Sarmi

Jayapura

Vanimo

Aitape

Wewak

Maprik

Pegunungan Van Rees

Taritatu

NEW

FEDERATED STATES

OF MICRONESIA

Ulithi

Fais

Yap

Ngulu

PALAU

Koror

Sorol

Ngulu

Wuvulu I.

Equator

Tg d'Urville

Macassar Strait

Kolaka

Kendari

Raha

Wowoni

Singkang

Sinjai

*Teluk
Bone*

*Kepulauan
Tukangbesi*

Kolaka

Wakatobi

Makassar

G. Lompobattang

Bulukumba

Bontosunggu

Benteng

Bantaeng

Salayar

Muna

Buton

Baubau

*Kepulauan
Banda*

*Kepulauan
Watubela*

Banda Sea

Wokam

Dobo

Benjina

Kobroor

*Kepulauan
Aru*

Trangan

Sia

*Kepulauan
Kai*

Tual
Kai
Besar

Kai
Kecil

*Kepulauan
Tanimbar*

Saumlakki

Larat

*Arafura
Sea*

Tg Deyong

Tg Vals

P. Dolak

Merauke

Morehead

Badu I.

Moa I.

AUSTRALIA

C. York

INDONESIA

ONESIA

*Flores
Sea*

Dompu
Raba
Bima

Sumbawa

Sumbawa

Waikabubak

Sumba

*Sawu
Sea*

Waingapu

Selat Sumba

Savu (Sawu)

Reo

Ruteng

Flores

Maumere

Ende

Larantuka

Kalabahi

Kepulauan Solor

G. Tata Mailau

Alor

Atauro

Manatuto

Dili

EAST TIMOR

Panfui

Kefamenanu

**EAST
TIMOR**

*East
Timor*

Kupang

Rote (Roti)

Kepulauan Alor

Wetar

Kepulauan Barat Daya

Damar

Roma

*Kepulauan
Leti*

*Kepulauan
Sermata*

Tepa

Babar

Babar

Selaru

*Kepulauan
Tanimbar*

Pegunungan Maoke

5030
Pk Jaya
Pk Trikora
5019
Pk Mandala
4700
4750

**IRIAN

JAYA**

Lake
Murray

4000

Tari

Mendi

PAPUA

NEW

GUINEA

Central Ra.

Balimo

Daru

Sepik

Digul

Strickland

Fly

Aramia

3074

2871

2964

2427

3000

Daet

© Collins Bartholomew Ltd

1:15M

KM   MILES
600

900   450

750   450

600   300

450

300   150

150

0

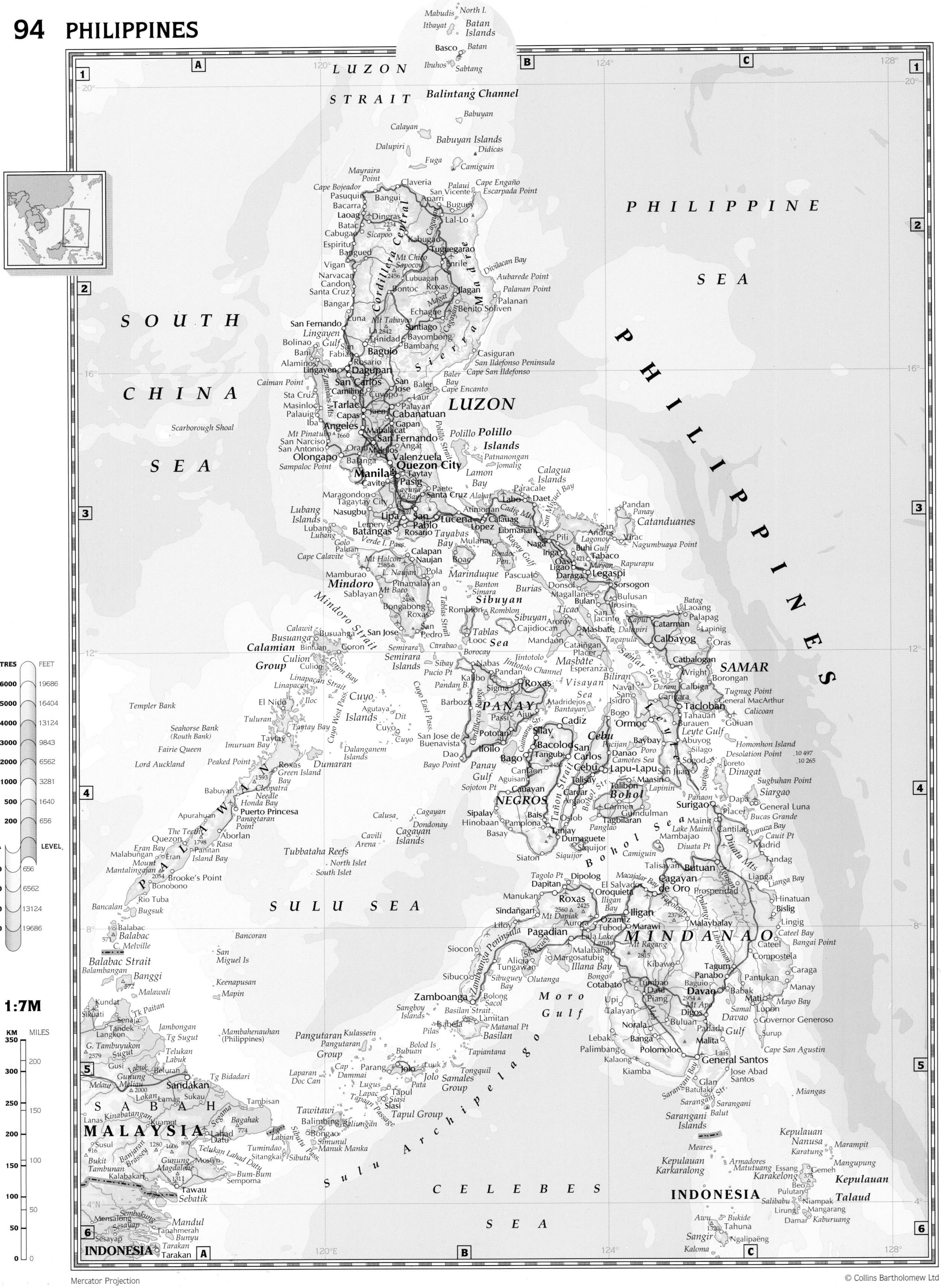

LUZON STRAIT

Balintang Channel

Mabudis *North I.*
Itbayat *Batan Islands*
Basco *Batan*
Ibuhos *Sabtang*

PHILIPPINE SEA

SOUTH CHINA SEA

Calayan
Dalupiri Babuyan *Didicas*
Fuga Babuyan Islands
Camiguin

Mayraira Point
Cape Bojeador Claveria
Pasuquin Palaui Cape Engaño
Bacarra San Vicente Escarpada Point
Laoag Dingras Aparri Buguey
Batac Lal-lo
Cabugao Sicapoo Kabugao Tuguegarao
Espiritu Enrile
Vigan Mt Chico Divilacan Bay
Narvacan Bangued Sapocoy Ilagan Aubarede Point
Candon Santiago Palanan Point
Santa Cruz Echague Palanan
Bangar Bontoc Roxas Benito Soliven

San Fernando Luna Bayombong Casiguran
Bolinao Lingayen Baguio Bambang San Ildefonso Peninsula
Bani Gulf Trinidad Cape San Ildefonso
Alaminos Lingayen Dagupan Baler
San Carlos San Jose Baler Bay
Caiman Point Camiling Cuyo Laur Cape Encanto
Sta Cruz Tarlac Palayan
Masinloc Capas Cabanatuan LUZON
Palauig Iba Jaen Gapan
Mt Pinatubo Angeles Mabalacat Polillo
San Narciso San Fernando Angat Polillo Islands
Olongapo Valenzuela Patnanongan
Sampaloc Point Bataan Quezon City Jomalig
Manila Pasig
Cavite Taytay Lamon Calagua Islands
Maragondon Paete Bay
Tagaytay City Santa Cruz Alabat
Laguna Bay Labo Paracale Daet
Lubang Islands Nasugbu Lipa San Pablo Lucena Atimonan Cadig Mts San Miguel Bay Pandan Panay
Lubang Lemery Batangas Rosario Lopez Libmanan Naga Pili Catanduanes
Lubang Verde I. Pass Tayabas Mulanay Iriga Buhi Virac
Golo Cape Calavite Bay Ragay Gulf Nagumbuaya Point
Mt Halcon Calapan Naujan Boac Oas Mayon Rapurapu
Mamburao Pola Marinduque Pascuato Ligao Daraga Legaspi
Mindoro Sablayan Baco Burias Magallanes Sorsogon
Pinamalayan Donsol Bulusan
Bongabong Banton Bulan Batag
Roxas Simara Irosin Laoang
Calawit San Jose Romblon San Jacinto Palapag
Busuanga Coron Tablas Sibuyan Ticao Lapinig
Calamian Bintuan Semirara Sea Masbate Catarman
Group Culion Semirara Islands Tablas Strait Mandaon Calbayog Oras
Linapacan Cuyo Cajidiocan Tagapula Catbalogan
Cuyo Islands Sibay Nabas Esperanza Biliran Wright SAMAR
El Nido Iloc Agutaya Dit Jintotolo Channel Masbate Naval San Calbiga Borongan
Tuluran Cuyo Kalibo Pandan Isidro Daram Tugnug Point
Templer Bank Tantay Bay Cuyo Panay B. Roxas Bogo Carigara General MacArthur
Seahorse Bank Imuruan Bay Barboza PANAY Ajuy Madridejos Ormoc Tacloban Calicoan
Fairie Queen Peaked Point Pototan Cadiz Bantayan Leyte Guiuan
Lord Auckland Roxas Green Island Sillay Danao Leyte Gulf
Dumaran Iloilo Bacolod San Cebu Baybay Abuyog Homonhon Island
Babuyan Bay Bago Tangub Carlos Lapu-Lapu Silago
PALAWAN Honda Bay Panay Talisay Camotes Sea Sogod Dinagat
Puerto Princesa Gulf Aguisan Cadiz Maasin Dapa
Apurahuan Panagtaran Point Bais NEGROS Talibon Bohol Surigao Siargao
The Teeth Rasa Sipalay Hinobaan Pamplona Carmen Gundulman Placer General Luna
Eran Bay Aborlan Basay Dumaguete Tagbilaran Lake Mainit Cantilan
Malabungan Panitan Calusa Cagayan Siaton Siquijor Panglao Mambajao Cauit Pt
Mount Island Bay Dondonay Tanjay Diuata Pt Madrid
Brooke's Point Cagayan Islands Camiguin Butuan Tandag
Rio Tuba Bonobono Cavili Arena Talisayan Cagayan Lianga
Bancalan Bugsuk Tubbataha Reefs Dapitan de Oro Prosperidad Lianga Bay
Balabac North Islet Dipolog El Salvador Hinatuan
C. Melville South Islet Manukan Oroquieta Iligan Bislig
Balabac Strait Roxas Iligan Malaybalay Cateel Bay
Balambangan Banggi SULU SEA Sindangan Bay Tubod MINDANAO Bangai Point
Malawali Bancoran Pagadian Mt Dapiak Marawi Mt Ragang Compostela
Mapin San Liloy Aurora Kibawe Babak Caraga
Kundat Miguel Is Keenapusan Siocon Lala Lake Tagum Pantukan Manay
Tandek Jambongan Mambahenauhan Zamboanga Peninsula Alicia Lanao Malabang Panabo
Langkon G. Tambuyukon (Philippines) Malangas Margosatubig Bongo Davao
Sandakan Pangutaran Sibuco Illana Bay Cotabato Datu Piang Davao
SABAH Telukan Labuk Pangutaran Group Tungawan Upi Talayan Digos Gulf
Lanas Kinabatangan Kulassein Bolong Moro Gulf Lebak Norala Governor Generoso
Zamboanga Sibuguey Banga Buluan
MALAYSIA Bagahak Tapiantana Bay Palimbang Polomoloc Cape San Agustin
Sandakan Isabela Basilan Kalaong Malita
Lahad Datu Basilan Strait Lamitan General Santos
Pilas Matanal Pt Jose Abad Santos
Tawau Jolo Samales Glan
Sebatik Doc Can Tapul Group Sarangani Bay
Laparan Lugus Siasi Miangas
INDONESIA Tawitawi Tapul Passage Sarangani Islands
Mandul Bongao Sibutu Sulu Archipelago Kepulauan Nanusa
CELEBES SEA Sangir INDONESIA Kepulauan Talaud

Mindoro Strait
Cuyo West Pass
Cuyo East Pass
Panay Gulf
Sulu Sea
Visayan Sea
Samar Sea
Bohol Sea
Leyte Gulf

Scarborough Shoal

© Collins Bartholomew Ltd

METRES	FEET
6000	19686
5000	16404
4000	13124
3000	9843
2000	6562
1000	3281
500	1640
200	656
SEA	LEVEL
200	656
2000	6562
4000	13124
6000	19686

1:7M

KM	MILES
350	
300	200
250	150
200	100
150	
100	50
50	
0	0

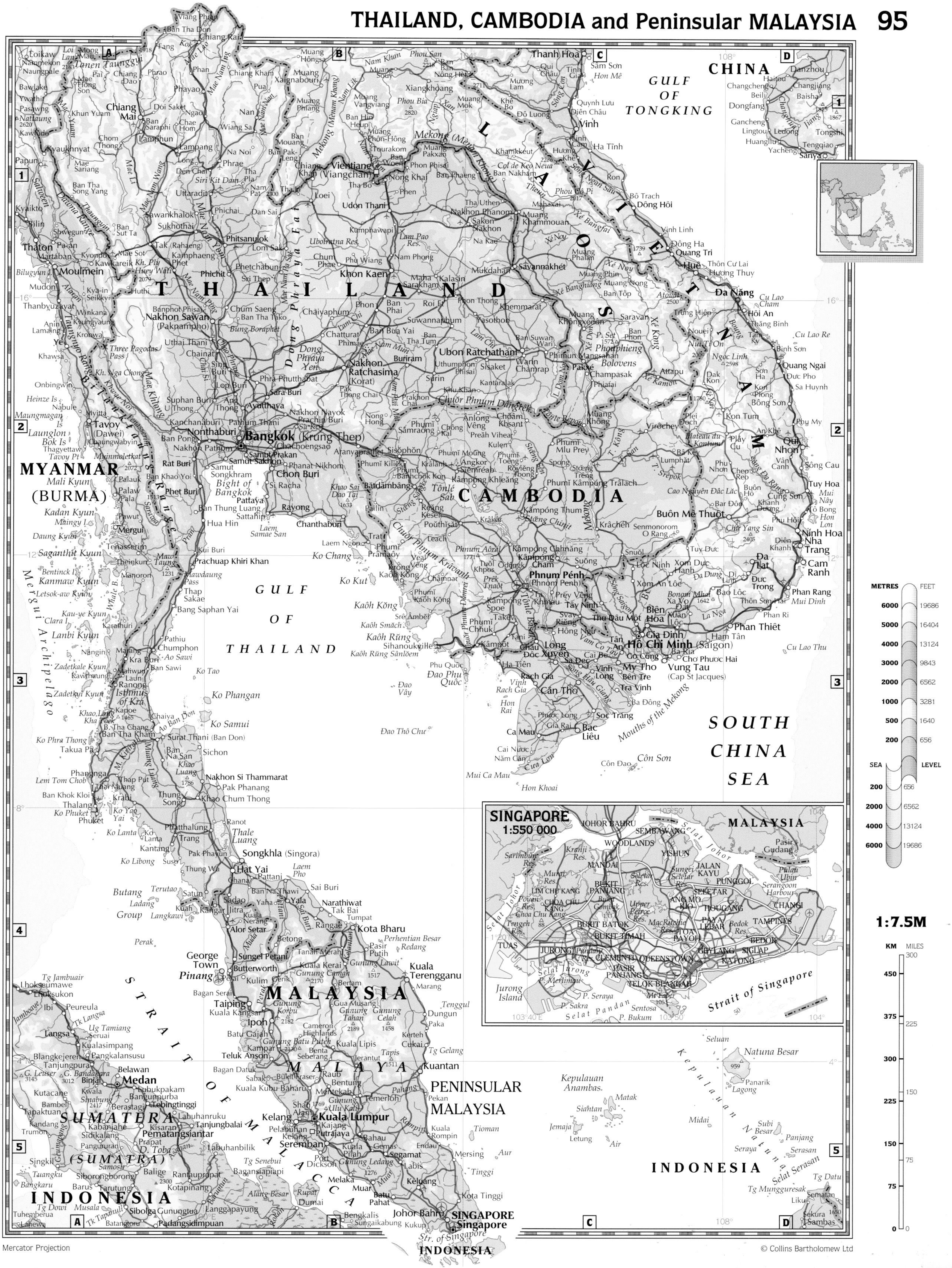

CHINA

GULF OF TONGKING

LAOS

VIETNAM

THAILAND

MYANMAR (BURMA)

CAMBODIA

GULF OF THAILAND

SOUTH CHINA SEA

Bangkok (Krung Thep)

Phnum Pénh (Phnom Penh)

Hô Chi Minh (Saigon)

Chiang Mai

Vientiane (Viangchan)

Nakhon Ratchasima (Korat)

Ubon Ratchathani

Đà Nẵng

Hon Mê

Cu Lao Cham

Hôi An

Quang Ngai

Kon Tum

Buôn Mê Thuột

Đà Lat

Nha Trang

Cam Ranh

Phan Rang

Phan Thiết

Vung Tau (Cap St Jacques)

Cân Thơ

Ca Mau

Bac Liêu

Soc Trăng

Mouths of the Mekong

Côn Sơn

Mui Ca Mau

Hon Khoai

SINGAPORE 1:550 000

JOHOR BAHRU

SEMBAWANG

WOODLANDS

YISHUN

MANDAI

BUKIT PANJANG

CHOA CHU KANG

SELETAR

PUNGGOL

CHANGI

TAMPINES

BEDOK

JURONG

BUKIT BATOK

BUKIT TIMAH

CLEMENTI

QUEENSTOWN

GEYLANG

SIGLAP

KATONG

Jurong Island

Sentosa

Strait of Singapore

Selat Pandan

MALAYSIA

PENINSULAR MALAYSIA

Kuala Lumpur

Putrajaya

Seremban

George Town Pinang

Butterworth

Ipoh

Taiping

Kuala Terengganu

Kota Bharu

Alor Setar

Hat Yai

Songkhla (Singora)

Nakhon Si Thammarat

Surat Thani (Ban Don)

Phuket

Krabi

Trang

Pattani

Yala

Narathiwat

SUMATERA (SUMATRA)

INDONESIA

Medan

Pematangsiantar

D. Toba

Strait of Singapore

Str. of Singapore

SINGAPORE

Johor Bahru

Kuantan

Melaka

Muar

STRAIT OF MALACCA

Natuna Besar

Kepulauan Anambas

Kepulauan Natuna

INDONESIA

METRES	FEET
6000	19686
5000	16404
4000	13124
3000	9843
2000	6562
1000	3281
500	1640
200	656
SEA	LEVEL
200	656
2000	6562
4000	13124
6000	19686

1:7.5M

KM	MILES
450	300
375	225
300	150
225	75
150	
75	
0	0

Mercator Projection

© Collins Bartholomew Ltd

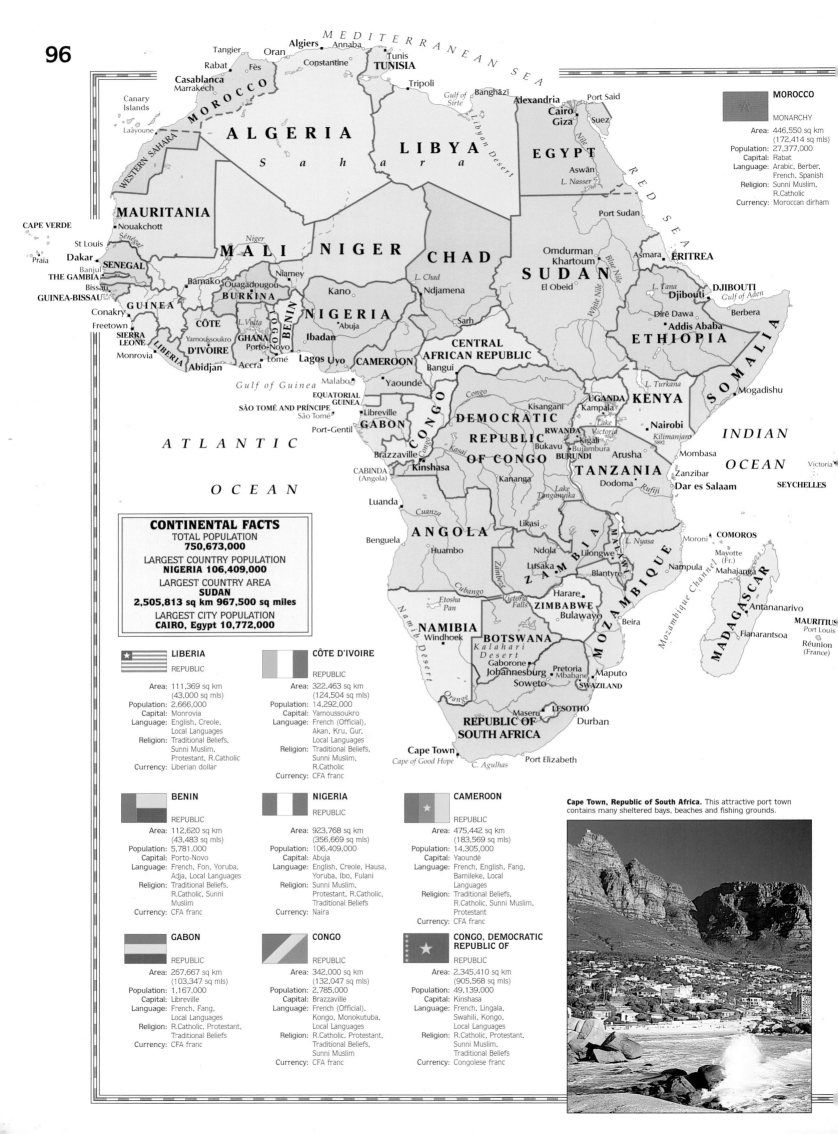

MEDITERRANEAN SEA

Tangier
Oran
Algiers
Annaba
Rabat
Fès
Constantine
Tunis
Casablanca
TUNISIA
Marrakech
Tripoli
Banghāzī
Gulf of Sirte
Alexandria
Port Said
Cairo
Giza
Suez
Canary Islands
MOROCCO
Aswān
L. Nasser

ALGERIA
Sahara
LIBYA
EGYPT

Laâyoune
WESTERN SAHARA

RED SEA

MAURITANIA
Nouakchott
Port Sudan

CAPE VERDE
St Louis
Senegal
Niger
MALI
NIGER
CHAD
Omdurman
Khartoum
Asmara
ERITREA
Praia
Dakar
Banjul
SENEGAL
Bamako
Ouagadougou
Niamey
L. Chad
El Obeid
SUDAN
Blue Nile
L. Tana
Djibouti
DJIBOUTI
Gulf of Aden
THE GAMBIA
Bissau
GUINEA-BISSAU
BURKINA
Kano
Ndjamena
Dirē Dawa
Berbera
Conakry
GUINEA
NIGERIA
Sarh
White Nile
Addis Ababa
Freetown
CÔTE
L. Volta
Abuja
ETHIOPIA
SIERRA LEONE
Yamoussoukro
GHANA
Ibadan
CENTRAL
Porto-Novo
D'IVOIRE
Lomé
Lagos Uyo
CAMEROON
AFRICAN REPUBLIC
Monrovia
LIBERIA
Abidjan
Accra
Bangui
L. Turkana
SOMALIA
BENIN
Gulf of Guinea
Malabo
Yaoundé
Mogadishu
EQUATORIAL GUINEA
UGANDA
KENYA
SÃO TOMÉ AND PRÍNCIPE
Libreville
Kisangani
Kampala
São Tomé
GABON
DEMOCRATIC
Lake Victoria
Nairobi
Port-Gentil
REPUBLIC
RWANDA
Kigali
Kilimanjaro 5892
INDIAN
Brazzaville
CONGO
OF CONGO
Bukavu
Bujumbura
Arusha
Mombasa
CABINDA (Angola)
Kinshasa
BURUNDI
OCEAN
Kanaga
TANZANIA
Zanzibar
Victoria
Luanda
Kananga
Lake Tanganyika
Dodoma
Dar es Salaam
SEYCHELLES
Cuanza
Rufiji
ATLANTIC
Likasi
COMOROS
Moroni
Benguela
ANGOLA
Ndola
Mayotte (Fr.)
Nampula
Mahajanga
OCEAN
Huambo
Lilongwe
L. Nyasa
Z A M B I A
Lusaka
Blantyre
MOZAMBIQUE
Zambezi
MAURITIUS
Etosha Pan
Victoria Falls
Harare
Beira
Port Louis
Réunion (France)
Namib Desert
Cubango
ZIMBABWE
Bulawayo
MADAGASCAR
Antananarivo
NAMIBIA
Windhoek
BOTSWANA
Fianarantsoa
Kalahari Desert
Gaborone
Pretoria
Mbabane
Maputo
Johannesburg
SWAZILAND
Soweto
Orange
Maseru
LESOTHO
Durban
REPUBLIC OF
Cape Town
SOUTH AFRICA
Cape of Good Hope
C. Agulhas
Port Elizabeth

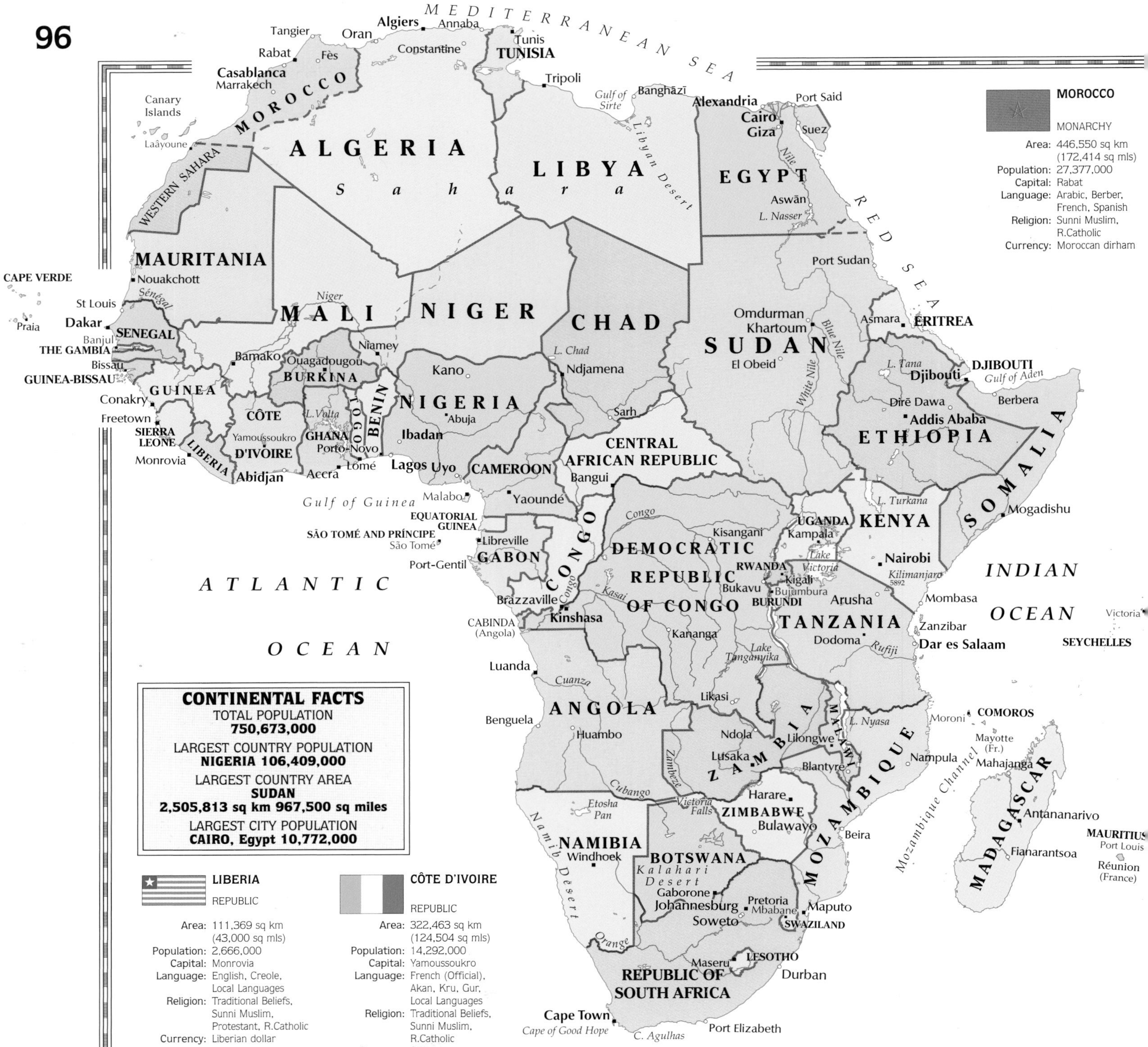

CONTINENTAL FACTS
TOTAL POPULATION
750,673,000
LARGEST COUNTRY POPULATION
NIGERIA 106,409,000
LARGEST COUNTRY AREA
SUDAN
2,505,813 sq km 967,500 sq miles
LARGEST CITY POPULATION
CAIRO, Egypt 10,772,000

MOROCCO
MONARCHY
Area: 446,550 sq km (172,414 sq mls)
Population: 27,377,000
Capital: Rabat
Language: Arabic, Berber, French, Spanish
Religion: Sunni Muslim, R.Catholic
Currency: Moroccan dirham

LIBERIA
REPUBLIC
Area: 111,369 sq km (43,000 sq mls)
Population: 2,666,000
Capital: Monrovia
Language: English, Creole, Local Languages
Religion: Traditional Beliefs, Sunni Muslim, Protestant, R.Catholic
Currency: Liberian dollar

CÔTE D'IVOIRE
REPUBLIC
Area: 322,463 sq km (124,504 sq mls)
Population: 14,292,000
Capital: Yamoussokro
Language: French (Official), Akan, Kru, Gur, Local Languages
Religion: Traditional Beliefs, Sunni Muslim, R.Catholic
Currency: CFA franc

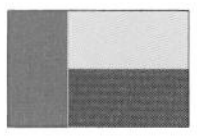

BENIN
REPUBLIC
Area: 112,620 sq km (43,483 sq mls)
Population: 5,781,000
Capital: Porto-Novo
Language: French, Fon, Yoruba, Adja, Local Languages
Religion: Traditional Beliefs, R.Catholic, Sunni Muslim
Currency: CFA franc

NIGERIA
REPUBLIC
Area: 923,768 sq km (356,669 sq mls)
Population: 106,409,000
Capital: Abuja
Language: English, Creole, Hausa, Yoruba, Ibo, Fulani
Religion: Sunni Muslim, Protestant, R.Catholic, Traditional Beliefs
Currency: Naira

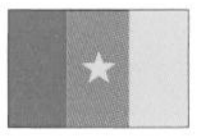

CAMEROON
REPUBLIC
Area: 475,442 sq km (183,569 sq mls)
Population: 14,305,000
Capital: Yaoundé
Language: French, English, Fang, Bamileke, Local Languages
Religion: Traditional Beliefs, R.Catholic, Sunni Muslim, Protestant
Currency: CFA franc

GABON
REPUBLIC
Area: 267,667 sq km (103,347 sq mls)
Population: 1,167,000
Capital: Libreville
Language: French, Fang, Local Languages
Religion: R.Catholic, Protestant, Traditional Beliefs
Currency: CFA franc

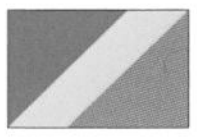

CONGO
REPUBLIC
Area: 342,000 sq km (132,047 sq mls)
Population: 2,785,000
Capital: Brazzaville
Language: French (Official), Kongo, Monokutuba, Local Languages
Religion: R.Catholic, Protestant, Traditional Beliefs, Sunni Muslim
Currency: CFA franc

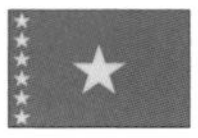

CONGO, DEMOCRATIC REPUBLIC OF
REPUBLIC
Area: 2,345,410 sq km (905,568 sq mls)
Population: 49,139,000
Capital: Kinshasa
Language: French, Lingala, Swahili, Kongo, Local Languages
Religion: R.Catholic, Protestant, Sunni Muslim, Traditional Beliefs
Currency: Congolese franc

Cape Town, Republic of South Africa. This attractive port town contains many sheltered bays, beaches and fishing grounds.

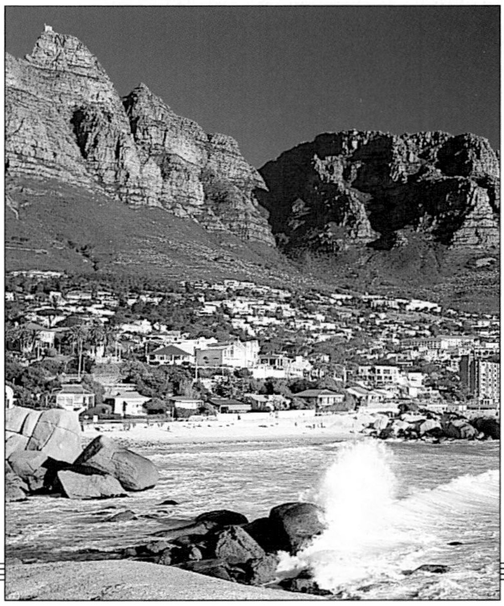

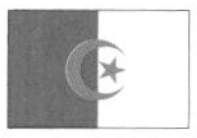

ALGERIA

REPUBLIC
Area: 2,381,741 sq km
(919,595 sq mls)
Population: 30,081,000
Capital: Algiers (Alger)
Language: Arabic, French, Berber
Religion: Sunni Muslim,
R.Catholic
Currency: Algerian dinar

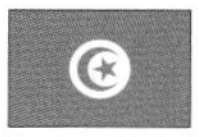

TUNISIA

REPUBLIC
Area: 164,150 sq km
(63,379 sq mls)
Population: 9,335,000
Capital: Tunis
Language: Arabic, French
Religion: Sunni Muslim
Currency: Tunisian dinar

LIBYA
REPUBLIC
Area: 1,759,540 sq km
(679,362 sq mls)
Population: 5,339,000
Capital: Tripoli (Tarābulus)
Language: Arabic, Berber
Religion: Sunni Muslim,
R.Catholic
Currency: Libyan dinar

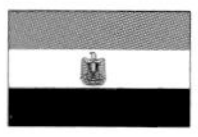

EGYPT

REPUBLIC
Area: 1,000,250 sq km
(386,199 sq mls)
Population: 65,978,000
Capital: Cairo (Al Qāhira)
Language: Arabic, French
Religion: Sunni Muslim,
Coptic Christian
Currency: Egyptian pound

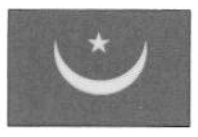

MAURITANIA

REPUBLIC
Area: 1,030,700 sq km
(397,955 sq mls)
Population: 2,529,000
Capital: Nouakchott
Language: Arabic, French,
Local Languages
Religion: Sunni Muslim
Currency: Ouguiya

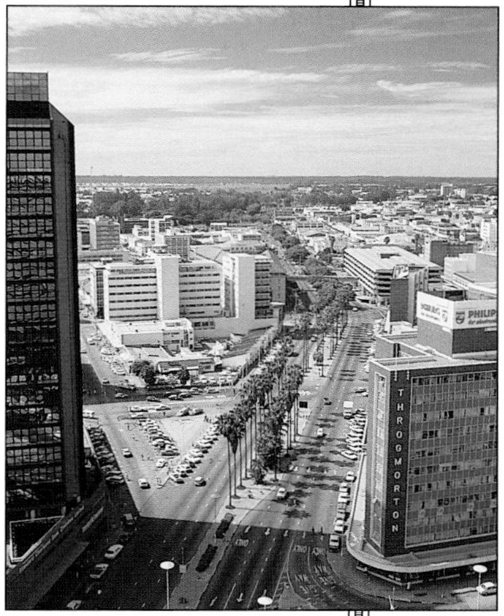

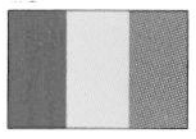

MALI

REPUBLIC
Area: 1,240,140 sq km
(478,821 sq mls)
Population: 10,694,000
Capital: Bamako
Language: French, Bambara,
Local Languages
Religion: Sunni Muslim,
Traditional Beliefs,
R.Catholic
Currency: CFA franc

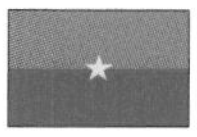

BURKINA

REPUBLIC
Area: 274,200 sq km
(105,869 sq mls)
Population: 11,305,000
Capital: Ouagadougou
Language: French, More (Mossi),
Fulani, Local Languages
Religion: Traditional Beliefs,
Sunni Muslim,
R.Catholic
Currency: CFA franc

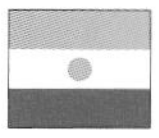

NIGER

REPUBLIC
Area: 1,267,000 sq km
(489,191 sq mls)
Population: 10,078,000
Capital: Niamey
Language: French (Official),
Hausa, Fulani,
Local Languages
Religion: Sunni Muslim,
Traditional Beliefs
Currency: CFA franc

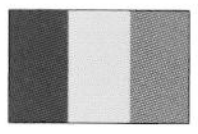

CHAD
REPUBLIC
Area: 1,284,000 sq km
(495,755 sq mls)
Population: 7,270,000
Capital: Ndjamena
Language: Arabic, French,
Local Languages
Religion: Sunni Muslim,
Traditional Beliefs,
R.Catholic
Currency: CFA franc

Harare. Following Zimbabwe's independence in 1980 this city became the focus for the population and the economy.

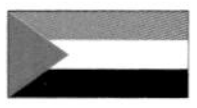

SUDAN

REPUBLIC
Area: 2,505,813 sq km
(967,500 sq mls)
Population: 28,292,000
Capital: Khartoum
Language: Arabic, Dinka, Nubian,
Beja, Nuer,
Local Languages
Religion: Sunni Muslim, Traditional
Beliefs, R.Catholic,
Protestant
Currency: Sudanese dinar

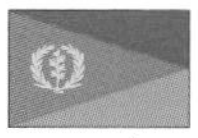

ERITREA

REPUBLIC
Area: 117,400 sq km
(45,328 sq mls)
Population: 3,577,000
Capital: Asmara
Language: Tigrinya, Arabic,
Tigre, English
Religion: Sunni Muslim,
Coptic Christian
Currency: Nakfa

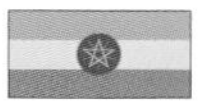

ETHIOPIA

REPUBLIC
Area: 1,133,880 sq km
(437,794 sq mls)
Population: 59,649,000
Capital: Addis Ababa
(Ādīs Ābeba)
Language: Amharic, Oromo,
Local Languages
Religion: Ethiopian Orthodox,
Sunni Muslim,
Traditional Beliefs
Currency: Birr

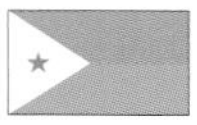

DJIBOUTI
REPUBLIC
Area: 23,200 sq km
(8,958 sq mls)
Population: 623,000
Capital: Djibouti
Language: Somali, French,
Arabic, Issa, Afar
Religion: Sunni Muslim,
R.Catholic
Currency: Djibouti franc

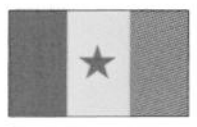

SENEGAL

REPUBLIC
Area: 196,720 sq km
(75,954 sq mls)
Population: 9,003,000
Capital: Dakar
Language: French (Official),
Wolof, Fulani,
Local Languages
Religion: Sunni Muslim,
R.Catholic,
Traditional Beliefs
Currency: CFA franc

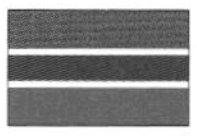

THE GAMBIA

REPUBLIC
Area: 11,295 sq km
(4,361 sq mls)
Population: 1,229,000
Capital: Banjul
Language: English (Official),
Malinke, Fulani,
Wolof
Religion: Sunni Muslim,
Protestant
Currency: Dalasi

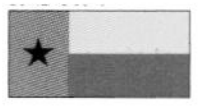

GUINEA-BISSAU

REPUBLIC
Area: 36,125 sq km
(13,948 sq mls)
Population: 1,161,000
Capital: Bissau
Language: Portuguese,
Portuguese Creole,
Local Languages
Religion: Traditional Beliefs,
Sunni Muslim,
R.Catholic
Currency: CFA franc

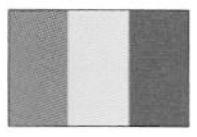

GUINEA
REPUBLIC
Area: 245,857 sq km
(94,926 sq mls)
Population: 7,337,000
Capital: Conakry
Language: French, Fulani,
Malinke, Local
Languages
Religion: Sunni Muslim,
Traditional Beliefs,
R.Catholic
Currency: Guinea franc

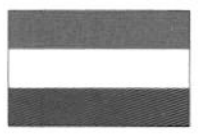

SIERRA LEONE
REPUBLIC
Area: 71,740 sq km
(27,699 sq mls)
Population: 4,568,000
Capital: Freetown
Language: English, Creole,
Mende, Temne,
Local Languages
Religion: Traditional Beliefs,
Sunni Muslim,
Protestant, R.Catholic
Currency: Leone

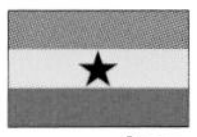

GHANA

REPUBLIC
Area: 238,537 sq km
(92,100 sq mls)
Population: 19,162,000
Capital: Accra
Language: English (Official),
Hausa, Akan,
Local Languages
Religion: Protestant, R.Catholic,
Sunni Muslim,
Traditional Beliefs
Currency: Cedi

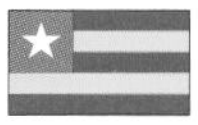

TOGO

REPUBLIC
Area: 56,785 sq km
(21,925 sq mls)
Population: 4,397,000
Capital: Lomé
Language: French, Ewe, Kabre,
Local Languages
Religion: Traditional Beliefs,
R.Catholic,
Sunni Muslim,
Protestant
Currency: CFA franc

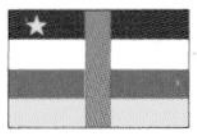

CENTRAL AFRICAN REPUBLIC

REPUBLIC
Area: 622,436 sq km
(240,324 sq mls)
Population: 3,485,000
Capital: Bangui
Language: French, Sango, Banda,
Baya, Local Languages
Religion: Protestant, R.Catholic,
Traditional Beliefs,
Sunni Muslim
Currency: CFA franc

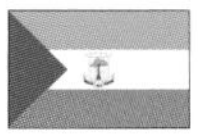

EQUATORIAL GUINEA
REPUBLIC
Area: 28,051 sq km
(10,831 sq mls)
Population: 431,000
Capital: Malabo
Language: Spanish, Fang
Religion: R.Catholic,
Traditional Beliefs
Currency: CFA franc

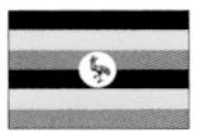

UGANDA

REPUBLIC
Area: 241,038 sq km
(93,065 sq mls)
Population: 20,554,000
Capital: Kampala
Language: English, Swahili
(Official), Luganda,
Local Languages
Religion: R.Catholic, Protestant,
Sunni Muslim,
Traditional Beliefs
Currency: Ugandan shilling

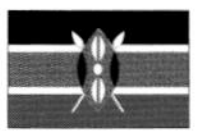

KENYA

REPUBLIC
Area: 582,646 sq km
(224,961 sq mls)
Population: 29,008,000
Capital: Nairobi
Language: Swahili (Official),
English,
Local Languages
Religion: R.Catholic,
Protestant,
Traditional Beliefs,
Currency: Kenyan shilling

POPULATION

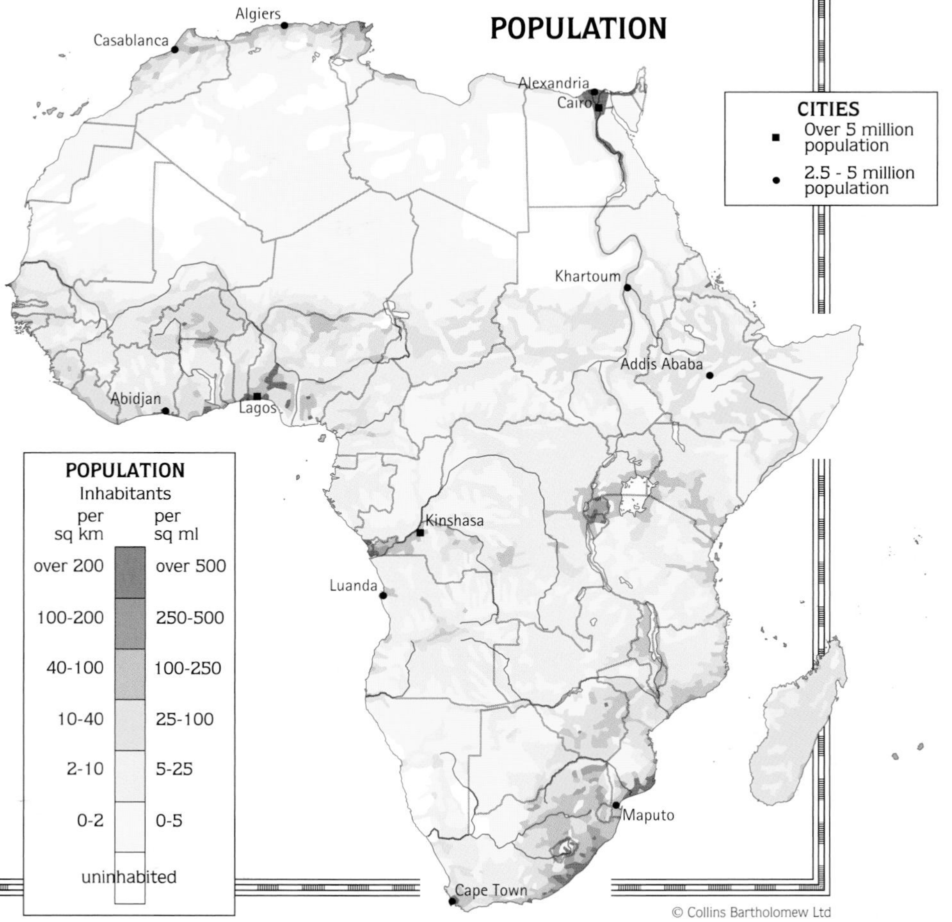

CITIES
- Over 5 million population
- 2.5 - 5 million population

POPULATION
Inhabitants

per sq km	per sq ml
over 200	over 500
100-200	250-500
40-100	100-250
10-40	25-100
2-10	5-25
0-2	0-5
uninhabited	

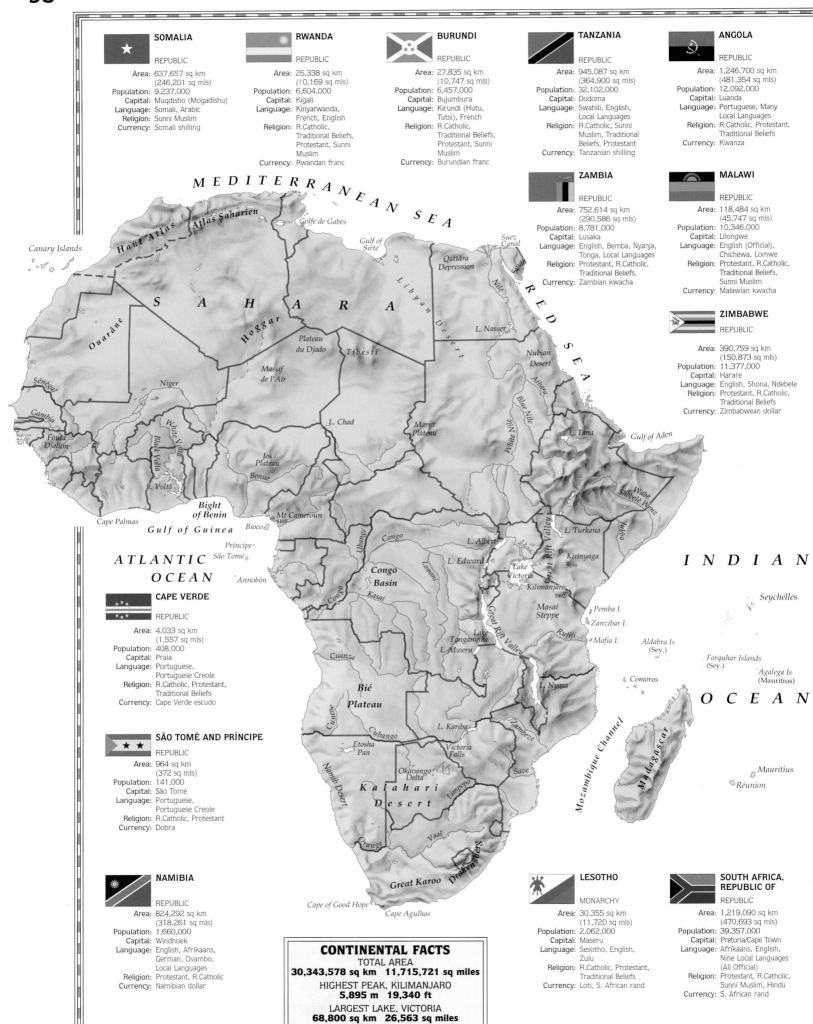

SOMALIA

REPUBLIC

Area: 637,657 sq km
(246,201 sq mls)
Population: 9,237,000
Capital: Muqdisho (Mogadishu)
Language: Somali, Arabic
Religion: Sunni Muslim
Currency: Somali shilling

RWANDA

REPUBLIC

Area: 26,338 sq km
(10,169 sq mls)
Population: 6,604,000
Capital: Kigali
Language: Kinyarwanda,
French, English
Religion: R.Catholic,
Traditional Beliefs,
Protestant, Sunni
Muslim
Currency: Rwandan franc

BURUNDI

REPUBLIC

Area: 27,835 sq km
(10,747 sq mls)
Population: 6,457,000
Capital: Bujumbura
Language: Kirundi (Hutu,
Tutsi), French
Religion: R.Catholic,
Traditional Beliefs,
Protestant, Sunni
Muslim
Currency: Burundian franc

TANZANIA

REPUBLIC

Area: 945,087 sq km
(364,900 sq mls)
Population: 32,102,000
Capital: Dodoma
Language: Swahili, English,
Local Languages
Religion: R.Catholic, Sunni
Muslim, Traditional
Beliefs, Protestant
Currency: Tanzanian shilling

ANGOLA

REPUBLIC

Area: 1,246,700 sq km
(481,354 sq mls)
Population: 12,092,000
Capital: Luanda
Language: Portuguese, Many
Local Languages
Religion: R.Catholic, Protestant,
Traditional Beliefs
Currency: Kwanza

ZAMBIA

REPUBLIC

Area: 752,614 sq km
(290,586 sq mls)
Population: 8,781,000
Capital: Lusaka
Language: English, Bemba, Nyanja,
Tonga, Local Languages
Religion: Protestant, R.Catholic,
Traditional Beliefs.
Currency: Zambian kwacha

MALAWI

REPUBLIC

Area: 118,484 sq km
(45,747 sq mls)
Population: 10,346,000
Capital: Lilongwe
Language: English (Official),
Chichewa, Lomwe
Religion: Protestant, R.Catholic,
Traditional Beliefs,
Sunni Muslim
Currency: Malawian kwacha

ZIMBABWE

REPUBLIC

Area: 390,759 sq km
(150,873 sq mls)
Population: 11,377,000
Capital: Harare
Language: English, Shona, Ndebele
Religion: Protestant, R.Catholic,
Traditional Beliefs
Currency: Zimbabwean dollar

CAPE VERDE

REPUBLIC

Area: 4,033 sq km
(1,557 sq mls)
Population: 408,000
Capital: Praia
Language: Portuguese,
Portuguese Creole
Religion: R.Catholic, Protestant,
Traditional Beliefs
Currency: Cape Verde escudo

SÃO TOMÉ AND PRÍNCIPE

REPUBLIC

Area: 964 sq km
(372 sq mls)
Population: 141,000
Capital: São Tomé
Language: Portuguese,
Portuguese Creole
Religion: R.Catholic, Protestant
Currency: Dobra

NAMIBIA

REPUBLIC

Area: 824,292 sq km
(318,261 sq mls)
Population: 1,660,000
Capital: Windhoek
Language: English, Afrikaans,
German, Ovambo,
Local Languages
Religion: Protestant, R.Catholic
Currency: Namibian dollar

LESOTHO

MONARCHY

Area: 30,355 sq km
(11,720 sq mls)
Population: 2,062,000
Capital: Maseru
Language: Sesotho, English,
Zulu
Religion: R.Catholic, Protestant,
Traditional Beliefs
Currency: Loti, S. African rand

SOUTH AFRICA, REPUBLIC OF

REPUBLIC

Area: 1,219,090 sq km
(470,693 sq mls)
Population: 39,357,000
Capital: Pretoria/Cape Town
Language: Afrikaans, English,
Nine Local Languages
(All Official)
Religion: Protestant, R.Catholic,
Sunni Muslim, Hindu
Currency: S. African rand

CONTINENTAL FACTS

TOTAL AREA
30,343,578 sq km   11,715,721 sq miles

HIGHEST PEAK, KILIMANJARO
5,895 m   19,340 ft

LARGEST LAKE, VICTORIA
68,800 sq km   26,563 sq miles

LONGEST RIVER, NILE
6,695 km   4,160 miles

CLIMATE

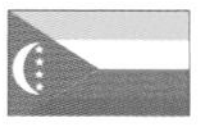

COMOROS

REPUBLIC

Area: 1,862 sq km
(719 sq mls)
Population: 658,000
Capital: Moroni
Language: Comorian, French,
Arabic
Religion: Sunni Muslim,
R.Catholic
Currency: Comoros franc

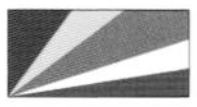

SEYCHELLES

REPUBLIC

Area: 455 sq km
(176 sq mls)
Population: 76,000
Capital: Victoria
Language: Seychellois (Seselwa,
French Creole),
English
Religion: R.Catholic, Protestant
Currency: Seychelles rupee

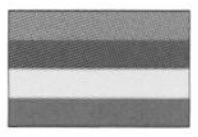

MAURITIUS

REPUBLIC

Area: 2,040 sq km
(788 sq mls)
Population: 1,141,000
Capital: Port Louis
Language: English, French Creole,
Hindi, Indian Languages
Religion: Hindu, R.Catholic,
Sunni Muslim,
Protestant
Currency: Mauritius rupee

MADAGASCAR

REPUBLIC

Area: 587,041 sq km
(226,658 sq mls)
Population: 15,057,000
Capital: Antananarivo
Language: Malagasy, French
Religion: Traditional Beliefs,
R.Catholic, Protestant,
Sunni Muslim,
Currency: Malagasy franc

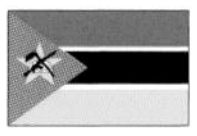

MOZAMBIQUE

REPUBLIC

Area: 799,380 sq km
(308,642 sq mls)
Population: 18,880,000
Capital: Maputo
Language: Portuguese, Makua,
Tsonga, Local Languages
Religion: Traditional Beliefs,
R.Catholic,
Sunni Muslim
Currency: Metical

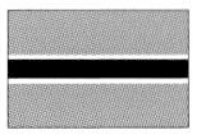

BOTSWANA

REPUBLIC

Area: 581,370 sq km
(224,468 sq mls)
Population: 1,570,000
Capital: Gaborone
Language: English, Setswana,
Shona, Local Languages
Religion: Traditional Beliefs,
Protestant, R.Catholic
Currency: Pula

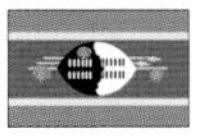

SWAZILAND

MONARCHY

Area: 17,364 sq km
(6,704 sq mls)
Population: 952,000
Capital: Mbabane
Language: Swazi (Siswati),
English
Religion: Protestant, R.Catholic,
Traditional Beliefs
Currency: Emalangeni,
S. African rand

Marrakesh

average monthly
temperature

colour refers to
climate type
shown on map

average monthly
rainfall

Aswān

CLIMATE TYPES
WARMER HUMID
Temperate
Mediterranean
DRY
Steppe
Desert
TROPICAL HUMID
Savanna
Rain forest

Freetown

Johannesburg

Livingstone

Zanzibar

Botswana. Elephants are one of the many types of native wildlife to be found in the Chobe National Park.

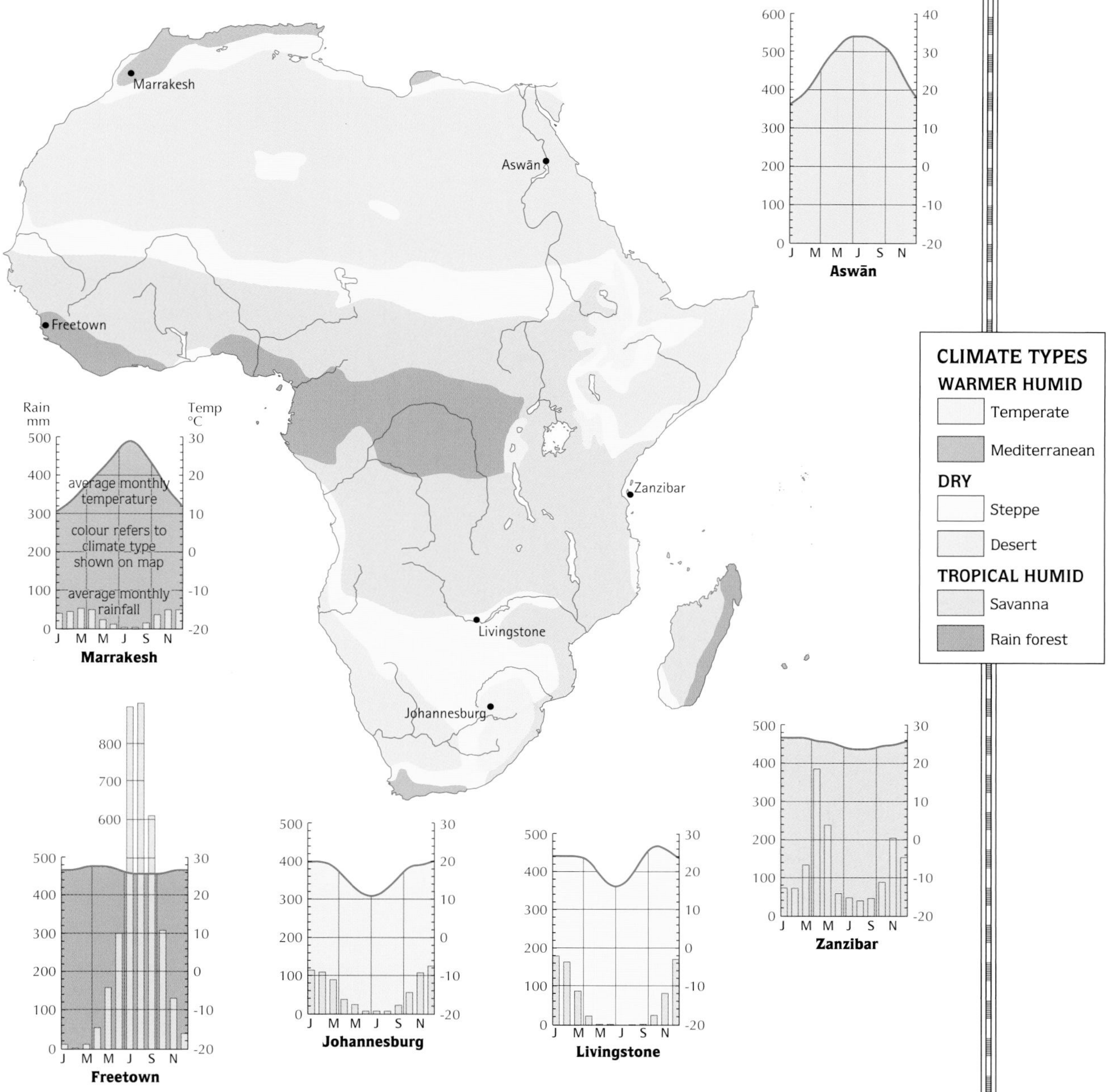

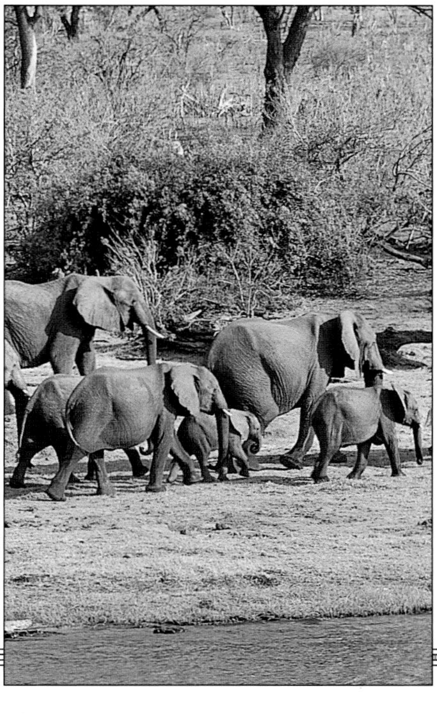

River Nile, Egypt. 96% of Egypt's population live in the Nile Delta and a 20km wide strip along the river.

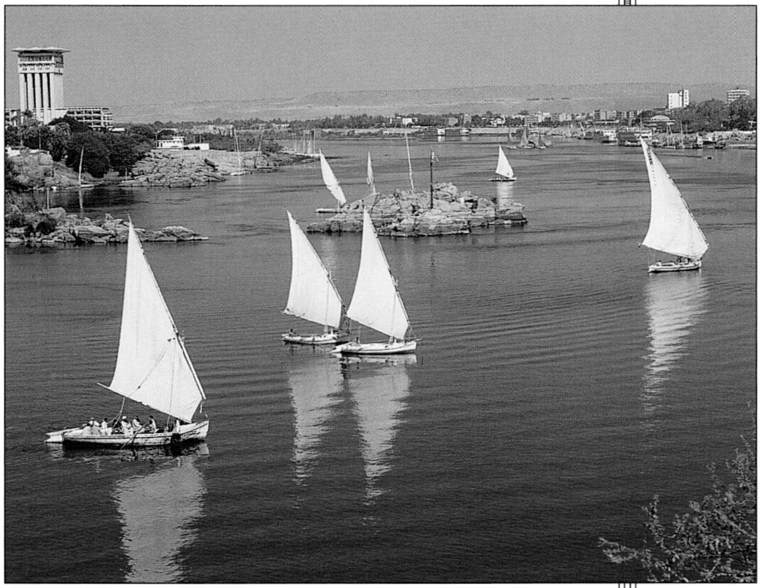

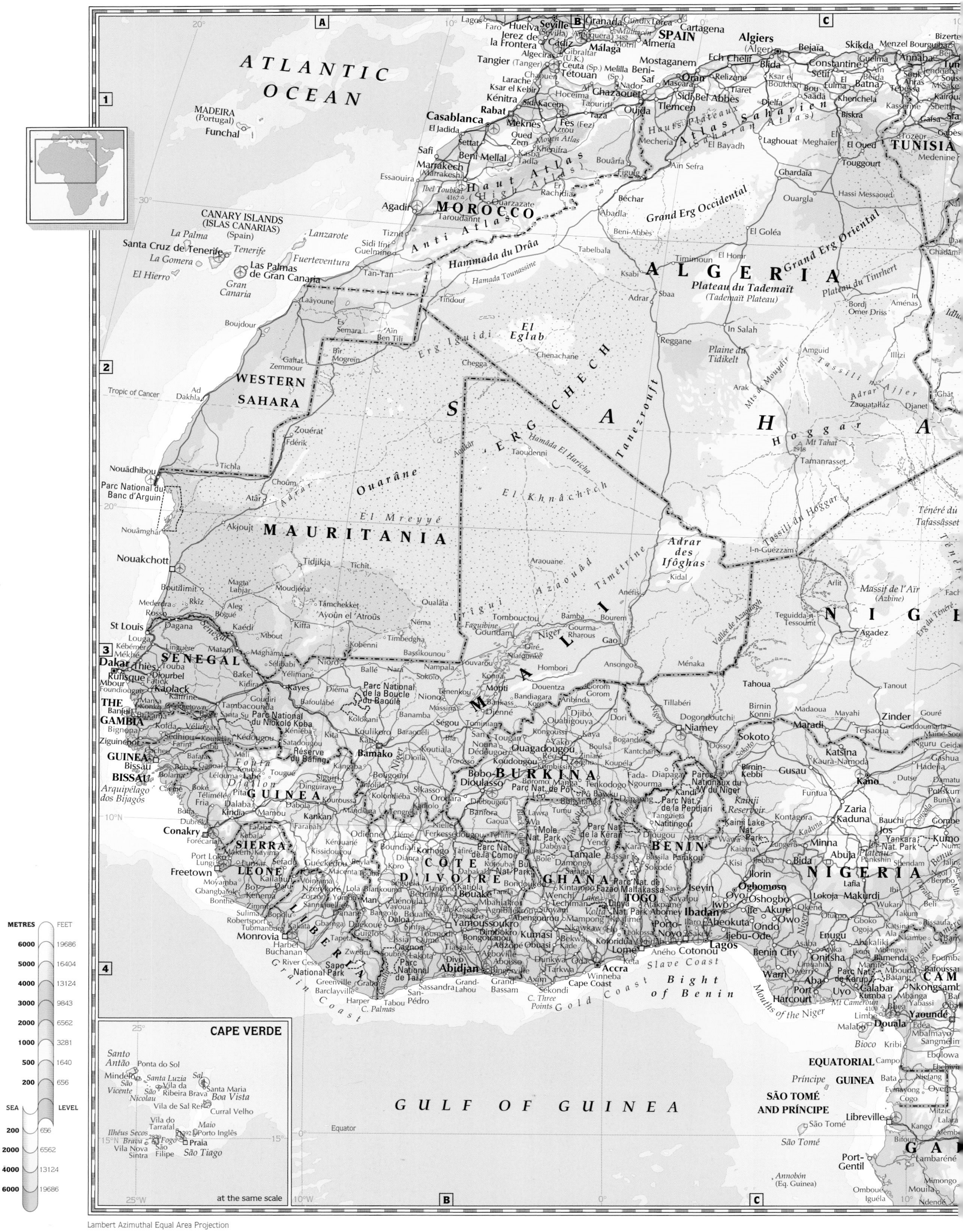

ATLANTIC
OCEAN

MADEIRA
(Portugal)
Funchal

CANARY ISLANDS
(ISLAS CANARIAS)
(Spain)

La Palma
Santa Cruz de Tenerife
La Gomera   Tenerife
El Hierro
Gran Canaria   Las Palmas
de Gran Canaria

Tropic of Cancer

WESTERN
SAHARA

MAURITANIA

Nouâdhibou
Parc National du
Banc d'Arguin
Nouâmghar
Nouakchott

SENEGAL
Dakar
Rufisque
Mbour
Kaolack
THE
GAMBIA
Banjul
GUINEA
BISSAU
BISSAU
Conakry
SIERRA
LEONE
Freetown
LIBERIA
Monrovia

SPAIN

MOROCCO
Casablanca
Rabat
Marrakech
Agadir

Haut Atlas   High Atlas
Anti Atlas

ALGERIA

Algiers (Alger)
Oran

Grand Erg Occidental
Grand Erg Oriental

TUNISIA

S A H A R A

MALI

Bamako

BURKINA
Ouagadougou
Bobo-
Dioulasso

CÔTE
D'IVOIRE
Yamoussoukro
Abidjan

GHANA
Accra

TOGO
BENIN
Porto-
Novo
Lomé
Cotonou

NIGER

Niamey

NIGERIA
Abuja
Ibadan
Lagos

Gulf of Guinea   Bight
of Benin

CAM

EQUATORIAL
GUINEA
Bata

SÃO TOMÉ
AND PRÍNCIPE

Príncipe

São Tomé

Libreville

GAB

GULF OF GUINEA

CAPE VERDE

Santo
Antão   Ponta do Sol
Mindelo   Santa Luzia   Sal
São   Vila da
Vicente   Ribeira Brava   Santa Maria
Nicolau   Boa Vista
Vila de Sal Rei
Vila do
Tarrafal   Curral Velho
Maio
Ilhéus Secos   Porto Inglês
Brava   Fogo   Praia   São Tiago
Vila Nova   Filipe
Sintra

at the same scale

METRES   FEET
6000   19686
5000   16404
4000   13124
3000   9843
2000   6562
1000   3281
500   1640
200   656
SEA   LEVEL
200   656
2000   6562
4000   13124
6000   19686

Lambert Azimuthal Equal Area Projection

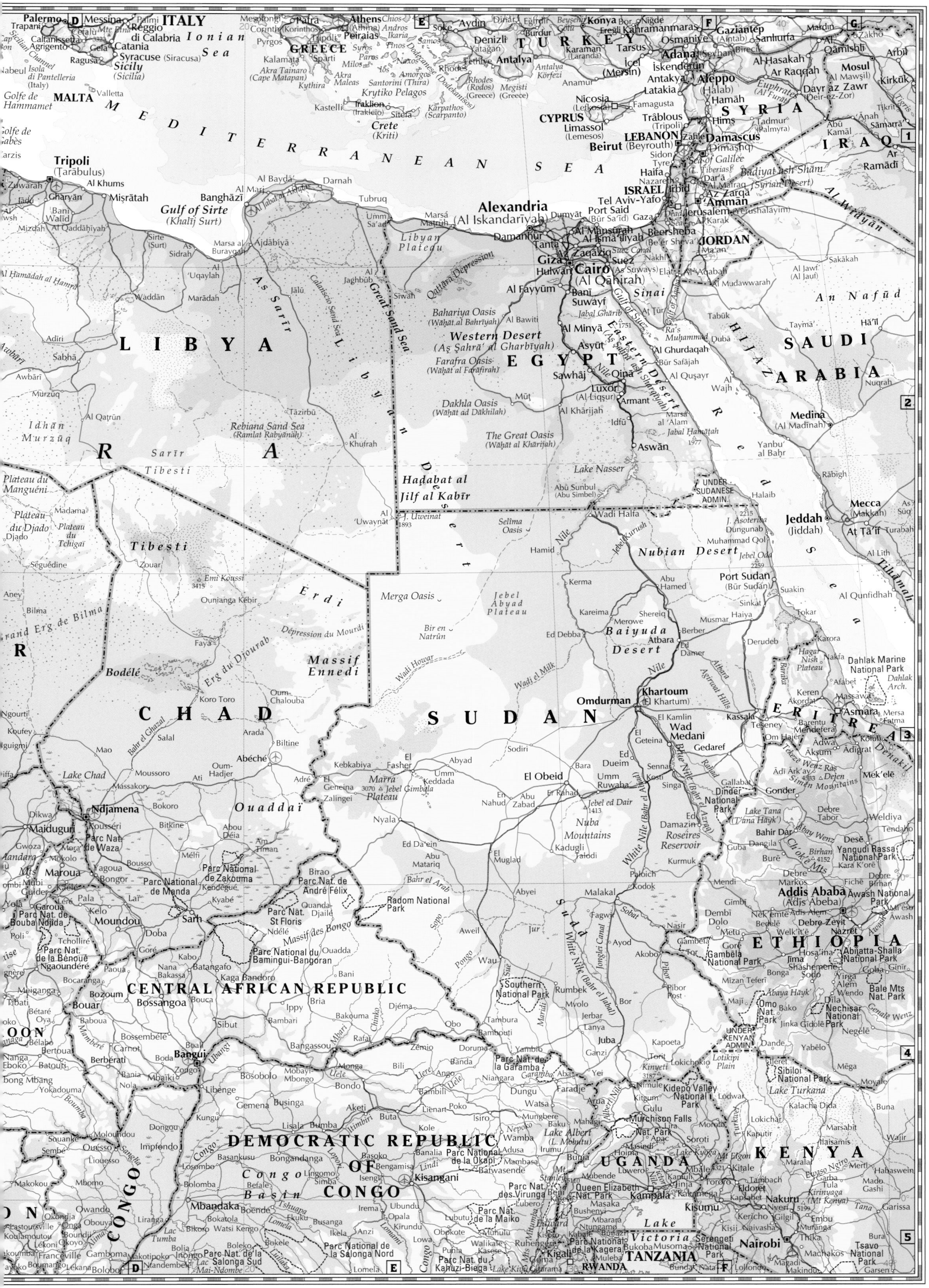

1:16M

KM   MILES
1000   600

800   500

600   400

400   200

200   100

0   0

© Collins Bartholomew Ltd

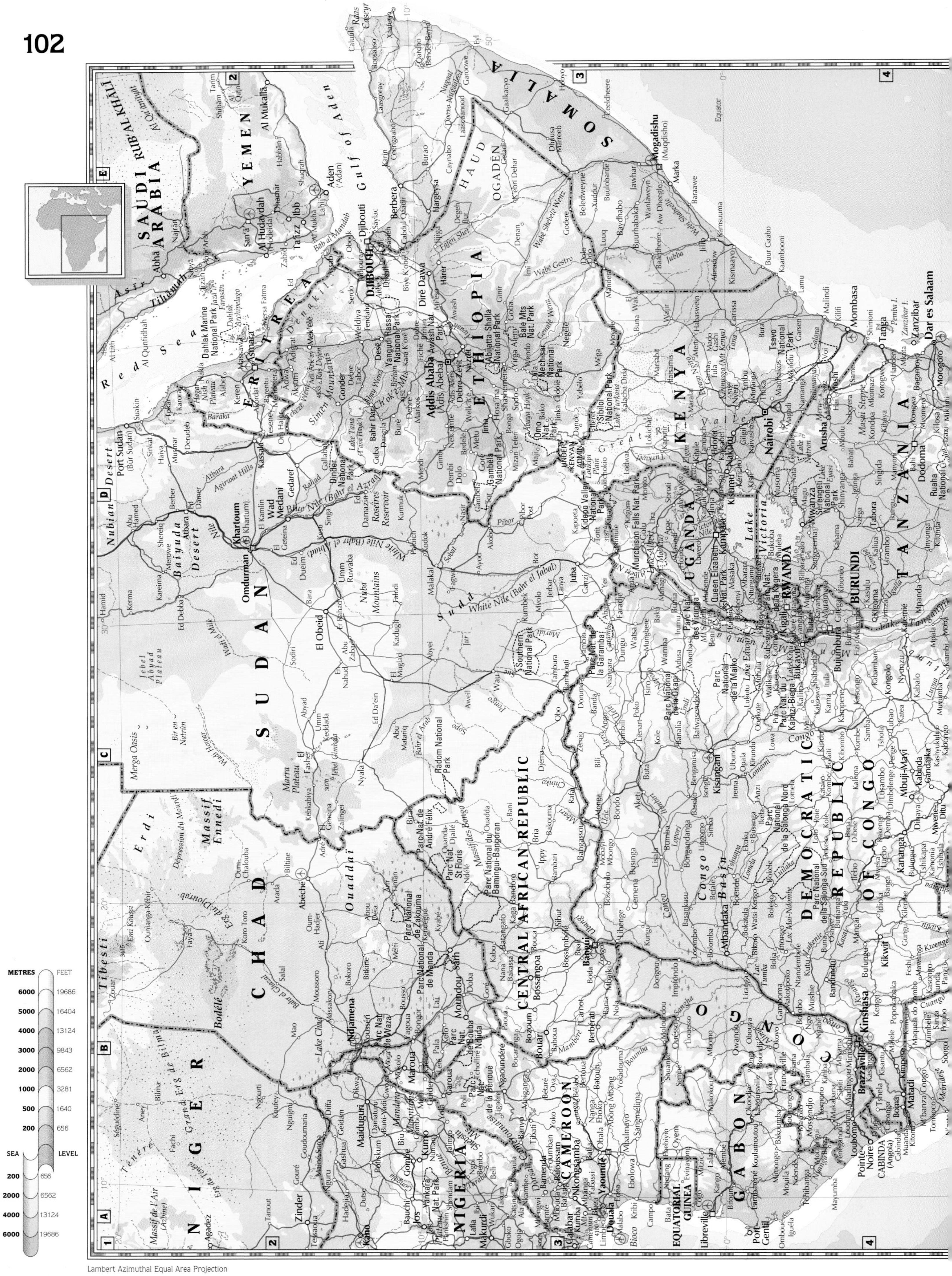

Lambert Azimuthal Equal Area Projection

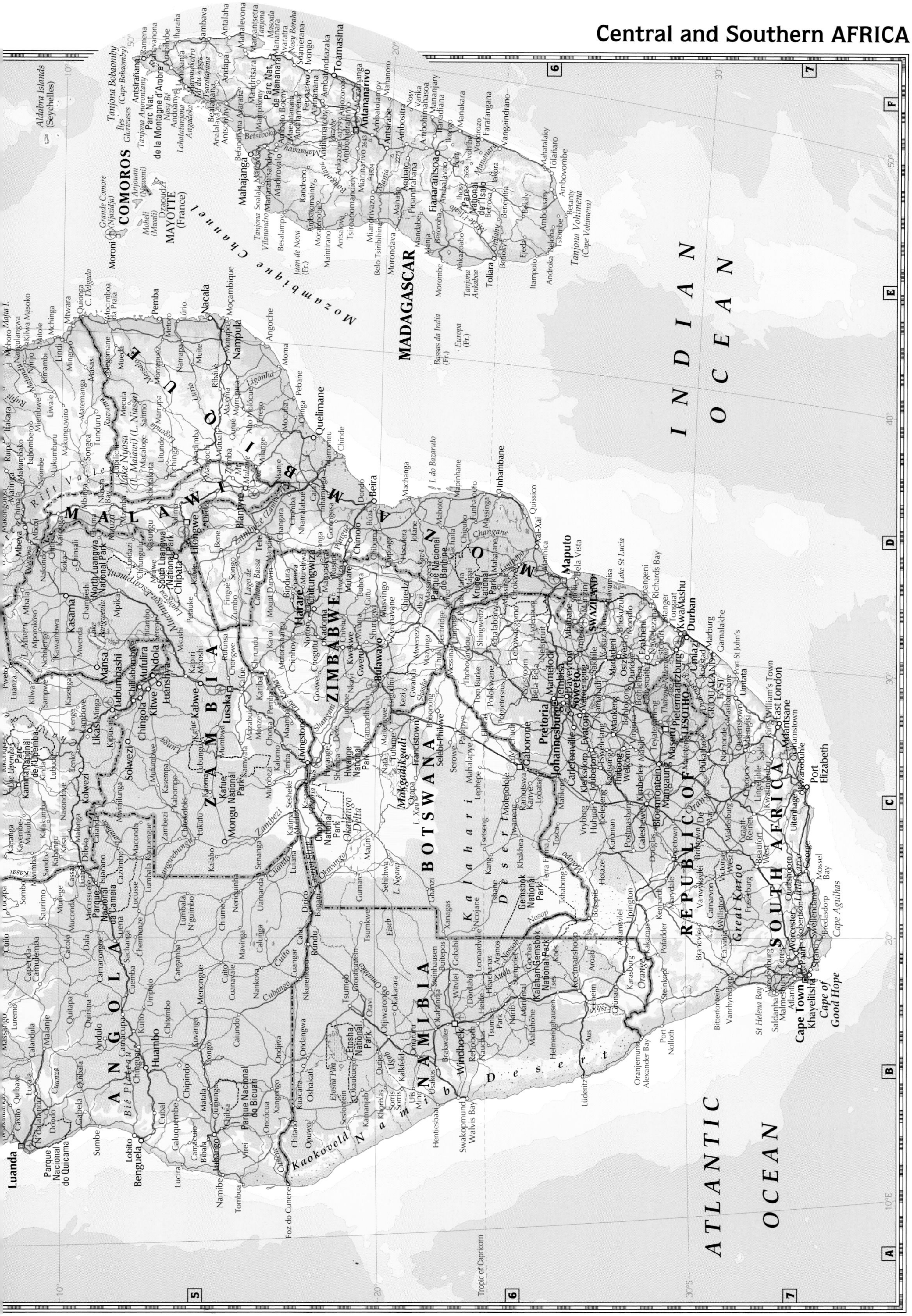

1:16M

KM	MILES
1000	600
800	500
	400
600	300
400	200
200	100
0	0

© Collins Bartholomew Ltd

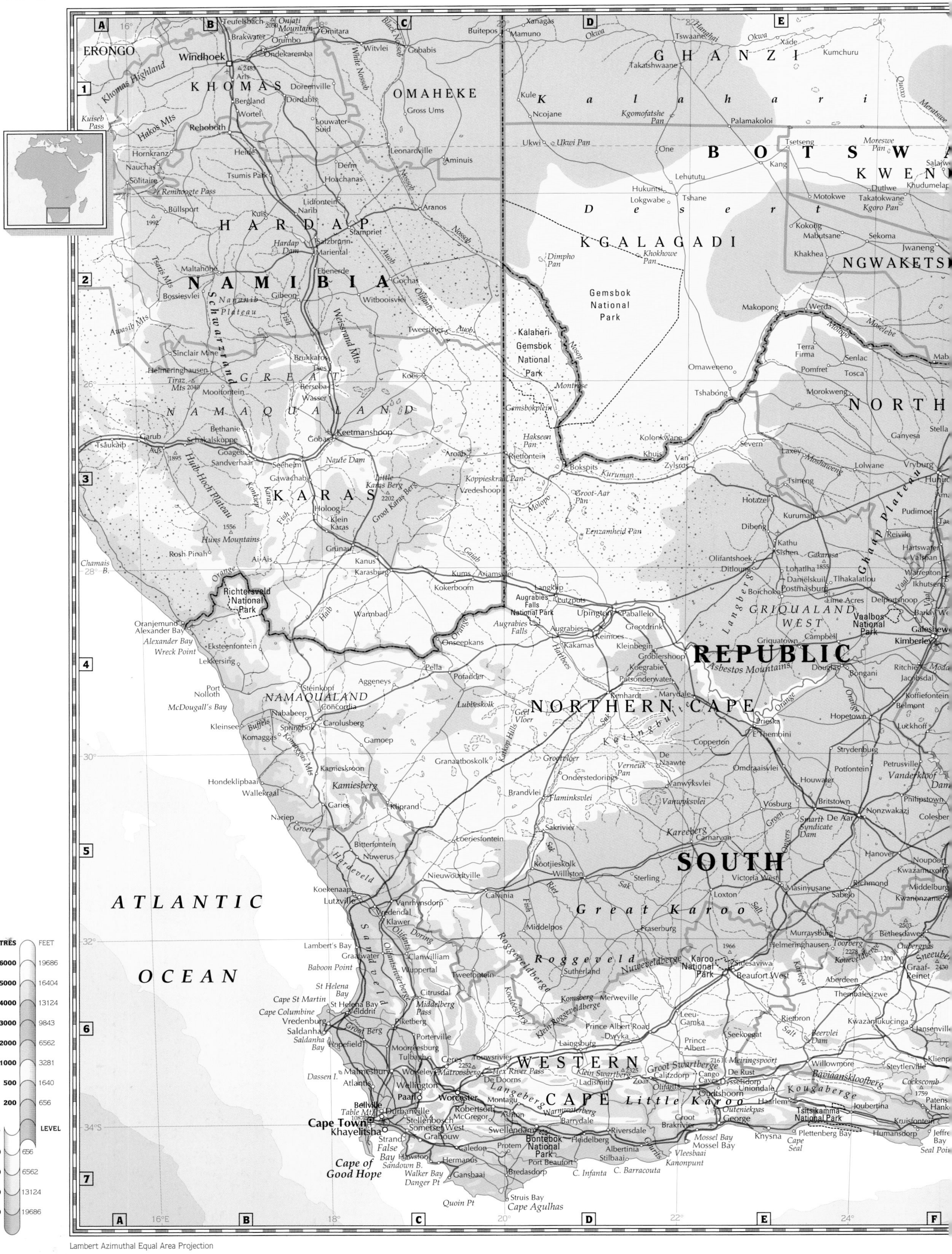
NAMIBIA
ERONGO
KHOMAS
OMAHEKE
HARDAP
KARAS
GREAT NAMAQUALAND
NAMAQUALAND
Windhoek
Rehoboth
Mariental
Keetmanshoop
Karasburg
Lüderitz
BOTSWANA
GHANZI
KGALAGADI
KWENENG
NGWAKETSE
Kalahari Desert
Gemsbok National Park
Kalahari Gemsbok National Park
Richtersveld National Park
Augrabies Falls National Park
REPUBLIC OF SOUTH AFRICA
NORTHERN CAPE
WESTERN CAPE
NORTH WEST
GRIQUALAND WEST
Great Karoo
Little Karoo
Roggeveld
Karoo National Park
Upington
Kimberley
Springbok
Calvinia
Beaufort West
Worcester
Paarl
Bellville
Cape Town
Khayelitsha
Stellenbosch
George
Mossel Bay
Oudtshoorn
Cape of Good Hope
Cape Agulhas
Bontebok National Park
Tsitsikamma National Park
Vaalbos National Park
ATLANTIC OCEAN
Orange
METRES
FEET
6000
19686
5000
16404
4000
13124
3000
9843
2000
6562
1000
3281
500
1640
200
656
SEA
LEVEL

Lambert Azimuthal Equal Area Projection

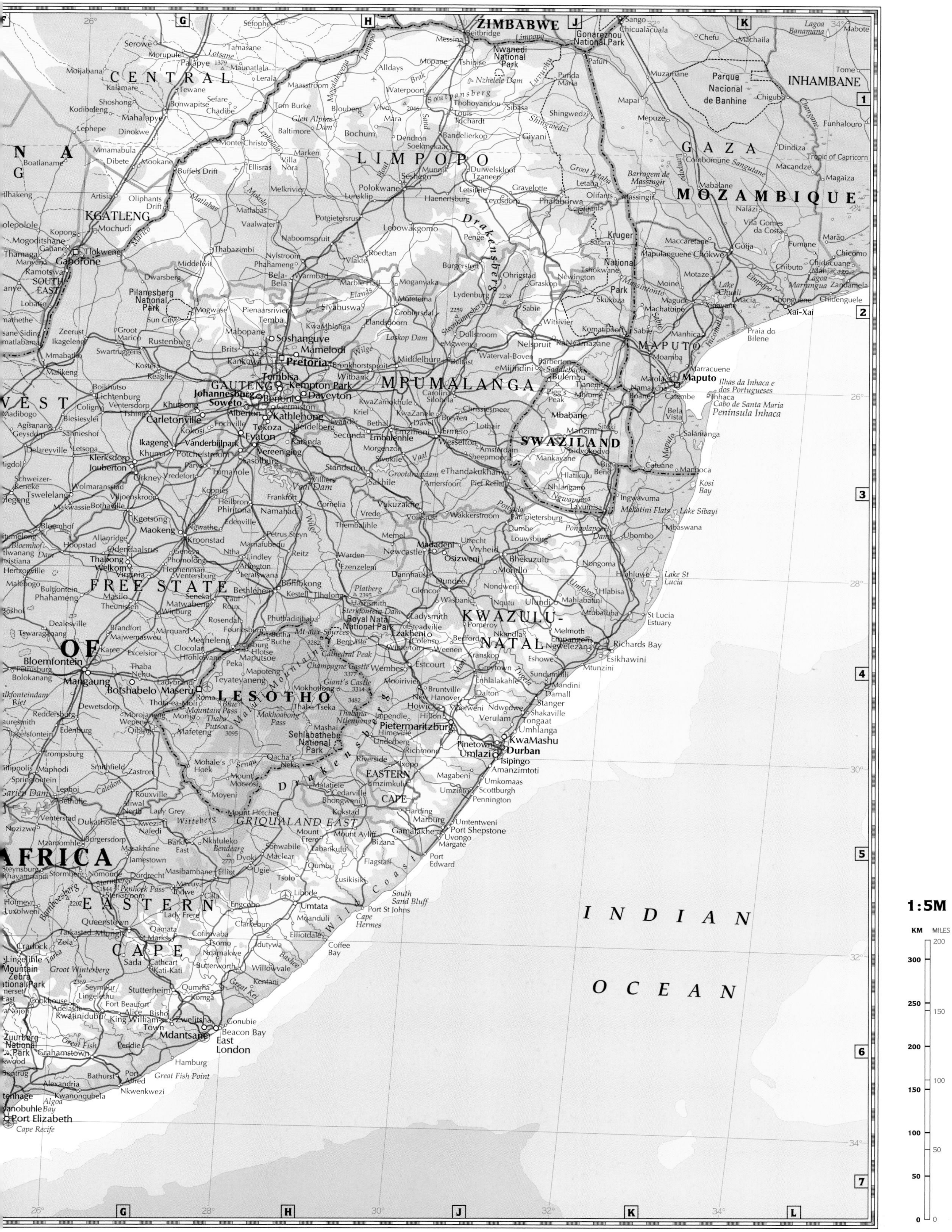
ZIMBABWE
MOZAMBIQUE
SWAZILAND
LESOTHO
LIMPOPO
MPUMALANGA
GAUTENG
KWAZULU-NATAL
FREE STATE
EASTERN CAPE
GAZA
MAPUTO
INHAMBANE
CENTRAL
KGATLENG
INDIAN OCEAN
Pretoria
Johannesburg
Soweto
Maputo
Durban
Pietermaritzburg
Bloemfontein
Maseru
Mbabane
Port Elizabeth
East London
Mdantsane
Umtata
Richards Bay
Gaborone
Drakensberg
Kruger National Park
Gonarezhou National Park
Parque Nacional de Banhine
Royal Natal National Park
Sehlabathebe National Park
Pilanesberg National Park
Wild Coast
Tropic of Capricorn
1:5M
KM
MILES
300
250
200
150
100
50
0
200
150
100
50
0

CONTINENTAL FACTS
TOTAL POPULATION
29,465,000
LARGEST COUNTRY POPULATION
AUSTRALIA 18,520,000
LARGEST COUNTRY AREA
AUSTRALIA
7,682,395 sq km 2,966,189 sq miles
LARGEST CITY POPULATION
SYDNEY, Australia 3,665,000

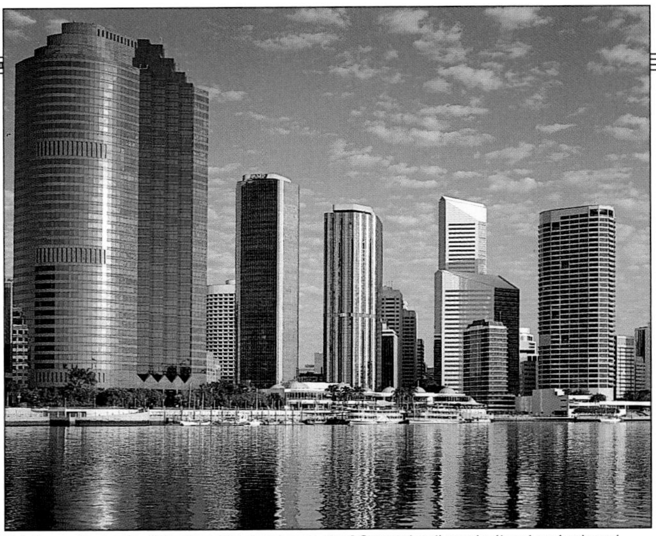

Brisbane, Australia. Following the development of Queensland's agricultural and mineral industries, its capital has become the third-largest city in Australia.

MARSHALL ISLANDS
REPUBLIC
Area: 181 sq km
(70 sq mls)
Population: 60,000
Capital: Delap-Uliga-Djarrit
Language: Marshallese, English
Religion: Protestant, R.Catholic
Currency: US dollar

SOLOMON ISLANDS
MONARCHY
Area: 28,370 sq km
(10,954 sq mls)
Population: 417,000
Capital: Honiara
Language: English, Solomon
Islands Pidgin,
Local Languages
Religion: Protestant, R.Catholic
Currency: Solomon Islands
dollar

FIJI
REPUBLIC
Area: 18,330 sq km
(7,077 sq mls)
Population: 796,000
Capital: Suva
Language: English, Fijian, Hindi
Religion: Protestant, Hindu,
R.Catholic,
Sunni Muslim
Currency: Fiji dollar

Wake I.
(U.S.A.)

Pagan

Northern Mariana
Islands
(U.S.A.)

Saipan
Rota Tinian

MARSHALL

ISLANDS
Bikini

Ratak Chain

Ralik Chain

Gaferut
Pikelot
Hall Is

Yap
Chuuk
Pohnpei
Palikir

Kosrae

Delap-Uliga-Djarrit

PALAU
C a r o l i n e   I s l a n d s

Nomoi Is

FEDERATED STATES OF MICRONESIA

Bairiki

Howland I.
(U.S.A.)
Baker I. (U.S.A.)

Gilbert
Islands

Yaren
NAURU

Phoenix Islands

Admiralty Is
New Ireland

K I R I B A T I

Wewak Bismarck
Sea Rabaul
Madang Sea

New

New Britain

Bougainville

Nanumea
Niutao

Tokelau
(N.Z.)

Mt Wilhelm
△4509 Lae
PAPUA

G u
i n e a

TUVALU Vaitupu
Nukufetau Vaiaku

Vaitupu

NEW GUINEA

Solomon

SOLOMON

Nukulaelae

G. of
Papua
Daru

Sea

Honiara
Malaita
Guadalcanal

ISLANDS

Santa Cruz
Is

Rotuma

American
Samoa

Port
Moresby

SAMOA
Savai'i
Apia
Upolu

Dange

Torres Strait

Manua Is
Tutuila

Banks Is

Wallis
and Futuna Is
(Fr.)

Melville I.
Bathurst I.
Darwin

Gulf of
Carpentaria

Timor Sea
C. Londonderry

Great Barrier Reef

Coral Sea
Islands
Territory
(Aust.)

C o r a l

S e a

Espiritu Santo
Malakula
VANUATU
Éfaté
Port Vila

Vanua Levu

FIJI
Viti Levu Suva

Vavau
Group

Palmersto

Niue (N.Z.)

C. Lévêque
Broome

Cairns

Tanna

New Caledonia
(Fr.)

Loyalty Is

Nouméa

TONGA
Nuku'alofa
Tongatapu
Group

Port Hedland
Barrow I.
North West C.

NORTHERN

TERRITORY **QUEENSLAND**
Alice
Springs

Townsville

Mackay

Rockhampton

S O U T H   P A C I F

Great Sandy
Desert

A U S

Charleville

Brisbane

Norfolk I.
(Aust.)

Raoul

WESTERN
Geraldton

T R A L I A

Kermadec Is
(N.Z.)

Kalgoorlie

AUSTRALIA

SOUTH

AUSTRALIA

Darling

Lord Howe I
(Aust.)

Great Barrier I.

Auckland

Port Augusta
Port
Pirie

NEW SOUTH
Newcastle

Rotorua
North
Island

Perth
Fremantle

Great
Australian

WALES
Sydney

A.C.T.
Adelaide Albury Canberra

T A S M A N

Blenheim
South Wellington

Chatham Is
(N.Z.)

Albany

Bight
Kangaroo I.

Murray
VICTORIA
Melbourne

S E A

Island

Christchurch

C. Leeuwin

Geelong
Bass
Strait
Launceston

NEW
Dunedin
ZEALAND

Hobart **TASMANIA**

Stewart I.

Bounty Is

Antipodes Is

Auckland Is

Campbell I.
(N.Z.)

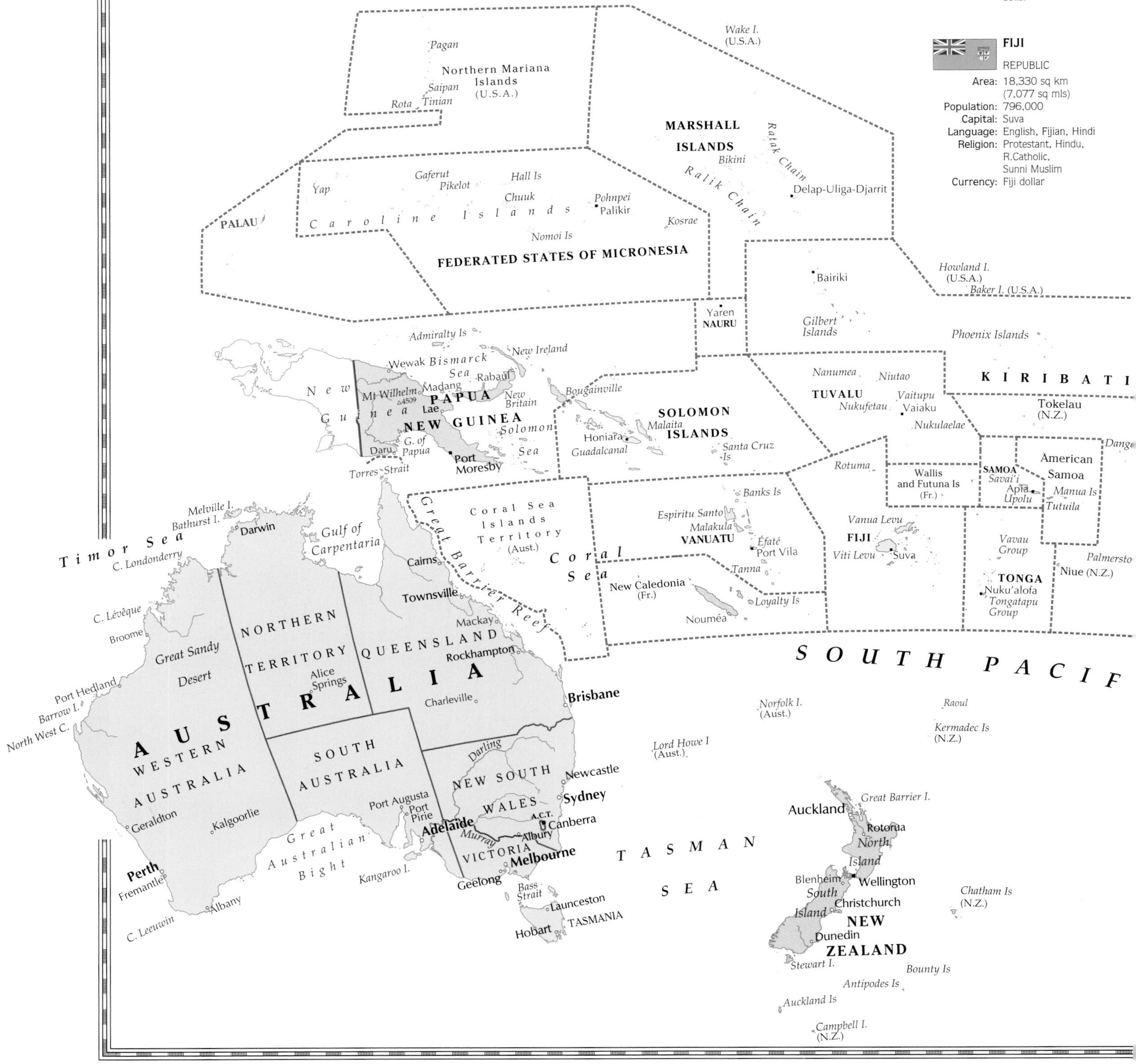

FED. STATES OF MICRONESIA
REPUBLIC
Area: 701 sq km
(271 sq mls)
Population: 114,000
Capital: Palikir
Language: English, Trukese,
Pohnpeian,
Local Languages
Religion: Protestant, R.Catholic
Currency: US dollar

PAPUA NEW GUINEA
MONARCHY
Area: 462,840 sq km
(178,704 sq mls)
Population: 4,600,000
Capital: Port Moresby
Language: English,
Tok Pisin (Pidgin),
Local Languages
Religion: Protestant, R.Catholic,
Traditional Beliefs
Currency: Kina

NAURU
REPUBLIC
Area: 21 sq km
(8 sq mls)
Population: 11,000
Capital: Yaren
Language: Nauruan,
Kiribati (Gilbertese,)
English
Religion: Protestant, R.Catholic
Currency: Australian dollar

KIRIBATI
REPUBLIC
Area: 717 sq km
(277 sq mls)
Population: 81,000
Capital: Bairiki
Language: Kiribati (Gilbertese),
English
Religion: R.Catholic, Protestant,
Baha'i, Mormon
Currency: Australian dollar

TONGA
MONARCHY
Area: 748 sq km
(289 sq mls)
Population: 98,000
Capital: Nuku'alofa
Language: Tongan, English
Religion: Protestant, R.Catholic,
Mormon
Currency: Pa'anga

TUVALU
MONARCHY
Area: 25 sq km
(10 sq mls)
Population: 11,000
Capital: Vaiaku
Language: Tuvaluan,
English (official)
Religion: Protestant
Currency: Australian dollar

VANUATU
REPUBLIC
Area: 12,190 sq km
(4,707 sq mls)
Population: 182,000
Capital: Port Vila
Language: English, Bislama
(English Creole),
French (all official)
Religion: Protestant, R.Catholic,
Traditional Beliefs
Currency: Vatu

SAMOA
MONARCHY
Area: 2,831 sq km
(1,093 sq mls)
Population: 174,000
Capital: Apia
Language: Samoan, English
Religion: Protestant, R.Catholic,
Sunni Muslim
Currency: Tala

POPULATION

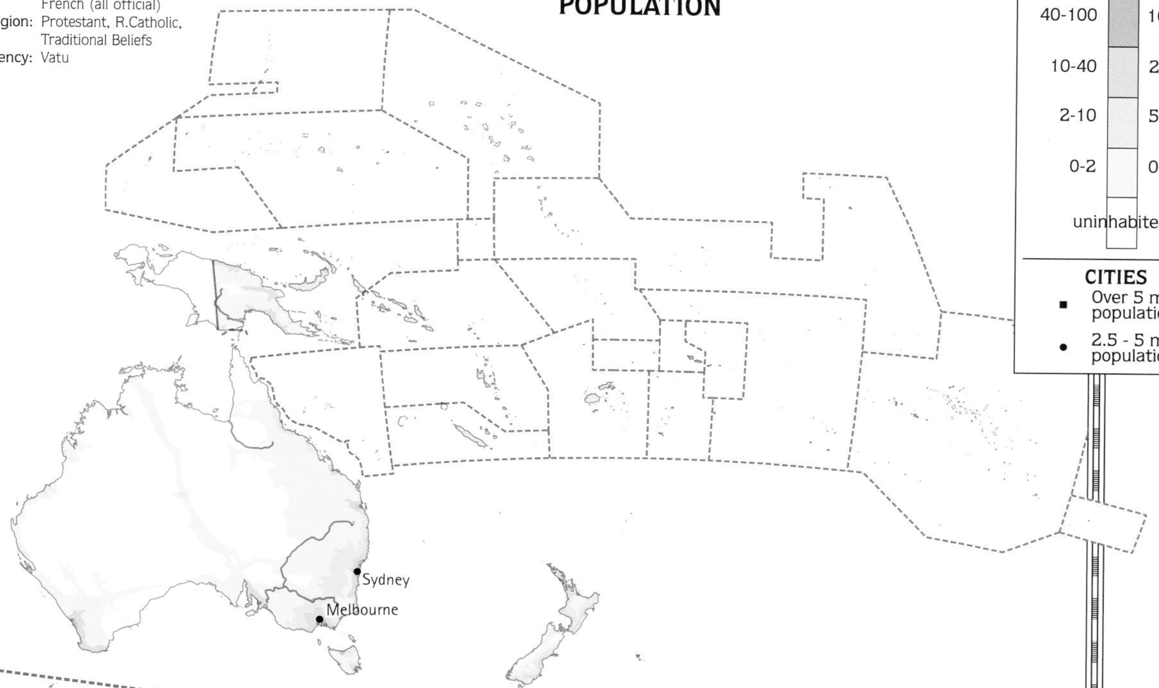

POPULATION
Inhabitants

per sq km	per sq ml
over 200	over 500
100-200	250-500
40-100	100-250
10-40	25-100
2-10	5-25
0-2	0-5
uninhabited	

CITIES
■ Over 5 million
population
● 2.5 - 5 million
population

Palmyra Atoll (U.S.A.)
Teraina
Tabuaeran
Kiritimati
vis I.
.S.A.)
Malden I.
Starbuck I.
Tongareva
Manihiki
(New Zealand)
vorov I.
Motu One
Rangiroa
Îles du Désappointement
Aitutaki
Papeete Tahiti
ok Is
Society Islands
F r e n c h
Tuamotu Archipelago
Hao
N.Z.)
otonga
P o l y n e s i a
Mururoa
Groupe Actéon
Tubuai Islands
Îles Gambier
Rapa
Henderson I.
(U.K.) Pitcairn I.
O C E A N

Sydney
Melbourne

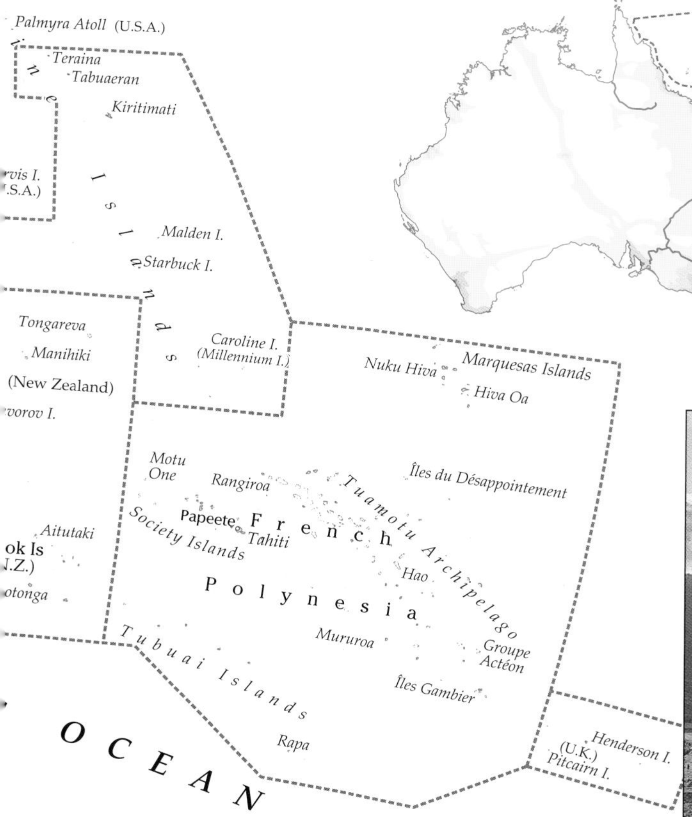

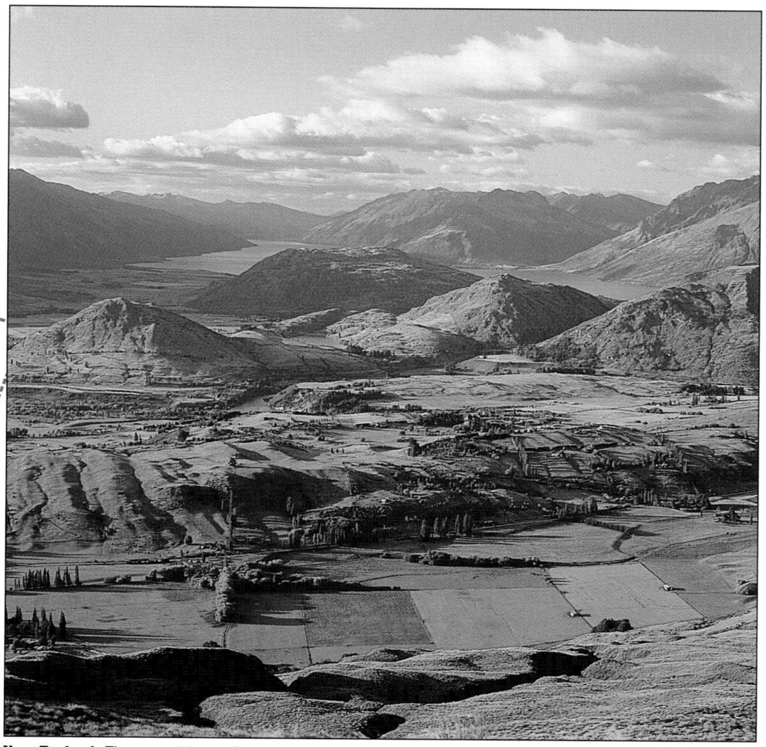

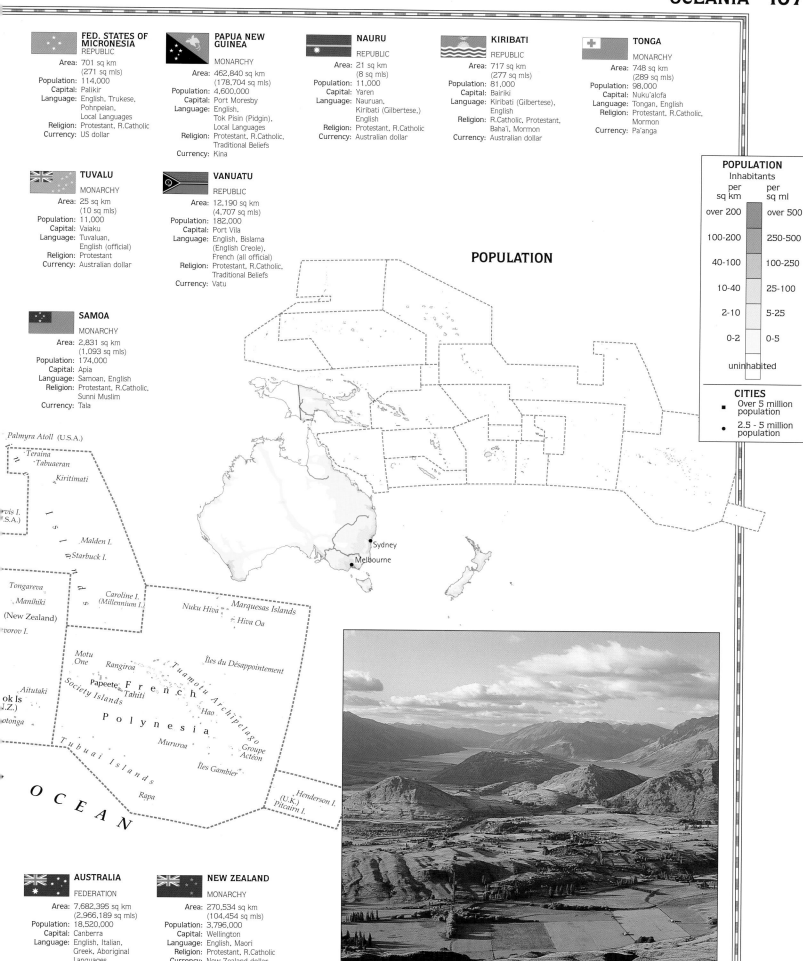

New Zealand. The mountainous South Island is fringed by extensive plains where cereals are grown and huge flocks of sheep are grazed.

AUSTRALIA
FEDERATION
Area: 7,682,395 sq km
(2,966,189 sq mls)
Population: 18,520,000
Capital: Canberra
Language: English, Italian,
Greek, Aboriginal
Languages
Religion: Protestant, R.Catholic,
Orthodox, Aboriginal
beliefs
Currency: Australian dollar

NEW ZEALAND
MONARCHY
Area: 270,534 sq km
(104,454 sq mls)
Population: 3,796,000
Capital: Wellington
Language: English, Maori
Religion: Protestant, R.Catholic
Currency: New Zealand dollar

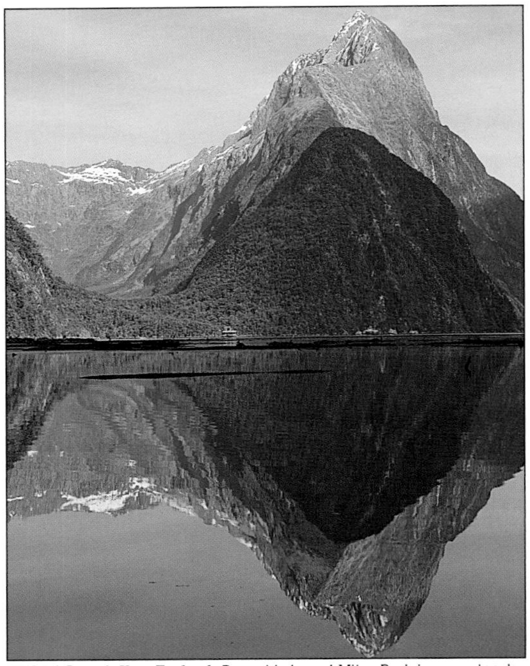

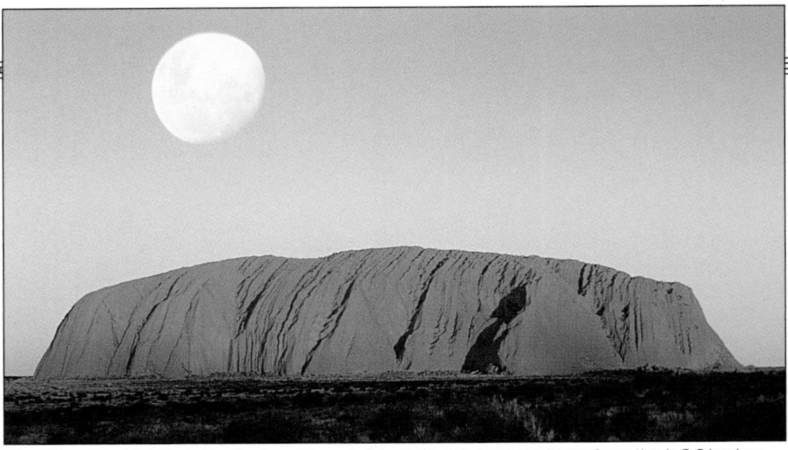

Uluru (Ayers Rock). Situated in the desert in central Australia, this huge sandstone formation is 3.6 km long and rises 348m above the surrounding area. It is famous for changing colour with the light.

Milford Sound, New Zealand. Pyramid-shaped Mitre Peak is a spectacular landmark in this 16km fjord which is up to 265m deep.

CONTINENTAL FACTS
TOTAL AREA
8,400,866 sq km   3,243,593 sq miles
HIGHEST PEAK, MT WILHELM
4,509 m   14,793 ft
LARGEST LAKE, EYRE (salt)
0 to 8,900 sq km   0 to 3,436 sq miles
LONGEST RIVER, MURRAY-DARLING
3,750 km   2,330 miles

Wake I.

Saipan
Rota   Tinian

Marshal
Islands
Bikini
Ralik Chain
Ratak Chain

Gaferut
Pikelot   Hall Is
Yap   Chuuk   Pohnpei
Palau   Caroline Islands   Kosrae
Nomoi Is

Howland I.
Baker I.

Nauru   Banaba   Nonouti   Beru
Tabiteuea   Nukunau
Onotoa
Gilbert   Arorae
Islands
Phoenix Islands   Kanton
McKean   Rawaki
Nikumaroro   Manra
Orona

Admiralty Is   New Hanover
Bismarck   New Ireland
Sea   Tauu Is   Nukumanu Is
New
Britain   Bougainville   Solomon
New   Islands
Georgia   Choiseul   Santa Isabel
Malaita
Guadalcanal
San Cristobal

Nanumea
Nanumanga   Niutao
Nui   Vaitupu
Nukufetau
Funafuti   Nukulaelae   Nukunono
Niulakita

Atafu   Tokelau
Fakaofo
Swains I.   Danger

New
Guinea   Mt Wilhelm
Mt Victoria
Owen Stanley
Range
G. of
Papua
Torres Strait
C. York
Louisiade Arch.

Solomon
Sea

Santa Cruz
Is

Rotuma   Íles Wallis
Íles de Hoorn

Samoa
Islands   Nass
Savai'i
Upolu   Manua Is   Rose I.
Tutuila

TIMOR
SEA
C. Londonderry   Melville I.
Bathurst I.   C. Arnhem   Gulf
Arnhem   of
Land   Carpentaria   Cape
York   Wellesley Is
Peninsula

Great Barrier Reef

CORAL
SEA

Banks Is
Espiritu Santo
Malakula   Éfaté
Erromango
Tanna   Anatom

Vanua Levu   Niuatoputopu
Fiji   Koro
Viti Levu   Gau
Kadavu
Ono-i-Lau

Tafahi
Vavau
Group   Niue   Palmersto

Tongatapu
'Ata   Group

New Caledonia   Loyalty Is

SOUTH   PACI

C. Levêque   Kimberley
Plateau   Lake
Argyle
Mitchell
Flinders

Eighty Mile Beach
Barrow I.
North West C.   Hamersley
Range
Ashburton   Gibson
Desert   Great Sandy
Desert
Macdonnell
Ranges   867
Uluru
(Ayers Rock)   Simpson
Desert

Great   Lake
Eyre
Lake
Torrens

Great Victoria Desert

Darling   Great Dividing Range

Norfolk I.   Raoul
Kermadec Is

Lord Howe I.

Great Barrier I.
North
Island

C. Leeuwin   Nullarbor Plain
Great
Australian
Bight   Kangaroo I.
Murray   Mt Kosciuszko
2230

TASMAN
SEA

South
Island   Southern Alps   Chatham Is

Bass
Strait   Flinders I.
King I.   Tasmania

Pitt I.

Snares Is   Stewart I.   Bounty Is
Antipodes Is

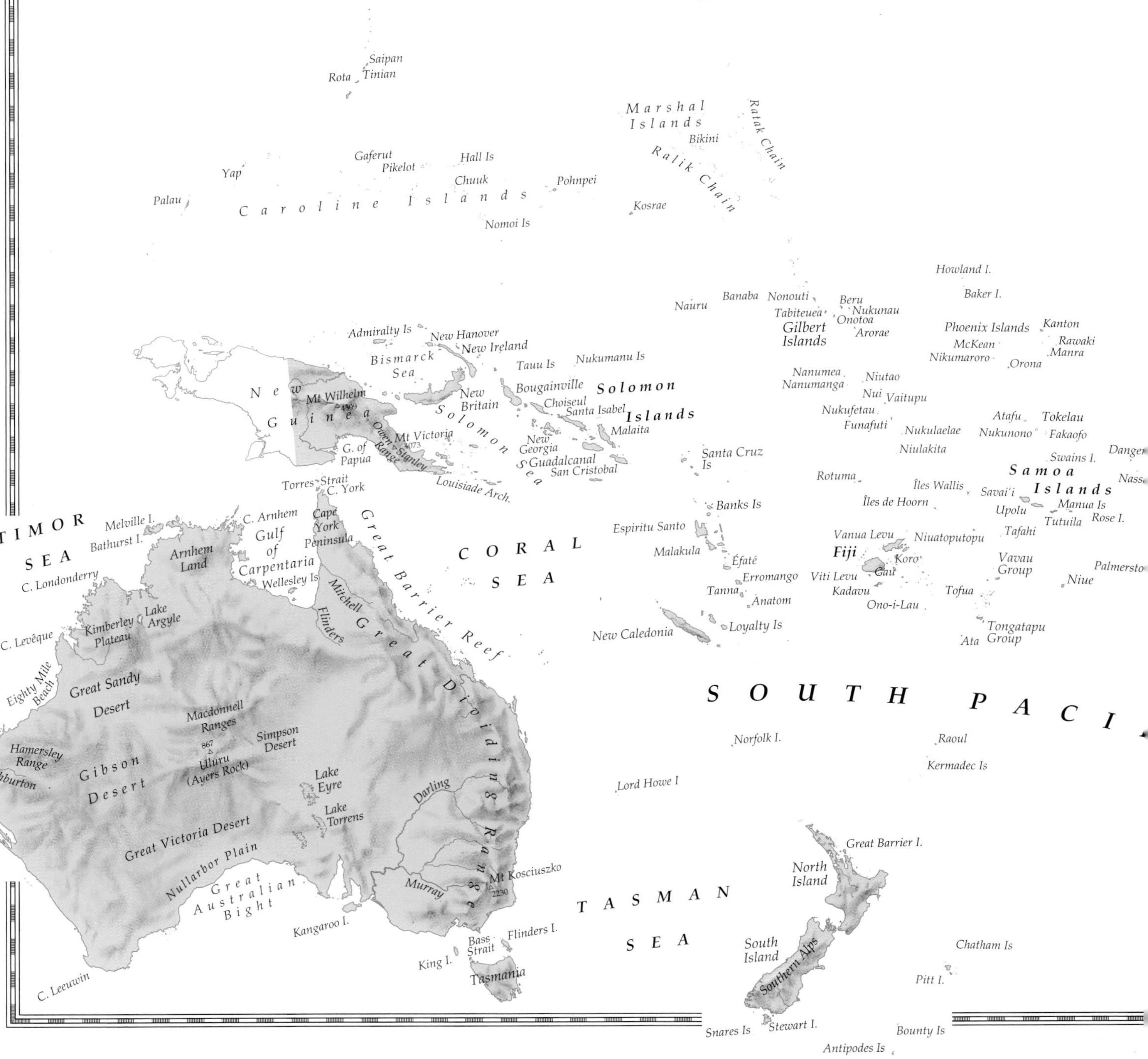

CLIMATE

Suva

Darwin

Rain
mm
Temp
°C

average monthly
temperature

colour refers to
climate type
shown on map

average monthly
rainfall

Mackay

CLIMATE TYPES

WARMER HUMID

Temperate

Humid
subtropical

Mediterranean

DRY

Steppe

Desert

TROPICAL HUMID

Savanna

Rain forest

Darwin

Mackay

Suva

Alice Springs

Bourke

Perth

Wellington

Bourke

Perth

Alice Springs

Wellington

Palmyra Atoll
Teraina
Tabuaeran
Kiritimati
arvis I.
Malden I.
Starbuck I.
Tongareva
Caroline I.
(Millennium I.)
Rakahanga
Manihiki
Vostok I.
Nuku Hiva
Marquesas Islands
Flint I.
Hiva Oa
vorov I.

Motu
One
Rangiroa
Îles du Désappointement
Fenua Ura
Raroia
Pukapuka
Raiatea
Huahine
Fakarava
ok Is
Hervey Is
Tahiti
Anaa
Hao
Aitutaki
Atiu
Mauke
Méhétia
Hérehérétué
rotonga
Îles Maria
Mangaia
Rurutu
Mururoa
Rimatara
Tubuai
Groupe
Actéon
Raivavae
Îles Gambier

Society Islands

Tuamotu Archipelago

Tubuai Islands

Oeno
Henderson I.
Rapa
Marotiri
Pitcairn I.
Ducie I.

C
O C E A N

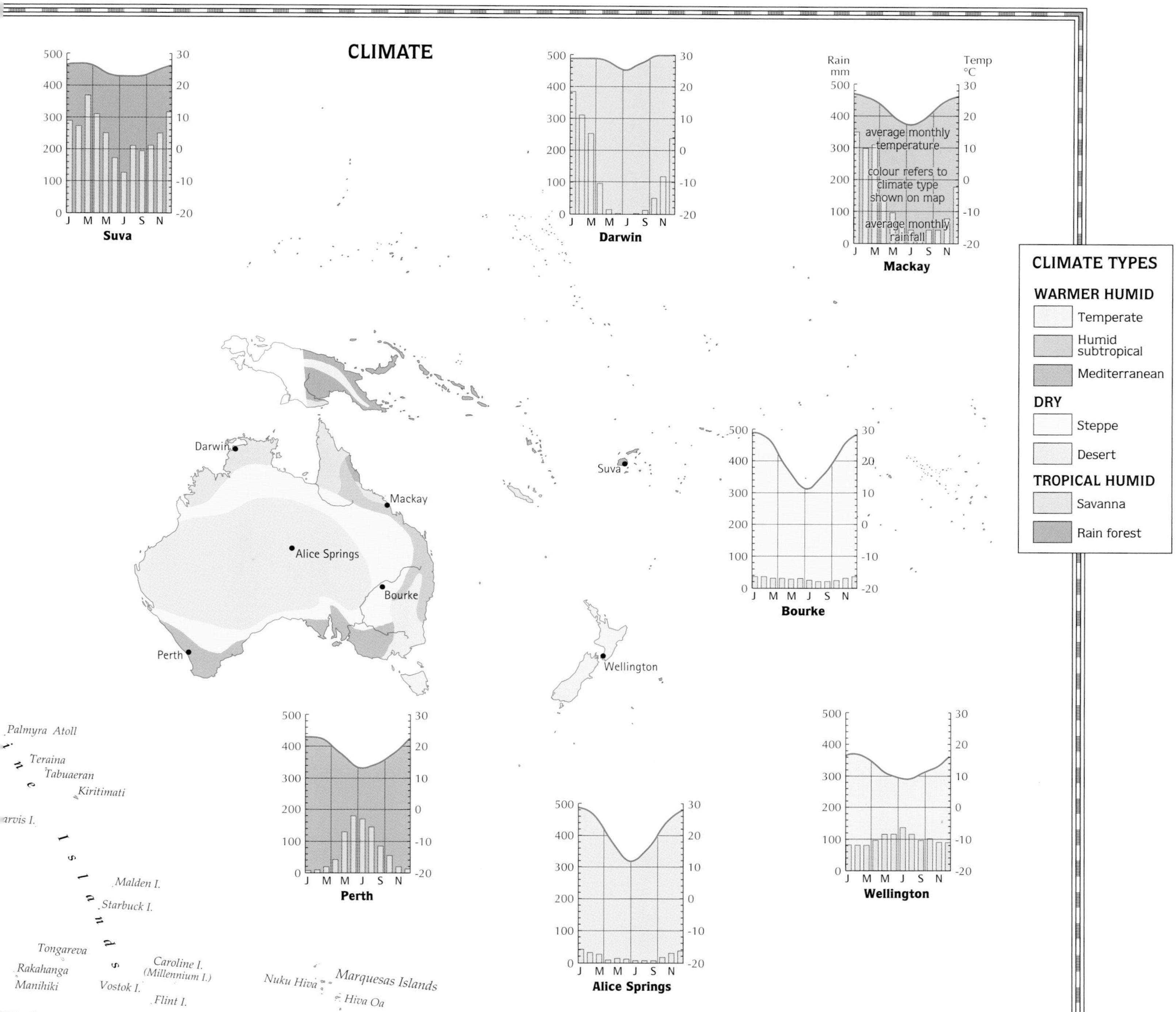

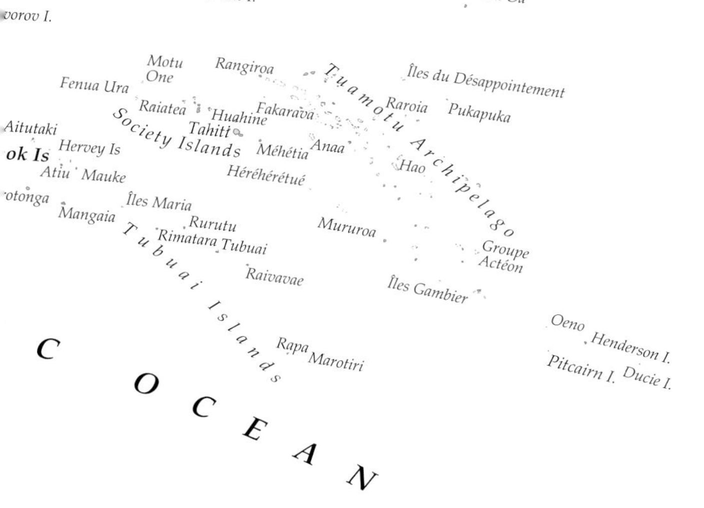

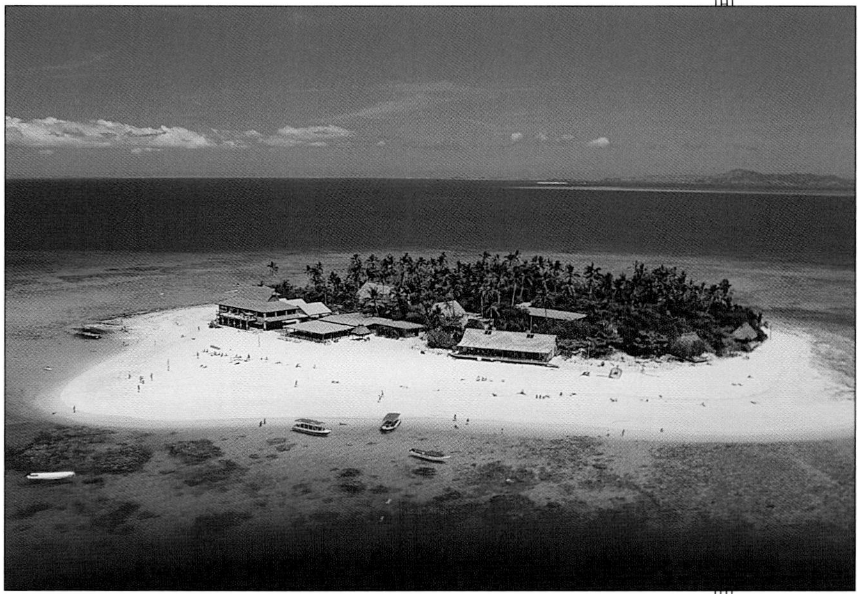

Beachcomber Island, Fiji. Tourists are attracted to the sandy beach and beautiful coral reef which surround the island.

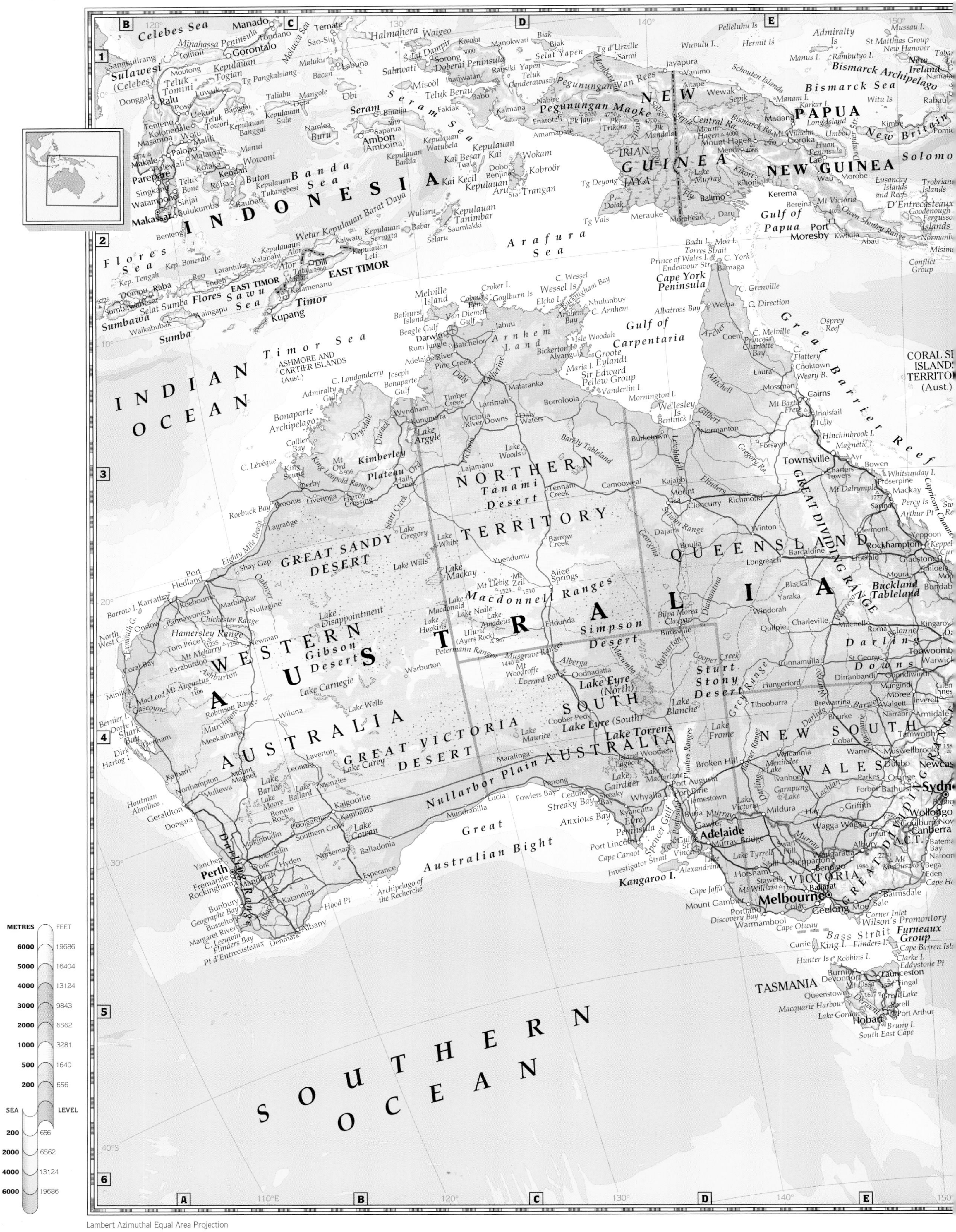
INDONESIA
AUSTRALIA
NORTHERN TERRITORY
WESTERN AUSTRALIA
SOUTH AUSTRALIA
QUEENSLAND
NEW SOUTH WALES
VICTORIA
TASMANIA
PAPUA NEW GUINEA
NEW GUINEA
IRIAN JAYA
EAST TIMOR
INDIAN OCEAN
SOUTHERN OCEAN
Timor Sea
Arafura Sea
Banda Sea
Flores Sea
Seram Sea
Celebes Sea
Bismarck Sea
Coral Sea Islands Territory (Aust.)
Gulf of Carpentaria
Great Australian Bight
Bass Strait
Great Barrier Reef
Great Dividing Range
Great Sandy Desert
Great Victoria Desert
Gibson Desert
Simpson Desert
Tanami Desert
Sturt Stony Desert
Nullarbor Plain
Kimberley Plateau
Cape York Peninsula
Arnhem Land
Macdonnell Ranges
Lake Eyre (North)
Lake Eyre (South)
Lake Torrens
Darwin
Perth
Adelaide
Melbourne
Canberra
Hobart
Townsville
Rockhampton
Alice Springs
Kalgoorlie
Port Moresby
Sulawesi (Celebes)
Timor
Sumba
Sumbawa
Kangaroo I.
METRES
FEET
6000
19686
5000
16404
4000
13124
3000
9843
2000
6562
1000
3281
500
1640
200
656
SEA
LEVEL

Lambert Azimuthal Equal Area Projection

KIRIBATI

Lyra Reef
Tanga Is
Nuguria Is
Feni Is
Kilinailau Is
C. St George
Buka I.
Sohano
Bougainville Island
Arawa
Treasury
Choiseul
Vella Lavella
New Georgia Is
Kolombangara
New Georgia Is (Solomon Is)
Rendova
Russell Is
Woodlark I.
Honiara
Guadalcanal
Avuavu
San Cristobal
Santa Ana
Rennell
Louisiade Arch.
Rossel I.
Tagula I.

Nukumanu Is (Mortlock Is)
Tauu Islands
Ontong Java Atoll
Roncador Reef
Santa Isabel
Buala
Malu'u
Malaita
Maramasike
Ulawa I.
Kirakira
Stewart Is
Florida Is
New Sound
Marovo

SOLOMON ISLANDS

Duff Is
Nupani
Swallow Is
Ndeni
Santa Cruz Islands (Solomon Is)
Utupua
Cherry Island
Vanikoro Is
Tikopia
Mitre Island

SEA

CORAL SEA

Torres Islands
Uréparapara
Vanua Lava
Banks Islands
Santa María I.
Espíritu Santo
Mt Tabwémasana 1879
Aoba
Maéwo
Malo
Pentecost I.
Norsup
Ambrym
Malakula
Émaé
Epi
Shepherd Is
Efaté
Port Vila
Erromango
Tanna
Aniwa
Anatom (Vanuatu)
Futuna

VANUATU

Îles Chesterfield (New Caledonia)
Récifs d'Entrecasteaux
Îles Bélep
Grand Passage
Récif des Français
Grand Récif de Cook
Koumac
Ouvéa
Îs Loyauté (Loyalty Is) (Fr.)
Lifou
Tadine
Yaté
Maré
Nouméa
Grand Récif du Sud
Î. des Pins

NEW CALEDONIA (NOUVELLE CALÉDONIE) (Fr.)

I. de Sable

Matthew I. (Fr.)
Hunter I. (Fr.)
Ceva-i-Ra (Fiji)

Rotuma (Fiji)

WALLIS AND FUTUNA IS (Fr.)
Îles Wallis
Îles de Hoorn

SAMOA
Savai'i
Apia
Upolu
Tutuila (U.S.A.)

Yasawa Group
Great Sea Reef
Labasma
Bligh Water
Vanua Levu
Koro
Lautoka
Tomaniivi 1324
Koro Sea
Viti Levu
Ovalau
Suva
Beqa
Gau
Kadavu Passage
Moala
Lakeba
Kadavu
Matuku

FIJI

Niuatoputopu (Tonga)
Tafahi (Tonga)

Vava'u Group
Tofua
TONGA

Ono-i-Lau (Fiji)

Ata (Tonga)

NIUE (N.Z.)

Nanumea
Nanumanga
Niutao
Nui
Vaitupu
Nukufetau
Funafuti
Vaiaku
Nukulaelae
Niulakita

TUVALU

Atafu
TOKELAU (N.Z.)
Nukunonu
Fakaofo

Equator

Gilbert Islands (Kiribati)
Nonouti
Tabiteuea
Beru
Nikunau
Onotoa
Nikunau
Tamana
Arorae
Kingsmill Group

Howland Island (U.S.A.)
Baker Island (U.S.A.)

Phoenix Islands
McKean
Nikumaroro
Orona (Kiribati)
Kanton
Manra

NAURU
Yaren
Banaba (Kiribati)
Aránuka

SOUTH PACIFIC OCEAN

Sandy Cape
Hervey Bay
Fraser Island
Maryborough
Gympie
Tewantin
Nambour
Caboolture
Brisbane
Beenleigh
Gold Coast
Byron Bay
Ballina
Casino
Grafton
Coffs Harbour
Macksville
Port Macquarie
Taree

Lord Howe Island (Aust.)

Norfolk Island (Aust.)

Raoul
Kermadec Is (N.Z.)

Horizon Deep •10882
Tropic of Capricorn

TASMAN SEA

Three Kings Is
Cape Maria van Diemen
North Cape
Whangarei
Kaipara Harbour
Takapuna
Manukau
Auckland
Great Barrier Island
Bay of Plenty
Tauranga
Hamilton
Tokoroa
East Cape
1754 Hikurangi
Gisborne
Lake Taupo
Napier
Wairoa
Mahia Peninsula
Hawke Bay
Hastings
Palmerston North
Masterton
Nelson
Lower Hutt
Wellington
Cape Palliser
Blenheim
NORTH ISLAND
North Taranaki Bight
New Plymouth
Mt Taranaki (Mt Egmont)
South Taranaki Bight
Wanganui
Cape Farewell
Mt Ruapehu

NEW ZEALAND

Karamea Bight
Westport
Greymouth
Hokitika
Cook Strait
Aoraki (Mt Cook)
Mt Aspiring
Southern Alps
Lake Te Anau
Resolution Island
Cape Providence
Lake Wanaka
Lake Wakatipu
Lake Tekapo
Lake Pukaki
Christchurch
Pegasus Bay
Banks Peninsula
Canterbury Bight
Timaru
Oamaru
SOUTH ISLAND
Otago Peninsula
Dunedin
Invercargill
Foveaux Strait
Stewart Island
South West Cape
Snares Is

Chatham Islands (N.Z.)
Pitt I.

Bounty Islands

Auckland Is

1:20M

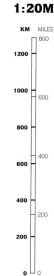

KM   MILES

© Collins Bartholomew Ltd

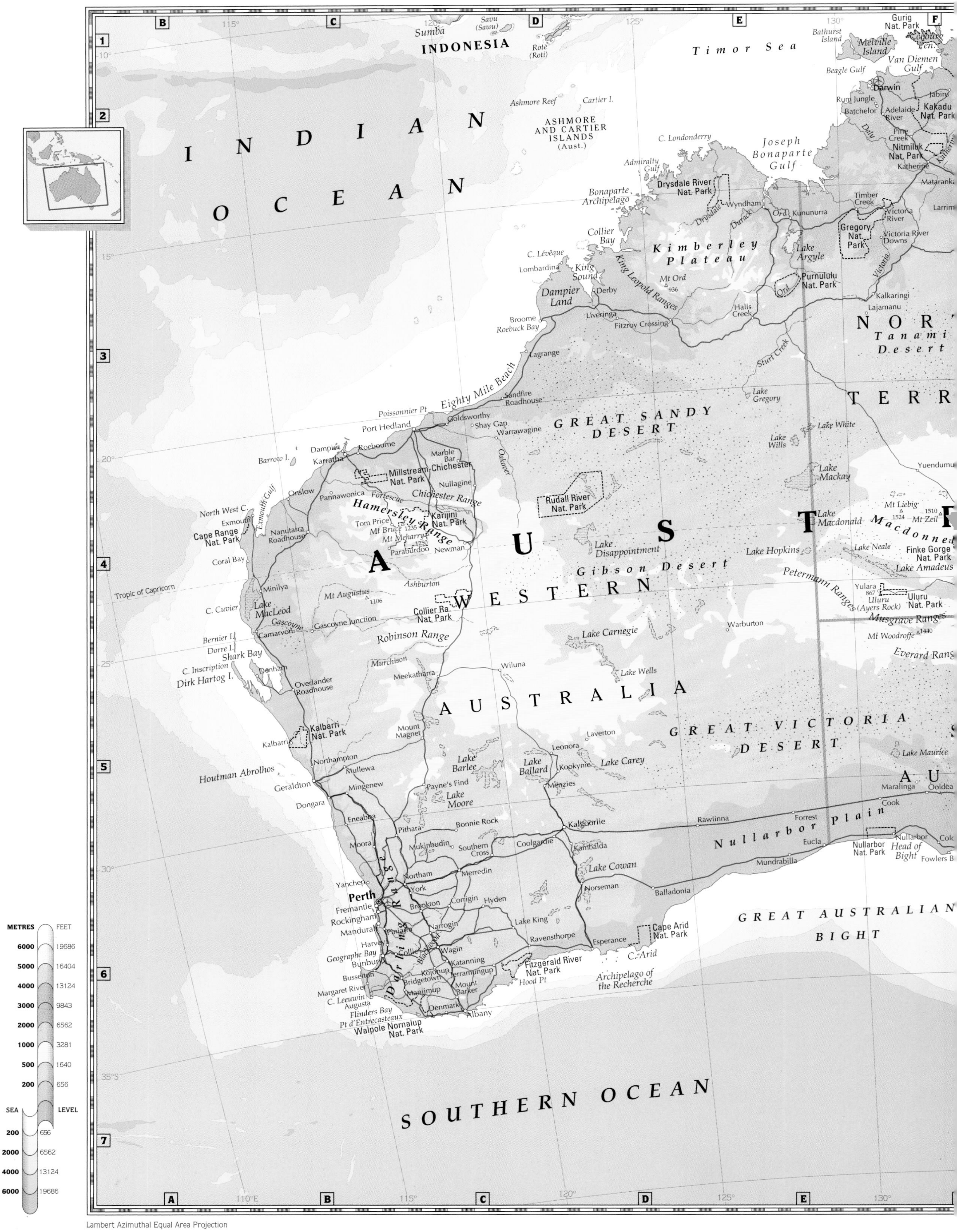
INDIAN OCEAN
SOUTHERN OCEAN
INDONESIA
Timor Sea
Sumba
Savu (Sawu)
Rote (Roti)
Ashmore Reef
Cartier I.
ASHMORE AND CARTIER ISLANDS (Aust.)
Bathurst Island
Melville Island
Gurig Nat. Park
Cobourg Pen.
Van Diemen Gulf
Beagle Gulf
Darwin
Rum Jungle
Batchelor
Adelaide River
Jabiru
Kakadu Nat. Park
Pine Creek
Nitmiluk Nat. Park
Katherine
Mataranka
Larrimah
Daly
C. Londonderry
Joseph Bonaparte Gulf
Admiralty Gulf
Drysdale River Nat. Park
Bonaparte Archipelago
Wyndham
Drysdale
Durack
Ord
Kununurra
Timber Creek
Victoria River
Gregory Nat. Park
Victoria River Downs
Victoria
Collier Bay
Kimberley Plateau
Lake Argyle
Purnululu Nat. Park
C. Lévêque
Lombardina
King Sound
Mt Ord
936
Dampier Land
Derby
King Leopold Ranges
Halls Creek
Kalkaringi
Lajamanu
Broome
Roebuck Bay
Liveringa
Fitzroy Crossing
NORTHERN TERRITORY
Tanami Desert
Lagrange
Sturt Creek
Eighty Mile Beach
Sandfire Roadhouse
Lake Gregory
Poissonnier Pt
Goldsworthy
Shay Gap
Warrawagine
Port Hedland
GREAT SANDY DESERT
Lake White
Lake Wills
Dampier
Karratha
Roebourne
Marble Bar
Barrow I.
Millstream-Chichester Nat. Park
Nullagine
Oakover
Yuendumu
Lake Mackay
Onslow
Pannawonica
Fortescue
Chichester Range
Rudall River Nat. Park
Mt Liebig
1524
1510
Mt Zeil
North West C.
Exmouth
Exmouth Gulf
Hamersley Range
Karijini Nat. Park
Tom Price
Mt Bruce
1235
Mt Meharry
1250
Paraburdoo
Newman
Lake Macdonald
Macdonnell Ranges
Cape Range Nat. Park
Nanutarra Roadhouse
AUSTRALIA
WESTERN AUSTRALIA
Lake Disappointment
Lake Hopkins
Lake Neale
Finke Gorge Nat. Park
Lake Amadeus
Coral Bay
Gibson Desert
Petermann Ranges
Yulara
867
Uluru (Ayers Rock)
Uluru Nat. Park
Tropic of Capricorn
Minilya
Ashburton
Mt Augustus
1106
C. Cuvier
Lake MacLeod
Collier Ra. Nat. Park
Musgrave Ranges
Gascoyne
Gascoyne Junction
Carnarvon
Warburton
Mt Woodroffe
1440
Bernier I.
Dorre I.
Robinson Range
Lake Carnegie
Shark Bay
Everard Ranges
C. Inscription
Dirk Hartog I.
Denham
Murchison
Wiluna
Meekatharra
Lake Wells
Overlander Roadhouse
Kalbarri Nat. Park
Kalbarri
Mount Magnet
GREAT VICTORIA DESERT
Laverton
Leonora
Lake Maurice
Northampton
Lake Barlee
Lake Ballard
Kookynie
Lake Carey
Houtman Abrolhos
Mullewa
Geraldton
Mingenew
Payne's Find
Menzies
Lake Moore
Maralinga
Ooldea
Dongara
Cook
Eneabba
Pithara
Bonnie Rock
Kalgoorlie
Rawlinna
Forrest
Nullarbor Plain
Moora
Mukinbudin
Southern Cross
Coolgardie
Kambalda
Eucla
Nullarbor Nat. Park
Nullarbor
Head of Bight
Fowlers Bay
Mundrabilla
Northam
Merredin
Lake Cowan
Yanchep
Perth
York
Norseman
Balladonia
Darling Range
Fremantle
Brookton
Corrigin
Hyden
Rockingham
Mandurah
Pinjarra
Narrogin
Lake King
Cape Arid Nat. Park
GREAT AUSTRALIAN BIGHT
Harvey
Geographe Bay
Bunbury
Collie
Wagin
Ravensthorpe
Esperance
C. Arid
Busselton
Katanning
Kojonup
Jerramungup
Fitzgerald River Nat. Park
Hood Pt
Archipelago of the Recherche
Margaret River
C. Leeuwin
Augusta
Bridgetown
Manjimup
Mount Barker
Denmark
Albany
Flinders Bay
Pt d'Entrecasteaux
Walpole Nornalup Nat. Park
METRES
FEET
6000
19686
5000
16404
4000
13124
3000
9843
2000
6562
1000
3281
500
1640
200
656
SEA
LEVEL
200
656
2000
6562
4000
13124
6000
19686
A
B
C
D
E
F
1
2
3
4
5
6
7
10°
15°
20°
25°
30°
35°S
110°E
115°
120°
125°
130°

Lambert Azimuthal Equal Area Projection

PAPUA
NEW GUINEA
CORAL SEA
TASMAN SEA
Q U E E N S L A N D
N E W S O U T H W A L E S
V I C T O R I A
A L I A
GREAT DIVIDING RANGE
GREAT BARRIER REEF
Gulf of Carpentaria
Cape York Peninsula
Arnhem Land
Great Barrier Reef Marine Park (Far North Section)
Great Barrier Reef Marine Park (Cairns Section)
Great Barrier Reef Marine Park (Central Section)
Great Barrier Reef Marine Park (Capricorn Section)
Capricorn Channel
Louisiade Archipelago
Conflict Group
Normanby I.
Misima I.
Samarai
Alotau
Tagula I.
Rossel I.
Bwagaoia
Abau
Badu I.
Moa I.
Prince of Wales I.
Endeavour Str.
C. York
Bamaga
Jardine River Nat. Park
Cullen Pt
C. Grenville
Weipa
Albatross Bay
Archer Bend Nat. Park
C. Direction
Aurukun
Archer
Coen
Rokeby Nat. Park
C. Keer-weer
Princess Charlotte Bay
C. Melville
Osprey Reef
Lakefield Nat. Park
Musgrave
C. Flattery
Cooktown
Laura
Weary B.
Mossman
Cairns
Mareeba
Atherton
Mt Bartle Frere 1612
Innisfail
Ravenshoe
Tully
Inkerman
Mitchell
Gamboola
Staaten River Nat. Park
Gilbert
Karumba
Normanton
Burketown
Croydon
Georgetown
Forsayth
Gregory Range
Hinchinbrook I.
Ingham
Great Palm I.
Townsville
Ayr
Burdekin
Bowen
Whitsunday I.
Charters Towers
Lake Dalrymple
Proserpine
Mt Dalrymple 1277
Mackay
Sarina
Percy Is
Swain Reefs
Arthur Pt
Clermont
Emerald
Rockhampton
Yeppoon
Keppel B.
Curtis I.
Gladstone
Blackwater
Springsure
Laleham
Biloela
Moura
Buckland Tableland
Carnarvon Nat. Park
Warrego
Bundaberg
Monto
Hervey Bay
Sandy Cape
Fraser Island
Gayndah
Maryborough
Murgon
Gympie
Kingaroy
Nambour
Tewantin
Maroochydore
Caboolture
Moreton I.
Dalby
Ipswich
Brisbane
North Stradbroke I.
Toowoomba
Beaudesert
Beenleigh
Gold Coast
Warwick
Inglewood
Stanthorpe
Murwillumbah
Lismore
Byron Bay
Tenterfield
Casino
Ballina
Roma
Miles
Chinchilla
Condamine
Balonne
Glenmorgan
Darling Downs
Mitchell
St George
Dirranbandi
Goondiwindi
Texas
Mungindi
Moree
Warialda
Glen Innes
Inverell
Grafton
Wee Waa
Narrabri
Armidale
New England Range
Round Mt 1615
Coffs Harbour
Macksville
Gunnedah
Tamworth
Kempsey
Port Macquarie
Murrurundi
Mt Barrington 1585
Taree
Forster
Muswellbrook
Singleton
Maitland
Newcastle
Cessnock
Gosford
Lithgow
Katoomba
Sydney
Wollongong
Botany Bay
Goulburn
Moss Vale
Nowra
Yass
Canberra
A.C.T.
Beecroft Pen.
Ulladulla
Batemans Bay
Moruya
Narooma
Cooma
Wadbilliga Nat. Park
Bega
Bombala
Eden
Cape Howe
Mallacoota Inlet
Croajingolong Nat. Park
Orbost
Snowy Mts
Kosciusko Nat. Park
Mt Kosciuszko 2230
Tumut
Tumbarumba
Hume Res.
Albury
Wodonga
Wangaratta
Benalla
Mt Bogong 1986
Mt Bogong Nat. Park
Wonnangatta-Moroka Nat. Park
Bairnsdale
Sale
Ninety Mile Beach
Moe
Wonthaggi
Corner Inlet
Wilson's Promontory
Melbourne
Geelong
Port Phillip Bay
Colac
Cape Otway
Phillip I.
Bass Strait
Kent Group
Flinders I.
Furneaux Group
Whitemark
King I.
Currie
Hunter I.
Warrnambool
Portland
Discovery Bay
Cape Nelson
Mount Gambier
Cape Jaffa
Naracoorte
Mt William 1167
Ararat
Ballarat
Stawell
Horsham
Maryborough
Castlemaine
Bendigo
Macedon 1011
Shepparton
Echuca
Cobram
Deniliquin
Kerang
Swan Hill
Charlton
Lake Tyrrell
Nhill
Little Desert Nat. Park
Wagga Wagga
Burrinjuck Res.
Temora
Young
Cowra
Bathurst
Orange
Parkes
Forbes
Mudgee
Wellington
Dubbo
Burrendong Reservoir
Narromine
West Wyalong
Lake Cargelligo
Hillston
Griffith
Leeton
Narrandera
Hay
Murrumbidgee
Lachlan
Booligal
Balranald
Robinvale
Ouyen
Mildura
Wentworth
Renmark
Berri
Lake Victoria
Murray
Darling
Garnpung Lake
Ivanhoe
Menindee
Menindee Lake
Wilcannia
Broken Hill
Barrier Range
Cobar
Nyngan
Warren
Gilgandra
Coonabarabran
Coonamble
Macquarie
Walgett
Barwon
Lightning Ridge
Brewarrina
Bourke
Goodooga
Warrego
Hungerford
Cunnamulla
Thargomindah
Grey Range
Sturt Nat. Park
Tibooburra
Quilpie
Charleville
Yaraka
Windorah
Currawilla
Blackall
Barcaldine
Longreach
Winton
Hughenden
Richmond
Julia Creek
Cloncurry
Kajabbi
Mount Isa
Selwyn Range
Dajarra
Boulia
Georgina
Diamantina
Cluny
Flinders
Leichhardt
Gregory Downs
Camooweal
Wellesley Is
Mornington I.
Bentinck I.
Gununa
Barkly Tableland
Calvert Hills
Borroloola
Sir Edward Pellew Group
Vanderlin I.
Limmen Bight
Maria I.
Numbulwar
Bickerton I.
Groote Eylandt
Alyangula
Isle Woodah
Arnhem Bay
C. Arnhem
Melville Bay
Nhulunbuy
Buckingham Bay
Elcho I.
Maningrida
C. Wessel
Wessel Is
Goulburn Is
Tennant Creek
Banka Banka
Barrow Creek
Lake Woods
Newcastle Waters
Daly Waters
Alice Springs
Simpson Desert
Simpson Desert Nat. Park
Bilpa Morea Claypan
Birdsville
Witjira Nat. Park
Alberga
Macumba
Oodnadatta
Marla
Warburton
Cooper Creek
Sturt Stony Desert
Lake Eyre (North)
Lake Eyre Nat. Park
Lake Eyre (South)
Lake Blanche
Marree
Goober Pedy
Lake Torrens
Leigh Creek
Lake Frome
Flinders Ranges
Tarcoola
Woomera
Island Lagoon
Pernatty Lagoon
Lake Macfarlane
Lake Gairdner
Ceduna
Port Augusta
Quorn
Whyalla
Port Pirie
Streaky Bay
Kyancutta
Anxious Bay
Eyre Peninsula
Spencer Gulf
Yorke Peninsula
Gulf St Vincent
Peterborough
Jamestown
Burra
Wallaroo
Port Lincoln
Cape Carnot
Gambier Is
Investigator Strait
Yorketown
Adelaide
Gawler
Murray Bridge
Tailem Bend
Lake Alexandrina
Victor Harbor
Kingscote
Flinders Chase Nat. Park
Kangaroo I.
1:12M
KM
MILES
600
500
400
300
200
100
0
300
200
100
0

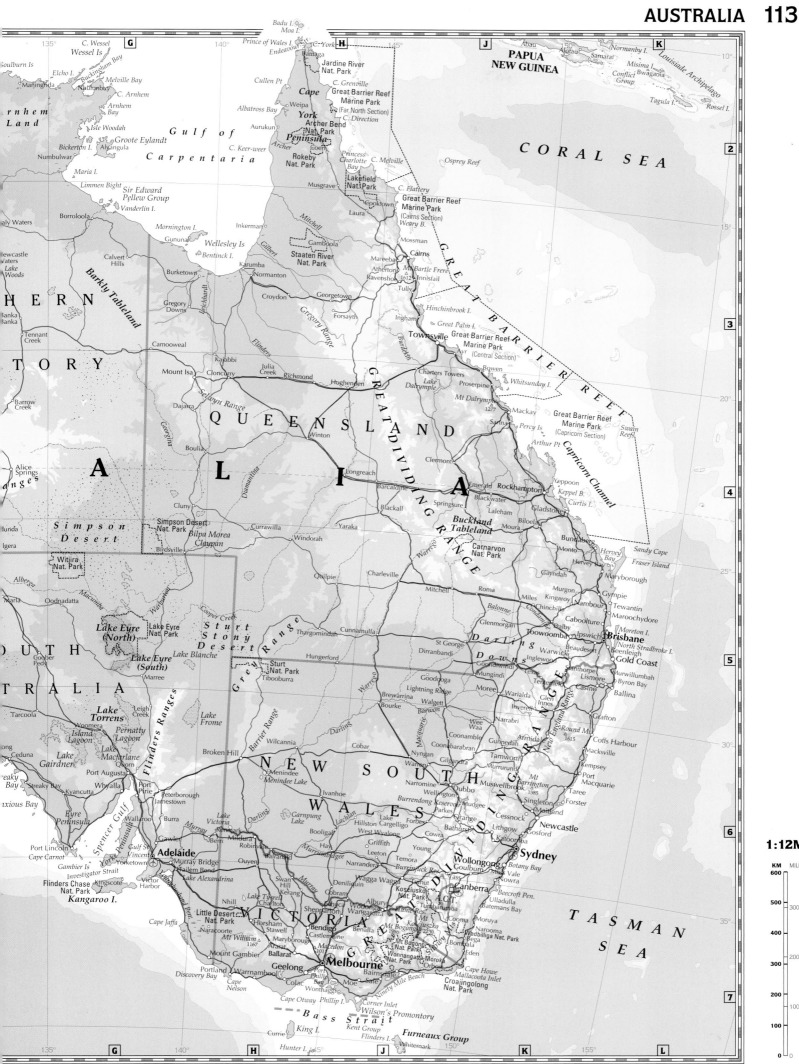

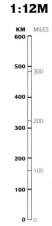

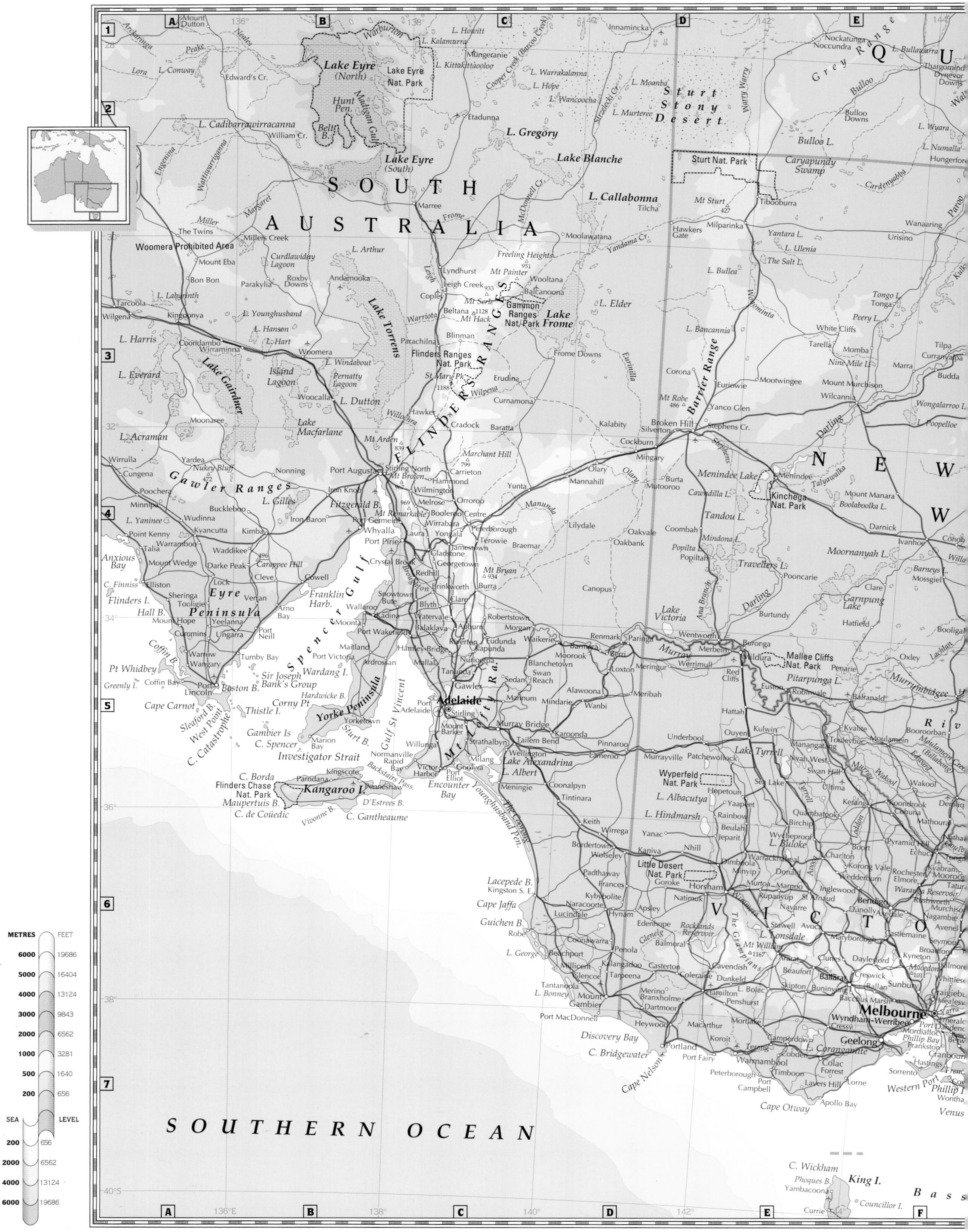

SOUTH AUSTRALIA

NEW SOUTH WALES

VICTORIA

SOUTHERN OCEAN

METRES	FEET
6000	19686
5000	16404
4000	13124
3000	9843
2000	6562
1000	3281
500	1640
200	656
SEA LEVEL	
200	656
2000	6562
4000	13124
6000	19686

Lambert Azimuthal Equal Area Projection

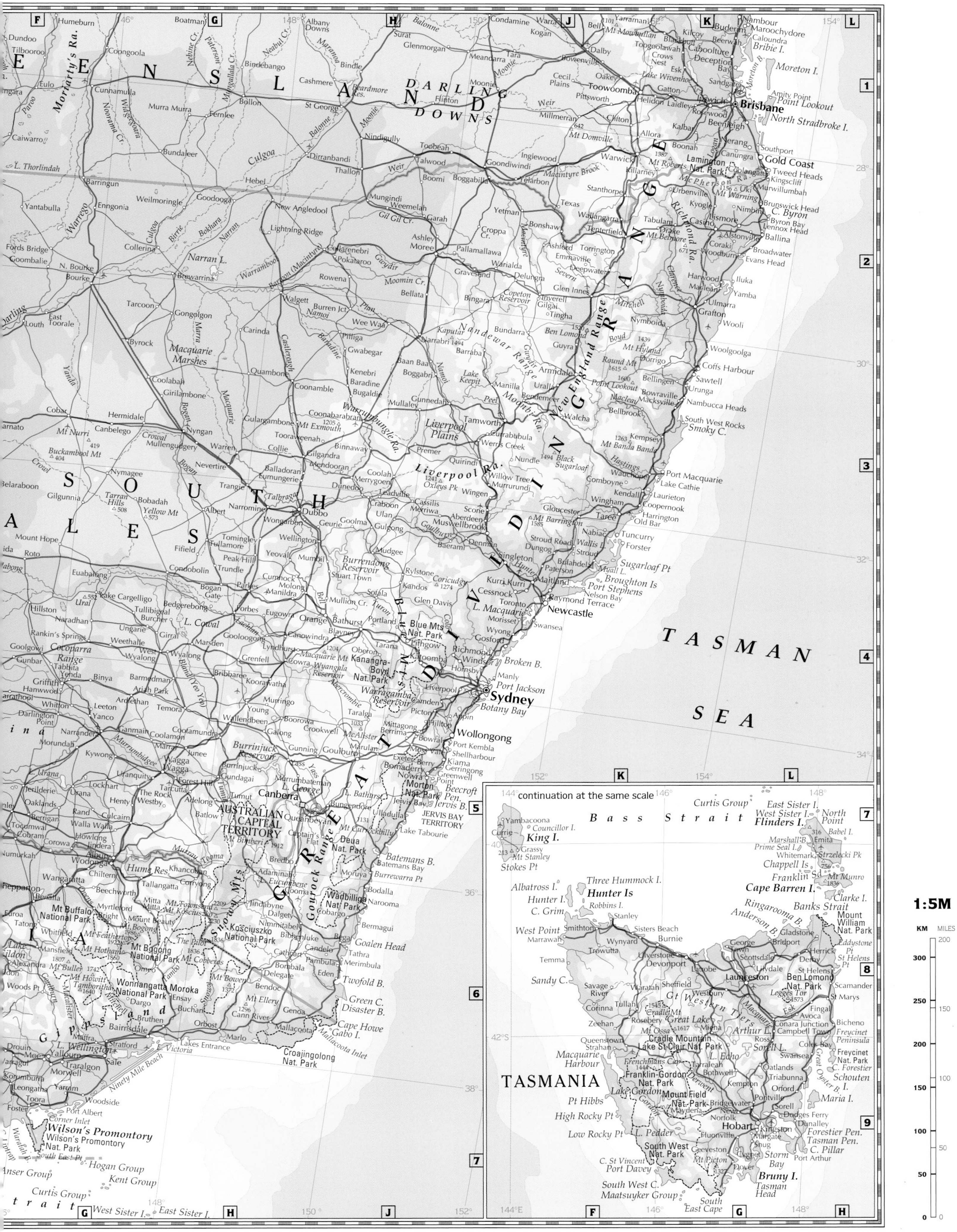
TASMAN SEA
DARLING DOWNS
NEW SOUTH WALES
GREAT DIVIDING RANGE
Brisbane
Gold Coast
Toowoomba
Sydney
Newcastle
Wollongong
Canberra
AUSTRALIAN CAPITAL TERRITORY
JERVIS BAY TERRITORY
Port Jackson
Botany Bay
Broken B.
Port Stephens
Port Macquarie
Coffs Harbour
Grafton
Tamworth
Armidale
Dubbo
Orange
Bathurst
Wagga Wagga
Albury
Goulburn
Moreton I.
North Stradbroke I.
Point Lookout
Tweed Heads
C. Byron
Batemans B.
Jervis B.
Twofold B.
Gabo I.
Cape Howe
Green C.
Wilson's Promontory
Kosciuszko National Park
Blue Mts Nat. Park
Liverpool Ra.
Nandewar Range
New England Range
Macquarie Marshes
Liverpool Plains
Warrumbungle Ra.
Gippsland
Ninety Mile Beach
Lakes Entrance
Croajingolong Nat. Park
Hogan Group
Kent Group
Curtis Group
West Sister I.
East Sister I.
continuation at the same scale
Bass Strait
King I.
Flinders I.
Cape Barren I.
Hunter Is
Three Hummock I.
TASMANIA
Launceston
Hobart
Devonport
Burnie
Cradle Mountain Lake St Clair Nat. Park
Franklin-Gordon Nat. Park
Mount Field Nat. Park
South West Nat. Park
Macquarie Harbour
Bruny I.
Tasman Pen.
Forestier Pen.
Freycinet Nat. Park
Maria I.
Schouten I.
South West C.
South East Cape
Maatsuyker Group
1:5M
KM
MILES

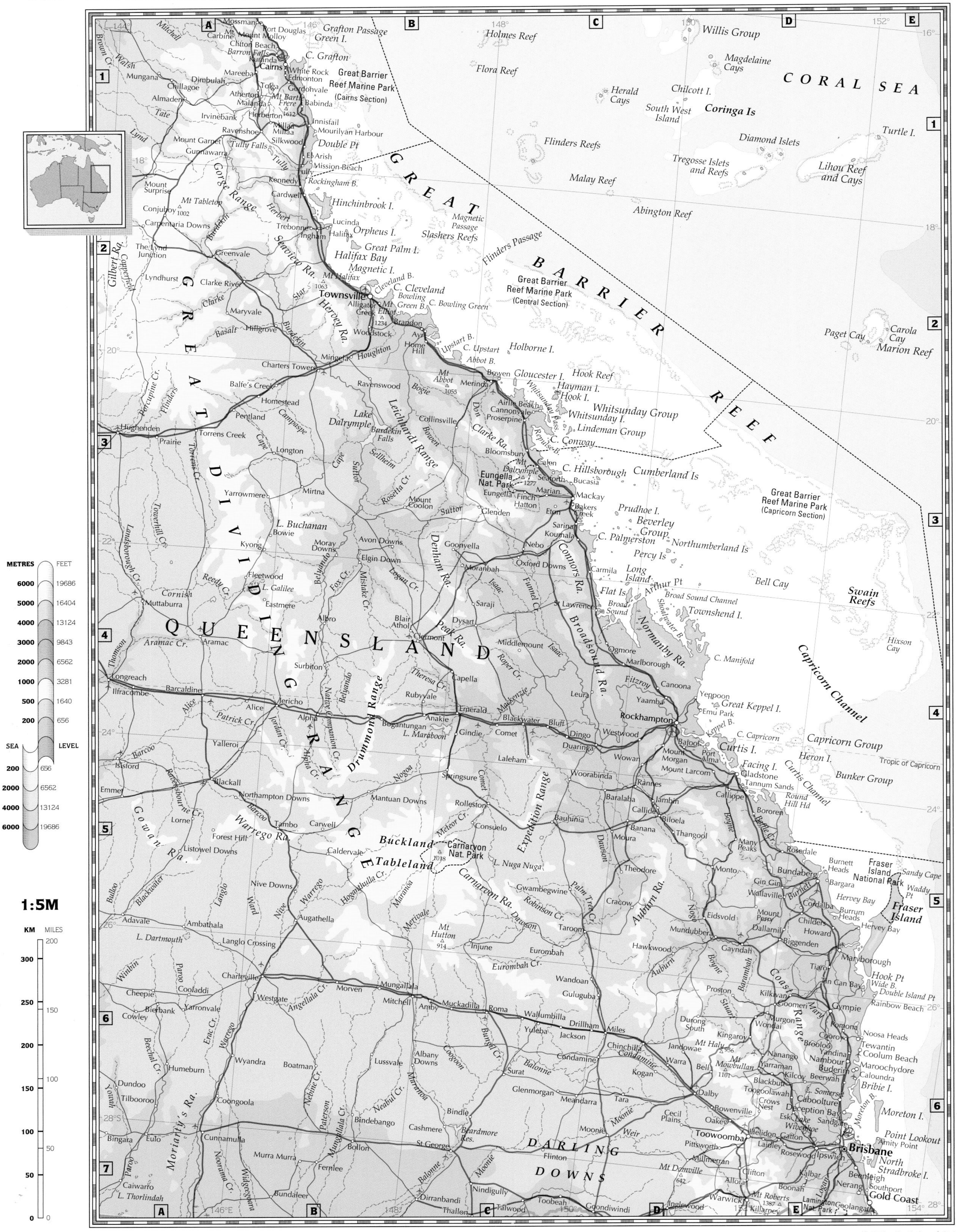

METRES **FEET**

METRES	FEET
6000	19686
5000	16404
4000	13124
3000	9843
2000	6562
1000	3281
500	1640
200	656

SEA **LEVEL**

200	656
2000	6562
4000	13124
6000	19686

1:5M

KM	MILES
300	200
250	150
200	100
150	50
100	0
50	
0	

Lambert Azimuthal Equal Area Projection

© Collins Bartholomew Ltd

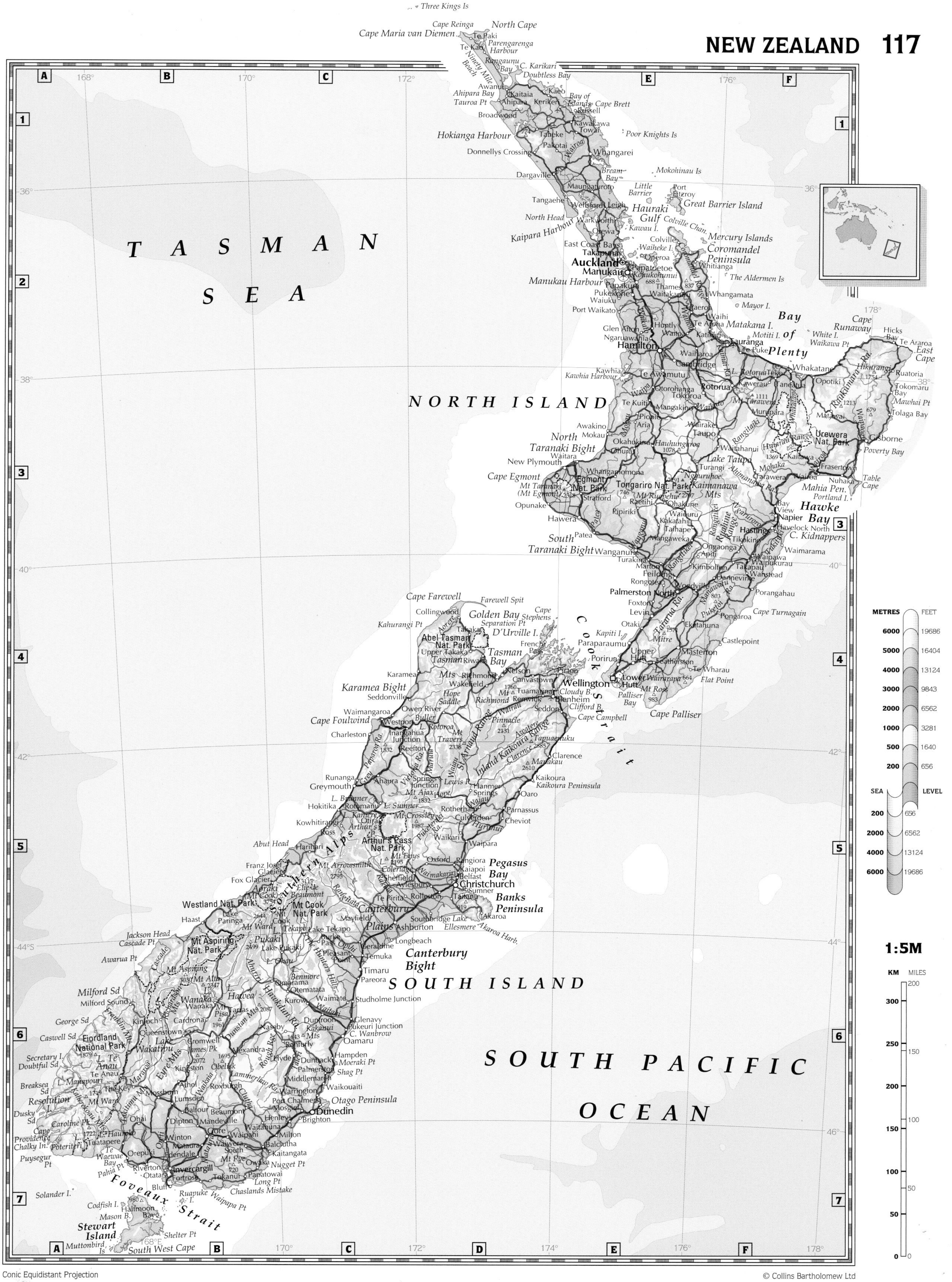

Three Kings Is

Cape Maria van Diemen · Cape Reinga · North Cape
Te Paki · Parengarenga Harbour
Te Kao · Rangaunu Bay · C. Karikari · Doubtless Bay
Awanui · Kaeo · Bay of Islands · Cape Brett
Ahipara Bay · Kaitaia · Kerikeri · Russell
Tauroa Pt · Ahipara · Kawakawa · Towai
Broadwood · Poor Knights Is
Hokianga Harbour · Taheke · Pakotai · Whangarei
Donnellys Crossing · Kaikohe
Dargaville · Maungaturoto · Bream Bay · Mokohinau Is
Tangaehe · Little Barrier · Port Fitzroy · Great Barrier Island
North Head · Wellsford · Leigh · Hauraki Gulf · Colville Chan.
Warkworth · Mercury Islands
Kaipara Harbour · Orewa · Colville · Coromandel Peninsula
East Coast Bays · Waiheke I. · Whitianga
Takapuna · Omaha · Coromandel
Auckland · Papatoetoe · The Aldermen Is
Manukau · Kohukohunui · Thames · 837 · Whangamata
Manukau Harbour · Papakura · 688 · Mayor I.
Pukekohe · Waitakaruru · Mercury Islands
Waiuku · Waihi · Bay of Plenty
Port Waikato · Paeroa · Matakana I. · Cape Runaway
Glen Afton · Huntly · Te Aroha · Tauranga · Motiti I. · White I. · Hicks Bay
Ngaruawahia · Katikati · Te Puke · Waikawa Pt · Te Araroa
Hamilton · Waihaora · Whakatane · East Cape
Cambridge · L. Rotorua · Te Teko · Hikurangi · Ruatoria
NORTH ISLAND · Te Awamutu · **Rotorua** · Kawerau · Tokomaru Bay
Otorohanga · Mt Tarawera · Murupara · Opotiki · Mawhai Pt
Kawhia · Te Kuiti · Mangakino · Waiotapu · 1213 · Matawai · Tolaga Bay
Kawhia Harbour · Piopio · Mt Tarawera · Ruatahuna · Urewera Nat. Park
Awakino · Aria · Okahukura · Hauhungaroa · Waitahanui · Rangitaiki · Poverty Bay
North Taranaki Bight · Mokau · 1078 · Lake Taupo · 1369 · Kaitawa · Gisborne
Waitara · Ohura · Nihotupu · Turangi · Mohaka · Frasertown
New Plymouth · Whangamomona · Ngaruhoe · Rangitikei · Wairoa
Cape Egmont · Egmont Nat. Park · Tongariro Nat. Park · Kaimanawa Mts · Nuhaka · Table Cape
Mt Taranaki · 746 · Mt Ruapehu · Mahia Pen.
(Mt Egmont) 2518 · Stratford · Ohakune · Portland I.
Opunake · Raetihi · Waiouru · Bay View · Napier
Hawera · Pipiriki · Waiuru · Hastings · Hawke Bay
South Taranaki Bight · Patea · Kakatahi · Taihape · Havelock North
Wanganui · Tikokino · C. Kidnappers
Turakina · Mangaweka · Ongaonga · Waimarama
Marton · Kimbolton · Waipawa · Waipukurau
Feilding · Rongotea · Ashhurst · 803 · Dannevirke · Wanstead
Palmerston North · Woodville · Porangahau
Foxton · Levin · Pahiatua · Cape Turnagain
Otaki · Eketahuna
Kapiti I. · Ekatahuna
Paraparaumu · Masterton · Castlepoint
Porirua · Upper Hutt · Carterton
Cape Farewell · Farewell Spit · **Wellington** · Greytown · Te Wharau
Collingwood · Cape Stephens · Lower Hutt · 664 · Wairarapa · Flat Point
Golden Bay · Separation Pt · D'Urville I. · Mt Ross · 983
Kahurangi Pt · Takaka · French Pass · Palliser Bay
Abel Tasman Nat. Park · Tasman Bay · Picton · Cape Palliser
Upper Takaka · Riwaka · Nelson · Cloudy B.
Karamea · Mts · Richmond · Canvastown · Tuamarina
Karamea Bight · Wakefield · Renwick · Blenheim
Hope Saddle · Richmond Ra. · Seddon · Clifford B.
Waimangaroa · Owen River · Wairau · Cape Campbell
Cape Foulwind · Westport · Buller · Pinnacle · 2131
Charleston · Inangahua Junction · 1532 · Mt Travers · 2338 · Awatere · Inland Kaikoura Range
Reefton · Victoria Ra. · 2885 · Tapuaenuku
Lewis R. · Clarence · Manaia · Kaikoura
Runanga · Ahaura · Springs Junction · Mt Ajax · Hanmer Springs · 2610
Greymouth · L. Brunner · Hope · Clarence · Kaikoura Peninsula
Hokitika · Rotomanu · L. Sumner · Rotherham · Parnassus · Oaro
Kowhitirangi · Kaniere · Mt Crossley · Culverden · Cheviot
Ross · Otira · Arthur's · 1987 · Waiau
Abut Head · Arthur's Pass Nat. Park · Waikari · Waipara
Harihari · Mt Enys · Oxford · Rangiora · Pegasus Bay
Franz Josef Glacier · 2195 · Coleridge · Kaiapoi
Fox Glacier · Mt Arrowsmith · Sheffield · Belfast · Banks Peninsula
Westland Nat. Park · 2795 · Wylesbury · **Christchurch**
Aoraki · Elfield · Waimakariri · Sumner
Mt Cook · Beaumont · Rolleston · Akaroa
Mt Cook Nat. Park · Te Pirita · Tirahi · Canterbury Plains
2644 · Cook · Mayfield · 919 · Lincoln Lake
Haast · Lake Paringa · Rangitata · Ashburton · Southbridge Lake · Ellesmere
Jackson Head · Mt Ward · Lake Tekapo · Akaroa Harb.
Cascade Pt · Mt Aspiring · 2099 · Canterbury Bight
Awarua Pt · Mt Aspiring Nat. Park · Geraldine · Longbeach
3027 Mt Aspiring · Lake Pukaki · Fairlie · Opihi · Pleasant Point · Temuka
Milford Sd · 2347 Mt Aspiring · L. Ohau · Pareora · Timaru
Milford Sound · Wanaka · Benmore · Waimate
George Sd · Kinloch · Hawea · Otematata
Queenstown · Dunstan Mts · 2087 · Waitaki · Kurow · SOUTH ISLAND
Caswell Sd · Lake Wakatipu · Cardrona · 1961 · Glenavy · Studholme Junction
Secretary I. · Fiordland National Park · 1879 · Cromwell · James Pk · 1413 · Kakanui Mts · Pukeuri Junction
Doubtful Sd · 2072 · 1695 · C. Wanbrow
Te Anau · Alexandra · Roxburgh Ra. · Naseby · Obelisk · Oamaru
Breaksea Sd · L. Te Anau · The Key · Flyde · Dunback
Resolution I. · Mossburn · Athol · Lammerlaw Ra. · Hampden · Moeraki Pt · Shag Pt
1215 · Mt Ward · Lumsden · Roxburgh · Middlemarch · Waikouaiti
Dusky Sd · Caroline · Dipton · Beaumont · Warrington
Secretary I. · Mandeville · Mosgiel · Port Chalmers · Otago Peninsula
Providence · Chalky Inlet · Balfour · Gore · Milton · Brighton
Puysegur Pt · Ohai · Winton · Kaitangata · **Dunedin**
Te Waewae Bay · Waianiwa · Waipahi · Balclutha
Pahia · Orepuki · Otautau · Clinton · Kaitangata
Riverton · Otatara · Edendale · Waiwera · Owaka
Foveaux Strait · Waewae · Mt Fyfe · 720 · South · Nugget Pt
Otara · **Invercargill** · Tokanui · Papatowai
Solander I. · Toetoes Bay · Long Pt · Chaslands Mistake
Codfish I. · 980 · Halfmoon Bay · Ruapuke I. · Waipapa Pt
Mason B. · Shelter Pt
Stewart Island · 168°E
Muttonbird Is · South West Cape

TASMAN SEA

NORTH ISLAND

SOUTH ISLAND

SOUTH PACIFIC OCEAN

Cook Strait

METRES	FEET
6000	19686
5000	16404
4000	13124
3000	9843
2000	6562
1000	3281
500	1640
200	656
SEA	LEVEL
200	656
2000	6562
4000	13124
6000	19686

1:5M

KM	MILES
	200
300	
250	150
200	100
150	
100	50
50	
0	0

Conic Equidistant Projection

© Collins Bartholomew Ltd

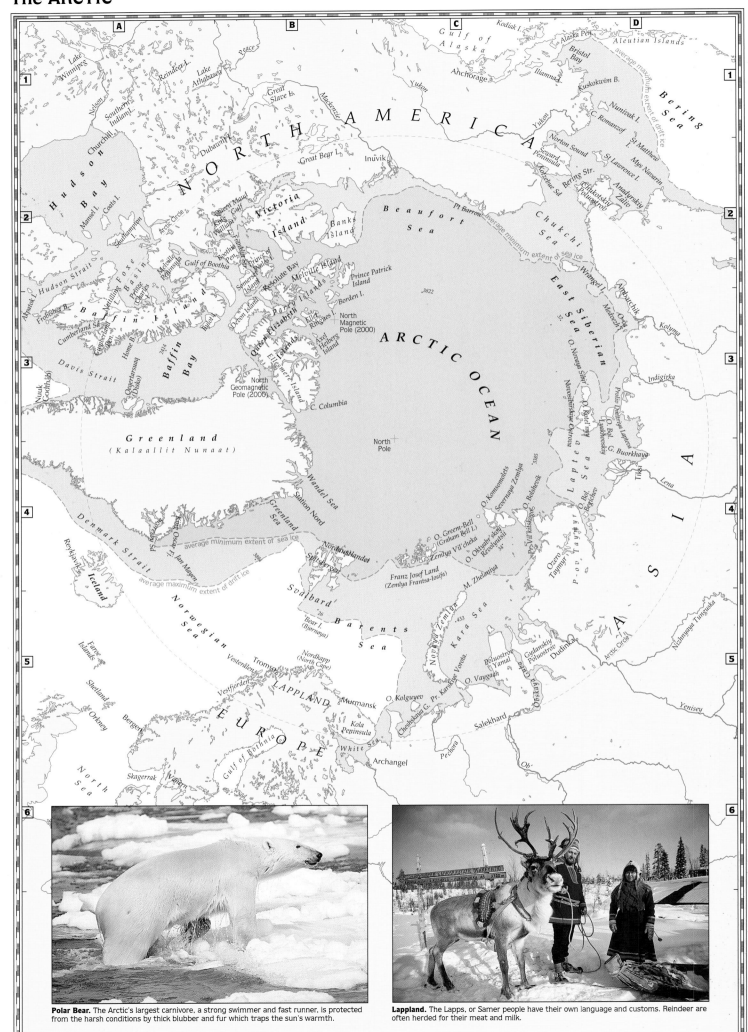

1:32M

KM MILES
800
1200
1000
600
800
400
600
400
200
200
0 0

Polar Bear. The Arctic's largest carnivore, a strong swimmer and fast runner, is protected from the harsh conditions by thick blubber and fur which traps the sun's warmth.

Lappland. The Lapps, or Samer people have their own language and customs. Reindeer are often herded for their meat and milk.

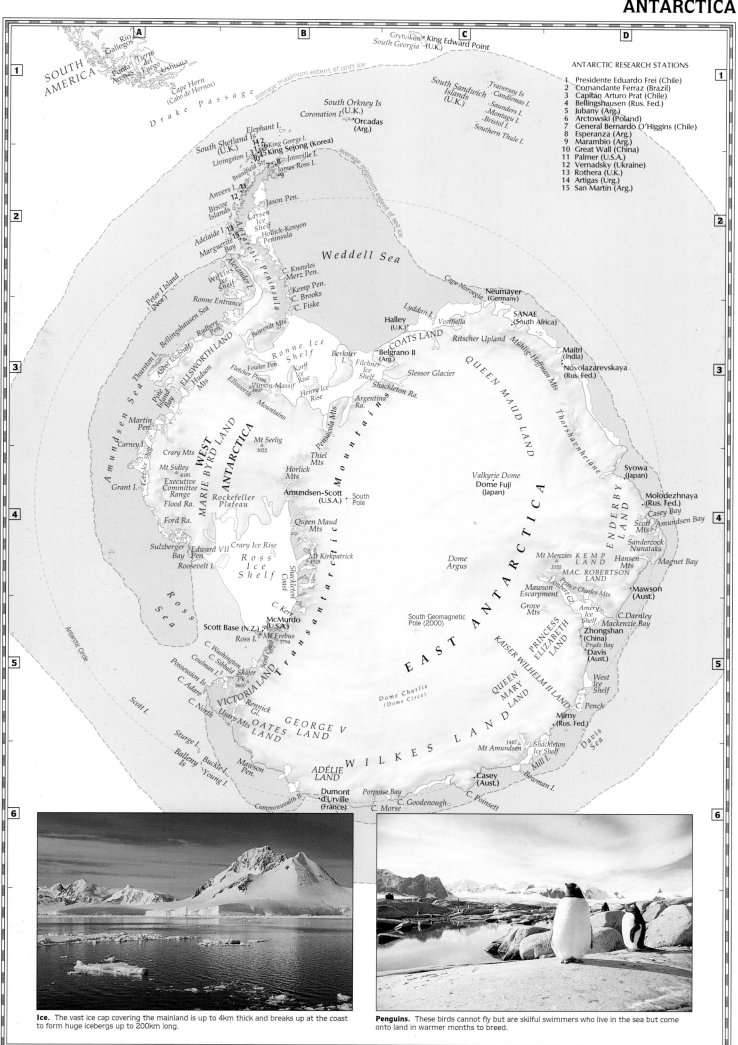

ANTARCTIC RESEARCH STATIONS

1. Presidente Eduardo Frei (Chile)
2. Comandante Ferraz (Brazil)
3. Capitán Arturo Prat (Chile)
4. Bellingshausen (Rus. Fed.)
5. Jubany (Arg.)
6. Arctowski (Poland)
7. General Bernardo O'Higgins (Chile)
8. Esperanza (Arg.)
9. Marambio (Arg.)
10. Great Wall (China)
11. Palmer (U.S.A.)
12. Vernadsky (Ukraine)
13. Rothera (U.K.)
14. Artigas (Urg.)
15. San Martín (Arg.)

1:32M

Ice. The vast ice cap covering the mainland is up to 4km thick and breaks up at the coast to form huge icebergs up to 200km long.

Penguins. These birds cannot fly but are skilful swimmers who live in the sea but come onto land in warmer months to breed.

Polar Stereographic Projection

© Collins Bartholomew Ltd

THE INDEX includes the names on the maps in the ATLAS. The names are generally indexed to the largest scale map on which they appear, and can be located using the grid reference letters and numbers around the map frame. Names on insets have a symbol: □, followed by the inset number.

Abbreviations used to describe features in the index and on the maps are explained below.

ABBREVIATIONS AND GLOSSARY

A. Alp Alpen Alpi *alp*
　Alt *upper*
A.C.T. Australian Capital Territory
Afgh. Afghanistan
Afr. Africa African
Aig. Aiguille *peak*
AK Alaska
AL Alabama
Alg. Algeria
Alta Alberta
AR Arkansas
Arch. Archipelago
Arg. Argentina
Arr. Arrecife *reef*
Austr. Australia
AZ Arizona
Azer. Azerbaijan

B. Bad *spa*
　Ban *village*
　Bay
Bangl. Bangladesh
B.C. British Columbia
Bg Berg *mountain*
Bge. Barragem *reservoir*
Bgt Bight Bugt *bay*
Bj Burj *hills*
Bol. Bolivia
Bos.-Herz. Bosnia Herzegovina
Br. Burun Burnu *point, cape*
Bt Bukit *bay*
Bü. Büyük *big*
Bulg. Bulgaria

C. Cape
　Col *high pass*
Ç. Çay *river*
CA California
Cabo Cabeço *summit*
Can. Canada
　Canal Canale *canal, channel*
　Cañon Canyon *canyon*
C.A.R. Central African Republic
Cat. Cataract
　Catena *mountains*
Cd Ciudad *town city*
Ch. Chaung *stream*
　Chott *salt lake, marsh*
Chan. Channel
Che Chaîne *mountain chain*
Cma Cima *summit*
Cno Corno *peak*
Co Cerro *hill, peak*
CO Colorado
Col. Colombia
Cord. Cordillera *mountain chain*
Cr. Creek
CT Connecticut
Cuch. Cuchilla *chain of mountains*

D. Da *big, river*
　Dag Dagh Dağı *mountain*
　Dağları *mountains*
-d. -dake *peak*
DE Delaware
Dem. Rep. Congo Democratic Republic of Congo
Dj. Djebel *mountain*
Dom. Rep. Dominican Republic

Eil. Eiland *island*
　Eilanden *islands*
Emb. Embalse *reservoir*
Equat. Equatorial
Escarp. Escarpment
Est. Estuary
Eth. Ethiopia
Etg Etang *lake, lagoon*

F. Firth
Fin. Finland
Fj. Fjell *mountain*

　Fjord Fjördur *fjord*
Fl. Fleuve *river*
FL Florida
Fr. French
F.Y.R.O.M. Former Yugoslav Republic of Macedonia

G. Gebel *mountain*
　Göl Gölö Gôl *lake*
G. Golfe Golfo Gulf Guba *gulf, bay*
　Gunung *mountain*
-g. -gawa *river*
GA Georgia
Gd Grand *big*
Gde Grande *big*
Geb. Gebergte *mountain range*
　Gebirge *mountains*
Gl. Glacier
Ger. Germany
Gr. Graben *trench, ditch*
　Gross Grosse
　Grande *big*
Grp Group
Gt Great Groot Groote *big*
Gy Góry Gory *mountains*

H. Hawr *lake*
　Hill Hills
　Hoch *high*
　Hora *mountain*
　Hory *mountains*
Harb. Harbour
Hd Head
Hgts Heights
HI Hawaii
Ht Haut *high*
Hte Haute *high*

I. Île Ilha Insel Isla
　Island Isle *island, isle*
　Isola Isole *island*
IA Iowa
ID Idaho
IL Illinois
IN Indiana
Indon. Indonesia
Is Islas Îles Ilhas
　Islands Isles
　islands, isles
Isr. Israel
Isth. Isthmus

J. Jabal Jebel *mountain*
　Jibāl *mountains*
　Jrvi Jaure Jezero
　Jezioro *lake*
　Jökull *glacier*

K. Kaap Kap Kapp *cape*
　Kaikyō *strait*
　Kato Káto *lower*
　Kiang *river or stream*
　Ko *island, lake, inlet*
　Koh Kūh Kūhha *island*
　Kolpos *gulf*
　Kopf *hill*
　Kuala *estuary*
　Kyst *coast*
　Küçük *small*
Kan. Kanal Kanaal *canal*
Kazak. Kazakhstan
Kep. Kepulauan *archipelago, islands*
Kg Kampong *village*
Khr Khrebet *mountain range*
Kl. Klein Kleine *small*
Kör. Körfez Körfezi *bay, gulf*
KS Kansas
KY Kentucky
Kyrg. Kyrgyzstan

L. Lac Lago Lake
　Liqen Loch Lough *lake, loch*
　Lam *stream*
LA Louisiana
Lag. Lagoon Laguna
　Lagôa *lagoon*
Lith. Lithuania

Lux. Luxembourg

M. Mae *river*
　Me *great, chief, mother*
　Meer *lake, sea*
　Muang *kingdom, province, town*
　Muong *town*
　Mys *cape*
　Maloye *small*
MA Massachusetts
Madag. Madagascar
Man. Manitoba
Maur. Mauritania
MD Maryland
ME Maine
Mex. Mexico
Mf Massif *mountains, upland*
Mgna Montagna *mountain*
Mgne Montagne *mountain*
Mgnes Montagnes *mountains*
MI Michigan
MN Minnesota
MO Missouri
Mon. Monasterio Monastery *monastery*
　Monument *monument*
Moz. Mozambique
MS Mississippi
Mt Mont Mount *mountain*
Mt. Mountain
MT Montana
Mte Monte *mountain*
Mtes Montes *mountains*
Mti Monti Munţi *mountains*
Mtii Munţii *mountains*
Mth Mouth
Mths Mouths
Mtn Mountain
Mts Monts Mountains

N. Nam *south(ern), river*
　Neu Ny *new*
　Nevado *peak*
　Nudo *mountain*
　Noord Nord Nörre
　Norre North *north(ern)*
　Nos *spit, point*
Nac. Nacional *national*
Nat. National
N.B. New Brunswick
NC North Carolina
ND North Dakota
NE Nebraska
Neth. Netherlands
Nfld and Newfoundland
Lab. and Labrador
NH New Hampshire
Nic. Nicaragua
Nizh. Nizhneye Nizhniy
　Nizhnyaya *lower*
Nizm. Nizmennost' *lowland*
NJ New Jersey
NM New Mexico
N.O. Noord Oost Nord Ost *northeast*
Nov. Novyy Novaya
　Noviye
　Novoye *new*
N.S. Nova Scotia
N.S.W. New South Wales
N.T. Northern Territory
NV Nevada
Nva Nueva *new*
N.W.T. Northwest Territories
NY New York
N.Z. New Zealand

O. Oost Ost *east*
　Ostrov *island*
Ø Østre *east*
Ob. Ober *upper, higher*
Oc. Ocean
Ode Oude *old*
Ogl. Oglat *well*
OH Ohio
OK Oklahoma
Ont. Ontario
Or. Óri Óros Ori *mountains*
　Oros *mountain*
OR Oregon
Orm. Ormos *bay*
O-va Ostrova *islands*
Ot Olet *mountain*
Öv. Över Övre *upper*
Oz. Ozero *lake*
　Ozera *lakes*

P. Pass
　Pic Pico Piz *peak, summit*
　Pou *mountain*
　Pulau *island*
PA Pennsylvania
Pak. Pakistan
Para. Paraguay
Pass. Passage
Peg. Pegunungan *mountain range*
P.E.I. Prince Edward Island
Pen. Peninsula Penisola *peninsula*
Per. Pereval *pass*
Phil. Philippines
Phn. Phnom *hill, mountain*
Pgio Poggio *hill*
Pl. Planina Planinski *mountain(s)*
Pla Playa *beach*
Plat. Plateau
Plosk. Ploskogor'ye *plateau*
P.N.G. Papua New Guinea
Pno Pantano *reservoir, swamp*
Pol. Poland
Por. Porog *rapids*
Port. Portugal
P-ov Poluostrov *peninsula*
P.P. Pulau-pulau *islands*
Pr. Proliv *strait*
　Przylądek *cape*
Presq. Presqu'île *peninsula*
Prom. Promontory
Prov. Province Provincial
Psa Presa *dam*
Pso Passo *dam*
Pt Point
　Pont *bridge*
　Petit *small*
Pta Ponta Punta *cape, point*
　Puerta *narrow pass*
Pte Pointe *cape, point*
　Ponte Puente *bridge*
Pto Porto Puerto *harbour, port*
Pzo Pizzo *mountain peak, mountain*

Qld. Queensland
Que. Quebec

R. Reshteh *mountain range*
　Rio Río Rivière Rūd *river*
Ra. Range
Rca Rocca *rock, fortress*
Reg. Region
Rep. Republic
Res. Reserve
Resr Reservoir
Resp. Respublika *republic*
Rf Reef
Rge Ridge
RI Rhode Island
Riba Ribeira *coast, bottom of the river valley*
Rte Route
Rus. Fed. Russian Federation

S. Salar Salina *salt pan*
　San São *saint*
　See *lake*
　Seto *strait, channel*
　Sjö *lake*
　Sör Süd Sud Syd *south*
　sur *on*
Sa Serra Sierra *mountain range*
S.A. South Australia
Sab. Sabkhat *salt flat*
Sask. Saskatchewan
SC South Carolina
Sc. Scoglio *rock, reef*
Sd Sound Sund *sound*
SD South Dakota
Seb. Sebjet Sebkhat Sebkra *salt flat*
Serb. and Serbia and
Mont. Montenegro
Serr. Serranía *mountain range*
Sev. Severnaya Severnyy *north(ern)*
Sh. Shā'ib *watercourse*
　Shatt *river (-mouth)*
　Shima *island*
　Shankou *pass*
Si Sidi *lord, master*
Sing. Singapore

Sk. Shuiku *reservoir*
Skt Sankt *saint*
Smt Seamount
Snra Senhora *Mrs, lady*
Snro Senhoro *Mr, gentleman*
Sp. Spain Spanish
　Spitze *peak*
Sr Sönder Sonder *southern*
Sr. Sredniy Srednyaya *middle*
St Saint Sint
　Staryy *old*
St. Stor Store *big*
　Stung *river*
Sta Santa *saint*
Ste Sainte *saint*
　Store *big*
Sto Santo *saint*
Str. Strait Stretta *strait*
Sv. Sväty Sveti *holy, saint*
Switz. Switzerland

T. Tal *valley*
　Tall Tell *hill*
　Tepe Tepesi *hill, peak*
Tajik. Tajikistan
Tanz. Tanzania
Tas. Tasmania
Terr. Territory
Tg Tanjung Tanjong *cape, point*
Thai. Thailand
Tk Teluk *bay*
Tmt Tablemount
TN Tennessee
Tr. Trench Trough
Tre Torre *tower, fortress*
Tte Teniente *lieutenant*
Turkm. Turkmenistan
TX Texas

U.A.E. United Arab Emirates
Ug Ujung *point, cape*
U.K. United Kingdom
Ukr. Ukraine
Unt. Unter *lower*
Upr Upper
Uru. Uruguay
U.S.A. United States of America
UT Utah
Uzbek. Uzbekistan

V. Val Valle Valley *valley*
　Väster Vest Vester *west(ern)*
　Vatn *lake*
　Ville *town*
Va Vila *small town*
VA Virginia
Venez. Venezuela
Vic. Victoria
Volc. Volcán Volcan Volcano *volcano*
Vdkhr. Vodokhranilishche *reservoir*
Vdskh. Vodoskhovyshche Vodaskhovyshcha *reservoir*
Vel. Velikiy Velikaya Velikiye *big*
Verkh. Verkhniy Verkhneye Verkhne *upper* Verkhnyaya *upper*
Vost. Vostochnyy *eastern*
Vozv. Vozvyshennost' *hills, upland*
VT Vermont

W. Wadi *watercourse*
　Wald *forest*
　Wan *bay*
　Water *water*
WA Washington
W.A. Western Australia
Wr Wester
WV West Virginia
WY Wyoming

-y. -yama *mountain*
Yt. Ytre Ytter Ytri *outer*
Yuzh. Yuzhnaya Yuzhno Yuzhnyy *southern*

Zal. Zaliv *bay*
Zap. Zapadnyy Zapadnaya Zapadno Zapadnoye *western*
Zem. Zemlya *land*

A

62 C5 Aachen Ger.
62 E6 Aalen Ger.
61 C2 Aalsmeer Neth.
61 C4 Aalst Belgium
61 C4 Aarschot Belgium
88 A3 Aba China
102 D3 Aba Dem. Rep. Congo
100 C4 Aba Nigeria
81 M6 Ābādān Iran
79 G3 Ābādeh Iran
100 B1 Abadla Alg.
46 D2 Abaeté r. Brazil
43 J4 Abaetetuba Brazil
25 E4 Abajo Pk summit U.S.A.
100 C4 Abakaliki Nigeria
86 F1 Abakan Rus. Fed.
86 E1 Abakanskiy Khrebet mts Rus. Fed.
69 E7 Abana Turkey
42 D6 Abancay Peru
79 G3 Abarqū Iran
90 J2 Abashiri Japan
90 J2 Abashiri-wan b. Japan
110 E3 Abau P.N.G.
102 D3 Ābaya Hāyk' l. Eth.
Ābay Wenz r. see Blue Nile
86 F1 Abaza Rus. Fed.
66 C4 Abbasanta Italy
30 C2 Abbaye, Pt pt U.S.A.
61 A5 Abbaye de Chaalis France
61 D5 Abbaye d'Orval Belgium
102 E2 Abbe, L. l. Eth.
64 E1 Abbeville France
27 E6 Abbeville LA U.S.A.
29 D5 Abbeville SC U.S.A.
60 B5 Abbeyfeale Rep. of Ireland
57 E6 Abbey Head hd U.K.
60 D5 Abbeyleix Rep. of Ireland
58 D3 Abbeytown U.K.
54 Q4 Abborrträsk Sweden
116 B3 Abbot, Mt mt Austr.
116 B2 Abbot B. b. Austr.
119 A3 Abbot Ice Shelf ice feature Antarctica
20 E5 Abbotsford Can.
30 B3 Abbotsford U.S.A.
25 F4 Abbott U.S.A.
84 C2 Abbottabad Pak.
81 H3 'Abd al 'Azīz, J. h. Syria
81 L5 Ābdānān Iran
101 E3 Abéché Chad
117 D4 Abel Tasman National Park nat. park N.Z.
100 B4 Abengourou Côte d'Ivoire
55 L9 Åbenrå Denmark
100 C4 Abeokuta Nigeria
59 C5 Aberaeron U.K.
57 F3 Aberchirder U.K.
115 H5 Abercrombie r. Austr.
59 D6 Aberdare U.K.
59 C5 Aberdaron U.K.
115 J4 Aberdeen Austr.
21 H4 Aberdeen Can.
89 □ Aberdeen China
104 F6 Aberdeen S. Africa
57 F3 Aberdeen U.K.
33 E5 Aberdeen MD U.S.A.
27 F5 Aberdeen MS U.S.A.
26 D2 Aberdeen SD U.S.A.
24 B2 Aberdeen WA U.S.A.
21 J2 Aberdeen Lake l. Can.
59 C5 Aberdyfi U.K.
57 E4 Aberfeldy U.K.
58 F4 Aberford U.K.
57 D4 Aberfoyle U.K.
59 D6 Abergavenny U.K.
27 C5 Abernathy U.S.A.
59 C5 Aberporth U.K.
59 C5 Abersoch U.K.
59 C5 Aberystwyth U.K.
78 E6 Abhā Saudi Arabia
81 M3 Abhar Iran
81 M4 Abhar Rūd r. Iran
Abiad, Bahr el r. see White Nile
45 A2 Abibe, Serranía de mts Col.
100 B4 Abidjan Côte d'Ivoire
84 B2 Ab-i-Istada l. Afgh.
102 D3 Abijatta-Shalla National Park nat. park Eth.
26 D4 Abilene KS U.S.A.
27 D5 Abilene TX U.S.A.
59 F6 Abingdon U.K.
30 B5 Abingdon IL U.S.A.
32 C6 Abingdon VA U.S.A.
116 C2 Abington Reef rf Coral Sea Is Terr.
69 F6 Abinsk Rus. Fed.
42 C5 Abiseo, Parque Nacional nat. park Peru
21 H2 Abitau Lake l. Can.
22 D4 Abitibi r. Can.
22 E4 Abitibi, Lake l. Can.
81 K5 Āb Naft r. Iraq
84 C3 Abohar India
100 B4 Aboisso Côte d'Ivoire
100 C4 Abomey Benin
101 D4 Abong Mbang Cameroon
94 A4 Aborlan Phil.
101 D3 Abou Déia Chad
81 K1 Abovyan Armenia
57 F3 Aboyne U.K.
79 F4 Abqaiq Saudi Arabia
47 D4 Abra, L. del l. Arg.
65 B3 Abrantes Port.
44 C2 Abra Pampa Arg.
46 E2 Abrolhos, Arquipélago dos is Brazil
24 E2 Absaroka Range mts U.S.A.
78 E6 Abū 'Arīsh Saudi Arabia
79 G5 Abu Dhabi U.A.E.
101 F3 Abu Hamed Sudan
100 C4 Abuja Nigeria
81 H4 Abū Kamāl Syria
101 E3 Abu Matariq Sudan
42 E6 Abunã r. Bol.
42 E5 Abunã Brazil
78 D7 Ābune Yosēf mt Eth.
80 C6 Abū Qīr, Khalīj b. Egypt
82 D6 Abu Road India
Abu Simbel see Abū Sunbul
81 K6 Abū Şukhayr Iraq
78 C5 Abū Sunbul Egypt
117 C5 Abut Head hd N.Z.
94 C4 Abuyog Phil.
101 E3 Abu Zabad Sudan
Abū Ẓabī see Abu Dhabi
81 M6 Abūzam Iran
101 E3 Abyad Sudan
101 E4 Abyei Sudan
33 J2 Acadia Nat. Park nat. park U.S.A.
36 D4 Acambaro Mex.
45 A2 Acandí Col.
65 B1 A Cañiza Spain
36 C4 Acaponeta Mex.
36 E5 Acapulco Mex.
43 J4 Acará Brazil
43 K4 Acaraú r. Brazil
46 A4 Acaray r. Para.
44 E3 Acaray, Represa de resr Para.
45 C2 Acarigua Venez.
36 F5 Acayucán Mex.
100 B4 Accra Ghana
58 E4 Accrington U.K.
45 C3 Achaguas Venez.
84 D5 Achalpur India
77 T3 Achayvayam Rus. Fed.
60 A4 Achill Island i. Rep. of Ireland
60 B4 Achill Sound Rep. of Ireland
57 C2 Achiltibuie U.K.
76 L4 Achinsk Rus. Fed.
57 C3 Achnasheen U.K.
57 C3 A'Chralaig mt U.K.
69 F6 Achuyevo Rus. Fed.
80 B3 Acıgöl l. Turkey
80 B3 Acıpayam Turkey
66 F6 Acireale Italy
26 E3 Ackley U.S.A.
37 K4 Acklins Island i. Bahamas
59 J5 Acle U.K.
47 B2 Aconcagua r. Chile
47 B2 Aconcagua, Cerro mt Arg.
43 L5 Acopiara Brazil
65 B1 A Coruña Spain
66 C2 Acqui Terme Italy
114 A4 Acraman, L. salt flat Austr.
80 E5 Acre Israel
66 G5 Acri Italy
62 J7 Ács Hungary
109 Actéon, Groupe atolls Pac. Oc.
32 B4 Ada OH U.S.A.
27 D5 Ada OK U.S.A.
65 D2 Adaja r. Spain
44 E8 Adam, Mt h. Falkland Is
115 H6 Adaminaby Austr.
33 G3 Adams MA U.S.A.
30 C4 Adams WV U.S.A.
24 B2 Adams, Mt mt U.S.A.
20 F4 Adams L. l. Can.
35 E2 Adams McGill Reservoir resr U.S.A.
20 C3 Adams Mt. mt U.S.A.
Adam's Peak mt see Sri Pada
34 B2 Adams Peak mt U.S.A.
'Adan see Aden
80 E3 Adana Turkey
60 C5 Adare Rep. of Ireland
119 A5 Adare, C. c. Antarctica
116 A5 Adavale Austr.
35 E2 Adaven U.S.A.
81 K5 Ad Daghghārah Iraq
78 F5 Ad Dahnā' des. Saudi Arabia
100 A2 Ad Dakhla Western Sahara
79 G4 Ad Dammām Saudi Arabia
Ad Dawḩah see Doha
81 J4 Ad Dawr Iraq
78 F5 Ad Dir'īyah Saudi Arabia
102 D3 Addis Ababa Eth.
33 K2 Addison U.S.A.
81 K6 Ad Dīwānīyah Iraq
59 G6 Addlestone U.K.
13 J4 Addu Atoll atoll Maldives
81 J6 Ad Duwayd w. Saudi Arabia
29 D6 Adel GA U.S.A.
26 E3 Adel IA U.S.A.
114 C5 Adelaide Austr.
105 G6 Adelaide S. Africa
29 E7 Adelaide Bahamas
119 B2 Adelaide I i. Antarctica
112 F2 Adelaide River Austr.
34 D4 Adelanto U.S.A.
119 B6 Adélie Land reg. Antarctica
115 H5 Adelong Austr.
78 E7 Aden Yemen
102 E2 Aden, Gulf of g. Somalia/Yemen
93 J7 Adi i. Indon.
102 D2 Ādī Ārk'ay Eth.
102 D2 Ādīgrat Eth.
84 D6 Adilabad India
81 J2 Adilcevaz Turkey
24 B3 Adin U.S.A.
101 D2 Adīrī Libya
33 F2 Adirondack Mountains mts U.S.A.
Ādīs Ābeba see Addis Ababa
102 D3 Ādīs Alem Eth.
80 G3 Adıyaman Turkey
63 N7 Adjud Romania
23 J3 Adlavik Islands is Can.
112 E2 Admiralty Gulf b. Austr.
20 C3 Admiralty Island i. U.S.A.
20 C3 Admiralty Island National Monument - Kootznoowoo Wilderness res. U.S.A.
110 E2 Admiralty Islands is P.N.G.
119 A5 Admiralty Mts mts Antarctica
83 E7 Adoni India
64 D5 Adour r. France
65 E4 Adra Spain
66 F6 Adrano Italy
100 B2 Adrar Alg.
100 C2 Adrar mts Alg.
101 E3 Adré Chad
31 E5 Adrian MI U.S.A.
27 C5 Adrian TX U.S.A.
52 Adriatic Sea sea Europe
102 C3 Adusa Dem. Rep. Congo
102 D2 Ādwa Eth.
77 P3 Adycha r. Rus. Fed.
69 F6 Adygeya, Respublika div. Rus. Fed.
69 F6 Adygeysk Rus. Fed.
69 H6 Adyk Rus. Fed.
100 B4 Adzopé Côte d'Ivoire
52 Aegean Sea sea Greece/Turkey
65 B1 A Estrada Spain
102 D2 Afabet Eritrea
81 K3 Afan Iran
70 Afghanistan country Asia
54 M5 Åfjord Norway
102 E3 Afmadow Somalia
65 C1 A Fonsagrada Spain
80 F3 'Afrīn, Nahr r. Syria/Turkey
80 F2 Afşin Turkey
61 D2 Afsluitdijk barrage Neth.
24 E3 Afton U.S.A.
43 H4 Afuá Brazil
80 E5 'Afula Israel
80 C2 Afyon Turkey
100 C3 Agadez Niger
100 B1 Agadir Morocco
82 D1 Agadyr' Kazak.
85 G5 Agartala India
84 C6 Agashi India
31 F2 Agate Can.
67 M6 Agathonisi i. Greece
83 D8 Agatti i. India
100 B4 Agboville Côte d'Ivoire
81 L1 Ağcabädi Azer.
81 L2 Ağdam Azer.
64 F5 Agde France
64 E4 Agen France
104 C4 Aggeneys S. Africa
61 F4 Agger r. Ger.
84 D1 Aghil Pass pass China
60 C3 Aghla Mountain h. Rep. of Ireland
67 L7 Agia Vervara Greece
80 G2 Ağın Turkey
67 K6 Agios Dimitrios Greece
67 L5 Agios Efstratios i. Greece
67 M5 Agios Fokas, Akra pt Greece
67 K5 Agios Konstantinos Greece
67 L7 Agios Nikolaos Greece
67 K4 Agiou Orous, Kolpos b. Greece
101 F3 Agirwat Hills h. Sudan
105 F3 Agisanang S. Africa
100 B4 Agnibilékrou Côte d'Ivoire
67 L2 Agnita Romania
88 A2 Agong China
84 D4 Agra India
69 H7 Agrakhanskiy Poluostrov pen. Rus. Fed.
84 B1 Agram Pass pass Pak.
65 F2 Agreda Spain
81 J2 Ağrı Turkey
67 K7 Agria Gramvousa i. Greece
66 E6 Agrigento Italy
93 L3 Agrihan i. N. Mariana Is
67 J5 Agrinio Greece
83 B3 Agrio r. Arg.
66 F4 Agropoli Italy
81 K1 Ağstafa Azer.
81 M1 Ağsu Azer.
45 B3 Aguadas Col.
45 B3 Agua de Dios Col.
37 L5 Aguadilla Puerto Rico
47 D4 Aguado Cecilio Arg.
37 H7 Aguadulce Panama
47 C3 Agua Escondida Arg.
36 D4 Aguanaval r. Mex.
47 C1 Agua Negra, Paso del pass Arg./Chile
46 B3 Aguapeí r. Brazil
36 C2 Agua Prieta Mex.
46 A3 Aguaray Guazú r. Para.
45 D2 Aguaro-Guariquito, Parque Nacional nat. park Venez.
36 D4 Aguascalientes Mex.
46 E2 Águas Formosas Brazil
46 C3 Agudos Brazil
35 F5 Aguila U.S.A.
65 D1 Aguilar de Campóo Spain
65 F4 Águilas Spain
94 B4 Aguisan Phil.
104 D7 Agulhas, Cape c. S. Africa
13 F7 Agulhas Basin sea feature Indian Ocean
46 D3 Agulhas Negras mt Brazil
13 F6 Agulhas Plateau sea feature Indian Ocean
92 □ Agung, G. vol. Indon.
94 C4 Agusan r. Phil.
94 B4 Agutaya Phil.
81 L2 Ahar Iran
117 C5 Ahaura N.Z.
61 F2 Ahaus Ger.
117 F3 Ahimanawa Ra. mts N.Z.
117 D1 Ahipara N.Z.
117 D1 Ahipara Bay b. N.Z.
81 J2 Ahlat Turkey
84 C5 Ahmadabad India
83 D7 Ahmadnagar India
84 B3 Ahmadpur East Pak.
79 L3 Ahmadpur Sial Pak.
54 T5 Ähtäri Fin.
55 U7 Ahtme Estonia
81 M6 Āhū Iran
64 F3 Ahun France
117 B6 Ahuriri r. N.Z.
81 M6 Ahvāz Iran
84 C5 Ahwa India
Ahwāz see Ahvāz
104 B3 Ai-Ais Namibia
88 D1 Aibag Gol r. China
34 □1 Aiea U.S.A.
80 E4 Aigialousa Cyprus
67 K6 Aigina i. Greece
67 K5 Aigio Greece
64 H4 Aigle de Chambeyron mt France
47 F2 Aiguá Uru.
91 F5 Aikawa Japan
29 D5 Aiken U.S.A.
45 A2 Ailigandi Panama
31 G4 Ailsa Craig Can.
57 C5 Ailsa Craig i. U.K.
46 E2 Aimorés, Sa dos h. Brazil
100 C1 Aïn Beïda Alg.
100 B2 'Aïn Ben Tili Maur.
65 H4 Aïn Defla Alg.
65 H5 Aïn el Hadjel Alg.
100 B1 Aïn Sefra Alg.
23 H4 Ainslie, Lake l. Can.
26 D3 Ainsworth U.S.A.
Aintab see Gaziantep
65 H4 Aïn Taya Alg.
65 G5 Aïn Tédélès Alg.
45 B4 Aipe Col.
95 C5 Air i. Indon.
20 G4 Airdrie Can.
57 E5 Airdrie U.K.
64 D5 Aire-sur-l'Adour France
88 D1 Airgin Sum China
116 C3 Airlie Beach Austr.
21 H3 Air Ronge Can.
88 F2 Ai Shan h. China
20 B2 Aishihik Can.
20 B2 Aishihik Lake l. Can.
64 G2 Aisne r. France
65 F3 Aitana mt Spain
110 E2 Aitape P.N.G.
26 E2 Aitkin U.S.A.
63 L7 Aiud Romania
64 G5 Aix-en-Provence France
64 G4 Aix-les-Bains France
85 F5 Aiyar Res. resr India
85 H5 Aizawl India
55 T8 Aizkraukle Latvia
55 R8 Aizpute Latvia
91 F6 Aizu-wakamatsu Japan
66 C4 Ajaccio France
45 B4 Ajajú r. Col.
Ajanta h. see Sahyadriparvat Range
54 O4 Ajaureforsen Sweden
117 D5 Ajax, Mt mt N.Z.
101 E1 Ajdābiyā Libya
a-Jiddét gravel area see Ḩarāsīs, Jiddat al
90 G4 Ajigasawa Japan
80 E5 'Ajlūn Jordan
84 C4 Ajmer India
35 F5 Ajo U.S.A.
35 F5 Ajo, Mt mt U.S.A.
94 B4 Ajuy Phil.
90 H3 Akabira Japan
90 J3 Akan National Park Japan
80 D4 Akanthou Cyprus
117 D5 Akaroa N.Z.
117 D5 Akaroa Har in. N.Z.
85 H4 Akas reg. India
84 B2 Akbar Afgh.
85 E4 Akbarpur India
65 J4 Akbou Alg.
76 G4 Akbulak Rus. Fed.
80 F2 Akçadağ Turkey
81 G3 Akçakale Turkey
80 C1 Akçakoca Turkey
80 D3 Akçali D. mt Turkey
80 C3 Ak D. mts Turkey
81 H2 Ak D. mts Turkey
80 C3 Akdağ mt Turkey
80 E2 Akdağmadeni Turkey
55 Q7 Åkersberga Sweden
61 C2 Akersloot Neth.
102 C3 Aketi Dem. Rep. Congo
81 J1 Akhalk'alak'i Georgia
69 G7 Akhalts'ikhe Georgia
85 G5 Akhaura Bangl.
101 E1 Akhḑar, Al Jabal al mts Libya
79 H5 Akhḑar, Jabal mts Oman
80 A2 Akhisar Turkey
80 F3 Akhtarīn Syria
69 H5 Akhtubinsk Rus. Fed.
81 J1 Akhuryan Armenia
91 C8 Aki Japan
22 D3 Akimiski Island i. Can.
80 E3 Akıncı Burun pt Turkey
80 G1 Akıncılar Turkey
90 G5 Akita Japan
100 A3 Akjoujt Maur.
54 P3 Akkajaure l. Sweden
90 J3 Akkeshi Japan
'Akko see Acre
76 J4 Akkol' Kazak.
80 F1 Akkuş Turkey
84 D4 Aklera India
55 R8 Akmeņrags pt Latvia
84 D1 Akmeqit China
Akmola see Astana
91 D7 Akō Japan
101 F4 Akobo Sudan
84 D5 Akola India
102 D2 Akordat Eritrea
80 D3 Akören Turkey
84 D5 Akot India
23 G1 Akpatok Island i. Can.
54 B4 Akranes Iceland
69 C7 Akrathos, Akra pt Greece
55 J7 Åkrehamn Norway
84 A2 Ak Robat Pass pass Afgh.
24 G3 Akron CO U.S.A.
32 C4 Akron OH U.S.A.
32 C4 Akron City Reservoir resr U.S.A.
84 D2 Aksai Chin terr. China/India
80 E2 Aksaray Turkey
69 F6 Aksay Rus. Fed.
84 D2 Aksayqin Hu l. China/Jammu and Kashmir
80 C2 Akşehir Turkey
80 C2 Akşehir Gölü l. Turkey
80 C3 Akseki Turkey
76 H5 Akshiganak Kazak.
82 F2 Aksu China
80 C3 Aksu r. Turkey
102 D2 Āksum Eth.
85 F1 Aktag mt China
81 K2 Aktaş D. mt Turkey
76 G5 Aktau Kazak.
82 E1 Aktogay Kazak.
63 O4 Aktsyabrski Belarus
76 G4 Aktyubinsk Kazak.
91 B8 Akune Japan
100 C4 Akure Nigeria
54 D4 Akureyri Iceland
85 G1 Akxokesay China
Akyab see Sittwe
80 G3 Akziyaret Turkey
55 L6 Ål Norway
29 C5 Alabama div. U.S.A.
29 C6 Alabama r. U.S.A.
29 C5 Alabaster U.S.A.
94 B3 Alabat i. Phil.
81 K7 Al 'Abţīyah w. Iraq
80 E1 Alaca Turkey
80 F2 Alacahan Turkey
80 E1 Alaçam Turkey
80 B2 Alaçam Dağları mts Turkey
81 J2 Ala Dag mt Turkey
81 J2 Ala Dağlar mts Turkey
80 E3 Ala Dağları mts Turkey
69 H7 Alagir Rus. Fed.
43 L6 Alagoinhas Brazil
65 F2 Alagón Spain
94 C5 Alah r. Phil.
54 S5 Alahärmä Fin.
81 L7 Al Aḩmadī Kuwait
54 S5 Alajärvi Fin.
37 H6 Alajuela Costa Rica
81 L2 Alajujeh Iran
84 D3 Alaknanda r. India
82 F1 Alakol', Ozero salt l. Kazak.
54 W3 Alakurtti Rus. Fed.
80 B6 Al 'Alamayn Egypt
42 F4 Alalaú r. Brazil
81 J3 Al 'Amādīyah Iraq
93 L3 Alamagan i. N. Mariana Is
81 L6 Al 'Amārah Iraq
85 H3 Alamdo China
81 K7 Al Amghar waterhole Iraq
94 A2 Alaminos Phil.
80 B6 Al 'Āmirīyah Egypt
35 E3 Alamo U.S.A.
35 F4 Alamo Dam dam U.S.A.
25 F5 Alamogordo U.S.A.
27 D6 Alamo Heights U.S.A.
25 E6 Alamos Mex.
25 F4 Alamosa U.S.A.
54 O4 Alanäs Sweden
55 Q6 Åland is Fin.
81 K2 Aland r. Iran
95 B5 Alang Besar i. Indon.
30 E3 Alanson U.S.A.
80 D3 Alanya Turkey
80 C1 Alaplı Turkey
Alappuzha see Alleppey
80 E7 Al 'Aqabah Jordan
65 E3 Alarcón, Embalse de resr Spain
80 D6 Al 'Arīsh Egypt
78 F4 Al Arţāwīyah Saudi Arabia
80 B2 Alaşehir Turkey
81 J6 Al 'Āshūrīyah w. Iraq
16 Alaska div. North America
118 C1 Alaska, Gulf of g. U.S.A.
20 E3 Alaska Highway Can./U.S.A.
118 D1 Alaska Peninsula pen. U.S.A.
18 Alaska Range mts U.S.A.
81 M2 Ālāt Azer.
81 J6 Al 'Athāmīn h. Iraq
68 H4 Alatyr' Rus. Fed.
68 H4 Alatyr' r. Rus. Fed.
42 C4 Alausí Ecuador
81 K1 Alaverdi Armenia
54 T4 Alavieska Fin.
54 S5 Alavus Fin.
114 D5 Alawoona Austr.
81 L1 Alazani r. Azer./Georgia
81 K5 Al 'Azīzīyah Iraq
66 C2 Alba Italy
80 F3 Al Bāb Syria
65 F3 Albacete Spain
114 D5 Albacutya, L. l. Austr.
81 K6 Al Bādiyah al Janūbīyah h. Iraq
67 K1 Alba Iulia Romania
81 M6 Albājī Iran
22 F3 Albanel, L. l. Can.
49 Albania country Europe
112 C7 Albany Austr.
22 C3 Albany r. Can.
29 C6 Albany GA U.S.A.
30 E5 Albany IN U.S.A.
28 C4 Albany KY U.S.A.
33 G3 Albany NY U.S.A.
24 B2 Albany OR U.S.A.
115 H1 Albany Downs Austr.
47 G2 Albardão do João Maria coastal area Brazil
Al Başrah see Basra
81 K6 Al Baţḩa' marsh Iraq
113 H2 Albatross Bay b. Austr.
115 F8 Albatross I. i. Austr.
78 B4 Al Bawiti Egypt
101 E1 Al Bayḑā' Libya
42 □ Albemarle, Pta pt Ecuador
29 E5 Albemarle Sd chan. U.S.A.
66 C2 Albenga Italy
65 D3 Alberche r. Spain
113 F5 Alberga watercourse Austr.
65 B2 Albergaria-a-Velha Port.
115 G4 Albert Austr.
64 F2 Albert France
114 C5 Albert, Lake l. Austr.
102 D3 Albert, Lake l. Uganda/Dem. Rep. Congo
20 F4 Alberta div. Can.
32 E6 Alberta U.S.A.
20 F4 Alberta, Mt mt Can.
104 D7 Albertinia S. Africa
61 D4 Albert Kanaal canal Belgium
26 E3 Albert Lea U.S.A.
101 F4 Albert Nile r. Sudan/Uganda
44 B8 Alberto de Agostini, Parque Nacional nat. park Chile
105 H3 Alberton S. Africa
64 H4 Albertville France
64 F5 Albi France
43 H2 Albina Suriname
34 A2 Albion CA U.S.A.
33 J2 Albion ME U.S.A.
30 E4 Albion MI U.S.A.
32 D3 Albion NY U.S.A.
65 E5 Alborán, Isla de i. Spain
55 L8 Ålborg Denmark
55 M8 Ålborg Bugt b. Denmark
79 G2 Alborz, Reshteh-ye mts Iran
20 F4 Albreda Can.
116 B4 Albro Austr.
65 B4 Albufeira Port.
25 F5 Albuquerque U.S.A.
79 H5 Al Buraymī Oman
65 C3 Alburquerque Spain
115 G6 Albury Austr.
81 H4 Al Buşayrah Syria
80 G7 Al Busayţā' plain Saudi Arabia
81 L6 Al Buşayyah Iraq
65 B3 Alcácer do Sal Port.
65 E2 Alcalá de Henares Spain
65 E4 Alcalá la Real Spain
66 E6 Alcamo Italy
65 F2 Alcañiz Spain
65 C3 Alcántara Spain
65 E3 Alcaraz Spain
65 D4 Alcaudete Spain
65 E3 Alcázar de San Juan Spain
69 F5 Alchevs'k Ukr.
47 D2 Alcira Arg.
46 E2 Alcobaça Brazil
65 F2 Alcora Spain
47 E2 Alcorta Arg.
65 F3 Alcoy Spain
65 H3 Alcúdia Spain
103 E4 Aldabra Islands is Seychelles
27 B6 Aldama Mex.
77 O4 Aldan Rus. Fed.
77 P3 Aldan r. Rus. Fed.
59 J5 Aldeburgh U.K.
56 E7 Alderney i. U.K.
34 B4 Alder Peak summit U.S.A.
59 G6 Aldershot U.K.
32 C6 Alderson U.S.A.
58 D3 Aldingham U.K.
59 F5 Aldridge U.K.
30 B5 Aledo U.S.A.

58 F2 Ashington U.K.
68 J3 Ashit r. Rus. Fed.
91 C8 Ashizuri-misaki pt Japan
27 D4 Ashland KS U.S.A.
32 B5 Ashland KY U.S.A.
33 J1 Ashland ME U.S.A.
24 F2 Ashland MT U.S.A.
33 H3 Ashland NH U.S.A.
32 B4 Ashland OH U.S.A.
24 B3 Ashland OR U.S.A.
32 E6 Ashland VA U.S.A.
30 B2 Ashland WV U.S.A.
115 H2 Ashley Austr.
26 D2 Ashley U.S.A.
112 D2 Ashmore and Cartier Islands terr. Austr.
112 D2 Ashmore Reef rf Ashmore and Cartier Is
68 C4 Ashmyany Belarus
35 H5 Ash Peak U.S.A.
80 E6 Ashqelon Israel
81 J6 Ash Shabakah Iraq
81 H3 Ash Shaddādah Syria
81 K6 Ash Shanāfīyah Iraq
81 H7 Ash Shaqīq w. Saudi Arabia
81 J4 Ash Sharqāṭ Iraq
81 L6 Ash Shaṭrah Iraq
80 D7 Ash Shaṭṭ Egypt
80 E6 Ash Shawbak Jordan
79 F7 Ash Shiḥr Yemen
32 C4 Ashtabula U.S.A.
81 K1 Ashtarak Armenia
84 D5 Ashti India
104 D6 Ashton S. Africa
24 E2 Ashton U.S.A.
58 E4 Ashton-under-Lyne U.K.
22 F4 Ashuapmushuan r. Can.
29 C5 Ashville U.S.A.
80 F4 'Āṣī, Nahr al r. Asia
85 F6 Āsika India
66 C4 Asinara, Golfo dell' b. Italy
76 K4 Asino Rus. Fed.
68 D4 Asipovichy Belarus
78 E5 'Asīr reg. Saudi Arabia
81 H2 Aşkale Turkey
55 M7 Asker Norway
55 O7 Askersund Sweden
55 M7 Askim Norway
86 F1 Askiz Rus. Fed.
81 L2 Aşlāndūz Iran
102 D2 Asmara Eritrea
55 O8 Åsnen l. Sweden
84 C4 Asop India
78 D5 Asoteriba, J. mt Sudan
81 M3 Aspar Iran
58 D3 Aspatria U.K.
25 F4 Aspen U.S.A.
27 C5 Aspermont U.S.A.
117 B6 Aspiring, Mt mt N.Z.
21 H4 Asquith Can.
80 F4 As Sa'an Syria
102 E2 Assab Eritrea
80 C7 Aş Şaff Egypt
80 E6 Aş Şāfī Jordan
80 F3 As Safīrah Syria
Aş Şaḥrā' al Gharbīyah see Western Desert
Aş Şaḥrā' ash Sharqīyah see Eastern Desert
80 D6 Aş Şāliḥīyah Egypt
81 H4 Aş Şāliḥīyah Syria
81 K6 As Salmān Iraq
80 E5 As Salṭ Jordan
85 H4 Assam div. India
81 K6 As Samāwah Iraq
80 F5 Aş Şanamayn Syria
101 E2 As Sarīr reg. Libya
33 F5 Assateague I. i. U.S.A.
33 F6 Assateague Island National Seashore res. U.S.A.
61 E1 Assen Neth.
61 D4 Assesse Belgium
85 F5 Assia Hills h. India
101 D1 As Sidrah Libya
21 H5 Assiniboia Can.
21 K5 Assiniboine r. Can.
20 F4 Assiniboine, Mt mt Can.
46 B3 Assis Brazil
66 E3 Assisi Italy
81 L7 Aş Şubayḥīyah Kuwait
81 G4 As Sukhnah Syria
81 K4 As Sulaymānīyah Iraq
78 F5 As Sulayyil Saudi Arabia
78 E5 As Sūq Saudi Arabia
81 H4 Aş Şuwar Syria
80 F5 As Suwaydā' Syria
81 K5 Aş Şuwayrah Iraq
As Suways see Suez
57 C2 Assynt, Loch l. U.K.
67 M7 Astakida i. Greece
76 J4 Astana Kazak.
81 M3 Astaneh Iran
81 M2 Astara Azer.
66 C2 Asti Italy
34 A2 Asti U.S.A.
47 C1 Astica Arg.
Astin Tag mts see Altun Shan
84 C2 Astor Jammu and Kashmir
84 C2 Astor r. Pak.
65 C1 Astorga Spain
24 B2 Astoria U.S.A.
55 N8 Åstorp Sweden
69 J6 Astrakhan' Rus. Fed.
Astrakhan' Bazar see Cälilabad
69 H6 Astrakhanskaya Oblast' div. Rus. Fed.
68 C4 Astravyets Belarus
65 C1 Asturias div. Spain
67 M6 Astypalaia i. Greece
93 L3 Asuncion i. N. Mariana Is
44 E3 Asunción Para.
78 C5 Aswān Egypt
78 C4 Asyūṭ Egypt
111 J4 Ata i. Tonga
45 D4 Atabapo r. Col./Venez.
44 C2 Atacama, Desierto de des. Chile
44 C2 Atacama, Salar de salt flat Chile
111 J2 Atafu i. Tokelau
100 C4 Atakpamé Togo
67 K5 Atalanti Greece
42 D6 Atalaya Peru
100 A2 Atâr Maur.
95 A1 Ataran r. Myanmar
35 H4 Atarque U.S.A.
34 B4 Atascadero U.S.A.
82 D1 Atasu Kazak.
93 H8 Atauro i. Indon.
101 F3 Atbara Sudan
101 F3 Atbara r. Sudan
76 H4 Atbasar Kazak.
27 F6 Atchafalaya Bay b. U.S.A.
26 E4 Atchison U.S.A.
66 E3 Aterno r. Italy
66 F3 Atessa Italy
61 B4 Ath Belgium
20 G4 Athabasca Can.
21 G3 Athabasca, Lake l. Can.
60 E4 Athboy Rep. of Ireland
60 C4 Athenry Rep. of Ireland
31 K3 Athens Can.
67 K6 Athens Greece
29 C5 Athens AL U.S.A.
29 D5 Athens GA U.S.A.
32 B5 Athens OH U.S.A.
29 C5 Athens TN U.S.A.
27 E5 Athens TX U.S.A.
59 F5 Atherstone U.K.
116 A1 Atherton Austr.
Athina see Athens
60 C4 Athleague Rep. of Ireland
60 D4 Athlone Rep. of Ireland
117 B6 Athol N.Z.
33 G3 Athol U.S.A.
57 E4 Atholl, Forest of reg. U.K.
67 L4 Athos mt Greece
80 E7 Ath Thamad Egypt
60 E5 Athy Rep. of Ireland
101 D3 Ati Chad
42 D7 Atico Peru
22 B4 Atikokan Can.
23 H3 Atikonak L. l. Can.
94 B3 Atimonan Phil.
77 R3 Atka Rus. Fed.
69 H5 Atkarsk Rus. Fed.
29 C5 Atlanta GA U.S.A.
30 C5 Atlanta IL U.S.A.
31 E3 Atlanta MI U.S.A.
80 D2 Atlantı Turkey
26 E3 Atlantic U.S.A.
33 F5 Atlantic City U.S.A.
13 D7 Atlantic-Indian-Antarctic Basin sea feature Atlantic Ocean
12 J9 Atlantic-Indian Ridge sea feature Indian Ocean
4 Atlantic Ocean
104 C6 Atlantis S. Africa
12 G3 Atlantis Fracture sea feature Atlantic Ocean
100 C1 Atlas Saharien mts Alg.
20 C3 Atlin Can.
20 C3 Atlin Lake l. Can.
20 C3 Atlin Prov. Park Can.
80 E5 'Atlit Israel
27 G6 Atmore U.S.A.
27 D5 Atoka U.S.A.
95 C1 Atouat mt Laos
85 G4 Atrai r. India
45 A3 Atrato r. Col.
33 F5 Atsion U.S.A.
80 E6 Aṭ Ṭafīlah Jordan
78 E5 Aṭ Ṭā'if Saudi Arabia
29 C5 Attalla U.S.A.
95 C2 Attapu Laos
67 M6 Attavyros mt Greece
22 D3 Attawapiskat Can.
22 C3 Attawapiskat r. Can.
22 C3 Attawapiskat L. l. Can.
81 G7 Aṭ Ṭawīl mts Saudi Arabia
62 F7 Attersee l. Austria
30 D5 Attica IN U.S.A.
32 B4 Attica OH U.S.A.
33 H3 Attleboro U.S.A.
59 J5 Attleborough U.K.
80 F7 Aṭ Ṭubayq reg. Saudi Arabia
14 G2 Attu Island i. U.S.A.
78 C4 Aṭ Ṭūr Egypt
47 C2 Atuel r. Arg.
55 O7 Åtvidaberg Sweden
32 C4 Atwood Lake l. U.S.A.
76 G5 Atyrau Kazak.
64 G5 Aubagne France
94 B2 Aubarede Point pt Phil.
64 G4 Aubenas France
35 F4 Aubrey Cliffs cliff U.S.A.
114 C5 Auburn Austr.
116 D5 Auburn r. Austr.
31 G4 Auburn Can.
29 C5 Auburn AL U.S.A.
34 B2 Auburn CA U.S.A.
30 E5 Auburn IN U.S.A.
33 H2 Auburn ME U.S.A.
26 E3 Auburn NE U.S.A.
32 E3 Auburn NY U.S.A.
24 B2 Auburn WA U.S.A.
116 D5 Auburn Ra. h. Austr.
64 F4 Aubusson France
47 C3 Auca Mahuida, Sa de mt Arg.
64 E5 Auch France
57 E4 Auchterarder U.K.
117 E2 Auckland N.Z.
111 G7 Auckland Islands is N.Z.
33 H2 Audet Can.
59 J7 Audresselles France
116 B5 Augathella Austr.
60 D3 Augher U.K.
60 E3 Aughnacloy U.K.
60 E5 Aughrim Rep. of Ireland
104 D4 Augrabies S. Africa
104 D4 Augrabies Falls waterfall S. Africa
104 D4 Augrabies Falls National Park nat. park S. Africa
31 F3 Au Gres U.S.A.
62 E6 Augsburg Ger.
112 C6 Augusta Austr.
66 F6 Augusta Italy
29 D5 Augusta GA U.S.A.
27 D4 Augusta KS U.S.A.
33 J2 Augusta ME U.S.A.
30 B3 Augusta WV U.S.A.
45 B2 Augustín Cadazzi Col.
112 C4 Augustus, Mt mt Austr.
61 B4 Aulnoye-Aymeries France
59 J7 Ault France
103 B6 Auob r. Namibia
23 G2 Aupaluk Can.
95 C5 Aur i. Malaysia
55 S6 Aura Fin.
84 D4 Auraiya India
84 C6 Aurangābād India
62 C4 Aurich Ger.
46 B2 Aurilândia Brazil
64 F4 Aurillac France
94 B5 Aurora Phil.
24 F4 Aurora CO U.S.A.
30 C5 Aurora IL U.S.A.
33 J2 Aurora ME U.S.A.
27 E4 Aurora MO U.S.A.
113 H2 Aurukun Austr.
103 B6 Aus Namibia
31 F3 Au Sable U.S.A.
31 E3 Au Sable r. U.S.A.
33 G2 Ausable r. U.S.A.
33 G2 Ausable Forks U.S.A.
30 D2 Au Sable Pt pt MI U.S.A.
31 F3 Au Sable Pt pt MI U.S.A.
57 F1 Auskerry i. U.K.
54 D4 Austari-Jökulsá r. Iceland
26 E3 Austin MN U.S.A.
34 D2 Austin NV U.S.A.
27 D6 Austin TX U.S.A.
109 Australes, Îles is Pac. Oc.
106 Australia country Australasia
115 H5 Australian Capital Territory div. Austr.
48 Austria country Europe
54 O2 Austvågøy i. Norway
54 U3 Autti Fin.
64 G3 Autun France
64 F4 Auvergne reg. France
64 F3 Auxerre France
64 G3 Auxonne France
33 F3 Ava U.S.A.
64 F3 Avallon France
34 C5 Avalon U.S.A.
23 K4 Avalon Peninsula pen. Can.
81 L2 Avān Iran
80 E2 Avanos Turkey
46 C3 Avaré Brazil
81 L2 Āvārsīn Iran
34 D4 Avawatz Mts mts U.S.A.
43 G4 Aveiro Brazil
65 B2 Aveiro Port.
65 B2 Aveiro, Ria de est. Port.
81 M4 Āvej Iran
47 E2 Avellaneda Arg.
66 F4 Avellino Italy
34 B3 Avenal U.S.A.
114 F6 Avenel Austr.
66 F4 Aversa Italy
61 B4 Avesnes-sur-Helpe France
55 P6 Avesta Sweden
64 F4 Aveyron r. France
66 E3 Avezzano Italy
57 E3 Aviemore U.K.
66 F4 Avigliano Italy
64 G5 Avignon France
65 D2 Ávila Spain
65 D1 Avilés Spain
68 H2 Avnyugskiy Rus. Fed.
115 G8 Avoca Tas. Austr.
114 E6 Avoca Vic. Austr.
114 E6 Avoca r. Austr.
60 E5 Avoca Rep. of Ireland
26 E3 Avoca U.S.A.
66 F6 Avola Italy
59 F5 Avon r. Eng. U.K.
59 F7 Avon r. Eng. U.K.
30 B5 Avon U.S.A.
35 F5 Avondale U.S.A.
116 B3 Avon Downs Austr.
59 E6 Avonmouth U.K.
29 D7 Avon Park U.S.A.
64 D2 Avranches France
61 A5 Avre r. France
111 G2 Avuavu Solomon Is
91 D7 Awaji-shima i. Japan
117 E3 Awakino N.Z.
117 D1 Awanui N.Z.
117 B6 Awarua Pt pt N.Z.
102 E3 Āwash Eth.
102 E2 Āwash r. Eth.
90 F5 Awa-shima i. Japan
102 D3 Āwash National Park nat. park Eth.
104 A2 Awasib Mts mts Namibia
117 D4 Awatere r. N.Z.
101 D2 Awbārī Libya
60 C5 Awbeg r. Rep. of Ireland
81 L6 'Awdah, Hawr al l. Iraq
102 E3 Aw Dheegle Somalia
57 C4 Awe, Loch l. U.K.
101 E4 Aweil Sudan
100 C4 Awka Nigeria
94 C6 Awu mt Indon.
114 F6 Axedale Austr.
118 B3 Axel Heiberg Island i. Can.
100 B4 Axim Ghana
59 E7 Axminster U.K.
91 D7 Ayabe Japan
47 E3 Ayacucho Arg.
42 D6 Ayacucho Peru
82 F1 Ayagoz Kazak.
86 E4 Ayakkum Hu salt l. China
65 C4 Ayamonte Spain
77 P4 Ayan Rus. Fed.
69 F7 Ayancık Turkey
45 B2 Ayapel Col.
80 D1 Ayaş Turkey
42 D6 Ayaviri Peru
84 B1 Āybak Afgh.
69 F5 Aydar r. Ukr.
79 K1 Aydarkul', Ozero l. Uzbek.
80 A3 Aydın Turkey
80 A2 Aydın Dağları mts Turkey
95 □ Ayer Chawan, P. i. Sing.
95 □ Ayer Merbau, P. i. Sing.
Ayers Rock h. see Uluru
77 N3 Aykhal Rus. Fed.
68 J2 Aykino Rus. Fed.
117 D5 Aylesbury N.Z.
59 G6 Aylesbury U.K.
32 E6 Aylett U.S.A.
65 E2 Ayllón Spain
31 G4 Aylmer Can.
21 H2 Aylmer Lake l. Can.
79 K2 Aynī Tajik.
80 G3 'Ayn 'Īsá Syria
101 F4 Ayod Sudan
77 S3 Ayon, O. i. Rus. Fed.
100 B3 'Ayoûn el 'Atroûs Maur.
116 B2 Ayr Austr.
57 D5 Ayr U.K.
57 D5 Ayr r. U.K.
80 D3 Ayrancı Turkey
58 C3 Ayre, Point of pt Isle of Man
82 B1 Ayteke Bi Kazak.
67 M3 Aytos Bulg.
95 B2 Ayutthaya Thai.
67 M5 Ayvacık Turkey
80 F2 Ayvalı Turkey
67 M5 Ayvalık Turkey
85 E4 Azamgarh India
100 B3 Azaouâd reg. Mali
100 C3 Azaouagh, Vallée de watercourse Mali/Niger
Azbine mts see L'Aïr, Massif de
76 G4 Azdavay Turkey
70 Azerbaijan country Asia
31 G2 Azilda Can.
33 H2 Aziscohos Lake l. U.S.A.
42 C4 Azogues Ecuador
76 F3 Azopol'ye Rus. Fed.
48 Azores terr. Port.
12 H3 Azores - Cape St Vincent Ridge sea feature Atlantic Ocean
69 F6 Azov Rus. Fed.
69 F6 Azov, Sea of sea Rus. Fed./Ukr.
100 B1 Azrou Morocco
25 F4 Aztec U.S.A.
65 D3 Azuaga Spain
44 B3 Azúcar r. Chile
37 H7 Azuero, Península de pen. Panama
47 E3 Azul Arg.
47 B4 Azul, Cerro mt Arg.
42 C5 Azul, Cordillera mts Peru
46 A1 Azul, Serra h. Brazil
91 G6 Azuma-san vol. Japan
67 F8 Azurduy Bol.
66 B6 Azzaba Alg.
80 F5 Az Zabadānī Syria
81 J6 Az Ẓafīrī reg. Iraq
Az Ẓahrān see Dhahran
78 C3 Az Zaqāzīq Egypt
80 F5 Az Zarqā' Jordan
81 L6 Az Zubayr Iraq

B

80 E5 Ba'abda Lebanon
80 F4 Ba'albek Lebanon
115 H3 Baan Baa Austr.
102 E3 Baardheere Somalia
84 B2 Bābā, Kūh-e mts Afgh.
67 M5 Baba Burnu pt Turkey
81 M1 Babadağ mt Azer.
67 N2 Babadag Romania
69 C7 Babaeski Turkey
42 C4 Babahoyo Ecuador
85 E3 Babai r. Nepal
88 B1 Babai Gaxun China
81 L2 Bābā Jān Iran
94 C5 Babak Phil.
78 E7 Bāb al Mandab str. Africa/Asia
93 H8 Babar i. Indon.
93 H8 Babar, Kepulauan is Indon.
102 D4 Babati Tanz.
68 E3 Babayevo Rus. Fed.
69 H7 Babayurt Rus. Fed.
30 B2 Babbitt U.S.A.
115 H7 Babel I. i. Austr.
116 A1 Babinda Austr.
20 D4 Babine Lake l. Can.
93 J7 Babo Indon.
79 G2 Bābol Iran
104 C6 Baboon Point pt S. Africa
35 G6 Baboquivari Peak summit U.S.A.
102 B3 Baboua C.A.R.
68 D4 Babruysk Belarus
84 B4 Babuhri India
84 C2 Babusar Pass pass Pak.
86 J1 Babushkin Rus. Fed.
94 A4 Babuyan Phil.
94 B2 Babuyan i. Phil.
89 F7 Babuyan Channel chan. Phil.
94 B2 Babuyan Islands is Phil.
81 K5 Babylon Iraq
43 K4 Bacabal Brazil
80 C1 Bacakliyayla T. mt Turkey
93 H7 Bacan i. Indon.
94 B2 Bacarra Phil.
63 N7 Bacău Romania
114 F6 Bacchus Marsh Austr.
89 C6 Bắc Giang Vietnam
25 F6 Bachiniva Mex.
89 C6 Bach Long Vi, Đao i. Vietnam
82 E3 Bachu China
21 J1 Back r. Can.
67 H2 Bačka Palanka Serb. and Mont.
20 D2 Backbone Ranges mts Can.
54 P5 Backe Sweden
114 B5 Backstairs Pass. chan. Austr.
57 E4 Backwater Reservoir resr U.K.
89 B6 Bac Lac Vietnam
95 C3 Bac Liêu Vietnam
89 C6 Bắc Ninh Vietnam
94 B3 Baco, Mt mt Phil.
25 E6 Bacoachi Mex.
94 B4 Bacolod Phil.
89 B6 Bắc Quang Vietnam
22 F2 Bacqueville, Lac l. Can.
83 E8 Badagara India
88 A1 Badain Jaran Shamo des. China
42 F4 Badajós, Lago l. Brazil
65 C3 Badajoz Spain
81 H6 Badanah Saudi Arabia
85 H4 Badarpur India
31 F4 Bad Axe U.S.A.
23 H4 Baddeck Can.
80 C3 Bademli Geçidi pass Turkey
62 H6 Baden Austria
62 D7 Baden Switz.
62 D6 Baden-Baden Ger.
57 D4 Badenoch reg. U.K.
23 J4 Badger Can.
62 D5 Bad Hersfeld Ger.
62 F7 Bad Hofgastein Austria
66 D2 Badia Polesine Italy
84 B4 Badin Pak.
62 F7 Bad Ischl Austria
Bādiyat ash Shām des. see Syrian Desert
62 E5 Bad Kissingen Ger.
62 C6 Bad Kreuznach Ger.
26 C2 Badlands reg. U.S.A.
26 C3 Badlands Nat. Park nat. park U.S.A.
62 D6 Bad Mergentheim Ger.
61 F4 Bad Neuenahr-Ahrweiler Ger.
88 D4 Badong China
95 C3 Ba Đông Vietnam
81 K5 Badrah Iraq
62 F7 Bad Reichenhall Ger.
84 D3 Badrinath Peaks mts India
62 E5 Bad Salzungen Ger.
62 E4 Bad Schwartau Ger.
62 E4 Bad Segeberg Ger.
113 H2 Badu I. i. Austr.
83 F9 Badulla Sri Lanka
54 B3 Bæir Iceland
115 J4 Baerami Austr.
65 E4 Baeza Spain
100 D4 Bafang Cameroon
100 A3 Bafatá Guinea-Bissau
118 A3 Baffin Bay b. Can.
118 A3 Baffin Island i. Can.
116 D5 Baffle Cr. r. Austr.
100 D4 Bafia Cameroon
100 A3 Bafing, Réserve du nat. park Mali
100 A3 Bafoulabé Mali
100 D4 Bafoussam Cameroon
79 H3 Bāfq Iran
80 E1 Bafra Turkey
69 E7 Bafra Burnu pt Turkey
79 H4 Bāft Iran
102 C3 Bafwasende Dem. Rep. Congo
85 F4 Bagaha India
94 A5 Bagahak h. Malaysia
83 E7 Bagalkot India
102 D4 Bagamoyo Tanz.
92 C6 Bagan Datuk Malaysia
103 C5 Bagani Namibia
95 B4 Bagan Serai Malaysia
95 B5 Baganslapiapi Indon.
35 F4 Bagdad U.S.A.
47 F1 Bagé Brazil
84 D3 Bageshwar India
24 F3 Baggs U.S.A.
59 C6 Baggy Point pt U.K.
84 C5 Bagh India
81 K5 Baghdād Iraq
84 B1 Baghlān Afgh.
26 E2 Bagley U.S.A.
85 E3 Baglung Nepal
65 G1 Bagnères-de-Luchon France
64 G4 Bagnols-sur-Cèze France
85 F4 Bagnuiti r. Nepal
88 C2 Bag Nur l. China
Bago see Pegu
94 B4 Bago Phil.
63 K3 Bagrationovsk Rus. Fed.
94 C5 Baguio Phil.
94 B2 Baguio Phil.
84 D3 Bahadurgarh India
85 G4 Baharampur India
78 B4 Bahariya Oasis oasis Egypt
92 C6 Bahau Malaysia
84 C3 Bahawalnagar Pak.
84 B3 Bahawalpur Pak.
80 F3 Bahçe Turkey
88 C4 Ba He r. China
84 D3 Baheri India
102 D4 Bahi Tanz.
46 E1 Bahia div. Brazil
47 D3 Bahía Blanca Arg.
25 E6 Bahía Kino Mex.
44 C7 Bahía Laura Arg.
44 E2 Bahía Negra Para.
25 D7 Bahía Tortugas Mex.
102 D2 Bahir Dar Eth.
85 E4 Bahraich India
70 Bahrain country Asia
81 M3 Bahrāmābād Iran
81 M3 Bahrām Beyg Iran
Bahr el Azraq r. see Blue Nile
63 L7 Baia Mare Romania
87 M2 Baicheng China
23 G4 Baie-Comeau Can.
Baie du Poste see Mistissini
23 F4 Baie-St-Paul Can.
23 J4 Baie Verte Can.
82 J3 Baigou r. China
84 E5 Baihar India
87 N3 Baihe Jilin China
88 D3 Baihe Shaanxi China
Baikal, Lake l. see Baykal, Ozero
67 K2 Băileşti Romania
67 K2 Băileştilor, Câmpia plain Romania
88 D1 Bailingmiao China
61 A4 Bailleul France
21 H2 Baillie r. Can.
60 E4 Baillieborough Rep. of Ireland
88 B3 Bailong Jiang r. China
82 K4 Baima China
59 G4 Bain r. U.K.
82 G5 Bainang China
29 C6 Bainbridge GA U.S.A.
33 F3 Bainbridge NY U.S.A.
85 G3 Baingoin China
80 F6 Bā'ir Jordan
80 F6 Bā'ir, Wādī watercourse Jordan
85 E2 Bairab Co l. China
85 F4 Bairagnia India
88 F1 Bairin Qiao China
Bairin Youqi see Daban
Bairin Zuoqi see Lindong
115 G6 Bairnsdale Austr.
94 B4 Bais Phil.
89 C7 Baisha Hainan China
89 E5 Baisha Jiangxi China
88 C4 Baisha Sichuan China
87 N3 Baishan China
87 N3 Baishan China
88 B3 Baishui Jiang r. China
89 B7 Bai Thương Vietnam
88 E1 Baitle r. China
88 F1 Baixingt China
88 B2 Baiyin China
101 F3 Baiyuda Desert des. Sudan
67 H1 Baja Hungary
25 D6 Baja, Punta pt Mex.
36 A2 Baja California pen. Mex.
35 E6 Baja California Norte div. Mex.
81 M3 Bājalān Iran
27 C7 Bajan Mex.
84 E3 Bajang Nepal
85 G5 Baj Baj India
45 A3 Bajo Baudó Col.
47 D1 Bajo Hondo Arg.
116 D4 Bajool Austr.
100 A3 Bakel Senegal
34 D4 Baker CA U.S.A.
24 F2 Baker MT U.S.A.
35 E2 Baker NV U.S.A.
24 C2 Baker OR U.S.A.
24 B1 Baker, Mt vol. U.S.A.
35 G4 Baker Butte summit U.S.A.
20 C3 Baker I. i. U.S.A.
111 J1 Baker Island i. Pac. Oc.
21 K2 Baker Lake Can.
21 K2 Baker Lake l. Can.
116 C3 Bakers Creek Austr.
22 E2 Bakers Dozen Islands is Can.
34 C4 Bakersfield U.S.A.
95 C2 Ba Kêv Cambodia
84 B4 Bakhasar India
69 E6 Bakhchysaray Ukr.
79 H2 Bakherden Turkm.
69 E5 Bakhmach Ukr.
79 G3 Bakhtegan, Daryācheh-ye salt pan Iran
Bakı see Baku

30 D3 Brussels U.S.A.
63 O5 Brusyliv Ukr.
115 G6 Bruthen Austr.
Bruxelles see Brussels
32 A4 Bryan OH U.S.A.
27 D6 Bryan TX U.S.A.
114 C4 Bryan, Mt h. Austr.
68 E4 Bryansk Rus. Fed.
68 E4 Bryanskaya Oblast' div. Rus. Fed.
69 H6 Bryanskoye Rus. Fed.
35 H5 Bryce, Mt. mt U.S.A.
35 F3 Bryce Canyon Nat. Park nat. park U.S.A.
55 J7 Bryne Norway
69 F6 Bryukhovetskaya Rus. Fed.
62 H5 Brzeg Pol.
111 F2 Buala Solomon Is
100 A3 Buba Guinea-Bissau
81 M7 Būbīyān I. i. Kuwait
94 B5 Bubuan i. Phil.
80 C3 Bucak Turkey
45 B3 Bucaramanga Col.
94 C4 Bucas Grande i. Phil.
116 C3 Bucasia Austr.
115 H6 Buchan Austr.
100 A4 Buchanan Liberia
30 D5 Buchanan MI U.S.A.
32 D6 Buchanan VA U.S.A.
116 A3 Buchanan, L. salt flat Austr.
27 D6 Buchanan, L. l. U.S.A.
23 J4 Buchans Can.
67 M2 Bucharest Romania
34 B4 Buchon, Point pt U.S.A.
63 M7 Bucin, Pasul pass Romania
115 F3 Buckambool Mt h. Austr.
35 F5 Buckeye U.S.A.
32 B5 Buckeye Lake l. U.S.A.
32 C5 Buckhannon U.S.A.
32 C5 Buckhannon r. U.S.A.
57 E4 Buckhaven U.K.
31 H3 Buckhorn Can.
35 H5 Buckhorn U.S.A.
31 H3 Buckhorn Lake l. Can.
32 B6 Buckhorn Lake l. U.S.A.
57 F3 Buckie U.K.
31 K3 Buckingham Can.
59 G5 Buckingham U.K.
32 D6 Buckingham U.S.A.
113 G2 Buckingham Bay b. Austr.
116 B5 Buckland Tableland reg. Austr.
114 B4 Buckleboo Austr.
119 A6 Buckle I. i. Antarctica
35 F4 Buckskin Mts mts U.S.A.
34 B2 Bucks Mt mt U.S.A.
33 J2 Bucksport U.S.A.
București see Bucharest
32 B4 Bucyrus U.S.A.
63 P4 Buda-Kashalyova Belarus
63 J7 Budapest Hungary
84 D3 Budaun India
114 F3 Budda Austr.
57 F4 Buddon Ness pt U.K.
66 C4 Buddusò Italy
59 C7 Bude U.K.
27 F6 Bude U.S.A.
69 H6 Budennovsk Rus. Fed.
115 K1 Buderim Austr.
84 D5 Budni India
68 E3 Budogoshch' Rus. Fed.
85 H2 Budongquan China
66 C4 Budoni Italy
100 C4 Buea Cameroon
34 B4 Buellton U.S.A.
47 D2 Buena Esperanza Arg.
45 A4 Buenaventura Col.
36 C3 Buenaventura Mex.
45 A4 Buenaventure, B. de b. Col.
25 F4 Buena Vista CO U.S.A.
32 D6 Buena Vista VA U.S.A.
65 E2 Buendia, Embalse de resr Spain
47 B4 Bueno r. Chile
47 E2 Buenos Aires Arg.
47 E3 Buenos Aires div. Arg.
44 B7 Buenos Aires, L. l. Arg./Chile
44 C7 Buen Pasto Arg.
27 B7 Búfalo Mex.
20 G3 Buffalo r. Can.
32 D3 Buffalo NY U.S.A.
27 D4 Buffalo OK U.S.A.
26 C2 Buffalo SD U.S.A.
27 D6 Buffalo TX U.S.A.
30 B3 Buffalo WV U.S.A.
24 F2 Buffalo WY U.S.A.
30 B3 Buffalo r. U.S.A.
115 G6 Buffalo, Mt mt Austr.
20 F3 Buffalo Head Hills h. Can.
20 F2 Buffalo Lake l. Can.
21 H3 Buffalo Narrows Can.
104 B4 Buffels watercourse S. Africa
105 G1 Buffels Drift S. Africa
29 D5 Buford U.S.A.
67 L2 Buftea Romania
63 K4 Bug r. Pol.
45 A4 Buga Col.
45 A3 Bugalagrande Col.
115 H3 Bugaldie Austr.
92 □ Bugel, Tanjung pt Indon.
66 G2 Bugojno Bos.-Herz.
94 A4 Bugsuk i. Phil.
94 B2 Buguey Phil.
103 D5 Buhera Zimbabwe
94 B3 Buhi Phil.
24 D3 Buhl ID U.S.A.
30 A2 Buhl MN U.S.A.
81 J3 Bühtan r. Turkey
63 N7 Buhuși Romania
59 D5 Builth Wells U.K.
100 B4 Bui National Park nat. park Ghana
68 J4 Buinsk Rus. Fed.
81 L4 Bu'in Soflā Iran
87 L2 Buir Nur l. Mongolia
103 B6 Buitepos Namibia
67 J3 Bujanovac Serb. and Mont.
102 C4 Bujumbura Burundi
87 L1 Bukachacha Rus. Fed.
111 F2 Buka I. i. P.N.G.
102 C4 Bukavu Dem. Rep. Congo
79 J2 Bukhara Uzbek.
94 C6 Bukide i. Indon.
95 □ Bukit Batok Sing.
95 B5 Bukit Fraser Malaysia
95 □ Bukit Panjang Sing.
95 □ Bukit Timah Sing.
92 C7 Bukittinggi Indon.
102 D4 Bukoba Tanz.
95 □ Bukum, P. i. Sing.
93 J7 Bula Indon.
68 J4 Bula r. Rus. Fed.
62 D7 Bülach Switz.
115 K4 Bulahdelal Austr.
94 B3 Bulan Phil.
80 G1 Bulancak Turkey
84 D3 Bulandshahr India
81 J2 Bulanık Turkey
103 C6 Bulawayo Zimbabwe
80 F3 Bulbul Syria
80 B2 Buldan Turkey
84 D5 Buldana India
105 J2 Bulembu Swaziland
86 H2 Bulgan Hövsgöl Mongolia
88 B1 Bulgan Ömnögovĭ Mongolia
49 Bulgaria country Europe
114 E1 Bullawarra, Lake salt flat Austr.
114 D3 Bullea, Lake salt flat Austr.
117 D4 Buller r. N.Z.
115 G6 Buller, Mt mt Austr.
35 E4 Bullhead City U.S.A.
34 D4 Bullion Mts mts U.S.A.
114 E2 Bulloo watercourse Austr.
114 E2 Bulloo Downs Austr.
114 E2 Bulloo L. salt flat Austr.
104 B2 Büllsport Namibia
114 E6 Buloke, Lake l. Austr.
105 G4 Bultfontein S. Africa
94 C5 Buluan Phil.
93 G8 Bulukumba Indon.
77 O2 Bulun Rus. Fed.
102 B4 Bulungu Bandundu Dem. Rep. Congo
102 C4 Bulungu Kasai-Occidental Dem. Rep. Congo
94 C3 Bulusan Phil.
102 C3 Bumba Dem. Rep. Congo
88 B1 Bumbat Sum China
35 F4 Bumble Bee U.S.A.
94 A5 Bum-Bum i. Malaysia
102 B4 Buna Dem. Rep. Congo
102 D3 Buna Kenya
102 D4 Bunazi Tanz.
60 C2 Bunbeg Rep. of Ireland
112 C6 Bunbury Austr.
60 E5 Bunclody Rep. of Ireland
60 D2 Buncrana Rep. of Ireland
102 D4 Bunda Tanz.
116 E5 Bundaberg Austr.
115 G2 Bundaleer Austr.
115 J3 Bundarra Austr.
84 C4 Bundi India
60 C3 Bundoran Rep. of Ireland
85 F5 Bundu India
59 J5 Bungay U.K.
95 B2 Bung Boraphet l. Thai.
115 H5 Bungendore Austr.
116 C6 Bungil Cr. r. Austr.
Bungle Bungle National Park nat. park see Purnululu National Park
91 C8 Bungo-suidō chan. Japan
102 D3 Bunia Dem. Rep. Congo
102 C4 Bunianga Dem. Rep. Congo
114 E6 Buninyong Austr.
100 D3 Buni-Yadi Nigeria
84 C2 Bunji Jammu and Kashmir
116 E4 Bunker Group atolls Austr.
35 E3 Bunkerville U.S.A.
27 E6 Bunkie U.S.A.
29 D6 Bunnell U.S.A.
80 E2 Bünyan Turkey
94 A6 Bunyu i. Indon.
95 D2 Buôn Hô Vietnam
95 D2 Buôn Mê Thuột Vietnam
77 P2 Buorkhaya, Guba b. Rus. Fed.
102 D4 Bura Kenya
83 E3 Burang China
46 E2 Buranhaém r. Brazil
102 E3 Burao Somalia
94 C4 Burauen Phil.
78 E4 Buraydah Saudi Arabia
34 C4 Burbank U.S.A.
115 G4 Burcher Austr.
116 B3 Burdekin r. Austr.
116 B3 Burdekin Falls waterfall Austr.
80 C3 Burdur Turkey
102 D2 Burē Eth.
59 J5 Bure r. U.K.
54 R4 Bureå Sweden
87 O1 Bureinskiy Khrebet mts Rus. Fed.
67 M3 Burgas Bulg.
29 E5 Burgaw U.S.A.
23 J4 Burgeo Can.
105 G5 Burgersdorp S. Africa
105 J2 Burgersfort S. Africa
59 G7 Burgess Hill U.K.
62 F6 Burghausen Ger.
57 E3 Burghead U.K.
61 B3 Burgh-Haamstede Neth.
66 F6 Burgio, Serra di h. Italy
65 E1 Burgos Spain
55 Q8 Burgsvik Sweden
Burgundy reg. see Bourgogne
82 J3 Burhan Budai Shan mts China
67 M5 Burhaniye Turkey
84 D5 Burhanpur India
85 E5 Burhar-Dhanpuri India
85 F4 Burhi Gandak r. India
94 B3 Burias i. Phil.
85 H4 Buri Dihing r. India
85 E4 Buri Gandak r. Nepal
23 J4 Burin Peninsula pen. Can.
95 B2 Buriram Thai.
43 K5 Buriti Bravo Brazil
46 C1 Buritis Brazil
117 C6 Burke Pass N.Z.
113 G3 Burketown Austr.
96 Burkina country Africa
31 H3 Burk's Falls Can.
24 D3 Burley U.S.A.
31 H4 Burlington Can.
26 C4 Burlington CO U.S.A.
30 B5 Burlington IA U.S.A.
30 D5 Burlington IN U.S.A.
33 J2 Burlington ME U.S.A.
33 G2 Burlington VT U.S.A.
30 C4 Burlington WV U.S.A.
Burma country see Myanmar
27 D6 Burnet U.S.A.
116 E5 Burnett r. Austr.
116 E5 Burnett Heads Austr.
24 B3 Burney U.S.A.
33 J2 Burnham U.S.A.
115 F8 Burnie Austr.
58 G3 Burniston U.K.
58 E4 Burnley U.K.
24 C3 Burns U.S.A.
21 H1 Burnside r. Can.
32 C5 Burnsville Lake l. U.S.A.
57 E4 Burntisland U.K.
21 K3 Burntwood r. Can.
21 J3 Burntwood Lake l. Can.
114 E5 Buronga Austr.
82 G1 Burqin China
80 G5 Burqu' Jordan
114 C4 Burra Austr.
57 □ Burra i. U.K.
57 □ Burravoe U.K.
57 F2 Burray i. U.K.
67 J4 Burrel Albania
115 H4 Burrendong Reservoir resr Austr.
115 H3 Burren Jct. Austr.
115 J5 Burrewarra Pt pt Austr.
65 F3 Burriana Spain
115 H5 Burrinjuck Austr.
115 H5 Burrinjuck Reservoir resr Austr.
36 D3 Burro, Serranías del mts Mex.
32 B5 Burr Oak Reservoir resr U.S.A.
57 D6 Burrow Head hd U.K.
116 E5 Burrum Heads Austr.
35 G2 Burrville U.S.A.
80 B1 Bursa Turkey
78 C4 Būr Safājah Egypt
Būr Sa'īd see Port Said
Būr Sudan see Port Sudan
114 D4 Burta Austr.
30 E3 Burt Lake l. U.S.A.
31 F4 Burton U.S.A.
22 E3 Burton, Lac l. Can.
60 C3 Burtonport Rep. of Ireland
59 F5 Burton upon Trent U.K.
54 R4 Burträsk Sweden
33 K1 Burtts Corner Can.
114 E4 Burtundy Austr.
93 H7 Buru i. Indon.
80 C6 Burullus, Bahra el lag. Egypt
102 D4 Burundi country Africa
102 C4 Bururi Burundi
20 B2 Burwash Landing Can.
57 F2 Burwick U.K.
69 E5 Buryn' Ukr.
59 H5 Bury St Edmunds U.K.
84 C2 Burzil Pass pass Jammu and Kashmir
102 C4 Busanga Dem. Rep. Congo
60 E2 Bush r. U.K.
79 G4 Būshehr Iran
85 E2 Bushêngcaka China
102 D4 Bushenyi Uganda
60 E2 Bushmills U.K.
30 B5 Bushnell U.S.A.
95 □ Busing, P. i. Sing.
102 C3 Businga Dem. Rep. Congo
80 F5 Buşrá ash Shām Syria
112 C6 Busselton Austr.
61 D2 Bussum Neth.
27 C7 Bustamante Mex.
25 F6 Bustillos, Lago l. Mex.
66 C2 Busto Arsizio Italy
94 A3 Busuanga Phil.
94 A3 Busuanga i. Phil.
102 C3 Buta Dem. Rep. Congo
95 A4 Butang Group is Thai.
47 C3 Buta Ranquil Arg.
102 C4 Butare Rwanda
114 B4 Bute Austr.
57 C5 Bute i. U.K.
57 C5 Bute, Sound of chan. U.K.
20 D4 Butedale Can.
20 D4 Bute In. in. Can.
105 H4 Butha Buthe Lesotho
30 E5 Butler IN U.S.A.
32 D4 Butler PA U.S.A.
60 D3 Butlers Bridge Rep. of Ireland
93 G7 Buton i. Indon.
24 D2 Butte U.S.A.
34 B1 Butte Meadows U.S.A.
92 C5 Butterworth Malaysia
105 H6 Butterworth S. Africa
60 C5 Buttevant Rep. of Ireland
20 D5 Buttle L. l. Can.
57 B2 Butt of Lewis hd U.K.
34 C4 Buttonwillow U.S.A.
94 C4 Butuan Phil.
89 B5 Butuo China
69 G5 Buturlinovka Rus. Fed.
85 E4 Butwal Nepal
102 E3 Buulobarde Somalia
102 E4 Buur Gaabo Somalia
102 E3 Buurhabaka Somalia
85 F4 Buxar India
59 F4 Buxton U.K.
68 G3 Buy Rus. Fed.
30 A1 Buyck U.S.A.
69 H7 Buynaksk Rus. Fed.
Büyük Ağri mt see Ararat, Mt
80 A3 Büyükmenderes r. Turkey
88 G1 Buyun Shan mt China
67 M2 Buzău Romania
103 D5 Búzi Moz.
76 G4 Buzuluk Rus. Fed.
69 G5 Buzuluk r. Rus. Fed.
33 H4 Buzzards Bay b. U.S.A.
113 K2 Bwagaoia P.N.G.
67 L3 Byala Bulg.
67 K3 Byala Slatina Bulg.
63 O4 Byalynichy Belarus
68 D4 Byarezina r. Belarus
68 C4 Byaroza Belarus
80 E4 Byblos Lebanon
62 H4 Bydgoszcz Pol.
68 D4 Byerazino Belarus
24 F4 Byers U.S.A.
63 O3 Byeshankovichy Belarus
55 K7 Bygland Norway
68 D4 Bykhaw Belarus
55 K7 Bykle Norway
118 A3 Bylot I. i. Can.
31 G3 Byng Inlet Can.
55 K6 Byrkjelo Norway
115 G3 Byrock Austr.
30 C4 Byron IL U.S.A.
33 H2 Byron ME U.S.A.
115 K2 Byron, C. hd Austr.
115 K2 Byron Bay Austr.
77 M2 Byrranga, Gory mts Rus. Fed.
54 R4 Byske Sweden
77 P3 Bytantay r. Rus. Fed.
63 J5 Bytom Pol.
62 H3 Bytów Pol.

C

44 E3 Caacupé Para.
46 A4 Caaguazú Para.
46 A4 Caaguazú, Cordillera de h. Para.
46 A3 Caarapó Brazil
46 A4 Caazapá Para.
42 C6 Caballas Peru
42 D4 Caballococha Peru
94 B3 Cabanatuan Phil.
23 G4 Cabano Can.
102 E2 Cabdul Qaadir Somalia
46 A1 Cabeceira Rio Manso Brazil
43 M5 Cabedelo Brazil
65 D3 Cabeza del Buey Spain
42 F7 Cabezas Bol.
47 E3 Cabildo Arg.
42 C2 Cabimas Venez.
102 B4 Cabinda Angola
102 B4 Cabinda div. Angola
24 C1 Cabinet Mts mts U.S.A.
45 B3 Cable Way pass Col.
46 D3 Cabo Frio Brazil
46 E3 Cabo Frio, Ilha do i. Brazil
22 E4 Cabonga, Réservoir resr Can.
27 E4 Cabool U.S.A.
115 K1 Caboolture Austr.
43 H3 Cabo Orange, Parque Nacional de nat. park Brazil
42 C4 Cabo Pantoja Peru
36 B2 Caborca Mex.
31 G3 Cabot Head pt Can.
23 J4 Cabot Strait str. Can.
42 D2 Cabral, Serra do mts Brazil
81 L2 Cäbrayıl Azer.
65 H3 Cabrera i. Spain
65 F3 Cabriel r. Spain
45 D3 Cabruta Venez.
94 B2 Cabugao Phil.
46 B4 Caçador Brazil
67 J3 Čačak Serb. and Mont.
47 G1 Caçapava do Sul Brazil
32 D5 Cacapon r. U.S.A.
46 B3 Cáceres Col.
66 C4 Caccia, Capo pt Italy
43 G7 Cáceres Brazil
65 C3 Cáceres Spain
24 D3 Cache Peak summit U.S.A.
100 A3 Cacheu Guinea-Bissau
44 C3 Cachi r. Arg.
44 C2 Cachi, Nevados de mt Arg.
43 H5 Cachimbo, Serra do h. Brazil
45 B3 Cáchira Col.
46 E1 Cachoeira Brazil
46 B2 Cachoeira Alta Brazil
47 G1 Cachoeira do Sul Brazil
46 E3 Cachoeiro de Itapemirim Brazil
100 A3 Cacine Guinea-Bissau
43 H3 Caciporé, Cabo pt Brazil
103 B5 Cacolo Angola
102 B4 Cacongo Angola
34 D3 Cactus Range mts U.S.A.
46 B2 Caçu Brazil
46 D1 Caculé Brazil
63 J6 Čadca Slovakia
114 A2 Cadibarrawirracanna, L. salt flat Austr.
94 B3 Cadig Mountains mts Phil.
31 H1 Cadillac Que. Can.
21 H5 Cadillac Sask. Can.
30 E3 Cadillac U.S.A.
94 B4 Cadiz Phil.
65 C4 Cádiz Spain
65 C4 Cádiz, Golfo de g. Spain
35 E4 Cadiz Lake l. U.S.A.
64 D2 Caen France
59 C4 Caernarfon U.K.
59 C4 Caernarfon Bay b. U.K.
59 D6 Caerphilly U.K.
32 B5 Caesar Creek Lake l. U.S.A.
80 E5 Caesarea Israel
46 D1 Caetité Brazil
44 C3 Cafayate Arg.
94 B4 Cagayan i. Phil.
94 B2 Cagayan r. Phil.
94 C4 Cagayan de Oro Phil.
94 B4 Cagayan Islands is Phil.
66 E3 Cagli Italy
66 C5 Cagliari Italy
66 C5 Cagliari, Golfo di b. Italy
45 B4 Caguán r. Col.
60 B6 Caha h. Rep. of Ireland
29 C5 Cahaba r. U.S.A.
60 B6 Caha Mts h. Rep. of Ireland
60 A6 Cahermore Rep. of Ireland
60 A6 Cahersiveen Rep. of Ireland
60 D5 Cahir Rep. of Ireland
103 D5 Cahora Bassa, Lago de resr Moz.
60 E5 Cahore Point pt Rep. of Ireland
64 E4 Cahors France
42 C5 Cahuapanas Peru
69 D6 Cahul Moldova
103 D5 Caia Moz.
43 G6 Caiabis, Serra dos h. Brazil
103 C5 Caianda Angola
46 B2 Caiapó r. Brazil
46 B2 Caiapó, Serra do mts Brazil
46 B2 Caiapônia Brazil
37 J4 Caibarién Cuba
89 C6 Cai Bâu, Đao i. Vietnam
95 C3 Cai Be Vietnam
45 D3 Caicara Venez.
37 K4 Caicos Is is Turks and Caicos Is
89 E4 Caidian China
47 B1 Caimanes Chile
94 A3 Caiman Point pt Phil.
65 F2 Caimodorro mt Spain
95 C3 Cai Nước Vietnam
57 E3 Cairn Gorm mt U.K.
57 E3 Cairngorm Mountains mts U.K.
57 C6 Cairnryan U.K.
116 A1 Cairns Austr.
57 E3 Cairn Toul mt U.K.
78 C4 Cairo Egypt
29 C6 Cairo U.S.A.
66 C2 Cairo Montenotte Italy
103 B5 Caiundo Angola
115 F2 Caiwarro Austr.
42 C5 Cajamarca Peru
94 B3 Cajidiocan Phil.
66 G1 Čakovec Croatia
80 B2 Çal Turkey
105 G5 Cala S. Africa
100 C4 Calabar Nigeria
31 J3 Calabogie Can.
45 D2 Calabozo Venez.
67 K3 Calafat Romania
44 B8 Calafate Arg.
94 B3 Calagua Islands is Phil.
65 F1 Calahorra Spain
103 B5 Calai Angola
64 E1 Calais France
33 K2 Calais U.S.A.
42 F5 Calama Brazil
44 C2 Calama Chile
45 B2 Calamar Bolívar Col.
45 B4 Calamar Guaviare Col.
94 A4 Calamian Group is Phil.
65 F2 Calamocha Spain
103 B4 Calandula Angola
101 E2 Calanscio Sand Sea des. Libya
94 B3 Calapan Phil.
67 M2 Călărași Romania
65 F2 Calatayud Spain
94 B3 Calauag Phil.
94 B3 Calavite, Cape pt Phil.
94 A3 Calawit i. Phil.
94 B2 Calayan i. Phil.
94 C3 Calbayog Phil.
94 C4 Calbiga Phil.
47 B4 Calbuco Chile
43 L5 Calcanhar, Ponta do pt Brazil
27 E6 Calcasieu L. l. U.S.A.
43 H3 Calçoene Brazil
Calcutta see Kolkata
65 B3 Caldas da Rainha Port.
46 C2 Caldas Novas Brazil
44 B3 Caldera Chile
116 B5 Caldervale Austr.
81 J2 Çaldıran Turkey
24 C3 Caldwell U.S.A.
32 D3 Caledon Can.
105 G5 Caledon r. Lesotho/S. Africa
104 C7 Caledon S. Africa
31 H4 Caledonia Can.
30 B4 Caledonia U.S.A.
116 C3 Calen Austr.
44 C7 Caleta Olivia Arg.
35 E5 Calexico U.S.A.
58 C3 Calf of Man i. U.K.
20 G4 Calgary Can.
29 C5 Calhoun U.S.A.
45 A4 Cali Col.
94 C4 Calicoan i. Phil.
83 E8 Calicut India
34 C4 Caliente CA U.S.A.
35 E3 Caliente NV U.S.A.
34 B3 California div. U.S.A.
36 B2 California, Golfo de g. Mex.
34 B3 California Aqueduct canal U.S.A.
34 C4 California Hot Springs U.S.A.
81 M2 Cälilabad Azer.
25 D5 Calipatria U.S.A.
34 A2 Calistoga U.S.A.
104 D6 Calitzdorp S. Africa
114 D2 Callabonna, L. salt flat Austr.
34 D2 Callaghan, Mt mt U.S.A.
29 D6 Callahan U.S.A.
60 D5 Callan Rep. of Ireland
31 H2 Callander Can.
57 D4 Callander U.K.
42 C6 Callao Peru
35 F2 Callao U.S.A.
33 F4 Callicoon U.S.A.
116 D5 Callide Austr.
59 C7 Callington U.K.
116 D5 Calliope Austr.
31 G2 Callum Can.
20 G4 Calmar Can.
30 B4 Calmar U.S.A.
35 E4 Cal-Nev-Ari U.S.A.
29 D7 Caloosahatchee r. U.S.A.
115 K1 Caloundra Austr.
34 B2 Calpine U.S.A.
66 F6 Caltanissetta Italy
30 C2 Calumet U.S.A.
103 B5 Calunga Angola
103 B5 Caluquembe Angola
94 B4 Calusa i. Phil.
102 F2 Caluula Somalia
35 G5 Calva U.S.A.
113 G3 Calvert Hills Austr.
20 D4 Calvert I. i. Can.
66 C3 Calvi France
65 H3 Calvià Spain
104 C5 Calvinia S. Africa
66 F4 Calvo, Monte mt Italy
59 H5 Cam r. U.K.
46 E1 Camaçari Brazil
34 B2 Camache Reservoir resr U.S.A.
103 B5 Camacuio Angola
103 B5 Camacupa Angola
45 D2 Camaguán Venez.
37 J4 Camagüey Cuba
37 J4 Camagüey, Arch. de is Cuba
95 B4 Camah, Gunung mt Malaysia
Çamalan see Gülek
42 D7 Camana Peru
103 C5 Camanongue Angola
46 B2 Camapuã Brazil
47 G1 Camaquã Brazil
47 G1 Camaquã r. Brazil
80 E3 Çamardı Turkey
36 E3 Camargo Mex.
44 C6 Camarones Arg.
44 C6 Camarones, Bahía b. Arg.
24 B2 Camas U.S.A.
95 C3 Ca Mau Vietnam
Cambay see Khambhat
Cambay, Gulf of g. see Khambhat, Gulf of
59 G6 Camberley U.K.
70 Cambodia country Asia
59 B7 Camborne U.K.
64 F1 Cambrai France
34 B4 Cambria U.S.A.
59 D5 Cambrian Mountains reg. U.K.
31 G4 Cambridge Can.
117 E2 Cambridge N.Z.
59 H5 Cambridge U.K.
30 B5 Cambridge IL U.S.A.
33 H3 Cambridge MA U.S.A.
33 E5 Cambridge MD U.S.A.
26 E2 Cambridge MN U.S.A.
33 G3 Cambridge NY U.S.A.
32 C4 Cambridge OH U.S.A.
23 G2 Cambrien, Lac l. Can.
115 J5 Camden Austr.
29 C5 Camden AL U.S.A.
27 E5 Camden AR U.S.A.

33 H2 Dead r. U.S.A.
29 F7 Deadman's Cay Bahamas
35 E4 Dead Mts mts U.S.A.
80 E6 Dead Sea salt l. Asia
59 J6 Deal U.K.
105 F4 Dealesville S. Africa
20 D4 Dean r. Can.
89 E4 De'an China
59 E6 Dean, Forest of forest U.K.
47 D1 Deán Funes Arg.
31 F4 Dearborn U.S.A.
20 D3 Dease r. Can.
20 C3 Dease Lake Can.
34 D3 Death Valley v. U.S.A.
34 D3 Death Valley Junction U.S.A.
34 D3 Death Valley National Park res. U.S.A.
64 E2 Deauville France
92 E6 Debak Malaysia
89 C6 Debao China
67 J4 Debar Macedonia
21 H4 Debden Can.
59 J5 Debenham U.K.
35 H2 De Beque U.S.A.
61 C3 De Biesbosch, Nationaal Park nat. park Neth.
33 J2 Deblois U.S.A.
102 D3 Debre Birhan Eth.
63 K7 Debrecen Hungary
102 D2 Debre Markos Eth.
102 D2 Debre Tabor Eth.
102 D3 Debre Zeyit Eth.
29 C5 Decatur AL U.S.A.
29 C5 Decatur GA U.S.A.
30 C6 Decatur IL U.S.A.
30 E5 Decatur IN U.S.A.
30 E4 Decatur MI U.S.A.
83 E7 Deccan plat. India
31 H2 Decelles, Lac resr Can.
115 K1 Deception Bay Austr.
62 G5 Děčín Czech Rep.
30 B4 Decorah U.S.A.
59 F6 Deddington U.K.
46 C4 Dedo de Deus mt Brazil
104 C6 De Doorns S. Africa
81 L1 Dedop'listsqaro Georgia
100 B3 Dédougou Burkina
68 D3 Dedovichi Rus. Fed.
103 D5 Dedza Malawi
59 D4 Dee est. U.K.
59 E4 Dee r. England/Wales U.K.
57 F3 Dee r. Scot. U.K.
60 C5 Deel r. Rep. of Ireland
60 D3 Deele r. Rep. of Ireland
32 D5 Deep Creek Lake l. U.S.A.
35 F2 Deep Creek Range mts U.S.A.
31 J2 Deep River Can.
33 G4 Deep River U.S.A.
21 K1 Deep Rose Lake l. Can.
34 D3 Deep Springs U.S.A.
115 J2 Deepwater Austr.
32 B5 Deer Creek Lake l. U.S.A.
33 K2 Deer I. i. Can.
33 J2 Deer I. i. U.S.A.
33 J2 Deer Isle U.S.A.
22 B3 Deer L. l. Can.
23 J4 Deer Lake Nfld and Lab. Can.
22 B3 Deer Lake Ont. Can.
24 D2 Deer Lodge U.S.A.
44 D2 Defensores del Chaco, Parque Nacional nat. park Para.
32 A4 Defiance U.S.A.
29 C6 De Funiak Springs U.S.A.
82 J4 Dêgê China
102 E3 Degeh Bur Eth.
85 G3 Dêgên China
62 F6 Deggendorf Ger.
84 C3 Degh r. Pak.
61 D3 De Groote Peel, Nationaal Park nat. park Neth.
81 N3 Dehgāh Iran
81 L4 Deh Golān Iran
81 L5 Dehlorān Iran
84 D3 Dehra Dun India
85 F4 Dehri India
81 K4 Deh Sheykh Iran
89 F5 Dehua China
87 N3 Dehui China
61 B4 Deinze Belgium
80 E5 Deir el Qamer Lebanon
Deir-ez-Zor see Dayr az Zawr
63 L7 Dej Romania
89 C4 Dejiang China
30 C5 De Kalb IL U.S.A.
27 E5 De Kalb TX U.S.A.
33 F2 De Kalb Junction U.S.A.
87 Q1 De-Kastri Rus. Fed.
78 D6 Dekemhare Eritrea
102 C4 Dekese Dem. Rep. Congo
34 C4 Delano U.S.A.
35 F2 Delano Peak summit U.S.A.
79 J3 Delārām Afgh.
105 F3 Delareyville S. Africa
21 H4 Delaronde Lake l. Can.
30 C5 Delavan IL U.S.A.
30 C4 Delavan WV U.S.A.
32 B4 Delaware U.S.A.
33 F5 Delaware div. U.S.A.
33 F4 Delaware r. U.S.A.
33 F5 Delaware Bay b. U.S.A.
32 B4 Delaware Lake l. U.S.A.
33 F4 Delaware Water Gap National Recreational Area res. U.S.A.
115 H6 Delegate Austr.
62 C7 Delémont Switz.
61 C2 Delft Neth.
61 E1 Delfzijl Neth.
103 E5 Delgado, Cabo pt Moz.
31 G4 Delhi Can.
82 J3 Delhi China
84 D3 Delhi India
25 F4 Delhi CO U.S.A.
33 F3 Delhi NY U.S.A.
92 □ Deli i. Indon.
81 J2 Deli r. Turkey
80 E2 Delice Turkey
80 E1 Delice r. Turkey
20 E1 Déline Can.
21 H4 Delisle Can.
26 D3 Dell Rapids U.S.A.
65 H4 Dellys Alg.
34 D5 Del Mar U.S.A.
35 E3 Delmar L. l. U.S.A.
62 D4 Delmenhorst Ger.
77 R2 De-Longa, O-va is Rus. Fed.
21 J5 Deloraine Can.
30 D5 Delphi U.S.A.
32 A4 Delphos U.S.A.
104 F4 Delportshoop S. Africa
29 D7 Delray Beach U.S.A.
25 E6 Del Río Mex.
27 C6 Del Rio U.S.A.
55 P6 Delsbo Sweden
35 H2 Delta CO U.S.A.
30 A5 Delta IA U.S.A.
35 F2 Delta UT U.S.A.
33 F3 Delta Reservoir resr U.S.A.
29 D6 Deltona U.S.A.
115 J2 Delungra Austr.
60 D4 Delvin Rep. of Ireland
67 J5 Delvinë Albania
102 C4 Demba Dem. Rep. Congo
102 D3 Dembī Dolo Eth.
68 D4 Demidov Rus. Fed.
25 F5 Deming U.S.A.
45 E4 Demini r. Brazil
80 B2 Demirci Turkey
67 M4 Demirköy Turkey
62 F4 Demmin Ger.
29 C5 Demopolis U.S.A.
30 D5 Demotte U.S.A.
92 C7 Dempo, G. vol. Indon.
84 D2 Dêmqog China/India
68 H2 Dem'yanovo Rus. Fed.
63 Q2 Demyansk Rus. Fed.
104 D5 De Naawte S. Africa
102 E2 Denakil reg. Eritrea
102 E3 Denan Eth.
21 J4 Denare Beach Can.
79 K2 Denau Uzbek.
31 J3 Denbigh Can.
59 D4 Denbigh U.K.
61 C1 Den Burg Neth.
95 B1 Den Chai Thai.
61 D2 Den Dolder Neth.
105 H1 Dendron S. Africa
88 C1 Dengkou China
85 H3 Dêngqên China
88 D3 Dengzhou China
Den Haag see The Hague
112 B5 Denham Austr.
116 B3 Denham Ra. mts Austr.
61 C2 Den Helder Neth.
65 G3 Denia Spain
114 F5 Deniliquin Austr.
24 C3 Denio U.S.A.
26 E3 Denison IA U.S.A.
27 D5 Denison TX U.S.A.
80 B3 Denizli Turkey
115 J4 Denman Austr.
112 C6 Denmark Austr.
48 Denmark country Europe
118 A4 Denmark Strait str. Greenland/Iceland
35 H3 Dennehotso U.S.A.
33 H4 Dennis Port U.S.A.
57 E4 Denny U.K.
33 K2 Dennysville U.S.A.
92 □ Denpasar Indon.
33 F5 Denton MD U.S.A.
27 D5 Denton TX U.S.A.
112 C6 D'Entrecasteaux, Point pt Austr.
111 G3 D'Entrecasteaux, Récifs rf New Caledonia
110 F2 D'Entrecasteaux Islands is P.N.G.
24 F4 Denver U.S.A.
85 F4 Deo India
84 D3 Deoband India
85 F5 Deogarh India
85 E5 Deogarh mt India
85 F4 Deoghar India
84 D5 Deori India
85 E4 Deoria India
84 C2 Deosai, Plains of plain Pak.
85 E5 Deosil India
61 D3 De Peel reg. Neth.
30 C3 De Pere U.S.A.
33 F3 Deposit U.S.A.
31 J2 Depot-Forbes Can.
31 J2 Depot-Rowanton Can.
30 C5 Depue U.S.A.
77 P3 Deputatskiy Rus. Fed.
82 J5 Dêqên China
89 D6 Deqing Guangdong China
89 F4 Deqing Zhejiang China
27 E5 De Queen U.S.A.
84 B3 Dera Bugti Pak.
84 B3 Dera Ghazi Khan Pak.
84 B3 Dera Ismail Khan Pak.
84 B3 Derawar Fort Pak.
69 J7 Derbent Rus. Fed.
115 G8 Derby Tas. Austr.
112 D3 Derby W.A. Austr.
59 F5 Derby U.K.
33 G4 Derby CT U.S.A.
27 D4 Derby KS U.S.A.
60 D3 Derg r. Rep. of Ireland/U.K.
60 C5 Derg, Lough l. Rep. of Ireland
69 J5 Dergachi Rus. Fed.
69 F5 Derhachi Ukr.
27 E6 De Ridder U.S.A.
81 H3 Derik Turkey
80 E2 Derinkuyu Turkey
69 F5 Derkul r. Rus. Fed./Ukr.
104 C1 Derm Namibia
60 D4 Derravaragh, Lough l. Rep. of Ireland
60 E5 Derry r. Rep. of Ireland
33 H3 Derry U.S.A.
60 C3 Derryveagh Mts h. Rep. of Ireland
88 A1 Derstei China
101 F3 Derudeb Sudan
104 E6 De Rust S. Africa
66 G2 Derventa Bos.-Herz.
115 G9 Derwent r. Austr.
58 G4 Derwent r. U.K.
57 G6 Derwent Reservoir resr U.K.
58 D3 Derwent Water l. U.K.
76 H4 Derzhavinsk Kazak.
47 C2 Desaguadero r. Arg.
42 E7 Desaguadero r. Bol.
34 D2 Desatoya Mts mts U.S.A.
31 F2 Desbarats Can.
21 J3 Deschambault L. l. Can.
21 J4 Deschambault Lake Can.
24 B2 Deschutes r. U.S.A.
102 D2 Desē Eth.
44 C7 Deseado Arg.
44 C7 Deseado r. Arg.
25 D6 Desemboque Mex.
35 F1 Deseret Peak summit U.S.A.
31 J3 Deseronto Can.
84 B3 Desert Canal canal Pak.
35 E5 Desert Center U.S.A.
26 E3 Des Moines IA U.S.A.
25 G4 Des Moines NM U.S.A.
30 A5 Des Moines r. U.S.A.
68 E5 Desna r. Rus. Fed.
69 D5 Desna Ukr.
68 E4 Desnogorsk Rus. Fed.
94 C4 Desolation Point pt Phil.
30 D4 Des Plaines U.S.A.
62 F5 Dessau Ger.
31 H1 Destor Can.
114 B5 D'Estrees B. b. Austr.
20 B2 Destruction Bay Can.
67 J2 Deta Romania
20 G2 Detah Can.
103 C5 Dete Zimbabwe
62 D5 Detmold Ger.
30 D3 Detour, Pt pt U.S.A.
31 F3 De Tour Village U.S.A.
31 F4 Detroit U.S.A.
26 E2 Detroit Lakes U.S.A.
115 H5 Deua Nat. Park nat. park Austr.
66 F1 Deutschlandsberg Austria
31 H2 Deux-Rivières Can.
67 K2 Deva Romania
80 E2 Develi Turkey
61 E2 Deventer Neth.
62 H6 Devět Skal h. Czech Rep.
84 B4 Devikot India
60 D5 Devil's Bit Mountain h. Rep. of Ireland
59 D5 Devil's Bridge U.K.
34 C4 Devils Den U.S.A.
34 C2 Devil's Gate pass U.S.A.
30 B2 Devil's Island i. U.S.A.
26 D1 Devil's Lake U.S.A.
34 C3 Devil's Peak summit U.S.A.
34 C3 Devils Postpile National Monument res. U.S.A.
29 F7 Devil's Pt Bahamas
59 F6 Devizes U.K.
84 C4 Devli India
67 M3 Devnya Bulg.
20 G4 Devon Can.
59 C5 Devon r. U.K.
118 B3 Devon I. i. Can.
115 G8 Devonport Austr.
80 C1 Devrek Turkey
80 D1 Devrekâni Turkey
80 E1 Devrez r. Turkey
84 D5 Dewas India
61 E2 De Weerribben, Nationaal Park nat. park Neth.
105 G4 Dewetsdorp S. Africa
32 B6 Dewey Lake l. U.S.A.
27 F5 De Witt AR U.S.A.
30 B5 De Witt IA U.S.A.
58 F4 Dewsbury U.K.
89 E4 Dexing China
33 J2 Dexter ME U.S.A.
27 F4 Dexter MO U.S.A.
33 E2 Dexter NY U.S.A.
88 B4 Deyang China
81 M3 Deylaman Iran
93 K8 Deyong, Tanjung pt Indon.
81 M6 Dez r. Iran
81 M5 Dezfūl Iran
88 E2 Dezhou China
79 G4 Dhahran Saudi Arabia
85 G4 Dhaka Bangl.
85 G5 Dhaleswari r. Bangl.
85 H4 Dhaleswari r. India
78 E7 Dhamār Yemen
85 F5 Dhāmara India
84 C5 Dhamnod India
85 E5 Dhamtari India
84 B3 Dhana Sar Pak.
85 F5 Dhanbad India
84 C5 Dhandhuka India
85 E3 Dhang Ra. mts Nepal
84 C5 Dhar India
85 F4 Dharan Bazar Nepal
84 B5 Dhari India
83 E8 Dharmavaram India
84 D2 Dharmshala India
83 E7 Dhārwād India
84 D4 Dhasan r. India
85 E3 Dhaulagiri mt Nepal
84 D4 Dhaulpur India
84 C4 Dhebar L. l. India
85 H4 Dhekiajuli India
80 E6 Dhībān Jordan
85 H4 Dhing India
84 B5 Dhoraji India
84 B5 Dhrangadhra India
84 C5 Dhule India
85 F4 Dhulian India
85 F4 Dhunche Nepal
84 D4 Dhund r. India
102 E3 Dhuusa Marreeb Somalia
67 L7 Dia i. Greece
34 B3 Diablo, Mt mt U.S.A.
25 D6 Diablo, Picacho del mt Mex.
34 B3 Diablo Range mts U.S.A.
47 E2 Diamante Arg.
47 C2 Diamante r. Arg.
113 H4 Diamantina watercourse Austr.
46 D2 Diamantina Brazil
43 K6 Diamantina, Chapada plat. Brazil
46 A1 Diamantino Brazil
34 □1 Diamond Head hd U.S.A.
116 D1 Diamond Islets is Coral Sea Is Terr.
35 E2 Diamond Peak summit U.S.A.
89 D6 Dianbai China
89 B5 Dian Chi l. China
89 C4 Dianjiang China
43 J6 Dianópolis Brazil
100 B4 Dianra Côte d'Ivoire
90 B2 Diaoling China
100 C3 Diapaga Burkina
102 C4 Dibaya Dem. Rep. Congo
104 E3 Dibeng S. Africa
22 F2 D'Iberville, Lac l. Can.
105 G1 Dibete Botswana
85 H4 Dibrugarh India
27 C5 Dickens U.S.A.
33 J1 Dickey U.S.A.
26 C2 Dickinson U.S.A.
29 C4 Dickson U.S.A.
33 F4 Dickson City U.S.A.
Dicle r. see Tigris
94 B2 Didicas i. Phil.
84 C4 Didwana India
67 M4 Didymoteicho Greece
64 G4 Die France
100 B3 Diébougou Burkina
21 H4 Diefenbaker, L. l. Can.
13 J4 Diego Garcia i. British Indian Ocean Territory
61 E5 Diekirch Lux.
100 B3 Diéma Mali
89 B6 Điện Biên Phu Vietnam
95 C1 Diên Châu Vietnam
95 D2 Diên Khanh Vietnam
64 E2 Dieppe France
88 C2 Di'er Nonchang Qu r. China
61 D3 Diessen Neth.
61 D4 Diest Belgium
62 D7 Dietikon Switz.
101 D3 Diffa Niger
23 G5 Digby Can.
85 F5 Digha India
64 H4 Digne-les-Bains France
64 F3 Digoin France
94 C5 Digos Phil.
84 D5 Digras India
84 B4 Digri Pak.
93 K8 Digul r. Indon.
100 B4 Digya National Park nat. park Ghana
64 G3 Dijon France
102 E2 Dikhil Djibouti
67 M5 Dikili Turkey
61 A3 Diksmuide Belgium
76 K2 Dikson Rus. Fed.
101 D3 Dikwa Nigeria
102 D3 Dīla Eth.
93 H8 Dili Indon.
81 K1 Dilijan Armenia
95 D3 Di Linh Vietnam
27 D6 Dilley U.S.A.
62 E6 Dillingen an der Donau Ger.
21 H3 Dillon Can.
24 D2 Dillon MT U.S.A.
29 E5 Dillon SC U.S.A.
103 C5 Dilolo Dem. Rep. Congo
81 K5 Diltāwa Iraq
85 H4 Dimapur India
Dimashq see Damascus
102 C4 Dimbelenge Dem. Rep. Congo
100 B4 Dimbokro Côte d'Ivoire
114 E6 Dimboola Austr.
116 A1 Dimbulah Austr.
67 L3 Dimitrovgrad Bulg.
68 J4 Dimitrovgrad Rus. Fed.
80 E6 Dīmona Israel
104 D2 Dimpho Pan salt pan Botswana
94 C4 Dinagat i. Phil.
85 G4 Dinajpur Bangl.
64 C2 Dinan France
84 C2 Dinanagar India
61 C4 Dinant Belgium
85 F4 Dinapur India
80 C2 Dinar Turkey
66 G2 Dinara Planina mts Croatia
102 D2 Dinder National Park nat. park Sudan
83 E8 Dindigul India
105 K1 Dindiza Moz.
84 E5 Dindori India
80 D3 Dinek Turkey
85 H4 Dingba Qu r. India
88 C2 Dingbian China
102 B4 Dinge Angola
85 F4 Dingla Nepal
60 A5 Dingle Rep. of Ireland
60 A5 Dingle Bay b. Rep. of Ireland
89 E5 Dingnan China
116 C4 Dingo Austr.
94 B2 Dingras Phil.
88 E3 Dingtao China
100 A3 Dinguiraye Guinea
57 D3 Dingwall U.K.
88 B3 Dingxi China
88 E2 Dingxing China
88 E3 Dingyuan China
88 E2 Dingzhou China
88 F2 Dingzi Gang harbour China
89 C6 Dinh Lâp Vietnam
35 G3 Dinnebito Wash r. U.S.A.
85 F3 Dinngyê China
105 G1 Dinokwe Botswana
21 L5 Dinorwic Lake U.S.A.
35 H1 Dinosaur U.S.A.
24 E3 Dinosaur Nat. Mon. res. U.S.A.
100 B3 Dioïla Mali
46 B4 Dionísio Cerqueira Brazil
100 A3 Diourbel Senegal
85 H4 Diphu India
84 B4 Diplo Pak.
94 B4 Dipolog Phil.
117 B6 Dipton N.Z.
79 L2 Dir Pak.
80 F2 Dirckli Turkey
100 B3 Diré Mali
113 H2 Direction, C. c. Austr.
102 E3 Dirē Dawa Eth.
103 C5 Dirico Angola
112 B5 Dirk Hartog I. i. Austr.
115 H2 Dirranbandi Austr.
81 M6 Dīrsīyeh Iran
35 G2 Dirty Devil r. U.S.A.
84 C4 Dīsa India
44 □ Disappointment, C. c. Atlantic Ocean
24 A2 Disappointment, C. c. U.S.A.
112 D4 Disappointment, L. salt flat Austr.
115 H6 Disaster B. b. Austr.
114 D7 Discovery Bay b. Austr.
Disko i. see Qeqertarsuaq
33 E6 Dismal Swamp swamp U.S.A.
85 G4 Dispur India
59 J5 Diss U.K.
46 C1 Distrito Federal div. Brazil
80 C6 Disūq Egypt
94 B4 Dit i. Phil.
104 E4 Ditloung S. Africa
66 F6 Dittaino r. Italy
84 B5 Diu India
94 C4 Diuata Mountains mts Phil.
94 C4 Diuata Pt pt Phil.
81 L4 Dīvān Darreh Iran
68 G4 Diveyevo Rus. Fed.
94 B2 Divilacan Bay b. Phil.
46 D3 Divinópolis Brazil
69 G6 Divnoye Rus. Fed.
100 B4 Divo Côte d'Ivoire
80 G2 Divriği Turkey
33 H2 Dixfield U.S.A.
33 J2 Dixmont U.S.A.
34 B2 Dixon CA U.S.A.
30 C5 Dixon IL U.S.A.
20 C4 Dixon Entrance chan. Can./U.S.A.
29 F7 Dixon's Bahamas
20 F3 Dixonville Can.
33 H2 Dixville Can.
81 J2 Diyadin Turkey
81 K5 Diyālā, Nahr r. Iraq
81 H3 Diyarbakır Turkey
84 B4 Diyodar India
101 D2 Djado Niger
101 D2 Djado, Plateau du plat. Niger
102 B4 Djambala Congo
100 C2 Djanet Alg.
100 C1 Djelfa Alg.
102 C3 Djéma C.A.R.
100 B3 Djenné Mali
100 B3 Djibo Burkina
96 Djibouti country Africa
102 E2 Djibouti Djibouti
60 E4 Djouce Mountain h. Rep. of Ireland
100 C4 Djougou Benin
54 F4 Djúpivogur Iceland
55 O6 Djurås Sweden
81 K1 Dmanisi Georgia
77 Q2 Dmitriya Lapteva, Proliv chan. Rus. Fed.
90 C2 Dmitriyevka Rus. Fed.
68 G4 Dmitriyevka Rus. Fed.
69 E4 Dmitriyev-L'govskiy Rus. Fed.
68 F3 Dmitrov Rus. Fed.
Dnepr r. see Dnieper
63 P5 Dnieper r. Europe
63 P3 Dnieper r. Rus. Fed.
76 E5 Dnieper r. Ukr.
63 N6 Dniester r. Ukr.
Dnipro r. see Dnieper
69 E5 Dniprodzerzhyns'k Ukr.
69 E5 Dnipropetrovs'k Ukr.
69 E6 Dniprorudne Ukr.
68 D3 Dno Rus. Fed.
Dnyapro r. see Dnieper
101 D4 Doba Chad
31 G3 Dobbinton Can.
55 S8 Dobele Latvia
93 J7 Doberai Peninsula pen. Indon.
47 D3 Doblas Arg.
93 J8 Dobo Indon.
67 H2 Doboj Bos.-Herz.
67 M3 Dobrich Bulg.
69 G4 Dobrinka Rus. Fed.
69 D4 Dobrush Belarus
94 A5 Doc Can rf Phil.
46 E2 Doce r. Brazil
59 H5 Docking U.K.
25 F6 Doctor Belisario Domínguez Mex.
67 M6 Dodecanese is Greece
Dodekanisos is see Dodecanese
24 C2 Dodge U.S.A.
30 A3 Dodge Center U.S.A.
27 C4 Dodge City U.S.A.
115 G9 Dodges Ferry Austr.
30 B4 Dodgeville U.S.A.
59 C7 Dodman Point pt U.K.
102 D4 Dodoma Tanz.
61 E3 Doetinchem Neth.
93 H7 Dofa Indon.
85 G2 Dogai Coring salt l. China
85 G2 Dogaicoring Qangco salt l. China
81 J2 Doğançay Dağı mt Turkey
80 F2 Doğanşehir Turkey
20 E4 Dog Creek Can.
85 G3 Dogên Co l. China
23 H2 Dog Island i. Can.
21 K4 Dog L. l. Can.
31 E1 Dog Lake l. Can.
91 C6 Dōgo i. Japan
100 C3 Dogondoutchi Niger
91 C7 Dōgo-yama mt Japan
81 K2 Doğubeyazıt Turkey
85 F3 Dogxung Zangbo r. China
85 G3 Do'gyaling China
79 G4 Doha Qatar
Dohad see Dāhod
85 H5 Dohazari Bangl.
85 G3 Doilungdêqên China
95 A1 Doi Saket Thai.
43 K5 Dois Irmãos, Serra dos h. Brazil
67 K4 Dojran, Lake l. Greece/Macedonia
55 M6 Dokka Norway
61 D1 Dokkum Neth.
84 B4 Dokri Pak.
63 N3 Dokshytsy Belarus
69 F6 Dokuchayevs'k Ukr.
93 K8 Dolak, Pulau i. Indon.
23 F4 Dolbeau Can.
59 C5 Dolbenmaen U.K.
64 D2 Dol-de-Bretagne France
64 G3 Dole France
59 D5 Dolgellau U.K.
33 F3 Dolgeville U.S.A.
69 F4 Dolgorukovo Rus. Fed.
69 F4 Dolgoye Rus. Fed.
66 C5 Dolianova Italy
87 Q2 Dolinsk Rus. Fed.
66 D1 Dolomiti mts Italy
102 E3 Dolo Odo Eth.
47 F3 Dolores Arg.
47 E2 Dolores Uru.
35 H2 Dolores r. U.S.A.
89 B7 Đô Lương Vietnam
69 B5 Dolyna Ukr.
80 B2 Domaniç Turkey
84 E2 Domar China
62 F6 Domažlice Czech Rep.
85 H2 Domba China
81 L5 Dom Bākh Iran
55 L5 Dombås Norway
62 J7 Dombóvár Hungary
119 C4 Dome Argus ice feature Antarctica
119 C5 Dome Charlie ice feature Antarctica
Dome Circe ice feature see Dome Charlie
20 E4 Dome Creek Can.
119 C4 Dome Fuji Japan Base Antarctica
20 D2 Dome Pk summit Can.
35 E5 Dome Rock Mts mts U.S.A.
64 D2 Domfront France
16 Dominica country Caribbean Sea
16 Dominican Republic country Caribbean Sea
95 C2 Dom Noi, L. r. Thai.
66 C1 Domodossola Italy
67 K5 Domokos Greece
47 F1 Dom Pedrito Brazil
93 F8 Dompu Indon.
47 B3 Domuyo, Volcán vol. Arg.
115 J2 Domville, Mt h. Austr.
116 C3 Don r. Austr.

69 G5 Don r. Rus. Fed.
57 F3 Don r. U.K.
95 C2 Don, Xé r. Laos
60 F3 Donaghadee U.K.
60 E3 Donaghmore U.K.
114 E6 Donald Austr.
Donau r. see Danube
62 D7 Donaueschingen Ger.
62 E6 Donauwörth Ger.
65 D3 Don Benito Spain
58 F4 Doncaster U.K.
103 B4 Dondo Angola
103 D5 Dondo Moz.
94 B4 Dondonay i. Phil.
60 C3 Donegal Rep. of Ireland
60 C3 Donegal Bay g. Rep. of Ireland
69 F6 Donets'k Ukr.
69 F5 Donets'kyy Kryazh h. Rus. Fed./Ukr.
89 D5 Dong'an China
112 B5 Dongara Austr.
84 E5 Dongargarh India
89 B5 Dongchuan China
85 F2 Dongco China
89 C7 Dongfang China
90 C1 Dongfanghong China
93 F7 Donggala Indon.
89 E5 Donggu China
89 D6 Dongguan China
95 C1 Đông Ha Vietnam
88 F3 Donghai China
89 D6 Donghai Dao i. China
88 C4 Dong He r. China
88 A1 Dong He watercourse China
95 C1 Đông Hồi Vietnam
90 A2 Dongjingcheng China
85 H3 Dongjug Xizang Zizhiqu China
85 H3 Dongjug Xizang Zizhiqu China
89 D5 Dongkou China
85 G4 Dongkya La pass India
89 C5 Donglan China
88 A2 Dongle China
88 G1 Dongliao r. China
90 B3 Dongning China
103 B5 Dongo Angola
102 B3 Dongou Congo
95 B1 Dong Phraya Fai mts Thai.
95 B2 Dong Phraya Yen escarpment Thai.
89 D6 Dongping Guangdong China
88 E3 Dongping Shandong China
85 G3 Dongqiao China
89 E6 Dongshan China
89 E6 Dongshan Dao i. China
88 D2 Dongsheng China
88 F3 Dongtai China
88 F3 Dongtai r. China
89 D4 Dongting Hu l. China
89 F5 Dongtou China
Dong Ujimqin Qi see Uliastai
89 E4 Dongxiang China
89 F4 Dongyang China
88 F2 Dongying China
88 B2 Dongzhen China
89 E4 Dongzhi China
20 B2 Donjek r. Can.
85 G5 Donmanick Islands is Bangl.
23 F4 Donnacona Can.
20 F3 Donnelly Can.
117 D1 Donnellys Crossing N.Z.
34 B2 Donner Pass pass U.S.A.
Donostia-San Sebastián see San Sebastián
67 L6 Donoussa i. Greece
68 F4 Donskoy Rus. Fed.
69 G6 Donskoye Rus. Fed.
94 B3 Donsol Phil.
60 A4 Dooagh Rep. of Ireland
57 D5 Doon, Loch l. U.K.
60 B5 Doonbeg r. Rep. of Ireland
30 D3 Door Peninsula pen. U.S.A.
102 E3 Dooxo Nugaaleed v. Somalia
27 C5 Dora U.S.A.
66 C2 Dora Baltea r. Italy
59 E7 Dorchester U.K.
103 B6 Dordabis Namibia
64 E4 Dordogne r. France
61 C3 Dordrecht Neth.
105 G5 Dordrecht S. Africa
104 C1 Doreenville Namibia
21 H4 Doré L. l. Can.
21 H4 Doré Lake Can.
66 C4 Dorgali Italy
100 B3 Dori Burkina
104 C5 Doring r. S. Africa
59 G6 Dorking U.K.
57 D3 Dornoch Firth est. U.K.
88 C1 Dornogovĭ div. Mongolia
68 E4 Dorogobuzh Rus. Fed.
63 N7 Dorohoi Romania
86 F2 Döröö Nuur salt l. Mongolia
54 P4 Dorotea Sweden
112 B5 Dorre I. i. Austr.
115 K3 Dorrigo Austr.
24 B3 Dorris U.S.A.
100 D4 Dorsale Camerounaise slope Cameroon/Nigeria
31 H3 Dorset Can.
62 C5 Dortmund Ger.
61 F3 Dortmund-Ems-Kanal canal Ger.
32 B6 Dorton U.S.A.
80 F3 Dörtyol Turkey
102 C3 Doruma Dem. Rep. Congo
44 C6 Dos Bahías, C. pt Arg.
35 H5 Dos Cabezas U.S.A.
42 C5 Dos de Mayo Peru
89 C6 Đo Son Vietnam
34 B3 Dos Palos U.S.A.
100 C3 Dosso Niger
29 C6 Dothan U.S.A.
64 F1 Douai France
100 C4 Douala Cameroon
64 B2 Douarnenez France
116 E5 Double Island Pt pt Austr.
34 C4 Double Peak summit U.S.A.
116 B1 Double Pt pt Austr.
64 H3 Doubs r. France
117 A6 Doubtful Sound in. N.Z.
117 D1 Doubtless Bay b. N.Z.
100 B3 Douentza Mali
58 C3 Douglas Isle of Man
104 E4 Douglas S. Africa
57 E5 Douglas U.K.
20 C3 Douglas AK U.S.A.
35 H6 Douglas AZ U.S.A.
29 D6 Douglas GA U.S.A.
24 F3 Douglas WY U.S.A.
20 D4 Douglas Chan. chan. Can.
35 H2 Douglas Creek r. U.S.A.
64 F1 Doullens France
57 D4 Doune U.K.
46 C2 Dourada, Cach. waterfall Brazil
46 B2 Dourada, Serra h. Brazil
46 C1 Dourada, Serra mts Brazil
46 A3 Dourados Brazil
46 A3 Dourados r. Brazil
46 B3 Dourados, Serra dos h. Brazil
65 C2 Douro r. Port.
59 F4 Dove r. Eng. U.K.
59 J5 Dove r. Eng. U.K.
23 J3 Dove Brook Can.
35 H3 Dove Creek U.S.A.
115 G9 Dover Austr.
59 J6 Dover U.K.
33 F5 Dover DE U.S.A.
33 H3 Dover NH U.S.A.
33 F4 Dover NJ U.S.A.
32 C4 Dover OH U.S.A.
59 J7 Dover, Strait of str. France/U.K.
33 J2 Dover-Foxcroft U.S.A.
81 M6 Doveyrīch, Rūd-e r. Iran/Iraq
30 D5 Dowagiac U.S.A.
95 A5 Dowi, Tg pt Indon.
34 B2 Downieville U.S.A.
60 F3 Downpatrick U.K.
33 F3 Downsville U.S.A.
81 M5 Dow Rūd Iran
81 L4 Dow Sar Iran
79 K2 Dowshī Afgh.
34 B1 Doyle U.S.A.
33 F4 Doylestown U.S.A.
91 C6 Dōzen is Japan
31 J2 Dozois, Réservoir resr Can.
46 B3 Dracena Brazil
61 E1 Drachten Neth.
67 L2 Drăgănești-Olt Romania
67 L2 Drăgășani Romania
45 E2 Dragon's Mouths str. Trinidad/Venez.
55 S6 Dragsfjärd Fin.
64 H5 Draguignan France
69 C4 Drahichyn Belarus
115 K2 Drake Austr.
35 F4 Drake AZ U.S.A.
21 J5 Drake ND U.S.A.
105 H5 Drakensberg mts Lesotho/S. Africa
105 J2 Drakensberg mts S. Africa
119 A1 Drake Passage str. Antarctica
67 L4 Drama Greece
55 M7 Drammen Norway
55 L7 Drangedal Norway
60 E3 Draperstown U.K.
84 C2 Dras Jammu and Kashmir
62 F7 Drau r. Austria
20 G4 Drayton Valley Can.
66 B6 Dréan Alg.
62 F5 Dresden Ger.
68 D4 Dretun' Belarus
64 E2 Dreux France
55 N6 Drevsjø Norway
32 D4 Driftwood U.S.A.
116 D6 Drillham Austr.
60 B6 Drimoleague Rep. of Ireland
66 G3 Drniš Croatia
67 K2 Drobeta - Turnu Severin Romania
60 E4 Drogheda Rep. of Ireland
69 B5 Drohobych Ukr.
Droichead Átha see Drogheda
59 E5 Droitwich U.K.
85 G4 Drokung India
60 D4 Dromod Rep. of Ireland
60 E3 Dromore Co. Down U.K.
60 D3 Dromore Co. Tyrone U.K.
59 F4 Dronfield U.K.
119 C3 Dronning Maud Land reg. Antarctica
84 B2 Drosh Pak.
69 F4 Droskovo Rus. Fed.
115 F7 Drouin Austr.
44 D2 Dr Pedro P. Peña Para.
20 G4 Drumheller Can.
24 D2 Drummond MT U.S.A.
30 B2 Drummond WV U.S.A.
31 F3 Drummond Island i. U.S.A.
116 B5 Drummond Range h. Austr.
23 F4 Drummondville Can.
57 D6 Drummore U.K.
57 D4 Drumochter Pass pass U.K.
55 T10 Druskininkai Lith.
77 Q3 Druzhina Rus. Fed.
67 L3 Dryanovo Bulg.
20 B3 Dry Bay b. U.S.A.
21 L5 Dryberry L. l. Can.
30 E2 Dryburg U.S.A.
22 B4 Dryden Can.
34 D2 Dry Lake l. U.S.A.
57 D4 Drymen U.K.
112 E3 Drysdale r. Austr.
112 E3 Drysdale River National Park nat. park Austr.
81 M4 Dūāb r. Iran
89 C6 Du'an China
33 F2 Duane U.S.A.
116 C4 Duaringa Austr.
85 G4 Duars reg. India
78 D4 Ḍubā Saudi Arabia
79 H4 Dubai U.A.E.
21 J2 Dubawnt r. Can.
21 J2 Dubawnt Lake l. Can.
Dubayy see Dubai
78 D4 Dubbagh, J. ad mt Saudi Arabia
115 H4 Dubbo Austr.
30 D1 Dublin Can.
60 E4 Dublin Rep. of Ireland
29 D5 Dublin U.S.A.
68 F3 Dubna Rus. Fed.
69 C5 Dubno Ukr.
24 D2 Dubois ID U.S.A.
24 E3 Dubois WY U.S.A.
32 D4 Du Bois U.S.A.
69 H5 Dubovka Rus. Fed.
69 G6 Dubovskoye Rus. Fed.
81 M1 Dübrar P. pass Azer.
100 A4 Dubréka Guinea
67 H3 Dubrovnik Croatia
69 C5 Dubrovytsya Ukr.
68 D4 Dubrowna Belarus
30 B4 Dubuque U.S.A.
55 S9 Dubysa r. Lith.
89 E4 Duchang China
35 G1 Duchesne U.S.A.
29 C5 Duck r. U.S.A.
21 J4 Duck Bay Can.
21 H4 Duck Lake Can.
30 E4 Duck Lake U.S.A.
35 E2 Duckwater U.S.A.
35 E2 Duckwater Peak summit U.S.A.
95 D2 Đưc Pho Vietnam
95 D3 Đưc Trong Vietnam
45 B4 Duda r. Col.
85 E4 Dudhi India
85 G4 Dudhnai India
76 K3 Dudinka Rus. Fed.
59 E5 Dudley U.K.
84 D6 Dudna r. India
57 F3 Dudwick, Hill of h. U.K.
100 B4 Duékoué Côte d'Ivoire
65 C2 Duero r. Spain
31 H1 Dufault, Lac l. Can.
22 E2 Dufferin, Cape hd Can.
32 B6 Duffield U.S.A.
111 G2 Duff Is is Solomon Is
57 E3 Dufftown U.K.
22 E1 Dufrost, Pte pt Can.
66 F3 Dugi Otok i. Croatia
88 C2 Dugui Qarag China
88 D3 Du He r. China
45 D4 Duida, Co mt Venez.
42 E3 Duída-Marahuaca, Parque Nacional nat. park Venez.
62 C5 Duisburg Ger.
45 B3 Duitama Col.
105 J1 Duiwelskloof S. Africa
88 B4 Dujiangyan China
81 K4 Dukān Dam dam Iraq
105 G5 Dukathole S. Africa
20 C4 Duke I. i. U.S.A.
79 G4 Dukhān Qatar
63 Q3 Dukhovshchina Rus. Fed.
84 B3 Duki Pak.
55 U9 Dūkštas Lith.
82 J3 Dulan China
Dulawan see Datu Piang
44 D3 Dulce r. Arg.
85 E2 Dulishi Hu salt l. China
105 J2 Dullstroom S. Africa
61 F3 Dülmen Ger.
67 M3 Dulovo Bulg.
30 A2 Duluth U.S.A.
30 A2 Duluth/Superior airport U.S.A.
59 D6 Dulverton U.K.
80 F5 Dūmā Syria
94 B4 Dumaguete Phil.
92 C6 Dumai Indon.
94 B4 Dumaran i. Phil.
27 F5 Dumas AR U.S.A.
27 C5 Dumas TX U.S.A.
80 F5 Ḍumayr Syria
57 D5 Dumbarton U.K.
105 J3 Dumbe S. Africa
63 J6 Ďumbier mt Slovakia
84 D2 Dumchele Jammu and Kashmir
85 H4 Dum Duma India
57 E5 Dumfries U.K.
85 F4 Dumka India
22 E4 Dumoine, L. l. Can.
119 B6 Dumont d'Urville France Base Antarctica
119 B6 Dumont d'Urville Sea sea Antarctica
78 C3 Dumyāṭ Egypt
Duna r. see Danube
62 H7 Dunajská Streda Slovakia
63 J7 Dunakeszi Hungary
115 G9 Dunalley Austr.
60 E4 Dunany Point pt Rep. of Ireland
67 N2 Dunării, Delta delta Romania
63 J7 Dunaújváros Hungary
Dunav r. see Danube
69 C5 Dunayivtsi Ukr.
117 C6 Dunback N.Z.
57 F4 Dunbar U.K.
57 E4 Dunblane U.K.
60 E4 Dunboyne Rep. of Ireland
20 E5 Duncan Can.
35 H5 Duncan AZ U.S.A.
27 D5 Duncan OK U.S.A.
22 D3 Duncan, Cape c. Can.
22 E3 Duncan, L. l. Can.
32 E4 Duncannon U.S.A.
57 E2 Duncansby Head hd U.K.
30 B5 Duncans Mills U.S.A.
60 E5 Duncormick Rep. of Ireland
55 S8 Dundaga Latvia
31 G3 Dundalk Can.
60 E3 Dundalk Rep. of Ireland
32 E5 Dundalk U.S.A.
60 E4 Dundalk Bay b. Rep. of Ireland
20 C4 Dundas I. i. Can.
Dun Dealgan see Dundalk
105 J4 Dundee S. Africa
57 F4 Dundee U.K.
31 F5 Dundee MI U.S.A.
32 E3 Dundee NY U.S.A.
88 E1 Dund Hot China
60 F3 Dundonald U.K.
115 F1 Dundoo Austr.
57 E6 Dundrennan U.K.
60 F3 Dundrum U.K.
60 F3 Dundrum Bay b. U.K.
85 E4 Dundwa Range mts India/Nepal
22 F2 Dune, Lac l. Can.
117 C6 Dunedin N.Z.
29 D6 Dunedin U.S.A.
115 H4 Dunedoo Austr.
57 E4 Dunfermline U.K.
60 E3 Dungannon U.K.
84 C5 Dungarpur India
60 D5 Dungarvan Rep. of Ireland
59 H7 Dungeness hd U.K.
44 C8 Dungeness, Pta pt Arg.
60 E3 Dungiven U.K.
60 C3 Dungloe Rep. of Ireland
115 J4 Dungog Austr.
102 C3 Dungu Dem. Rep. Congo
92 C6 Dungun Malaysia
101 F2 Dungunab Sudan
87 N3 Dunhua China
82 H2 Dunhuang China
114 E6 Dunkeld Austr.
57 E4 Dunkeld U.K.
Dunkerque see Dunkirk
59 D6 Dunkery Beacon h. U.K.
64 F1 Dunkirk France
32 D3 Dunkirk U.S.A.
100 B4 Dunkwa Ghana
60 E4 Dún Laoghaire Rep. of Ireland
60 E4 Dunlavin Rep. of Ireland
60 E4 Dunleer Rep. of Ireland
60 E2 Dunloy U.K.
60 B6 Dunmanus Bay b. Rep. of Ireland
60 B6 Dunmanway Rep. of Ireland
60 C4 Dunmore Rep. of Ireland
29 E7 Dunmore Town Bahamas
34 D3 Dunmovin U.S.A.
60 F3 Dunmurry U.K.
29 E5 Dunn U.S.A.
57 E2 Dunnet Bay b. U.K.
57 E2 Dunnet Head hd U.K.
34 B2 Dunnigan U.S.A.
26 C3 Dunning U.S.A.
31 H4 Dunnville Can.
114 E6 Dunolly Austr.
57 D5 Dunoon U.K.
57 F5 Duns U.K.
26 C1 Dunseith U.S.A.
24 B3 Dunsmuir U.S.A.
59 G6 Dunstable U.K.
117 B6 Dunstan Mts mts N.Z.
117 C6 Duntroon N.Z.
57 B3 Dunvegan, Loch in. U.K.
84 B3 Dunyapur Pak.
88 E1 Duolun China
89 D5 Dupang Ling mts China
31 H1 Duparquet, Lac l. Can.
67 K3 Dupnitsa Bulg.
26 C2 Dupree U.S.A.
28 B4 Du Quoin U.S.A.
112 E3 Durack r. Austr.
Dura Europos see Aş Şālihīyah
80 E1 Durağan Turkey
64 G5 Durance r. France
30 E4 Durand MI U.S.A.
30 B3 Durand WI U.S.A.
27 B7 Durango div. Mex.
36 D4 Durango Mex.
65 E1 Durango Spain
25 F4 Durango U.S.A.
27 D5 Durant U.S.A.
47 F2 Durazno Uru.
47 F1 Durazno, Cuchilla Grande del h. Uru.
105 J4 Durban S. Africa
64 F5 Durban-Corbières France
104 C6 Durbanville S. Africa
32 D5 Durbin U.S.A.
61 D4 Durbuy Belgium
61 E4 Düren Ger.
84 E5 Durg India
85 F5 Durgapur India
31 G3 Durham Can.
58 F3 Durham U.K.
34 B2 Durham CA U.S.A.
29 E4 Durham NC U.S.A.
33 H3 Durham NH U.S.A.
69 D6 Durlești Moldova
67 H3 Durmitor mt Serb. and Mont.
57 D2 Durness U.K.
116 D6 Durong South Austr.
67 H4 Durrës Albania
59 F6 Durrington U.K.
60 A6 Dursey Island i. Rep. of Ireland
80 B2 Dursunbey Turkey
80 F5 Durūz, Jabal ad mt Syria
93 K7 D'Urville, Tanjung pt Indon.
117 D4 D'Urville Island i. N.Z.
89 C5 Dushan China
79 K2 Dushanbe Tajik.
69 H7 Dushet'i Georgia
117 A6 Dusky Sound in. N.Z.
62 C5 Düsseldorf Ger.
35 F1 Dutch Mt mt U.S.A.
104 E1 Dutlwe Botswana
100 C3 Dutse Nigeria
114 B3 Dutton, Lake salt flat Austr.
35 F2 Dutton, Mt mt U.S.A.
68 H3 Duvannoye Rus. Fed.
23 F2 Duvert, Lac l. Can.
89 C5 Duyun China
80 C1 Düzce Turkey
Dvina, Western r. see Zapadnaya Dvina
69 F5 Dvorichna Ukr.
90 B2 Dvoryanka Rus. Fed.
84 B5 Dwarka India
105 G2 Dwarsberg S. Africa
30 C5 Dwight U.S.A.
61 E2 Dwingelderveld, Nationaal Park nat. park Neth.
24 C2 Dworshak Res. resr U.S.A.
104 D6 Dwyka S. Africa
68 E4 Dyat'kovo Rus. Fed.
57 F3 Dyce U.K.
30 D5 Dyer IN U.S.A.
34 C3 Dyer NV U.S.A.
31 G3 Dyer Bay Can.
29 B4 Dyersburg U.S.A.
30 B4 Dyersville U.S.A.
59 D5 Dyfi r. U.K.
57 E3 Dyke U.K.
69 G7 Dykh Tau mt Georgia/Rus. Fed.
63 J4 Dylewska Góra h. Pol.
114 F2 Dynevor Downs Austr.
105 H5 Dyoki S. Africa
116 C4 Dysart Austr.
30 A4 Dysart U.S.A.
104 E6 Dysselsdorp S. Africa
87 K3 Dzamïn Üüd Mongolia
103 E5 Dzaoudzi Africa
68 G3 Dzerzhinsk Rus. Fed.
63 N5 Dzerzhyns'k Ukr.
Dzhambul see Taraz
79 G1 Dzhanga Turkm.
69 E6 Dzhankoy Ukr.
69 H5 Dzhanybek Rus. Fed.
77 R3 Dzhigudzhak Rus. Fed.
79 K1 Dzhizak Uzbek.
77 P4 Dzhugdzhur, Khrebet mts Rus. Fed.
Dzhul'fa see Culfa
82 E2 Dzhungarskiy Alatau, Khr. mts China/Kazak.
82 B1 Dzhusaly Kazak.
63 K4 Działdowo Pol.
Dzungarian Basin basin see Junggar Pendi
86 J2 Dzuunmod Mongolia
68 C4 Dzyaniskavichy Belarus
68 C4 Dzyarzhynsk Belarus
63 N4 Dzyatlavichy Belarus

E

22 C3 Eabamet L. l. Can.
35 H4 Eagar U.S.A.
23 J3 Eagle r. Can.
25 F4 Eagle U.S.A.
33 F3 Eagle Bay U.S.A.
21 H4 Eagle Cr. r. Can.
34 D4 Eagle Crags summit U.S.A.
21 L5 Eagle L. l. Can.
24 B3 Eagle L. l. U.S.A.
33 J1 Eagle Lake U.S.A.
33 J1 Eagle Lake l. U.S.A.
30 B2 Eagle Mtn h. U.S.A.
27 C6 Eagle Pass U.S.A.
30 C2 Eagle River MI U.S.A.
30 C3 Eagle River WV U.S.A.
20 F3 Eaglesham Can.
35 F5 Eagle Tail Mts mts U.S.A.
22 B3 Ear Falls Can.
34 C4 Earlimart U.S.A.
57 F5 Earlston U.K.
31 H2 Earlton Can.
57 E4 Earn r. U.K.
57 D4 Earn, L. l. U.K.
27 C5 Earth U.S.A.
58 H4 Easington U.K.
29 D5 Easley U.S.A.
119 C5 East Antarctica reg. Antarctica
33 F4 East Ararat U.S.A.
32 D3 East Aurora U.S.A.
27 F6 East Bay b. U.S.A.
33 G2 East Berkshire U.S.A.
59 H7 Eastbourne U.K.
32 D4 East Branch Clarion River Reservoir resr U.S.A.
33 H4 East Brooklyn U.S.A.
117 G2 East Cape c. N.Z.
35 G2 East Carbon City U.S.A.
30 D5 East Chicago U.S.A.
87 M6 East China Sea sea Asia
33 G2 East Corinth U.S.A.
59 H5 East Dereham U.K.
15 M7 Easter Island is Pac. Oc.
15 M7 Easter Island Fracture Zone sea feature Pac. Oc.
105 G5 Eastern Cape div. S. Africa
78 C4 Eastern Desert des. Egypt
85 E6 Eastern Ghats mts India
84 B4 Eastern Nara canal Pak.
Eastern Transvaal div. see Mpumalanga
21 K4 Easterville Can.
44 E8 East Falkland i. Falkland Is
33 H4 East Falmouth U.S.A.
62 C4 East Frisian Islands is Ger.
34 D2 Eastgate U.S.A.
26 D2 East Grand Forks U.S.A.
59 G6 East Grinstead U.K.
33 G4 East Hampton U.S.A.
33 G3 Easthampton U.S.A.
32 D4 East Hickory U.S.A.
33 G3 East Jamaica U.S.A.
12 K1 East Jan Mayen Ridge sea feature Atlantic Ocean
30 E3 East Jordan U.S.A.
57 D5 East Kilbride U.K.
30 D3 East Lake U.S.A.
59 F7 Eastleigh U.K.
32 C4 East Liverpool U.S.A.
57 B3 East Loch Tarbert b. U.K.
105 G6 East London S. Africa
32 B5 East Lynn Lake l. U.S.A.
22 E3 Eastmain Can.
22 F3 Eastmain r. Can.
33 G2 Eastman Can.
29 D5 Eastman U.S.A.
116 A4 Eastmere Austr.
33 J2 East Millinocket U.S.A.
30 B5 East Moline U.S.A.
30 C5 Easton IL U.S.A.
33 E5 Easton MD U.S.A.
33 F4 Easton PA U.S.A.
15 M8 East Pacific Ridge sea feature Pac. Oc.
15 N5 East Pacific Rise sea feature Pac. Oc.
34 A2 East Park Res. resr U.S.A.
23 H4 East Point pt Can.
29 C5 East Point U.S.A.
33 K2 Eastport ME U.S.A.
30 E3 Eastport MI U.S.A.
34 D1 East Range mts U.S.A.
East Retford see Retford
77 Q2 East Siberian Sea sea Rus. Fed.
115 H7 East Sister I. i. Austr.
28 B4 East St Louis U.S.A.
93 H8 East Timor country Asia
85 F4 East Tons r. India
115 F3 East Toorale Austr.
30 C4 East Troy U.S.A.
33 F6 Eastville U.S.A.
34 C2 East Walker r. U.S.A.
33 G3 East Wallingford U.S.A.
29 D5 Eatonton U.S.A.
30 B3 Eau Claire U.S.A.
30 B3 Eau Claire r. U.S.A.
14 E5 Eauripik Rise-New Guinea Rise sea feature Pac. Oc.
36 E4 Ebano Mex.
59 D6 Ebbw Vale U.K.
100 D4 Ebebiyin Equatorial Guinea
104 B2 Ebenerde Namibia
32 D4 Ebensburg U.S.A.
80 C2 Eber Gölü l. Turkey
62 F4 Eberswalde-Finow Ger.
31 F4 Eberts Can.
90 G3 Ebetsu Japan
89 B4 Ebian China
86 D3 Ebinur Hu salt l. China
66 F4 Eboli Italy
100 D4 Ebolowa Cameroon
81 K3 Ebrāhīm Ḩeşār Iran
65 G2 Ebro r. Spain
67 M4 Eceabat Turkey
94 B2 Echague Phil.
65 E1 Echarri-Aranaz Spain
100 C1 Ech Chélif Alg.
65 E1 Echegárate, Puerto pass Spain
115 G9 Echo, L. l. Austr.
20 F1 Echo Bay N.W.T. Can.
31 E2 Echo Bay Ont. Can.
35 G3 Echo Cliffs cliff U.S.A.
22 B3 Echoing r. Can.
31 K2 Échouani, Lac l. Can.
61 E5 Echternach Lux.
114 F6 Echuca Austr.
65 D4 Écija Spain
30 E2 Eckerman U.S.A.
62 D3 Eckernförde Ger.

139

64 D3 Fontenay-le-Comte France
54 F3 Fontur *pt* Iceland
31 H3 Foot's Bay Can.
88 C3 Foping China
115 H4 Forbes Austr.
24 C1 Forbes, Mt *mt* Can.
62 E6 Forchheim Ger.
23 G2 Ford *r.* Can.
30 D2 Ford *r.* U.S.A.
55 J6 Førde Norway
21 K2 Forde Lake *l.* Can.
59 H5 Fordham U.K.
59 F7 Fordingbridge U.K.
119 A4 Ford Ra. *mts* Antarctica
115 F2 Fords Bridge Austr.
27 E5 Fordyce U.S.A.
100 A4 Forécariah Guinea
59 F7 Foreland *hd* U.K.
59 D6 Foreland Point *pt* U.K.
20 D4 Foresight Mtn *mt* Can.
31 G4 Forest Can.
27 F5 Forest *MS* U.S.A.
32 B4 Forest *OH* U.S.A.
33 G3 Forest Dale U.S.A.
115 G5 Forest Hill *N.S.W.* Austr.
116 A5 Forest Hill *Qld.* Austr.
34 B2 Forestdale U.S.A.
115 H9 Forestier, C. *hd* Austr.
115 H9 Forestier Pen. *pen.* Austr.
30 A3 Forest Lake U.S.A.
29 C5 Forest Park U.S.A.
23 G4 Forestville Can.
57 F4 Forfar U.K.
24 A2 Forks U.S.A.
33 J2 Forks, The U.S.A.
32 E4 Forksville U.S.A.
66 E2 Forlì Italy
58 D4 Formby U.K.
65 G3 Formentera *i.* Spain
65 H3 Formentor, Cap de *pt* Spain
46 D3 Formiga Brazil
44 E3 Formosa Arg.
Formosa *country see* Taiwan
46 C1 Formosa Brazil
43 G6 Formosa, Serra *h.* Brazil
46 D1 Formoso *r.* Brazil
57 E3 Forres U.K.
114 E7 Forrest *Vic.* Austr.
112 E4 Forrest *W.A.* Austr.
30 C5 Forrest U.S.A.
27 F5 Forrest City U.S.A.
30 C4 Forreston U.S.A.
54 P5 Fors Sweden
113 H3 Forsayth Austr.
54 S3 Forsnäs Sweden
55 S6 Forssa Fin.
115 K4 Forster Austr.
27 E5 Forsyth *MO* U.S.A.
24 F2 Forsyth *MT* U.S.A.
31 J1 Forsythe Can.
84 C3 Fort Abbas Pak.
22 D3 Fort Albany Can.
43 L4 Fortaleza Brazil
35 H5 Fort Apache U.S.A.
20 G4 Fort Assiniboine Can.
30 C4 Fort Atkinson U.S.A.
57 D3 Fort Augustus U.K.
105 G4 Fort Beaufort S. Africa
24 E2 Fort Benton U.S.A.
21 H3 Fort Black Can.
34 A2 Fort Bragg U.S.A.
Fort-Chimo *see* Kuujjuaq
21 G3 Fort Chipewyan Can.
27 D5 Fort Cobb Res. *resr* U.S.A.
24 F3 Fort Collins U.S.A.
31 J3 Fort-Coulonge Can.
33 F2 Fort Covington U.S.A.
27 C6 Fort Davis U.S.A.
37 M6 Fort-de-France Martinique
29 C5 Fort Deposit U.S.A.
26 E3 Fort Dodge U.S.A.
112 C4 Fortescue *r.* Austr.
26 E1 Fort Frances U.S.A.
22 E3 Fort George Can.
57 D4 Forth *r.* U.K.
57 F4 Forth, Firth of *est.* U.K.
Fort Hertz *see* Putao
35 E2 Fortification Range *mts* U.S.A.
44 D2 Fortín Capitán Demattei Para.
44 D2 Fortín General Mendoza Para.
44 D2 Fortín Madrejón Para.
44 D2 Fortín Pilcomayo Arg.
42 F7 Fortín Ravelo Bol.
42 F7 Fortín Suárez Arana Bol.
33 J1 Fort Kent U.S.A.
29 D7 Fort Lauderdale U.S.A.
20 E2 Fort Liard Can.
21 G3 Fort Mackay Can.
20 G5 Fort Macleod Can.
30 B5 Fort Madison U.S.A.
30 B3 Fort McCoy U.S.A.
21 G3 Fort McMurray Can.
24 G3 Fort Morgan U.S.A.
29 D7 Fort Myers U.S.A.
20 E3 Fort Nelson Can.
20 E3 Fort Nelson *r.* Can.
Fort Norman *see* Tulit'a
29 C5 Fort Payne U.S.A.
24 F1 Fort Peck U.S.A.
24 F2 Fort Peck Res. *resr* U.S.A.
29 D7 Fort Pierce U.S.A.
26 C2 Fort Pierre U.S.A.
20 F2 Fort Providence Can.
21 J4 Fort Qu'Appelle Can.
20 G2 Fort Resolution Can.
117 B7 Fortrose N.Z.
57 D3 Fortrose U.K.

34 A2 Fort Ross U.S.A.
22 E3 Fort Rupert Can.
Fort Sandeman *see* Zhob
20 G4 Fort Saskatchewan Can.
27 E4 Fort Scott U.S.A.
22 C2 Fort Severn Can.
20 E2 Fort Simpson Can.
21 G2 Fort Smith Can.
27 E5 Fort Smith U.S.A.
20 E4 Fort St James Can.
20 E3 Fort St John Can.
27 C6 Fort Stockton U.S.A.
25 F5 Fort Sumner U.S.A.
24 A3 Fortuna Can.
26 C1 Fortuna U.S.A.
23 J4 Fortune B. *b.* Can.
20 F3 Fort Vermilion Can.
29 C6 Fort Walton Beach U.S.A.
30 E5 Fort Wayne U.S.A.
57 C4 Fort William U.K.
27 D5 Fort Worth U.S.A.
54 N4 Forvik Norway
89 D6 Foshan China
89 □ Fo Shek Chau *i.* China
66 B2 Fossano Italy
115 G7 Foster Austr.
20 B3 Foster, Mt *mt* Can./U.S.A.
32 B4 Fostoria U.S.A.
59 G4 Fotherby U.K.
64 D2 Fougères France
57 □ Foula *i.* U.K.
59 H6 Foulness Point *pt* U.K.
117 C4 Foulwind, Cape *c.* N.Z.
100 C4 Foumban Cameroon
100 A3 Foundiougne Senegal
30 A4 Fountain U.S.A.
64 G2 Fourches, Mont des *h.* France
34 D4 Four Corners U.S.A.
105 H4 Fouriesburg S. Africa
67 M6 Fournoi *i.* Greece
30 C2 Fourteen Mile Pt *pt* U.S.A.
100 A3 Fouta Djallon *reg.* Guinea
117 A7 Foveaux Strait *str.* N.Z.
29 E7 Fowl Cay *i.* Bahamas
25 F4 Fowler *CO* U.S.A.
30 D5 Fowler *IN* U.S.A.
30 E4 Fowler *MI* U.S.A.
119 B3 Fowler Pen. *pen.* Antarctica
112 F6 Fowlers Bay Austr.
81 M3 Fowman Iran
21 L3 Fox *r.* Can.
30 C4 Fox *r.* U.S.A.
116 B4 Fox Cr. *r.* Austr.
20 F4 Fox Creek Can.
58 C3 Foxdale U.K.
118 A2 Foxe Basin *basin* Can.
117 C5 Fox Glacier N.Z.
20 G3 Fox Lake Can.
30 C4 Fox Lake U.S.A.
117 E4 Foxton N.Z.
57 D3 Foyers U.K.
60 D3 Foyle *r.* Rep. of Ireland/U.K.
60 D3 Foyle, Lough *b.* Rep. of Ireland/U.K.
60 B5 Foynes Rep. of Ireland
103 B5 Foz do Cunene Angola
46 A4 Foz do Iguaçu Brazil
65 G2 Fraga Spain
46 C3 Franca Brazil
111 G3 Français, Récif des *rf* New Caledonia
48 France *country* Europe
114 D6 Frances Austr.
20 D2 Frances *r.* Can.
20 D2 Frances Lake Can.
20 D2 Frances Lake *l.* Can.
102 B4 Franceville Gabon
33 H2 Francis, Lake *l.* U.S.A.
26 D3 Francis Case, Lake *l.* U.S.A.
27 D4 Francisco I. Madero Mex.
46 D2 Francisco Sá Brazil
103 C6 Francistown Botswana
20 D4 François Lake *l.* Can.
24 E3 Francs Peak *summit* U.S.A.
31 H4 Frankenmuth U.S.A.
105 H3 Frankfort S. Africa
30 D5 Frankfort *IN* U.S.A.
28 C4 Frankfort *KY* U.S.A.
30 D3 Frankfort *MI* U.S.A.
62 D5 Frankfurt am Main Ger.
62 G4 Frankfurt an der Oder Ger.
35 E1 Frankin Lake *l.* U.S.A.
62 E6 Fränkische Alb *reg.* Ger.
62 E6 Fränkische Schweiz *reg.* Ger.
28 E3 Franklin *ID* U.S.A.
28 C4 Franklin *IN* U.S.A.
27 F6 Franklin *LA* U.S.A.
33 H3 Franklin *MA* U.S.A.
29 D5 Franklin *NC* U.S.A.
33 H3 Franklin *NH* U.S.A.
33 F4 Franklin *NJ* U.S.A.
32 D4 Franklin *PA* U.S.A.
32 C5 Franklin *TN* U.S.A.
32 E6 Franklin *VA* U.S.A.
32 C6 Franklin *WV* U.S.A.
24 C1 Franklin D. Roosevelt Lake *l.* U.S.A.
115 F9 Franklin-Gordon National Park *nat. park* Austr.
114 A4 Franklin Harbor *b.* Austr.
20 E2 Franklin Mountains *mts* Can.
117 A6 Franklin Mts *mts* N.Z.
115 G8 Franklin Sd *chan.* Austr.

118 B2 Franklin Strait *sea chan.* Can.
114 F7 Frankston Austr.
55 P5 Fränsta Sweden
30 E1 Franz Can.
117 C5 Franz Josef Glacier N.Z.
76 G2 Franz Josef Land *is* Rus. Fed.
66 C5 Frasca, Capo della *pt* Italy
66 E4 Frascati Italy
20 E4 Fraser *r. B.C.* Can.
23 H2 Fraser *r.* Nfld and Lab.
104 D5 Fraserburg S. Africa
57 F3 Fraserburgh U.K.
22 D4 Fraserdale Can.
116 E5 Fraser Island *i.* Austr.
116 E5 Fraser Island National Park Austr.
20 E4 Fraser Lake Can.
20 E4 Fraser Plateau *plat.* Can.
117 F3 Frasertown N.Z.
30 E2 Frater Can.
62 D7 Frauenfeld Switz.
47 E2 Fray Bentos Uru.
58 E4 Freckleton U.K.
30 E3 Frederic *WI* U.S.A.
30 A3 Frederic *WV* U.S.A.
55 L9 Fredericia Denmark
32 E5 Frederick *MD* U.S.A.
27 D5 Frederick *OK* U.S.A.
27 D6 Fredericksburg *TX* U.S.A.
32 E5 Fredericksburg *VA* U.S.A.
20 C3 Frederick Sound *chan.* U.S.A.
27 F4 Fredericktown U.S.A.
23 G4 Fredericton Can.
55 M8 Frederikshavn Denmark
55 N9 Frederiksværk Denmark
35 H5 Fredonia *AZ* U.S.A.
32 D3 Fredonia *NY* U.S.A.
54 Q4 Fredrika Sweden
55 M7 Fredrikstad Norway
33 H4 Freehold U.S.A.
33 H4 Freeland U.S.A.
114 C3 Freeling Heights *mt* Austr.
34 C2 Freel Peak *summit* U.S.A.
26 D3 Freeman U.S.A.
30 D5 Freeman, Lake *l.* U.S.A.
30 C4 Freeport *IL* U.S.A.
33 H3 Freeport *ME* U.S.A.
33 G4 Freeport *NY* U.S.A.
27 E6 Freeport *TX* U.S.A.
29 E7 Freeport City Bahamas
27 D7 Freer U.S.A.
105 G4 Free State *div.* S. Africa
100 A4 Freetown Sierra Leone
65 C4 Fregenal de la Sierra Spain
64 C2 Fréhel, Cap *pt* France
62 C6 Freiburg im Breisgau Ger.
62 E6 Freising Ger.
62 G6 Freistadt Austria
64 H5 Fréjus France
112 C6 Fremantle Austr.
30 E4 Fremont *MI* U.S.A.
26 D3 Fremont *NE* U.S.A.
32 B4 Fremont *OH* U.S.A.
35 G2 Fremont *r.* U.S.A.
32 B6 Frenchburg U.S.A.
32 C4 French Creek *r.* U.S.A.
38 French Guiana *terr.* S. America
114 F7 French I. *i.* Austr.
21 K3 Frenchman *r.* Can./U.S.A.
34 C2 Frenchman Can.
34 B2 Frenchman L. *l. CA* U.S.A.
35 E3 Frenchman L. *l. NV* U.S.A.
115 F9 Frenchmans Cap *mt* Austr.
60 C4 Frenchpark Rep. of Ireland
117 D4 French Pass N.Z.
33 J1 Frenchville U.S.A.
60 D5 Freshford Rep. of Ireland
35 G6 Freshal Canyon U.S.A.
36 D4 Fresnillo Mex.
34 C3 Fresno U.S.A.
34 C3 Fresno *r.* U.S.A.
65 H3 Freu, Cap des *pt* Spain
62 D6 Freudenstadt Ger.
115 H9 Freycinet Nat. Park *nat. park* Austr.
115 H9 Freycinet Peninsula *pen.* Austr.
64 H2 Freyming-Merlebach France
47 D5 Freyre Arg.
100 A3 Fria Guinea
34 C3 Friant U.S.A.
44 C3 Frias Arg.
62 C7 Fribourg Switz.
62 D7 Friedrichshafen Ger.
33 J3 Friendship U.S.A.
61 D1 Friese Wad *tidal flats* Neth.
59 J6 Frinton-on-Sea U.K.
27 D6 Frio *r.* U.S.A.
57 B4 Frisa, Loch *l.* U.K.
35 F2 Frisco Mt *mt* U.S.A.
118 A3 Frobisher Bay *b.* Can.
21 H3 Frobisher Lake *l.* Can.
54 L5 Frohavet *b.* Norway
69 G5 Frolovo Rus. Fed.
68 K2 Frolovskaya Rus. Fed.
114 C2 Frome *watercourse* Austr.
59 E6 Frome U.K.
114 C3 Frome, Lake *salt flat* Austr.
114 C3 Frome Downs Austr.
36 F5 Frontera Mex.
25 E6 Fronteras Mex.

32 D5 Front Royal U.S.A.
66 E4 Frosinone Italy
32 D5 Frostburg U.S.A.
54 L5 Frøya *i.* Norway
35 H2 Fruita U.S.A.
35 G1 Fruitland U.S.A.
Frunze *see* Bishkek
62 C7 Frutigen Switz.
63 J6 Frýdek-Místek Czech Rep.
33 H2 Fryeburg U.S.A.
89 F5 Fu'an China
89 E5 Fuchuan China
89 F4 Fuchun Jiang *r.* China
57 A3 Fuday *i.* U.K.
89 E5 Fude China
89 F5 Fuding China
65 E2 Fuenlabrada Spain
65 D3 Fuente Obejuna Spain
44 E2 Fuerte Olimpo Para.
100 A2 Fuerteventura *i.* Canary Is
94 B3 Fuga *i.* Phil.
88 E3 Fugou China
88 D2 Fugu China
82 G1 Fuhai China
81 J4 Fuḥaymī Iraq
79 H4 Fujairah U.A.E.
91 F7 Fuji Japan
89 E5 Fujian *div.* China
88 C4 Fu Jiang *r.* China
91 F7 Fuji-Hakone-Izu National Park Japan
90 B1 Fujin China
91 F7 Fujinomiya Japan
91 F7 Fuji-san *vol.* Japan
90 H3 Fukagawa Japan
91 D7 Fukuchiyama Japan
91 A8 Fukue Japan
91 A8 Fukue-jima *i.* Japan
91 E6 Fukui Japan
91 B8 Fukuoka Japan
91 G6 Fukushima Japan
91 B9 Fukuyama Japan
62 D5 Fulda Ger.
59 G6 Fulham U.K.
88 E3 Fuliji China
89 C4 Fuling China
21 M2 Fullerton, Cape *hd* Can.
30 B5 Fulton *IL* U.S.A.
28 B4 Fulton *KY* U.S.A.
26 F4 Fulton *MO* U.S.A.
33 E3 Fulton *NY* U.S.A.
105 K2 Fumane Moz.
61 C5 Fumay France
91 F7 Funabashi Japan
111 H2 Funafuti *i.* Tuvalu
100 A1 Funchal Port.
45 D2 Fundación Col.
45 D2 Fundão Port.
23 G5 Fundy, Bay of *g.* Can.
23 G4 Fundy Nat. Park *nat. park* Can.
34 D3 Funeral Peak *summit* U.S.A.
103 D6 Funhalouro Moz.
88 F3 Funing *Jiangsu* China
89 B6 Funing *Yunnan* China
88 D3 Funiu Shan *mts* China
116 C4 Funnel Cr. *r.* Austr.
100 C4 Funtua Nigeria
57 □ Funzie U.K.
89 F5 Fuqing China
90 H3 Fuqun Japan
79 H4 Fürgun, Küh-e *mt* Iran
68 G3 Furmanov Rus. Fed.
90 D3 Furmanovo Rus. Fed.
34 D3 Furnace Creek U.S.A.
46 C3 Furnas, Represa *resr* Brazil
113 J7 Furneaux Group *is* Austr.
62 G4 Fürstenwalde Ger.
62 E6 Fürth Ger.
90 G3 Furubira Japan
90 G5 Furukawa Japan
45 B3 Fusagasugá Col.
88 G1 Fushan *Liaoning* China
89 B4 Fushun *Sichuan* China
87 N3 Fusong China
89 C6 Fusui China
91 B8 Futago-san *vol.* Japan
111 H3 Futuna *i.* Vanuatu
89 E5 Futun Xi *r.* China
88 C3 Fuxian China
87 M3 Fuxing *Liaoning* China
88 F1 Fuxin *Liaoning* China
90 F5 Fuya Japan
88 E3 Fuyang *Anhui* China
89 F4 Fuyang *Zhejiang* China
88 E2 Fuyang *r.* China
87 M2 Fuyu China
89 B5 Fuyuan China
82 G1 Fuyun China
89 F5 Fuzhou China
Fuzhou *see* Linchuan
81 L2 Füzuli Azer.
55 M9 Fyn *i.* Denmark
57 C5 Fyne, Loch *in.* U.K.
F.Y.R.O.M. *country see* Macedonia

G

66 C6 Gaâfour Tunisia
102 E3 Gaalkacyo Somalia
105 F2 Gabane Botswana
34 D2 Gabbs U.S.A.
34 C2 Gabbs Valley Range *mts* U.S.A.
103 B5 Gabela Angola
100 D1 Gabès Tunisia

101 D1 Gabès, Golfe de *g.* Tunisia
115 H6 Gabo I. *i.* Austr.
96 Gabon *country* Africa
103 C6 Gaborone Botswana
67 L3 Gabrovo Bulg.
100 A3 Gabú Guinea-Bissau
83 E7 Gadag India
54 O4 Gäddede Sweden
84 B5 Gadhra India
84 B4 Gadra Pak.
29 C5 Gadsden U.S.A.
83 E7 Gadwal India
54 S2 Gæi'dnuvuop'pi Norway
59 D6 Gaer U.K.
67 L2 Găești Romania
66 E4 Gaeta Italy
66 E4 Gaeta, Golfo di *g.* Italy
29 D5 Gaffney U.S.A.
100 C1 Gafsa Tunisia
68 E4 Gagarin Rus. Fed.
68 H4 Gagino Rus. Fed.
100 B4 Gagnoa Côte d'Ivoire
23 G3 Gagnon Can.
69 G7 Gagra Georgia
81 L4 Gahväreh Iran
104 C4 Gaiab *watercourse* Namibia
85 G3 Gaibandha Bangl.
64 E5 Gaillac France
29 D6 Gainesville *FL* U.S.A.
29 D5 Gainesville *GA* U.S.A.
27 D5 Gainesville *TX* U.S.A.
59 G4 Gainsborough U.K.
114 A3 Gairdner, Lake *salt flat* Austr.
57 C3 Gairloch U.K.
57 C3 Gair Loch *in.* U.K.
88 G1 Gaizhou China
104 E3 Gakarosa *mt* S. Africa
84 C1 Gakuch Jammu and Kashmir
85 G3 Gala China
57 F5 Galashiels U.K.
67 M3 Galata, Nos *pt* Bulg.
67 N2 Galați Romania
67 H4 Galatina Italy
32 C6 Galax U.S.A.
60 C5 Galbally Rep. of Ireland
55 L6 Galdhøpiggen *summit* Norway
30 A4 Galena U.S.A.
45 E2 Galeota Pt *pt* Trinidad and Tobago
45 E2 Galera, Punta *pt* Chile
45 E2 Galera Pt *pt* Trinidad and Tobago
30 B5 Galesburg U.S.A.
104 F4 Galeshewe S. Africa
30 B3 Galesville U.S.A.
32 E4 Galeton U.S.A.
69 G7 Gali Georgia
68 G3 Galich Rus. Fed.
68 G2 Galichskaya Vozvyshennost' *reg.* Rus. Fed.
65 C1 Galicia *div.* Spain
116 A4 Galilee, Lake *salt flat* Austr.
80 E3 Galilee, Sea of *l.* Israel
32 B4 Galion U.S.A.
35 H3 Galiuro Mts *mts* U.S.A.
101 F3 Gallabat Sudan
29 C4 Gallatin Rus. Fed.
24 E2 Gallatin *r.* U.S.A.
83 F9 Galle Sri Lanka
44 B8 Gallegos *r.* Arg.
45 C1 Galinas, Pta *pt* Col.
66 H4 Gallipoli Italy
32 B5 Gallipolis U.S.A.
54 R3 Gällivare Sweden
54 O5 Gällö Sweden
33 G3 Gallo *l.* U.K.
35 H4 Gallo Mts *mts* U.S.A.
35 H4 Gallup U.S.A.
57 B4 Galmisdale U.K.
115 H5 Galong Austr.
57 D5 Galston U.K.
34 B2 Galt U.S.A.
100 A2 Galtat Zemmour Western Sahara
60 C5 Galtee Mountains *h.* Rep. of Ireland
60 C5 Galtymore *h.* Rep. of Ireland
30 A3 Galva U.S.A.
27 E6 Galveston U.S.A.
27 E6 Galveston Bay *b.* U.S.A.
47 E2 Galvez Arg.
85 E3 Galwa Nepal
60 B4 Galway Rep. of Ireland
60 B4 Galway Bay *g.* Rep. of Ireland
89 B6 Gâm *r.* Vietnam
59 J8 Gamaches France
105 J5 Gamalakhe S. Africa
45 B2 Gamarra Col.
85 G3 Gamba China
102 D3 Gambēla Eth.
102 D3 Gambēla National Park *nat. park* Eth.
84 D2 Gambhir *r.* India
109 Gambier, Îles *is* Pac. Oc.
114 B5 Gambier Is *is* Austr.
23 K4 Gambo Can.
102 B4 Gamboma Congo
113 H3 Gamboola Austr.
35 H4 Gamerco U.S.A.
55 P8 Gamleby Sweden
54 S4 Gammelstaden Sweden
113 G3 Gammon Ranges Nat. Park *nat. park* Austr.
90 B3 Gamova, Mys *pt* Rus. Fed.
35 H4 Ganado U.S.A.

31 J3 Gananoque Can.
81 L1 Gäncä Azer.
89 C7 Gancheng China
93 F7 Gandadiwata, Bukit *mt* Indon.
85 G3 Gandaingoin China
102 C4 Gandajika Dem. Rep. Congo
85 E4 Gandak Dam *dam* Nepal
84 B3 Gandari Mountain *mt* Pak.
84 A3 Gandava Pak.
23 K4 Gander Can.
65 G2 Gandesa Spain
84 C5 Gandevi India
84 B5 Gandhidham India
84 C4 Gandhinagar India
84 C4 Gāndhī Sāgar *resr* India
84 C4 Gāndhī Sāgar Dam *dam* India
65 F3 Gandia Spain
79 J4 Gand-i-Zureh *plain* Afgh.
46 E1 Gandu Brazil
Ganga *r. see* Ganges
47 C4 Gangán Arg.
84 D4 Ganganagar India
85 H5 Gangaw Myanmar
88 C3 Gangca China
84 E3 Gangdisê Shan *mts* China
64 F5 Ganges France
85 G4 Ganges *r.* India
85 G5 Ganges, Mouths of the *est.* Bangl./India
84 D3 Gangoh India
84 D3 Gangotri *mt* India
85 G4 Gangtok India
88 B3 Gangu China
83 G7 Ganjam India
89 B4 Gan Jiang *r.* China
88 G1 Ganjig China
89 B4 Ganluo China
115 G5 Ganmain Austr.
64 F3 Gannat France
24 E3 Gannett Peak *summit* U.S.A.
84 C5 Ganora India
88 C2 Ganquan China
104 C7 Gansbaai S. Africa
88 B3 Gansu *div.* China
88 B2 Gantang China
114 B6 Gantheaume, C. *hd* Austr.
69 G7 Gant'iadi Georgia
89 C6 Ganxian China
88 F3 Ganyu China
89 E4 Ganzhou China
101 F4 Ganzi Sudan
100 B3 Gao Mali
89 B4 Gao'an China
88 D3 Gaocheng China
88 C4 Gaochun China
89 E4 Gaohebu China
88 B2 Gaolan China
88 F2 Gaomi China
89 D5 Gaomutang China
88 D3 Gaoping China
88 A2 Gaotai China
88 E2 Gaotang China
88 C2 Gaotouyao China
100 B3 Gaoua Burkina
100 A3 Gaoual Guinea
88 E2 Gaoyang China
88 F3 Gaoyou China
88 F3 Gaoyou Hu *l.* China
89 D6 Gaozhou China
64 H4 Gap France
94 B3 Gapan Phil.
65 F5 Gap Carbon *hd* Alg.
84 E2 Gar China
60 C4 Gara, Lough *l.* Rep. of Ireland
115 H2 Garah Austr.
102 C3 Garamba *r.* Dem. Rep. Congo
43 L5 Garanhuns Brazil
105 G2 Ga-Rankuwa S. Africa
102 D3 Garba Tula Kenya
34 A1 Garberville U.S.A.
62 D4 Garbsen Ger.
46 C3 Garça Brazil
46 B1 Garças, Rio das *r.* Brazil
85 G2 Garco China
66 D2 Garda, Lago di *l.* Italy
81 K1 Gardabani Georgia
65 G5 Garde, Cap de *hd* Alg.
26 C4 Garden City U.S.A.
30 D3 Garden Corners U.S.A.
34 C5 Garden Grove U.S.A.
21 L4 Garden Hill Can.
30 D3 Garden I. *i.* U.S.A.
28 B2 Garden Pen. *pen.* U.S.A.
84 B2 Gardez Afgh.
33 J2 Gardiner *ME* U.S.A.
24 E2 Gardiner *MT* U.S.A.
33 G4 Gardiners I. *i.* U.S.A.
30 C5 Gardner U.S.A.
33 K2 Gardner Lake *l.* U.S.A.
14 H4 Gardner Pinnacles *is* U.S.A.
34 C2 Gardnerville U.S.A.
57 E4 Garelochhead U.K.
30 E2 Gargantua, Cape *c.* Can.
81 M6 Gargar Iran
55 R9 Gargždai Lith.
84 D5 Garhakota India
84 D5 Garhchiroli India
84 A3 Garhi Khairo Pak.
84 D4 Garhi Malehra India
20 E5 Garibaldi, Mt *mt* Can.
20 E5 Garibaldi Prov. Park *nat. park* Can.

88 C4 Guanmian Shan *mts* China
88 D3 Guanpo China
45 D2 Guanta Venez.
37 J4 Guantánamo Cuba
88 E1 Guanting Sk. *resr* China
89 D5 Guanyang China
88 A4 Guanyinqiao China
88 F3 Guanyun China
45 A4 Guapí Col.
42 F6 Guaporé *r.* Bol./Brazil
42 E7 Guaqui Bol.
46 D1 Guará *r.* Brazil
43 L5 Guarabira Brazil
46 E3 Guarapari Brazil
46 B4 Guarapuava Brazil
46 C4 Guaraqueçaba Brazil
46 D3 Guaratinguetá Brazil
46 C4 Guaratuba, Baía de *b.* Brazil
65 C2 Guarda Port.
46 C2 Guarda Mor Brazil
65 D1 Guardo Spain
45 D2 Guárico *r.* Venez.
45 C3 Guarrojo *r.* Col.
46 C4 Guarujá Brazil
45 D4 Guasacavi *r.* Col.
45 C4 Guasacavi, Cerro *h.* Col.
45 B2 Guasare *r.* Venez.
36 C3 Guasave Mex.
45 C3 Guasdualito Venez.
45 E3 Guasipati Venez.
46 B4 Guassú *r.* Brazil
16 Guatemala *country* Central America
36 F6 Guatemala Guatemala
45 D2 Guatope, Parque Nacional *nat. park* Venez.
47 D3 Guatrache Arg.
45 C4 Guaviare *r.* Col.
46 C3 Guaxupé Brazil
45 B4 Guayabero *r.* Col.
45 D3 Guayapo *r.* Venez.
42 C4 Guayaquil Ecuador
42 B4 Guayaquil, Golfo de *g.* Ecuador
42 E6 Guayaramerín Bol.
36 B3 Guaymas Mex.
102 D2 Guba Eth.
66 E3 Gubbio Italy
69 F5 Gubkin Rus. Fed.
88 D3 Gucheng China
69 G7 Gudaut'a Georgia
55 M6 Gudbrandsdalen *v.* Norway
84 B3 Guddu Barrage *barrage* Pak.
69 H7 Gudermes Rus. Fed.
83 F7 Gudivada India
90 A3 Gudong *r.* China
80 D1 Güdül Turkey
83 E8 Gudur India
55 K6 Gudvangen Norway
100 A4 Guéckédou Guinea
31 J1 Guéguen, Lac *l.* Can.
45 B4 Güejar *r.* Col.
100 C1 Guelma Alg.
100 A2 Guelmine Morocco
31 G4 Guelph Can.
45 D2 Güera *r.* Venez.
23 G2 Guerard, Lac *l.* Can.
64 E3 Guéret France
56 E7 Guernsey *i.* U.K.
24 F3 Guernsey U.S.A.
27 D7 Guerrero Mex.
36 B3 Guerrero Negro Mex.
12 F5 Guiana Basin *sea feature* Atlantic Ocean
114 C6 Guichen B. *b.* Austr.
89 E4 Guichi China
47 F2 Guichón Uru.
88 A3 Guide China
101 D4 Guider Cameroon
89 C5 Guiding China
66 E4 Guidonia-Montecelio Italy
89 C6 Guigang China
100 B4 Guiglo Côte d'Ivoire
105 K2 Guija Moz.
89 D6 Gui Jiang *r.* China
89 F4 Guiji Shan *mts* China
59 G6 Guildford U.K.
33 J2 Guilford U.S.A.
89 D5 Guilin China
22 E2 Guillaume-Delisle, Lac *l.* Can.
65 B2 Guimarães Port.
94 B4 Guimaras Str. *chan.* Phil.
88 E3 Guimeng Ding *mt* China
88 A3 Guinan China
34 A2 Guinda U.S.A.
94 C4 Guindulman Phil.
96 Guinea *country* Africa
98 Guinea, Gulf of *g.* Africa
12 J5 Guinea Basin *sea feature* Atlantic Ocean
96 Guinea-Bissau *country* Africa
37 H4 Güines Cuba
64 C2 Guingamp France
64 B2 Guipavas France
89 D6 Guiping China
46 B2 Guiratinga Brazil
45 E2 Güiria Venez.
61 B5 Guise France
94 C4 Guiuan Phil.
89 E4 Guixi China
89 C5 Guiyang *Guizhou* China
89 D5 Guiyang *Hunan* China
89 C5 Guizhou *div.* China
84 B5 Gujarat *div.* India
84 C2 Gujar Khan Pak.
84 C2 Gujranwala Pak.
84 C2 Gujrat Pak.
69 F5 Gukovo Rus. Fed.
81 K3 Gük Tappeh Iran
84 D2 Gulabgarh Jammu and Kashmir
79 H1 Gulabie Uzbek.
88 B2 Gulang China
115 H3 Gulargambone Austr.
83 E7 Gulbarga India
55 U8 Gulbene Latvia
79 L1 Gülchö Kyrgyzstan
80 E3 Gülek Turkey
118 A2 Gulf of Boothia *gulf* Can.
27 F6 Gulfport U.S.A.
115 H4 Gulgong Austr.
87 M1 Gulian China
89 B5 Gulin China
79 K1 Gulistan Uzbek.
30 E3 Gull I. *i.* U.S.A.
21 H4 Gull Lake Can.
54 R3 Gullträsk Sweden
80 D3 Gülnar Turkey
69 G7 Gulrip'shi Georgia
80 E2 Gülşehir Turkey
102 D3 Gulu Uganda
116 D6 Guluguba Austr.
84 B3 Gumal *r.* Pak.
103 C5 Gumare Botswana
79 G2 Gumdag Turkm.
85 F5 Gumia India
85 F5 Gumla India
61 F3 Gummersbach Ger.
80 E1 Gümüşhacıköy Turkey
81 G1 Gümüşhane Turkey
84 D4 Guna India
115 F5 Gunbar Austr.
115 H5 Gundagai Austr.
80 D3 Gündoğmuş Turkey
80 B2 Güney Turkey
102 B4 Gungu Dem. Rep. Congo
69 H7 Gunib Rus. Fed.
21 K4 Gunisao *r.* Can.
116 A1 Gunnawarra Austr.
115 J3 Gunnedah Austr.
115 H5 Gunning Austr.
25 F4 Gunnison *CO* U.S.A.
35 G2 Gunnison *UT* U.S.A.
25 E4 Gunnison *r.* U.S.A.
83 E7 Guntakal India
29 C5 Guntersville U.S.A.
29 C5 Guntersville L. *l.* U.S.A.
83 F7 Guntur India
113 G3 Gununa Austr.
92 B6 Gunungsitoli Indon.
95 A5 Gunungtua Indon.
62 E6 Günzburg Ger.
62 E6 Gunzenhausen Ger.
88 E1 Guojiatun China
88 E3 Guoyang China
88 A2 Gurban Hudag China
88 D1 Gurban Obo China
80 B2 Güre Turkey
84 D3 Gurgaon India
43 K5 Gurgueia *r.* Brazil
84 B4 Gurha India
45 E3 Guri, Embalse de *resr* Venez.
112 F2 Gurig National Park *nat. park* Austr.
46 C2 Gurinhatã Brazil
69 H7 Gurjaani Georgia
81 J2 Gürpınar Turkey
85 G3 Guru China
103 D5 Guruè Moz.
80 F2 Gürün Turkey
43 J4 Gurupi *r.* Brazil
84 C4 Guru Sikhar *mt* India
68 B4 Gur'yevsk Rus. Fed.
100 C3 Gusau Nigeria
68 B4 Gusev Rus. Fed.
88 G2 Gushan China
35 H1 Gusher U.S.A.
79 J2 Gushgy Turkm.
88 E3 Gushi China
94 A5 Gusi Malaysia
77 M2 Gusikha Rus. Fed.
68 D4 Gusino Rus. Fed.
86 J1 Gusinoozersk Rus. Fed.
85 F5 Guskara India
68 G4 Gus'-Khrustal'nyy Rus. Fed.
66 C5 Guspini Italy
20 B3 Gustavus U.S.A.
34 B3 Gustine U.S.A.
62 F4 Güstrow Ger.
85 H3 Gutang China
62 D5 Gütersloh Ger.
35 H5 Guthrie *AZ* U.S.A.
28 C4 Guthrie *KY* U.S.A.
27 D5 Guthrie *OK* U.S.A.
27 C5 Guthrie *TX* U.S.A.
89 E5 Gutian *Fujian* China
89 F5 Gutian *Fujian* China
61 E5 Gutland *reg.* Ger./Lux.
85 F3 Gutsuo China
30 B4 Guttenberg U.S.A.
103 D5 Gutu Zimbabwe
85 G4 Guwahati India
81 J3 Guwēr Iraq
38 Guyana *country* S. America
88 D1 Guyang China
27 C4 Guymon U.S.A.
115 J3 Guyra Austr.
88 E1 Guyuan *Hebei* China
88 C3 Guyuan *Ningxia* China
79 K2 Guzar Uzbek.
89 C4 Guzhang China
88 E3 Guzhen China
25 E6 Guzmán Mex.
25 F6 Guzmán, Lago de *l.* Mex.
63 K3 Gvardeysk Rus. Fed.
115 H3 Gwabegar Austr.
79 J4 Gwadar Pak.
84 D4 Gwalior India
116 C5 Gwambegwine Austr.
103 C6 Gwanda Zimbabwe
60 C3 Gweebarra Bay *b.* Rep. of Ireland
60 C2 Gweedore Rep. of Ireland
103 C5 Gweru Zimbabwe
30 D2 Gwinn U.S.A.
101 D3 Gwoza Nigeria
115 H2 Gwydir *r.* Austr.
85 H3 Gyaca China
88 B3 Gyagartang China
85 F2 Gyangnyi Caka *salt l.* China
85 F3 Gyangrang China
85 G3 Gyangzê China
85 G3 Gyaring Co *l.* China
82 J4 Gyaring Hu *l.* China
67 L6 Gyaros *i.* Greece
85 H3 Gyarubtang China
76 J2 Gydanskiy Poluostrov *pen.* Rus. Fed.
85 H3 Gyimda China
85 F3 Gyirong *Xizang Zizhiqu* China
85 F3 Gyirong *Xizang Zizhiqu* China
85 H2 Gyiza China
116 E6 Gympie Austr.
63 J7 Gyöngyös Hungary
62 H7 Győr Hungary
21 K4 Gypsumville Can.
23 G2 Gyrfalcon Is *i.* Can.
67 K6 Gytheio Greece
63 K7 Gyula Hungary
81 J1 Gyumri Armenia
79 H2 Gyzylarbat Turkm.

H

54 T5 Haapajärvi Fin.
54 T4 Haapavesi Fin.
55 S7 Haapsalu Estonia
61 C2 Haarlem Neth.
104 E6 Haarlem S. Africa
117 B5 Haast *r.* N.Z.
82 G1 Habahe China
102 D3 Habaswein Kenya
23 F3 Habay Can.
78 F7 Ḩabbān Yemen
81 J5 Ḩabbānīyah, Hawr al *l.* Iraq
85 G4 Habiganj Bangl.
88 E1 Habirag China
85 G5 Habra India
45 B5 Hacha Col.
47 B3 Hachado, P. de *pass* Arg./Chile
91 F8 Hachijō-jima *i.* Japan
90 G4 Hachinohe Japan
91 F7 Hachiōji Japan
80 E2 Hacıbektaş Turkey
81 H2 Hacıömer Turkey
114 C3 Hack, Mt *mt* Austr.
103 D6 Hacufera Moz.
78 B5 Ḩadabat al Jilf al Kabīr *plat.* Egypt
79 H5 Ḩadd, Ra's al *pt* Oman
57 F5 Haddington U.K.
100 D3 Hadejia Nigeria
80 E5 Hadera Israel
55 L9 Haderslev Denmark
83 D10 Hadhdhunmathi Atoll *atoll* Maldives
80 D3 Hadım Turkey
59 H5 Hadleigh U.K.
80 F6 Ḩadraj, Wādī *watercourse* Saudi Arabia
78 F6 Ḩadramawt *reg.* Yemen
55 M8 Hadsund Denmark
69 E5 Hadyach Ukr.
47 F1 Haedo, Cuchilla de *h.* Uru.
87 N4 Haeju N. Korea
87 N4 Haeju-man *b.* N. Korea
105 H1 Haenertsburg S. Africa
21 H4 Hafford Can.
80 F2 Hafik Turkey
84 C2 Hafizabad Pak.
85 H4 Hāflong India
54 C4 Hafnarfjörður Iceland
54 B4 Hafursfjörður *b.* Iceland
31 G2 Hagar Can.
102 D2 Hagar Nish Plateau *plat.* Eritrea
93 L4 Hagåtña Guam
61 C4 Hageland *reg.* Belgium
62 C5 Hagen Ger.
110 E2 Hagen, Mount *mt* P.N.G.
32 E5 Hagerstown U.S.A.
64 D5 Hagetmau France
55 N6 Hagfors Sweden
24 D2 Haggin, Mount *mt* U.S.A.
91 B7 Hagi Japan
89 B6 Ha Giang Vietnam
59 E5 Hagley U.K.
60 B5 Hag's Head *hd* Rep. of Ireland
21 H4 Hague Can.
64 H2 Haguenau France
88 E2 Hai *r.* China
102 D4 Hai Tanz.
88 F3 Hai'an China
104 B4 Haib *watercourse* Namibia
88 G1 Haicheng China
89 C6 Hai Dương Vietnam
80 E5 Haifa Israel
80 E5 Haifa, Bay of *b.* Israel
89 E6 Haifeng China
89 D6 Haikou China
78 E4 Ḩā'īl Saudi Arabia
87 L2 Hailar China
31 H2 Haileybury Can.
90 A2 Hailin China
59 H7 Hailsham U.K.
54 T4 Hailuoto Fin.
88 F4 Haimen China
89 C7 Hainan *div.* China
89 D7 Hainan *i.* China
20 B3 Haines U.S.A.
20 B2 Haines Junction Can.
89 C6 Hai Phong Vietnam
88 A2 Hairag China
88 B1 Hairhan Namag China
89 F5 Haitan Dao *i.* China
16 Haiti *country* Caribbean Sea
89 C7 Haitou China
35 G5 Haivana Nakya U.S.A.
34 D3 Haiwee Reservoir U.S.A.
88 E2 Haixing China
101 F3 Haiya Sudan
88 A2 Haiyan *Qinghai* China
89 F4 Haiyan *Zhejiang* China
88 F2 Haiyang China
88 B2 Haiyuan China
88 F3 Haizhou Wan *b.* China
63 K7 Hajdúböszörmény Hungary
66 C7 Hajeb El Ayoun Tunisia
79 G7 Ḩajhir *mt* Yemen
90 F5 Hajiki-zaki *pt* Japan
85 F4 Hajipur India
85 H5 Haka Myanmar
34 □2 Hakalau U.S.A.
47 C4 Hakelhuincul, Altiplanicie de *plat.* Arg.
Hakha *see* Haka
81 J3 Hakkârı Turkey
54 R3 Hakkas Sweden
91 D7 Hakken-zan *mt* Japan
90 H2 Hako-dake *mt* Japan
90 G4 Hakodate Japan
104 B1 Hakos Mts *mts* Namibia
104 D3 Hakseen Pan *salt pan* S. Africa
91 E6 Hakui Japan
91 E6 Haku-san *vol.* Japan
91 E6 Haku-san National Park Japan
84 B4 Hala Pak.
Ḩalab *see* Aleppo
81 K4 Halabja Iraq
101 F2 Halaib Sudan
79 H6 Ḩalāniyāt, Juzur al *is* Oman
34 □2 Halawa U.S.A.
80 F4 Halba Lebanon
86 G2 Halban Mongolia
62 E5 Halberstadt Ger.
94 B3 Halcon, Mt *mt* Phil.
54 □ Haldarsvik Faroe Is
55 M7 Halden Norway
62 E4 Haldensleben Ger.
85 G5 Haldi *r.* India
85 G5 Haldia India
85 G4 Haldibari India
84 D3 Haldwani India
31 F3 Hale U.S.A.
34 □1 Haleiwa U.S.A.
59 E5 Halesowen U.K.
59 J5 Halesworth U.K.
80 F3 Halfeti Turkey
117 B7 Halfmoon Bay N.Z.
20 E3 Halfway *r.* Can.
60 C6 Halfway Rep. of Ireland
61 C2 Halfweg Neth.
85 E4 Halia India
81 G4 Ḩalībīyah Syria
31 H3 Haliburton Can.
116 B2 Halifax Austr.
23 H5 Halifax Can.
58 F4 Halifax U.K.
32 D6 Halifax U.S.A.
116 B2 Halifax, Mt *mt* Austr.
116 B2 Halifax Bay *b.* Austr.
57 E2 Halkirk U.K.
54 P5 Hälla Sweden
114 A5 Hall Bay *b.* Austr.
61 C4 Halle Belgium
62 E5 Halle Ger.
55 O7 Hällefors Sweden
62 F7 Hallein Austria
119 C3 Halley *U.K. Base* Antarctica
54 Q4 Hällnäs Sweden
26 D1 Hallock U.S.A.
55 O7 Hallsberg Sweden
112 E3 Halls Creek Austr.
31 H3 Halls Lake Can.
54 O5 Hallviken Sweden
93 H6 Halmahera *i.* Indon.
55 N8 Halmstad Sweden
84 C5 Halol India
55 M8 Hals Denmark
54 T5 Halsua Fin.
61 F3 Haltern Ger.
58 E3 Haltwhistle U.K.
116 D6 Haly, Mount *h.* Austr.
61 B5 Ham France
91 C7 Hamada Japan
100 B2 Ḩamâda El Ḩaricha *des.* Mali
81 M4 Hamadān Iran
100 B2 Hamada Tounassine *des.* Alg.
80 F4 Ḩamāh Syria
90 G3 Hamamasu Japan
91 E7 Hamamatsu Japan
55 M6 Hamar Norway
54 O2 Hamarøy Norway
78 C5 Ḩamāţah, Jabal *mt* Egypt
90 H2 Hamatonbetsu Japan
83 F9 Hambantota Sri Lanka
58 F3 Hambleton Hills *h.* U.K.
62 D4 Hamburg Ger.
105 G6 Hamburg S. Africa
27 F5 Hamburg *AR* U.S.A.
32 D3 Hamburg *NY* U.S.A.
33 F4 Hamburg *PA* U.S.A.
33 G4 Hamden U.S.A.
55 T6 Hämeenlinna Fin.
62 D4 Hameln Ger.
112 C4 Hamersley Range *mts* Austr.
87 N4 Hamhŭng N. Korea
82 H2 Hami China
81 M6 Ḩamīd Iran
101 F2 Hamid Sudan
114 E6 Hamilton Austr.
37 M2 Hamilton Bermuda
31 H4 Hamilton Can.
117 E2 Hamilton N.Z.
57 D5 Hamilton U.K.
29 C5 Hamilton *AL* U.S.A.
30 B5 Hamilton *IL* U.S.A.
24 D2 Hamilton *MT* U.S.A.
33 F3 Hamilton *NY* U.S.A.
32 A5 Hamilton *OH* U.S.A.
34 B3 Hamilton, Mt *mt* *CA* U.S.A.
35 E2 Hamilton, Mt *mt* *NV* U.S.A.
34 A2 Hamilton City U.S.A.
55 U6 Hamina Fin.
81 H6 Ḩāmir, Wādī al *watercourse* Saudi Arabia
84 D3 Hamirpur India
23 J3 Hamilton Inlet *in.* Can.
114 C5 Hamley Bridge Austr.
30 D3 Hamlin Lake *l.* U.S.A.
62 C5 Hamm Ger.
100 B2 Hammada du Drâa *plat.* Alg.
81 J3 Ḩammām al 'Alīl Iraq
66 D6 Hammamet Tunisia
101 D1 Hammamet, Golfe de *b.* Tunisia
81 L6 Ḩammār, Hawr al *l.* Iraq
54 P5 Hammarstrand Sweden
54 O5 Hammerdal Sweden
54 S1 Hammerfest Norway
61 E3 Hamminkeln Ger.
114 C4 Hammond Austr.
30 D5 Hammond *IN* U.S.A.
27 F6 Hammond *LA* U.S.A.
24 F2 Hammond *MT* U.S.A.
31 E3 Hammond Bay *b.* U.S.A.
32 E3 Hammondsport U.S.A.
33 F5 Hammonton U.S.A.
117 C6 Hampden N.Z.
59 F6 Hampshire Downs *h.* U.K.
23 G4 Hampton Can.
27 E5 Hampton *AR* U.S.A.
33 H3 Hampton *NH* U.S.A.
33 E6 Hampton *VA* U.S.A.
81 K4 Ḩamrīn, Jabal *h.* Iraq
95 C3 Ham Tân Vietnam
84 D2 Hamta Pass *pass* India
79 H4 Hāmūn-e Jaz Mūrīān *salt marsh* Iran
79 K4 Hamun-i-Lora *l.* Pak.
79 J4 Hamun-i-Mashkel *salt flat* Pak.
81 J2 Hamur Turkey
61 D4 Han, Grotte de *cave* Belgium
34 □2 Hana U.S.A.
104 E1 Hanahai *watercourse* Botswana/Namibia
34 □2 Hanalei U.S.A.
90 G5 Hanamaki Japan
88 D3 Hancheng China
32 D5 Hancock *MD* U.S.A.
30 C2 Hancock *MI* U.S.A.
33 F4 Hancock *NY* U.S.A.
57 C2 Handa Island *i.* U.K.
88 E2 Handan China
102 D4 Handeni Tanz.
34 C3 Hanford U.S.A.
86 G2 Hangayn Nuruu *mts* Mongolia
Hanggin Houqi *see* Xamba
Hanggin Qi *see* Xin
88 E2 Hangu China
84 B2 Hangu Pak.
89 D5 Hanguang China
89 F4 Hangzhou China
89 F4 Hangzhou Wan *b.* China
81 H2 Hani Turkey
88 B2 Hanjiaoshui China
104 F6 Hankey S. Africa
55 S7 Hanko Fin.
35 G2 Hanksville U.S.A.
84 D2 Hanle Jammu and Kashmir
117 D5 Hanmer Springs N.Z.
21 G4 Hanna Can.
22 D3 Hannah Bay *b.* Can.
30 B6 Hannibal U.S.A.
62 D4 Hannover Ger.
55 O9 Hanöbukten *b.* Sweden
89 B6 Ha Nôi Vietnam
Hanoi *see* Ha Nôi
31 G3 Hanover Can.
104 F5 Hanover S. Africa
33 G3 Hanover *NH* U.S.A.
32 E5 Hanover *PA* U.S.A.
119 D4 Hansen Mts *mts* Antarctica
89 D4 Hanshou China
88 E4 Han Shui *r.* China
84 D3 Hansi India
54 Q2 Hansnes Norway
114 B3 Hanson, L. *salt flat* Austr.
32 B6 Hansonville U.S.A.
55 L8 Hanstholm Denmark
68 C4 Hantsavichy Belarus
84 C3 Hanumangarh India
115 G5 Hanwwod Austr.
88 C3 Hanyin China
89 B4 Hanyuan China
88 C3 Hanzhong China
109 Hao *atoll* Pac. Oc.
85 G5 Hāora India
54 T4 Haparanda Sweden
85 H4 Hāpoli India
23 H3 Happy Valley-Goose Bay Can.
90 A4 Hapsu N. Korea
84 D3 Hapur India
78 C4 Ḩaql Saudi Arabia
68 D4 Haradok Belarus
91 G6 Haramachi Japan
84 C2 Haramukh *mt* India
84 C3 Harappa Road Pak.
103 D5 Harare Zimbabwe
79 H6 Ḩarāsīs, Jiddat al *gravel area* Oman
87 J2 Har-Ayrag Mongolia
100 A4 Harbel Liberia
87 N2 Harbin China
31 F4 Harbor Beach U.S.A.
30 E3 Harbor Springs U.S.A.
23 J4 Harbour Breton Can.
44 E8 Harbours, B. of *b.* Falkland Is
35 F5 Harcuvar Mts *mts* U.S.A.
84 D5 Harda Khās India
55 K6 Hardangervidda *plat.* Norway
55 K6 Hardangervidda Nasjonalpark *nat. park* Norway
104 B2 Hardap *div.* Namibia
104 B2 Hardap Dam *dam* Namibia
61 E2 Hardenberg Neth.
61 D2 Harderwijk Neth.
104 C5 Hardeveld *mts* S. Africa
24 F2 Hardin U.S.A.
105 H5 Harding S. Africa
21 G4 Hardisty Can.
20 F2 Hardisty Lake *l.* Can.
84 E4 Hardoi India
33 G2 Hardwick U.S.A.
114 B5 Hardwicke B. *b.* Austr.
27 F4 Hardy U.S.A.
30 E4 Hardy Reservoir *resr* U.S.A.
61 F2 Haren (Ems) Ger.
102 E3 Hārer Eth.
33 F4 Harford U.S.A.
102 E3 Hargeysa Somalia
63 M7 Harghita-Mădăraș, Vârful *mt* Romania
81 H2 Harhal D. *mts* Turkey
88 C2 Harhatan China
82 J3 Har Hu *l.* China
84 D3 Haridwar India
117 C5 Harihari N.Z.
91 D7 Harima-nada *b.* Japan
85 G5 Haringhat *r.* Bangl.
61 C3 Haringvliet *est.* Neth.
79 L3 Haripur Pak.
55 S6 Harjavalta Fin.
26 E3 Harlan *IA* U.S.A.
32 B6 Harlan *KY* U.S.A.
59 C5 Harlech U.K.
24 E1 Harlem U.S.A.
59 J5 Harleston U.K.
61 D1 Harlingen Neth.
27 D7 Harlingen U.S.A.
59 H6 Harlow U.K.
24 E2 Harlowton U.S.A.
33 J2 Harmony *ME* U.S.A.
30 A4 Harmony *MN* U.S.A.
84 A3 Harnai Pak.
24 B3 Harney Basin *basin* U.S.A.
24 C3 Harney L. *l.* U.S.A.
55 P5 Härnösand Sweden
87 M2 Har Nur China
86 F2 Har Nuur *l.* Mongolia
57 □ Haroldswick U.K.
100 B4 Harper Liberia
34 D4 Harper Lake *l.* U.S.A.
32 E5 Harpers Ferry U.S.A.
23 H2 Harp Lake *l.* Can.
81 G2 Harput Turkey
Harqin Qi *see* Jinshan
35 F5 Harquahala Mts *mts* U.S.A.
81 G3 Harran Turkey
22 E3 Harricanaw *r.* Can.
29 C5 Harriman U.S.A.
33 G3 Harriman Reservoir *resr* U.S.A.
115 K3 Harrington Austr.
33 F5 Harrington U.S.A.
23 J3 Harrington Harbour Can.
57 B3 Harris U.K.
114 A3 Harris, Lake *salt flat* Austr.
57 A3 Harris, Sound of *chan.* U.K.
28 B4 Harrisburg *IL* U.S.A.
32 E4 Harrisburg *PA* U.S.A.
105 H4 Harrismith S. Africa
27 E4 Harrison *AR* U.S.A.
30 E3 Harrison *MI* U.S.A.
23 J3 Harrison, Cape *c.* Can.
32 D5 Harrisonburg U.S.A.
20 E5 Harrison L. *l.* Can.
26 E4 Harrisonville U.S.A.
31 F3 Harrisville *MI* U.S.A.
33 F2 Harrisville *NY* U.S.A.
32 C5 Harrisville *WV* U.S.A.
58 F4 Harrogate U.K.
81 L4 Harsīn Iran
80 G1 Harşit *r.* Turkey
67 M2 Hârșova Romania
54 P2 Harstad Norway
30 D4 Hart U.S.A.
114 B3 Hart, L. *salt flat* Austr.
88 G1 Hartao China

104 D4 Hartbees *watercourse* S. Africa
62 G7 Hartberg Austria
55 K6 Harteigan *mt* Norway
57 E5 Hart Fell *h.* U.K.
33 G4 Hartford *CT* U.S.A.
30 D4 Hartford *MI* U.S.A.
26 D3 Hartford *SD* U.S.A.
30 C4 Hartford *WV* U.S.A.
20 E3 Hart Highway Can.
23 G4 Hartland Can.
59 C7 Hartland U.K.
33 J2 Hartland U.S.A.
59 C6 Hartland Point *pt* U.K.
58 F3 Hartlepool U.K.
27 C5 Hartley U.S.A.
20 D4 Hartley Bay Can.
55 U6 Hartola Fin.
20 E4 Hart Ranges *mts* Can.
62 E6 Härtsfeld *h.* Ger.
104 F3 Hartswater S. Africa
29 D5 Hartwell Res. *resr* U.S.A.
86 F2 Har Us Nuur *l.* Mongolia
30 C4 Harvard U.S.A.
25 F4 Harvard, Mt *mt* U.S.A.
112 C6 Harvey Austr.
33 K2 Harvey Can.
30 D2 Harvey *MI* U.S.A.
26 C2 Harvey *ND* U.S.A.
59 J6 Harwich U.K.
115 K2 Harwood Austr.
84 C3 Haryana *div.* India
80 F6 Ḥaṣāh, Wādī al *watercourse* Jordan
84 C2 Hasan Abdal Pak.
80 E2 Hasan Dağı *mts* Turkey
81 H3 Hasankeyf Turkey
81 L3 Ḥasan Sālārān Iran
80 E5 Ḥasbani *r.* Lebanon
80 E2 Hasbek Turkey
85 E5 Hasdo *r.* India
61 F2 Hase *r.* Ger.
61 F2 Haselünne Ger.
81 M3 Hashtpar Iran
81 L3 Hashtrud Iran
27 D5 Haskell U.S.A.
59 G6 Haslemere U.K.
63 M7 Hăşmaşul Mare *mt* Romania
83 E8 Hassan India
81 K4 Hassan Iraq
35 F5 Hassayampa *r.* U.S.A.
61 D4 Hasselt Belgium
100 C1 Hassi Messaoud Alg.
55 N8 Hässleholm Sweden
114 F7 Hastings Austr.
115 K3 Hastings *r.* Austr.
117 F3 Hastings N.Z.
59 H7 Hastings U.K.
30 E4 Hastings *MI* U.S.A.
30 A3 Hastings *MN* U.S.A.
26 D3 Hastings *NE* U.S.A.
Hatay *see* Antakya
35 F3 Hatch U.S.A.
21 J3 Hatchet Lake *l.* Can.
29 B5 Hatchie *r.* U.S.A.
114 E4 Hatfield Austr.
58 G4 Hatfield U.K.
86 H1 Hatgal Mongolia
84 D4 Hathras India
85 F4 Hatia Nepal
95 C3 Ha Tiên Vietnam
95 C1 Ha Tĩnh Vietnam
114 E5 Hattah Austr.
29 F5 Hatteras, Cape *c.* U.S.A.
54 N4 Hattfjelldal Norway
85 E6 Hatti *r.* India
29 B6 Hattiesburg U.S.A.
95 B4 Hat Yai Thai.
102 E3 Haud *reg.* Eth.
55 K7 Hauge Norway
55 J7 Haugesund Norway
95 C3 Hâu Giang, Sông *r.* Vietnam
117 E3 Hauhungaroa *mt* N.Z.
55 K7 Haukeligrend Norway
54 T4 Haukipudas Fin.
55 V5 Haukivesi *l.* Fin.
21 H3 Haultain *r.* Can.
117 E2 Hauraki Gulf *g.* N.Z.
117 A7 Hauroko, L. *l.* N.Z.
33 J3 Haut, Isle au *i.* U.S.A.
100 B1 Haut Atlas *mts* Morocco
23 G4 Hauterive Can.
61 E4 Hautes Fagnes *moorland* Belgium
61 D5 Haut-Fourneau, Étang du *l.* France
100 B1 Hauts Plateaux *plat.* Alg.
34 □1 Hauula U.S.A.
30 B5 Havana U.S.A.
59 G7 Havant U.K.
35 E4 Havasu Lake *l.* U.S.A.
62 F4 Havel *r.* Ger.
31 J3 Havelock Can.
29 E5 Havelock U.S.A.
117 F3 Havelock North N.Z.
59 C6 Haverfordwest U.K.
33 H3 Haverhill U.S.A.
62 G6 Havlíčkův Brod Czech Rep.
54 T1 Havøysund Norway
67 M5 Havran Turkey
24 E1 Havre U.S.A.
23 H4 Havre Aubert, Île du *i.* Can.
33 E5 Havre de Grace U.S.A.
23 H3 Havre-St-Pierre Can.
67 M4 Havsa Turkey
80 E1 Havza Turkey
34 □2 Hawaii *i.* U.S.A.
14 H4 Hawaiian Islands *is* Pac. Oc.
14 H4 Hawaiian Ridge *sea feature* Pac. Oc.
34 □2 Hawaii Volcanoes National Park *nat. park* U.S.A.
81 L7 Ḥawallī Kuwait
59 D4 Hawarden U.K.
117 B6 Hawea, L. *l.* N.Z.
117 E3 Hawera N.Z.
58 E3 Hawes U.K.
34 □2 Hawi U.S.A.
57 F5 Hawick U.K.
81 L6 Ḥawīzah, Hawr al *l.* Iraq
117 B6 Hawkdun Range *mts* N.Z.
117 F3 Hawke Bay *b.* N.Z.
23 J3 Hawke Island *i.* Can.
114 C3 Hawker Austr.
114 D2 Hawkers Gate Austr.
33 F2 Hawkesbury Can.
35 F3 Hawkins Peak *summit* U.S.A.
31 F3 Hawks U.S.A.
33 K2 Hawkshaw Can.
116 D5 Hawkwood Austr.
33 F4 Hawley U.S.A.
81 J5 Ḥawrān, Wādī *watercourse* Iraq
104 C7 Hawston S. Africa
34 C2 Hawthorne U.S.A.
58 F3 Haxby U.K.
114 F5 Hay Austr.
20 F2 Hay *r.* Can.
30 B3 Hay *r.* U.S.A.
88 B1 Haya China
90 G5 Hayachine-san *mt* Japan
61 E5 Hayange France
81 K3 Haydarābad Iran
35 G5 Hayden *AZ* U.S.A.
24 C2 Hayden *ID* U.S.A.
21 L3 Hayes *r.* Can.
59 B7 Hayle U.K.
79 H6 Haymā' Oman
80 D2 Haymana Turkey
116 C3 Hayman I. *i.* Austr.
32 E5 Haymarket U.S.A.
33 J2 Haynesville U.S.A.
59 D5 Hay-on-Wye U.K.
69 C7 Hayrabolu Turkey
20 F2 Hay River Can.
26 D4 Hays U.S.A.
69 D5 Haysyn Ukr.
34 A3 Hayward *CA* U.S.A.
30 B2 Hayward *WV* U.S.A.
59 G7 Haywards Heath U.K.
79 K3 Hazarajat *reg.* Afgh.
32 B6 Hazard U.S.A.
85 F5 Hazāribāg India
85 E5 Hazaribagh Range *mts* India
61 A4 Hazebrouck France
20 D3 Hazelton Can.
61 C2 Hazerswoude-Rijndijk Neth.
33 F4 Hazleton U.S.A.
81 G6 Ḥazm al Jalāmid *ridge* Saudi Arabia
84 A1 Hazrat Sultan Afgh.
81 H2 Hazro Turkey
47 D2 H. Bouchard Arg.
60 B4 Headford Rep. of Ireland
112 F6 Head of Bight *b.* Austr.
34 A2 Healdsburg U.S.A.
114 F6 Healesville Austr.
59 F4 Heanor U.K.
13 J7 Heard *i.* Indian Ocean
27 D6 Hearne U.S.A.
22 D4 Hearst Can.
59 H7 Heathfield U.K.
33 E6 Heathsville U.S.A.
27 D7 Hebbronville U.S.A.
88 E2 Hebei *div.* China
115 G2 Hebel Austr.
27 E5 Heber Springs U.S.A.
88 E3 Hebi China
23 H2 Hebron Can.
30 D5 Hebron *IN* U.S.A.
26 D3 Hebron *NE* U.S.A.
33 G3 Hebron *NY* U.S.A.
80 E6 Hebron West Bank
23 H2 Hebron Fiord *in.* Can.
20 C4 Hecate Strait *chan.* Can.
23 C3 Heceta I. *i.* U.S.A.
89 C5 Hechi China
89 C4 Hechuan China
55 N5 Hede Sweden
55 O6 Hedemora Sweden
89 D6 Hede Sk. *resr* China
24 C2 He Devil Mt. *mt* U.S.A.
30 A5 Hedrick U.S.A.
61 D2 Heerenveen Neth.
61 C2 Heerhugowaard Neth.
61 D4 Heerlen Neth.
Hefa *see* Haifa
88 E4 Hefei China
89 D4 Hefeng China
90 B1 Hegang China
91 E6 Hegura-jima *i.* Japan
62 D3 Heide Ger.
103 B6 Heide Namibia
62 D6 Heidelberg Ger.
105 H3 Heidelberg *Gauteng* S. Africa
104 D7 Heidelberg *Western Cape* S. Africa
Heihe *see* Heihe
87 N1 Heihe China
105 G3 Heilbron S. Africa
62 D6 Heilbronn Ger.
62 E3 Heiligenhafen Ger.
89 □ Hei Ling Chau *i.* China
87 N2 Heilongjiang *div.* China
87 P1 Heilong Jiang *r.* China/Rus. Fed.
54 M5 Heimdal Norway
55 U6 Heinola Fin.
95 A2 Heinze Is *is* Myanmar
88 G1 Heishan China
61 C3 Heist-op-den-Berg Belgium
88 E2 Hejian China
89 B4 Hejiang China
89 D6 He Jiang *r.* China
88 D3 Hejin China
80 F2 Hekimhan Turkey
54 D5 Hekla *vol.* Iceland
88 B2 Hekou *Gansu* China
89 B6 Hekou *Yunnan* China
54 N5 Helagsfjället *mt* Sweden
88 B2 Helan Shan *mts* China
85 H4 Helem India
34 D3 Helen, Mt *mt* U.S.A.
27 F5 Helena *AR* U.S.A.
24 E2 Helena *MT* U.S.A.
57 D4 Helensburgh U.K.
89 D7 Helen Shoal *sand bank* Paracel Is
80 E6 Ḥelez Israel
62 C3 Helgoland *i.* Ger.
62 D3 Helgoländer Bucht *b.* Ger.
115 K1 Helidon Austr.
54 C5 Hella Iceland
54 P2 Helland Norway
61 C3 Hellevoetsluis Neth.
54 R2 Helligskogen Norway
65 F3 Hellín Spain
24 C2 Hells Canyon *gorge* U.S.A.
84 3 Helmand *r.* Afgh.
103 B6 Helmeringhausen Namibia
61 D3 Helmond Neth.
57 E2 Helmsdale U.K.
57 E2 Helmsdale *r.* U.K.
62 E4 Helmstedt Ger.
87 N3 Helong China
35 G2 Helper U.S.A.
55 N8 Helsingborg Sweden
55 N8 Helsingør Denmark
55 T6 Helsinki Fin.
59 B7 Helston U.K.
58 D3 Helvellyn *mt* U.K.
60 D5 Helvick Head *hd* Rep. of Ireland
59 G6 Hemel Hempstead U.K.
34 D5 Hemet U.S.A.
32 E3 Hemlock Lake *l.* U.S.A.
33 G2 Hemmingford Can.
27 D6 Hempstead U.S.A.
59 J5 Hemsby U.K.
55 Q8 Hemse Sweden
88 A3 Henan China
88 D3 Henan *div.* China
65 E2 Henares *r.* Spain
90 F4 Henashi-zaki *pt* Japan
80 C1 Hendek Turkey
47 E3 Henderson Arg.
28 C4 Henderson *KY* U.S.A.
29 E4 Henderson *NC* U.S.A.
35 E3 Henderson *NV* U.S.A.
33 E3 Henderson *NY* U.S.A.
27 E5 Henderson *TX* U.S.A.
29 D5 Hendersonville *NC* U.S.A.
29 C4 Hendersonville *TN* U.S.A.
59 G6 Hendon U.K.
82 J5 Hengduan Shan *mts* China
61 E2 Hengelo Neth.
89 D5 Hengshan *Hunan* China
88 C2 Hengshan *Shaanxi* China
90 B2 Hengshan China
88 D2 Heng Shan *mt Shanxi* China
89 D5 Heng Shan *mt Hunan* China
88 E2 Hengshui China
89 C6 Hengxian China
89 D5 Hengyang *Hunan* China
89 D5 Hengyang *Hunan* China
69 E6 Heniches'k Ukr.
117 C6 Henley N.Z.
59 G6 Henley-on-Thames U.K.
33 F5 Henlopen, Cape *pt* U.S.A.
61 F4 Hennef (Sieg) Ger.
105 G3 Hennenman S. Africa
33 H3 Henniker U.S.A.
27 D5 Henrietta U.S.A.
22 D2 Henrietta Maria, Cape *c.* Can.
35 G3 Henrieville U.S.A.
30 C5 Henry U.S.A.
119 B3 Henry Ice Rise *ice feature* Antarctica
35 G2 Henry Mts *mts* U.S.A.
31 G4 Hensall Can.
103 B6 Hentiesbaai Namibia
115 G5 Henty Austr.
83 J7 Henzada Myanmar
21 H4 Hepburn Can.
89 E5 Heping China
89 C6 Hepu China
88 D2 Hequ China
116 C1 Herald Cays *atolls* Coral Sea Is Terr.
79 J3 Herāt Afgh.
64 F5 Hérault *r.* France
116 A2 Herbert *r.* Austr.
21 H4 Herbert Can.
116 A1 Herberton Austr.
59 E5 Hereford U.K.
27 C5 Hereford U.S.A.
62 D4 Herford Ger.
26 D4 Herington U.S.A.
81 L2 Herīs Iran
62 D7 Herisau Switz.
61 E3 Herkenbosch Neth.
33 F3 Herkimer U.S.A.
27 C7 Hermanas Mex.
57 □ Herma Ness *hd* U.K.
104 C7 Hermanus S. Africa
105 H5 Hermes, Cape *pt* S. Africa
115 G3 Hermidale Austr.
24 C2 Hermiston U.S.A.
44 C9 Hermite, Is *i.* Chile
110 E2 Hermit Is *is* P.N.G.
80 E5 Hermon, Mount *mt* Lebanon/Syria
47 B2 Hermosa, P. de V. *pass* Chile
27 D7 Hermosa, Valle *v.* Arg.
36 B3 Hermosillo Mex.
44 F3 Hernandarias Para.
61 F3 Herne Ger.
59 J6 Herne Bay U.K.
55 L8 Herning Denmark
30 D1 Heron Bay Can.
116 D4 Heron I. *i.* Austr.
65 D3 Herrera del Duque Spain
27 B7 Herreras Mex.
115 G8 Herrick Austr.
32 E4 Hershey U.S.A.
59 G6 Hertford U.K.
61 E4 Hertogenwald *forest* Belgium
105 F4 Hertzogville S. Africa
116 E5 Hervey Bay Austr.
116 E5 Hervey Bay *b.* Austr.
116 B2 Hervey Ra. *mts* Austr.
81 M4 Ḥeşar Iran
61 C4 Hesbaye *reg.* Belgium
89 C6 Heshan China
88 C3 Heshui China
88 D2 Heshun China
34 D4 Hesperia U.S.A.
20 C2 Hess *r.* Can.
89 B6 Het *r.* Laos
34 B3 Hetch Hetchy Aqueduct *canal* U.S.A.
61 D3 Heteren Neth.
26 C2 Hettinger U.S.A.
58 E3 Hetton U.K.
62 E5 Hettstedt Ger.
61 D3 Heusden Belgium
58 E3 Hexham U.K.
88 F4 Hexian *Anhui* China
89 D5 Hexian *Guangxi* China
Hexigten Qi *see* Jingpeng
88 B2 Hexipu China
104 C6 Hex River Pass *pass* S. Africa
88 D3 Heyang China
58 E3 Heysham U.K.
89 E6 Heyuan China
114 D7 Heywood Austr.
58 E4 Heywood U.K.
30 C5 Heyworth U.S.A.
88 E3 Heze China
89 B5 Hezhang China
88 B3 Hezheng China
88 B3 Hezuozhen China
29 D7 Hialeah U.S.A.
26 E4 Hiawatha U.S.A.
30 A2 Hibbing U.S.A.
115 F9 Hibbs, Pt *hd* Austr.
29 D5 Hickory U.S.A.
117 G2 Hicks Bay N.Z.
21 K2 Hicks L. *l.* Can.
32 A4 Hicksville U.S.A.
27 D5 Hico U.S.A.
90 H3 Hidaka-sanmyaku *mts* Japan
27 D7 Hidalgo Mex.
36 C3 Hidalgo del Parral Mex.
46 C2 Hidrolândia Brazil
91 C7 Higashi-Hiroshima Japan
90 G5 Higashine Japan
91 D7 Higashi-ōsaka Japan
91 A8 Higashi-suidō *chan.* Japan
33 F3 Higgins Bay U.S.A.
30 E3 Higgins Lake *l.* U.S.A.
High Atlas *mts see* Haut Atlas
24 B3 High Desert *des.* U.S.A.
30 C3 High Falls Reservoir *resr* U.S.A.
30 E3 High I. *i.* U.S.A.
89 □ High Island Reservoir *resr* China
30 D4 Highland Park U.S.A.
34 C2 Highland Peak *summit CA* U.S.A.
35 E3 Highland Peak *summit NV* U.S.A.
20 F3 High Level Can.
85 F5 High Level Canal *canal* India
29 E5 High Point U.S.A.
20 F3 High Prairie Can.
20 G4 High River Can.
29 E7 High Rock Bahamas
21 J3 Highrock Lake *l.* Can.
115 F9 High Rocky Pt *hd* Austr.
58 E3 High Seat *h.* U.K.
33 F4 Hightstown U.S.A.
59 G6 High Wycombe U.K.
45 D2 Higuerote Venez.
55 S7 Hiiumaa *i.* Estonia
78 D4 Hijaz *reg.* Saudi Arabia
35 E3 Hiko U.S.A.
91 E7 Hikone Japan
117 G2 Hikurangi *mt* N.Z.
35 F3 Hildale U.S.A.
62 D4 Hildesheim Ger.
85 G4 Hili Bangl.
26 D4 Hill City U.S.A.
35 H2 Hill Creek *r.* U.S.A.
55 N9 Hillerød Denmark
116 A2 Hillgrove Austr.
26 D2 Hillsboro *ND* U.S.A.
33 H3 Hillsboro *NH* U.S.A.
32 B5 Hillsboro *OH* U.S.A.
27 D5 Hillsboro *TX* U.S.A.
32 C5 Hillsboro *WV* U.S.A.
30 B4 Hillsboro *WV* U.S.A.
116 C3 Hillsborough, C. *pt* Austr.
30 E5 Hillsdale *MI* U.S.A.
33 G3 Hillsdale *NY* U.S.A.
32 E4 Hillsgrove U.S.A.
57 F4 Hillside U.K.
35 F4 Hillside U.S.A.
115 F4 Hillston Austr.
32 C6 Hillsville U.S.A.
115 J5 Hilltop Austr.
34 □2 Hilo U.S.A.
105 J4 Hilton S. Africa
32 E3 Hilton U.S.A.
31 F2 Hilton Beach Can.
29 D5 Hilton Head Island U.S.A.
81 G3 Hilvan Turkey
61 D2 Hilversum Neth.
84 D3 Himachal Pradesh *div.* India
74 Himalaya *mts* Asia
85 F3 Himalchul *mt* Nepal
54 S4 Himanka Fin.
67 H4 Himarë Albania
84 C5 Himatnagar India
91 D7 Himeji Japan
90 G5 Himekami-dake *mt* Japan
105 H4 Himeville S. Africa
91 E6 Himi Japan
80 F4 Ḥimş Syria
94 C4 Hinatuan Phil.
116 B2 Hinchinbrook I. *i.* Austr.
59 F5 Hinckley U.K.
30 A2 Hinckley *MN* U.S.A.
35 F2 Hinckley *UT* U.S.A.
33 F3 Hinckley Reservoir *resr* U.S.A.
84 D3 Hindan *r.* India
84 D4 Hindaun India
58 G3 Hinderwell U.K.
58 E4 Hindley U.K.
32 B6 Hindman U.S.A.
114 D6 Hindmarsh, L. *l.* Austr.
85 F5 Hindola India
84 B2 Hindu Kush *mts* Afgh./Pak.
83 E8 Hindupur India
20 F3 Hines Creek Can.
29 D6 Hinesville U.S.A.
84 D5 Hinganghat India
84 D6 Hingoli India
81 H2 Hınıs Turkey
34 D4 Hinkley U.S.A.
54 O2 Hinnøya *i.* Norway
94 B4 Hinobaan Phil.
65 D3 Hinojosa del Duque Spain
91 C7 Hino-misaki *pt* Japan
33 G3 Hinsdale U.S.A.
20 F4 Hinton Can.
32 C6 Hinton U.S.A.
81 K2 Hirabit Dağ *mt* Turkey
91 A8 Hirado Japan
91 A8 Hirado-shima *i.* Japan
85 E5 Hirakud Reservoir India
90 H3 Hiroo Japan
90 G4 Hirosaki Japan
91 C7 Hiroshima Japan
62 E7 Hirschberg *mt* Ger.
64 G2 Hirson France
55 L8 Hirtshals Denmark
84 C3 Hisar India
81 M3 Hisar Iran
80 D1 Hisarönü Turkey
81 K6 Ḥisb, Sha'īb *watercourse* Iraq
80 E6 Hisban Jordan
37 K4 Hispaniola *i.* Caribbean Sea
85 F4 Hisua India
81 J5 Hīt Iraq
91 G6 Hitachi Japan
91 G6 Hitachi-ōta Japan
91 B8 Hitoyoshi Japan
54 L5 Hitra *i.* Norway
91 C7 Hiuchi-nada *b.* Japan
20 E4 Hixon Can.
116 E4 Hixson Cay *rf* Austr.
81 J2 Hizan Turkey
55 O7 Hjälmaren *l.* Sweden
21 H2 Hjalmar Lake *l.* Can.
55 L5 Hjerkinn Norway
55 O7 Hjo Sweden
55 M8 Hjørring Denmark
105 J4 Hlabisa S. Africa
105 J3 Hlatikulu Swaziland
69 E5 Hlobyne Ukr.
105 G4 Hlohlowane S. Africa
105 H4 Hlotse Lesotho
105 K4 Hluhluwe S. Africa
69 E5 Hlukhiv Ukr.
63 O4 Hlusha Belarus
68 C4 Hlybokaye Belarus
100 C4 Ho Ghana
103 B6 Hoachanas Namibia
115 G9 Hobart Austr.
27 D5 Hobart U.S.A.
27 C5 Hobbs U.S.A.
29 D7 Hobe Sound U.S.A.
88 D1 Hobor China
55 L8 Hobro Denmark
102 E3 Hobyo Somalia
95 C3 Hô Chi Minh Vietnam
62 G7 Hochschwab *mt* Austria
32 B5 Hocking *r.* U.S.A.
84 D4 Hodal India
58 E4 Hodder *r.* U.K.
59 G6 Hoddesdon U.K.
Hodeida *see* Al Ḥudaydah
33 K1 Hodgdon U.S.A.
63 K7 Hódmezővásárhely Hungary
65 J5 Hodna, Chott el *salt l.* Alg.
61 C3 Hoek van Holland Neth.
61 D4 Hoensbroek Neth.
90 A3 Hoeryŏng N. Korea
62 E5 Hof Ger.
105 F5 Hofmeyr S. Africa
54 F4 Höfn Iceland
55 P6 Hofors Sweden
54 D4 Hofsjökull *ice cap* Iceland
91 B7 Hōfu Japan
55 N8 Höganäs Sweden
115 G7 Hogan Group *is* Austr.
116 B5 Hoganthulla Cr. *r.* Austr.
100 C2 Hoggar *plat.* Alg.
33 F6 Hog I. *i.* U.S.A.
55 P8 Högsby Sweden
62 F7 Hohe Tauern *mts* Austria
61 E4 Hohe Venn *moorland* Belgium
88 D1 Hohhot China
85 G2 Hoh Xil Hu *salt l.* China
85 G2 Hoh Xil Shan *mts* China
95 D2 Hôi An Vietnam
102 D3 Hoima Uganda
89 B6 Hôi Xuân Vietnam
85 H4 Hojai India
91 C8 Hōjo Japan
117 D1 Hokianga Harbour *in.* N.Z.
117 C5 Hokitika N.Z.
90 H3 Hokkaidō *i.* Japan
55 L7 Hokksund Norway
81 K1 Hoktemberyan Armenia
55 L6 Hol Norway
55 M9 Holbæk Denmark
59 H5 Holbeach U.K.
116 C2 Holborne I. *i.* Austr.
35 G4 Holbrook U.S.A.
30 B3 Holcombe Flowage *resr* U.S.A.
21 G4 Holden Can.
35 F2 Holden U.S.A.
27 D5 Holdenville U.S.A.
26 D3 Holdrege U.S.A.
37 J4 Holguín Cuba
55 N6 Höljes Sweden
30 D4 Holland U.S.A.
119 B2 Hollick-Kenyon Peninsula *pen.* Antarctica
32 D4 Hollidaysburg U.S.A.
20 C3 Hollis *AK* U.S.A.
27 D5 Hollis *OK* U.S.A.
34 B3 Hollister U.S.A.
31 F4 Holly U.S.A.
27 F5 Holly Springs U.S.A.
29 D7 Hollywood U.S.A.
54 N4 Holm Norway
116 B1 Holmes Reef *rf* Coral Sea Is Terr.
55 M7 Holmestrand Norway
54 R5 Holmön *i.* Sweden
54 R5 Holmsund Sweden
104 B3 Holoog Namibia
55 L8 Holstebro Denmark
29 D4 Holston *r.* U.S.A.
32 C6 Holston Lake *l.* U.S.A.
59 C7 Holsworthy U.K.
59 J5 Holt U.K.
30 E4 Holt U.S.A.
26 E4 Holton U.S.A.
60 D5 Holycross Rep. of Ireland
59 C4 Holyhead U.K.
59 C4 Holyhead Bay *b.* U.K.
58 F2 Holy Island *i. Eng.* U.K.
59 C4 Holy Island *i. Wales* U.K.
33 G3 Holyoke U.S.A.
59 D4 Holywell U.K.
62 E7 Holzkirchen Ger.
100 B3 Hombori Mali
61 F5 Homburg Ger.
118 A3 Home Bay *b.* Can.
116 B2 Home Hill Austr.
27 E5 Homer U.S.A.
29 D6 Homerville U.S.A.
116 A3 Homestead Austr.
29 D7 Homestead U.S.A.
29 C5 Homewood U.S.A.
94 C4 Homonhon Island *i.* Phil.
Homs *see* Ḥimş
69 D4 Homyel' Belarus
45 B3 Honda Col.
94 A4 Honda Bay *b.* Phil.
35 H4 Hon Dah U.S.A.
104 B5 Hondeklipbaai S. Africa
88 C1 Hondlon Ju China
27 D6 Hondo U.S.A.
61 E1 Hondsrug *reg.* Neth.
16 Honduras *country* Central America
55 M6 Hønefoss Norway
33 F4 Honesdale U.S.A.
34 B1 Honey Lake *l.* U.S.A.
33 E3 Honeyoye Lake *l.* U.S.A.
64 E2 Honfleur France
89 C6 Hong, Mouths of the *est.* Vietnam
89 C6 Hông, Sông *r.* Vietnam
88 E4 Hong'an China
89 C6 Hông Gai Vietnam
89 E6 Honghai Wan *b.* China
89 B6 Honghe China
88 E3 Hong He *r.* China
89 D4 Honghu China
89 C5 Hongjiang China
89 □ Hong Kong China
89 □ Hong Kong *aut. reg.* China
89 □ Hong Kong Island *i.* China
88 C2 Hongliu *r.* China
88 B2 Hongliuyuan China
95 C3 Hông Ngư Vietnam
88 B2 Hongshansi China
89 D6 Hongshui He *r.* China
88 D2 Hongtong China

55 V6 Imatra Fin.
91 E7 Imazu Japan
44 G3 Imbituba Brazil
46 B4 Imbituva Brazil
68 G3 imeni Babushkina Rus. Fed.
102 E3 Īmī Eth.
81 M2 İmişli Azer.
66 D2 Imola Italy
105 H4 Impendle S. Africa
43 J5 Imperatriz Brazil
66 C3 Imperia Italy
26 C3 Imperial U.S.A.
34 D5 Imperial Beach U.S.A.
35 E5 Imperial Valley v. U.S.A.
102 B3 Impfondo Congo
85 H4 Imphal India
67 L4 İmroz Turkey
80 F5 Imtān Syria
25 E6 Imuris Mex.
94 A4 Imuruan Bay b. Phil.
91 E7 Ina Japan
42 E6 Inambari r. Peru
100 C2 In Aménas Alg.
117 C4 Inangahua Junction N.Z.
93 J7 Inanwatan Indon.
54 U2 Inari Fin.
54 U2 Inarijärvi l. Fin.
54 T2 Inarijoki r. Fin./Norway
65 H3 Inca Spain
69 E7 İnce Burnu pt Turkey
69 C7 İnce Burnu pt Turkey
80 D3 İncekum Burnu pt Turkey
80 E2 İncesu Turkey
60 E5 Inch Rep. of Ireland
57 C2 Inchard, Loch b. U.K.
57 E4 Inchkeith i. U.K.
87 N4 Inch'ŏn S. Korea
105 K2 Incomati r. Moz.
57 B5 Indaal, Loch in. U.K.
46 D2 Indaiá r. Brazil
46 B2 Indaiá Grande r. Brazil
54 P5 Indalsälven r. Sweden
55 J6 Indalstø Norway
34 C3 Independence CA U.S.A.
30 B4 Independence IA U.S.A.
27 E4 Independence KS U.S.A.
30 A2 Independence MN U.S.A.
26 E4 Independence MO U.S.A.
32 C6 Independence VA U.S.A.
30 B3 Independence WV U.S.A.
24 C3 Independence Mts mts U.S.A.
76 G5 Inderborskiy Kazak.
70 India country Asia
30 D2 Indian r. U.S.A.
32 D4 Indiana U.S.A.
30 D5 Indiana div. U.S.A.
30 D5 Indiana Dunes National Lakeshore res. U.S.A.
13 O7 Indian-Antarctic Ridge sea feature Pac. Oc.
30 D6 Indianapolis U.S.A.
Indian Desert des. see Thar Desert
23 J3 Indian Harbour Can.
33 F3 Indian Lake U.S.A.
30 D3 Indian Lake l. MI U.S.A.
32 B4 Indian Lake l. OH U.S.A.
32 D4 Indian Lake l. PA U.S.A.
5 Indian Ocean
26 E3 Indianola IA U.S.A.
27 F5 Indianola MS U.S.A.
35 F2 Indian Peak summit U.S.A.
30 E3 Indian River U.S.A.
35 E3 Indian Springs U.S.A.
35 G4 Indian Wells U.S.A.
77 Q2 Indigirka r. Rus. Fed.
67 J2 Inđija Serb. and Mont.
20 F2 Indin Lake l. Can.
34 D5 Indio U.S.A.
111 G3 Indispensable Reefs rf Solomon Is
71 Indonesia country Asia
84 C5 Indore India
92 □ Indramayu, Tanjung pt Indon.
64 E3 Indre r. France
Indur see Nizamabad
84 B4 Indus r. Pak.
84 A5 Indus, Mouths of the est. Pak.
105 G5 Indwe S. Africa
69 E7 İnebolu Turkey
80 B1 İnegöl Turkey
32 B6 Inez U.S.A.
104 D7 Infanta, Cape hd S. Africa
36 D5 Infiernillo, Presa l. Mex.
95 B1 Ing, Mae Nam r. Thai.
30 D3 Ingalls U.S.A.
34 B2 Ingalls, Mt mt U.S.A.
21 J2 Ingalls Lake l. Can.
47 C4 Ingeniero Jacobacci Arg.
31 G4 Ingersoll Can.
116 B2 Ingham Austr.
58 E3 Ingleborough h. U.K.
58 E3 Ingleton U.K.
115 J2 Inglewood Qld. Austr.
114 E6 Inglewood Vic. Austr.
59 H4 Ingoldmells U.K.
62 E6 Ingolstadt Ger.
23 H4 Ingonish Can.
85 G4 Ingrāj Bāzār India
20 F2 Ingray Lake l. Can.
100 C3 I-n-Guezzam Alg.
69 H7 Ingushskaya Respublika div. Rus. Fed.
105 K3 Ingwavuma S. Africa
105 K2 Inhaca Moz.
105 K3 Inhaca, Peninsula pen. Moz.
103 D6 Inhambane Moz.
105 K1 Inhambane div. Moz.
103 D5 Inhaminga Moz.
46 B3 Inhanduízinho r. Brazil
46 D1 Inhaúmas Brazil
45 C4 Inírida r. Col.
60 A4 Inishark i. Rep. of Ireland
60 A4 Inishbofin i. Rep. of Ireland
60 A3 Inishkea North i. Rep. of Ireland
60 A3 Inishkea South i. Rep. of Ireland
60 B4 Inishmaan i. Rep. of Ireland
60 B4 Inishmore i. Rep. of Ireland
60 C3 Inishmurray i. Rep. of Ireland
60 D2 Inishowen pen. Rep. of Ireland
60 E2 Inishowen Head hd Rep. of Ireland
60 D2 Inishtrahull i. Rep. of Ireland
60 D2 Inishtrahull Sound chan. Rep. of Ireland
60 A4 Inishturk i. Rep. of Ireland
116 C5 Injune Austr.
113 H3 Inkerman Austr.
117 D5 Inland Kaikoura Range mts N.Z.
114 D1 Innamincka Austr.
54 O3 Inndyr Norway
Inner Mongolian Aut. Region div. see Nei Mongol Zizhiqu
57 C3 Inner Sound chan. U.K.
116 B1 Innisfail Austr.
62 E7 Innsbruck Austria
60 D4 Inny r. Rep. of Ireland
102 B4 Inongo Dem. Rep. Congo
62 J4 Inowrocław Pol.
100 C2 In Salah Alg.
68 H4 Insar Rus. Fed.
57 F3 Insch U.K.
112 B5 Inscription, C. c. Austr.
76 H3 Inta Rus. Fed.
47 D2 Intendente Alvear Arg.
62 C7 Interlaken Switz.
26 E1 International Falls U.S.A.
91 G7 Inubō-zaki pt Japan
22 E2 Inukjuak Can.
118 C2 Inuvik Can.
57 C4 Inveraray U.K.
57 F4 Inverbervie U.K.
117 B7 Invercargill N.Z.
115 J2 Inverell Austr.
57 D3 Invergordon U.K.
57 E4 Inverkeithing U.K.
23 H4 Inverness Can.
57 D3 Inverness U.K.
29 D6 Inverness U.S.A.
57 F3 Inverurie U.K.
114 B5 Investigator Strait chan. Austr.
86 E1 Inya Rus. Fed.
25 C5 Inyokern U.S.A.
34 C3 Inyo Mts mts U.S.A.
102 D4 Inyonga Tanz.
68 H4 Inza Rus. Fed.
69 G4 Inzhavino Rus. Fed.
67 J5 Ioannina Greece
93 L2 Iō-jima i. Japan
27 E4 Iola U.S.A.
57 B4 Iona i. U.K.
24 C1 Ione U.S.A.
30 E4 Ionia U.S.A.
67 H5 Ionian Islands is Greece
66 G6 Ionian Sea sea Greece/Italy
Ionoi Nisoi is see Ionian Islands
81 L1 Iori r. Georgia
67 L6 Ios i. Greece
91 B9 Iō-shima i. Japan
30 A4 Iowa div. U.S.A.
30 B5 Iowa r. U.S.A.
30 B5 Iowa City U.S.A.
26 E3 Iowa Falls U.S.A.
46 C2 Ipameri Brazil
42 D5 Iparía Peru
42 D2 Ipatinga Brazil
69 G6 Ipatovo Rus. Fed.
105 F3 Ipelegeng S. Africa
45 A4 Ipiales Col.
46 E1 Ipiaú Brazil
46 B4 Ipiranga Brazil
92 C6 Ipoh Malaysia
43 L5 Ipojuca r. Brazil
46 B2 Iporá Brazil
102 C3 Ippy C.A.R.
67 M4 İpsala Turkey
115 K1 Ipswich Austr.
59 J5 Ipswich U.K.
44 B2 Iquique Chile
42 D4 Iquitos Peru
91 E7 Irago-misaki pt Japan
67 L6 Irakleia i. Greece
Irakleio see Iraklion
67 L7 Iraklion Greece
46 E1 Iramaia Brazil
70 Iran country Asia
81 L3 Īrānshāh Iran
79 J4 Īrānshahr Iran
36 D4 Irapuato Mex.
70 Iraq country Asia
33 G2 Irasville U.S.A.
46 B4 Irati Brazil
80 E5 Irbid Jordan
76 H4 Irbit Rus. Fed.
43 K6 Irecê Brazil
48 Ireland, Republic of country Europe
102 C4 Irema Dem. Rep. Congo
76 H5 Irgiz Kazak.
93 K8 Irian Jaya div. Indon.
110 D2 Irian Jaya reg. Indon.
81 L2 Īrī Dagh mt Iran
94 B3 Iriga Phil.
100 B3 Irîgui reg. Mali/Maur.
103 D4 Iringa Tanz.
43 H4 Iriri r. Brazil
56 D5 Irish Sea sea Rep. of Ireland
43 J4 Irituia Brazil
86 H1 Irkutsk Rus. Fed.
80 D2 Irmak Turkey
114 B4 Iron Baron Austr.
31 F2 Iron Bridge Can.
32 E3 Irondequoit U.S.A.
114 B4 Iron Knob Austr.
30 C3 Iron Mountain U.S.A.
35 F3 Iron Mountain mt U.S.A.
30 C2 Iron River U.S.A.
27 F4 Ironton MO U.S.A.
32 B5 Ironton OH U.S.A.
30 B2 Ironwood U.S.A.
33 F2 Iroquois Can.
30 D5 Iroquois r. U.S.A.
94 C3 Irosin Phil.
91 F7 Irō-zaki pt Japan
69 D5 Irpin' Ukr.
83 J7 Irrawaddy r. China/Myanmar
83 H7 Irrawaddy, Mouths of the est. Myanmar
68 J2 Irta Rus. Fed.
58 E3 Irthing r. U.K.
86 C1 Irtysh r. Kazak./Rus. Fed.
102 C3 Irumu Dem. Rep. Congo
65 F1 Irún Spain
57 D5 Irvine U.K.
34 D5 Irvine CA U.S.A.
32 B6 Irvine KY U.S.A.
116 A1 Irvinebank Austr.
27 D5 Irving U.S.A.
116 C4 Isaac r. Austr.
94 B5 Isabela Phil.
42 □ Isabela, Isla i. Ecuador
37 G6 Isabelia, Cordillera mts Nic.
30 B2 Isabella U.S.A.
34 C4 Isabella Lake l. U.S.A.
30 D2 Isabelle, Pt pt U.S.A.
54 B3 Ísafjarðardjúp est. Iceland
54 B3 Ísafjörður Iceland
91 B8 Isahaya Japan
84 B2 Isà Khel Pak.
68 G1 Isakogorka Rus. Fed.
45 C4 Isana r. Col.
57 □ Isbister U.K.
66 E4 Ischia, Isola d' i. Italy
45 A4 Iscuande r. Col.
91 E7 Ise Japan
102 C3 Isengi Dem. Rep. Congo
64 H4 Isère r. France
61 F3 Iserlohn Ger.
66 F4 Isernia Italy
91 F6 Isesaki Japan
91 E7 Ise-shima National Park Japan
91 E7 Ise-wan b. Japan
100 C4 Iseyin Nigeria
Isfahan see Eşfahān
79 L1 Isfara Tajik.
81 K5 Isḩāq Iraq
68 J4 Isheyevka Rus. Fed.
90 G3 Ishikari-gawa r. Japan
90 G3 Ishikari-wan b. Japan
90 G5 Ishinomaki Japan
90 G5 Ishinomaki-wan b. Japan
91 G6 Ishioka Japan
91 C8 Ishizuchi-san mt Japan
84 C1 Ishkuman Pak.
30 D2 Ishpeming U.S.A.
85 G4 Ishurdi Bangl.
42 E7 Isiboro Sécure, Parque Nacional nat. park Bol.
80 B2 Işıklı Turkey
80 B2 Işıklı Barajı resr Turkey
76 J4 Isil'kul' Rus. Fed.
105 J4 Isipingo S. Africa
102 C3 Isiro Dem. Rep. Congo
116 A5 Isisford Austr.
80 F3 İskenderun Turkey
80 E1 İskilip Turkey
76 K4 Iskitim Rus. Fed.
67 L3 Iskŭr r. Bulg.
20 C3 Iskut Can.
20 C3 Iskut r. Can.
80 F3 İslahiye Turkey
84 C2 Islamabad Pak.
84 C3 Islam Barrage barrage Pak.
84 B4 Islamgarh Pak.
84 B4 Islamkot Pak.
29 D7 Islamorada U.S.A.
94 A4 Island Bay b. Phil.
33 J1 Island Falls U.S.A.
21 L4 Island L. l. Can.
114 B3 Island Lagoon salt flat Austr.
21 L4 Island Lake Can.
30 A2 Island Lake l. U.S.A.
60 F3 Island Magee pen. U.K.
34 A1 Island Mountain U.S.A.
24 E2 Island Park U.S.A.
33 H2 Island Pond U.S.A.
117 E1 Islands, Bay of b. N.Z.
57 B5 Islay i. U.K.
32 E6 Isle of Wight U.S.A.
30 C2 Isle Royale National Park nat. park U.S.A.
81 M1 İsmayıllı Azer.
55 R5 Isojoki Fin.
103 D5 Isoka Zambia
54 U3 Isokylä Fin.
66 G5 Isola di Capo Rizzuto Italy
80 C3 Isparta Turkey
67 M3 Isperikh Bulg.
81 H1 İspir Turkey
70 Israel country Asia
68 H4 Issa Rus. Fed.
100 B4 Issia Côte d'Ivoire
81 K6 Issin Iraq
64 F4 Issoire France
81 J4 Isṭablāt Iraq
80 B1 İstanbul Turkey
İstanbul Boğazı str. see Bosporus
81 M5 Īstgāh-e Eznā Iran
67 K5 Istiaia Greece
45 A3 Istmina Col.
29 D7 Istokpoga, L. l. U.S.A.
66 E2 Istra pen. Croatia
64 G5 Istres France
Istria pen. see Istra
85 G5 Iswaripur Bangl.
43 L6 Itabaianinha Brazil
43 K6 Itaberaba Brazil
46 D2 Itabira Brazil
46 D3 Itabirito Brazil
46 E1 Itabuna Brazil
43 G4 Itacoatiara Brazil
46 B3 Itaguajé Brazil
46 C3 Itaí Brazil
46 A4 Itaimbey r. Para.
43 G4 Itaituba Brazil
44 G3 Itajaí Brazil
46 D3 Itajubá Brazil
85 F5 Itaki India
42 F6 Italia, Laguna l. Bol.
48 Italy country Europe
43 L7 Itamaraju Brazil
46 D2 Itamarandiba Brazil
46 E2 Itambacuri Brazil
46 E2 Itambacuri r. Brazil
46 D2 Itambé, Pico de mt Brazil
103 E6 Itampolo Madag.
85 H4 Itanagar India
46 D1 Itanguari r. Brazil
46 C4 Itanhaém Brazil
46 E2 Itanhém Brazil
46 E2 Itanhém r. Brazil
46 E2 Itaobim Brazil
46 C2 Itapajipe Brazil
46 E1 Itaparica, Ilha i. Brazil
46 E1 Itapebi Brazil
46 E3 Itapemirim Brazil
46 D3 Itaperuna Brazil
46 E1 Itapetinga Brazil
46 C3 Itapetininga Brazil
46 C3 Itapeva Brazil
43 L6 Itapicuru r. Bahia Brazil
43 K5 Itapicuru r. Maranhão Brazil
43 K4 Itapicuru Mirim Brazil
43 L4 Itapipoca Brazil
46 C4 Itararé Brazil
46 C3 Itararé r. Brazil
84 D5 Itarsi India
46 B2 Itarumã Brazil
94 B1 Itbayat i. Phil.
20 G1 Itchen Lake l. Can.
45 B3 Ité r. Col.
67 K5 Itea Greece
30 E4 Ithaca MI U.S.A.
32 E3 Ithaca NY U.S.A.
80 F6 Ithrah Saudi Arabia
91 B8 Itihusa-yama mt Japan
102 C3 Itimbiri r. Dem. Rep. Congo
46 E2 Itinga Brazil
46 A2 Itiquira Brazil
46 A2 Itiquira r. Brazil
91 F7 Itō Japan
91 E6 Itoigawa Japan
66 C4 Ittiri Italy
46 C3 Itu Brazil
45 B3 Ituango Col.
42 D5 Ituí r. Brazil
46 C2 Ituiutaba Brazil
102 C4 Itula Dem. Rep. Congo
46 C2 Itumbiara Brazil
43 G2 Ituni Guyana
46 D3 Itupiranga Brazil
46 B2 Iturama Brazil
46 A4 Iturbe Para.
77 Q5 Iturup, Ostrov i. Rus. Fed.
42 E5 Ituxi r. Brazil
62 D4 Itzehoe Ger.
45 C4 Iuaretê Brazil
77 V3 Iul'tin Rus. Fed.
45 C4 Iutica Brazil
46 B3 Ivaí r. Brazil
54 U2 Ivalo Fin.
54 U2 Ivalojoki r. Fin.
69 C4 Ivanava Belarus
114 F4 Ivanhoe Austr.
31 F1 Ivanhoe r. Can.
21 H2 Ivanhoe Lake l. N.W.T. Can.
31 F1 Ivanhoe Lake l. Ont. Can.
63 O5 Ivankiv Ukr.
69 C5 Ivano-Frankivs'k Ukr.
68 G3 Ivanovo Rus. Fed.
68 G3 Ivanovskaya Oblast' div. Rus. Fed.
35 E4 Ivanpah Lake l. U.S.A.
68 J4 Ivanteyevka Rus. Fed.
68 C4 Ivatsevichy Belarus
67 M4 Ivaylovgrad Bulg.
76 H3 Ivdel' Rus. Fed.
46 B3 Ivinheima Brazil
46 B3 Ivinheima r. Brazil
103 E6 Ivohibe Madag.
66 B2 Ivrea Italy
67 M5 İvrindi Turkey
69 H7 Ivris Ugheltekhili pass Georgia
63 N4 Ivyanyets Belarus
90 G5 Iwaizumi Japan
91 G6 Iwaki Japan
90 G4 Iwaki-san vol. Japan
91 C7 Iwakuni Japan
90 G3 Iwamizawa Japan
90 G5 Iwate-san vol. Japan
100 C4 Iwo Nigeria
Iwo Jima i. see Iō-jima
68 C4 Iwye Belarus
36 E4 Ixmiquilpán Mex.
105 J5 Ixopo S. Africa
59 H5 Ixworth U.K.
86 H1 Iya r. Rus. Fed.
91 C8 Iyo Japan
91 C8 Iyo-nada b. Japan
36 G5 Izabal, L. de l. Guatemala
90 G3 Izari-dake mt Japan
102 D4 Izazi Tanz.
69 H7 Izberbash Rus. Fed.
63 Q3 Izdeshkovo Rus. Fed.
76 G4 Izhevsk Rus. Fed.
76 G3 Izhma Rus. Fed.
68 K1 Izhma r. Rus. Fed.
69 F4 Izmalkovo Rus. Fed.
69 D6 Izmayil Ukr.
67 M5 İzmir Turkey
67 M5 İzmir Körfezi g. Turkey
80 B1 İznik Gölü l. Turkey
69 G6 Izobil'nyy Rus. Fed.
91 F7 Izu-hantō pen. Japan
91 A7 Izuhara Japan
91 D7 Izumisano Japan
91 C7 Izumo Japan
91 F7 Izu-shotō is Japan
69 C5 Izyaslav Ukr.
69 F5 Izyum Ukr.

J

Jabal, Bahr el r. see White Nile
65 E3 Jabalón r. Spain
84 D5 Jabalpur India
80 F3 Jabbūl Syria
112 F2 Jabiru Austr.
80 E4 Jablah Syria
66 G3 Jablanica Bos.-Herz.
43 M5 Jaboatão Brazil
46 C3 Jaboticabal Brazil
65 F1 Jaca Spain
43 K6 Jacaré r. Brazil
43 G5 Jacareacanga Brazil
46 C3 Jacareí Brazil
47 C1 Jáchal r. Arg.
42 E2 Jacinto Brazil
42 F5 Jaciparaná r. Brazil
30 D1 Jackfish Can.
31 H3 Jack Lake l. Can.
33 H2 Jackman U.S.A.
27 D5 Jacksboro U.S.A.
116 C6 Jackson Austr.
27 G6 Jackson AL U.S.A.
34 B2 Jackson CA U.S.A.
32 B6 Jackson KY U.S.A.
30 E4 Jackson MI U.S.A.
26 E3 Jackson MN U.S.A.
27 F4 Jackson MO U.S.A.
27 F5 Jackson MS U.S.A.
32 B5 Jackson OH U.S.A.
29 B5 Jackson TN U.S.A.
24 E3 Jackson WY U.S.A.
117 B5 Jackson Head hd N.Z.
24 E2 Jackson L. l. U.S.A.
30 D3 Jacksonport U.S.A.
27 E5 Jacksonville AR U.S.A.
29 D6 Jacksonville FL U.S.A.
30 B6 Jacksonville IL U.S.A.
29 E5 Jacksonville NC U.S.A.
27 E6 Jacksonville TX U.S.A.
29 D6 Jacksonville Beach U.S.A.
37 K5 Jacmel Haiti
84 B3 Jacobabad Pak.
43 K6 Jacobina Brazil
35 F3 Jacob Lake U.S.A.
104 F4 Jacobsdal S. Africa
23 H4 Jacques-Cartier, Détroit de chan. Can.
23 G4 Jacques Cartier, Mt mt Can.
23 G4 Jacquet River Can.
47 G1 Jacuí r. Brazil
43 L6 Jacuípe r. Brazil
43 J4 Jacunda Brazil
46 C4 Jacupiranga Brazil
45 C2 Jacura Venez.
66 G2 Jadovnik mt Bos.-Herz.
101 D1 Jādū Libya
42 C5 Jaén Peru
94 B3 Jaen Phil.
65 E4 Jaén Spain
81 M4 Ja'farābād Iran
Jaffa see Tel Aviv-Yafo
114 C6 Jaffa, C. pt Austr.
83 E9 Jaffna Sri Lanka
33 G3 Jaffrey U.S.A.
84 D3 Jagadhri India
83 F7 Jagdalpur India
105 F4 Jagersfontein S. Africa
84 D2 Jaggang China
Jagok Tso salt l. see Urru Co
84 C3 Jagraon India
47 G2 Jaguarão Brazil
47 G2 Jaguarão r. Brazil/Uru.
46 C4 Jaguariaíva Brazil
85 F4 Jahanabad India
81 M3 Jahan Dagh mt Iran
84 C4 Jahazpur India
81 K7 Jahmah w. Iraq
79 G4 Jahrom Iran
88 B3 Jainca China
84 C4 Jaipur India
84 B4 Jaisalmer India
84 E5 Jaisinghnagar India
84 D5 Jaitgarh mt India
85 E3 Jajarkot Nepal
66 G2 Jajce Bos.-Herz.
85 G4 Jakar Bhutan
92 □ Jakarta Indon.
20 C2 Jakes Corner Can.
84 B5 Jakhan India
54 P3 Jäkkvik Sweden
54 S5 Jakobstad Fin.
27 C5 Jal U.S.A.
84 B2 Jalālābād Afgh.
79 L1 Jalal-Abad Kyrgyzstan
80 C7 Jalālah al Baḩarīya, Jabal plat. Egypt
84 C3 Jalandhar India
36 E5 Jalapa Enríquez Mex.
55 S5 Jalasjärvi Fin.
81 K4 Jalawlā' Iraq
85 G4 Jaldhaka r. Bangl.
46 B3 Jales Brazil
85 F5 Jaleshwar India
84 C5 Jalgaon Maharashtra India
84 D5 Jalgaon Maharashtra India
81 L6 Jalībah Iraq
100 D4 Jalingo Nigeria
84 C6 Jalna India
65 F2 Jalón r. Spain
85 G4 Jalpaiguri India
101 E2 Jālū Libya
16 Jamaica country Caribbean Sea
37 J5 Jamaica Channel chan. Haiti/Jamaica
81 L3 Jamalabad Iran
81 M5 Jamālābād Iran
85 G4 Jamalpur Bangl.
85 F4 Jamalpur India
43 G5 Jamanxim r. Brazil
92 C7 Jambi Indon.
116 D5 Jambin Austr.
84 C4 Jambo India
95 A4 Jamboaye r. Indon.
94 A5 Jambongan i. Malaysia
95 A4 Jambuair, Tg pt Indon.
81 K4 Jambūr Iraq
26 D2 James r. ND U.S.A.
32 D6 James r. VA U.S.A.
84 B4 Jamesabad Pak.
22 D3 James Bay b. Can.
29 E7 James Cistern Bahamas
47 D2 James Craik Arg.
117 B6 James Pk mt N.Z.
119 B2 James Ross I. i. Antarctica
114 C4 Jamestown Austr.
105 G5 Jamestown S. Africa
26 D2 Jamestown ND U.S.A.
32 D3 Jamestown NY U.S.A.
81 M4 Jamīlābād Iran
84 C2 Jammu Jammu and Kashmir
84 C2 Jammu and Kashmir terr. Asia
84 B5 Jamnagar India
84 D4 Jamni r. India
84 B3 Jampur Pak.
55 T6 Jämsä Fin.
55 T6 Jämsänkoski Fin.
85 F5 Jamshedpur India
85 G5 Jamuna r. Bangl.
82 G5 Janakpur Nepal
46 D1 Janaúba Brazil
46 B2 Jandaia Brazil
79 G3 Jandaq Iran
84 B2 Jandola Pak.
116 D6 Jandowae Austr.
34 B1 Janesville CA U.S.A.
30 C4 Janesville WV U.S.A.
85 G4 Jangipur India
81 L2 Jānī Beyglū Iran
12 J1 Jan Mayen i. Arctic Ocean
81 L5 Jannah Iraq
25 E6 Janos Mex.
104 F6 Jansenville S. Africa
46 D1 Januária Brazil
84 C5 Jaora India
71 Japan country Asia
90 C5 Japan, Sea of sea Pac. Oc.
Japan Alps Nat. Park see Chibu-Sangaku Nat. Park
14 E4 Japan Tr. sea feature Pac. Oc.
42 E4 Japurá r. Brazil
85 H4 Jāpvo Mount mt India
45 A3 Jaqué Panama
80 G3 Jarābulus Syria
46 A3 Jaraguari Brazil
80 E5 Jarash Jordan
46 A3 Jardim Brazil
113 H2 Jardine River National Park nat. park Austr.
87 L2 Jargalant Mongolia
81 K4 Jarmo Iraq
55 P7 Järna Sweden
62 H5 Jarocin Pol.
63 L5 Jarosław Pol.
54 N5 Järpen Sweden
88 B2 Jartai China
42 F6 Jarú Brazil
55 T7 Järvakandi Estonia
55 T6 Järvenpää Fin.

84 B5 Jasdan India
79 H4 Jāsk Iran
63 K6 Jasło Pol.
44 D8 Jason Is is Falkland Is
119 B2 Jason Pen. pen. Antarctica
20 F4 Jasper Can.
29 C5 Jasper AL U.S.A.
27 E4 Jasper AR U.S.A.
29 D6 Jasper FL U.S.A.
28 C4 Jasper IN U.S.A.
32 E3 Jasper NY U.S.A.
32 B5 Jasper OH U.S.A.
27 E6 Jasper TX U.S.A.
20 F4 Jasper Nat. Park nat. park Can.
81 K5 Jaşşān Iraq
63 J6 Jastrzębie-Zdrój Pol.
84 C4 Jaswantpura India
63 J7 Jászberény Hungary
46 B2 Jataí Brazil
43 G4 Jatapu r. Brazil
84 B4 Jati Pak.
84 B3 Jatoi Pak.
46 C3 Jaú Brazil
42 F4 Jaú r. Brazil
42 F4 Jaú, Parque Nacional do nat. park Brazil
45 E5 Jauaperi r. Brazil
45 D3 Jaua Sarisariñama, Parque Nacional nat. park Venez.
55 S8 Jaunlutriņi Latvia
55 U8 Jaunpiebalga Latvia
85 E4 Jaunpur India
46 A2 Jauru Brazil
46 B2 Jauru r. Brazil
69 G7 Java Georgia
92 □ Java i. Indon.
13 M4 Java Ridge sea feature Indian Ocean
87 K2 Javarthushuu Mongolia
92 D7 Java Sea sea Indon.
13 M4 Java Trench sea feature Indian Ocean
Jawa i. see Java
92 □ Jawa Barat div. Indon.
84 C4 Jawad India
84 B4 Jawai r. India
92 □ Jawa Tengah div. Indon.
92 □ Jawa Timur div. Indon.
80 F3 Jawbān Bayk Syria
84 C6 Jawhar India
102 E3 Jawhar Somalia
62 H5 Jawor Pol.
93 K7 Jaya, Pk mt Indon.
93 L7 Jayapura Indon.
85 F4 Jaynagar India
80 F5 Jayrūd Syria
81 M3 Jazvān Iran
30 D5 J. C. Murphey Lake l. U.S.A.
35 E4 Jean U.S.A.
20 E2 Jean Marie River Can.
23 G2 Jeannin, Lac l. Can.
100 C4 Jebba Nigeria
101 E3 Jebel Abyad Plateau plat. Sudan
84 C3 Jech Doab lowland Pak.
57 F5 Jedburgh U.K.
78 D5 Jeddah Saudi Arabia
66 C6 Jedeida Tunisia
33 F3 Jefferson NY U.S.A.
30 C4 Jefferson WV U.S.A.
24 D2 Jefferson r. U.S.A.
34 D2 Jefferson, Mt mt U.S.A.
24 B2 Jefferson, Mt vol. U.S.A.
26 E4 Jefferson City U.S.A.
28 C4 Jeffersonville U.S.A.
104 F7 Jeffrey's Bay S. Africa
44 E2 Jejuí Guazú r. Para.
55 T8 Jēkabpils Latvia
62 G5 Jelenia Góra Pol.
85 G4 Jelep La pass China
55 S8 Jelgava Latvia
32 A6 Jellico U.S.A.
95 C5 Jemaja i. Indon.
92 □ Jember Indon.
62 E5 Jena Ger.
100 C1 Jendouba Tunisia
80 E5 Jenīn West Bank
32 B6 Jenkins U.S.A.
34 A2 Jenner U.S.A.
27 E6 Jennings U.S.A.
21 K4 Jenpeg Can.
114 E6 Jeparit Austr.
46 E1 Jequié Brazil
46 D2 Jequitaí Brazil
46 D2 Jequitaí r. Brazil
46 E2 Jequitinhonha Brazil
46 E1 Jequitinhonha r. Brazil
95 B5 Jerantut Malaysia
101 F4 Jerbar Sudan
37 K5 Jérémie Haiti
65 C4 Jerez de la Frontera Spain
65 C3 Jerez de los Caballeros Spain
54 T2 Jerggul Norway
67 J5 Jergucat Albania
116 B4 Jericho Austr.
80 E6 Jericho West Bank
115 F5 Jerilderie Austr.
81 K2 Jermuk Armenia
24 D3 Jerome U.S.A.
112 C6 Jerramungup Austr.
56 E7 Jersey i. U.K.
33 F4 Jersey City U.S.A.
32 E4 Jersey Shore U.S.A.
28 B4 Jerseyville U.S.A.
43 K5 Jerumenha Brazil
80 E6 Jerusalem Israel/West Bank
115 J5 Jervis B. b. Austr.
115 J5 Jervis Bay Austr.
115 J5 Jervis Bay Territory div. Austr.
66 F1 Jesenice Slovenia
66 E3 Jesi Italy
55 M6 Jessheim Norway
85 G5 Jessore Bangl.
29 D6 Jesup U.S.A.
36 F5 Jesús Carranza Mex.
47 D1 Jesús María Arg.
84 B5 Jetalsar India
26 D4 Jetmore U.S.A.
85 F4 Jha Jha India
84 D3 Jhajjar India
84 C4 Jhajju India
84 A3 Jhal Pak.
85 G5 Jhalakati Bangl.
82 E6 Jhalawar India
84 C3 Jhang Pak.
84 D4 Jhansi India
85 F5 Jharia India
85 F5 Jharkhand admin. div. India
85 F5 Jharsuguda India
84 B3 Jhatpat Pak.
84 C2 Jhelum Pak.
84 C2 Jhelum r. Pak.
85 G5 Jhenida Bangl.
84 B4 Jhudo Pak.
85 F4 Jhumritilaiya India
84 C3 Jhunjhunūn India
88 C3 Jiachuan China
88 F4 Jiading China
89 D5 Jiahe China
89 B4 Jiajiang China
88 B3 Jialing Jiang r. China
90 B1 Jiamusi China
89 E5 Ji'an Jiangxi China
89 E5 Ji'an Jiangxi China
87 N3 Ji'an Jilin China
88 F1 Jianchang China
89 F4 Jiande China
89 B4 Jiang'an China
89 A6 Jiangcheng China
89 B5 Jiangchuan China
88 B4 Jiange China
89 C4 Jiangjin China
89 C5 Jiangkou China
89 E5 Jiangle China
88 B3 Jiangluozhen China
89 D6 Jiangmen China
89 F4 Jiangshan China
88 F3 Jiangsu div. China
89 E5 Jiangxi div. China
88 D3 Jiangxian China
88 F3 Jiangyan China
88 F4 Jiangyin China
89 D5 Jiangyong China
88 B4 Jiangyou China
88 F3 Jianhu China
89 D6 Jian Jiang r. China
89 D4 Jianli China
89 E5 Jianning China
89 F5 Jian'ou China
88 F1 Jianping Liaoning China
88 F1 Jianping Liaoning China
89 C4 Jianshi China
89 B6 Jianshui China
89 F5 Jianyang Fujian China
89 B4 Jianyang Sichuan China
88 D2 Jiaocheng China
88 E2 Jiaohe Hebei China
87 N3 Jiaohe Jilin China
Jiaojiang see Taizhou
88 F2 Jiaolai r. China
88 G1 Jiaolai r. China
89 E5 Jiaoling China
88 F3 Jiaonan China
88 F2 Jiaozhou China
88 F2 Jiaozhou Wan b. China
88 D3 Jiaozuo China
88 D2 Jiaxian China
88 F4 Jiaxing China
89 D4 Jiayu China
82 J3 Jiayuguan China
89 E6 Jiazi China
Jiddah see Jeddah
80 D6 Jiddī, Jabal al h. Egypt
90 B2 Jidong China
88 B2 Jieheba China
54 Q2 Jiehkkevarri mt Norway
89 E6 Jieshi China
89 E6 Jieshi Wan b. China
88 E3 Jieshou China
54 T2 Iešjávri l. Norway
89 E6 Jiexi China
88 D2 Jiexiu China
89 E6 Jieyang China
55 T9 Jieznas Lith.
88 A3 Jigzhi China
62 G6 Jihlava Czech Rep.
102 E3 Jijiga Eth.
89 A4 Jiju China
84 B2 Jilga r. Afgh.
102 E3 Jilib Somalia
87 N3 Jilin China
87 N3 Jilin div. China
88 A2 Jiling China
102 D3 Jīma Eth.
27 C6 Jiménez Mex.
36 D3 Jiménez Chihuahua Mex.
36 E4 Jiménez Tamaulipas Mex.
88 F2 Jimo China
82 G2 Jimsar China
33 F4 Jim Thorpe U.S.A.
88 E2 Jinan China
88 B2 Jinchang China
88 D3 Jincheng China
88 B4 Jinchuan China
84 D3 Jind India
115 H6 Jindabyne Austr.
115 G5 Jindera Austr.
62 G6 Jindřichův Hradec Czech Rep.
88 C3 Jing r. China
89 E4 Jing'an China
88 C2 Jingbian China
88 C3 Jingchuan China
89 F4 Jingde China
89 E4 Jingdezhen China
85 E5 Jinggangshan China
89 E4 Jinggongqiao China
88 E2 Jinghai China
83 K6 Jinghong China
88 F3 Jingjiang China
88 D2 Jingle China
88 D4 Jingmen China
88 B3 Jingning China
88 E1 Jingpeng China
90 A3 Jingpo China
90 A3 Jingpo Hu resr China
89 D4 Jingsha China
88 B2 Jingtai China
89 C6 Jingxi China
89 F4 Jingxian China
88 B2 Jingyuan China
89 C5 Jingzhou Hunan China
89 D4 Jingzhou China
89 F3 Jinhu China
89 F4 Jinhua China
88 D1 Jining Nei Mongol Zizhiqu China
88 E3 Jining Shandong China
102 D3 Jinja Uganda
89 F5 Jinjiang China
89 E4 Jin Jiang r. China
102 D3 Jinka Eth.
88 F1 Jinlingsi China
89 C7 Jinmu Jiao pt China
36 G6 Jinotepe Nic.
89 C5 Jinping Guizhou China
89 B6 Jinping Yunnan China
89 A5 Jinping Shan mts China
89 C5 Jinsha China
Jinsha Jiang r. see Yangtze
88 F1 Jinshan China
88 F4 Jinshan China
89 D4 Jinshi China
88 B4 Jintang China
94 B4 Jintotolo i. Phil.
94 B4 Jintotolo Channel chan. Phil.
84 D6 Jintur India
89 E5 Jinxi China
88 E4 Jinxian China
88 E3 Jinxiang Shandong China
89 F5 Jinxiang Zhejiang China
89 B5 Jinyang China
89 F4 Jinyun China
88 E4 Jinzhai China
88 F1 Jinzhou China
88 F2 Jinzhou China
42 F6 Ji-Paraná Brazil
42 F5 Jiparaná r. Brazil
42 B4 Jipijapa Ecuador
89 C4 Jishou China
89 E5 Jishui China
80 F4 Jisr ash Shughūr Syria
95 B4 Jitra Malaysia
88 C2 Jiudengkou China
88 B4 Jiuding Shan mt China
88 C3 Jiufoping China
89 E4 Jiujiang Jiangxi China
89 E4 Jiujiang Jiangxi China
89 E4 Jiuling Shan mts China
89 A4 Jiulong China
88 F1 Jiumiao China
82 J3 Jiuquan China
89 C5 Jiuxu China
79 J4 Jiwani Pak.
89 F4 Jixi Anhui China
87 O2 Jixi Heilongjiang China
90 B1 Jixian China
88 D3 Jiyuan China
78 E6 Jīzān Saudi Arabia
88 E2 Jizhou China
91 C7 Jizō-zaki pt Japan
43 M5 João Pessoa Brazil
46 C2 João Pinheiro Brazil
34 C2 Job Peak summit U.S.A.
85 F5 Joda India
84 C4 Jodhpur India
54 V5 Joensuu Fin.
91 F6 Jōetsu Japan
103 D6 Jofane Moz.
20 F4 Joffre, Mt mt Can.
55 U7 Jõgeva Estonia
55 U7 Jõgua Estonia
105 G3 Johannesburg S. Africa
34 D4 Johannesburg U.S.A.
84 E5 Johilla r. India
24 C2 John Day U.S.A.
24 B2 John Day r. U.S.A.
20 F3 John D'or Prairie Can.
33 G4 John F. Kennedy airport U.S.A.
32 D6 John H. Kerr Res. resr U.S.A.
57 E2 John o'Groats U.K.
29 D4 Johnson City U.S.A.
20 C2 Johnson's Crossing Can.
29 D5 Johnston U.S.A.
14 H4 Johnston Atoll Pac. Oc.
57 D5 Johnstone U.K.
60 D5 Johnstown Rep. of Ireland
33 F3 Johnstown NY U.S.A.
32 D4 Johnstown PA U.S.A.
31 F3 Johnswood U.S.A.
92 C6 Johor Bahru Malaysia
55 U7 Jõhvi Estonia
63 G3 Joinville Brazil
64 G2 Joinville France
119 B2 Joinville I. i. Antarctica
54 Q3 Jokkmokk Sweden
54 F4 Jökulsá á Dál r. Iceland
54 E3 Jökulsá á Fjöllum r. Iceland
54 F4 Jökulsá í Fljótsdal r. Iceland
81 K2 Jolfa Iran
30 C5 Joliet U.S.A.
22 F4 Joliette Can.
94 B5 Jolo Phil.
94 B5 Jolo i. Phil.
94 B3 Jomalig i. Phil.
92 □ Jombang Indon.
82 J4 Jomda China
55 T9 Jonava Lith.
88 B3 Jonê China
27 F5 Jonesboro AR U.S.A.
33 K2 Jonesboro ME U.S.A.
33 K2 Jonesport U.S.A.
32 B6 Jonesville U.S.A.
101 F4 Jonglei Canal canal Sudan
85 E5 Jonk r. India
55 O8 Jönköping Sweden
23 F4 Jonquière Can.
27 E4 Joplin U.S.A.
33 E5 Joppatowne U.S.A.
84 D4 Jora India
70 Jordan country Asia
80 E6 Jordan r. Asia
24 F2 Jordan U.S.A.
24 E3 Jordan r. U.S.A.
116 B4 Jordan Cr. watercourse Austr.
24 C3 Jordan Valley U.S.A.
46 B4 Jordão r. Brazil
55 N6 Jordet Norway
85 H4 Jorhat India
54 R4 Jörn Sweden
55 U5 Joroinen Fin.
55 K7 Jørpeland Norway
100 C4 Jos Nigeria
94 C5 Jose Abad Santos Phil.
44 B6 José de San Martin Arg.
46 A2 Joselândia Brazil
47 F2 José Pedro Varela Uru.
23 G3 Joseph, Lac l. Can.
112 E2 Joseph Bonaparte Gulf g. Austr.
35 G4 Joseph City U.S.A.
91 F6 Jōshinetsu-kōgen National Park Japan
35 E5 Joshua Tree National Park res. U.S.A.
100 C4 Jos Plateau plat. Nigeria
55 K6 Jostedalsbreen Nasjonalpark nat. park Norway
55 L6 Jotunheimen Nasjonalpark nat. park Norway
104 E6 Joubertina S. Africa
105 G3 Jouberton S. Africa
55 U6 Joutsa Fin.
55 V6 Joutseno Fin.
85 H4 Jowai India
60 B4 Joyce's Country reg. Rep. of Ireland
24 A1 Juan de Fuca Strait chan. U.S.A.
103 E5 Juan de Nova i. Indian Ocean
15 O8 Juan Fernández, Islas is Chile
54 V5 Juankoski Fin.
27 C7 Juaréz Mex.
34 D5 Juárez, Sierra de mts Mex.
43 K5 Juàzeiro Brazil
43 L5 Juàzeiro do Norte Brazil
101 F4 Juba Sudan
102 E3 Jubba r. Somalia
34 D4 Jubilee Pass pass U.S.A.
65 F3 Júcar r. Spain
36 E5 Juchitán Mex.
46 E2 Jucuruçu r. Brazil
55 J7 Judaberg Norway
81 H6 Judaidat al Hamir Iraq
81 G4 Judaydah Syria
81 H6 Judayyidat 'Ar'ar w. Iraq
62 G7 Judenburg Austria
55 M9 Juelsminde Denmark
88 C2 Juh China
88 F1 Juhua Dao i. China
37 G6 Juigalpa Nic.
61 F1 Juist i. Ger.
46 D3 Juiz de Fora Brazil
42 E8 Julaca Bol.
26 C3 Julesburg U.S.A.
42 D7 Juliaca Peru
113 H4 Julia Creek Austr.
43 G3 Juliana Top summit Suriname
66 E1 Julijske Alpe mts Slovenia
47 E2 Julio, 9 de Arg.
42 C5 Jumbilla Peru
65 F3 Jumilla Spain
85 E3 Jumla Nepal
84 B5 Junagadh India
85 E6 Junagarh India
88 F3 Junan China
47 B2 Juncal mt Chile
47 D4 Juncal, L. l. Arg.
27 D6 Junction TX U.S.A.
35 F2 Junction UT U.S.A.
26 D4 Junction City U.S.A.
46 C3 Jundiaí Brazil
20 C3 Juneau U.S.A.
115 G5 Junee Austr.
62 C7 Jungfrau mt Switz.
86 E2 Junggar Pendi basin China
84 A4 Jungshahi Pak.
32 E4 Juniata r. U.S.A.
47 E2 Junín Arg.
47 B3 Junín de los Andes Arg.
33 K1 Juniper Can.
34 B3 Junipero Serro Peak summit U.S.A.
89 B4 Junlian China
54 P5 Junsele Sweden
24 C3 Juntura U.S.A.
55 T8 Juodupė Lith.
46 C4 Juquiá Brazil
101 E4 Jur r. Sudan
64 H3 Jura mts France/Switz.
57 C4 Jura i. U.K.
57 C5 Jura, Sound of chan. U.K.
46 E1 Juraci Brazil
45 A3 Juradó Col.
55 S9 Jurbarkas Lith.
80 E6 Jurf ad Darāwīsh Jordan
85 G2 Jurhen Ul Shan mts China
55 S8 Jūrmala Latvia
54 U4 Jurmu Fin.
88 F4 Jurong China
95 □ Jurong Sing.
42 E4 Juruá r. Brazil
43 G5 Juruena r. Brazil
54 R5 Jurva Fin.
47 D2 Justo Daract Arg.
42 E4 Jutaí r. Brazil
46 A3 Juti Brazil
36 G6 Jutiapa Guatemala
36 G6 Juticalpa Honduras
54 P3 Jutis Sweden
54 V5 Juuka Fin.
55 U6 Juva Fin.
88 F3 Juxian China
88 A1 Juyan China
88 E3 Juye China
103 C6 Jwaneng Botswana
55 T5 Jyväskylä Fin.

K

84 D2 K2 mt China/Jammu and Kashmir
34 □1 Kaala mt U.S.A.
102 E4 Kaambooni Kenya
55 S6 Kaarina Fin.
54 V5 Kaavi Fin.
93 G8 Kabaena i. Indon.
100 A4 Kabala Sierra Leone
102 C4 Kabale Uganda
102 C4 Kabalo Dem. Rep. Congo
102 C4 Kabambare Dem. Rep. Congo
103 C5 Kabangu Dem. Rep. Congo
95 A5 Kabanjahe Indon.
69 G7 Kabardino-Balkarskaya Respublika div. Rus. Fed.
102 C4 Kabare Dem. Rep. Congo
54 R3 Kåbdalis Sweden
30 E1 Kabenung Lake l. Can.
22 D4 Kabinakagami Lake l. Can.
102 C4 Kabinda Dem. Rep. Congo
81 L5 Kabīrkūh mts Iran
84 B3 Kabirwala Pak.
102 B3 Kabo C.A.R.
103 C5 Kabompo Zambia
102 C4 Kabongo Dem. Rep. Congo
81 M4 Kabūd Rāhang Iran
94 B2 Kabugao Phil.
84 B2 Kābul Afgh.
84 C2 Kabul r. Afgh.
94 C6 Kaburuang i. Indon.
103 C5 Kabwe Zambia
69 H5 Kachalinskaya Rus. Fed.
84 B5 Kachchh, Gulf of g. India
84 C1 Kach Pass pass Afgh.
86 J1 Kachug Rus. Fed.
81 H1 Kaçkar Dağı mt Turkey
84 A3 Kadanai r. Afgh./Pak.
95 A2 Kadan Kyun i. Myanmar
111 H3 Kadavu i. Fiji
111 H3 Kadavu Passage chan. Fiji
100 B4 Kade Ghana
84 C5 Kadi India
80 B1 Kadıköy Turkey
114 B4 Kadina Austr.
80 D2 Kadınhanı Turkey
100 B3 Kadiolo Mali
80 F3 Kadirli Turkey
83 D8 Kadmat i. India
26 C3 Kadoka U.S.A.
103 C5 Kadoma Zimbabwe
101 E3 Kadugli Sudan
100 C3 Kaduna Nigeria
100 C4 Kaduna r. Nigeria
85 J3 Kadusam mt China
68 F3 Kaduy Rus. Fed.
68 G3 Kadyy Rus. Fed.
76 G3 Kadzherom Rus. Fed.
100 A3 Kaédi Maur.
101 D3 Kaélé Cameroon
34 □1 Kaena Pt pt U.S.A.
117 D1 Kaeo N.Z.
87 N4 Kaesŏng N. Korea
80 F6 Kāf Saudi Arabia
103 C4 Kafakumba Dem. Rep. Congo
100 A3 Kaffrine Senegal
67 L5 Kafireas, Akra pt Greece
80 C6 Kafr ash Shaykh Egypt
103 C5 Kafue Zambia
103 C5 Kafue r. Zambia
103 C5 Kafue National Park nat. park Zambia
91 E6 Kaga Japan
102 B3 Kaga Bandoro C.A.R.
69 G6 Kagal'nitskaya Rus. Fed.
79 J2 Kagan Uzbek.
31 F3 Kagawong Can.
54 R4 Kåge Sweden
102 D4 Kagera, Parc National de la nat. park Rwanda
81 J1 Kağızman Turkey
91 B9 Kagoshima Japan
81 M3 Kahak Iran
34 □1 Kahaluu U.S.A.
102 D4 Kahama Tanz.
34 □1 Kahana U.S.A.
69 D5 Kaharlyk Ukr.
92 E7 Kahayan r. Indon.
102 B4 Kahemba Dem. Rep. Congo
117 A6 Kaherekoau Mts mts N.Z.
30 B5 Kahoka U.S.A.
34 □2 Kahoolawe i. U.S.A.
80 F3 Kahramanmaraş Turkey
84 B3 Kahror Pak.
80 G3 Kahta Turkey
34 □1 Kahuku U.S.A.
34 □1 Kahuku Pt pt U.S.A.
34 □2 Kahului U.S.A.
117 D4 Kahurangi Point pt N.Z.
84 C2 Kahuta Pak.
102 C4 Kahuzi-Biega, Parc National du nat. park Dem. Rep. Congo
93 J8 Kai, Kepulauan is Indon.
100 C4 Kaiama Nigeria
117 D5 Kaiapoi N.Z.
35 F3 Kaibab U.S.A.
25 D4 Kaibab Plat. plat. U.S.A.
93 J8 Kai Besar i. Indon.
35 G3 Kaibito U.S.A.
35 G3 Kaibito Plateau plat. U.S.A.
88 E3 Kaifeng Henan China
88 E3 Kaifeng Henan China
89 F4 Kaihua China
104 D4 Kaiingveld reg. S. Africa
88 C4 Kaijiang China
93 J8 Kai Kecil i. Indon.
89 □ Kai Keung Leng China
117 D5 Kaikoura N.Z.
117 D5 Kaikoura Peninsula pen. N.Z.
100 A4 Kailahun Sierra Leone
Kailas mt see Kangrinboqê Feng
85 G4 Kailāshahar India
Kailas Range mts see Gangdisê Shan
89 C5 Kaili China
88 F1 Kailu China
34 □1 Kailua U.S.A.
34 □2 Kailua Kona U.S.A.
117 E2 Kaimai Range h. N.Z.
93 J7 Kaimana Indon.
117 E3 Kaimanawa Mountains mts N.Z.
85 H2 Kaimar China
84 E4 Kaimur Range h. India
55 S7 Käina Estonia
91 D8 Kainan Japan
91 D7 Kainan Japan
100 C3 Kainji Lake National Park nat. park Nigeria
100 C3 Kainji Reservoir resr Nigeria
117 E2 Kaipara Harbour in. N.Z.
35 G3 Kaiparowits Plateau plat. U.S.A.
89 D6 Kaiping China
23 J3 Kaipokok Bay in. Can.
84 D3 Kairana India
100 D1 Kairouan Tunisia
119 C5 Kaiser Wilhelm II Land reg. Antarctica
90 A3 Kaishantun China
117 D1 Kaitaia N.Z.
117 B7 Kaitangata N.Z.
117 F3 Kaitawa N.Z.
84 D3 Kaithal India
54 R3 Kaitum Sweden
93 H8 Kaiwatu Indon.
34 □2 Kaiwi Channel chan. U.S.A.
88 C4 Kaixian China
89 C5 Kaiyang China
88 G1 Kaiyuan Liaoning China
89 B6 Kaiyuan Yunnan China
54 U4 Kajaani Fin.
113 H4 Kajabbi Austr.
95 B5 Kajang Malaysia
84 B3 Kajanpur Pak.
81 L2 K'ajaran Armenia
81 L3 Kaju Iran
22 C4 Kakabeka Falls Can.
112 F2 Kakadu National Park nat. park Austr.
104 D4 Kakamas S. Africa
102 D3 Kakamega Kenya
117 C6 Kakanui Mts mts N.Z.
100 A4 Kakata Liberia
117 E3 Kakatahi N.Z.
85 H4 Kakching India
91 C7 Kake Japan
20 C3 Kake U.S.A.
102 C4 Kakenge Dem. Rep. Congo
69 E6 Kakhovka Ukr.
69 E6 Kakhovs'ke Vodoskhovyshche resr Ukr.
83 F7 Kākināda India
20 F2 Kakisa Can.
20 F2 Kakisa r. Can.
20 F2 Kakisa Lake l. Can.
91 D7 Kakogawa Japan
102 C4 Kakoswa Dem. Rep. Congo
84 D4 Kakrala India
91 G6 Kakuda Japan
20 F4 Kakwa r. Can.
84 B3 Kala Pak.
66 D7 Kalaâ Kebira Tunisia

80 D3 Kazancı Turkey
68 J4 Kazanka r. Rus. Fed.
67 L3 Kazanlŭk Bulg.
93 L1 Kazan-rettō is Japan
69 G5 Kazanskaya Rus. Fed.
69 H7 Kazbek mt Georgia/Rus. Fed.
67 M5 Kaz Dağı mts Turkey
79 G4 Kāzerūn Iran
68 J2 Kazhim Rus. Fed.
63 K6 Kazincbarcika Hungary
69 H7 Kazret'i Georgia
69 J5 Kaztalovka Kazak.
90 G4 Kazuno Japan
76 H3 Kazymskiy Mys Rus. Fed.
67 L6 Kea i. Greece
60 E3 Keady U.K.
34 □2 Kealakekua Bay b. U.S.A.
35 G4 Keams Canyon U.S.A.
26 D3 Kearney U.S.A.
35 G5 Kearny U.S.A.
80 G2 Keban Turkey
80 G2 Keban Barajı resr Turkey
100 A3 Kébémèr Senegal
80 F4 Kebīr, Nahr al r. Lebanon/Syria
101 E3 Kebkabiya Sudan
54 Q3 Kebnekaise mt Sweden
57 B2 Kebock Head hd U.K.
102 E3 K'ebrī Dehar Eth.
92 □ Kebumen Indon.
20 D3 Kechika r. Can.
80 C3 Keçiborlu Turkey
63 J7 Kecskemét Hungary
81 H1 K'eda Georgia
55 S9 Kėdainiai Lith.
84 D3 Kedar Kanta mt India
84 D3 Kedarnath Peak mt India
23 G4 Kedgwick Can.
92 □ Kediri Indon.
100 A3 Kédougou Senegal
20 D2 Keele r. Can.
20 C2 Keele Pk summit Can.
25 C4 Keeler U.S.A.
57 F4 Keen, Mount mt U.K.
94 A5 Keenapusan i. Phil.
33 G3 Keene U.S.A.
115 J3 Keepit, Lake resr Austr.
61 C3 Keerbergen Belgium
113 H2 Keer-weer, C. pt Austr.
103 B6 Keetmanshoop Namibia
21 L6 Keewatin Can.
21 L5 Keewatin U.S.A.
67 J5 Kefallonia i. Greece
93 G8 Kefamenanu Indon.
54 B4 Keflavík Iceland
82 E2 Kegen Kazak.
23 G2 Keglo, Baie de b. Can.
69 H6 Kegul'ta Rus. Fed.
55 T7 Kehra Estonia
83 J6 Kehsi Mansam Myanmar
58 F4 Keighley U.K.
55 T7 Keila Estonia
104 D4 Keimoes S. Africa
54 U5 Keitele Fin.
54 T5 Keitele l. Fin.
114 D6 Keith Austr.
57 F3 Keith U.K.
20 E1 Keith Arm b. Can.
23 G5 Kejimkujik National Park nat. park Can.
34 □2 Kekaha U.S.A.
63 K7 Kékes mt Hungary
84 C4 Kekri India
83 D9 Kelai i. Maldives
88 D2 Kelan China
95 B5 Kelang Malaysia
95 B4 Kelantan r. Malaysia
62 E6 Kelheim Ger.
66 D6 Kelibia Tunisia
79 J2 Kelifskiy Uzboy marsh Turkm.
81 G1 Kelkit Turkey
80 F1 Kelkit r. Turkey
22 E2 Keller Lake l. Can.
32 B4 Kelleys I. i. U.S.A.
24 C2 Kellogg U.S.A.
54 V3 Kelloselkä Fin.
60 E4 Kells Rep. of Ireland
55 S9 Kelmė Lith.
101 D4 Kelo Chad
20 F5 Kelowna Can.
34 A2 Kelseyville U.S.A.
57 F5 Kelso U.K.
35 E4 Kelso CA U.S.A.
24 B2 Kelso WA U.S.A.
92 C6 Keluang Malaysia
21 J4 Kelvington Can.
68 E1 Kem' Rus. Fed.
68 E1 Kem' r. Rus. Fed.
81 G2 Kemah Turkey
80 G2 Kemaliye Turkey
67 M5 Kemalpaşa Turkey
20 D4 Kemano Can.
80 C3 Kemer Antalya Turkey
80 B3 Kemer Muğla Turkey
80 B3 Kemer Barajı resr Turkey
76 K4 Kemerovo Rus. Fed.
54 T4 Kemi Fin.
54 U3 Kemijärvi Fin.
54 U3 Kemijärvi l. Fin.
54 T3 Kemijoki r. Fin.
61 A4 Kemmelberg h. Belgium
24 E3 Kemmerer U.S.A.
57 F3 Kemnay U.K.
27 D5 Kemp, L. l. U.S.A.
54 T4 Kempele Fin.
61 C3 Kempen reg. Belgium
119 D4 Kemp Land reg. Antarctica
119 B2 Kemp Pen. pen. Antarctica
29 E7 Kemp's Bay Bahamas
115 K3 Kempsey Austr.
22 F4 Kempt, L. l. Can.
62 F7 Kempten Ger.
115 G9 Kempton Austr.
105 H3 Kempton Park S. Africa
31 K3 Kemptville Can.
92 □ Kemujan i. Indon.
84 E4 Ken r. India
58 E3 Kendal U.K.
115 K3 Kendall Austr.
21 M2 Kendall, Cape hd Can.
30 E5 Kendallville U.S.A.
93 G7 Kendari Indon.
92 E7 Kendawangan Indon.
101 D3 Kendégué Chad
85 F5 Kendrāparha India
24 C2 Kendrick U.S.A.
35 G4 Kendrick Peak summit U.S.A.
83 G6 Kendujhargarh India
115 H3 Kenebri Austr.
27 D6 Kenedy U.S.A.
100 A4 Kenema Sierra Leone
102 B4 Kenge Dem. Rep. Congo
83 J6 Kengtung Myanmar
104 D4 Kenhardt S. Africa
100 A3 Kéniéba Mali
100 B1 Kénitra Morocco
88 F2 Kenli China
60 B6 Kenmare Rep. of Ireland
26 C1 Kenmare U.S.A.
60 A6 Kenmare River in. Rep. of Ireland
25 G5 Kenna U.S.A.
33 J2 Kennebec r. U.S.A.
33 H3 Kennebunk U.S.A.
33 H3 Kennebunkport U.S.A.
116 A2 Kennedy Austr.
89 □ Kennedy Town China
27 F6 Kenner U.S.A.
59 F6 Kennet r. U.K.
27 F4 Kennett U.S.A.
24 C2 Kennewick U.S.A.
31 G1 Kenogami Lake Can.
31 G1 Kenogamissi Lake l. Can.
20 B2 Keno Hill Can.
21 L5 Kenora Can.
30 D4 Kenosha U.S.A.
68 F2 Kenozero, Ozero l. Rus. Fed.
58 E3 Kent r. U.K.
33 G4 Kent CT U.S.A.
27 B6 Kent TX U.S.A.
24 B2 Kent WA U.S.A.
105 H6 Kentani S. Africa
82 C2 Kentau Kazak.
115 G7 Kent Group is Austr.
30 D5 Kentland U.S.A.
32 B4 Kenton U.S.A.
32 A6 Kentucky div. U.S.A.
29 B4 Kentucky Lake l. U.S.A.
23 H4 Kentville Can.
27 F6 Kentwood LA U.S.A.
30 E4 Kentwood MI U.S.A.
96 Kenya country Africa
Kenya, Mount mt see Kirinyaga
30 A3 Kenyon U.S.A.
34 □2 Keokea U.S.A.
30 B5 Keokuk U.S.A.
95 C1 Keo Neua, Col de pass Laos/Vietnam
30 B5 Keosauqua U.S.A.
116 D4 Keppel Bay b. Austr.
95 □ Keppel Harbour chan. Sing.
80 B2 Kepsut Turkey
83 E8 Kerala div. India
114 E5 Kerang Austr.
55 T6 Kerava Fin.
65 G4 Kerba Alg.
69 F6 Kerch Ukr.
110 E2 Kerema P.N.G.
20 F5 Keremeos Can.
69 E7 Kerempe Burun pt Turkey
102 D2 Keren Eritrea
81 L4 Kerend Iran
13 J7 Kerguelen Plateau sea feature Indian Ocean
102 D4 Kericho Kenya
117 D1 Kerikeri N.Z.
55 V6 Kerimäki Fin.
92 C7 Kerinci, G. vol. Indon.
85 E2 Keriya Shankou pass China
79 K2 Kerki Turkm.
67 K4 Kerkinitis, Limni l. Greece
67 H5 Kerkyra Greece
Kerkyra i. see Corfu
101 F3 Kerma Sudan
14 J5 Kermadec Islands is Pac. Oc.
14 H8 Kermadec Tr. sea feature Pac. Oc.
79 H3 Kermān Iran
34 B3 Kerman U.S.A.
81 L4 Kermānshāh Iran
27 C6 Kermit U.S.A.
25 C5 Kern r. U.S.A.
34 C4 Kern, South Fork r. U.S.A.
23 G2 Kernertut, Cap pt Can.
34 C4 Kernville U.S.A.
67 L6 Keros i. Greece
68 K2 Keros Rus. Fed.
100 B4 Kérouané Guinea
61 E4 Kerpen Ger.
119 B5 Kerr, C. c. Antarctica
21 H4 Kerrobert Can.
27 D6 Kerrville U.S.A.
60 B5 Kerry Head hd Rep. of Ireland
95 B4 Kerteh Malaysia
55 M9 Kerteminde Denmark
80 D4 Keryneia Cyprus
68 H3 Kerzhenets r. Rus. Fed.
22 D3 Kesagami Lake l. Can.
55 V6 Kesälahti Fin.
69 C7 Keşan Turkey
80 G1 Keşap Turkey
90 G5 Kesennuma Japan
84 B1 Keshem Afgh.
84 A1 Keshendeh-ye Bala Afgh.
84 B5 Keshod India
81 M5 Keshvar Iran
80 D2 Keskin Turkey
68 E2 Keskozero Rus. Fed.
61 E3 Kessel Neth.
105 H4 Kestell S. Africa
54 W4 Kesten'ga Rus. Fed.
54 U4 Kestilä Fin.
31 H3 Keswick Can.
58 D3 Keswick U.K.
62 H7 Keszthely Hungary
76 K4 Ket' r. Rus. Fed.
100 C4 Keta Ghana
95 □ Ketam, P. i. Sing.
92 E7 Ketapang Indon.
20 C3 Ketchikan U.S.A.
61 D2 Ketelmeer l. Neth.
86 D3 Ketmen', Khrebet mts China/Kazak.
59 G5 Kettering U.K.
32 A5 Kettering U.S.A.
20 F5 Kettle r. Can.
30 A2 Kettle r. U.S.A.
32 E4 Kettle Creek r. U.S.A.
34 C3 Kettleman City U.S.A.
24 C1 Kettle River Ra. mts U.S.A.
32 E3 Keuka Lake l. U.S.A.
55 T5 Keuruu Fin.
61 E3 Kevelaer Ger.
30 C5 Kewanee U.S.A.
30 D3 Kewaunee U.S.A.
30 C2 Keweenaw Bay b. U.S.A.
30 C2 Keweenaw Peninsula pen. U.S.A.
30 D2 Keweenaw Pt pt U.S.A.
45 E3 Keweigek Guyana
60 C3 Key, Lough l. Rep. of Ireland
22 F3 Keyano Can.
31 G3 Key Harbour Can.
29 D7 Key Largo U.S.A.
59 E6 Keynsham U.K.
32 D5 Keyser U.S.A.
32 D5 Keysers Ridge U.S.A.
35 G6 Keystone Peak summit U.S.A.
32 D6 Keysville U.S.A.
81 M4 Keytū Iran
29 D7 Key West FL U.S.A.
30 B4 Key West IA U.S.A.
33 H3 Kezar Falls U.S.A.
103 C6 Kezi Zimbabwe
63 K6 Kežmarok Slovakia
104 D2 Kgalagadi div. Botswana
105 G2 Kgatleng div. Botswana
104 D1 Kgomofatshe Pan salt pan Botswana
104 F2 Kgoro Pan salt pan Botswana
105 G3 Kgotsong S. Africa
87 P2 Khabarovsk Rus. Fed.
81 H4 Khābūr, Nahr al r. Syria
81 J7 Khadd, W. al watercourse Saudi Arabia
84 E4 Khaga India
85 G5 Khagrachari Bangl.
84 B3 Khairgarh Pak.
84 B4 Khairpur Pak.
84 D4 Khajurāho India
103 C6 Khakhea Botswana
81 M4 Khalajestan reg. Iran
84 D2 Khalatse Jammu and Kashmir
84 A3 Khalifat mt Pak.
81 M3 Khalkhāl Iran
85 F6 Khallikot India
68 D4 Khalopyenichy Belarus
86 H1 Khamar-Daban, Khrebet mts Rus. Fed.
84 C5 Khambhat India
84 B6 Khambhat, Gulf of g. India
84 D5 Khamgaon India
95 C1 Khamkkeut Laos
83 F7 Khammam India
77 N3 Khamra Rus. Fed.
81 M4 Khamseh reg. Iran
95 B1 Khan, Nam r. Laos
84 B1 Khānābād Afgh.
81 J5 Khān al Baghdādī Iraq
81 K5 Khān al Maḩāwīl Iraq
81 K5 Khān al Mashāhidah Iraq
81 K5 Khān al Muşallá Iraq
81 K3 Khānaqāh Iran
81 K4 Khānaqīn Iraq
81 K6 Khān ar Raḩbah Iraq
81 K2 Khanasur Pass pass Iran/Turkey
80 F6 Khān az Zabīb Jordan
84 C2 Khanbari Pass pass Jammu and Kashmir
115 H6 Khancoban Austr.
84 B2 Khand Pass pass Afgh./Pak.
84 D5 Khandwa India
77 P3 Khandyga Rus. Fed.
84 B3 Khanewal Pak.
95 D2 Khanh Dương Vietnam
84 D4 Khaniadhana India
81 K5 Khān Jadwal Iraq
90 C2 Khanka, Lake l. China/Rus. Fed.
Khanka, Ozero l. see Khanka, Lake
84 C2 Khanki Weir barrage Pak.
84 D3 Khanna India
84 B3 Khanpur Pak.
80 F4 Khān Shaykhūn Syria
82 D2 Khantau Kazak.
76 L3 Khantayskoye, Ozero l. Rus. Fed.
76 H3 Khanty-Mansiysk Rus. Fed.
80 E6 Khān Yūnis Gaza
95 A3 Khao Chum Thong Thai.
84 D5 Khapa India
82 E3 Khapalu Pak.
87 K2 Khapcheranga Rus. Fed.
69 H6 Kharabali Rus. Fed.
85 F5 Kharagpur India
Kharari see Abu Road
84 C6 Khardi India
84 D2 Khardung La pass India
81 L6 Kharfiyah Iraq
84 C5 Khargon India
84 C4 Khari r. Rajasthan India
84 C4 Khari r. Rajasthan India
84 C2 Kharian Pak.
85 E5 Khariar India
69 F5 Kharkiv Ukr.
Khar'kov see Kharkiv
67 L4 Kharmanli Bulg.
68 G3 Kharovsk Rus. Fed.
81 M4 Khar Rūd r. Iran
85 E5 Kharsia India
101 F3 Khartoum Sudan
69 H7 Khasav'yurt Rus. Fed.
79 J4 Khāsh Iran
78 D7 Khashm el Girba Sudan
69 G7 Khashuri Georgia
85 G4 Khāsi Hills h. India
67 L4 Khaskovo Bulg.
77 M2 Khatanga Rus. Fed.
77 M2 Khatangskiy Zaliv b. Rus. Fed.
84 B1 Khatinza Pass pass Pak.
80 D6 Khatmia Pass pass Egypt
77 T3 Khatyrka Rus. Fed.
79 K1 Khavast Uzbek.
84 B5 Khavda India
84 B2 Khawak Pass pass Afgh.
95 A2 Khawsa Myanmar
105 F5 Khayamnandi S. Africa
79 L2 Khaydarken Kyrgyzstan
104 C7 Khayelitsha S. Africa
81 J3 Khāzir r. Iraq
95 C1 Khê Bo Vietnam
84 C4 Khedbrahma India
83 E3 Khela India
65 H4 Khemis Miliana Alg.
95 C1 Khemmarat Thai.
100 C1 Khenchela Alg.
100 B1 Khenifra Morocco
84 D4 Kherli India
69 E6 Kherson Ukr.
77 L2 Kheta r. Rus. Fed.
84 D4 Khilchipur India
87 K1 Khilok Rus. Fed.
80 F4 Khirbat Isrīyah Syria
84 D2 Khitai P. pass China/Jammu and Kashmir
81 L2 Khīyāv Iran
55 V6 Khiytola Rus. Fed.
95 B2 Khlong, Mae r. Thai.
69 C5 Khmel'nyts'kyy Ukr.
69 C5 Khmil'nyk Ukr.
81 L2 Khodā Āfarīn Iran
79 H1 Khodzheyli Uzbek.
104 D2 Khokhowe Pan salt pan Botswana
84 B4 Khokhropar Pak.
79 K2 Kholm Afgh.
68 G1 Kholmogory Rus. Fed.
87 Q2 Kholmsk Rus. Fed.
63 Q3 Kholm-Zhirkovskiy Rus. Fed.
81 M3 Khoman Iran
104 B1 Khomas div. Namibia
104 A1 Khomas Highland reg. Namibia
81 M4 Khondāb Iran
69 G7 Khoni Georgia
95 B1 Khon Kaen Thai.
77 Q3 Khonuu Rus. Fed.
69 G5 Khoper r. Rus. Fed.
87 O2 Khor Rus. Fed.
87 O2 Khor r. Rus. Fed.
84 B4 Khora Pak.
85 F5 Khordha India
87 J1 Khorinsk Rus. Fed.
103 B6 Khorixas Namibia
69 C2 Khorol Rus. Fed.
69 E5 Khorol Ukr.
81 L2 Khoroslū Dāgh h. Iran
81 M5 Khorramābād Iran
81 M3 Khorram Darreh Iran
81 M6 Khorramshahr Iran
79 L2 Khorugh Tajik.
69 H6 Khosheutovo Rus. Fed.
81 M6 Khosravī Iran
81 M6 Khosrowābād Iran
81 K4 Khosrowvī Iran
84 C1 Khotgaz pass Afgh.
84 B2 Khowst Afgh.
85 H5 Khreum Myanmar
85 G4 Khri r. India
68 H2 Khristoforovo Rus. Fed.
76 Q2 Khroma r. Rus. Fed.
76 G4 Khromtau Kazak.
90 D2 Khrustalnyy Rus. Fed.
63 O6 Khrystynivka Ukr.
104 F1 Khudumelapye Botswana
104 D3 Khuis Botswana
79 K1 Khŭjand Tajik.
95 C2 Khu Khan Thai.
84 A1 Khulm r. Afgh.
85 G5 Khulna Bangl.
81 J1 Khulo Georgia
105 G3 Khuma S. Africa
84 C2 Khunjerab Pass pass China/Jammu and Kashmir
79 G3 Khunsar Iran
85 F5 Khunti India
95 A1 Khun Yuam Thai.
84 D4 Khurai India
84 D3 Khurja India
81 J6 Khurr, Wādī al watercourse Saudi Arabia
84 C2 Khushab Pak.
81 M3 Khūshāvar Iran
69 B5 Khust Ukr.
105 G3 Khutsong S. Africa
68 J4 Khvalynsk Rus. Fed.
81 L3 Khvosh Maqām Iran
81 K2 Khvoy Iran
68 E3 Khvoynaya Rus. Fed.
95 A2 Khwae Noi r. Thai.
84 B2 Khwaja Kuram mt Afgh.
84 B1 Khwaja Muhammad Ra. mts Afgh.
84 B2 Khyber Pass pass Afgh./Pak.
115 J5 Kiama Austr.
94 C5 Kiamba Phil.
102 C4 Kiambi Dem. Rep. Congo
27 E5 Kiamichi r. U.S.A.
54 V4 Kiantajärvi l. Fin.
84 D2 Kibar India
94 C5 Kibawe Phil.
102 D4 Kibaya Tanz.
103 D4 Kibiti Tanz.
102 C4 Kibombo Dem. Rep. Congo
102 D4 Kibondo Tanz.
67 J4 Kičevo Macedonia
68 H3 Kichmengskiy Gorodok Rus. Fed.
100 C3 Kidal Mali
59 E5 Kidderminster U.K.
102 D3 Kidepo Valley National Park nat. park Uganda
100 A3 Kidira Senegal
84 D2 Kidmang Jammu and Kashmir
117 F3 Kidnappers, Cape c. N.Z.
59 E4 Kidsgrove U.K.
62 E3 Kiel Ger.
30 C4 Kiel U.S.A.
63 K5 Kielce Pol.
58 E2 Kielder Water resr U.K.
62 E3 Kieler Bucht b. Ger.
103 C5 Kienge Dem. Rep. Congo
61 F3 Kierspe Ger.
69 D5 Kiev Ukr.
100 A3 Kiffa Maur.
67 K5 Kifisia Greece
81 K4 Kifrī Iraq
102 D4 Kigali Rwanda
81 H2 Kiğı Turkey
23 H2 Kiglapait Mts mts Can.
102 C4 Kigoma Tanz.
54 S3 Kihlanki Fin.
55 S5 Kihniö Fin.
54 T4 Kiiminki Fin.
91 D8 Kii-sanchi mts Japan
91 D8 Kii-suidō chan. Japan
67 J2 Kikinda Serb. and Mont.
68 H3 Kiknur Rus. Fed.
90 G4 Kikonai Japan
103 C4 Kikondja Dem. Rep. Congo
110 E2 Kikori P.N.G.
110 E2 Kikori r. P.N.G.
102 B4 Kikwit Dem. Rep. Congo
55 P6 Kilafors Sweden
84 D2 Kilar India
34 □2 Kilauea U.S.A.
34 □2 Kilauea Crater crater U.S.A.
57 C5 Kilbrannan Sound chan. U.K.
90 A4 Kilchu N. Korea
60 E4 Kilcoole Rep. of Ireland
60 D4 Kilcormac Rep. of Ireland
115 K1 Kilcoy Austr.
60 E4 Kildare Rep. of Ireland
54 X2 Kil'dinstroy Rus. Fed.
102 B4 Kilembe Dem. Rep. Congo
57 C5 Kilfinan U.K.
27 E5 Kilgore U.S.A.
58 E2 Kilham U.K.
102 D4 Kilifi Kenya
102 D4 Kilimanjaro mt Tanz.
111 F2 Kilinailau Is is P.N.G.
103 D4 Kilindoni Tanz.
55 T7 Kilingi-Nõmme Estonia
80 F3 Kilis Turkey
69 D6 Kiliya Ukr.
60 B5 Kilkee Rep. of Ireland
60 F3 Kilkeel U.K.
60 D5 Kilkenny Rep. of Ireland
59 C7 Kilkhampton U.K.
67 K4 Kilkis Greece
116 E6 Kilkivan Austr.
60 B3 Killala Rep. of Ireland
60 B3 Killala Bay b. Rep. of Ireland
60 C5 Killaloe Rep. of Ireland
31 J3 Killaloe Station Can.
21 G4 Killam Can.
115 K2 Killarney Austr.
31 G3 Killarney Can.
60 B5 Killarney Rep. of Ireland
60 B6 Killarney National Park nat. park Rep. of Ireland
31 G2 Killarney Provincial Park nat. park Can.
60 B4 Killary Harbour b. Rep. of Ireland
27 D6 Killeen U.S.A.
60 D5 Killenaule Rep. of Ireland
60 C4 Killimor Rep. of Ireland
57 D4 Killin U.K.
60 F3 Killinchy U.K.
60 E5 Killinick Rep. of Ireland
23 H1 Killiniq Can.
23 H1 Killiniq Island i. Can.
60 B5 Killorglin Rep. of Ireland
60 E5 Killurin Rep. of Ireland
60 C3 Killybegs Rep. of Ireland
60 D2 Kilmacrenan Rep. of Ireland
60 B4 Kilmaine Rep. of Ireland
60 C5 Kilmallock Rep. of Ireland
57 B3 Kilmaluag U.K.
57 D5 Kilmarnock U.K.
57 C4 Kilmelford U.K.
68 J3 Kil'mez' Rus. Fed.
68 J3 Kil'mez' r. Rus. Fed.
60 C6 Kilmona Rep. of Ireland
114 F6 Kilmore Austr.
60 E5 Kilmore Quay Rep. of Ireland
102 D4 Kilosa Tanz.
54 R2 Kilpisjärvi Fin.
54 X2 Kilp"yavr Rus. Fed.
60 E3 Kilrea U.K.
60 B5 Kilrush Rep. of Ireland
57 D5 Kilsyth U.K.
83 D8 Kiltān i. India
60 C4 Kiltullagh Rep. of Ireland
103 C4 Kilwa Dem. Rep. Congo
103 D4 Kilwa Masoko Tanz.
57 D5 Kilwinning U.K.
103 D4 Kimambi Tanz.
114 B4 Kimba Austr.
102 B4 Kimba Congo
26 C3 Kimball U.S.A.
110 F2 Kimbe P.N.G.
20 F5 Kimberley Can.
104 F4 Kimberley S. Africa
112 E3 Kimberley Plateau plat. Austr.
117 E4 Kimbolton N.Z.
87 N3 Kimch'aek N. Korea
55 S6 Kimito Fin.
67 L6 Kimolos i. Greece
68 F4 Kimovsk Rus. Fed.
102 B4 Kimpese Dem. Rep. Congo
91 F5 Kimpoku-san mt Japan
68 F3 Kimry Rus. Fed.
102 B4 Kimvula Dem. Rep. Congo
92 F5 Kinabalu, Gunung mt Malaysia
94 A5 Kinabatangan r. Malaysia
67 M6 Kinaros i. Greece
57 E2 Kinbrace U.K.
31 G3 Kincardine Can.
57 E4 Kincardine U.K.
114 E4 Kinchega National Park nat. park Austr.
20 D3 Kincolith Can.
103 C4 Kinda Dem. Rep. Congo
85 H5 Kindat Myanmar
27 E6 Kinder U.S.A.
59 F4 Kinder Scout h. U.K.
21 H4 Kindersley Can.
100 A3 Kindia Guinea
102 C4 Kindu Dem. Rep. Congo
68 G3 Kineshma Rus. Fed.
116 D6 Kingaroy Austr.
18 King Christian IX Land reg. Greenland
18 King Christian X Land reg. Greenland
34 B3 King City U.S.A.
119 C1 King Edward Point U.K. Base Antarctica
32 E3 King Ferry U.S.A.
33 H2 Kingfield U.S.A.
27 D5 Kingfisher U.S.A.
18 King Frederik VI Coast reg. Greenland
18 King Frederik VIII Land reg. Greenland
119 B1 King George I. i. Antarctica
22 E2 King George Islands is Can.
20 D4 King I. i. Can.
68 D3 Kingisepp Rus. Fed.
115 F8 King Island i. Austr.
31 H1 King Kirkland Can.
112 D3 King Leopold Ranges h. Austr.
35 E4 Kingman AZ U.S.A.
27 D4 Kingman KS U.S.A.
33 J2 Kingman ME U.S.A.
20 D3 King Mtn mt Can.
114 A3 Kingoonya Austr.
18 King Oscar Fjord fjord Greenland
60 D5 Kings r. Rep. of Ireland
34 C3 Kings r. U.S.A.
59 D7 Kingsbridge U.K.
34 C3 Kingsburg U.S.A.
33 J2 Kingsbury U.S.A.
34 C3 Kings Canyon National Park nat. park U.S.A.
115 K2 Kingscliff Austr.
114 B5 Kingscote Austr.
60 E4 Kingscourt Rep. of Ireland
119 B2 King Sejong Korea Base Antarctica
30 C3 Kingsford U.S.A.
29 D6 Kingsland GA U.S.A.
30 E5 Kingsland IN U.S.A.
59 H5 King's Lynn U.K.
111 H2 Kingsmill Group is Kiribati
59 H6 Kingsnorth U.K.
112 D3 King Sound b. Austr.
24 E3 Kings Peak summit U.S.A.
32 B6 Kingsport U.S.A.
31 J3 Kingston Can.
37 J5 Kingston Jamaica
117 B6 Kingston N.Z.
30 B6 Kingston IL U.S.A.

114 C4 Mannahill Austr.
83 E9 Mannar Sri Lanka
83 E9 Mannar, Gulf of *g.* India/Sri Lanka
62 D6 Mannheim Ger.
60 A4 Mannin Bay *b.* Rep. of Ireland
20 F3 Manning Can.
29 D5 Manning U.S.A.
59 J6 Manningtree U.K.
66 C4 Mannu, Capo *pt* Italy
114 C5 Mannum Austr.
93 J7 Manokwari Indon.
102 C4 Manono Dem. Rep. Congo
95 A3 Manoron Myanmar
64 G5 Manosque France
111 J2 Manra *i.* Kiribati
65 G2 Manresa Spain
84 C3 Mānsa India
103 C5 Mansa Zambia
100 A3 Mansa Konko The Gambia
84 C2 Mansehra Pak.
118 A2 Mansel I. *i.* Can.
115 G6 Mansfield Austr.
59 F4 Mansfield U.K.
27 E5 Mansfield *LA* U.S.A.
32 B4 Mansfield *OH* U.S.A.
32 E4 Mansfield *PA* U.S.A.
20 E3 Manson Creek Can.
81 M6 Manşūrī Iran
80 E3 Mansurlu Turkey
42 B4 Manta Ecuador
42 B4 Manta, B. de *b.* Ecuador
94 A4 Mantalingajan, Mount *mt* Phil.
34 B3 Manteca U.S.A.
45 C3 Mantecal Venez.
29 F5 Manteo U.S.A.
64 E2 Mantes-la-Jolie France
35 G2 Manti U.S.A.
46 D3 Mantiqueira, Serra da *mts* Brazil
30 E3 Manton U.S.A.
66 D2 Mantova Italy
55 T6 Mäntsälä Fin.
55 T5 Mänttä Fin.
Mantua *see* Mantova
116 B5 Mantuan Downs Austr.
68 H3 Manturovo Rus. Fed.
55 U6 Mäntyharju Fin.
54 U3 Mäntyjärvi Fin.
42 D6 Manu, Parque Nacional *nat. park* Peru
35 H4 Manuelito U.S.A.
47 F2 Manuel J. Cobo Arg.
46 E1 Manuel Vitorino Brazil
43 H5 Manuelzinho Brazil
93 G7 Manui *i.* Indon.
94 B4 Manukan Phil.
117 E2 Manukau N.Z.
117 E2 Manukau Harbour *in.* N.Z.
94 A5 Manuk Manka *i.* Phil.
114 C4 Manunda *watercourse* Austr.
110 E2 Manus I. *i.* P.N.G.
105 F2 Manyana Botswana
69 G6 Manych-Gudilo, Ozero *l.* Rus. Fed.
35 H3 Many Farms U.S.A.
102 D4 Manyoni Tanz.
116 D5 Many Peaks Austr.
80 D6 Manzala, Bahra el *l.* Egypt
65 E3 Manzanares Spain
37 J4 Manzanillo Cuba
36 D5 Manzanillo Mex.
87 L2 Manzhouli China
105 J3 Manzini Swaziland
101 D3 Mao Chad
Maó *see* Mahón
88 D4 Maocifan China
88 C2 Maojiachuan China
93 K7 Maoke, Pegunungan *mts* Indon.
105 G3 Maokeng S. Africa
88 B2 Maomao Shan *mt* China
89 D6 Maoming China
89 □ Ma On Shan *h.* China
103 D6 Mapai Moz.
84 E3 Mapam Yumco *l.* China
93 G7 Mapane Indon.
105 F5 Maphodi S. Africa
27 C7 Mapimí Mex.
36 D3 Mapimí, Bolsón de *des.* Mex.
94 A5 Mapin *i.* Phil.
103 D6 Mapinhane Moz.
45 D3 Mapire Venez.
30 E4 Maple *r.* U.S.A.
21 H5 Maple Creek Can.
105 G4 Mapoteng Lesotho
115 J7 Maprik P.N.G.
43 G4 Mapuera *r.* Brazil
105 K2 Mapulanguene Moz.
103 D6 Maputo Moz.
105 K2 Maputo *div.* Moz.
105 K3 Maputo *r.* Moz.
105 G4 Maputsoe Lesotho
81 H6 Maqar an Na'am *w.* Iraq
88 B3 Maqu China
85 F3 Maquan He *r.* China
102 B4 Maquela do Zombo Angola
47 C4 Maquinchao Arg.
47 C4 Maquinchao *r.* Arg.
30 B4 Maquoketa U.S.A.
30 B4 Maquoketa *r.* U.S.A.
46 D3 Mar, Serra do *mts* Brazil
21 H1 Mara *r.* Can.
85 E5 Māra India
105 H1 Mara S. Africa
45 C2 Mara Venez.
42 E4 Maraã Brazil
43 J5 Maraba Brazil
116 C4 Maraboon, L. *resr* Austr.
43 H3 Maracá, Ilha de *i.* Brazil
45 C2 Maracaibo Venez.
45 C2 Maracaibo, Lago de *l.* Venez.
46 A3 Maracaju Brazil
46 A3 Maracaju, Serra de *h.* Brazil
46 E1 Maracás, Chapada de *reg.* Brazil
45 D2 Maracay Venez.
101 D2 Marādah Libya
100 C3 Maradi Niger
81 L3 Marāgheh Iran
46 E1 Maragogipe Brazil
94 B3 Maragondon Phil.
45 D4 Marahuaca, Co *mt* Venez.
43 J4 Marajó, Baía de *est.* Brazil
43 J3 Marajó, Ilha de *i.* Brazil
102 D3 Maralal Kenya
84 C2 Marala Weir *barrage* Pak.
81 J1 Maralik Armenia
112 F6 Maralinga Austr.
111 G2 Maramasike *i.* Solomon Is
94 C5 Marampit *i.* Indon.
81 K4 Marāna Iraq
35 G5 Marana U.S.A.
81 K2 Marand Iran
95 B4 Marang Malaysia
95 A3 Marang Myanmar
46 C1 Maranhão *r.* Brazil
116 C6 Maranoa *r.* Austr.
42 D4 Marañón *r.* Peru
105 L2 Marão Moz.
65 C2 Marão *mt* Port.
45 D4 Marari *r.* Brazil
117 A6 Mararoa *r.* N.Z.
30 D1 Marathon Can.
29 D7 Marathon *FL* U.S.A.
27 C6 Marathon *TX* U.S.A.
46 E1 Maraú Brazil
45 D4 Marauiá *r.* Brazil
94 C4 Marawi Phil.
81 M1 Märäzä Azer.
65 D4 Marbella Spain
112 C4 Marble Bar Austr.
35 G3 Marble Canyon U.S.A.
35 G3 Marble Canyon *gorge* U.S.A.
105 H2 Marble Hall S. Africa
33 H3 Marblehead U.S.A.
21 L2 Marble I. *i.* Can.
105 J5 Marburg S. Africa
33 E5 Marburg, Lake *l.* U.S.A.
62 D5 Marburg an der Lahn Ger.
62 H7 Marcali Hungary
59 H5 March U.K.
114 D4 Marchant Hill *h.* Austr.
61 D4 Marche-en-Famenne Belgium
65 D4 Marchena Spain
42 □ Marchena, Isla *i.* Ecuador
47 D1 Mar Chiquita, L. *l.* Arg.
62 G6 Marchtrenk Austria
29 D7 Marco U.S.A.
22 E2 Marcopeet Islands *is* Can.
47 D2 Marcos Juárez Arg.
33 G2 Marcy, Mt *mt* U.S.A.
84 C2 Mardan Pak.
47 F3 Mar del Plata Arg.
81 H3 Mardin Turkey
111 G4 Maré *i.* New Caledonia
57 C3 Maree, Loch *l.* U.K.
116 A1 Mareeba Austr.
30 A5 Marengo *IA* U.S.A.
30 C4 Marengo *IL* U.S.A.
66 E6 Marettimo, Isola *i.* Italy
68 E3 Marevo Rus. Fed.
27 B6 Marfa U.S.A.
114 B2 Margaret *watercourse* Austr.
112 C6 Margaret River Austr.
45 E2 Margarita, Isla de *i.* Venez.
90 D3 Margaritovo Rus. Fed.
115 G9 Margate Austr.
105 J5 Margate S. Africa
59 J6 Margate U.K.
79 L1 Margilan Uzbek.
79 J3 Margo, Dasht-i *des.* Afgh.
94 B5 Margosatubig Phil.
61 D4 Margraten Neth.
30 E3 Margrethe, Lake *l.* U.S.A.
20 E4 Marguerite Can.
119 B2 Marguerite Bay *b.* Antarctica
85 G3 Margyang China
81 L5 Marhaj Khalīl Iraq
81 J3 Marhan D. *h.* Iraq
69 E6 Marhanets' Ukr.
15 J7 Maria *is* Pac. Oc.
44 C2 María Elena Chile
113 G2 Maria I. *i.* *N.T.* Austr.
115 H9 Maria I. *i.* *Tas.* Austr.
47 E3 María Ignacia Arg.
116 C3 Marian Austr.
14 E4 Mariana Ridge *sea feature* Pac. Oc.
14 E5 Mariana Trench *sea feature* Pac. Oc.
85 H4 Mariani India
20 F2 Marian Lake *l.* Can.
27 F5 Marianna *AR* U.S.A.
29 C6 Marianna *FL* U.S.A.
62 F6 Mariánské Lázně Czech Rep.
36 C4 Marías, Islas *is* Mex.
37 H7 Mariato, Pta *pt* Panama
117 D1 Maria van Diemen, Cape *c.* N.Z.
66 F1 Maribor Slovenia
35 F5 Maricopa *AZ* U.S.A.
34 C4 Maricopa *CA* U.S.A.
35 F5 Maricopa Mts *mts* U.S.A.
101 E4 Maridi *watercourse* Sudan
119 A4 Marie Byrd Land *reg.* Antarctica
37 M5 Marie-Galante *i.* Guadeloupe
55 Q6 Mariehamn Fin.
46 B1 Mariembero *r.* Brazil
103 B6 Mariental Namibia
55 N7 Mariestad Sweden
29 C5 Marietta *GA* U.S.A.
32 C5 Marietta *OH* U.S.A.
64 G5 Marignane France
76 K4 Mariinsk Rus. Fed.
55 S9 Marijampolė Lith.
46 C3 Marília Brazil
27 C7 Marín Mex.
65 B1 Marín Spain
66 G5 Marina di Gioiosa Ionica Italy
68 D4 Mar''ina Horka Belarus
94 B3 Marinduque *i.* Phil.
30 D3 Marinette U.S.A.
46 B3 Maringá Brazil
65 B3 Marinha Grande Port.
28 B4 Marion *IL* U.S.A.
30 E5 Marion *IN* U.S.A.
33 K2 Marion *ME* U.S.A.
32 B4 Marion *OH* U.S.A.
29 E5 Marion *SC* U.S.A.
32 C6 Marion *VA* U.S.A.
29 D5 Marion, L. *l.* U.S.A.
114 B5 Marion Bay Austr.
116 E2 Marion Reef *rf* Coral Sea Is Terr.
45 D3 Maripa Venez.
34 C3 Mariposa U.S.A.
44 D2 Mariscal Estigarribia Para.
64 H4 Maritime Alps *mts* France/Italy
67 L3 Maritsa *r.* Bulg.
68 J3 Mari-Turek Rus. Fed.
69 F6 Mariupol' Ukr.
81 L4 Marīvān Iran
68 J3 Mariy El, Respublika *div.* Rus. Fed.
102 E3 Marka Somalia
82 J5 Markam China
81 K2 Markān Iran
55 N8 Markaryd Sweden
31 G3 Markdale Can.
61 D2 Marken *i.* Neth.
105 H1 Marken S. Africa
61 D2 Markermeer *l.* Neth.
59 G5 Market Deeping U.K.
59 E5 Market Drayton U.K.
59 G5 Market Harborough U.K.
60 E3 Markethill U.K.
58 G4 Market Weighton U.K.
77 N3 Markha *r.* Rus. Fed.
31 H4 Markham Can.
69 F5 Markivka Ukr.
77 T3 Markovo Rus. Fed.
69 H5 Marks Rus. Fed.
62 D6 Marktheidenfeld Ger.
62 E7 Marktoberdorf Ger.
30 B6 Mark Twain Lake *l.* U.S.A.
61 F3 Marl Ger.
113 F5 Marla Austr.
116 C4 Marlborough Austr.
33 H3 Marlborough U.S.A.
59 F6 Marlborough Downs *h.* U.K.
27 D6 Marlin U.S.A.
32 C5 Marlinton U.S.A.
115 H6 Marlo Austr.
64 E4 Marmande France
80 B1 Marmara, Sea of *g.* Turkey
Marmara Denizi *g. see* Marmara, Sea of
80 B2 Marmara Gölü *l.* Turkey
80 B3 Marmaris Turkey
26 C2 Marmarth U.S.A.
32 C5 Marmet U.S.A.
22 B4 Marmion L. *l.* Can.
66 D1 Marmolada *mt* Italy
64 F2 Marne-la-Vallée France
81 K1 Marneuli Georgia
114 E6 Marnoo Austr.
103 E5 Maroantsetra Madag.
103 E5 Maromokotro *mt* Madag.
103 D5 Marondera Zimbabwe
43 H2 Maroni *r.* Fr. Guiana
115 K1 Maroochydore Austr.
109 Marotiri *is* Pac. Oc.
101 D3 Maroua Cameroon
103 E5 Marovoay Madag.
81 H4 Marqādah Syria
88 A3 Mar Qu *r.* China
105 G4 Marquard S. Africa
29 D7 Marquesas Keys *is* U.S.A.
30 D2 Marquette U.S.A.
109 Marquises, Îles *is* Pac. Oc.
114 E3 Marra Austr.
115 G3 Marra *r.* Austr.
105 K2 Marracuene Moz.
100 B1 Marrakech Morocco
Marrakesh *see* Marrakech
105 L2 Marrangua, Lagoa *l.* Moz.
101 E3 Marra Plateau *plat.* Sudan
115 G5 Marrar Austr.
115 F8 Marrawah Austr.
114 C2 Marree Austr.
27 F6 Marrero U.S.A.
103 D5 Marromeu Moz.
103 D5 Marrupa Moz.
78 C4 Marsá al 'Alam Egypt
101 D1 Marsa al Burayqah Libya
102 D3 Marsabit Kenya
66 E6 Marsala Italy
78 B3 Marsá Maţrūḩ Egypt
66 G3 Marsciano Italy
115 G4 Marsden Austr.
61 C2 Marsdiep *chan.* Neth.
64 G5 Marseille France
30 C5 Marseilles U.S.A.
54 O4 Marsfjället *mt* Sweden
21 H4 Marshall Can.
27 E5 Marshall *AR* U.S.A.
28 C4 Marshall *IL* U.S.A.
30 E4 Marshall *MI* U.S.A.
26 E2 Marshall *MN* U.S.A.
26 E4 Marshall *MO* U.S.A.
27 E5 Marshall *TX* U.S.A.
115 G7 Marshall B. *b.* Austr.
106 Marshall Islands *is* Pac. Oc.
26 E3 Marshalltown U.S.A.
30 B3 Marshfield U.S.A.
29 E7 Marsh Harbour Bahamas
33 K1 Mars Hill U.S.A.
27 F6 Marsh Island *i.* U.S.A.
20 C2 Marsh Lake *l.* Can.
81 M3 Marshūn Iran
24 C3 Marsing U.S.A.
55 P7 Märsta Sweden
85 F4 Marsyangdi *r.* Nepal
95 A1 Martaban Myanmar
83 J7 Martaban, Gulf of *g.* Myanmar
92 E7 Martapura Indon.
92 C7 Martapura Indon.
31 H2 Marten River Can.
21 H4 Martensville Can.
27 D7 Marte R. Gómez, Presa *resr* Mex.
27 D7 Marte R. Gómez, Presa
33 H4 Martha's Vineyard *i.* U.S.A.
62 C7 Martigny Switz.
63 J6 Martin Slovakia
26 C3 Martin *SD* U.S.A.
29 B4 Martin *TN* U.S.A.
35 C5 Martin, L. *l.* U.S.A.
35 E5 Martinez Lake U.S.A.
37 M6 Martinique *terr.* Caribbean
119 A3 Martin Pen. *pen.* Antarctica
32 D4 Martinsburg *PA* U.S.A.
32 E5 Martinsburg *WV* U.S.A.
32 C4 Martins Ferry U.S.A.
32 D6 Martinsville U.S.A.
12 H7 Martin Vas, Ilhas *is* Atlantic Ocean
117 E4 Marton N.Z.
65 G2 Martorell Spain
65 E4 Martos Spain
76 G4 Martuk Kazak.
81 K1 Martuni Armenia
91 C7 Marugame Japan
117 D5 Maruia *r.* N.Z.
43 L6 Maruim Brazil
69 G7 Marukhis Ugheltekhili *pass* Georgia/Rus. Fed.
115 H5 Marulan Austr.
64 F4 Marvejols France
35 G2 Marvine, Mt *mt* U.S.A.
21 G4 Marwayne Can.
116 E6 Mary *r.* Austr.
79 J2 Mary Turkm.
116 E5 Maryborough *Qld.* Austr.
114 E6 Maryborough *Vic.* Austr.
104 E4 Marydale S. Africa
68 J4 Mar'yevka Rus. Fed.
21 H2 Mary Frances Lake *l.* Can.
33 E5 Maryland *div.* U.S.A.
58 D3 Maryport U.K.
23 J3 Mary's Harbour Can.
23 K4 Marystown Can.
35 F2 Marysvale U.S.A.
23 G4 Marysville Can.
34 B2 Marysville *CA* U.S.A.
26 D4 Marysville *KS* U.S.A.
32 B4 Marysville *OH* U.S.A.
116 A2 Maryvale Austr.
37 H1 Maryville Tennessee
23 E5 Maryville U.S.A.
102 D4 Masai Steppe *plain* Tanz.
102 D4 Masaka Uganda
105 G5 Masakhane S. Africa
81 M2 Masallı Azer.
93 G7 Masamba Indon.
87 N4 Masan S. Korea
33 J1 Masardis U.S.A.
103 D5 Masasi Tanz.
42 F7 Masaví Bol.
94 B3 Masbate Phil.
94 B4 Masbate *i.* Phil.
100 C1 Mascara Alg.
13 H4 Mascarene Basin *sea feature* Indian Ocean
13 J4 Mascarene Ridge *sea feature* Indian Ocean
33 G2 Mascouche Can.
105 G4 Maseru Lesotho
105 H4 Mashai Lesotho
89 C6 Mashan China
84 D2 Masherbrum *mt* Pak.
79 H2 Mashhad Iran
84 C4 Mashi *r.* India
81 L2 Mashīrān Iran
54 S2 Masi Norway
105 G5 Masibambane S. Africa
105 G4 Masilo S. Africa
102 D3 Masindi Uganda
94 A3 Masinloc Phil.
104 E5 Masinyusane S. Africa
79 H6 Maşīrah, Gulf of *b.* Oman
79 H5 Maşīrah, Jazīrat *i.* Oman
81 K1 Masis Armenia
81 M6 Masjed Soleymān Iran
60 B4 Mask, Lough *l.* Rep. of Ireland
80 G3 Maskanah Syria
103 F5 Masoala, Tanjona *c.* Madag.
30 E4 Mason *MI* U.S.A.
34 C2 Mason *NV* U.S.A.
27 D6 Mason *TX* U.S.A.
117 A7 Mason Bay *b.* N.Z.
26 E3 Mason City *IA* U.S.A.
30 C5 Mason City *IL* U.S.A.
32 D5 Masontown U.S.A.
Masqaţ *see* Muscat
66 D2 Massa Italy
33 G3 Massachusetts *div.* U.S.A.
33 H3 Massachusetts Bay *b.* U.S.A.
35 H1 Massadona U.S.A.
66 G4 Massafra Italy
101 D3 Massakory Chad
66 D3 Massa Marittimo Italy
103 D6 Massangena Moz.
103 B4 Massango Angola
102 D2 Massawa Eritrea
33 G2 Massawippi, Lac *l.* Can.
33 F2 Massena U.S.A.
20 C4 Masset Can.
31 F2 Massey Can.
64 F4 Massif Central *mts* France
32 C4 Massillon U.S.A.
100 B3 Massina Mali
103 D6 Massinga Moz.
103 D6 Massingir Moz.
105 K1 Massingir, Barragem de *resr* Moz.
105 K2 Massintonto *r.* Moz./S. Africa
31 K3 Masson Can.
81 M1 Maştağa Azer.
117 E4 Masterton N.Z.
67 M5 Masticho, Akra *pt* Greece
29 E7 Mastic Point Bahamas
84 C1 Mastuj Pak.
79 K4 Mastung Pak.
68 C4 Masty Belarus
91 B7 Masuda Japan
81 M3 Masuleh Iran
103 D6 Masvingo Zimbabwe
80 F4 Maşyāf Syria
31 G2 Matachewan Can.
25 F6 Matachic Mex.
45 D4 Matacuni *r.* Venez.
102 B4 Matadi Dem. Rep. Congo
37 G6 Matagalpa Nic.
22 E4 Matagami Can.
22 E4 Matagami, Lac *l.* Can.
27 D6 Matagorda I. *i.* U.S.A.
95 C5 Matak *i.* Indon.
117 F2 Matakana Island *i.* N.Z.
103 B5 Matala Angola
100 A3 Matam Senegal
36 D3 Matamoros *Coahuila* Mex.
36 E3 Matamoros *Tamaulipas* Mex.
94 B5 Matanal Point *pt* Phil.
103 D4 Matandu *r.* Tanz.
23 G4 Matane Can.
84 B2 Matanui Pak.
37 H4 Matanzas Cuba
Matapan, Cape *pt see* Tainaro, Akra
23 G4 Matapédia *r.* Can.
47 B2 Mataquito *r.* Chile
83 F9 Matara Sri Lanka
92 F8 Mataram Indon.
42 D7 Matarani Peru
112 F2 Mataranka Austr.
65 H2 Mataró Spain
105 H5 Matatiele S. Africa
117 B7 Mataura N.Z.
117 B7 Mataura *r.* N.Z.
45 D3 Mataveni *r.* Col.
117 F3 Matawai N.Z.
42 F6 Mategua Bol.
36 D4 Matehuala Mex.
103 D5 Matemanga Tanz.
66 G4 Matera Italy
66 C6 Mateur Tunisia
22 D4 Matheson Can.
27 D6 Mathis U.S.A.
114 F5 Mathoura Austr.
84 D4 Mathura India
94 C5 Mati Phil.
85 G4 Matiali India
89 D5 Matianxu China
84 B4 Matiari Pak.
36 E5 Matías Romero Mex.
23 G3 Matimekosh Can.
31 F2 Matinenda Lake *l.* Can.
33 J3 Matinicus I. *i.* U.S.A.
85 G5 Matla *r.* India
105 G1 Matlabas *r.* S. Africa
84 B4 Matli Pak.
59 F4 Matlock U.K.
45 D3 Mato *r.* Venez.
45 D3 Mato, Co *mt* Venez.
42 G7 Mato Grosso Brazil
46 A1 Mato Grosso *div.* Brazil
40 Mato Grosso, Planalto do *plat.* Brazil
46 B3 Mato Grosso do Sul *div.* Brazil
105 K2 Matola Moz.
65 B2 Matosinhos Port.
79 H5 Maţraḩ Oman
104 C6 Matroosberg *mt* S. Africa
91 C7 Matsue Japan
90 G4 Matsumae Japan
91 E6 Matsumoto Japan
91 E7 Matsusaka Japan
89 F5 Matsu Tao *i.* Taiwan
91 C8 Matsuyama Japan
22 D4 Mattagami *r.* Can.
31 H2 Mattawa Can.
33 J2 Mattawamkeag U.S.A.
62 C7 Matterhorn *mt* Italy/Switz.
24 D3 Matterhorn *mt* U.S.A.
111 H4 Matthew Island *i.* New Caledonia
45 E3 Matthews Ridge Guyana
37 K4 Matthew Town Bahamas
28 B4 Mattoon U.S.A.
111 H3 Matuku *i.* Fiji
45 E2 Maturín Venez.
94 C5 Matutuang *i.* Indon.
105 G4 Matwabeng S. Africa
84 E4 Mau *Uttar Pradesh* India
85 E4 Mau *Uttar Pradesh* India
85 E4 Mau Aimma India
61 B4 Maubeuge France
64 E5 Maubourguet France
57 D5 Mauchline U.K.
43 G4 Maués Brazil
85 E4 Mauganj India
93 L2 Maug Islands *is* N. Mariana Is
34 □2 Maui *i.* U.S.A.
47 B2 Maule *div.* Chile
47 B2 Maule *r.* Chile
47 B4 Maullín Chile
60 B3 Maumakeogh *h.* Rep. of Ireland
32 B4 Maumee U.S.A.
32 B4 Maumee *r.* U.S.A.
31 F5 Maumee Bay *b.* U.S.A.
93 G8 Maumere Indon.
60 B4 Maumturk Mts *h.* Rep. of Ireland
103 C5 Maun Botswana
34 □2 Mauna Kea *vol.* U.S.A.
34 □2 Mauna Loa *vol.* U.S.A.
34 □1 Maunalua B. *b.* U.S.A.
105 G1 Maunatlala Botswana
117 E2 Maungaturoto N.Z.
85 H5 Maungdaw Myanmar
95 A2 Maungmagan Is *is* Myanmar
114 B5 Maupertuis B. *b.* Austr.
112 F5 Maurice, L. *salt flat* Austr.
61 D3 Maurik Neth.
96 Mauritania *country* Africa
96 Mauritius *country* Africa
30 B4 Mauston U.S.A.
45 D4 Mavaca *r.* Venez.
103 C5 Mavinga Angola
105 G5 Mavuya S. Africa
84 D3 Mawana India
102 B4 Mawanga Dem. Rep. Congo
89 D4 Ma Wang Dui China
95 A3 Mawdaung Pass *pass* Myanmar/Thai.
117 G3 Mawhai Point *pt* N.Z.
83 H6 Mawlaik Myanmar
119 D4 Mawson *Austr. Base* Antarctica
119 D4 Mawson Escarpment *escarpment* Antarctica
119 B6 Mawson Pen. *pen.* Antarctica
95 A3 Maw Taung *mt* Myanmar
26 C2 Max U.S.A.
66 C5 Maxia, Punta *mt* Italy
30 D5 Maxinkuckee, Lake *l.* U.S.A.
54 S5 Maxmo Fin.
31 F2 Maxton U.S.A.
34 A2 Maxwell U.S.A.
57 F4 May, Isle of *i.* U.K.
77 P3 Maya *r.* Rus. Fed.
37 K4 Mayaguana *i.* Bahamas
37 L5 Mayagüez Puerto Rico
100 C3 Mayahi Niger
102 B4 Mayama Congo
79 H2 Mayamey Iran
36 G5 Maya Mountains *mts* Belize/Guatemala
89 C5 Mayang China
88 B3 Mayanhe China
90 F5 Maya-san *mt* Japan
57 D5 Maybole U.K.
81 K4 Maydān Sarāy Iraq
84 B2 Maydā Shahr Afgh.
115 G9 Maydena Austr.
61 F4 Mayen Ger.
64 D2 Mayenne France
64 D2 Mayenne *r.* France
35 F4 Mayer U.S.A.
20 F4 Mayerthorpe Can.
117 C5 Mayfield N.Z.
28 B4 Mayfield U.S.A.
25 F5 Mayhill U.S.A.
90 A2 Mayi *r.* China
69 G6 Maykop Rus. Fed.
83 J6 Maymyo Myanmar
86 F1 Mayna Rus. Fed.
31 J3 Maynooth Can.
20 B2 Mayo Can.
47 E2 Mayo, 25 de *Buenos Aires* Arg.
47 C3 Mayo, 25 de *La Pampa* Arg.
94 C5 Mayo Bay *b.* Phil.
102 B4 Mayoko Congo
20 B2 Mayo Lake *l.* Can.
94 B3 Mayon *vol.* Phil.
47 D3 Mayor Buratovich Arg.
117 F2 Mayor I. *i.* N.Z.
44 D1 Mayor Pablo Lagerenza Para.

103 E5 **Mayotte** *terr.* Africa
94 B2 **Mayraira Point** *pt* Phil.
87 N1 **Mayskiy** Rus. Fed.
32 B5 **Maysville** U.S.A.
102 B4 **Mayumba** Gabon
85 E3 **Mayum La** *pass* China
31 F4 **Mayville** *MI* U.S.A.
26 D2 **Mayville** *ND* U.S.A.
32 D3 **Mayville** *NY* U.S.A.
30 C4 **Mayville** *WV* U.S.A.
26 C3 **Maywood** U.S.A.
47 D3 **Maza** Arg.
68 F3 **Maza** Rus. Fed.
103 C5 **Mazabuka** Zambia
43 H4 **Mazagão** Brazil
61 C5 **Mazagran** France
64 F5 **Mazamet** France
84 D1 **Mazar** China
66 E6 **Mazara del Vallo** Italy
79 K2 **Mazār-e Sharīf** Afgh.
45 E3 **Mazaruni** *r.* Guyana
25 E6 **Mazatán** Mex.
36 F6 **Mazatenango** Guatemala
36 C4 **Mazatlán** Mex.
35 G4 **Mazatzal Peak** *summit* U.S.A.
55 S8 **Mažeikiai** Lith.
81 G2 **Mazgirt** Turkey
55 S8 **Mazirbe** Latvia
25 E6 **Mazocahui** Mex.
102 D4 **Mazomora** Tanz.
81 M3 **Mazr'eh** Iran
81 M5 **Māzū** Iran
103 C6 **Mazunga** Zimbabwe
69 D4 **Mazyr** Belarus
105 J3 **Mbabane** Swaziland
100 B4 **Mbahiakro** Côte d'Ivoire
102 B3 **Mbaïki** C.A.R.
103 D4 **Mbala** Zambia
102 D3 **Mbale** Uganda
100 D4 **Mbalmayo** Cameroon
102 B4 **Mbandaka** Dem. Rep. Congo
100 C4 **Mbanga** Cameroon
102 B4 **M'banza Congo** Angola
102 D4 **Mbarara** Uganda
102 C3 **Mbari** *r.* C.A.R.
100 D4 **Mbengwi** Cameroon
103 D4 **Mbeya** Tanz.
103 D5 **Mbinga** Tanz.
103 D6 **Mbizi** Zimbabwe
102 B3 **Mbomo** Congo
100 D4 **Mbouda** Cameroon
100 A3 **Mbour** Senegal
100 A3 **Mbout** Maur.
103 D4 **Mbozi** Tanz.
102 C4 **Mbuji-Mayi** Dem. Rep. Congo
102 D4 **Mbulu** Tanz.
102 D4 **Mbuyuni** Tanz.
33 K2 **McAdam** Can.
27 E5 **McAlester** U.S.A.
32 E4 **McAlevys Fort** U.S.A.
115 H5 **McAlister** *mt* Austr.
27 D7 **McAllen** U.S.A.
32 B5 **McArthur** U.S.A.
31 J3 **McArthur Mills** Can.
20 B2 **McArthur Wildlife Sanctuary** *res.* Can.
20 E4 **McBride** Can.
24 C2 **McCall** U.S.A.
27 C6 **McCamey** U.S.A.
24 D3 **McCammon** U.S.A.
20 C4 **McCaulay I.** *i.* Can.
34 B3 **McClure, L.** *l.* U.S.A.
27 F6 **McComb** U.S.A.
26 C3 **McConaughy, L.** *l.* U.S.A.
32 E5 **McConnellsburg** U.S.A.
32 C5 **McConnelsville** U.S.A.
26 C3 **McCook** U.S.A.
21 K4 **McCreary** Can.
35 E4 **McCullough Range** *mts* U.S.A.
20 D3 **McDame** Can.
24 C3 **McDermitt** U.S.A.
24 D2 **McDonald Peak** *summit* U.S.A.
114 C2 **McDonnell Creek** *watercourse* Austr.
104 B4 **McDougall's Bay** *b.* S. Africa
35 G5 **McDowell Peak** *summit* U.S.A.
34 C4 **McFarland** U.S.A.
21 H3 **McFarlane** *r.* Can.
35 E2 **McGill** U.S.A.
20 E4 **McGregor** *r.* Can.
104 C6 **McGregor** S. Africa
30 A2 **McGregor** U.S.A.
31 G2 **McGregor Bay** Can.
24 D2 **McGuire, Mt** *mt* U.S.A.
103 D4 **Mchinga** Tanz.
33 G2 **McIndoe Falls** U.S.A.
26 C2 **McIntosh** U.S.A.
111 J2 **McKean** *i.* Kiribati
32 A6 **McKee** U.S.A.
32 D4 **McKeesport** U.S.A.
33 F3 **McKeever** U.S.A.
29 B4 **McKenzie** U.S.A.
18 **McKinley, Mt** *mt* U.S.A.
27 D5 **McKinney** U.S.A.
34 C4 **McKittrick** U.S.A.
26 C2 **McLaughlin** U.S.A.
20 F3 **McLennan** Can.
20 F4 **McLeod** *r.* Can.
20 E3 **McLeod Lake** Can.
24 B3 **McLoughlin, Mt** *mt* U.S.A.
30 E2 **McMillan** U.S.A.
24 B2 **McMinnville** *OR* U.S.A.
29 C5 **McMinnville** *TN* U.S.A.
119 B5 **McMurdo** *U.S.A. Base* Antarctica
35 H4 **McNary** U.S.A.
20 F4 **McNaughton Lake** *l.* Can.
35 H6 **McNeal** U.S.A.
26 D4 **McPherson** U.S.A.
115 K2 **McPherson Ra.** *mts* Austr.
20 B2 **McQuesten** *r.* Can.
29 D5 **McRae** U.S.A.
20 E1 **McVicar Arm** *b.* Can.
105 G6 **Mdantsane** S. Africa
66 B6 **M'Daourouch** Alg.
35 E3 **Mead, Lake** *l.* U.S.A.
27 C4 **Meade** U.S.A.
21 H4 **Meadow Lake** Can.
21 H4 **Meadow Lake Provincial Park** *res.* Can.
35 E3 **Meadow Valley Wash** *r.* U.S.A.
32 C4 **Meadville** U.S.A.
31 G3 **Meaford** Can.
90 J3 **Meaken-dake** *vol.* Japan
57 A2 **Mealasta Island** *i.* U.K.
65 B2 **Mealhada** Port.
57 D4 **Meall a'Bhuiridh** *mt* U.K.
23 J3 **Mealy Mountains** *mts* Can.
115 H1 **Meandarra** Austr.
20 F3 **Meander River** Can.
94 C5 **Meares** *i.* Indon.
64 F2 **Meaux** France
102 B4 **Mebridege** *r.* Angola
78 D5 **Mecca** Saudi Arabia
33 H2 **Mechanic Falls** U.S.A.
32 B4 **Mechanicsburg** U.S.A.
30 B5 **Mechanicsville** U.S.A.
61 C3 **Mechelen** Belgium
61 D4 **Mechelen** Neth.
100 B1 **Mecheria** Alg.
61 E4 **Mechernich** Ger.
80 E1 **Mecitözü** Turkey
61 F4 **Meckenheim** Ger.
62 E3 **Mecklenburger Bucht** *b.* Ger.
103 D5 **Mecula** Moz.
65 C2 **Meda** Port.
92 B6 **Medan** Indon.
47 D3 **Médanos** Arg.
47 C3 **Medanosa, Pta** *pt* Arg.
33 K2 **Meddybemps L.** *l.* U.S.A.
65 H4 **Médéa** Alg.
45 B3 **Medellín** Col.
59 F4 **Meden** *r.* U.K.
100 D1 **Medenine** Tunisia
100 A3 **Mederdra** Maur.
24 B3 **Medford** *OR* U.S.A.
30 B3 **Medford** *WV* U.S.A.
33 F5 **Medford Farms** U.S.A.
67 N2 **Medgidia** Romania
30 B5 **Media** U.S.A.
47 C2 **Media Luna** Arg.
63 M7 **Mediaș** Romania
24 C2 **Medical Lake** U.S.A.
24 F3 **Medicine Bow** U.S.A.
24 F3 **Medicine Bow Mts** *mts* U.S.A.
24 F3 **Medicine Bow Peak** *summit* U.S.A.
21 G4 **Medicine Hat** Can.
27 D4 **Medicine Lodge** U.S.A.
46 E2 **Medina** Brazil
78 D5 **Medina** Saudi Arabia
32 D3 **Medina** *NY* U.S.A.
32 C4 **Medina** *OH* U.S.A.
65 E2 **Medinaceli** Spain
65 D2 **Medina del Campo** Spain
65 D2 **Medina de Rioseco** Spain
85 F5 **Medinīpur** India
52 **Mediterranean Sea** *sea* Africa/Europe
76 G4 **Mednogorsk** Rus. Fed.
64 D4 **Médoc** *reg.* France
68 H3 **Medvedevo** Rus. Fed.
69 H5 **Medveditsa** *r.* Rus. Fed.
66 F2 **Medvednica** *mts* Croatia
77 S2 **Medvezh'i, O-va** *is* Rus. Fed.
87 P2 **Medvezh'ya, Gora** *mt* China/Rus. Fed.
68 E2 **Medvezh'yegorsk** Rus. Fed.
59 H6 **Medway** *r.* U.K.
112 C5 **Meekatharra** Austr.
35 H1 **Meeker** U.S.A.
34 B2 **Meeks Bay** U.S.A.
23 J4 **Meelpaeg Res.** *resr* Can.
61 E3 **Meerlo** Neth.
84 D3 **Meerut** India
24 E2 **Meeteetse** U.S.A.
102 D3 **Mēga** Eth.
85 G4 **Meghalaya** *div.* India
85 F5 **Meghāsani** *mt* India
85 G5 **Meghna** *r.* Bangl.
81 L2 **Meghri** Armenia
80 B3 **Megisti** *i.* Greece
54 U1 **Mehamn** Norway
112 C4 **Meharry, Mt** *mt* Austr.
81 L4 **Mehdīkhān** Iran
84 D5 **Mehekar** India
85 G5 **Meherpur** Bangl.
32 E6 **Meherrin** *r.* U.S.A.
81 L2 **Mehrābān** Iran
81 L5 **Mehrān** Iraq
84 B2 **Mehtar Lām** Afgh.
46 C2 **Meia Ponte** *r.* Brazil
101 D4 **Meiganga** Cameroon
89 B4 **Meigu** China
87 N3 **Meihekou** China
89 E5 **Mei Jiang** *r.* China
57 D5 **Meikle Millyea** *h.* U.K.
83 J6 **Meiktila** Myanmar
62 E5 **Meiningen** Ger.
104 E6 **Meiringspoort** *pass* S. Africa
89 B4 **Meishan** China
62 F5 **Meißen** Ger.
89 C5 **Meitan** China
88 C3 **Meixian** China
89 E5 **Meizhou** China
84 D4 **Mej** *r.* India
44 C3 **Mejicana** *mt* Arg.
44 B2 **Mejillones** Chile
102 D2 **Mek'elē** Eth.
100 A3 **Mékhé** Senegal
84 B3 **Mekhtar** Pak.
66 C7 **Meknassy** Tunisia
100 B1 **Meknès** Morocco
95 C3 **Mekong** *r.* Asia
82 K6 **Mekong** *r.* China
95 C3 **Mekong, Mouths of the** *est.* Vietnam
92 C6 **Melaka** Malaysia
14 G6 **Melanesia** *is* Pac. Oc.
94 A5 **Melaut** *r.* Malaysia
114 F6 **Melbourne** Austr.
29 D6 **Melbourne** U.S.A.
57 □ **Melby** U.K.
62 D3 **Meldorf** Ger.
31 F3 **Meldrum Bay** Can.
80 E2 **Melendiz Dağı** *mt* Turkey
68 G4 **Melenki** Rus. Fed.
23 F2 **Mélèzes, Rivière aux** *r.* Can.
101 D3 **Mélfi** Chad
66 F4 **Melfi** Italy
21 J4 **Melfort** Can.
54 M5 **Melhus** Norway
94 A5 **Meliau, Gunung** *mt* Malaysia
65 C1 **Melide** Spain
100 B1 **Melilla** Spain
47 E2 **Melincué** Arg.
47 B2 **Melipilla** Chile
61 B3 **Meliskerke** Neth.
21 J5 **Melita** Can.
69 E6 **Melitopol'** Ukr.
62 G6 **Melk** Austria
105 H1 **Melkrivier** S. Africa
59 E6 **Melksham** U.K.
54 T3 **Mellakoski** Fin.
54 Q5 **Mellansel** Sweden
30 B2 **Mellen** U.S.A.
55 N7 **Mellerud** Sweden
105 J4 **Melmoth** S. Africa
47 F2 **Melo** Uru.
114 C4 **Melrose** Austr.
57 F5 **Melrose** U.K.
59 G5 **Melton Mowbray** U.K.
64 F2 **Melun** France
21 J4 **Melville** Can.
113 H2 **Melville, C.** *c.* Austr.
94 A5 **Melville, C.** *c.* Phil.
23 J3 **Melville, Lake** *l.* Can.
113 G2 **Melville Bay** *b.* Austr.
118 B2 **Melville I.** *i.* Can.
112 F2 **Melville Island** *i.* Austr.
118 A2 **Melville Peninsula** *pen.* Can.
60 C3 **Melvin, Lough** *l.* Rep. of Ireland/U.K.
77 T3 **Melyuveyem** Rus. Fed.
85 E2 **Mêmar Co** *salt l.* China
93 K7 **Memberamo** *r.* Indon.
93 F8 **Memboro** Indon.
105 H3 **Memel** S. Africa
62 E7 **Memmingen** Ger.
61 C5 **Mémorial Américain** *h.* France
92 D6 **Mempawah** Indon.
80 C7 **Memphis** Egypt
30 A5 **Memphis** *MO* U.S.A.
29 B5 **Memphis** *TN* U.S.A.
27 C5 **Memphis** *TX* U.S.A.
33 G2 **Memphrémagog, Lac** *l.* Can.
90 H3 **Memuro-dake** *mt* Japan
69 E5 **Mena** Ukr.
27 E5 **Mena** U.S.A.
100 C3 **Ménaka** Mali
Mènam Khong *r. see* **Mekong**
27 D6 **Menard** U.S.A.
30 C3 **Menasha** U.S.A.
64 F4 **Mende** France
102 D2 **Mendefera** Eritrea
81 M3 **Mendejīn** Iran
20 C3 **Mendenhall Glacier** *gl.* U.S.A.
102 D3 **Mendī** Eth.
110 E2 **Mendi** P.N.G.
59 E6 **Mendip Hills** *h.* U.K.
34 A2 **Mendocino** U.S.A.
24 A3 **Mendocino, C.** *c.* U.S.A.
30 E4 **Mendon** U.S.A.
115 H3 **Mendooran** Austr.
34 B3 **Mendota** *CA* U.S.A.
30 C5 **Mendota** *IL* U.S.A.
30 C4 **Mendota, Lake** *l.* U.S.A.
47 C2 **Mendoza** Arg.
47 C2 **Mendoza** *div.* Arg.
47 C2 **Mendoza** *r.* Arg.
45 C2 **Mene de Mauroa** Venez.
45 C2 **Mene Grande** Venez.
67 M5 **Menemen** Turkey
88 E3 **Mengcheng** China
80 D1 **Mengen** Turkey
92 D7 **Menggala** Indon.
89 D5 **Mengshan** China
88 F3 **Meng Shan** *mts* China
88 E3 **Mengyin** China
89 B6 **Mengzi** China
23 G3 **Menihek** Can.
23 G3 **Menihek Lakes** *lakes* Can.
114 E4 **Menindee** Austr.
114 E4 **Menindee Lake** *l.* Austr.
114 C5 **Meningie** Austr.
81 M4 **Menjān** Iran
77 O3 **Menkere** Rus. Fed.
64 F2 **Mennecy** France
30 D3 **Menominee** U.S.A.
30 D3 **Menominee** *r.* U.S.A.
30 C4 **Menomonee Falls** U.S.A.
30 B3 **Menomonie** U.S.A.
103 B5 **Menongue** Angola
65 J2 **Menorca** *i.* Spain
94 A6 **Mensalong** Indon.
92 B7 **Mentawai, Kepulauan** *is* Indon.
Mentawai Islands *is see* **Mentawai, Kepulauan**
95 B5 **Mentekab** Malaysia
35 H4 **Mentmore** U.S.A.
92 D7 **Mentok** Indon.
64 H5 **Menton** France
32 C4 **Mentor** U.S.A.
61 D5 **Menuchenet** Belgium
100 C1 **Menzel Bourguiba** Tunisia
66 D6 **Menzel Temime** Tunisia
112 D5 **Menzies** Austr.
119 D4 **Menzies, Mt** *mt* Antarctica
27 B6 **Meoqui** Mex.
61 E2 **Meppel** Neth.
62 C4 **Meppen** Ger.
105 K1 **Mepuze** Moz.
105 G4 **Meqheleng** S. Africa
68 G3 **Mera** *r.* Rus. Fed.
54 M5 **Meråker** Norway
26 F4 **Meramec** *r.* U.S.A.
66 D1 **Merano** Italy
45 E3 **Merari, Sa.** *mt* Brazil
104 F1 **Meratswe** *r.* Botswana
93 L8 **Merauke** Indon.
114 E5 **Merbein** Austr.
34 B3 **Merced** U.S.A.
47 B1 **Mercedario, Cerro** *mt* Arg.
47 E2 **Mercedes** *Buenos Aires* Arg.
44 E3 **Mercedes** *Corrientes* Arg.
47 D2 **Mercedes** *San Luis* Arg.
47 E2 **Mercedes** Uru.
32 A4 **Mercer** *OH* U.S.A.
30 B2 **Mercer** *WV* U.S.A.
20 F4 **Mercoal** Can.
117 E2 **Mercury Islands** *is* N.Z.
59 E6 **Mere** U.K.
33 H3 **Meredith** U.S.A.
27 C5 **Meredith, Lake** *l.* U.S.A.
27 C5 **Meredith Nat. Recreation Area, Lake** *res.* U.S.A.
30 B6 **Meredosia** U.S.A.
69 F5 **Merefa** Ukr.
101 E3 **Merga Oasis** *oasis* Sudan
95 A2 **Mergui** Myanmar
95 A3 **Mergui Archipelago** *is* Myanmar
114 D5 **Meribah** Austr.
67 M4 **Meriç** *r.* Greece/Turkey
36 G4 **Mérida** Mex.
65 C3 **Mérida** Spain
45 C2 **Mérida** Venez.
45 C2 **Mérida, Cordillera de** *mts* Venez.
33 G4 **Meriden** U.S.A.
34 B2 **Meridian** *CA* U.S.A.
27 F5 **Meridian** *MS* U.S.A.
64 D4 **Mérignac** France
54 T4 **Merijärvi** Fin.
55 R6 **Merikarvia** Fin.
115 H6 **Merimbula** Austr.
116 C3 **Merinda** Austr.
114 D5 **Meringur** Austr.
114 D6 **Merino** Austr.
116 B5 **Merivale** *r.* Austr.
27 C5 **Merkel** U.S.A.
95 □ **Merlimau, P.** *i.* Sing.
101 F3 **Merowe** Sudan
85 F3 **Mêrqung Co** *salt l.* China
112 C6 **Merredin** Austr.
57 D5 **Merrick** *h.* U.K.
31 K3 **Merrickville** Can.
30 C3 **Merrill** U.S.A.
30 D5 **Merrillville** U.S.A.
33 C3 **Merriman** U.S.A.
20 E4 **Merritt** Can.
29 D6 **Merritt Island** U.S.A.
115 J4 **Merriwa** Austr.
115 H3 **Merrygoen** Austr.
102 E2 **Mersa Fatma** Eritrea
61 E5 **Mersch** Lux.
59 E4 **Mersey** *est.* U.K.
Mersin *see* **İçel**
92 C6 **Mersing** Malaysia
55 S8 **Mērsrags** Latvia
84 C4 **Merta** India
59 D6 **Merthyr Tydfil** U.K.
102 D3 **Merti** Kenya
65 C4 **Mértola** Port.
102 D4 **Meru** *vol.* Tanz.
104 D6 **Merweville** S. Africa
80 E1 **Merzifon** Turkey
62 C6 **Merzig** Ger.
119 B2 **Merz Pen.** *pen.* Antarctica
35 G5 **Mesa** U.S.A.
26 A2 **Mesabi Range** *h.* U.S.A.
66 G4 **Mesagne** Italy
67 L7 **Mesara, Ormos** *b.* Greece
35 H3 **Mesa Verde Nat. Park** *nat. park* U.S.A.
45 B4 **Mesay** *r.* Col.
54 P4 **Meselefors** Sweden
22 F3 **Mesgouez L.** *l.* Can.
68 J2 **Meshchura** Rus. Fed.
Meshed *see* **Mashhad**
69 G5 **Meshkovskaya** Rus. Fed.
30 E3 **Mesick** U.S.A.
67 K4 **Mesimeri** Greece
67 J5 **Mesolongi** Greece
81 J4 **Mesopotamia** *reg.* Iraq
35 E3 **Mesquite** *NV* U.S.A.
27 D5 **Mesquite** *TX* U.S.A.
35 E4 **Mesquite Lake** *l.* U.S.A.
103 D5 **Messalo** *r.* Moz.
66 F5 **Messina** Italy
105 J1 **Messina** S. Africa
66 F5 **Messina, Stretta di** *str.* Italy
31 J2 **Messines** Can.
67 K6 **Messini** Greece
67 K6 **Messiniakos Kolpos** *b.* Greece
67 L5 **Meston, Akra** *pt* Greece
66 E2 **Mestre** Italy
80 F1 **Mesudiye** Turkey
45 C3 **Meta** *r.* Col./Venez.
31 G2 **Metagama** Can.
27 F6 **Metairie** U.S.A.
30 C5 **Metamora** U.S.A.
44 C3 **Metán** Arg.
116 C5 **Meteor Creek** *r.* Austr.
12 H9 **Meteor Depth** *depth* Atlantic Ocean
67 J6 **Methoni** Greece
33 H3 **Methuen** U.S.A.
57 E4 **Methven** U.K.
66 G3 **Metković** Croatia
20 C3 **Metlakatla** U.S.A.
103 D5 **Metoro** Moz.
92 D8 **Metro** Indon.
28 B4 **Metropolis** U.S.A.
34 C4 **Mettler** U.S.A.
102 D3 **Metu** Eth.
64 H2 **Metz** France
64 G2 **Meuse** *r.* Belgium/France
59 C7 **Mevagissey** U.K.
88 B3 **Mêwa** China
27 D6 **Mexia** U.S.A.
36 A2 **Mexicali** Mex.
35 H3 **Mexican Hat** U.S.A.
35 H3 **Mexican Water** U.S.A.
16 **Mexico** *country* Central America
36 E5 **México** Mex.
33 H2 **Mexico** *ME* U.S.A.
26 F4 **Mexico** *MO* U.S.A.
33 E3 **Mexico** *NY* U.S.A.
18 **Mexico, Gulf of** *g.* Mex./U.S.A.
79 J2 **Meymaneh** Afgh.
81 L5 **Meymeh, Rūdkhāneh-ye** *r.* Iran
67 K3 **Mezdra** Bulg.
76 F3 **Mezen'** Rus. Fed.
64 G4 **Mézenc, Mont** *mt* France
68 J2 **Mezhdurechensk** Rus. Fed.
86 E1 **Mezhdurechensk** Rus. Fed.
76 G2 **Mezhdusharskiy, O.** *i.* Rus. Fed.
63 K7 **Mezőtúr** Hungary
36 C4 **Mezquital** *r.* Mex.
55 U8 **Mežvidi** Latvia
103 D5 **Mfuwe** Zambia
105 J3 **Mhlume** Swaziland
84 C5 **Mhow** India
85 H5 **Mi** *r.* Myanmar
36 E5 **Miahuatlán** Mex.
65 D3 **Miajadas** Spain
35 G5 **Miami** *AZ* U.S.A.
29 D7 **Miami** *FL* U.S.A.
27 E4 **Miami** *OK* U.S.A.
29 D7 **Miami Beach** U.S.A.
81 M6 **Mīān Āb** Iran
81 L3 **Miandowāb** Iran
103 E5 **Miandrivazo** Madag.
81 L3 **Mīāneh** Iran
94 C5 **Miangas** *i.* Phil.
89 B4 **Mianning** China
84 B2 **Mianwali** Pak.
88 C3 **Mianxian** China
88 B4 **Mianyang** China
88 B4 **Mianzhu** China
88 F2 **Miao Dao** *i.* China
88 F2 **Miaodao Qundao** *is* China
89 F5 **Miaoli** Taiwan
103 E5 **Miarinarivo** Madag.
76 H4 **Miass** Rus. Fed.
35 G5 **Mica Mt** *mt* U.S.A.
88 C3 **Micang Shan** *mts* China
63 K6 **Michalovce** Slovakia
21 H3 **Michel** Can.
30 C2 **Michigamme Lake** *l.* U.S.A.
30 C2 **Michigamme Reservoir** *resr* U.S.A.
30 D2 **Michigan** *div.* U.S.A.
30 D4 **Michigan, Lake** *l.* U.S.A.
30 D5 **Michigan City** U.S.A.
30 E2 **Michipicoten Bay** *b.* Can.
30 E2 **Michipicoten I.** *i.* Can.
30 E1 **Michipicoten River** Can.
68 G4 **Michurinsk** Rus. Fed.
37 H6 **Mico** *r.* Nic.
14 E5 **Micronesia** *is* Pac. Oc.
95 C5 **Midai** *i.* Indon.
12 F4 **Mid-Atlantic Ridge** *sea feature* Atlantic Ocean
104 C6 **Middelberg Pass** *pass* S. Africa
61 B3 **Middelburg** Neth.
104 F5 **Middelburg** *Eastern Cape* S. Africa
105 H2 **Middelburg** *Mpumalanga* S. Africa
55 L9 **Middelfart** Denmark
61 C3 **Middelharnis** Neth.
104 D5 **Middelpos** S. Africa
105 G2 **Middelwit** S. Africa
24 C3 **Middle Alkali Lake** *l.* U.S.A.
14 N5 **Middle America Trench** *sea feature* Pac. Oc.
92 A4 **Middle Andaman** *i.* Andaman and Nicobar Is
33 H4 **Middleboro** U.S.A.
32 E4 **Middleburg** U.S.A.
33 F3 **Middleburgh** U.S.A.
33 G2 **Middlebury** U.S.A.
117 C6 **Middlemarch** N.Z.
116 C4 **Middlemount** Austr.
32 B6 **Middlesboro** U.S.A.
58 F3 **Middlesbrough** U.K.
34 A2 **Middletown** *CA* U.S.A.
33 G4 **Middletown** *CT* U.S.A.
33 F5 **Middletown** *DE* U.S.A.
33 F4 **Middletown** *NY* U.S.A.
32 A5 **Middletown** *OH* U.S.A.
30 E4 **Middleville** U.S.A.
59 G7 **Midhurst** U.K.
13 K4 **Mid-Indian Basin** *sea feature* Indian Ocean
13 K6 **Mid-Indian Ridge** *sea feature* Indian Ocean
31 H3 **Midland** Can.
31 E4 **Midland** *MI* U.S.A.
27 C5 **Midland** *TX* U.S.A.
60 C6 **Midleton** Rep. of Ireland
14 F4 **Mid-Pacific Mountains** *sea feature* Pac. Oc.
54 □ **Miðvágur** Faroe Is
Midway *see* **Thamarīt**
14 H4 **Midway Islands** *is* Pac. Oc.
24 F3 **Midwest** U.S.A.
27 D5 **Midwest City** U.S.A.
61 D2 **Midwoud** Neth.
81 H3 **Midyat** Turkey
57 □ **Mid Yell** U.K.
67 K3 **Midzhur** *mt* Bulg./Serb. and Mont.
55 U6 **Miehikkälä** Fin.
54 T3 **Miekojärvi** *l.* Fin.
63 K5 **Mielec** Pol.
103 D4 **Miembwe** Tanz.
115 G8 **Miena** Austr.
54 U2 **Mieraslompolo** Fin.
63 M7 **Miercurea-Ciuc** Romania
65 D1 **Mieres** Spain
102 E3 **Mī'ēso** Eth.
32 E4 **Mifflinburg** U.S.A.
32 E4 **Mifflintown** U.S.A.
88 C3 **Migang Shan** *mt* China
105 F3 **Migdol** S. Africa
85 H3 **Miging** India
36 E5 **Miguel Alemán, Presa** *resr* Mex.
36 C3 **Miguel Hidalgo, Presa** *resr* Mex.
80 C2 **Mihaliççık** Turkey
91 C7 **Mihara** Japan
91 F7 **Mihara-yama** *vol.* Japan
65 F2 **Mijares** *r.* Spain
61 C2 **Mijdrecht** Neth.
31 F3 **Mikado** U.S.A.
63 N4 **Mikashevichy** Belarus
64 F4 **Mikhaylov** Rus. Fed.
90 C3 **Mikhaylovka** Rus. Fed.
69 G5 **Mikhaylovka** Rus. Fed.
86 C1 **Mikhaylovskiy** Rus. Fed.
85 H4 **Mikīr Hills** *mts* India
55 U6 **Mikkeli** Fin.
55 U6 **Mikkelin mlk** Fin.
20 G3 **Mikkwa** *r.* Can.
102 D4 **Mikumi** Tanz.
68 J2 **Mikun'** Rus. Fed.
91 F6 **Mikuni-sanmyaku** *mts* Japan
91 F8 **Mikura-jima** *i.* Japan
26 E2 **Milaca** U.S.A.
83 D9 **Miladhunmadulu Atoll** *atoll* Maldives
66 C2 **Milan** Italy
29 B5 **Milan** U.S.A.
114 C5 **Milang** Austr.
103 D5 **Milange** Moz.
Milano *see* **Milan**
80 A3 **Milas** Turkey
66 F5 **Milazzo** Italy
26 D2 **Milbank** U.S.A.
59 H5 **Mildenhall** U.K.
114 E5 **Mildura** Austr.
89 B5 **Mile** China
116 D6 **Miles** Austr.
24 F2 **Miles City** U.S.A.
60 C5 **Milestone** Rep. of Ireland
66 F4 **Miletto, Monte** *mt* Italy
60 D2 **Milford** Rep. of Ireland
34 B1 **Milford** *CA* U.S.A.
33 G4 **Milford** *CT* U.S.A.
33 F5 **Milford** *DE* U.S.A.
30 D5 **Milford** *IL* U.S.A.
33 H3 **Milford** *MA* U.S.A.
33 J2 **Milford** *ME* U.S.A.
33 H3 **Milford** *NH* U.S.A.
33 F3 **Milford** *NY* U.S.A.
35 F2 **Milford** *UT* U.S.A.
59 B6 **Milford Haven** U.K.
117 A6 **Milford Sound** N.Z.
117 A6 **Milford Sound** *in.* N.Z.
65 H4 **Miliana** Alg.
24 F1 **Milk** *r.* Can./U.S.A.
101 F3 **Milk, Wadi el** *watercourse* Sudan
77 R4 **Mil'kovo** Rus. Fed.
116 A1 **Millaa Millaa** Austr.
65 F2 **Millárs** *r.* Spain
64 F4 **Millau** France
34 B1 **Mill Creek** *r.* U.S.A.
29 D5 **Milledgeville** *GA* U.S.A.
30 C5 **Milledgeville** *IL* U.S.A.
26 E2 **Mille Lacs** *l.* U.S.A.
22 B4 **Mille Lacs, Lac des** *l.* Can.
Millennium I. *i. see* **Caroline Island**
114 A2 **Miller** *watercourse* Austr.
26 D2 **Miller** U.S.A.

30 B3 Miller Dam Flowage resr U.S.A.
31 G3 Miller Lake Can.
69 G5 Millerovo Rus. Fed.
35 G6 Miller Peak summit U.S.A.
32 C4 Millersburg OH U.S.A.
32 E4 Millersburg PA U.S.A.
114 B3 Millers Creek Austr.
32 E6 Millers Tavern U.S.A.
34 C3 Millerton Lake l. U.S.A.
57 C5 Milleur Point pt U.K.
119 C6 Mill I. i. Antarctica
114 D6 Millicent Austr.
31 F4 Millington MI U.S.A.
29 B5 Millington TN U.S.A.
33 J2 Millinocket U.S.A.
115 J1 Millmerran Austr.
58 D3 Millom U.K.
57 D5 Millport U.K.
33 F5 Millsboro U.S.A.
20 F2 Mills Lake l. Can.
32 C5 Millstone U.S.A.
112 C4 Millstream-Chichester National Park nat. park Austr.
23 G4 Milltown Can.
60 B5 Milltown Malbay Rep. of Ireland
33 K1 Millville Can.
33 F5 Millville U.S.A.
33 J2 Milo U.S.A.
90 D3 Milogradovo Rus. Fed.
67 L6 Milos i. Greece
68 F4 Miloslavskoye Rus. Fed.
114 D2 Milparinka Austr.
32 E4 Milroy U.S.A.
31 H4 Milton Can.
117 B7 Milton N.Z.
29 C6 Milton FL U.S.A.
30 A5 Milton IA U.S.A.
32 E4 Milton PA U.S.A.
33 G2 Milton VT U.S.A.
32 C4 Milton, Lake l. U.S.A.
24 C2 Milton-Freewater U.S.A.
59 G5 Milton Keynes U.K.
89 D4 Miluo China
30 D4 Milwaukee U.S.A.
69 G5 Milyutinskaya Rus. Fed.
64 D4 Mimizan France
102 B4 Mimongo Gabon
27 C7 Mina Mex.
34 C2 Mina U.S.A.
79 H4 Mīnāb Iran
93 G6 Minahassa Peninsula pen. Indon.
21 L4 Minaki Can.
91 B8 Minamata Japan
91 E7 Minami Alps National Park Japan
92 C6 Minas Indon.
47 F2 Minas Uru.
81 M7 Mīnā' Sa'ūd Kuwait
23 H4 Minas Basin b. Can.
47 F1 Minas de Corrales Uru.
46 D2 Minas Gerais div. Brazil
46 D2 Minas Novas Brazil
36 F5 Minatitlán Mex.
85 H5 Minbu Myanmar
85 H5 Minbya Myanmar
44 B6 Minchinmávida vol. Chile
66 D2 Mincio r. Italy
81 L2 Mincivan Azer.
94 C5 Mindanao i. Phil.
114 D5 Mindarie Austr.
100 □ Mindelo Cape Verde
31 H3 Minden Can.
62 D4 Minden Ger.
27 E5 Minden LA U.S.A.
34 C2 Minden NV U.S.A.
85 H6 Mindon Myanmar
114 E4 Mindona L. l. Austr.
94 B3 Mindoro i. Phil.
94 A3 Mindoro Strait str. Phil.
102 B4 Mindouli Congo
60 D6 Mine Head hd Rep. of Ireland
59 D6 Minehead U.K.
46 B2 Mineiros Brazil
27 E5 Mineola U.S.A.
31 B1 Mineral U.S.A.
34 C3 Mineral King U.S.A.
69 G6 Mineral'nyye Vody Rus. Fed.
30 B4 Mineral Point U.S.A.
27 D5 Mineral Wells U.S.A.
35 F2 Minersville U.S.A.
66 G4 Minervino Murge Italy
85 E1 Minfeng China
103 C5 Minga Dem. Rep. Congo
81 L1 Mingäçevir Azer.
81 L1 Mingäçevir Su Anbarı resr Azer.
23 H3 Mingan Can.
114 D4 Mingary Austr.
116 B2 Mingela Austr.
112 C5 Mingenew Austr.
88 E3 Minggang China
88 F3 Mingguang China
65 F3 Minglanilla Spain
103 D5 Mingoyo Tanz.
89 B4 Mingshan China
87 N2 Mingshui China
57 A4 Mingulay i. U.K.
89 E5 Mingxi China
88 B2 Minhe China
89 F5 Minhou China
93 D3 Minicoy i. India
112 B4 Minilya Austr.
23 H3 Minipi Lake l. Can.
21 J4 Minitonas Can.
89 F5 Min Jiang r. China
88 B4 Min Jiang r. China
88 A2 Minle China
100 C4 Minna Nigeria
55 O5 Minne Sweden
26 E2 Minneapolis U.S.A.
21 K4 Minnedosa Can.
30 A2 Minnesota div. U.S.A.
114 A4 Minnipa Austr.
22 B4 Minnitaki L. l. Can.
65 B2 Miño r. Port./Spain
30 C3 Minocqua U.S.A.
30 B2 Minong U.S.A.
30 C5 Minonk U.S.A.
Minorca i. see Menorca
26 C1 Minot U.S.A.
88 B2 Minqin China
89 F5 Minqing China
88 B3 Min Shan mts China
84 H4 Minsin Myanmar
68 C4 Minsk Belarus
63 K4 Mińsk Mazowiecki Pol.
59 E5 Minsterley U.K.
84 C1 Mintaka Pass pass China/Jammu and Kashmir
88 A3 Mintang China
23 G4 Minto Can.
22 F2 Minto, Lac l. Can.
25 F4 Minturn U.S.A.
80 C6 Minūf Egypt
86 F1 Minusinsk Rus. Fed.
85 J3 Minutang India
88 B3 Minxian China
114 E6 Minyip Austr.
31 E3 Mio U.S.A.
22 E4 Miquelon Can.
23 J4 Miquelon i. N. America
45 A4 Mira r. Col.
33 F2 Mirabel Can.
46 D2 Mirabela Brazil
43 J5 Miracema do Norte Brazil
43 J5 Mirador, Parque Nacional de nat. park Brazil
45 B4 Miraflores Col.
81 H5 Mīrah, Wādī al watercourse Iraq/S. Arabia
46 D2 Miralta Brazil
47 F3 Miramar Arg.
64 G5 Miramas France
23 G4 Miramichi r. Can.
67 L7 Mirampelou, Kolpos b. Greece
46 A3 Miranda Brazil
46 A3 Miranda r. Brazil
34 A1 Miranda U.S.A.
65 E1 Miranda de Ebro Spain
65 C2 Mirandela Port.
66 D2 Mirandola Italy
46 B3 Mirandópolis Brazil
79 G6 Mirbāṭ Oman
64 E5 Mirepoix France
92 E6 Miri Malaysia
47 G2 Mirim, Lagoa l. Brazil
119 D5 Mirnyy Rus. Fed. Base Antarctica
77 N3 Mirnyy Rus. Fed.
68 G2 Mirnyy Rus. Fed.
21 J3 Mirond L. l. Can.
84 C2 Mirpur Pak.
84 B4 Mirpur Batoro Pak.
84 B4 Mirpur Khas Pak.
84 B4 Mirpur Sakro Pak.
20 G4 Mirror Can.
116 B3 Mirtna Austr.
67 K6 Mirtoö Pelagos sea Greece
91 A7 Miryang S. Korea
85 E4 Mirzapur India
91 C8 Misaki Japan
90 G4 Misawa Japan
23 H4 Miscou I. i. Can.
84 C1 Misgar Pak.
90 B2 Mishan China
30 D5 Mishawaka U.S.A.
30 E1 Mishibishu Lake l. Can.
91 B7 Mi-shima i. Japan
85 H3 Mishmi Hills mts India
110 F3 Misima I. i. P.N.G.
37 H6 Miskitos, Cayos atolls Nic.
63 K6 Miskolc Hungary
93 J7 Misoöl i. Indon.
30 B2 Misquah Hills h. U.S.A.
101 D1 Miṣrātah Libya
84 E4 Misrikh India
31 E1 Missanabie Can.
22 D3 Missinaibi r. Can.
31 F1 Missinaibi Lake l. Can.
21 J3 Missinipe Can.
20 E5 Mission Can.
26 C3 Mission U.S.A.
116 B1 Mission Beach Austr.
22 D3 Missisa L. l. Can.
31 F2 Missisagi r. Can.
31 H4 Mississauga Can.
30 E5 Mississinewa Lake l. U.S.A.
31 J3 Mississippi r. Can.
27 F5 Mississippi div. U.S.A.
27 F6 Mississippi r. U.S.A.
27 F6 Mississippi Delta delta U.S.A.
24 D2 Missoula U.S.A.
30 A6 Missouri div. U.S.A.
26 C2 Missouri r. U.S.A.
26 E3 Missouri Valley U.S.A.
116 B4 Mistake Cr. r. Austr.
23 F4 Mistassini Can.
23 F4 Mistassini r. Can.
22 F3 Mistassini, L. l. Can.
23 H2 Mistastin Lake l. Can.
62 H6 Mistelbach Austria
23 H2 Mistinibi, Lac l. Can.
22 F3 Mistissini Can.
20 C3 Misty Fiords National Monument Wilderness res. U.S.A.
116 B6 Mitchell Austr.
115 K2 Mitchell r. N.S.W. Austr.
113 H3 Mitchell r. Qld. Austr.
115 G6 Mitchell r. Vic. Austr.
31 G4 Mitchell Can.
26 D3 Mitchell U.S.A.
30 E3 Mitchell, Lake l. U.S.A.
29 D5 Mitchell, Mt mt U.S.A.
60 C5 Mitchelstown Rep. of Ireland
80 C6 Mīt Ghamr Egypt
84 B3 Mithankot Pak.
84 B4 Mithi Pak.
84 B4 Mithrani Canal canal Pak.
67 M5 Mithymna Greece
20 C3 Mitkof I. i. U.S.A.
91 G6 Mito Japan
103 D4 Mitole Tanz.
117 E4 Mitre mt N.Z.
111 H3 Mitre Island i. Solomon Is
115 J5 Mittagong Austr.
115 G6 Mitta Mitta Austr.
62 D4 Mittellandkanal canal Ger.
45 C4 Mitú Col.
45 C4 Mituas Col.
103 C5 Mitumba, Chaîne des mts Dem. Rep. Congo
102 C4 Mitumba, Monts mts Dem. Rep. Congo
102 B3 Mitzic Gabon
91 F7 Miura Japan
81 G4 Miyāh, Wādī al watercourse Syria
91 F7 Miyake-jima i. Japan
90 G5 Miyako Japan
91 B9 Miyakonojō Japan
88 B4 Miyaluo China
84 B5 Miyāni India
91 B9 Miyazaki Japan
91 D7 Miyazu Japan
89 B5 Miyi China
91 C7 Miyoshi Japan
88 E1 Miyun China
88 E1 Miyun Sk. resr China
102 D3 Mīzan Teferī Eth.
101 D1 Mizdah Libya
60 B6 Mizen Head hd Rep. of Ireland
69 B5 Mizhhir"ya Ukr.
88 D2 Mizhi China
85 H5 Mizoram div. India
90 G5 Mizusawa Japan
55 O7 Mjölby Sweden
102 D4 Mkata Tanz.
102 D4 Mkomazi Tanz.
103 C5 Mkushi Zambia
62 G5 Mladá Boleslav Czech Rep.
67 J2 Mladenovac Serb. and Mont.
63 K4 Mława Pol.
66 G3 Mljet i. Croatia
105 G5 Mlungisi S. Africa
63 M5 Mlyniv Ukr.
105 F2 Mmabatho S. Africa
105 G1 Mmamabula Botswana
105 F2 Mmathethe Botswana
55 J6 Mo Norway
35 H2 Moab U.S.A.
113 H2 Moa I. i. Austr.
111 H3 Moala i. Fiji
105 K2 Moamba Moz.
114 D2 Moanba, Lake salt flat Austr.
35 E3 Moapa U.S.A.
60 D4 Moate Rep. of Ireland
102 C4 Moba Dem. Rep. Congo
91 G7 Mobara Japan
102 C3 Mobayi-Mbongo Dem. Rep. Congo
26 E4 Moberly U.S.A.
29 B6 Mobile AL U.S.A.
35 F5 Mobile AZ U.S.A.
29 B6 Mobile Bay b. U.S.A.
26 C2 Mobridge U.S.A.
Mobutu, Lake l. see Albert, Lake
43 J4 Mocajuba Brazil
103 E5 Moçambique Moz.
45 D2 Mocapra r. Venez.
89 B6 Môc Châu Vietnam
45 D2 Mochirma, Parque Nacional nat. park Venez.
103 C6 Mochudi Botswana
103 E5 Mocimboa da Praia Moz.
54 R4 Mockträsk Sweden
45 A4 Mocoa Col.
46 C3 Mococa Brazil
25 F6 Moctezuma Chihuahua Mex.
25 E6 Moctezuma Sonora Mex.
103 D5 Mocuba Moz.
64 H4 Modane France
84 C5 Modasa India
104 F4 Modder r. S. Africa
66 D2 Modena Italy
35 F3 Modena U.S.A.
34 B3 Modesto U.S.A.
115 G7 Moe Austr.
59 D5 Moel Sych h. U.K.
55 M6 Moelv Norway
54 Q2 Moen Norway
35 G3 Moenkopi U.S.A.
117 C6 Moeraki Pt pt N.Z.
57 E5 Moffat U.K.
84 C3 Moga India
Mogadishu see Muqdisho
32 C4 Mogadore Reservoir resr U.S.A.
105 H1 Mogalakwena r. S. Africa
105 H2 Moganyaka S. Africa
46 C3 Mogi-Mirim Brazil
87 L1 Mogocha Rus. Fed.
66 C6 Mogod mts Tunisia
105 F2 Mogoditshane Botswana
83 J6 Mogok Myanmar
35 H5 Mogollon Mts mts U.S.A.
35 G4 Mogollon Plateau plat. U.S.A.
105 G2 Mogwase S. Africa
67 H2 Mohács Hungary
117 F3 Mohaka r. N.Z.
105 G5 Mohale's Hoek Lesotho
21 J5 Mohall U.S.A.
65 G5 Mohammadia Alg.
84 E3 Mohan r. India/Nepal
35 E4 Mohave, L. l. U.S.A.
35 F5 Mohawk U.S.A.
33 F3 Mohawk r. U.S.A.
35 F5 Mohawk Mts mts U.S.A.
103 E5 Moheli i. Comoros
60 D4 Mohill Rep. of Ireland
35 F4 Mohon Peak summit U.S.A.
103 D4 Mohoro Tanz.
81 M5 Moh Reza Shah Pahlavi resr Iran
69 C5 Mohyliv Podil's'kyy Ukr.
55 K7 Moi Norway
105 G1 Moijabana Botswana
105 K2 Moine Moz.
63 N7 Moinești Romania
33 F2 Moira U.S.A.
54 O3 Mo i Rana Norway
85 H4 Moirang India
55 T7 Mõisaküla Estonia
47 E1 Moisés Ville Arg.
23 G3 Moisie Can.
23 G3 Moisie r. Can.
64 E4 Moissac France
34 C4 Mojave U.S.A.
34 D4 Mojave r. U.S.A.
34 D4 Mojave Desert des. U.S.A.
46 C3 Moji das Cruzes Brazil
46 C3 Moji-Guaçu r. Brazil
91 B8 Mojikō Japan
85 F4 Mokāma India
34 □1 Mokapu Pen. pen. U.S.A.
117 E3 Mokau N.Z.
117 E3 Mokau r. N.Z.
34 B2 Mokelumne r. U.S.A.
105 H4 Mokhoabong Pass pass Lesotho
105 H4 Mokhotlong Lesotho
66 D7 Moknine Tunisia
117 E1 Mokohinau Is is N.Z.
101 D3 Mokolo Cameroon
105 G1 Mokolo r. S. Africa
87 N5 Mokp'o S. Korea
68 G4 Moksha r. Rus. Fed.
68 H4 Mokshan Rus. Fed.
34 □1 Mokuauia I. i. U.S.A.
34 □1 Mokulua Is is U.S.A.
65 F3 Molatón mt Spain
54 K5 Molde Norway
54 O3 Moldjord Norway
48 Moldova country Europe
67 L2 Moldoveanu, Vârful mt Romania
59 D7 Mole r. U.K.
100 B4 Mole National Park nat. park Ghana
103 C6 Molepolole Botswana
55 T9 Molėtai Lith.
66 G4 Molfetta Italy
65 F2 Molina de Aragón Spain
30 B5 Moline U.S.A.
55 N7 Molkom Sweden
81 M4 Mollā Bodāgh Iran
85 H4 Mol Len mt India
42 D7 Mollendo Peru
55 N8 Mölnlycke Sweden
68 F3 Molochnoye Rus. Fed.
54 X2 Molochnyy Rus. Fed.
119 D4 Molodezhnaya Rus. Fed. Base Antarctica
68 E3 Molodoy Tud Rus. Fed.
34 □2 Molokai i. U.S.A.
15 K4 Molokai Fracture Zone sea feature Pac. Oc.
68 J3 Moloma r. Rus. Fed.
115 H4 Molong Austr.
104 F2 Molopo watercourse Botswana/S. Africa
101 D4 Moloundou Cameroon
21 K4 Molson L. l. Can.
93 H7 Moluccas is Indon.
93 H6 Molucca Sea g. Indon.
103 D5 Moma Moz.
114 E3 Momba Austr.
102 D4 Mombasa Kenya
85 H4 Mombi New India
46 B2 Mombuca, Serra da h. Brazil
69 C7 Momchilgrad Bulg.
30 D5 Momence U.S.A.
45 B2 Mompós Col.
55 N9 Møn i. Denmark
35 G2 Mona U.S.A.
37 L5 Mona, I. i. Puerto Rico
57 A3 Monach, Sound of chan. U.K.
57 A3 Monach Islands is U.K.
48 Monaco country Europe
57 D3 Monadhliath Mountains mts U.K.
60 E3 Monaghan Rep. of Ireland
27 C6 Monahans U.S.A.
37 L5 Mona Passage chan. Dom. Rep./Puerto Rico
103 E5 Monapo Moz.
57 C3 Monar, Loch l. U.K.
20 D4 Monarch Mt. mt Can.
25 F4 Monarch Pass pass U.S.A.
20 F4 Monashee Mts mts Can.
66 D7 Monastir Tunisia
63 P3 Monastyrshchina Rus. Fed.
69 D5 Monastyryshche Ukr.
90 H2 Monbetsu Japan
90 H3 Monbetsu Japan
66 B2 Moncalieri Italy
54 X3 Monchegorsk Rus. Fed.
62 C5 Mönchengladbach Ger.
65 B4 Monchique Port.
29 E5 Moncks Corner U.S.A.
36 D3 Monclova Mex.
23 H4 Moncton Can.
65 C2 Mondego r. Port.
105 J3 Mondlo S. Africa
66 B2 Mondovì Italy
30 B3 Mondovi U.S.A.
66 E4 Mondragone Italy
67 K6 Monemvasia Greece
90 G1 Moneron, Ostrov i. Rus. Fed.
32 D4 Monessen U.S.A.
31 K1 Monet Can.
60 D5 Moneygall Rep. of Ireland
60 E3 Moneymore U.K.
66 E2 Monfalcone Italy
65 C1 Monforte Spain
102 C3 Monga Dem. Rep. Congo
89 C6 Mông Cai Vietnam
95 A1 Mong Mau Myanmar
70 Mongolia country Asia
84 C2 Mongora Pak.
103 C5 Mongu Zambia
33 J3 Monhegan I. i. U.S.A.
57 E5 Moniaive U.K.
34 D2 Monitor Mt mt U.S.A.
34 D2 Monitor Range mts U.S.A.
60 C4 Monivea Rep. of Ireland
31 G4 Monkton Can.
85 F3 Mon La pass China
59 E6 Monmouth U.K.
30 B5 Monmouth IL U.S.A.
33 H2 Monmouth ME U.S.A.
20 E4 Monmouth Mt. mt Can.
59 E6 Monnow r. U.K.
100 C4 Mono r. Togo
34 C3 Mono Lake l. U.S.A.
33 H4 Monomoy Pt pt U.S.A.
30 D5 Monon U.S.A.
30 B4 Monona U.S.A.
66 G4 Monopoli Italy
32 C5 Monongahela r. U.S.A.
65 F2 Monreal del Campo Spain
66 E5 Monreale Italy
27 E5 Monroe LA U.S.A.
31 F5 Monroe MI U.S.A.
29 D5 Monroe NC U.S.A.
33 F4 Monroe NY U.S.A.
35 F2 Monroe UT U.S.A.
30 C4 Monroe WV U.S.A.
30 B6 Monroe City U.S.A.
29 C6 Monroeville U.S.A.
100 A4 Monrovia Liberia
61 B4 Mons Belgium
66 D2 Monselice Italy
104 D6 Montagu S. Africa
30 D4 Montague U.S.A.
119 C1 Montagu I. i. Atlantic Ocean
66 F5 Montalto mt Italy
66 G5 Montalto Uffugo Italy
67 K3 Montana Bulg.
24 E2 Montana div. U.S.A.
64 F3 Montargis France
64 E4 Montauban France
33 G4 Montauk U.S.A.
33 H4 Montauk Pt pt U.S.A.
64 G3 Montbard France
64 H4 Mont Blanc mt France/Italy
65 G2 Montblanc Spain
64 G4 Montbrison France
64 G3 Montceau-les-Mines France
64 D5 Mont-de-Marsan France
64 F2 Montdidier France
43 H4 Monte Alegre Brazil
46 C1 Monte Alegre de Goiás Brazil
46 D1 Monte Azul Brazil
22 E4 Montebello Can.
66 F6 Montebello Ionico Italy
66 E2 Montebelluna Italy
47 D2 Monte Buey Arg.
64 H5 Monte-Carlo Monaco
47 F1 Monte Caseros Arg.
105 G1 Monte Christo S. Africa
47 C2 Monte Comán Arg.
37 K5 Monte Cristi Dom. Rep.
66 D3 Montecristo, Isola di i. Italy
37 J5 Montego Bay Jamaica
64 G4 Montélimar France
44 E2 Monte Lindo r. Para.
66 F4 Montella Italy
30 C4 Montello U.S.A.
36 E3 Montemorelos Mex.
65 B3 Montemor-o-Novo Port.
67 H3 Montenegro div. Serb. and Mont.
103 D5 Montepuez Moz.
66 D3 Montepulciano Italy
64 F2 Montereau-faut-Yonne France
34 B3 Monterey CA U.S.A.
32 D5 Monterey VA U.S.A.
34 B3 Monterey Bay b. U.S.A.
45 B2 Montería Col.
42 F7 Montero Bol.
36 D3 Monterrey Mex.
66 F4 Montesano sulla Marcellana Italy
43 L6 Monte Santo Brazil
46 D2 Montes Claros Brazil
66 F3 Montesilvano Italy
66 D3 Montevarchi Italy
47 F2 Montevideo Uru.
26 E2 Montevideo U.S.A.
25 F4 Monte Vista U.S.A.
30 A5 Montezuma U.S.A.
35 G4 Montezuma Castle National Monument res. U.S.A.
35 H3 Montezuma Creek U.S.A.
34 D3 Montezuma Peak summit U.S.A.
59 D5 Montgomery U.K.
29 C5 Montgomery U.S.A.
62 C7 Monthey Switz.
27 F5 Monticello AR U.S.A.
29 D6 Monticello FL U.S.A.
30 B4 Monticello IA U.S.A.
30 D5 Monticello IN U.S.A.
33 K1 Monticello ME U.S.A.
30 B5 Monticello MO U.S.A.
33 F4 Monticello NY U.S.A.
35 H3 Monticello UT U.S.A.
30 C4 Monticello WV U.S.A.
47 E1 Montiel, Cuchilla de h. Arg.
64 E4 Montignac France
65 D4 Montilla Spain
23 G4 Mont-Joli Can.
31 K2 Mont-Laurier Can.
23 G4 Mont Louis Can.
64 F3 Montluçon France
23 F4 Montmagny Can.
61 D5 Montmédy France
30 D5 Montmorenci U.S.A.
23 F4 Montmorency Can.
64 E3 Montmorillon France
116 D5 Monto Austr.
24 E3 Montpelier ID U.S.A.
30 E5 Montpelier IN U.S.A.
32 A4 Montpelier OH U.S.A.
33 G2 Montpelier VT U.S.A.
64 F5 Montpellier France
22 F4 Montréal Can.
31 G2 Montreal r. Can.
31 F2 Montreal r. Can.
30 E2 Montreal I. i. Can.
21 H4 Montreal L. l. Can.
21 H4 Montreal Lake Can.
33 F2 Montréal-Mirabel Can.
30 E2 Montreal River Can.
62 C7 Montreux Switz.
104 D3 Montrose w. S. Africa
57 F4 Montrose U.K.
25 F4 Montrose CO U.S.A.
31 F4 Montrose MI U.S.A.
33 F4 Montrose PA U.S.A.
23 G4 Monts, Pte des pt Can.
37 M5 Montserrat terr. Caribbean
35 G3 Monument Valley reg. U.S.A.
83 J6 Monywa Myanmar
66 C2 Monza Italy
103 C5 Monze Zambia
65 G2 Monzón Spain
105 J4 Mooi r. S. Africa
104 B3 Mooifontein Namibia
105 J4 Mooirivier S. Africa
105 G1 Mookane Botswana
114 C2 Moolawatana Austr.
115 H2 Moomin Cr. r. Austr.
114 A3 Moonaree Austr.
115 J3 Moonbi Ra. mts Austr.
115 J1 Moonie Austr.
115 H2 Moonie r. Austr.
114 B5 Moonta Austr.
112 C6 Moora Austr.
24 F2 Moorcroft U.S.A.
112 C5 Moore, Lake salt flat Austr.
32 D5 Moorefield U.S.A.
29 E7 Moores I. i. Bahamas
33 K2 Moores Mills Can.
57 E5 Moorfoot Hills h. U.K.
26 D2 Moorhead U.S.A.
114 E4 Moornanyah Lake l. Austr.
114 D5 Moorook Austr.
114 F6 Mooroopna Austr.
104 C6 Moorreesburg S. Africa
22 D3 Moose r. Can.
22 D3 Moose Factory Can.
33 J2 Moosehead Lake l. U.S.A.
21 H4 Moose Jaw Can.
21 J4 Moose Lake l. Can.
30 A2 Moose Lake U.S.A.
33 H2 Mooselookmeguntic Lake l. U.S.A.
22 D3 Moose River Can.
21 J4 Moosomin Can.
22 D3 Moosonee Can.
114 E3 Mootwingee Austr.
105 H1 Mopane S. Africa
100 B3 Mopti Mali
84 A2 Moqor Afgh.
42 D7 Moquegua Peru
101 D3 Mora Cameroon
65 E3 Mora Spain
55 O6 Mora Sweden
47 B2 Mora, Cerro mt Arg./Chile
84 A3 Morad r. Pak.
84 D3 Moradabad India
103 E5 Morafenobe Madag.
103 E5 Moramanga Madag.
30 E3 Moran MI U.S.A.
24 E3 Moran WY U.S.A.

47 C3 Neuquén r. Arg.
62 F4 Neuruppin Ger.
29 E5 Neuse r. U.S.A.
62 H7 Neusiedler See l. Austria/Hungary
61 E3 Neuss Ger.
61 F4 Neustadt (Wied) Ger.
62 F4 Neustrelitz Ger.
62 C5 Neuwied Ger.
27 E4 Nevada U.S.A.
34 D2 Nevada div. U.S.A.
65 E4 Nevada, Sierra mts Spain
34 B1 Nevada, Sierra mts U.S.A.
47 C2 Nevado, Cerro mt Arg.
47 C3 Nevado, Sierra del mts Arg.
68 D3 Nevel' Rus. Fed.
64 F3 Nevers France
115 G3 Nevertire Austr.
67 H3 Nevesinje Bos.-Herz.
69 G6 Nevinnomyssk Rus. Fed.
57 C3 Nevis, Loch in. U.K.
80 E2 Nevşehir Turkey
90 C2 Nevskoye Rus. Fed.
35 E5 New r. CA U.S.A.
32 C6 New r. WV U.S.A.
20 D3 New Aiyansh Can.
28 C4 New Albany IN U.S.A.
27 F5 New Albany MS U.S.A.
33 E4 New Albany PA U.S.A.
43 G2 New Amsterdam Guyana
115 G2 New Angledool Austr.
33 F5 Newark DE U.S.A.
33 F5 Newark MD U.S.A.
33 F4 Newark NJ U.S.A.
32 E3 Newark NY U.S.A.
32 B4 Newark OH U.S.A.
33 F4 Newark airport U.S.A.
35 E2 Newark Lake l. U.S.A.
59 G4 Newark-on-Trent U.K.
33 E3 Newark Valley U.S.A.
33 H4 New Bedford U.S.A.
24 B2 Newberg U.S.A.
33 F3 New Berlin U.S.A.
29 E5 New Bern U.S.A.
30 E2 Newberry MI U.S.A.
29 D5 Newberry SC U.S.A.
34 D4 Newberry Springs U.S.A.
58 F2 Newbiggin-by-the-Sea U.K.
29 F7 New Bight Bahamas
31 J3 Newboro Can.
33 G3 New Boston MA U.S.A.
32 B5 New Boston OH U.S.A.
27 D6 New Braunfels U.S.A.
60 E4 Newbridge Rep. of Ireland
110 E2 New Britain i. P.N.G.
33 G4 New Britain U.S.A.
23 G4 New Brunswick div. Can.
33 F4 New Brunswick U.S.A.
30 D5 New Buffalo U.S.A.
57 F3 Newburgh U.K.
33 F4 Newburgh U.S.A.
59 F6 Newbury U.K.
33 H3 Newburyport U.S.A.
58 E3 Newby Bridge U.K.
106 New Caledonia terr. Pac. Oc.
14 F7 New Caledonia Trough sea feature Pac. Oc.
23 G4 New Carlisle Can.
115 J4 Newcastle Austr.
23 G4 Newcastle N.B. Can.
31 H4 Newcastle Ont. Can.
60 E4 Newcastle Rep. of Ireland
105 H3 Newcastle S. Africa
60 F3 Newcastle U.K.
34 B2 Newcastle CA U.S.A.
30 E6 New Castle IN U.S.A.
32 B4 Newcastle OH U.S.A.
32 C4 New Castle PA U.S.A.
35 F3 Newcastle UT U.S.A.
32 C6 New Castle VA U.S.A.
24 F3 Newcastle WY U.S.A.
59 C5 Newcastle Emlyn U.K.
59 E4 Newcastle-under-Lyme U.K.
58 F3 Newcastle upon Tyne U.K.
113 F3 Newcastle Waters Austr.
60 B5 Newcastle West Rep. of Ireland
33 F6 New Church U.S.A.
35 H3 Newcomb U.S.A.
57 D5 New Cumnock U.K.
57 F3 New Deer U.K.
84 D3 New Delhi India
33 K1 New Denmark Can.
34 B3 New Don Pedro Reservoir resr U.S.A.
115 J3 New England Range mts Austr.
59 E6 Newent U.K.
23 J4 Newfoundland and Labrador div. Can.
12 G2 Newfoundland Basin sea feature Atlantic Ocean
24 D3 Newfoundland Evaporation Basin salt l. U.S.A.
57 D5 New Galloway U.K.
111 F2 New Georgia i. Solomon Is
111 F2 New Georgia Islands is Solomon Is
23 H4 New Glasgow Can.
93 L7 New Guinea i. Asia
32 B4 New Hampshire U.S.A.
33 G3 New Hampshire div. U.S.A.
30 A4 New Hampton U.S.A.
110 F2 New Hanover i. P.N.G.
105 J4 New Hanover S. Africa
33 G4 New Haven U.S.A.
20 D3 New Hazelton Can.
34 B2 New Hogan Reservoir resr U.S.A.
30 C4 New Holstein U.S.A.
27 F6 New Iberia U.S.A.
105 J2 Newington S. Africa
60 D5 Newinn Rep. of Ireland
110 F2 New Ireland i. P.N.G.
33 F5 New Jersey div. U.S.A.
32 E6 New Kent U.S.A.
32 B5 New Lexington U.S.A.
30 B4 New Lisbon U.S.A.
31 H2 New Liskeard Can.
33 G4 New London CT U.S.A.
30 B5 New London IA U.S.A.
30 B6 New London MO U.S.A.
30 C3 New London WV U.S.A.
112 C4 Newman Austr.
30 D6 Newman U.S.A.
31 H3 Newmarket Can.
60 B5 Newmarket Rep. of Ireland
59 H5 Newmarket U.K.
32 D5 New Market U.S.A.
60 C5 Newmarket on-Fergus Rep. of Ireland
32 C5 New Martinsville U.S.A.
24 C2 New Meadows U.S.A.
34 B3 New Melanes L. l. U.S.A.
25 F5 New Mexico div. U.S.A.
29 C5 Newnan U.S.A.
115 G9 New Norfolk Austr.
27 F6 New Orleans U.S.A.
33 F4 New Paltz U.S.A.
32 C4 New Philadelphia U.S.A.
57 F3 New Pitsligo U.K.
117 E3 New Plymouth N.Z.
60 B4 Newport Mayo Rep. of Ireland
60 C5 Newport Tipperary Rep. of Ireland
59 E5 Newport Eng. U.K.
59 F7 Newport Eng. U.K.
59 D6 Newport Wales U.K.
27 F5 Newport AR U.S.A.
32 A5 Newport KY U.S.A.
33 J2 Newport ME U.S.A.
31 F5 Newport MI U.S.A.
33 G3 Newport NH U.S.A.
24 A2 Newport OR U.S.A.
33 H4 Newport RI U.S.A.
33 G2 Newport VT U.S.A.
24 C1 Newport WA U.S.A.
34 D5 Newport Beach U.S.A.
32 E6 Newport News U.S.A.
59 G5 Newport Pagnell U.K.
29 E7 New Providence i. Bahamas
59 B7 Newquay U.K.
23 G4 New Richmond Can.
30 A3 New Richmond U.S.A.
35 F5 New River U.S.A.
27 F6 New Roads U.S.A.
59 H7 New Romney U.K.
60 E5 New Ross Rep. of Ireland
60 E3 Newry U.K.
57 E4 New Scone U.K.
30 A5 New Sharon U.S.A.
New Siberia Islands is see Novosibirskiye Ostrova
29 D6 New Smyrna Beach U.S.A.
115 G4 New South Wales div. Austr.
58 E4 Newton U.K.
26 E3 Newton IA U.S.A.
26 D4 Newton KS U.S.A.
33 H3 Newton MA U.S.A.
27 F5 Newton MS U.S.A.
33 F4 Newton NJ U.S.A.
59 D7 Newton Abbot U.K.
57 F3 Newtonhill U.K.
57 D5 Newton Mearns U.K.
57 D6 Newton Stewart U.K.
60 C5 Newtown Rep. of Ireland
59 E5 Newtown Eng. U.K.
59 D5 Newtown Wales U.K.
26 C1 New Town U.S.A.
60 F3 Newtownabbey U.K.
60 F3 Newtownards U.K.
60 D3 Newtownbutler U.K.
60 E4 Newtownmountkennedy Rep. of Ireland
57 F5 Newtown St Boswells U.K.
60 D3 Newtownstewart U.K.
26 E2 New Ulm U.S.A.
34 A2 Newville U.S.A.
20 E5 New Westminster Can.
33 G4 New York U.S.A.
33 E3 New York div. U.S.A.
106 N.Z. country Australasia
68 G3 Neya Rus. Fed.
79 G4 Neyrīz Iran
79 H2 Neyshābūr Iran
36 F5 Nezahualcóyotl, Presa resr Mex.
102 B4 Ngabé Congo
95 A2 Nga Chong, Khao mt Myanmar/Thai.
94 C6 Ngalipaëng Indon.
103 C6 Ngami, Lake l. Botswana
85 F3 Ngamring China
85 E3 Ngangla Ringco salt l. China
84 E2 Nganglong Kangri mt China
84 E2 Nganglong Kangri mts China
85 F3 Ngangzê Co salt l. China
95 C1 Ngan Sau, Sông r. Vietnam
95 A1 Ngao Thai.
101 D4 Ngaoundéré Cameroon
117 E2 Ngaruawahia N.Z.
117 F3 Ngaruroro r. N.Z.
117 E3 Ngauruhoe vol. N.Z.
92 □ Ngawi Indon.
95 B1 Ngiap r. Laos
102 B4 Ngo Congo
95 C2 Ngoc Linh mt Vietnam
85 F3 Ngoin, Co salt l. China
100 D4 Ngol Bembo Nigeria
85 H2 Ngom Qu r. China
85 F2 Ngoqumaima China
82 J4 Ngoring Hu l. China
101 D3 Ngourti Niger
101 D3 Nguigmi Niger
93 K5 Ngulu i. Micronesia
95 B1 Ngum, Nam r. Laos
92 □ Ngunut Indon.
100 D3 Nguru Nigeria
89 B6 Nguyên Binh Vietnam
104 E2 Ngwaketse div. Botswana
105 G3 Ngwathe S. Africa
105 K3 Ngwavuma r. Swaziland
105 J4 Ngwelezana S. Africa
105 D5 Nhamalabué Moz.
95 D2 Nha Trang Vietnam
114 D6 Nhill Austr.
105 J3 Nhlangano Swaziland
89 B6 Nho Quan Vietnam
113 G2 Nhulunbuy Austr.
21 J4 Niacam Can.
100 B3 Niafounké Mali
30 D3 Niagara U.S.A.
31 H4 Niagara Falls Can.
32 D3 Niagara Falls U.S.A.
31 H4 Niagara River r. Can./U.S.A.
100 C3 Niamey Niger
94 C5 Niampak Indon.
103 D4 Niangandu Tanz.
102 C3 Niangara Dem. Rep. Congo
92 B6 Nias i. Indon.
Niassa, Lago l. see Nyasa, Lake
55 R8 Nīca Latvia
16 Nicaragua country Central America
37 G6 Nicaragua, Lago de l. Nic.
66 G5 Nicastro Italy
64 H5 Nice France
23 F3 Nichicun, Lac l. Can.
85 E4 Nichlaul India
29 E7 Nicholl's Town Bahamas
31 F2 Nicholson Can.
83 H9 Nicobar Islands is Andaman and Nicobar Is
80 D4 Nicosia Cyprus
37 H7 Nicoya, G. de b. Costa Rica
37 G7 Nicoya, Pen. de pen. Costa Rica
33 K1 Nictau Can.
55 R9 Nida Lith.
58 F4 Nidd r. U.K.
63 K4 Nidzica Pol.
62 D3 Niebüll Ger.
62 F7 Niedere Tauern mts Austria
61 F2 Niedersachsen div. Ger.
100 D4 Niefang Equatorial Guinea
100 B3 Niellé Côte d'Ivoire
62 D4 Nienburg (Weser) Ger.
61 E3 Niers r. Ger.
43 G2 Nieuw Amsterdam Suriname
61 C2 Nieuwe-Niedorp Neth.
61 C3 Nieuwerkerk aan de IJssel Neth.
43 G2 Nieuw Nickerie Suriname
104 C5 Nieuwoudtville S. Africa
61 A3 Nieuwpoort Belgium
61 C3 Nieuw-Vossemeer Neth.
80 E3 Niğde Turkey
96 Niger country Africa
100 C4 Niger r. Africa
100 C4 Niger, Mouths of the est. Nigeria
96 Nigeria country Africa
31 G1 Nighthawk Lake l. Can.
67 K4 Nigrita Greece
91 G6 Nihonmatsu Japan
91 F6 Niigata Japan
91 F6 Niigata-yake-yama vol. Japan
91 C8 Niihama Japan
34 □2 Niihau i. U.S.A.
91 F7 Nii-jima i. Japan
90 H3 Niikappu Japan
91 C7 Niimi Japan
91 F6 Niitsu Japan
61 D2 Nijkerk Neth.
61 D3 Nijmegen Neth.
61 E2 Nijverdal Neth.
54 W2 Nikel' Rus. Fed.
100 C4 Nikki Benin
91 F6 Nikkō Nat. Park Japan
68 H4 Nikolayevka Rus. Fed.
69 H5 Nikolayevsk Rus. Fed.
68 H4 Nikol'sk Penzen. Rus. Fed.
68 H3 Nikol'sk Vologod. Rus. Fed.
77 S4 Nikol'skoye Rus. Fed.
69 E6 Nikopol' Ukr.
81 M3 Nīk Pey Iran
80 F1 Niksar Turkey
67 H3 Nikšić Serb. and Mont.
111 J2 Nikumaroro i. Kiribati
111 H2 Nikunau i. Kiribati
84 C2 Nila Pak.
85 F5 Nilagiri India
35 E5 Niland U.S.A.
83 D10 Nilandhoo Atoll atoll Maldives
84 D3 Nilang India
78 C4 Nile r. Africa
30 D5 Niles U.S.A.
54 V5 Nilsiä Fin.
84 C4 Nimach India
115 K2 Nimbin Austr.
64 G5 Nîmes France
115 H6 Nimmitabel Austr.
101 F4 Nimule Sudan
81 J3 Nīnawá Iraq
115 H2 Nindigully Austr.
83 D9 Nine Degree Channel chan. India
114 E3 Nine Mile Lake salt flat Austr.
34 D2 Ninemile Peak summit U.S.A.
13 K5 Ninetyeast Ridge sea feature Indian Ocean
115 G7 Ninety Mile Beach beach Austr.
117 D1 Ninety Mile Beach beach N.Z.
33 F3 Nineveh U.S.A.
90 A2 Ning'an China
89 F4 Ningbo China
88 F1 Ningcheng China
89 F5 Ningde China
89 E5 Ningdu China
89 D5 Ninggang China
89 F4 Ningguo China
89 F4 Ninghai China
88 E2 Ninghe China
89 E5 Ninghua China
82 J4 Ningjing Shan mts China
88 E3 Ningling China
89 C6 Ningming China
89 B5 Ningnan China
88 C3 Ningqiang China
88 C3 Ningshan China
88 D2 Ningwu China
88 B2 Ningxia div. China
88 C3 Ningxian China
89 D4 Ningxiang China
88 E3 Ningyang China
89 D5 Ningyuan China
89 C6 Ninh Binh Vietnam
95 D2 Ninh Hoa Vietnam
90 G4 Ninohe Japan
46 A3 Nioaque Brazil
26 C3 Niobrara r. U.S.A.
85 H4 Nioko India
100 A3 Niokolo Koba, Parc National du nat. park Senegal
100 B3 Niono Mali
100 B3 Nioro Mali
64 D3 Niort France
21 J4 Nipawin Can.
22 C4 Nipigon Can.
22 C4 Nipigon, Lake l. Can.
30 C1 Nipigon Bay b. Can.
23 H3 Nipishish Lake l. Can.
31 H2 Nipissing Can.
31 G2 Nipissing, L. l. Can.
34 B4 Nipomo U.S.A.
81 K5 Nippur Iraq
35 E4 Nipton U.S.A.
46 C1 Niquelândia Brazil
81 L2 Nīr Iran
83 E7 Nirmal India
67 J3 Niš Serb. and Mont.
65 C3 Nisa Port.
66 F6 Niscemi Italy
Nīshāpūr see Neyshābūr
91 B9 Nishino-'omote Japan
91 C6 Nishino-shima i. Japan
91 A8 Nishi-Sonogi-hantō pen. Japan
91 D7 Nishiwaki Japan
20 B2 Nisling r. Can.
61 C4 Nismes, Forêt de forest Belgium
61 C3 Nispen Neth.
55 N8 Nissan r. Sweden
63 O7 Nistrului Inferior, Câmpia lowland Moldova
20 C2 Nisutlin r. Can.
67 M6 Nisyros i. Greece
23 F3 Nitchequon Can.
46 D3 Niterói Brazil
57 E5 Nith r. U.K.
57 E5 Nithsdale v. U.K.
84 D3 Niti Pass pass China
112 F2 Nitmiluk National Park nat. park Austr.
62 J6 Nitra Slovakia
32 C5 Nitro U.S.A.
111 J3 Niuatoputopu i. Tonga
106 Niue terr. Pac. Oc.
111 H3 Niulakita i. Tuvalu
89 B5 Niulan Jiang r. China
111 H2 Niutao i. Tuvalu
88 G1 Niuzhuang China
54 T5 Nivala Fin.
116 B5 Nive watercourse Austr.
116 B5 Nive Downs Austr.
61 C4 Nivelles Belgium
68 K2 Nivshera Rus. Fed.
84 C4 Niwāi India
34 C2 Nixon U.S.A.
85 E1 Niya He r. China
81 M1 Niyazoba Azer.
83 E7 Nizamabad India
68 H3 Nizhegorodskaya Oblast' div. Rus. Fed.
77 S3 Nizhnekolymsk Rus. Fed.
77 L4 Nizhneudinsk Rus. Fed.
76 J3 Nizhnevartovsk Rus. Fed.
77 P2 Nizhneyansk Rus. Fed.
68 G4 Nizhniy Lomov Rus. Fed.
68 G3 Nizhniy Novgorod Rus. Fed.
68 K2 Nizhniy Odes Rus. Fed.
68 H3 Nizhniy Yenangsk Rus. Fed.
54 W3 Nizhnyaya Pirenga, Ozero l. Rus. Fed.
77 K3 Nizhnyaya Tunguska r. Rus. Fed.
69 D5 Nizhyn Ukr.
63 K4 Nizina reg. Pol.
80 F3 Nizip Turkey
90 D3 Nizmennyy, Mys pt Rus. Fed.
54 R2 Njallavarri mt Norway
54 Q3 Njavve Sweden
Njazidja i. see Grande Comore
103 D4 Njinjo Tanz.
103 D4 Njombe Tanz.
55 P5 Njurundabommen Sweden
100 D4 Nkambe Cameroon
105 J4 Nkandla S. Africa
100 B4 Nkawkaw Ghana
103 C5 Nkayi Zimbabwe
103 D5 Nkhata Bay Malawi
103 D5 Nkhotakota Malawi
100 C4 Nkongsamba Cameroon
105 G5 Nkululeko S. Africa
103 B5 Nkurenkuru Namibia
105 G6 Nkwenkwezi S. Africa
85 J4 Noa Dihing r. India
85 G5 Noakhali Bangl.
85 F5 Noamundi India
60 E4 Nobber Rep. of Ireland
91 B8 Nobeoka Japan
90 G3 Noboribetsu Japan
46 A1 Nobres Brazil
114 E1 Noccundra Austr.
114 E1 Nockatunga Austr.
31 G2 Noelville Can.
36 B2 Nogales Arizona
36 B2 Nogales Mex.
91 B8 Nōgata Japan
64 E2 Nogent-le-Rotrou France
61 A5 Nogent-sur-Oise France
68 F4 Noginsk Rus. Fed.
116 D5 Nogo r. Austr.
116 B5 Nogoa r. Austr.
91 E7 Nōgōhaku-san mt Japan
47 E2 Nogoyá Arg.
47 E2 Nogoya r. Arg.
84 C3 Nohar India
90 G4 Noheji Japan
61 F5 Nohfelden Ger.
64 C3 Noirmoutier, Île de i. France
64 C3 Noirmoutier-en-l'Île France
91 F7 Nojima-zaki c. Japan
84 C4 Nokha India
79 J4 Nok Kundi Pak.
21 J3 Nokomis Lake l. Can.
102 B3 Nola C.A.R.
68 J3 Nolinsk Rus. Fed.
33 H4 No Mans Land i. U.S.A.
77 V3 Nome Alaska
88 B1 Nomgon Mongolia
85 J1 Nomhon China
105 G5 Nomonde S. Africa
91 A8 Nomo-zaki pt Japan
68 G3 Nomzha Rus. Fed.
21 H2 Nonacho Lake l. Can.
105 J4 Nondweni S. Africa
95 C1 Nông Hèt Laos
95 B2 Nong Hong Thai.
95 B1 Nong Khai Thai.
105 J3 Nongoma S. Africa
114 B4 Nonning Austr.
25 F7 Nonoava Mex.
111 H2 Nonouti i. Kiribati
95 B2 Nonthaburi Thai.
104 F5 Nonzwakazi S. Africa
115 G2 Nooroma Cr. watercourse Austr.
61 B3 Noordbeveland i. Neth.
61 C2 Noorderhaaks i. Neth.
61 D2 Noordoost Polder reclaimed land Neth.
116 E6 Noosa Heads Austr.
20 D5 Nootka I. i. Can.
79 K2 Norak Tajik.
94 C5 Norala Phil.
31 H1 Noranda Can.
55 O6 Norberg Sweden
76 D2 Nordaustlandet i. Svalbard
20 F4 Nordegg Can.
62 C4 Norden Ger.
76 L2 Nordenshel'da, Arkhipelag is Rus. Fed.
61 F1 Norderland reg. Ger.
61 F1 Norderney Ger.
61 F1 Norderney i. Ger.
62 E4 Norderstedt Ger.
55 J6 Nordfjordeid Norway
54 O3 Nordfold Norway
Nordfriesische Inseln is see North Frisian Islands
62 E5 Nordhausen Ger.
61 F2 Nordhorn Ger.
54 T1 Nordkapp c. Norway
54 Q2 Nordkjosbotn Norway
54 N4 Nordli Norway
62 E6 Nördlingen Ger.
54 Q5 Nordmaling Sweden
62 D3 Nord-Ostsee-Kanal canal Ger.
61 F3 Nordrhein-Westfalen div. Ger.
60 D5 Nore r. Rep. of Ireland
64 F5 Nore, Pic de mt France
26 D3 Norfolk NE U.S.A.
33 F2 Norfolk NY U.S.A.
111 G4 Norfolk Island terr. Pac. Oc.
14 G7 Norfolk Island Ridge sea feature Pac. Oc.
27 E4 Norfork L. l. U.S.A.
55 K6 Norheimsund Norway
91 E6 Norikura-dake vol. Japan
76 K3 Noril'sk Rus. Fed.
81 K1 Nor Kharberd Armenia
31 H3 Norland Can.
30 C5 Normal U.S.A.
27 D5 Norman U.S.A.
29 D5 Norman, L. l. U.S.A.
110 F2 Normanby I. i. P.N.G.
116 D4 Normanby Ra. h. Austr.
Normandes, Îles is see Channel Islands
56 F7 Normandie reg. France
Normandy reg. see Normandie
113 H3 Normanton Austr.
114 C5 Normanville Austr.
20 D1 Norman Wells Can.
47 B4 Ñorquinco Arg.
54 R5 Norra Kvarken str. Fin./Sweden
54 O4 Norra Storfjället mts Sweden
32 B6 Norris Lake l. U.S.A.
33 F4 Norristown U.S.A.
55 P7 Norrköping Sweden
55 Q7 Norrtälje Sweden
112 D6 Norseman Austr.
54 Q4 Norsjö Sweden
111 G3 Norsup Vanuatu
47 F3 Norte, Pta pt Buenos Aires Arg.
44 D6 Norte, Pta pt Chubut Arg.
119 A5 North, C. c. Antarctica
23 H4 North, C. c. Can.
33 G3 North Adams U.S.A.
58 F3 Northallerton U.K.
112 C6 Northam Austr.
112 B5 Northampton Austr.
59 G5 Northampton U.K.
33 G3 Northampton U.S.A.
116 A5 Northampton Downs Austr.
92 A4 North Andaman i. Andaman and Nicobar Is
32 E5 North Anna r. U.S.A.
33 J2 North Anson U.S.A.
20 G2 North Arm b. Can.
29 D5 North Augusta U.S.A.
23 H2 North Aulatsivik Island i. Can.
21 H4 North Battleford Can.
31 H2 North Bay Can.
22 E2 North Belcher Islands is Can.
24 A3 North Bend U.S.A.
57 F4 North Berwick U.K.
33 H3 North Berwick U.S.A.
115 F3 North Bourke Austr.
30 A3 North Branch U.S.A.
23 H4 North Cape pt Can.
North Cape c. see Nordkapp
117 D1 North Cape c. N.Z.
22 B3 North Caribou Lake l. Can.
29 D5 North Carolina div. U.S.A.
24 B1 North Cascades Nat. Park U.S.A.
31 F2 North Channel chan. Can.
60 E2 North Channel str. U.K.
33 H2 North Conway U.S.A.
26 C2 North Dakota div. U.S.A.
59 H6 North Downs h. U.K.
32 D3 North East U.S.A.
12 H2 North-Eastern Atlantic Basin sea feature Atlantic Ocean
29 E7 Northeast Providence Chan. chan. Bahamas
29 F7 North End Pt pt Bahamas
84 C1 Northern Areas div. Pak.
104 D4 Northern Cape div. S. Africa
21 K3 Northern Indian Lake l. Can.
56 C4 Northern Ireland div. U.K.
22 B4 Northern Light L. l. Can.
106 Northern Mariana Islands terr. Pac. Oc.
113 F3 Northern Territory div. Austr.
57 F4 North Esk r. U.K.
33 G3 Northfield MA U.S.A.
26 E2 Northfield MN U.S.A.
33 G2 Northfield VT U.S.A.
59 J6 North Foreland c. U.K.
35 E3 North Fork U.S.A.
30 E3 North Fox I. i. U.S.A.
22 D3 North French r. Can.
62 C3 North Frisian Islands is Ger.
118 B3 North Geomagnetic Pole Can.
58 G3 North Grimston U.K.
33 K2 North Head Can.
117 E2 North Head hd N.Z.
21 K2 North Henik Lake l. Can.
33 G3 North Hudson U.S.A.
117 E3 North Island i. N.Z.
94 B1 North Island i. Phil.
94 B4 North Islet rf Phil.
35 G4 North Jadito Canyon U.S.A.

30 D5 North Judson U.S.A.
21 K3 North Knife r. Can.
85 E4 North Koel r. India
35 G5 North Komelik U.S.A.
71 North Korea country Asia
85 H4 North Lakhimpur India
35 E3 North Las Vegas U.S.A.
27 E5 North Little Rock U.S.A.
103 D5 North Luangwa National Park nat. park Zambia
118 B3 North Magnetic Pole Can.
30 E5 North Manchester U.S.A.
30 D3 North Manitou I. i. U.S.A.
20 D2 North Nahanni r. Can.
21 L5 Northome U.S.A.
34 C3 North Palisade summit U.S.A.
26 C3 North Platte U.S.A.
26 C3 North Platte r. U.S.A.
115 G7 North Point pt Austr.
89 □ North Point pt China
28 D2 North Point pt U.S.A.
30 E3 Northport U.S.A.
35 F3 North Rim U.S.A.
57 F1 North Ronaldsay i. U.K.
57 F1 North Ronaldsay Firth chan. U.K.
34 B2 North San Juan U.S.A.
21 G4 North Saskatchewan r. Can.
52 North Sea sea Europe
21 J3 North Seal r. Can.
58 F2 North Shields U.K.
34 D2 North Shoshone Peak summit U.S.A.
59 H4 North Somercotes U.K.
115 K1 North Stradbroke I. i. Austr.
33 H2 North Stratford U.S.A.
58 F2 North Sunderland U.K.
117 E3 North Taranaki Bight b. N.Z.
20 F4 North Thompson r. Can.
57 A3 Northton U.K.
32 D3 North Tonawanda U.S.A.
117 A7 North Trap rf N.Z.
33 G2 North Troy U.S.A.
22 D3 North Twin I. i. Can.
58 E2 North Tyne r. U.K.
57 A3 North Uist i. U.K.
116 D3 Northumberland Is is Austr.
58 E2 Northumberland National Park nat. park U.K.
23 H4 Northumberland Strait chan. Can.
20 E5 North Vancouver Can.
33 F3 Northville U.S.A.
59 J5 North Walsham U.K.
104 F3 North West div. S. Africa
112 B4 North West C. c. Austr.
84 C2 North West Frontier div. Pak.
29 E7 Northwest Providence Chan. chan. Bahamas
23 J3 North West River Can.
21 G2 Northwest Territories div. Can.
59 E4 Northwich U.K.
33 F5 North Wildwood U.S.A.
33 H2 North Woodstock U.S.A.
58 G3 North York Moors reg. U.K.
58 G3 North York Moors National Park U.K.
23 G4 Norton Can.
58 G3 Norton U.K.
26 D4 Norton KS U.S.A.
32 B6 Norton VA U.S.A.
33 H2 Norton VT U.S.A.
103 D5 Norton Zimbabwe
77 V3 Norton Sound b. Alaska
119 C2 Norvegia, Kap c. Antarctica
33 G4 Norwalk CT U.S.A.
32 B4 Norwalk OH U.S.A.
48 Norway country Europe
33 H2 Norway U.S.A.
31 J3 Norway Bay Can.
21 K4 Norway House Can.
12 J1 Norwegian Basin sea feature Atlantic Ocean
52 Norwegian Sea sea Atlantic Ocean
31 G4 Norwich Can.
59 J5 Norwich U.K.
33 G4 Norwich CT U.S.A.
33 F3 Norwich NY U.S.A.
33 H3 Norwood MA U.S.A.
33 F2 Norwood NY U.S.A.
32 A5 Norwood OH U.S.A.
21 H1 Nose Lake l. Can.
90 G2 Noshappu-misaki hd Japan
90 G4 Noshiro Japan
69 D5 Nosivka Ukr.
68 H3 Noskovo Rus. Fed.
104 D2 Nosop r. Botswana/S. Africa
76 G3 Nosovaya Rus. Fed.
57 □ Noss, Isle of i. U.K.
46 A1 Nossa Senhora do Livramento Brazil
55 N7 Nossebro Sweden
104 C2 Nossob r. Namibia
103 E5 Nosy Bé i. Madag.
103 F5 Nosy Boraha i. Madag.
103 E6 Nosy Varika Madag.
35 F2 Notch Peak summit U.S.A.
62 H4 Noteć r. Pol.
66 F6 Noto, Golfo di g. Italy
55 L7 Notodden Norway
91 E6 Noto-hantō pen. Japan
23 G4 Notre Dame, Monts mts Can.
23 K4 Notre Dame Bay b. Can.
31 K3 Notre-Dame-de-la-Salette Can.
33 H2 Notre-Dame-des-Bois Can.
31 K2 Notre-Dame-du-Laus Can.
31 H2 Notre-Dame-du-Nord Can.
31 G3 Nottawasaga Bay b. Can.
22 E3 Nottaway r. Can.
59 F5 Nottingham U.K.
32 E6 Nottoway r. U.S.A.
21 H5 Notukeu Cr. r. Can.
100 A2 Nouâdhibou Maur.
100 A3 Nouakchott Maur.
100 A3 Nouâmghâr Maur.
95 C2 Nouei Vietnam
111 G4 Nouméa New Caledonia
100 B3 Nouna Burkina
104 F5 Noupoort S. Africa
54 V3 Nousu Fin.
Nouveau-Comptoir see Wemindji
Nouvelle Calédonie is see New Caledonia
46 C1 Nova América Brazil
46 B3 Nova Esperança Brazil
46 D3 Nova Friburgo Brazil
66 G2 Nova Gradiška Croatia
46 C3 Nova Granada Brazil
46 D3 Nova Iguaçu Brazil
69 E6 Nova Kakhovka Ukr.
46 D2 Nova Lima Brazil
68 D4 Novalukoml' Belarus
69 D6 Nova Odesa Ukr.
66 C2 Novara Italy
46 C1 Nova Roma Brazil
23 H5 Nova Scotia div. Can.
34 A2 Novato U.S.A.
46 E2 Nova Venécia Brazil
46 B1 Nova Xavantino Brazil
77 R2 Novaya Sibir', Ostrov i. Rus. Fed.
76 G2 Novaya Zemlya is Rus. Fed.
67 M3 Nova Zagora Bulg.
65 F3 Novelda Spain
62 J7 Nové Zámky Slovakia
68 E3 Novgorodskaya Oblast' div. Rus. Fed.
69 E5 Novhorod-Sivers'kyy Ukr.
67 K3 Novi Iskŭr Bulg.
66 C2 Novi Ligure Italy
67 M3 Novi Pazar Bulg.
67 J3 Novi Pazar Serb. and Mont.
67 H2 Novi Sad Serb. and Mont.
69 G6 Novoaleksandrovsk Rus. Fed.
69 G5 Novoanninskiy Rus. Fed.
42 F5 Novo Aripuanã Brazil
69 F6 Novoazovs'k Ukr.
68 H3 Novocheboksarsk Rus. Fed.
69 G6 Novocherkassk Rus. Fed.
68 G1 Novodvinsk Rus. Fed.
44 F3 Novo Hamburgo Brazil
46 B3 Novo Horizonte Brazil
62 G6 Novohradské Hory mts Czech Rep.
69 C5 Novohrad-Volyns'kyy Ukr.
69 G6 Novokubansk Rus. Fed.
76 K4 Novokuznetsk Rus. Fed.
119 D3 Novolazarevskaya Rus. Fed. Base Antarctica
77 M2 Novoletov'ye Rus. Fed.
66 F2 Novo Mesto Slovenia
68 F4 Novomichurinsk Rus. Fed.
69 F6 Novomikhaylovskiy Rus. Fed.
68 F4 Novomoskovsk Rus. Fed.
69 E5 Novomoskovs'k Ukr.
69 D6 Novomyrhorod Ukr.
69 G5 Novonikolayevskiy Rus. Fed.
69 E6 Novooleksiyivka Ukr.
90 D2 Novopokrovka Rus. Fed.
69 G6 Novopokrovskaya Rus. Fed.
69 J5 Novorepnoye Rus. Fed.
69 F6 Novorossiysk Rus. Fed.
77 M2 Novorybnaya Rus. Fed.
63 O2 Novorzhev Rus. Fed.
69 E6 Novoselivs'ke Ukr.
63 O1 Novosel'ye Rus. Fed.
69 F6 Novoshakhtinsk Rus. Fed.
90 C2 Novoshakhtinskiy Rus. Fed.
76 K4 Novosibirsk Rus. Fed.
77 Q2 Novosibirskiye Ostrova is Rus. Fed.
68 D3 Novosokol'niki Rus. Fed.
68 H4 Novospasskoye Rus. Fed.
69 E6 Novotroyits'ke Ukr.
69 D5 Novoukrayinka Ukr.
69 J5 Novouzensk Rus. Fed.
69 C5 Novovolyns'k Ukr.
69 F5 Novovoronezh Rus. Fed.
69 D4 Novozybkov Rus. Fed.
62 H6 Nový Jičín Czech Rep.
77 M2 Novyy Rus. Fed.
69 F5 Novyy Oskol Rus. Fed.
76 J3 Novyy Port Rus. Fed.
76 J3 Novyy Tor'yal Rus. Fed.
76 J3 Novyy Urengoy Rus. Fed.
77 P4 Novyy Urgal Rus. Fed.
27 E4 Nowata U.S.A.
81 M4 Nowbarān Iran
81 M3 Nowdī Iran
Nowgong see Nagaon
84 D4 Nowgong India
21 J2 Nowleye Lake l. Can.
62 G4 Nowogard Pol.
115 J5 Nowra Austr.
81 M2 Nowshahr Iran
79 G2 Now Shahr Iran
84 C2 Nowshera Pak.
63 K6 Nowy Sącz Pol.
63 K6 Nowy Targ Pol.
33 E4 Noxen U.S.A.
95 C1 Noy, Xé r. Laos
95 C1 Noy, Xé r. Laos
76 J3 Noyabr'sk r. Rus. Fed.
20 C3 Noyes I. i. U.S.A.
64 F2 Noyon France
105 F5 Nozizwe S. Africa
105 G6 Nqamakwe S. Africa
105 J4 Nqutu S. Africa
103 D5 Nsanje Malawi
102 B4 Ntandembele Dem. Rep. Congo
105 G3 Ntha S. Africa
102 D4 Ntungamo Uganda
101 F3 Nuba Mountains mts Sudan
81 K1 Nubarashen Armenia
101 F2 Nubian Desert des. Sudan
47 B3 Ñuble r. Chile
88 D1 Nüden Mongolia
42 D7 Nudo Coropuna mt Peru
27 D6 Nueces r. U.S.A.
45 C2 Nueva Florida Venez.
47 F2 Nueva Helvecia Uru.
47 B3 Nueva Imperial Chile
45 A4 Nueva Loja Ecuador
44 B6 Nueva Lubecka Arg.
36 D3 Nueva Rosita Mex.
37 J4 Nuevitas Cuba
47 D4 Nuevo, Golfo g. Arg.
36 C2 Nuevo Casas Grandes Mex.
36 E3 Nuevo Laredo Mex.
27 C7 Nuevo León div. Mex.
102 E3 Nugaal watercourse Somalia
116 C5 Nuga Nuga, L. l. Austr.
117 B7 Nugget Pt pt N.Z.
117 F2 Nuguria Is is P.N.G.
117 F3 Nuhaka N.Z.
111 H2 Nui i. Tuvalu
95 C2 Nui Ti On mt Vietnam
82 J5 Nu Jiang r. China
114 A4 Nukey Bluff h. Austr.
111 J4 Nuku'alofa Tonga
111 H2 Nukufetau i. Tuvalu
111 H2 Nukulaelae i. Tuvalu
111 F2 Nukumanu Is is P.N.G.
111 J2 Nukunonu i. Pac. Oc.
79 H1 Nukus Uzbek.
112 D4 Nullagine Austr.
112 F6 Nullarbor Austr.
112 F6 Nullarbor National Park nat. park Austr.
112 E6 Nullarbor Plain plain Austr.
88 F1 Nulu'erhu Shan mts China
114 F2 Numalla, Lake salt flat Austr.
100 D4 Numan Nigeria
91 F6 Numata Japan
91 F7 Numazu Japan
113 G2 Numbulwar Austr.
55 L6 Numedal v. Norway
93 J7 Numfoor i. Indon.
115 F6 Numurkah Austr.
23 H2 Nunaksaluk Island i. Can.
16 Nunavut reg. Can.
32 E3 Nunda U.S.A.
115 J3 Nundle Austr.
59 F5 Nuneaton U.K.
22 B3 Nungesser L. l. Can.
77 V4 Nunivak I. i. Alaska
84 D2 Nunkun mt India
77 U3 Nunligran Rus. Fed.
65 C2 Nuñomoral Spain
66 C4 Nuoro Italy
111 G3 Nupani i. Solomon Is
78 E4 Nuqrah Saudi Arabia
45 A3 Nuquí Col.
84 E1 Nur China
81 J2 Nurettin Turkey
25 E6 Nuri Mex.
114 C5 Nuriootpa Austr.
84 B2 Nuristan reg. Afgh.
68 J4 Nurlaty Rus. Fed.
54 V5 Nurmes Fin.
54 S5 Nurmo Fin.
62 E6 Nürnberg Ger.
Nürnberg see Nürnberg
115 G3 Nurri, Mt h. Austr.
85 H1 Nur Turu China
81 H3 Nusaybin Turkey
80 F4 Nuşayrīyah, Jabal an mts Syria
79 K4 Nushki Pak.
23 H2 Nutak Can.
35 H5 Nutrioso U.S.A.
84 B3 Nuttal Pak.
16 Nuuk Greenland
54 U3 Nuupas Fin.
104 C5 Nuwerus S. Africa
104 D6 Nuweveldberge mts S. Africa
81 K4 Nuzi Iraq
105 J1 Nwanedi National Park nat. park S. Africa
76 H3 Nyagan' Rus. Fed.
114 E5 Nyah West Austr.
85 G3 Nyainqêntanglha Feng mt China
85 G3 Nyainqêntanglha Shan mts China
85 H2 Nyainrong China
54 Q5 Nyåker Sweden
101 E3 Nyala Sudan
85 F3 Nyalam China
103 C5 Nyamandhiovu Zimbabwe
68 G2 Nyandoma Rus. Fed.
68 F2 Nyandomskiy Vozvyshennost' reg. Rus. Fed.
102 B4 Nyanga r. Gabon
103 D5 Nyanga Zimbabwe
85 H3 Nyang Qu r. Tibet China
85 G3 Nyang Qu r. Tibet China
84 D3 Nyar r. India
103 D5 Nyasa, Lake l. Africa
68 C4 Nyasvizh Belarus
55 M9 Nyborg Denmark
54 V1 Nyborg Norway
55 O8 Nybro Sweden
85 G3 Nyêmo China
102 D4 Nyeri Kenya
85 F3 Nyima China
86 F6 Nyingchi China
63 K7 Nyíregyháza Hungary
54 S5 Nykarleby Fin.
55 M9 Nykøbing Denmark
55 M9 Nykøbing Sjælland Denmark
55 P7 Nyköping Sweden
54 P5 Nyland Sweden
105 H2 Nylstroom S. Africa
115 G4 Nymagee Austr.
115 K2 Nymboida Austr.
115 K2 Nymboida r. Austr.
55 P7 Nynäshamn Sweden
115 G3 Nyngan Austr.
63 L4 Nyoman r. Belarus/Lith.
62 C7 Nyon Switz.
64 G4 Nyons France
76 G3 Nyrob Rus. Fed.
62 H5 Nysa Pol.
Nysa Łużycka r. see Neiße
68 J2 Nyuchpas Rus. Fed.
90 F5 Nyūdō-zaki pt Japan
102 C4 Nyunzu Dem. Rep. Congo
77 N3 Nyurba Rus. Fed.
68 J2 Nyuvchim Rus. Fed.
69 E6 Nyzhn'ohirs'kyy Ukr.
102 D4 Nzega Tanz.
100 B4 Nzérékoré Guinea
102 B4 N'zeto Angola
105 J1 Nzhelele Dam dam S. Africa
Nzwani i. see Anjouan

O

26 C2 Oahe, Lake l. U.S.A.
34 □1 Oahu i. U.S.A.
114 D4 Oakbank Austr.
35 F2 Oak City U.S.A.
27 E6 Oakdale U.S.A.
26 D2 Oakes U.S.A.
115 J1 Oakey Austr.
59 G5 Oakham U.K.
24 B1 Oak Harbor U.S.A.
32 C6 Oak Hill U.S.A.
33 G2 Oakhurst U.S.A.
30 B2 Oak I. i. U.S.A.
34 A3 Oakland CA U.S.A.
32 D5 Oakland MD U.S.A.
26 D3 Oakland NE U.S.A.
24 B3 Oakland OR U.S.A.
115 G5 Oaklands Austr.
30 D5 Oak Lawn U.S.A.
26 C4 Oakley U.S.A.
112 D4 Oakover r. Austr.
24 B3 Oakridge U.S.A.
29 C4 Oak Ridge U.S.A.
114 D4 Oakvale Austr.
31 H4 Oakville Can.
117 C6 Oamaru N.Z.
117 D5 Oaro N.Z.
94 B3 Oas Phil.
24 D3 Oasis U.S.A.
119 B5 Oates Land reg. Antarctica
115 G9 Oatlands Austr.
35 E4 Oatman U.S.A.
36 E5 Oaxaca Mex.
76 H3 Ob' r. Rus. Fed.
100 D4 Obala Cameroon
91 D7 Obama Japan
57 C4 Oban U.K.
90 G5 Obanazawa Japan
65 C1 O Barco Spain
22 F4 Obatogama L. l. Can.
61 C2 Obdam Neth.
20 F4 Obed Can.
117 B6 Obelisk mt N.Z.
26 C4 Oberlin KS U.S.A.
32 B4 Oberlin OH U.S.A.
115 H4 Oberon Austr.
62 F6 Oberpfälzer Wald mts Ger.
93 H7 Obi i. Indon.
43 G4 Óbidos Brazil
79 K2 Obigarm Tajik.
90 H3 Obihiro Japan
69 H6 Obil'noye Rus. Fed.
45 C2 Obispos Venez.
87 O2 Obluch'ye Rus. Fed.
68 F4 Obninsk Rus. Fed.
102 C3 Obo C.A.R.
88 A2 Obo China
102 E2 Obock Djibouti
90 A4 Obŏk N. Korea
102 C4 Obokote Dem. Rep. Congo
102 B4 Obouya Congo
69 F5 Oboyan' Rus. Fed.
68 G2 Obozerskiy Rus. Fed.
85 E4 Obra India
25 E7 Obregón, Presa resr Mex.
67 J2 Obrenovac Serb. and Mont.
80 D2 Obruk Turkey
76 J2 Obskaya Guba chan. Rus. Fed.
100 B4 Obuasi Ghana
69 D5 Obukhiv Ukr.
68 J2 Ob''yachevo Rus. Fed.
29 D6 Ocala U.S.A.
45 D4 Ocamo r. Venez.
27 C7 Ocampo Mex.
45 B2 Ocaña Col.
65 E3 Ocaña Spain
42 E7 Occidental, Cordillera mts Chile
45 A4 Occidental, Cordillera mts Col.
42 C6 Occidental, Cordillera mts Peru
20 B3 Ocean Cape pt U.S.A.
33 F5 Ocean City MD U.S.A.
33 F5 Ocean City NJ U.S.A.
20 D4 Ocean Falls Can.
12 G3 Oceanographer Fracture sea feature Atlantic Ocean
34 D5 Oceanside U.S.A.
27 F6 Ocean Springs U.S.A.
69 D6 Ochakiv Ukr.
69 G7 Och'amch'ire Georgia
57 E4 Ochil Hills h. U.K.
84 C1 Ochili Pass pass Afgh.
62 E6 Ochsenfurt Ger.
55 P6 Ockelbo Sweden
63 M7 Ocolaşul Mare, Vârful mt Romania
30 C4 Oconomowoc U.S.A.
30 D3 Oconto U.S.A.
34 D5 Ocotillo Wells U.S.A.
100 B4 Oda Ghana
91 C7 Ōda Japan
78 D5 Oda, Jebel mt Sudan
54 E4 Ódáðahraun lava Iceland
90 A4 Ŏdaejin N. Korea
90 G4 Ōdate Japan
91 F7 Odawara Japan
55 K6 Odda Norway
21 K3 Odei r. Can.
30 C5 Odell U.S.A.
65 B4 Odemira Port.
80 A2 Ödemiş Turkey
105 G3 Odendaalsrus S. Africa
55 M9 Odense Denmark
62 D6 Odenwald reg. Ger.
64 G4 Oder r. Ger.
62 G3 Oderbucht b. Ger.
69 D6 Odesa Ukr.
55 O7 Ödeshog Sweden
27 C6 Odessa U.S.A.
65 C4 Odiel r. Spain
100 B4 Odienné Côte d'Ivoire
68 F4 Odintsovo Rus. Fed.
95 C3 Ŏdôngk Cambodia
62 J6 Odra r. Ger./Pol.
43 K5 Oeiras Brazil
26 C3 Oelrichs U.S.A.
30 B4 Oelwein U.S.A.
61 D5 Oesling h. Lux.
81 H1 Of Turkey
66 G4 Ofanto r. Italy
62 D5 Offenbach am Main Ger.
62 C6 Offenburg Ger.
67 M6 Ofidoussa i. Greece
90 G5 Ōfunato Japan
90 F5 Oga Japan
102 E3 Ogadēn reg. Eth.
90 F5 Oga-hantō pen. Japan
91 E7 Ōgaki Japan
26 C3 Ogallala U.S.A.
31 H2 Ogascanane, Lac l. Can.
100 C4 Ogbomoso Nigeria
26 E3 Ogden IA U.S.A.
24 E3 Ogden UT U.S.A.
20 C3 Ogden, Mt mt Can.
33 F2 Ogdensburg U.S.A.
29 C5 Oglethorpe, Mt mt U.S.A.
66 D1 Oglio r. Italy
116 C4 Ogmore Austr.
100 C4 Ogoja Nigeria
22 C3 Ogoki r. Can.
22 C3 Ogoki Res. resr Can.
67 K3 Ogosta r. Bulg.
55 T8 Ogre Latvia
66 F2 Ogulin Croatia
81 L1 Oğuz Azer.
117 A6 Ohai N.Z.
117 E3 Ohakune N.Z.
90 G4 Ōhata Japan
117 B6 Ohau, L. l. N.Z.
47 B2 O'Higgins div. Chile
44 B7 O'Higgins, Lago l. Chile
32 B4 Ohio div. U.S.A.
28 C4 Ohio r. U.S.A.
67 J4 Ohrid Macedonia
67 J4 Ohrid, Lake l. Albania/Macedonia
105 J2 Ohrigstad S. Africa
117 E3 Ohura N.Z.
43 H3 Oiapoque Brazil
57 D3 Oich, Loch l. U.K.
85 H3 Oiga China
32 D4 Oil City U.S.A.
34 C4 Oildale U.S.A.
64 F2 Oise r. France
91 B8 Ōita Japan
67 K5 Oiti mt Greece
34 C4 Ojai U.S.A.
47 D2 Ojeda Arg.
30 B3 Ojibwa U.S.A.
27 B6 Ojinaga Mex.
91 F6 Ojiya Japan
25 F6 Ojo de Laguna Mex.
25 D7 Ojo de Liebre, Lago b. Mex.
44 C3 Ojos del Salado, Nevado mt Arg.
68 G4 Oka r. Rus. Fed.
103 B6 Okahandja Namibia
117 E3 Okahukura N.Z.
103 B6 Okakarara Namibia
23 H2 Okak Islands is Can.
20 F5 Okanagan Falls Can.
20 F4 Okanagan Lake l. Can.
24 C1 Okanogan r. Can./U.S.A.
20 F5 Okanogan U.S.A.
24 B1 Okanogan Range mts U.S.A.
84 C3 Okara Pak.
103 B5 Okaukuejo Namibia
103 C5 Okavango r. Botswana/Namibia
103 C5 Okavango Delta swamp Botswana
91 F6 Okaya Japan
91 C7 Okayama Japan
91 E7 Okazaki Japan
29 D7 Okeechobee U.S.A.
29 D7 Okeechobee, L. l. U.S.A.
29 D6 Okefenokee Swamp swamp U.S.A.
59 C7 Okehampton U.K.
100 C4 Okene Nigeria
84 B5 Okha India
77 Q4 Okha Rus. Fed.
85 F4 Okhaldhunga Nepal
84 B5 Okha Rann marsh India
77 Q3 Okhotka r. Rus. Fed.
77 Q4 Okhotsk Rus. Fed.
77 Q4 Okhotsk, Sea of g. Rus. Fed.
Okhotskoye More g. see Okhotsk, Sea of
69 E5 Okhtyrka Ukr.
87 N6 Okinawa i. Japan
87 N6 Okinawa-shotō is Japan
91 B7 Okino-shima i. Japan
77 P6 Oki-shotō i. Japan
91 C6 Oki-shotō is Japan
27 D5 Oklahoma div. U.S.A.
27 D5 Oklahoma City U.S.A.
27 D5 Okmulgee U.S.A.
102 B4 Okondja Gabon
20 G4 Okotoks Can.
68 E4 Okovskiy Les forest Rus. Fed.
102 B4 Okoyo Congo
54 S1 Øksfjord Norway
68 F2 Oksovskiy Rus. Fed.
68 J4 Oktyabr'sk Rus. Fed.
68 G2 Oktyabr'skiy Archangel. Rus. Fed.
69 G6 Oktyabr'skiy Volgograd. Rus. Fed.
77 R4 Oktyabr'skiy Rus. Fed.
76 G4 Oktyabr'skiy Rus. Fed.
76 H3 Oktyabr'skoye Rus. Fed.
77 L2 Oktyabr'skoy Revolyutsii, Ostrov i. Rus. Fed.
68 E3 Okulovka Rus. Fed.
90 F3 Okushiri-tō i. Japan
104 E1 Okwa watercourse Botswana
54 B4 Ólafsvík Iceland
34 C3 Olancha U.S.A.
34 C3 Olancha Peak summit U.S.A.
55 P8 Öland i. Sweden
54 W3 Olanga Rus. Fed.
114 D4 Olary Austr.
114 D4 Olary watercourse Austr.
26 E4 Olathe U.S.A.
47 E3 Olavarría Arg.
62 H5 Oława Pol.
35 G5 Olberg U.S.A.
66 C4 Olbia Italy
32 D3 Olcott U.S.A.
115 K3 Old Bar Austr.
60 D4 Oldcastle Rep. of Ireland
62 D4 Oldenburg Ger.
62 E3 Oldenburg in Holstein Ger.
61 E2 Oldenzaal Neth.
54 R2 Olderdalen Norway
33 F3 Old Forge NY U.S.A.
33 F4 Old Forge PA U.S.A.
58 E4 Oldham U.K.
60 C6 Old Head of Kinsale hd Rep. of Ireland
20 G4 Oldman r. Can.
57 F3 Oldmeldrum U.K.
33 H3 Old Orchard Beach U.S.A.
23 K4 Old Perlican Can.
20 G4 Olds Can.
33 J2 Old Town U.S.A.
21 H4 Old Wives L. l. Can.
35 E4 Old Woman Mts mts U.S.A.
32 D3 Olean U.S.A.
63 L3 Olecko Pol.
77 O4 Olekma r. Rus. Fed.
77 O3 Olekminsk Rus. Fed.
69 E5 Oleksandriya Ukr.
68 H1 Olema Rus. Fed.
55 J7 Ølen Norway
54 X2 Olenegorsk Rus. Fed.
77 N3 Olenek Rus. Fed.
77 O2 Olenek r. Rus. Fed.
77 O2 Olenekskiy Zaliv b. Rus. Fed.
68 E3 Olenino Rus. Fed.
69 C5 Olevs'k Ukr.
90 D3 Ol'ga Rus. Fed.
65 C4 Olhão Port.
104 C2 Olifants watercourse Namibia

105 J1 Olifants S. Africa
104 C6 Olifants r. S. Africa
104 D6 Olifants r. S. Africa
104 C5 Olifants r. S. Africa
104 E3 Olifantshoek S. Africa
104 C6 Olifantsrivierberge mts S. Africa
47 G2 Olimar Grande r. Uru.
46 C3 Olímpia Brazil
43 M5 Olinda Brazil
103 D5 Olinga Moz.
105 G2 Oliphants Drift Botswana
47 D2 Oliva Arg.
65 F3 Oliva Spain
44 C3 Oliva, Cordillera de mts Arg./Chile
47 C1 Olivares, Co del mt Chile
32 B5 Olive Hill U.S.A.
46 D3 Oliveira Brazil
65 C3 Olivenza Spain
26 E2 Olivia U.S.A.
68 G4 Ol'khi Rus. Fed.
44 C2 Ollagüe Chile
47 B1 Ollita, Cordillera de mts Arg./Chile
47 B1 Ollitas mt Arg.
42 C5 Olmos Peru
33 G3 Olmstedville U.S.A.
59 G5 Olney U.K.
28 C4 Olney U.S.A.
55 O8 Olofström Sweden
62 H6 Olomouc Czech Rep.
68 E2 Olonets Rus. Fed.
94 B3 Olongapo Phil.
64 D5 Oloron-Ste-Marie France
65 H1 Olot Spain
87 L1 Olovyannaya Rus. Fed.
84 C5 Olpad India
63 K4 Olsztyn Pol.
62 C7 Olten Switz.
67 M2 Oltenița Romania
81 H1 Oltu Turkey
94 B5 Olutanga i. Phil.
24 B2 Olympia U.S.A.
24 A2 Olympic Nat. Park U.S.A.
24 B2 Olympic Nat. Park nat. park U.S.A.
Olympus mt see Troödos, Mount
67 K4 Olympus mt Greece
24 B2 Olympus, Mt mt U.S.A.
77 S3 Olyutorskiy Rus. Fed.
77 T4 Olyutorskiy, Mys c. Rus. Fed.
77 S4 Olyutorskiy Zaliv b. Rus. Fed.
85 E2 Oma China
90 G4 Ōma Japan
91 E6 Ōmachi Japan
91 F7 Omae-zaki pt Japan
60 D3 Omagh U.K.
26 E3 Omaha U.S.A.
104 C1 Omaheke div. Namibia
24 C1 Omak U.S.A.
70 Oman country Asia
79 H4 Oman, Gulf of g. Asia
117 B6 Omarama N.Z.
103 B6 Omaruru Namibia
103 B5 Omatako watercourse Namibia
42 D7 Omate Peru
104 E2 Omaweneno Botswana
90 G4 Ōma-zaki c. Japan
102 A4 Omboué Gabon
66 D3 Ombrone r. Italy
85 F3 Ombu China
104 E5 Omdraaisvlei S. Africa
101 F3 Omdurman Sudan
66 C2 Omegna Italy
115 G6 Omeo Austr.
102 D2 Om Hajēr Eritrea
20 D3 Omineca Mountains mts Can.
104 B1 Omitara Namibia
91 F7 Ōmiya Japan
20 C3 Ommaney, Cape hd U.S.A.
61 E2 Ommen Neth.
88 B1 Ömnögovĭ div. Mongolia
77 S3 Omolon Rus. Fed.
77 R3 Omolon r. Rus. Fed.
102 D3 Omo National Park nat. park Eth.
90 G5 Omono-gawa r. Japan
76 J4 Omsk Rus. Fed.
77 R3 Omsukchan Rus. Fed.
90 H2 Ōmū Japan
67 L2 Omu, Vârful mt Romania
91 A8 Ōmura Japan
30 B4 Onalaska U.S.A.
33 F6 Onancock U.S.A.
22 D4 Onaping Lake l. Can.
25 E6 Onavas Mex.
31 E3 Onaway U.S.A.
95 A2 Onbingwin Myanmar
47 D1 Oncativo Arg.
58 C3 Onchan U.K.
103 B5 Oncócua Angola
103 B5 Ondangwa Namibia
104 B1 Ondekaremba Namibia
104 D5 Onderstedorings S. Africa
103 B5 Ondjiva Angola
100 C4 Ondo Nigeria
87 K2 Öndörhaan Mongolia
88 B1 Ondor Mod China
88 D1 Ondor Sum China
68 E2 Ondozero Rus. Fed.
104 D1 One Botswana
83 D10 One and a Half Degree Channel chan. Maldives
68 F2 Onega Rus. Fed.
68 F2 Onega r. Rus. Fed.
76 E3 Onega, Lake chan. Rus. Fed.
68 E2 Onega, Lake l. Rus. Fed.
20 E4 One Hundred Mile House Can.
33 F3 Oneida U.S.A.
33 F3 Oneida Lake l. U.S.A.
26 D3 O'Neill U.S.A.
77 R5 Onekotan, O. i. Rus. Fed.
33 F3 Oneonta U.S.A.
117 E2 Oneroa N.Z.
63 N7 Onești Romania
68 E1 Onezhskaya Guba g. Rus. Fed.
Onezhskove Ozero chan. see Onega, Lake
Onezhskoye Ozero l. see Onega, Lake
85 E5 Ong r. India
102 B4 Onga Gabon
117 F3 Ongaonga N.Z.
104 E4 Ongers watercourse S. Africa
Ongniud Qi see Wudan
83 F7 Ongole India
69 G7 Oni Georgia
103 E6 Onilahy r. Madag.
100 C4 Onitsha Nigeria
104 B1 Onjati Mountain mt Namibia
91 E7 Ōno Japan
111 J4 Ono-i-Lau i. Fiji
91 C7 Onomichi Japan
111 H2 Onotoa i. Kiribati
20 G4 Onoway Can.
104 C4 Onseepkans S. Africa
112 C4 Onslow Austr.
29 E5 Onslow Bay b. U.S.A.
90 B3 Onsong N. Korea
91 E7 Ontake-san vol. Japan
22 B3 Ontario div. Can.
24 C2 Ontario U.S.A.
31 H4 Ontario, Lake l. Can./U.S.A.
30 C2 Ontonagon U.S.A.
111 F2 Ontong Java Atoll atoll Solomon Is
113 G5 Oodnadatta Austr.
112 F6 Ooldea Austr.
27 E4 Oologah L. resr U.S.A.
61 B3 Oostakker Belgium
Oostende see Ostend
61 D2 Oostendorp Neth.
61 C3 Oosterhout Neth.
61 B3 Oosterschelde est. Neth.
61 B3 Oosterscheldekering barrage Neth.
61 A4 Oostvleteren Belgium
Ootacamund see Udagamandalam
20 D4 Ootsa Lake Can.
20 D4 Ootsa Lake l. Can.
32 E5 Opal U.S.A.
102 C4 Opala Dem. Rep. Congo
68 J3 Oparino Rus. Fed.
22 B3 Opasquia Can.
22 B3 Opasquia Provincial Park res. Can.
22 F3 Opataca L. l. Can.
62 H6 Opava Czech Rep.
29 C5 Opelika U.S.A.
27 E6 Opelousas U.S.A.
24 F1 Opheim U.S.A.
31 F2 Ophir Can.
117 C6 Opihi r. N.Z.
22 E3 Opinaca r. Can.
22 E3 Opinaca, Réservoir resr Can.
22 D3 Opinnagau r. Can.
81 K5 Opis Iraq
23 G3 Opiscotéo, Lac l. Can.
68 D3 Opochka Rus. Fed.
62 H5 Opole Pol.
65 B2 Oporto Port.
117 F3 Opotiki N.Z.
29 C6 Opp U.S.A.
54 L5 Oppdal Norway
117 D3 Opunake N.Z.
103 B5 Opuwo Namibia
30 B5 Oquawka U.S.A.
33 H2 Oquossoc U.S.A.
35 G5 Oracle U.S.A.
35 G5 Oracle Junction U.S.A.
63 K7 Oradea Romania
54 E4 Öræfajökull gl. Iceland
67 J3 Orahovac Serb. and Mont.
84 D4 Orai India
100 B1 Oran Alg.
44 D2 Orán Arg.
95 C2 O Rang Cambodia
90 A4 Ŏrang N. Korea
115 H4 Orange Austr.
64 G4 Orange France
103 B6 Orange r. Namibia/S. Africa
33 G3 Orange MA U.S.A.
27 E6 Orange TX U.S.A.
32 D5 Orange VA U.S.A.
43 H3 Orange, Cabo c. Brazil
29 D5 Orangeburg U.S.A.
Orange Free State div. see Free State
31 G3 Orangeville Can.
35 G2 Orangeville U.S.A.
36 G5 Orange Walk Belize
94 B3 Orani Phil.
103 B6 Oranjemund Namibia
45 C1 Oranjestad Aruba
60 C4 Oranmore Rep. of Ireland
103 C6 Orapa Botswana
94 C3 Oras Phil.
67 K2 Orăștie Romania
54 S5 Oravais Fin.
67 J2 Oravița Romania
84 E2 Orba Co l. China
66 D3 Orbetello Italy
65 D1 Orbigo r. Spain
115 H6 Orbost Austr.
119 B1 Orcadas Arg. Base Antarctica
35 H2 Orchard Mesa U.S.A.
45 D2 Orchila, Isla i. Venez.
34 B4 Orcutt U.S.A.
112 E3 Ord r. Austr.
112 E3 Ord, Mt h. Austr.
25 D4 Orderville U.S.A.
65 B1 Ordes Spain
34 D4 Ord Mt mt U.S.A.
80 F1 Ordu Turkey
81 L2 Ordubad Azer.
25 G4 Ordway U.S.A.
Ordzhonikidze see Vladikavkaz
69 E6 Ordzhonikidze Ukr.
34 C1 Oreana U.S.A.
55 O7 Örebro Sweden
30 C4 Oregon IL U.S.A.
32 B4 Oregon OH U.S.A.
30 C4 Oregon WV U.S.A.
24 B3 Oregon div. U.S.A.
24 B2 Oregon City U.S.A.
68 F4 Orekhovo-Zuyevo Rus. Fed.
68 F4 Orel Rus. Fed.
35 G1 Orem U.S.A.
80 A2 Ören Turkey
67 M6 Ören Turkey
76 G4 Orenburg Rus. Fed.
47 E3 Orense Arg.
117 A7 Orepuki N.Z.
55 N9 Öresund str. Denmark
117 E2 Orewa N.Z.
67 K4 Orfanou, Kolpos b. Greece
115 G9 Orford Austr.
59 J5 Orford U.K.
59 J5 Orford Ness spit U.K.
35 F5 Organ Pipe Cactus National Monument res. U.S.A.
84 B2 Orgūn Afgh.
80 B2 Orhaneli Turkey
69 D7 Orhangazi Turkey
68 J3 Orichi Rus. Fed.
33 K2 Orient U.S.A.
42 E7 Oriental, Cordillera mts Bol.
45 B3 Oriental, Cordillera mts Col.
42 D6 Oriental, Cordillera mts Peru
47 E3 Oriente Arg.
65 F3 Orihuela Spain
69 E6 Orikhiv Ukr.
31 H3 Orillia Can.
55 T6 Orimattila Fin.
45 E2 Orinoco r. Col./Venez.
45 E2 Orinoco Delta delta Venez.
85 F5 Orissa div. India
55 S7 Orissaare Estonia
66 C5 Oristano Italy
55 T6 Orivesi Fin.
54 V5 Orivesi l. Fin.
43 G4 Oriximiná Brazil
36 E5 Orizaba Mex.
36 E5 Orizaba, Pico de vol. Mex.
54 L5 Orkanger Norway
55 N8 Örkelljunga Sweden
54 L5 Orkla r. Norway
105 G3 Orkney S. Africa
56 E2 Orkney is U.K.
27 C6 Orla U.S.A.
34 A2 Orland U.S.A.
46 C3 Orlândia Brazil
29 D6 Orlando U.S.A.
64 E3 Orléans France
33 J4 Orleans MA U.S.A.
33 G2 Orleans VT U.S.A.
68 J3 Orlov Rus. Fed.
68 F4 Orlovskaya Oblast' div. Rus. Fed.
69 G6 Orlovskiy Rus. Fed.
94 C4 Ormoc Phil.
29 D6 Ormond Beach U.S.A.
58 E4 Ormskirk U.K.
33 G2 Ormstown Can.
64 D2 Orne r. France
54 N3 Ørnes Norway
54 Q5 Örnsköldsvik Sweden
45 C3 Orocué Col.
100 B3 Orodara Burkina
24 C2 Orofino U.S.A.
25 F5 Orogrande U.S.A.
23 G4 Oromocto Can.
80 E6 Oron Israel
111 J2 Orona i. Kiribati
33 J2 Orono U.S.A.
57 B4 Oronsay i. U.K.
Orontes r. see 'Āṣī, Nahr al
Oroqen Zizhiqi see Alihe
94 B4 Oroquieta Phil.
43 L5 Orós, Açude resr Brazil
66 C4 Orosei Italy
66 C4 Orosei, Golfo di b. Italy
63 K7 Orosháza Hungary
35 G5 Oro Valley U.S.A.
34 B2 Oroville CA U.S.A.
24 C1 Oroville WA U.S.A.
34 B2 Oroville, Lake l. U.S.A.
116 B2 Orpheus I. i. Austr.
114 C4 Orroroo Austr.
55 O6 Orsa Sweden
68 D4 Orsha Belarus
76 G4 Orsk Rus. Fed.
54 K5 Ørsta Norway
65 C1 Ortegal, Cabo c. Spain
64 D5 Orthez France
65 C1 Ortigueira Spain
25 E6 Ortiz Mex.
45 D2 Ortiz Venez.
66 D1 Ortles mt Italy
58 E3 Orton U.K.
66 F3 Ortona Italy
26 D2 Ortonville U.S.A.
77 O3 Orulgan, Khrebet mts Rus. Fed.
104 B1 Orumbo Namibia
81 K3 Orūmīyeh Iran
81 K3 Orūmīyeh, Daryācheh-ye salt l. Iran
42 E7 Oruro Bol.
66 E3 Orvieto Italy
32 C4 Orwell OH U.S.A.
33 G3 Orwell VT U.S.A.
55 M5 Os Norway
37 H7 Osa, Pen. de pen. Costa Rica
30 A4 Osage U.S.A.
26 E4 Osage r. U.S.A.
91 D7 Ōsaka Japan
61 E5 Osburger Hochwald forest Ger.
55 N8 Osby Sweden
27 F5 Osceola AR U.S.A.
26 E3 Osceola IA U.S.A.
66 C4 Oschiri Italy
31 F3 Oscoda U.S.A.
68 F4 Osetr r. Rus. Fed.
91 A8 Ōse-zaki pt Japan
31 K3 Osgoode Can.
79 L1 Osh Kyrgyzstan
103 B5 Oshakati Namibia
90 G3 Oshamanbe Japan
31 H4 Oshawa Can.
90 G5 Oshika-hantō pen. Japan
90 F4 Ō-shima i. Japan
91 F7 Ō-shima i. Japan
26 C3 Oshkosh NE U.S.A.
30 C3 Oshkosh WV U.S.A.
81 K3 Oshnovīyeh Iran
100 C4 Oshogbo Nigeria
81 M5 Oshtorān Kūh mt Iran
81 M5 Oshtorīnān Iran
102 B4 Oshwe Dem. Rep. Congo
67 H2 Osijek Croatia
66 E3 Osimo Italy
84 C4 Osiyān India
105 J3 Osizweni S. Africa
66 G2 Osječenica mt Bos.-Herz.
54 O5 Ösjön l. Sweden
26 E3 Oskaloosa U.S.A.
55 P8 Oskarshamn Sweden
31 K1 Oskélanéo Can.
69 F5 Oskol r. Rus. Fed.
55 M7 Oslo Norway
94 B4 Oslob Phil.
55 M7 Oslofjorden chan. Norway
80 E1 Osmancık Turkey
80 B1 Osmaneli Turkey
80 F3 Osmaniye Turkey
55 V7 Os'mino Rus. Fed.
62 D4 Osnabrück Ger.
67 K3 Osogovske Planine mts Bulg./Macedonia
47 B4 Osorno Chile
65 D1 Osorno Spain
47 B4 Osorno, Vol. vol. Chile
20 F5 Osoyoos Can.
55 J6 Osøyri Norway
113 J2 Osprey Reef rf Coral Sea Is Terr.
61 D3 Oss Neth.
115 G8 Ossa, Mt mt Austr.
30 B3 Osseo U.S.A.
31 F3 Ossineke U.S.A.
33 H3 Ossipee Lake l. U.S.A.
23 H3 Ossokmanuan Lake l. Can.
68 E3 Ostashkov Rus. Fed.
61 A3 Ostend Belgium
63 P5 Oster Ukr.
55 O8 Österbymo Sweden
55 N6 Österdalälven l. Sweden
55 M5 Østerdalen v. Norway
55 O5 Östersund Sweden
55 Q6 Östhammar Sweden
62 J6 Ostrava Czech Rep.
63 J4 Ostróda Pol.
69 F5 Ostrogozhsk Rus. Fed.
68 D3 Ostrov Rus. Fed.
63 K5 Ostrowiec Świętokrzyski Pol.
63 K4 Ostrów Mazowiecka Pol.
62 H5 Ostrów Wielkopolski Pol.
67 L3 Osŭm r. Bulg.
91 B9 Ōsumi-Kaikyō chan. Japan
91 B9 Ōsumi-shotō is Japan
65 D4 Osuna Spain
33 F2 Oswegatchie U.S.A.
30 C5 Oswego IL U.S.A.
33 E3 Oswego NY U.S.A.
32 E3 Oswego r. U.S.A.
59 D5 Oswestry U.K.
91 F6 Ōta Japan
117 C6 Otago Peninsula pen. N.Z.
117 E4 Otaki N.Z.
54 U4 Otanmäki Fin.
45 B4 Otare, Co h. Col.
90 G3 Otaru Japan
117 B7 Otatara N.Z.
42 C3 Otavalo Ecuador
103 B5 Otavi Namibia
91 G6 Ōtawara Japan
117 C6 Otematata N.Z.
55 U7 Otepää Estonia
24 C2 Othello U.S.A.
117 C5 Otira N.Z.
33 E3 Otisco Lake l. U.S.A.
23 F3 Otish, Monts mts Can.
103 B6 Otjiwarongo Namibia
58 F4 Otley U.K.
Otog Qi see Ulan
90 H2 Otoineppu Japan
117 E3 Otorohanga N.Z.
22 C3 Otoskwin r. Can.
67 H4 Otranto Italy
67 H4 Otranto, Strait of str. Albania/Italy
77 T3 Otrozhnyy Rus. Fed.
30 E4 Otsego U.S.A.
30 E3 Otsego Lake l. MI U.S.A.
33 F3 Otsego Lake l. NY U.S.A.
33 F3 Otselic U.S.A.
91 D7 Ōtsu Japan
55 L6 Otta Norway
31 K3 Ottawa Can.
31 H2 Ottawa r. Can.
30 C5 Ottawa IL U.S.A.
26 E4 Ottawa KS U.S.A.
32 A4 Ottawa OH U.S.A.
22 D2 Ottawa Islands is Can.
58 E2 Otterburn U.K.
35 G2 Otter Creek Reservoir resr U.S.A.
30 D1 Otter I. i. Can.
22 D3 Otter Rapids Can.
59 C7 Ottery r. U.K.
61 C4 Ottignies Belgium
30 A5 Ottumwa U.S.A.
100 C4 Otukpo Nigeria
44 D3 Otumpa Arg.
42 C5 Otuzco Peru
114 E7 Otway, C. c. Austr.
89 B6 Ou, Nam r. Laos
27 E5 Ouachita r. U.S.A.
27 E5 Ouachita, L. l. U.S.A.
27 E5 Ouachita Mts mts U.S.A.
102 C3 Ouadda C.A.R.
101 E3 Ouaddaï reg. Chad
100 B3 Ouagadougou Burkina
100 B3 Ouahigouya Burkina
100 B3 Oualâta Maur.
102 C3 Ouanda-Djailé C.A.R.
100 B2 Ouarâne reg. Maur.
100 C1 Ouargla Alg.
100 B1 Ouarzazate Morocco
104 F6 Oubergpas pass S. Africa
61 B4 Oudenaarde Belgium
104 E6 Oudtshoorn S. Africa
65 F5 Oued Tlélat Alg.
100 B1 Oued Zem Morocco
66 B6 Oued Zénati Alg.
64 B2 Ouessant, Île d' i. France
102 B3 Ouésso Congo
100 C4 Ouidah Benin
25 E7 Ouiriego Mex.
100 B1 Oujda Morocco
54 T4 Oulainen Fin.
65 G4 Ouled Farès Alg.
54 T4 Oulu Fin.
54 U4 Oulujärvi l. Fin.
54 U4 Oulujoki r. Fin.
54 T4 Oulunsalo Fin.
64 H4 Oulx Italy
101 E3 Oum-Chalouba Chad
100 B4 Oumé Côte d'Ivoire
101 D3 Oum-Hadjer Chad
54 T3 Ounasjoki r. Fin.
59 G5 Oundle U.K.
101 E3 Ounianga Kébir Chad
61 D4 Oupeye Belgium
61 E5 Our r. Lux.
62 C6 Our, Vallée de l' v. Ger./Lux.
25 F4 Ouray CO U.S.A.
35 H1 Ouray UT U.S.A.
65 C1 Ourense Spain
43 K5 Ouricurí Brazil
46 C3 Ourinhos Brazil
46 C1 Ouro r. Brazil
46 D3 Ouro Preto Brazil
61 D4 Ourthe r. Belgium
58 G4 Ouse r. Eng. U.K.
59 H7 Ouse r. Eng. U.K.
23 G3 Outardes r. Can.
104 E6 Outeniekpas pass S. Africa
57 A2 Outer Hebrides is U.K.
30 B2 Outer I. i. U.S.A.
34 C5 Outer Santa Barbara Channel chan. U.S.A.
103 B6 Outjo Namibia
54 V5 Outokumpu Fin.
57 □ Out Skerries is U.K.
111 G4 Ouvéa i. New Caledonia
89 D5 Ouyanghai Skuiku resr China
114 E5 Ouyen Austr.
59 G5 Ouzel r. U.K.
66 C4 Ovace, Pte d' mt France
81 G2 Ovacık Turkey
66 C2 Ovada Italy
111 H3 Ovalau i. Fiji
47 B1 Ovalle Chile
65 B2 Ovar Port.
47 D2 Oveja mt Arg.
115 G6 Ovens r. Austr.
54 S3 Överkalix Sweden
112 B5 Overlander Roadhouse Austr.
35 E3 Overton U.S.A.
54 S3 Övertorneå Sweden
55 P8 Överum Sweden
61 C2 Overveen Neth.
30 E4 Ovid U.S.A.
65 D1 Oviedo Spain
54 T2 Øvre Anarjokka Nasjonalpark nat. park Norway
54 Q2 Øvre Dividal Nasjonalpark nat. park Norway
55 M6 Øvre Rendal Norway
69 D5 Ovruch Ukr.
117 B7 Owaka N.Z.
102 B4 Owando Congo
91 E7 Owase Japan
26 E2 Owatonna U.S.A.
33 E3 Owego U.S.A.
13 H3 Owen Fracture sea feature Indian Ocean
60 B3 Owenmore r. Rep. of Ireland
117 D4 Owen River N.Z.
34 C3 Owens r. U.S.A.
28 C4 Owensboro U.S.A.
34 D3 Owens Lake l. U.S.A.
31 G3 Owen Sound Can.
31 G3 Owen Sound in. Can.
110 E2 Owen Stanley Range mts P.N.G.
100 C4 Owerri Nigeria
20 D4 Owikeno L. l. Can.
32 B5 Owingsville U.S.A.
33 J2 Owls Head U.S.A.
100 C4 Owo Nigeria
31 E4 Owosso U.S.A.
81 L4 Owrāmān, Kūh-e mts Iran/Iraq
24 C3 Owyhee U.S.A.
24 C3 Owyhee r. U.S.A.
24 C3 Owyhee Mts mts U.S.A.
42 C6 Oxapampa Peru
54 E3 Öxarfjörður b. Iceland
21 J5 Oxbow Can.
33 J1 Oxbow U.S.A.
55 P7 Oxelösund Sweden
117 D5 Oxford N.Z.
59 F6 Oxford U.K.
31 F4 Oxford MI U.S.A.
27 F5 Oxford MS U.S.A.
33 F3 Oxford NY U.S.A.
33 E5 Oxford PA U.S.A.
116 C3 Oxford Downs Austr.
21 K4 Oxford House Can.
21 K4 Oxford L. l. Can.
114 F5 Oxley Austr.
115 J3 Oxleys Pk mt Austr.
34 C4 Oxnard U.S.A.
31 H3 Oxtongue Lake Can.
54 N3 Øya Norway
91 F6 Oyama Japan
43 H3 Oyapock r. Brazil/Fr. Guiana
102 B3 Oyem Gabon
57 D3 Oykel r. U.K.
100 C4 Oyo Nigeria
64 G3 Oyonnax France
85 H5 Oyster I. i. Myanmar
81 J2 Özalp Turkey
94 B4 Ozamiz Phil.
29 C6 Ozark AL U.S.A.
30 E2 Ozark MI U.S.A.
27 E4 Ozark Plateau plat. U.S.A.
26 E4 Ozarks, Lake of the l. U.S.A.
77 R4 Ozernovskiy Rus. Fed.
68 E4 Ozernyy Rus. Fed.
63 L3 Ozersk Rus. Fed.
68 F4 Ozery Rus. Fed.
77 Q3 Ozhogino Rus. Fed.
66 C4 Ozieri Italy
27 C6 Ozona U.S.A.
91 B7 Ozuki Japan
69 G7 Ozurget'i Georgia

P

95 A1 Pa-an Myanmar
104 C6 Paarl S. Africa
104 D4 Paballelo S. Africa
90 A4 P'abal-li N. Korea
57 A4 Pabbay i. Scot. U.K.
57 A3 Pabbay i. Scot. U.K.
63 J5 Pabianice Pol.
85 G4 Pabna Bangl.
55 T9 Pabradė Lith.
79 K4 Pab Range mts Pak.
42 F6 Pacaás Novos, Parque Nacional nat. park Brazil
45 E4 Pacaraima, Serra mts Brazil
42 C5 Pacasmayo Peru
25 E6 Pacheco Mex.
68 H2 Pachikha Rus. Fed.
66 F6 Pachino Italy
84 D5 Pachor India
36 E4 Pachuca Mex.
34 B2 Pacific U.S.A.
91 F8 Pacific Ocean
94 C4 Pacijan i. Phil.
43 H4 Pacoval Brazil
46 D2 Pacuí r. Brazil
62 H5 Paczków Pol.
94 C5 Padada Phil.
45 D4 Padamo r. Venez.
92 C7 Padang Indon.
92 C7 Padangpanjang Indon.
95 A5 Padangsidimpuan Indon.
68 E2 Padany Rus. Fed.
81 M5 Padatha, Kūh-e mt Iran
45 D4 Padauiri r. Brazil
42 F8 Padcaya Bol.
20 F4 Paddle Prairie Can.
32 C5 Paden City U.S.A.
65 D5 Paderborn Ger.
67 K2 Padeşu, Vârful mt Romania
42 F7 Padilla Bol.
54 P3 Padjelanta Nationalpark nat. park Sweden
85 G5 Padma r. Bangl.
Padova see Padua

27 D7 **Padre Island** *i.* U.S.A.
66 C3 **Padro, Monte** *mt* France
59 C7 **Padstow** U.K.
63 N3 **Padsvillye** Belarus
114 D6 **Padthaway** Austr.
66 D2 **Padua** Italy
28 B4 **Paducah** *KY* U.S.A.
27 C5 **Paducah** *TX* U.S.A.
84 D2 **Padum** Jammu and Kashmir
90 A4 **Paegam** N. Korea
117 E2 **Paeroa** N.Z.
94 B3 **Paete** Phil.
80 D4 **Pafos** Cyprus
105 J1 **Pafúri** Moz.
66 F2 **Pag** Croatia
66 F2 **Pag** *i.* Croatia
94 B5 **Pagadian** Phil.
92 C7 **Pagai Selatan** *i.* Indon.
92 C7 **Pagai Utara** *i.* Indon.
93 L3 **Pagan** *i.* N. Mariana Is
92 F7 **Pagatan** Indon.
35 G3 **Page** U.S.A.
55 R9 **Pagėgiai** Lith.
44 □ **Paget, Mt** *mt* Atlantic Ocean
116 E2 **Paget Cay** *rf* Coral Sea Is Terr.
25 F4 **Pagosa Springs** U.S.A.
85 G4 **Pagri** China
22 C3 **Pagwa River** Can.
34 □2 **Pahala** U.S.A.
95 B5 **Pahang** *r.* Malaysia
84 B2 **Paharpur** Pak.
117 A7 **Pahia Pt** *pt* N.Z.
34 □2 **Pahoa** U.S.A.
29 D7 **Pahokee** U.S.A.
35 E3 **Pahranagat Range** *mts* U.S.A.
84 D4 **Pahuj** *r.* India
34 D3 **Pahute Mesa** *plat.* U.S.A.
95 A1 **Pai** Thai.
55 T7 **Paide** Estonia
59 D7 **Paignton** U.K.
55 T6 **Päijänne** *l.* Fin.
85 F3 **Paikü Co** *l.* China
95 B2 **Pailin** Cambodia
47 B4 **Paillaco** Chile
34 □2 **Pailolo Chan.** *chan.* U.S.A.
55 S6 **Paimio** Fin.
47 B2 **Paine** Chile
32 C4 **Painesville** U.S.A.
35 G3 **Painted Desert** *des.* U.S.A.
35 F5 **Painted Rock Reservoir** *resr* U.S.A.
114 C3 **Painter, Mount** *mt* Austr.
21 K3 **Paint Lake Provincial Recr. Park** *res.* Can.
32 B6 **Paintsville** U.S.A.
31 G3 **Paisley** Can.
57 D5 **Paisley** U.K.
42 B5 **Paita** Peru
94 A5 **Paitan, Teluk** *b.* Malaysia
89 D4 **Paizhou** China
54 S3 **Pajala** Sweden
43 L5 **Pajeú** *r.* Brazil
95 B4 **Paka** Malaysia
42 F2 **Pakaraima Mountains** *mts* Guyana
31 G3 **Pakesley** Can.
77 S3 **Pakhachi** Rus. Fed.
70 **Pakistan** *country* Asia
89 □ **Pak Ka Shan** *h.* China
Paknampho *see* **Nakhon Sawan**
83 J6 **Pakokku** Myanmar
117 D1 **Pakotai** N.Z.
83 C3 **Pakpattan** Pak.
95 B3 **Pak Phanang** Thai.
95 B4 **Pak Phayun** Thai.
55 S9 **Pakruojis** Lith.
63 J7 **Paks** Hungary
89 □ **Pak Tam Chung** China
95 B2 **Pak Thong Chai** Thai.
84 B2 **Paktīkā** Afgh.
95 C2 **Pakxé** Laos
101 D4 **Pala** Chad
95 A2 **Pala** Myanmar
66 G3 **Palagruža** *i.* Croatia
67 K7 **Palaiochora** Greece
64 F2 **Palaiseau** France
Palakkat *see* **Palghat**
104 E1 **Palamakoloi** Botswana
65 H2 **Palamós** Spain
84 C4 **Palana** India
77 R4 **Palana** Rus. Fed.
94 B2 **Palanan** Phil.
94 B2 **Palanan Point** *pt* Phil.
81 L4 **Palangān** Iran
84 C4 **Palanpur** India
94 C3 **Palapag** Phil.
103 C6 **Palapye** Botswana
85 G4 **Palasbari** India
77 R3 **Palatka** Rus. Fed.
71 **Palau** *country* Pac. Oc.
94 B2 **Palaui** *i.* Phil.
94 A3 **Palauig** Phil.
95 A2 **Palauk** Myanmar
14 E5 **Palau Tr.** *sea feature* Pac. Oc.
95 A2 **Palaw** Myanmar
94 A4 **Palawan** *i.* Phil.
94 B3 **Palayan** Phil.
55 T7 **Paldiski** Estonia
85 H5 **Pale** Myanmar
61 D2 **Paleis Het Loo** Neth.
92 C7 **Palembang** Indon.
44 B6 **Palena** Chile
65 D1 **Palencia** Spain
36 F5 **Palenque** Mex.
66 E5 **Palermo** Italy
27 E6 **Palestine** U.S.A.
85 H5 **Paletwa** Myanmar
83 E8 **Palghat** India
84 C4 **Pali** India
94 C5 **Palimbang** Phil.
66 F4 **Palinuro, Capo** *c.* Italy
35 H2 **Palisade** U.S.A.
61 D5 **Paliseul** Belgium
84 B5 **Palitana** India
55 S7 **Palivere** Estonia
68 D3 **Palkino** Rus. Fed.
83 E9 **Palk Strait** *str.* India/Sri Lanka
115 J2 **Pallamallawa** Austr.
60 C5 **Pallas Green** Rep. of Ireland
54 S2 **Pallas ja Ounastunturin Kansallispuisto** *nat. park* Fin.
69 H5 **Pallasovka** Rus. Fed.
117 E4 **Palliser, Cape** *c.* N.Z.
117 E4 **Palliser Bay** *b.* N.Z.
84 C3 **Pallu** India
65 D4 **Palma del Río** Spain
65 H3 **Palma de Mallorca** Spain
45 C2 **Palmar** *r.* Venez.
45 C3 **Palmarito** Venez.
100 B4 **Palmas, Cape** *c.* Liberia
46 D1 **Palmas de Monte Alto** Brazil
29 D7 **Palm Bay** U.S.A.
29 D7 **Palm Beach** U.S.A.
34 C4 **Palmdale** U.S.A.
46 B4 **Palmeira** Brazil
43 L5 **Palmeira dos Índios** Brazil
43 K5 **Palmeirais** Brazil
119 B2 **Palmer** *U.S.A. Base* Antarctica
117 C6 **Palmerston** N.Z.
108 **Palmerston** *i.* Pac. Oc.
116 C3 **Palmerston, C.** *pt* Austr.
117 E4 **Palmerston North** N.Z.
33 F4 **Palmerton** U.S.A.
29 E7 **Palmetto Pt** *pt* Bahamas
66 F5 **Palmi** Italy
45 A4 **Palmira** Col.
34 D5 **Palm Springs** U.S.A.
116 C5 **Palm Tree Cr.** *r.* Austr.
Palmyra *see* **Tadmur**
30 B6 **Palmyra** *MO* U.S.A.
32 E3 **Palmyra** *NY* U.S.A.
30 C4 **Palmyra** *WV* U.S.A.
109 **Palmyra Atoll** *i.* Pac. Oc.
85 F5 **Palmyras Point** *pt* India
34 A3 **Palo Alto** U.S.A.
45 A3 **Palo de las Letras** Col.
101 F3 **Paloich** Sudan
54 S2 **Palojärvi** Fin.
54 U2 **Palomaa** Fin.
34 D5 **Palomar Mt** *mt* U.S.A.
35 G6 **Palominas** U.S.A.
93 G7 **Palopo** Indon.
65 F4 **Palos, Cabo de** *c.* Spain
35 F5 **Palo Verde** *AZ* U.S.A.
35 E5 **Palo Verde** *CA* U.S.A.
54 U4 **Paltamo** Fin.
93 F7 **Palu** Indon.
81 G2 **Palu** Turkey
94 B3 **Paluan** Phil.
84 D3 **Palwal** India
77 T3 **Palyavaam** *r.* Rus. Fed.
115 H6 **Pambula** Austr.
92 □ **Pamekasan** Indon.
92 □ **Pameungpeuk** Indon.
64 E5 **Pamiers** France
82 D3 **Pamir** *mts* Asia
29 E5 **Pamlico Sound** *chan.* U.S.A.
27 C5 **Pampa** U.S.A.
42 F7 **Pampa Grande** Bol.
40 **Pampas** *reg.* Arg.
45 B3 **Pamplona** Col.
94 B4 **Pamplona** Phil.
65 F1 **Pamplona** Spain
80 C1 **Pamukova** Turkey
32 E6 **Pamunkey** *r.* U.S.A.
84 D2 **Pamzal** Jammu and Kashmir
28 B4 **Pana** U.S.A.
94 C5 **Panabo** Phil.
35 E3 **Panaca** U.S.A.
94 A4 **Panagtaran Point** *pt* Phil.
92 □ **Panaitan** *i.* Indon.
83 D7 **Panaji** India
16 **Panama** *country* Central America
37 J7 **Panamá** Panama
37 J7 **Panamá, Golfo de** *b.* Panama
37 J7 **Panama Canal** *canal* Panama
29 C6 **Panama City** U.S.A.
34 D3 **Panamint Range** *mts* U.S.A.
34 D3 **Panamint Springs** U.S.A.
34 D3 **Panamint Valley** U.S.A.
94 C4 **Panaon** *i.* Phil.
85 G4 **Panar** *r.* India
66 F5 **Panarea, Isola** *i.* Italy
95 D5 **Panarik** Indon.
94 B3 **Panay** *i.* Phil.
94 C3 **Panay** *i.* Phil.
94 B4 **Panay Gulf** *b.* Phil.
35 E2 **Pancake Range** *mts* U.S.A.
67 J2 **Pančevo** Serb. and Mont.
94 B4 **Pandan** Phil.
94 C3 **Pandan** Phil.
94 B4 **Pandan B.** *b.* Phil.
95 □ **Pandan Res.** *resr* Sing.
84 E5 **Pandaria** India
46 D1 **Pandeiros** *r.* Brazil
83 E7 **Pandharpur** India
84 D5 **Pandhurna** India
47 F2 **Pando** Uru.
59 E6 **Pandy** U.K.
55 T9 **Panevėžys** Lith.
92 □ **Pangandaran** Indon.
84 C2 **Pangi Range** *mts* Pak.
92 E7 **Pangkalanbuun** Indon.
92 B6 **Pangkalansusu** Indon.
92 D7 **Pangkalpinang** Indon.
93 G7 **Pangkalsiang, Tanjung** *pt* Indon.
94 B4 **Panglao** *i.* Phil.
76 J3 **Pangody** Rus. Fed.
84 D2 **Pangong Tso** *l.* India
92 □ **Pangrango** *vol.* Indon.
47 B3 **Panguipulli** Chile
47 B3 **Panguipulli, L.** *l.* Chile
35 F3 **Panguitch** U.S.A.
95 A5 **Pangururan** Indon.
94 B5 **Pangutaran** *i.* Phil.
94 B5 **Pangutaran Group** *is* Phil.
27 C5 **Panhandle** U.S.A.
102 C4 **Pania-Mwanga** Dem. Rep. Congo
84 B5 **Pānikoita** *i.* India
69 G5 **Panino** Rus. Fed.
84 D3 **Panipat** India
94 A4 **Panitan** Phil.
95 D5 **Panjang** *i.* Indon.
81 L5 **Panjbarār** Iran
79 J4 **Panjgur** Pak.
84 C5 **Panjhra** *r.* India
Panjim *see* **Panaji**
88 G1 **Panjin** China
84 B2 **Panjkora** *r.* Pak.
84 B3 **Panjnad** *r.* Pak.
54 W5 **Pankakoski** Fin.
100 C4 **Pankshin** Nigeria
90 B3 **Pan Ling** *mts* China
82 F6 **Panna** India
84 D4 **Panna** *reg.* India
112 C4 **Pannawonica** Austr.
46 B3 **Panorama** Brazil
Panshan *see* **Panjin**
87 N3 **Panshi** China
46 A2 **Pantanal de São Lourenço** *marsh* Brazil
46 A2 **Pantanal do Taquarí** *marsh* Brazil
43 G7 **Pantanal Matogrossense, Parque Nacional do** *nat. park* Brazil
66 D6 **Pantelleria** Italy
66 E6 **Pantelleria, Isola di** *i.* Italy
93 G8 **Pantemakassar** Indon.
94 C5 **Pantukan** Phil.
36 E4 **Pánuco** Mex.
89 B5 **Panxian** China
89 D6 **Panyu** China
89 A5 **Panzhihua** China
102 B4 **Panzi** Dem. Rep. Congo
45 E3 **Pao** *r.* Venez.
66 G5 **Paola** Italy
28 C4 **Paoli** U.S.A.
102 B3 **Paoua** C.A.R.
62 H7 **Pápa** Hungary
66 F4 **Papa, Monte del** *mt* Italy
117 E2 **Papakura** N.Z.
36 E4 **Papantla** Mex.
117 C5 **Paparoa Range** *mts* N.Z.
57 □ **Papa Stour** *i.* U.K.
117 E2 **Papatoetoe** N.Z.
117 B7 **Papatowai** N.Z.
57 F1 **Papa Westray** *i.* U.K.
62 C4 **Papenburg** Ger.
31 K2 **Papineau-Labelle, Réserve Faunique de** *res.* Can.
35 E3 **Papoose L.** *l.* U.S.A.
57 B5 **Paps of Jura** *h.* U.K.
110 E2 **Papua, Gulf of** *g.* P.N.G.
106 **Papua New Guinea** *country* Australasia
95 A1 **Papun** Myanmar
59 C7 **Par** U.K.
46 D2 **Pará** *r.* Brazil
43 J4 **Pará** *r.* Brazil
68 G4 **Para** *r.* Rus. Fed.
112 C4 **Paraburdoo** Austr.
94 B3 **Paracale** Phil.
46 C2 **Paracatu** Brazil
46 D2 **Paracatu** *r.* Brazil
114 C3 **Parachilna** Austr.
67 J3 **Paraćin** Serb. and Mont.
46 D2 **Pará de Minas** Brazil
31 J1 **Paradis** Can.
34 B2 **Paradise** *CA* U.S.A.
30 E2 **Paradise** *MI* U.S.A.
21 H4 **Paradise Hill** Can.
34 D2 **Paradise Peak** *summit* U.S.A.
23 J3 **Paradise River** Can.
27 F4 **Paragould** U.S.A.
42 F6 **Paragua** *r.* Bol.
45 E3 **Paragua** *r.* Venez.
43 G7 **Paraguai** *r.* Brazil
45 C2 **Paraguáipoa** Venez.
45 C1 **Paraguaná, Pen. de** *pen.* Venez.
44 E3 **Paraguay** *r.* Arg./Para.
38 **Paraguay** *country* S. America
43 L5 **Paraíba** *r.* Brazil
46 D3 **Paraíba do Sul** *r.* Brazil
100 C4 **Parakou** Benin
114 B3 **Parakylia** Austr.
84 E6 **Paralkot** India
43 G2 **Paramaribo** Suriname
45 B3 **Paramillo** *mt* Col.
45 A3 **Paramillo, Parque Nacional** *nat. park* Col.
46 D1 **Paramirim** Brazil
45 A3 **Paramo Frontino** *mt* Col.
33 F4 **Paramus** U.S.A.
77 R4 **Paramushir, O.** *i.* Rus. Fed.
47 E1 **Paraná** Arg.
43 J6 **Paraná** Brazil
46 B4 **Paraná** *div.* Brazil
46 C1 **Paraná** *r.* Brazil
47 E2 **Paraná** *r.* S. America
46 C1 **Paranã, Sa do** *h.* Brazil
46 C4 **Paranaguá** Brazil
46 B2 **Paranaíba** Brazil
46 B2 **Paranaíba** *r.* Brazil
47 E2 **Paraná Ibicuy** *r.* Arg.
46 B3 **Paranapanema** *r.* Brazil
46 C4 **Paranapiacaba, Serra** *mts* Brazil
46 B3 **Paranavaí** Brazil
84 B2 **Parandev Pass** *pass* Afgh.
94 B5 **Parang** Phil.
67 K2 **Parângul Mare, Vârful** *mt* Romania
84 C5 **Parantij** India
46 D2 **Paraopeba** *r.* Brazil
81 K4 **Pārāpāra** Iraq
117 E4 **Paraparaumu** N.Z.
45 D3 **Paraque, Co** *mt* Venez.
27 D7 **Paras** Mex.
84 D5 **Paratwada** India
81 L4 **Parāū, Kūh-e** *mt* Iraq
46 B2 **Paraúna** Brazil
64 G3 **Paray-le-Monial** France
84 D4 **Parbati** *r.* India
83 E7 **Parbhani** India
62 E4 **Parchim** Ger.
30 C4 **Pardeeville** U.S.A.
85 G2 **Parding** China
46 E1 **Pardo** *r.* Bahia/Minas Gerais Brazil
46 B3 **Pardo** *r.* Mato Grosso do Sul Brazil
46 D1 **Pardo** *r.* Minas Gerais Brazil
46 C3 **Pardo** *r.* São Paulo Brazil
62 G5 **Pardubice** Czech Rep.
92 □ **Pare** Indon.
84 D2 **Pare Chu** *r.* China
42 F6 **Parecis, Serra dos** *h.* Brazil
27 C7 **Paredón** Mex.
81 K2 **Pareh** Iran
117 D1 **Parengarenga Harbour** *in.* N.Z.
22 E4 **Parent, Lac** *l.* Can.
117 C6 **Pareora** N.Z.
93 F7 **Parepare** Indon.
47 D2 **Parera** Arg.
68 G3 **Parfen'yevo** Rus. Fed.
92 B2 **Parfino** Rus. Fed.
67 J5 **Parga** Greece
55 S6 **Pargas** Fin.
45 E2 **Paria, Gulf of** *g.* Trinidad/Venez.
45 E2 **Paria, Península de** *pen.* Venez.
45 D2 **Pariaguán** Venez.
35 F3 **Paria Plateau** *plat.* U.S.A.
55 V6 **Parikkala** Fin.
Parima *r. see* **Uatatás**
45 D4 **Parima, Serra** *mts* Brazil
45 D4 **Parima-Tapirapecó, Parque Nacional** *nat. park* Venez.
42 B4 **Pariñas, Pta** *pt* Peru
114 D5 **Paringa** Austr.
43 G4 **Parintins** Brazil
31 G4 **Paris** Can.
64 F2 **Paris** France
32 A5 **Paris** *KY* U.S.A.
29 B4 **Paris** *TN* U.S.A.
27 E5 **Paris** *TX* U.S.A.
30 E2 **Parisienne, Île** *i.* Can.
60 D3 **Park** U.K.
55 S5 **Parkano** Fin.
23 J3 **Parke Lake** *l.* Can.
35 E4 **Parker** U.S.A.
35 E4 **Parker Dam** *dam* U.S.A.
21 K2 **Parker Lake** *l.* Can.
30 A4 **Parkersburg** *IA* U.S.A.
32 C5 **Parkersburg** *WV* U.S.A.
115 H4 **Parkes** Austr.
30 B3 **Park Falls** U.S.A.
30 D5 **Park Forest** U.S.A.
31 F2 **Parkinson** Can.
26 E2 **Park Rapids** U.S.A.
20 E5 **Parksville** Can.
33 F4 **Parksville** U.S.A.
66 D2 **Parma** Italy
24 C3 **Parma** *ID* U.S.A.
32 C4 **Parma** *OH* U.S.A.
45 D3 **Parmana** Venez.
43 K4 **Parnaíba** Brazil
43 K4 **Parnaíba** *r.* Brazil
67 K5 **Parnassos** *mt* Greece
117 D5 **Parnassus** N.Z.
114 B5 **Parndana** Austr.
30 A5 **Parnell** U.S.A.
67 K6 **Parnon** *mts* Greece
55 T7 **Pärnu** Estonia
55 T7 **Pärnu-Jaagupi** Estonia
114 F2 **Paroo** *watercourse* Austr.
79 J3 **Paropamisus** *mts* Afgh.
67 L6 **Paros** Greece
67 L6 **Paros** *i.* Greece
35 F3 **Parowan** U.S.A.
47 B3 **Parral** Chile
33 F6 **Parramore I.** *i.* U.S.A.
36 D3 **Parras** Mex.
47 F3 **Parravicini** Arg.
59 E6 **Parrett** *r.* U.K.
23 H4 **Parrsboro** Can.
118 B3 **Parry Islands** *is* Can.
31 G3 **Parry Sound** Can.
27 E4 **Parsons** *KS* U.S.A.
32 D5 **Parsons** *WV* U.S.A.
64 D3 **Parthenay** France
90 C3 **Partizansk** Rus. Fed.
59 H4 **Partney** U.K.
60 B4 **Partry** Rep. of Ireland
60 B4 **Partry Mts** *h.* Rep. of Ireland
43 H4 **Paru** *r.* Brazil
45 D3 **Parucito** *r.* Venez.
84 C4 **Parvatsar** India
84 D4 **Parwan** *r.* India
85 E3 **Paryang** China
105 G3 **Parys** S. Africa
34 C4 **Pasadena** *CA* U.S.A.
27 E6 **Pasadena** *TX* U.S.A.
42 B4 **Pasado, C.** *pt* Ecuador
95 B2 **Pa Sak, Mae Nam** *r.* Thai.
95 A1 **Pasawng** Myanmar
27 F6 **Pascagoula** U.S.A.
31 J1 **Pascalis** Can.
63 N7 **Pașcani** Romania
24 C2 **Pasco** U.S.A.
46 E2 **Pascoal, Monte** *h.* Brazil
94 B3 **Pascual** Phil.
Pas de Calais *str. see* **Dover, Strait of**
62 G4 **Pasewalk** Ger.
21 H3 **Pasfield Lake** *l.* Can.
68 E2 **Pasha** Rus. Fed.
94 B3 **Pasig** Phil.
81 H2 **Pasinler** Turkey
95 □ **Pasir Gudang** Malaysia
95 □ **Pasir Panjang** Sing.
92 C5 **Pasir Putih** Malaysia
34 A2 **Paskenta** U.S.A.
79 J4 **Pasni** Pak.
47 F2 **Paso de los Toros** Uru.
44 B7 **Paso Río Mayo** Arg.
34 B4 **Paso Robles** U.S.A.
21 J4 **Pasquia Hills** *h.* Can.
33 J2 **Passadumkeag** U.S.A.
30 C1 **Passage I.** *i.* U.S.A.
62 F6 **Passau** Ger.
94 B4 **Passi** Phil.
44 F3 **Passo Fundo** Brazil
46 C3 **Passos** Brazil
68 C4 **Pastavy** Belarus
42 C4 **Pastaza** *r.* Peru
45 A4 **Pasto** Col.
35 H3 **Pastora Peak** *summit* U.S.A.
94 B2 **Pasuquin** Phil.
92 □ **Pasuruan** Indon.
55 T8 **Pasvalys** Lith.
94 B5 **Pata** *i.* Phil.
40 **Patagonia** *reg.* Arg.
35 G6 **Patagonia** U.S.A.
85 G4 **Patakata** India
84 D5 **Patan** India
84 C5 **Patan** India
Patan *see* **Somnath**
85 F4 **Patan** Nepal
114 E5 **Patchewollock** Austr.
117 E3 **Patea** N.Z.
117 E3 **Patea** *r.* N.Z.
58 F3 **Pateley Bridge** U.K.
85 G5 **Patenga Point** *pt* Bangl.
104 F6 **Patensie** S. Africa
66 F6 **Paternò** Italy
115 J4 **Paterson** Austr.
115 G1 **Paterson** *r.* Austr.
33 F4 **Paterson** U.S.A.
84 C2 **Pathankot** India
Pathein *see* **Bassein**
24 F3 **Pathfinder Res.** *resr* U.S.A.
95 A3 **Pathiu** Thai.
95 B2 **Pathum Thani** Thai.
92 □ **Pati** Indon.
45 A4 **Patía** *r.* Col.
84 D3 **Patiala** India
67 M6 **Patmos** *i.* Greece
85 F4 **Patna** India
85 E5 **Patnagarh** India
94 B3 **Patnanongan** *i.* Phil.
81 J2 **Patnos** Turkey
84 E3 **Paton** India
67 H4 **Patos** Albania
43 L5 **Patos** Brazil
44 F4 **Patos, Lagoa dos** *l.* Brazil
46 C2 **Patos de Minas** Brazil
47 C1 **Patquía** Arg.
67 J5 **Patra** Greece
54 B4 **Patreksfjörður** Iceland
116 A4 **Patrick Cr.** *watercourse* Austr.
46 C2 **Patrocínio** Brazil
54 V2 **Patsoyoki** *r.* Europe
95 B4 **Pattani** Thai.
95 B4 **Pattani** *r.* Thai.
95 B2 **Pattaya** Thai.
33 J2 **Patten** U.S.A.
34 B3 **Patterson** U.S.A.
32 D5 **Patterson** *r.* U.S.A.
20 C2 **Patterson, Mt** *mt* Can.
30 E3 **Patterson, Pt** *pt* U.S.A.
34 C3 **Patterson Mt** *mt* U.S.A.
54 T4 **Pattijoki** Fin.
54 R2 **Pättikkä** Fin.
20 D3 **Pattullo, Mt** *mt* Can.
85 G5 **Patuakhali** Bangl.
21 H3 **Patuanak** Can.
32 E5 **Patuxent** *r.* U.S.A.
36 D5 **Pátzcuaro** Mex.
64 D5 **Pau** France
64 D4 **Pauillac** France
85 H5 **Pauk** Myanmar
85 H5 **Paukkaung** Myanmar
35 F4 **Paulden** U.S.A.
32 A4 **Paulding** U.S.A.
23 H2 **Paul Island** *i.* Can.
43 K5 **Paulistana** Brazil
43 L5 **Paulo Afonso** Brazil
105 J3 **Paulpietersburg** S. Africa
105 G4 **Paul Roux** S. Africa
33 F2 **Paul Smiths** U.S.A.
27 D5 **Pauls Valley** U.S.A.
83 J7 **Paungde** Myanmar
45 C3 **Pauto** *r.* Col.
46 E2 **Pavão** Brazil
81 L4 **Pāveh** Iran
66 C2 **Pavia** Italy
55 R8 **Pāvilosta** Latvia
68 H3 **Pavino** Rus. Fed.
67 L3 **Pavlikeni** Bulg.
76 J4 **Pavlodar** Kazak.
69 E5 **Pavlohrad** Ukr.
68 H4 **Pavlovka** Rus. Fed.
68 G4 **Pavlovo** Rus. Fed.
69 G5 **Pavlovsk** Rus. Fed.
69 F6 **Pavlovskaya** Rus. Fed.
45 B4 **Pavon** Col.
84 E3 **Pawayan** India
30 E4 **Paw Paw** U.S.A.
33 H4 **Pawtucket** U.S.A.
95 A2 **Pawut** Myanmar
30 C5 **Paxton** U.S.A.
92 C7 **Payakumbuh** Indon.
95 □ **Paya Lebar** Sing.
24 C2 **Payette** U.S.A.
76 H3 **Pay-Khoy, Khrebet** *h.* Rus. Fed.
22 F2 **Payne, Lac** *l.* Can.
34 B1 **Paynes Creek** U.S.A.
112 C5 **Payne's Find** Austr.
47 E2 **Paysandú** Uru.
35 G4 **Payson** *AZ* U.S.A.
35 G1 **Payson** *UT* U.S.A.
47 C3 **Payún, Cerro** *vol.* Arg.
80 D1 **Pazar** Turkey
81 H1 **Pazar** Turkey
80 F3 **Pazarcık** Turkey
67 L3 **Pazardzhik** Bulg.
45 C3 **Paz de Ariporo** Col.
45 B3 **Paz de Rio** Col.
66 E2 **Pazin** Croatia
20 G3 **Peace** *r.* Can.
20 F3 **Peace River** Can.
35 F4 **Peach Springs** U.S.A.
59 F4 **Peak District National Park** U.K.
114 A2 **Peake** *watercourse* Austr.
23 G4 **Peaked Mt.** *h.* U.S.A.
94 A4 **Peaked Point** *pt* Phil.
115 H4 **Peak Hill** Austr.
116 C4 **Peak Ra.** *h.* Austr.
35 H2 **Peale, Mt** *mt* U.S.A.
35 H6 **Pearce** U.S.A.
30 C1 **Pearl** Can.
27 F6 **Pearl** *r.* U.S.A.
34 □1 **Pearl City** U.S.A.
34 □1 **Pearl Harbor** *in.* U.S.A.
27 D6 **Pearsall** U.S.A.
29 D6 **Pearson** U.S.A.
18 **Peary Land** *reg.* Greenland
22 C2 **Peawanuck** Can.
103 D5 **Pebane** Moz.
67 J3 **Peć** Serb. and Mont.
46 D2 **Peçanha** Brazil
54 W2 **Pechenga** Rus. Fed.
76 G3 **Pechora** Rus. Fed.
68 C3 **Pechory** Rus. Fed.
31 F4 **Peck** U.S.A.
27 C6 **Pecos** U.S.A.
27 C6 **Pecos** *r.* U.S.A.
67 H1 **Pécs** Hungary
115 G9 **Pedder, L.** *l.* Austr.
105 G6 **Peddie** S. Africa
25 F6 **Pedernales** Mex.
54 S5 **Pedersöre** Fin.
85 E3 **Pêdo La** *pass* China
46 E1 **Pedra Azul** Brazil
45 C3 **Pedraza la Vieja** Venez.
45 C2 **Pedregal** Venez.
46 C3 **Pedregulho** Brazil
43 K4 **Pedreiras** Brazil
43 J5 **Pedro Afonso** Brazil
45 C4 **Pedro Chico** Col.
44 C2 **Pedro de Valdivia** Chile
46 A2 **Pedro Gomes** Brazil
45 D4 **Pedro II, Ilha** *i.* Brazil
44 E2 **Pedro Juan Caballero** Para.
43 K4 **Pedroll** Brazil
47 G1 **Pedro Osório** Brazil
57 E5 **Peebles** U.K.
29 E5 **Pee Dee** *r.* U.S.A.
33 G4 **Peekskill** U.S.A.
115 J3 **Peel** *r.* Austr.
58 C3 **Peel** U.K.
20 F4 **Peers** Can.
114 E3 **Peery L.** *salt flat* Austr.
117 D5 **Pegasus Bay** *b.* N.Z.
83 J7 **Pegu** Myanmar
68 J2 **Pegysh** Rus. Fed.
47 E2 **Pehuajó** Arg.
89 F6 **Peikang** Taiwan
Peipsi Järve *l. see* **Peipus, Lake**
55 U7 **Peipus, Lake** *l.* Estonia/Rus. Fed.
67 K6 **Peiraias** Greece
88 E3 **Peitun** China
43 J6 **Peixe** Brazil
46 B1 **Peixe** *r.* Goiás Brazil
46 B3 **Peixe** *r.* São Paulo Brazil
88 E3 **Peixian** China
46 A2 **Peixo de Couro** *r.* Brazil
105 G4 **Peka** Lesotho
92 □ **Pekalongan** Indon.
95 B5 **Pekan** Malaysia
30 C5 **Pekin** U.S.A.
95 B5 **Pelabuhan Kelang** Malaysia
31 F5 **Pelee I.** *i.* Can.
31 F5 **Pelee Pt** *pt* Can.
93 G7 **Peleng** *i.* Indon.
68 J2 **Peles** Rus. Fed.
30 A1 **Pelican Lake** *l.* *MN* U.S.A.
30 C3 **Pelican Lake** *l.* *WV* U.S.A.
21 J3 **Pelican Narrows** Can.
54 U3 **Pelkosenniemi** Fin.
104 C4 **Pella** S. Africa

31 J3 Quyon Can.
88 E2 Quzhou Hebei China
89 F4 Quzhou Zhejiang China
69 H7 Qvareli Georgia
Qyteti Stalin see Kuçovë

R

62 H7 Raab r. Austria
54 T4 Raahe Fin.
54 V5 Rääkkylä Fin.
61 E2 Raalte Neth.
54 T3 Raanujärvi Fin.
92 □ Raas i. Indon.
57 B3 Raasay i. U.K.
57 B3 Raasay, Sound of chan. U.K.
93 F8 Raba Indon.
84 E2 Rabang China
66 F7 Rabat Malta
100 B1 Rabat Morocco
110 F2 Rabaul P.N.G.
20 D3 Rabbit r. Can.
78 D5 Rābigh Saudi Arabia
85 G5 Rabnabad Islands is Bangl.
69 D6 Râbniţa Moldova
85 B5 Raccoon Creek r. U.S.A.
23 K4 Race, C. c. Can.
33 H3 Race Pt pt U.S.A.
80 E5 Rachaïya Lebanon
27 D7 Rachal U.S.A.
35 E3 Rachel U.S.A.
95 C3 Rach Gia Vietnam
95 C3 Rach Gia, Vinh b. Vietnam
62 J5 Racibórz Pol.
30 D4 Racine U.S.A.
31 F1 Racine Lake l. Can.
30 E2 Raco U.S.A.
63 M7 Rădăuţi Romania
28 C4 Radcliff U.S.A.
32 C6 Radford U.S.A.
84 B5 Radhanpur India
22 E3 Radisson Can.
20 F4 Radium Hot Springs Can.
57 J3 Radnevo Bulg.
63 K5 Radom Pol.
67 K3 Radomir Bulg.
101 E4 Radom National Park nat. park Sudan
63 J5 Radomsko Pol.
69 D5 Radomyshl' Ukr.
67 K4 Radoviš Macedonia
59 E6 Radstock U.K.
68 C4 Radun' Belarus
55 S9 Radviliškis Lith.
63 M5 Radyvyliv Ukr.
84 E4 Rae Bareli India
20 F2 Rae-Edzo Can.
20 F2 Rae Lakes Can.
61 E4 Raeren Belgium
117 E3 Raetihi N.Z.
47 E1 Rafaela Arg.
80 E6 Rafaḥ Gaza
102 C3 Rafaï C.A.R.
78 E4 Rafḥā' Saudi Arabia
79 H3 Rafsanjān Iran
94 C5 Ragang, Mt vol. Phil.
94 B3 Ragay Gulf b. Phil.
33 J3 Ragged I. i. U.S.A.
66 F6 Ragusa Italy
88 A3 Ra'gyagoinba China
93 G7 Raha Indon.
68 D4 Rahachow Belarus
102 D2 Rahad r. Sudan
Rahaeng see Tak
84 B3 Rahimyar Khan Pak.
47 B3 Rahue mt Chile
87 E7 Raichur India
85 G4 Raiganj India
85 E5 Raigarh India
35 E2 Railroad Valley v. U.S.A.
23 G3 Raimbault, Lac l. Can.
114 E5 Rainbow Austr.
116 E5 Rainbow Beach Austr.
35 G3 Rainbow Bridge Nat. Mon. res. U.S.A.
20 F3 Rainbow Lake Can.
32 C6 Rainelle U.S.A.
84 B3 Raini r. Pak.
24 B2 Rainier, Mt vol. U.S.A.
22 B4 Rainy r. U.S.A.
21 L5 Rainy River Can.
85 E5 Raipur Madhya Pradesh India
84 C4 Raipur Rajasthan India
55 S6 Raisio Fin.
84 D5 Raitalai India
109 Raivavae i. Pac. Oc.
83 F7 Rajahmundry India
54 V2 Raja-Jooseppi Fin.
79 L4 Rajanpur Pak.
83 E9 Rajapalaiyam India
84 C4 Rajasthan div. India
84 C3 Rajasthan Canal canal India
85 F4 Rajauli India
85 G5 Rajbari Bangl.
84 D4 Rajgarh Rajasthan India
84 C3 Rajgarh Rajasthan India
80 F6 Rajil, W. watercourse Jordan
85 E5 Rajim India
84 B5 Rajkot India
85 F4 Rajmahal India
85 F4 Rajmahal Hills h. India
84 E5 Raj Nandgaon India
84 D3 Rajpura India
85 G4 Rajshahi Bangl.
85 F3 Raka China
117 C5 Rakaia r. N.Z.
84 C1 Rakaposhi mt Pak.
69 C5 Rakhiv Ukr.
84 B3 Rakhni Pak.
92 □ Rakit i. Indon.
90 D2 Rakitnoye Rus. Fed.
69 E5 Rakitnoye Rus. Fed.
55 U7 Rakke Estonia
55 M7 Rakkestad Norway
84 B3 Rakni r. Pak.
55 U7 Rakvere Estonia
29 E5 Raleigh U.S.A.
30 D2 Ralph U.S.A.
20 E2 Ram r. Can.
23 H2 Ramah Can.
35 H4 Ramah U.S.A.
46 D1 Ramalho, Serra do h. Brazil
80 E6 Ramallah West Bank
14 E3 Ramapo Deep sea feature N. Pacific Ocean
105 F2 Ramatlabama S. Africa
110 E2 Rambutyo I. i. P.N.G.
59 C7 Rame Head hd U.K.
103 E5 Ramena Madag.
68 F3 Rameshki Rus. Fed.
83 E9 Rameswaram India
84 D4 Ramganga r. India
85 G5 Ramgarh Bangl.
85 F5 Ramgarh Bihar India
84 B4 Ramgarh Rajasthan India
78 F3 Rāmhormoz Iran
80 E6 Ramla Israel
Ramlat Rabyānah des. see Rebiana Sand Sea
80 E7 Ramm, Jabal mt Jordan
84 D3 Ramnagar India
67 M2 Râmnicu Sărat Romania
67 L2 Râmnicu Vâlcea Romania
34 D5 Ramona U.S.A.
31 G1 Ramore Can.
103 C6 Ramotswa Botswana
84 D3 Rampur India
84 C4 Rampura India
Rampur Boalia see Rajshahi
85 F4 Rampur Hat India
85 H6 Ramree I. i. Myanmar
54 P5 Ramsele Sweden
31 F2 Ramsey Can.
58 C3 Ramsey Isle of Man
59 G5 Ramsey U.K.
59 B6 Ramsey Island i. U.K.
31 F2 Ramsey Lake l. Can.
59 J6 Ramsgate U.K.
84 D5 Ramtek India
55 T9 Ramygala Lith.
45 C4 Rana, Co h. Col.
85 G5 Ranaghat India
84 C5 Ranapur India
92 F5 Ranau Malaysia
47 B2 Rancagua Chile
85 F5 Ranchi India
47 B4 Ranco, Lago l. Chile
115 G5 Rand Austr.
60 E3 Randalstown U.K.
66 F6 Randazzo Italy
55 M8 Randers Denmark
33 H3 Randolph MA U.S.A.
33 G3 Randolph VT U.S.A.
55 N5 Randsjö Sweden
54 S4 Råneå Sweden
117 C6 Ranfurly N.Z.
95 B4 Rangae Thai.
85 H5 Rangamati Bangl.
117 D1 Rangaunu Bay b. N.Z.
33 H2 Rangeley U.S.A.
33 H2 Rangeley Lake l. U.S.A.
35 H1 Rangely U.S.A.
31 F2 Ranger Lake Can.
117 D5 Rangiora N.Z.
117 C5 Rangitata r. N.Z.
117 E4 Rangitikei r. N.Z.
92 □ Rangkasbitung Indon.
Rangoon see Yangôn
85 G4 Rangpur Bangl.
83 E8 Ranibennur India
85 F5 Raniganj India
85 E5 Ranijula Peak mt India
84 B4 Ranipur Pak.
27 C6 Rankin U.S.A.
21 L2 Rankin Inlet Can.
21 L2 Rankin Inlet in. Can.
115 G4 Rankin's Springs Austr.
55 U7 Ranna Estonia
116 D5 Rannes Austr.
57 D4 Rannoch, L. l. U.K.
57 D4 Rannoch Moor moorland U.K.
84 B4 Rann of Kachchh marsh India
95 A3 Ranong Thai.
95 B4 Ranot Thai.
68 G4 Ranova r. Rus. Fed.
81 M5 Rānsa Iran
55 N6 Ransby Sweden
93 J7 Ransiki Indon.
55 V5 Rantasalmi Fin.
92 B6 Rantauprapat Indon.
93 F7 Rantepao Indon.
30 C5 Rantoul U.S.A.
63 R2 Rantsevo Rus. Fed.
54 T4 Rantsila Fin.
54 U4 Ranua Fin.
81 K3 Rānya Iraq
90 C1 Raohe China
89 E6 Raoping China
109 Rapa i. Pac. Oc.
66 C2 Rapallo Italy
84 B5 Rapar India
47 B2 Rapel r. Chile
60 D3 Raphoe Rep. of Ireland
32 E5 Rapidan r. U.S.A.
114 C5 Rapid Bay Austr.
26 C2 Rapid City U.S.A.
31 H2 Rapide-Deux Can.
31 H2 Rapide-Sept Can.
30 D3 Rapid River U.S.A.
55 T7 Rapla Estonia
32 E5 Rappahannock r. U.S.A.
85 E4 Rapti r. India
84 B5 Rapur India
94 C3 Rapurapu i. Phil.
33 F2 Raquette r. U.S.A.
33 F3 Raquette Lake U.S.A.
33 F3 Raquette Lake l. U.S.A.
33 F4 Raritan Bay b. U.S.A.
15 J7 Rarotonga i. Pac. Oc.
94 A4 Rasa i. Phil.
47 D4 Rasa, Pta pt Arg.
80 E6 Ra's an Naqb Jordan
102 D2 Ras Dejen mt Eth.
55 S9 Raseiniai Lith.
80 C6 Rashīd Egypt
84 A3 Rashid Qala Afgh.
81 M3 Rasht Iran
84 C1 Raskam mts China
79 K4 Raskoh mts Pak.
101 F2 Ra's Muḥammad c. Egypt
44 C6 Raso, C. pt Arg.
68 D4 Rasony Belarus
85 E4 Rasra India
66 D6 Rass Jebel Tunisia
68 G4 Rasskazovo Rus. Fed.
79 G4 Ras Tannūrah Saudi Arabia
55 O5 Rätan Sweden
105 H3 Ratanda S. Africa
84 C3 Ratangarh India
85 E5 Ratanpur India
55 O5 Rätansbyn Sweden
95 A2 Rat Buri Thai.
84 D4 Rath India
60 E4 Rathangan Rep. of Ireland
60 D5 Rathdowney Rep. of Ireland
60 E5 Rathdrum Rep. of Ireland
85 H5 Rathedaung Myanmar
62 F4 Rathenow Ger.
60 E3 Rathfriland U.K.
60 C5 Rathkeale Rep. of Ireland
60 E2 Rathlin Island i. U.K.
60 C5 Rathluirc Rep. of Ireland
85 C3 Ratiya India
84 C5 Ratlam India
83 D7 Ratnagiri India
83 F9 Ratnapura Sri Lanka
69 C5 Ratne Ukr.
84 B4 Rato Dero Pak.
25 F4 Raton U.S.A.
57 G3 Rattray Head hd U.K.
55 O6 Rättvik Sweden
20 C3 Ratz, Mt mt Can.
95 B5 Raub Malaysia
47 E3 Rauch Arg.
81 L7 Raudhatain Kuwait
54 F3 Raufarhöfn Iceland
117 G2 Raukumara mt N.Z.
117 F3 Raukumara Range mts N.Z.
55 R6 Rauma Fin.
92 E8 Raung, G. vol. Indon.
85 F5 Raurkela India
90 J2 Rausu Japan
54 V5 Rautavaara Fin.
55 V6 Rautjärvi Fin.
24 D2 Ravalli U.S.A.
81 L4 Ravānsar Iran
33 G3 Ravena U.S.A.
58 D3 Ravenglass U.K.
66 E2 Ravenna Italy
116 A5 Ravensbourne Cr. watercourse Austr.
62 D7 Ravensburg Ger.
116 A1 Ravenshoe Austr.
112 D6 Ravensthorpe Austr.
116 B3 Ravenswood Austr.
32 C5 Ravenswood U.S.A.
84 C3 Ravi r. Pak.
81 H4 Rāwah Iraq
84 C2 Rawalpindi Pak.
81 K3 Rawāndiz Iraq
84 C3 Rawatsar India
62 H5 Rawicz Pol.
32 D5 Rawley Springs U.S.A.
112 E6 Rawlinna Austr.
24 F3 Rawlins U.S.A.
44 C6 Rawson Arg.
85 F4 Raxaul India
23 J4 Ray, C. hd Can.
83 F7 Rāyagarha India
80 F5 Rayak Lebanon
87 N2 Raychikhinsk Rus. Fed.
59 H6 Rayleigh U.K.
20 G5 Raymond Can.
33 H3 Raymond NH U.S.A.
24 B2 Raymond WA U.S.A.
115 J4 Raymond Terrace Austr.
27 D7 Raymondville U.S.A.
95 B2 Rayong Thai.
32 D4 Raystown Lake l. U.S.A.
64 B2 Raz, Pte du pt France
81 M4 Razan Iran
81 M5 Rāzān Iran
81 J5 Razāzah, Buḥayrat ar l. Iraq
Razdan see Hrazdan
90 B3 Razdol'noye Rus. Fed.
81 M5 Razeh Iran
67 M3 Razgrad Bulg.
67 N2 Razim, Lacul lag. Romania
67 K4 Razlog Bulg.
64 D3 Ré, Île de i. France
59 G6 Reading U.K.
33 F4 Reading U.S.A.
30 B4 Readstown U.S.A.
105 G2 Reagile S. Africa
47 D2 Realicó Arg.
64 F5 Réalmont France
95 B2 Reăng Kesei Cambodia
27 C7 Reata Mex.
101 E2 Rebiana Sand Sea des. Libya
68 D2 Reboly Rus. Fed.
90 G2 Rebun-tō i. Japan
112 D6 Recherche, Archipelago of the is Austr.
84 C3 Rechna Doab lowland Pak.
69 D4 Rechytsa Belarus
43 M5 Recife Brazil
105 F7 Recife, Cape c. S. Africa
62 C5 Recklinghausen Ger.
44 E3 Reconquista Arg.
44 C3 Recreo Arg.
21 K5 Red r. Can./U.S.A.
27 E6 Red r. U.S.A.
95 B4 Redang i. Malaysia
33 F4 Red Bank NJ U.S.A.
29 C5 Red Bank TN U.S.A.
23 J3 Red Bay Can.
34 A1 Red Bluff U.S.A.
35 F4 Red Butte summit U.S.A.
58 F3 Redcar U.K.
21 G4 Redcliff Can.
114 E5 Red Cliffs Austr.
26 D3 Red Cloud U.S.A.
20 G4 Red Deer Can.
21 G4 Red Deer r. Alta. Can.
21 J4 Red Deer r. Sask. Can.
21 J4 Red Deer L. l. Can.
33 F5 Redden U.S.A.
105 G4 Reddersburg S. Africa
24 B3 Redding U.S.A.
59 F5 Redditch U.K.
33 F3 Redfield NY U.S.A.
26 D2 Redfield SD U.S.A.
114 C4 Redhill Austr.
35 H4 Red Hill U.S.A.
27 D4 Red Hills h. U.S.A.
23 J4 Red Indian L. l. Can.
30 E5 Redkey U.S.A.
21 L4 Red L. l. Can.
35 E4 Red L. U.S.A.
21 L4 Red Lake Can.
26 E1 Red Lakes lakes U.S.A.
24 E2 Red Lodge U.S.A.
24 B2 Redmond U.S.A.
26 E3 Red Oak U.S.A.
65 C3 Redondo Port.
30 C1 Red Rock Can.
33 E4 Red Rock U.S.A.
98 Red Sea sea Africa/Asia
20 E4 Redstone Can.
20 D2 Redstone r. Can.
21 L4 Red Sucker L. l. Can.
20 G4 Redwater Can.
23 H3 Red Wine r. Can.
30 A3 Red Wing U.S.A.
34 A3 Redwood City U.S.A.
26 E2 Redwood Falls U.S.A.
24 B3 Redwood Nat. Park U.S.A.
34 A2 Redwood Valley U.S.A.
60 D4 Ree, Lough l. Rep. of Ireland
30 E4 Reed City U.S.A.
34 C3 Reedley U.S.A.
30 C4 Reedsburg U.S.A.
24 A3 Reedsport U.S.A.
33 E6 Reedville U.S.A.
116 A4 Reedy Cr. watercourse Austr.
117 C5 Reefton N.Z.
80 G2 Refahiye Turkey
27 D6 Refugio U.S.A.
62 F6 Regen Ger.
62 F6 Regensburg Ger.
100 C2 Reggane Alg.
66 F5 Reggio di Calabria Italy
66 D2 Reggio nell'Emilia Italy
63 M7 Reghin Romania
21 J4 Regina Can.
54 W4 Regozero Rus. Fed.
84 D5 Rehli India
103 B6 Rehoboth Namibia
35 H4 Rehoboth U.S.A.
33 F5 Rehoboth Bay b. U.S.A.
33 F5 Rehoboth Beach U.S.A.
80 E6 Rehovot Israel
57 C3 Reidh, Rubha pt U.K.
29 E4 Reidsville U.S.A.
59 G6 Reigate U.K.
35 G5 Reiley Peak summit U.S.A.
64 G2 Reims France
30 A4 Reinbeck U.S.A.
62 E4 Reinbek Ger.
21 J3 Reindeer r. Can.
21 K4 Reindeer I. i. Can.
21 J3 Reindeer Lake l. Can.
54 N3 Reine Norway
117 D1 Reinga, Cape c. N.Z.
65 D1 Reinosa Spain
54 B4 Reiphólsfjöll mt Iceland
54 R2 Reisaelva r. Norway
54 S2 Reisa Nasjonalpark nat. park Norway
54 T5 Reisjärvi Fin.
105 H3 Reitz S. Africa
104 F3 Reivilo S. Africa
45 D3 Rejunya Venez.
21 H2 Reliance Can.
100 C1 Relizane Alg.
114 C4 Remarkable, Mt mt Austr.
104 B1 Remhoogte Pass pass Namibia
62 C6 Remiremont France
84 D2 Remo Gl. gl. India
69 G6 Remontnoye Rus. Fed.
62 C5 Remscheid Ger.
30 E4 Remus U.S.A.
55 M6 Rena Norway
28 B4 Rend L. l. U.S.A.
111 F2 Rendova i. Solomon Is
62 D3 Rendsburg Ger.
31 J3 Renfrew Can.
57 D5 Renfrew U.K.
47 B2 Rengo Chile
88 C3 Ren He r. China
88 E4 Renheji China
89 D5 Renhua China
89 C5 Renhuai China
69 D6 Reni Ukr.
114 D5 Renmark Austr.
111 G3 Rennell i. Solomon Is
64 D2 Rennes France
119 B5 Rennick Gl. gl. Antarctica
21 H2 Rennie Lake l. Can.
66 D2 Reno r. Italy
34 C2 Reno U.S.A.
32 E4 Renovo U.S.A.
88 E2 Renqiu China
89 B4 Renshou China
30 D5 Rensselaer IN U.S.A.
33 G3 Rensselaer NY U.S.A.
61 D2 Renswoude Neth.
24 B2 Renton U.S.A.
85 E4 Renukut India
117 D4 Renwick N.Z.
100 B3 Réo Burkina
93 G8 Reo Indon.
24 C1 Republic U.S.A.
26 D3 Republican r. U.S.A.
116 C3 Repulse B. b. Austr.
42 D5 Requena Peru
65 F3 Requena Spain
80 F1 Reşadiye Turkey
81 J2 Reşadıye Turkey
46 B4 Reserva Brazil
44 E3 Resistencia Arg.
67 J2 Reşiţa Romania
118 B2 Resolute Bay Can.
117 A6 Resolution Island i. N.Z.
95 □ Retan Laut, P. i. Sing.
59 G4 Retford U.K.
64 G2 Rethel France
67 L7 Rethymno Greece
90 C2 Rettikhovka Rus. Fed.
98 Réunion i. Indian Ocean
65 G2 Reus Spain
62 D6 Reutlingen Ger.
34 D3 Reveille Peak summit U.S.A.
64 F5 Revel France
20 F4 Revelstoke Can.
36 B5 Revillagigedo, Islas is Mex.
20 C3 Revillagigedo I. i. U.S.A.
61 C5 Revin France
80 E6 Revivim Israel
84 E4 Rewa India
84 D3 Rewari India
24 E3 Rexburg U.S.A.
23 H4 Rexton Can.
34 A2 Reyes, Point pt U.S.A.
34 C4 Reyes Peak summit U.S.A.
80 F3 Reyhanlı Turkey
54 C4 Reykir Iceland
12 G2 Reykjanes Ridge sea feature Atlantic Ocean
54 B5 Reykjanestá pt Iceland
54 C4 Reykjavík Iceland
36 E3 Reynosa Mex.
55 U8 Rēzekne Latvia
81 M3 Rezvānshahr Iran
80 F5 Rharaz, W. watercourse Syria
59 D5 Rhayader U.K.
Rhein r. see Rhine
62 C4 Rheine Ger.
61 E4 Rheinisches Schiefergebirge h. Ger.
61 F5 Rheinland-Pfalz div. Ger.
Rhin r. see Rhine
62 C5 Rhine r. Europe
33 G4 Rhinebeck U.S.A.
30 C3 Rhinelander U.S.A.
66 C2 Rho Italy
33 H4 Rhode Island div. U.S.A.
67 N6 Rhodes Greece
67 N6 Rhodes i. Greece
24 D2 Rhodes Pk summit U.S.A.
67 L4 Rhodope Mountains mts Bulg./Greece
64 G4 Rhône r. France/Switz.
Rhum i. see Rum
59 D4 Rhyl U.K.
46 E2 Riacho Brazil
46 D1 Riacho de Santana Brazil
46 C1 Rialma Brazil
46 C1 Rianópolis Brazil
84 C2 Riasi Jammu and Kashmir
92 C6 Riau, Kepulauan is Indon.
65 C1 Ribadeo Spain
65 D1 Ribadesella Spain
46 B3 Ribas do Rio Pardo Brazil
103 D5 Ribáuè Moz.
58 E4 Ribble r. U.K.
55 L9 Ribe Denmark
46 C4 Ribeira r. Brazil
46 C3 Ribeirão Preto Brazil
64 E4 Ribérac France
42 E6 Riberalta Bol.
62 F3 Ribnitz-Damgarten Ger.
62 G6 Říčany Czech Rep.
25 F6 Ricardo Flores Magón Mex.
35 E4 Rice U.S.A.
31 F2 Rice Lake l. Can.
30 B3 Rice Lake U.S.A.
30 A4 Riceville IA U.S.A.
32 D4 Riceville PA U.S.A.
105 K4 Richards Bay S. Africa
21 G3 Richardson r. Can.
27 D5 Richardson U.S.A.
33 H2 Richardson Lakes l. U.S.A.
117 B6 Richardson Mts mts N.Z.
61 D1 Richel i. Neth.
35 F2 Richfield U.S.A.
33 F3 Richfield Springs U.S.A.
33 E3 Richford NY U.S.A.
33 G2 Richford VT U.S.A.
30 B5 Richland U.S.A.
30 B4 Richland Center U.S.A.
32 C6 Richlands U.S.A.
115 J4 Richmond N.S.W. Austr.
113 H4 Richmond Qld. Austr.
31 K3 Richmond Can.
117 D4 Richmond N.Z.
105 J4 Richmond Kwazulu-Natal S. Africa
104 E5 Richmond Northern Cape S. Africa
58 F3 Richmond U.K.
30 E6 Richmond IN U.S.A.
32 A6 Richmond KY U.S.A.
33 J2 Richmond ME U.S.A.
31 F4 Richmond MI U.S.A.
32 E6 Richmond VA U.S.A.
33 G2 Richmond VT U.S.A.
117 D4 Richmond, Mt mt N.Z.
31 H4 Richmond Hill Can.
115 K2 Richmond Ra. h. Austr.
104 B4 Richtersveld National Park nat. park S. Africa
32 B4 Richwood OH U.S.A.
32 C5 Richwood WV U.S.A.
31 K3 Rideau r. Can.
31 J3 Rideau Lakes l. Can.
34 D4 Ridgecrest U.S.A.
32 D4 Ridgway U.S.A.
21 J4 Riding Mountain Nat. Park nat. park Can.
62 D6 Riedlingen Ger.
62 F5 Riesa Ger.
44 B8 Riesco, Isla i. Chile
104 D5 Riet r. S. Africa
55 R9 Rietavas Lith.
104 D3 Rietfontein S. Africa
61 D3 Riethoven Neth.
66 E3 Rieti Italy
25 F4 Rifle U.S.A.
54 E3 Rifstangi pt Iceland
85 H3 Riga India
55 T8 Rīga Latvia
55 S8 Riga, Gulf of g. Estonia/Latvia
Rīgas Jūras Līcis g. see Riga, Gulf of
33 F2 Rigaud Can.
24 C2 Riggins U.S.A.
23 J3 Rigolet Can.
57 E5 Rigside U.K.
85 E4 Rihand r. India
85 E4 Rihand Dam dam India
Riia Laht g. see Riga, Gulf of
55 T6 Riihimäki Fin.
25 D5 Riito Mex.
66 F2 Rijeka Croatia
90 G5 Rikuzen-takata Japan
67 K3 Rila mts Bulg.
24 C3 Riley U.S.A.
64 G4 Rillieux-la-Pape France
63 K6 Rimavská Sobota Slovakia
20 G4 Rimbey Can.
66 E2 Rimini Italy
23 G4 Rimouski Can.
57 D2 Rimsdale, Loch l. U.K.
85 G3 Rinbung China
84 E4 Rind r. India
54 L5 Rindal Norway
115 G8 Ringarooma B. b. Austr.
84 C4 Ringas India
85 G2 Ring Co salt l. China
55 M6 Ringebu Norway
55 L8 Ringkøbing Denmark
60 E2 Ringsend U.K.
55 M9 Ringsted Denmark
54 Q2 Ringvassøy i. Norway
59 F7 Ringwood U.K.
47 B3 Riñihue Chile
47 B3 Riñihue, L. l. Chile
30 C4 Rio U.S.A.
46 A2 Rio Alegre Brazil
42 C4 Riobamba Ecuador
35 H2 Rio Blanco U.S.A.
42 E6 Rio Branco Brazil
45 E4 Rio Branco, Parque Nacional do nat. park Brazil
46 C4 Rio Branco do Sul Brazil
46 A3 Rio Brilhante Brazil
47 B4 Río Bueno Chile
45 E2 Río Caribe Venez.
47 D1 Río Ceballos Arg.
46 C3 Rio Claro Brazil
45 E2 Rio Claro Trinidad and Tobago
47 D3 Río Colorado Arg.
47 D2 Río Cuarto Arg.
46 D3 Rio de Janeiro Brazil
46 D3 Rio de Janeiro div. Brazil
44 G3 Rio do Sul Brazil
44 C8 Río Gallegos Arg.
44 C8 Río Grande Arg.
47 G2 Rio Grande Brazil
36 D4 Río Grande Mex.
36 C2 Rio Grande r. Mex./U.S.A.
37 H6 Rio Grande r. Mex./U.S.A.
27 D7 Rio Grande City U.S.A.
12 G7 Rio Grande Rise sea feature Atlantic Ocean
45 B2 Ríohacha Col.
42 C5 Rioja Peru
43 L5 Rio Largo Brazil
64 F4 Riom France
42 E7 Río Mulatos Bol.

47 C4 Río Negro *div.* Arg.
46 C4 Rio Negro Brazil
69 G7 Rioni *r.* Georgia
47 G1 Río Pardo Brazil
46 D1 Rio Pardo de Minas Brazil
47 D1 Río Primero Arg.
25 F5 Rio Rancho U.S.A.
35 G6 Rio Rico U.S.A.
47 D1 Río Segundo Arg.
45 A3 Ríosucio Col.
47 D2 Río Tercero Arg.
42 C4 Río Tigre Ecuador
94 A4 Rio Tuba Phil.
46 B2 Rio Verde Brazil
36 E4 Río Verde Mex.
46 A2 Rio Verde de Mato Grosso Brazil
34 B2 Rio Vista U.S.A.
46 A2 Riozinho *r.* Brazil
63 P5 Ripky Ukr.
58 F3 Ripley *Eng.* U.K.
59 F4 Ripley *Eng.* U.K.
32 B5 Ripley *OH* U.S.A.
29 B5 Ripley *TN* U.S.A.
32 C5 Ripley *WV* U.S.A.
65 H1 Ripoll Spain
58 F3 Ripon U.K.
34 B3 Ripon *CA* U.S.A.
30 C4 Ripon *WV* U.S.A.
59 D6 Risca U.K.
90 G2 Rishiri-tō *i.* Japan
80 E6 Rishon Le Ziyyon Israel
55 L7 Risør Norway
54 L5 Rissa Norway
55 U6 Ristiina Fin.
54 V4 Ristijärvi Fin.
54 W2 Ristikent Rus. Fed.
104 F4 Ritchie S. Africa
119 C3 Ritscher Upland *mts* Antarctica
54 P3 Ritsem Sweden
25 C4 Ritter, Mt *mt* U.S.A.
65 E2 Rituerto *r.* Spain
24 C2 Ritzville U.S.A.
47 C2 Rivadavia *Mendoza* Arg.
47 D2 Rivadavia *Pampas* Arg.
44 D2 Rivadavia *Salta* Arg.
47 B1 Rivadavia Chile
66 D2 Riva del Garda Italy
25 F6 Riva Palacio Mex.
37 G6 Rivas Nic.
47 D3 Rivera Arg.
47 F1 Rivera Uru.
100 B4 River Cess Liberia
33 G4 Riverhead U.S.A.
115 F5 Riverina *reg.* Austr.
104 D7 Riversdale S. Africa
105 H5 Riverside S. Africa
34 D5 Riverside U.S.A.
114 C5 Riverton Austr.
21 K4 Riverton Can.
117 B7 Riverton N.Z.
24 E3 Riverton U.S.A.
23 H4 Riverview Can.
64 F5 Rivesaltes France
29 D7 Riviera Beach U.S.A.
33 J1 Rivière Bleue Can.
23 G4 Rivière-du-Loup Can.
69 C5 Rivne Ukr.
117 D4 Riwaka N.Z.
82 J4 Riwoqê China
78 F5 Riyadh Saudi Arabia
88 A2 Riyue Shankou *pass* China
81 H1 Rize Turkey
88 F3 Rizhao China
80 E4 Rizokarpason Cyprus
55 L7 Rjukan Norway
55 K7 Rjuvbrokkene *mt* Norway
100 A3 Rkîz Maur.
55 M6 Roa Norway
59 G5 Roade U.K.
54 M4 Roan Norway
35 H2 Roan Cliffs *cliff* U.S.A.
64 G3 Roanne France
29 C5 Roanoke *AL* U.S.A.
30 C5 Roanoke *IL* U.S.A.
32 D6 Roanoke *VA* U.S.A.
28 E4 Roanoke *r.* U.S.A.
29 E4 Roanoke Rapids U.S.A.
35 H2 Roan Plateau *plat.* U.S.A.
60 B6 Roaringwater Bay *b.* Rep. of Ireland
54 R5 Röbäck Sweden
115 F8 Robbins I. *i.* Austr.
114 C6 Robe Austr.
60 B4 Robe *r.* Rep. of Ireland
114 D3 Robe, Mt *h.* Austr.
27 C6 Robert Lee U.S.A.
24 D3 Roberts U.S.A.
115 K2 Roberts, Mt *mt* Austr.
34 D2 Roberts Creek Mt *mt* U.S.A.
54 R4 Robertsfors Sweden
85 E4 Robertsganj India
27 E5 Robert S. Kerr Res. *resr* U.S.A.
104 C6 Robertson S. Africa
100 A4 Robertsport Liberia
114 C4 Robertstown Austr.
23 F4 Roberval Can.
58 G3 Robin Hood's Bay U.K.
28 C4 Robinson U.S.A.
116 C5 Robinson Cr. *r.* Austr.
112 C5 Robinson Range *h.* Austr.
114 E5 Robinvale Austr.
35 G5 Robles Junction U.S.A.
35 G5 Robles Pass *pass* U.S.A.
21 J4 Roblin Can.
20 F4 Robson, Mt *mt* Can.
27 D7 Robstown U.S.A.
66 E6 Rocca Busambra *mt* Italy
47 F2 Rocha Uru.
58 E4 Rochdale U.K.
46 A2 Rochedo Brazil
61 D4 Rochefort Belgium
64 D4 Rochefort France
22 F2 Rochefort, Lac *l.* Can.
68 G2 Rochegda Rus. Fed.
30 C5 Rochelle U.S.A.
114 F6 Rochester Austr.
59 H6 Rochester U.K.
30 D5 Rochester *IN* U.S.A.
30 A3 Rochester *MN* U.S.A.
33 H3 Rochester *NH* U.S.A.
32 E3 Rochester *NY* U.S.A.
59 H6 Rochford U.K.
64 C2 Roc'h Trévezel *h.* France
20 D2 Rock *r.* Can.
30 B5 Rock *r.* U.S.A.
12 H2 Rockall Bank *sea feature* Atlantic Ocean
119 B4 Rockefeller Plateau *plat.* Antarctica
30 C4 Rockford U.S.A.
21 H5 Rockglen Can.
116 D4 Rockhampton Austr.
30 C1 Rock Harbor U.S.A.
29 D5 Rock Hill U.S.A.
112 C6 Rockingham Austr.
29 E5 Rockingham U.S.A.
116 B2 Rockingham B. *b.* Austr.
33 G2 Rock Island Can.
30 B5 Rock Island U.S.A.
26 D1 Rocklake U.S.A.
33 F2 Rockland Can.
33 H3 Rockland *MA* U.S.A.
33 J2 Rockland *ME* U.S.A.
30 C2 Rockland *MI* U.S.A.
114 E6 Rocklands Reservoir *resr* Austr.
35 H3 Rock Point U.S.A.
33 H3 Rockport U.S.A.
26 D3 Rock Rapids U.S.A.
24 F2 Rock Springs *MT* U.S.A.
24 E3 Rock Springs *WY* U.S.A.
27 C6 Rocksprings U.S.A.
32 D3 Rockton Can.
30 D6 Rockville *IN* U.S.A.
32 E5 Rockville *MD* U.S.A.
33 J2 Rockwood U.S.A.
25 G4 Rocky Ford U.S.A.
32 B5 Rocky Fork Lake *l.* U.S.A.
31 F2 Rocky Island Lake *l.* Can.
29 E5 Rocky Mount *NC* U.S.A.
32 D6 Rocky Mount *VA* U.S.A.
20 G4 Rocky Mountain House Can.
24 F3 Rocky Mountain Nat. Park *nat. park* U.S.A.
18 Rocky Mountains *mts* Can./U.S.A.
20 F4 Rocky Mountains Forest Reserve *res.* Can.
61 C5 Rocroi France
55 L6 Rodberg Norway
55 M9 Rødbyhavn Denmark
23 J3 Roddickton Can.
58 B3 Rodel U.K.
47 C1 Rodeo Arg.
27 B7 Rodeo Mex.
35 H6 Rodeo U.S.A.
64 F4 Rodez France
68 G3 Rodniki Rus. Fed.
Rodos *see* Rhodes
Rodos *i. see* Rhodes
13 J5 Rodrigues Fracture *sea feature* Indian Ocean
112 C4 Roebourne Austr.
112 D3 Roebuck Bay *b.* Austr.
105 H2 Roedtan S. Africa
61 D3 Roermond Neth.
61 B4 Roeselare Belgium
27 E4 Rogers U.S.A.
31 F3 Rogers City U.S.A.
34 D4 Rogers Lake *l.* U.S.A.
24 D3 Rogerson U.S.A.
32 B6 Rogersville U.S.A.
22 E3 Roggan *r.* Can.
104 D6 Roggeveld *plat.* S. Africa
104 D6 Roggeveldberge *escarpment* S. Africa
54 O3 Rognan Norway
24 A3 Rogue *r.* U.S.A.
24 E1 Rohnert Park U.S.A.
62 F6 Rohrbach in Oberösterreich Austria
84 B4 Rohri Pak.
84 D3 Rohtak India
95 B1 Roi Et Thai.
15 K6 Roi Georges, Îles du *is* Pac. Oc.
55 S8 Roja Latvia
47 E2 Rojas Arg.
83 B3 Rojhan Pak.
95 B5 Rokan *r.* Indon.
113 H2 Rokeby National Park *nat. park* Austr.
55 T9 Rokiškis Lith.
54 R4 Roknäs Sweden
69 C5 Rokytne Ukr.
46 B3 Rolândia Brazil
26 F4 Rolla U.S.A.
55 L6 Rollag Norway
116 C5 Rolleston Austr.
117 D5 Rolleston N.Z.
31 H2 Rollet Can.
29 F7 Rolleville Bahamas
31 J2 Rolphton Can.
116 C6 Roma Austr.
93 H8 Roma *i.* Indon.
Roma *see* Rome
105 G4 Roma Lesotho
55 Q8 Roma Sweden
29 E5 Romain, Cape *c.* U.S.A.
23 H3 Romaine *r.* Can.
63 N7 Roman Romania
12 H6 Romanche Gap *sea feature* Atlantic Ocean
49 Romania *country* Europe
69 G5 Romanovka Rus. Fed.
87 K1 Romanovka Rus. Fed.
64 G4 Romans-sur-Isère France
118 D1 Romanzof, Cape *c.* U.S.A.
64 H2 Rombas France
94 B3 Romblon Phil.
94 B3 Romblon *i.* Phil.
66 E4 Rome Italy
29 C5 Rome *GA* U.S.A.
33 J2 Rome *ME* U.S.A.
33 F3 Rome *NY* U.S.A.
31 F4 Romeo U.S.A.
59 H6 Romford U.K.
64 F2 Romilly-sur-Seine France
32 D5 Romney U.S.A.
59 H6 Romney Marsh *reg.* U.K.
69 E5 Romny Ukr.
55 L9 Rømø *i.* Denmark
64 E3 Romorantin-Lanthenay France
95 B5 Rompin *r.* Malaysia
59 F7 Romsey U.K.
95 C1 Ron Vietnam
57 C3 Rona *i. Scot.* U.K.
57 C1 Rona *i. Scot.* U.K.
57 □ Ronas Hill *h.* U.K.
43 H6 Roncador, Serra do *h.* Brazil
111 F2 Roncador Reef *rf* Solomon Is
65 D4 Ronda Spain
55 L6 Rondane Nasjonalpark *nat. park* Norway
45 C3 Rondón Col.
46 A2 Rondonópolis Brazil
82 E3 Rondu Jammu and Kashmir
47 F2 Ró Negro, Embalse del *resr* Uru.
89 C5 Rong'an China
89 B4 Rongchang China
88 G2 Rongcheng Wan *b.* China
85 G3 Rong Chu *r.* China
89 C5 Rongjiang China
89 C6 Rong Jiang *r.* China
85 H5 Rongklang Range *mts* Myanmar
117 E4 Rongotea N.Z.
89 C5 Rongshui China
89 D6 Rongxian *Guangxi* China
89 B4 Rongxian *Sichuan* China
55 O9 Rønne Denmark
55 O8 Ronneby Sweden
119 B3 Ronne Entrance *str.* Antarctica
119 B3 Ronne Ice Shelf *ice feature* Antarctica
61 B4 Ronse Belgium
84 D3 Roorkee India
61 C3 Roosendaal Neth.
35 G5 Roosevelt *AZ* U.S.A.
35 G1 Roosevelt *UT* U.S.A.
20 D3 Roosevelt, Mt *mt* Can.
35 G5 Roosevelt Dam *dam* U.S.A.
119 A4 Roosevelt I. *i.* Antarctica
20 E2 Root *r.* Can.
30 B4 Root *r.* U.S.A.
68 K2 Ropcha Rus. Fed.
116 C4 Roper Cr. *r.* Austr.
64 D4 Roquefort France
45 E4 Roraima *div.* Brazil
42 F2 Roraima, Mt *mt* Guyana
54 M5 Røros Norway
54 M4 Rørvik Norway
63 P6 Ros' *r.* Ukr.
42 □ Rosa, C. *pt* Ecuador
37 K4 Rosa, Lake *l.* Bahamas
34 C4 Rosamond U.S.A.
34 C4 Rosamond Lake *l.* U.S.A.
47 E2 Rosario Arg.
25 E7 Rosario Mex.
36 A2 Rosario *Baja California* Mex.
27 C7 Rosario *Coahuila* Mex.
94 B3 Rosario Phil.
94 B2 Rosario Phil.
45 B2 Rosario Venez.
47 E2 Rosario del Tala Arg.
47 F1 Rosário do Sul Brazil
46 A1 Rosário Oeste Brazil
34 D5 Rosarito Mex.
66 F5 Rosarno Italy
33 F4 Roscoe U.S.A.
64 C2 Roscoff France
60 C4 Roscommon Rep. of Ireland
30 E3 Roscommon U.S.A.
60 D5 Roscrea Rep. of Ireland
34 C2 Rose, Mt *mt* U.S.A.
37 M5 Roseau Dominica
21 K5 Roseau U.S.A.
115 F8 Rosebery Austr.
23 J4 Rose Blanche Can.
24 B3 Roseburg U.S.A.
31 E3 Rose City U.S.A.
116 D5 Rosedale Austr.
58 G3 Rosedale Abbey U.K.
101 F3 Roseires Reservoir *resr* Sudan
27 E6 Rosenberg U.S.A.
55 K7 Rosendal Norway
105 G4 Rosendal S. Africa
62 F7 Rosenheim Ger.
20 C4 Rose Pt *pt* Can.
66 F3 Roseto degli Abruzzi Italy
21 H4 Rosetown Can.
Rosetta *see* Rashīd
116 B3 Rosetta Cr. *r.* Austr.
21 J4 Rose Valley Can.
34 B2 Roseville *CA* U.S.A.
30 B5 Roseville *IL* U.S.A.
115 K1 Rosewood Austr.
90 D2 Roshchino Rus. Fed.
68 D2 Roshchino Rus. Fed.
104 B3 Rosh Pinah Namibia
66 D3 Rosignano Marittimo Italy
67 L2 Roșiori de Vede Romania
55 N9 Roskilde Denmark
68 E4 Roslavl' Rus. Fed.
54 X2 Roslyakovo Rus. Fed.
115 G9 Ross Austr.
20 C2 Ross *r.* Can.
117 C5 Ross N.Z.
117 E4 Ross, Mt *mt* N.Z.
66 G5 Rossano Italy
60 C3 Rossan Point *pt* Rep. of Ireland
27 F5 Ross Barnett Res. *l.* U.S.A.
23 G3 Ross Bay Junction Can.
60 B6 Ross Carbery Rep. of Ireland
111 F3 Rossel Island *i.* P.N.G.
119 B4 Ross Ice Shelf *ice feature* Antarctica
23 H5 Rossignol, L. *l.* Can.
119 B5 Ross Island *i.* Antarctica
60 E5 Rosslare Rep. of Ireland
59 A5 Rosslare Harbour Rep. of Ireland
31 J3 Rossmore Can.
100 A3 Rosso Maur.
66 C3 Rosso, Capo *pt* France
59 E6 Ross-on-Wye U.K.
69 F5 Rossosh' Rus. Fed.
30 D1 Rossport Can.
20 C2 Ross River Can.
119 A5 Ross Sea *sea* Antarctica
54 O4 Røssvatnet *l.* Norway
30 D5 Rossville U.S.A.
20 D3 Rosswood Can.
81 K3 Rōst Iraq
21 H4 Rosthern Can.
62 F3 Rostock Ger.
68 F3 Rostov Rus. Fed.
69 F6 Rostov-na-Donu Rus. Fed.
69 G6 Rostovskaya Oblast' *div.* Rus. Fed.
54 R4 Rosvik Sweden
29 C5 Roswell *GA* U.S.A.
25 F5 Roswell *NM* U.S.A.
93 L4 Rota *i.* N. Mariana Is
93 G9 Rote *i.* Indon.
62 E6 Roth Ger.
58 F2 Rothbury U.K.
58 F2 Rothbury Forest *forest* U.K.
62 E6 Rothenburg ob der Tauber Ger.
59 G7 Rother *r.* U.K.
119 B2 Rothera *U.K. Base* Antarctica
117 D5 Rotherham N.Z.
59 F4 Rotherham U.K.
57 E3 Rothes U.K.
57 C5 Rothesay U.K.
30 C3 Rothschild U.S.A.
59 G5 Rothwell U.K.
Roti *i. see* Rote
115 F4 Roto Austr.
117 C5 Rotomanu N.Z.
66 C3 Rotondo, Monte *mt* France
117 D4 Rotoroa, L. *l.* N.Z.
117 F3 Rotorua N.Z.
117 F3 Rotorua, L. *l.* N.Z.
62 F6 Rott *r.* Ger.
62 G7 Rottenmann Austria
61 C3 Rotterdam Neth.
61 E1 Rottumeroog *i.* Neth.
61 E1 Rottumerplaat *i.* Neth.
62 D6 Rottweil Ger.
111 H3 Rotuma *i.* Fiji
54 O5 Rötviken Sweden
64 F1 Roubaix France
64 E2 Rouen France
117 B6 Rough Ridge *ridge* N.Z.
Roulers *see* Roeselare
23 F3 Roundeyed, Lac *l.* Can.
58 F3 Round Hill *h.* U.K.
116 D5 Round Hill Hd *hd* Austr.
34 D2 Round Mountain U.S.A.
115 K3 Round Mt *mt* Austr.
35 H3 Round Rock U.S.A.
24 E2 Roundup U.S.A.
57 E1 Rousay *i.* U.K.
33 G2 Rouses Point U.S.A.
64 F5 Roussillon *reg.* France
Routh Bank *sand bank see* Seahorse Bank
105 G5 Rouxville S. Africa
31 H1 Rouyn Can.
54 T3 Rovaniemi Fin.
69 F5 Roven'ki Rus. Fed.
66 D2 Rovereto Italy
95 C2 Rôviĕng Tbong Cambodia
66 D2 Rovigo Italy
66 E2 Rovinj Croatia
69 H5 Rovnoye Rus. Fed.
115 H2 Rowena Austr.
94 B2 Roxas Phil.
94 A4 Roxas Phil.
94 B3 Roxas Phil.
94 B4 Roxas Phil.
94 B4 Roxas Phil.
29 E4 Roxboro U.S.A.
117 B6 Roxburgh N.Z.
114 B3 Roxby Downs Austr.
25 F4 Roy U.S.A.
60 E4 Royal Canal *canal* Rep. of Ireland
30 C1 Royale, Isle *i.* U.S.A.
105 H4 Royal Natal National Park *nat. park* S. Africa
31 F4 Royal Oak U.S.A.
64 D4 Royan France
61 A5 Roye France
59 G5 Royston U.K.
69 D6 Rozdil'na Ukr.
69 E6 Rozdol'ne Ukr.
69 F6 Rozivka Ukr.
69 G4 Rtishchevo Rus. Fed.
59 D5 Ruabon U.K.
103 B5 Ruacana Namibia
102 D4 Ruaha National Park *nat. park* Tanz.
117 F3 Ruahine Range *mts* N.Z.
117 E3 Ruapehu, Mt *vol.* N.Z.
117 B7 Ruapuke I. *i.* N.Z.
117 G2 Ruatoria N.Z.
68 D4 Ruba Belarus
78 F6 Rub' al Khālī *des.* Saudi Arabia
90 H3 Rubeshibe Japan
34 B2 Rubicon *r.* U.S.A.
69 F5 Rubizhne Ukr.
86 D1 Rubtsovsk Rus. Fed.
35 E1 Ruby Lake *l.* U.S.A.
35 E1 Ruby Mountains *mts* U.S.A.
116 B4 Rubyvale Austr.
89 D5 Rucheng China
32 D5 Ruckersville U.S.A.
112 D4 Rudall River National Park *nat. park* Austr.
85 E4 Rudauli India
81 M3 Rūdbār Iran
55 M9 Rudkøbing Denmark
87 P3 Rudnaya Pristan' China
77 P5 Rudnaya Pristan' Rus. Fed.
68 K3 Rudnichnyy Rus. Fed.
68 D4 Rudnya Rus. Fed.
76 H4 Rudnyy Kazak.
90 D2 Rudnyy Rus. Fed.
76 G1 Rudol'fa, Ostrov *i.* Rus. Fed.
88 F3 Rudong China
32 A2 Rudyard U.S.A.
103 D4 Rufiji *r.* Tanz.
47 D2 Rufino Arg.
100 A3 Rufisque Senegal
103 C5 Rufunsa Zambia
88 F3 Rugao China
59 F5 Rugby U.K.
26 C1 Rugby U.S.A.
59 F5 Rugeley U.K.
62 F3 Rügen *i.* Ger.
32 B4 Ruggles U.S.A.
102 C4 Ruhengeri Rwanda
55 S8 Ruhnu *i.* Estonia
61 E3 Ruhr *r.* Ger.
89 F5 Rui'an China
25 F5 Ruidoso U.S.A.
89 E5 Ruijin China
21 N2 Ruin Point *pt* Can.
103 D4 Ruipa Tanz.
45 B3 Ruiz, Nevado del *vol.* Col.
80 F5 Rujaylah, Ḥarrat ar *lava* Jordan
55 T8 Rūjiena Latvia
85 E3 Rukumkot Nepal
102 D4 Rukwa, Lake *l.* Tanz.
56 C3 Rum *i.* U.K.
67 H2 Ruma Serb. and Mont.
101 E4 Rumbek Sudan
29 F7 Rum Cay *i.* Bahamas
33 H2 Rumford U.S.A.
64 G4 Rumilly France
112 F2 Rum Jungle Austr.
90 G3 Rumoi Japan
88 E3 Runan China
117 C5 Runanga N.Z.
117 F2 Runaway, Cape *c.* N.Z.
59 E4 Runcorn U.K.
103 B5 Rundu Namibia
54 Q5 Rundvik Sweden
95 B3 Rŭng, Kaôh *i.* Cambodia
95 B3 Rŭng Sânlŏem, Kaôh *i.* Cambodia
88 C3 Runheji China
55 V6 Ruokolahti Fin.
88 G3 Ruoqiang China
85 H4 Rupa India
47 B4 Rupanco, L. *l.* Chile
114 E6 Rupanyup Austr.
95 B5 Rupat *i.* Indon.
22 E3 Rupert *r.* Can.
24 D3 Rupert U.S.A.
22 E3 Rupert Bay *b.* Can.
61 E4 Rurstausee *resr* Ger.
103 D5 Rusape Zimbabwe
67 L3 Ruse Bulg.
59 G5 Rushden U.K.
30 B4 Rushford U.S.A.
30 C4 Rush Lake *l.* U.S.A.
85 H3 Rushon India
79 L2 Rushon Tajik.
30 B5 Rushville *IL* U.S.A.
26 C3 Rushville *NE* U.S.A.
114 F6 Rushworth Austr.
27 E6 Rusk U.S.A.
29 D7 Ruskin U.S.A.
21 J4 Russell *Man.* Can.
33 F2 Russell *Ont.* Can.
117 E1 Russell N.Z.
26 D4 Russell U.S.A.
20 F2 Russell Lake *l.* Can.
111 F2 Russell Is *is* Solomon Is
29 C4 Russellville *AL* U.S.A.
27 E5 Russellville *AR* U.S.A.
28 C4 Russellville *KY* U.S.A.
62 D5 Rüsselsheim Ger.
70 Russian Federation *country* Asia/Europe
90 C3 Russkiy, Ostrov *i.* Rus. Fed.
81 K1 Rust'avi Georgia
105 G2 Rustenburg S. Africa
27 E5 Ruston U.S.A.
93 G8 Ruteng Indon.
35 E2 Ruth U.S.A.
31 H2 Rutherglen Can.
59 D4 Ruthin U.K.
68 H3 Rutka *r.* Rus. Fed.
33 G3 Rutland U.S.A.
59 G5 Rutland Water *resr* U.K.
21 G2 Rutledge Lake *l.* Can.
84 D2 Rutog China
31 G2 Rutter Can.
54 T4 Ruukki Fin.
103 D5 Ruvuma *r.* Moz./Tanz.
80 F5 Ruwayshid, Wādī *watercourse* Jordan
89 D5 Ruyuan China
76 H4 Ruzayevka Kazak.
68 H4 Ruzayevka Rus. Fed.
88 D3 Ruzhou China
63 J6 Ružomberok Slovakia
102 C4 Rwanda *country* Africa
68 H2 Ryadovo Rus. Fed.
57 C5 Ryan, Loch *b.* U.K.
68 F4 Ryazan' Rus. Fed.
68 G4 Ryazanskaya Oblast' *div.* Rus. Fed.
68 G4 Ryazhsk Rus. Fed.
76 E2 Rybachiy, Poluostrov *pen.* Rus. Fed.
Rybach'ye *see* Balykchy
68 F3 Rybinsk Rus. Fed.
68 F3 Rybinskoye Vdkhr. *resr* Rus. Fed.
68 J4 Rybnaya Sloboda Rus. Fed.
63 J5 Rybnik Pol.
68 F4 Rybnoye Rus. Fed.
20 F3 Rycroft Can.
55 O8 Ryd Sweden
119 B3 Rydberg Pen. *pen.* Antarctica
59 F7 Ryde U.K.
59 H7 Rye U.K.
58 G3 Rye *r.* U.K.
69 E5 Ryl'sk Rus. Fed.
115 H4 Rylstone Austr.
91 F5 Ryōtsu Japan
Ryuku Islands *is see* Nansei-shotō
63 L5 Rzeszów Pol.
69 G4 Rzhaksa Rus. Fed.
68 E3 Rzhev Rus. Fed.

S

62 E5 Saalfeld Ger.
61 E5 Saar *r.* Ger.
62 C6 Saarbrücken Ger.
61 E5 Saarburg Ger.
55 S7 Saaremaa *i.* Estonia
54 T3 Saarenkylä Fin.
61 E5 Saargau *reg.* Ger.
54 T5 Saarijärvi Fin.
54 U3 Saari-Kämä Fin.
54 R2 Saarikoski Fin.
61 E5 Saarland *div.* Ger.
62 C6 Saarlouis Ger.
81 M2 Saatlı Azer.
47 D3 Saavedra Arg.
80 F5 Sab' Ābār Syria
67 H2 Šabac Serb. and Mont.
65 H2 Sabadell Spain
91 E7 Sabae Japan
93 F5 Sabah *div.* Malaysia
95 B5 Sabak Malaysia
81 L2 Sabalan, Kūhhā-ye *mts* Iran
84 D4 Sabalgarh India
37 H4 Sabana, Arch. de *is* Cuba
45 B2 Sabanalarga Col.
80 D1 Şabanözü Turkey
46 D2 Sabará Brazil
84 C5 Sabarmati *r.* India
66 E4 Sabaudia Italy
104 E5 Sabelo S. Africa
101 D2 Sabhā Libya
84 D3 Sabi *r.* India
105 K2 Sabie Moz.
105 K2 Sabie *r.* Moz./S. Africa
105 J2 Sabie S. Africa
25 F6 Sabinal Mex.
36 D3 Sabinas Mex.
27 C7 Sabinas Hidalgo Mex.
27 E6 Sabine L. *l.* U.S.A.
81 M1 Sabirabad Azer.
94 B3 Sablayan Phil.
29 D7 Sable, Cape *c.* U.S.A.
111 F3 Sable, Île de *i.* New Caledonia
23 J5 Sable Island *i.* Can.
31 F2 Sables, River aux *r.* Can.
94 B1 Sabtang *i.* Phil.
65 C2 Sabugal Port.
30 B4 Sabula U.S.A.
78 E6 Şabyā Saudi Arabia
Sabzanar *see* Shīndand
79 H2 Sabzevār Iran
67 N2 Sacalinul Mare, Insula *i.* Romania
67 L2 Săcele Romania
103 B5 Sachanga Angola
22 B3 Sachigo *r.* Can.
22 B3 Sachigo L. *l.* Can.
84 C5 Sachin India
84 D2 Sach Pass *pass* India
33 E3 Sackets Harbor U.S.A.
23 H4 Sackville Can.
33 H3 Saco *ME* U.S.A.
24 F1 Saco *MT* U.S.A.
94 B5 Sacol *i.* Phil.

34 B2 **Sacramento** U.S.A.
34 B2 **Sacramento** *r.* U.S.A.
25 F5 **Sacramento Mts** *mts* U.S.A.
24 B3 **Sacramento Valley** *v.* U.S.A.
105 G6 **Sada** S. Africa
65 F1 **Sádaba** Spain
80 F4 **Şadad** Syria
95 B4 **Sadao** Thai.
81 K5 **Saddat al Hindīyah** Iraq
105 J2 **Saddleback** *pass* S. Africa
95 C3 **Sa Đec** Vietnam
85 H3 **Sadêng** China
84 B3 **Sadiqabad** Pak.
84 C1 **Sad Istragh** *mt* Afgh./Pak.
82 J5 **Sadiya** India
81 L5 **Sa'dīyah, Hawr as** *l.* Iraq
65 B3 **Sado** *r.* Port.
91 F6 **Sadoga-shima** *i.* Japan
65 H3 **Sa Dragonera** *i.* Spain
55 M8 **Sæby** Denmark
Safad *see* **Zefat**
81 L6 **Safayal Maqūf** *w.* Iraq
55 N7 **Säffle** Sweden
35 H5 **Safford** U.S.A.
59 H5 **Saffron Walden** U.K.
100 B1 **Safi** Morocco
81 M3 **Safīd** *r.* Iran
81 M5 **Safid Dasht** Iran
80 F4 **Şāfītā** Syria
54 X2 **Safonovo** *Murmansk.* Rus. Fed.
68 E4 **Safonovo** *Smolensk.* Rus. Fed.
76 F3 **Safonovo** Rus. Fed.
80 D1 **Safranbolu** Turkey
81 L6 **Safwān** Iraq
85 F3 **Saga** China
91 B8 **Saga** Japan
91 F7 **Sagamihara** Japan
91 F7 **Sagami-nada** *g.* Japan
91 F7 **Sagami-wan** *b.* Japan
45 B3 **Sagamoso** *r.* Col.
95 A2 **Saganthit Kyun** *i.* Myanmar
84 D5 **Sagar** India
69 H7 **Sagarejo** Georgia
85 G5 **Sagar I.** *i.* India
77 O2 **Sagastyr** Rus. Fed.
31 F4 **Saginaw** U.S.A.
31 F4 **Saginaw Bay** *b.* U.S.A.
23 H2 **Saglek Bay** *b.* Can.
66 C3 **Sagone, Golfe de** *b.* France
65 B4 **Sagres** Port.
85 H5 **Sagu** Myanmar
25 F4 **Saguache** U.S.A.
37 H4 **Sagua la Grande** Cuba
35 G5 **Saguaro National Monument** *res.* U.S.A.
23 F4 **Saguenay** *r.* Can.
65 F3 **Sagunto** Spain
84 C5 **Sagwara** India
45 B2 **Sahagún** Col.
65 D1 **Sahagún** Spain
81 L3 **Sahand, Kūh-e** *mt* Iran
98 **Sahara** *des.* Africa
Saharan Atlas *mts see* **Atlas Saharien**
84 D3 **Saharanpur** India
85 F4 **Saharsa** India
84 D3 **Sahaswan** India
84 C3 **Sahiwal** Pak.
81 L4 **Şahneh** Iran
81 K6 **Şaḩrā al Ḩijārah** *reg.* Iraq
25 E6 **Sahuaripa** Mex.
35 G6 **Sahuarita** U.S.A.
95 D2 **Sa Huynh** Vietnam
Sahyadri *mts see* **Western Ghats**
84 C5 **Sahyadriparvat Range** *h.* India
84 E4 **Sai** *r.* India
95 B4 **Sai Buri** Thai.
95 B4 **Sai Buri** *r.* Thai.
Saïda *see* **Sidon**
95 B2 **Sai Dao Tai, Khao** *mt* Thai.
85 G4 **Saidpur** Bangl.
84 C2 **Saidu** Pak.
91 C6 **Saigō** Japan
Saigon *see* **Hô Chi Minh**
95 C3 **Saigon, Sông** *r.* Vietnam
85 H5 **Saiha** India
88 D1 **Saihan Tal** China
88 A1 **Saihan Toroi** China
91 C8 **Saijō** Japan
91 B8 **Saiki** Japan
89 □ **Sai Kung** China
55 V6 **Saimaa** *l.* Fin.
80 F2 **Saimbeyli** Turkey
81 L3 **Sa'īndezh** Iran
57 F5 **St Abb's Head** *hd* U.K.
59 B7 **St Agnes** U.K.
59 A8 **St Agnes** *i.* U.K.
23 J4 **St Alban's** Can.
59 G6 **St Albans** U.K.
33 G2 **St Albans** *VT* U.S.A.
32 C5 **St Albans** *WV* U.S.A.
59 E7 **St Alban's Head** *hd* U.K.
20 G4 **St Albert** Can.
61 B4 **St-Amand-les-Eaux** France
64 F3 **St-Amand-Montrond** France
64 G3 **St-Amour** France
33 K2 **St Andrews** Can.
57 F4 **St Andrews** U.K.
37 J5 **St Ann's Bay** Jamaica
60 F6 **St Ann's Head** *hd* Wales
23 J3 **St Anthony** Can.
24 E3 **St Anthony** U.S.A.
114 E6 **St Arnaud** Austr.
117 D5 **St Arnaud Range** *mts* N.Z.
23 J3 **St-Augustin** Can.
29 D6 **St Augustine** U.S.A.
59 C7 **St Austell** U.K.
64 E3 **St-Avertin** France
61 E5 **St-Avold** France
37 M5 **St Barthélémy** *i.* Guadeloupe
58 D3 **St Bees** U.K.
58 D3 **St Bees Head** *hd* U.K.
59 B6 **St Bride's Bay** *b.* U.K.
64 C2 **St-Brieuc** France
35 G5 **St Carlos Lake** *l.* U.S.A.
31 H4 **St Catharines** Can.
29 D6 **St Catherines I.** *i.* U.S.A.
59 F7 **St Catherine's Point** *pt* U.K.
64 E4 **St-Céré** France
33 G2 **St-Césaire** Can.
64 G4 **St-Chamond** France
24 E3 **St Charles** *ID* U.S.A.
32 E5 **St Charles** *MD* U.S.A.
30 A4 **St Charles** *MN* U.S.A.
26 F4 **St Charles** *MO* U.S.A.
31 F4 **St Clair** U.S.A.
31 F4 **St Clair Shores** U.S.A.
64 G3 **St-Claude** France
59 C6 **St Clears** U.K.
26 E2 **St Cloud** U.S.A.
23 G4 **St Croix** *r.* Can.
30 A2 **St Croix** *r.* U.S.A.
37 M5 **St Croix** *i.* Virgin Is
30 A3 **St Croix Falls** U.S.A.
35 G6 **St David** U.S.A.
59 B6 **St David's** Wales
59 B6 **St David's Head** *hd* U.K.
64 H2 **St-Dié** France
64 G2 **St-Dizier** France
21 K5 **Ste Anne** Can.
23 G3 **Ste Anne, L.** *l.* Can.
23 F4 **Ste-Anne-de-Beaupré** Can.
33 J1 **Sainte-Anne-de-Madawaska** Can.
31 K2 **Sainte-Anne-du-Lac** Can.
33 H1 **Ste-Camille-de-Lellis** Can.
64 G4 **St-Égrève** France
33 H1 **Sainte-Justine** Can.
33 J1 **St-Éleuthère** Can.
20 B2 **St Elias Mountains** *mts* Can.
23 G3 **Ste Marguerite** *r.* Can.
64 H5 **Ste-Maxime** France
64 D4 **Saintes** France
33 G2 **Ste-Thérèse** Can.
64 G4 **St-Étienne** France
33 F2 **St Eugene** Can.
33 G2 **St-Eustache** Can.
37 M5 **St Eustatius** *i.* Neth. Ant.
23 F4 **St-Félicien** Can.
60 F3 **Saintfield** U.K.
66 C3 **St-Florent** France
64 F3 **St-Florent-sur-Cher** France
102 C3 **St Floris, Parc National** *nat. park* C.A.R.
33 J1 **St-Francis** *r.* Can./U.S.A.
26 C4 **St Francis** *KS* U.S.A.
33 J1 **St Francis** *ME* U.S.A.
27 F4 **St Francis** *r.* U.S.A.
23 K4 **St Francis, C.** *c.* Can.
33 J1 **St Froid Lake** *l.* U.S.A.
62 D7 **St Gallen** Switz.
64 E5 **St-Gaudens** France
33 H2 **St-Gédéon** Can.
115 H2 **St George** Austr.
33 K2 **St George** Can.
29 D5 **St George** *SC* U.S.A.
35 F3 **St George** *UT* U.S.A.
111 F2 **St George, C.** *pt* P.N.G.
24 A3 **St George, Pt** *pt* U.S.A.
29 C6 **St George I.** *i.* U.S.A.
23 F4 **St-Georges** Can.
37 M6 **St George's** Grenada
23 J4 **St George's B.** *b.* Can.
110 F2 **St George's Channel** *chan.* P.N.G.
56 C6 **St George's Channel** *chan.* Rep. of Ireland/U.K.
59 C6 **St Govan's Head** *hd* U.K.
30 E3 **St Helen** U.S.A.
12 J7 **St Helena** *i.* Atlantic Ocean
34 A2 **St Helena** U.S.A.
104 C6 **St Helena Bay** S. Africa
104 C6 **St Helena Bay** *b.* S. Africa
12 J7 **St Helena Fracture** *sea feature* Atlantic Ocean
115 H8 **St Helens** Austr.
59 E4 **St Helens** U.K.
24 B2 **St Helens** U.S.A.
24 B2 **St Helens, Mt** *vol.* U.S.A.
115 H8 **St Helens Pt** *pt* Austr.
56 E7 **St Helier** U.K.
61 D4 **St-Hubert** Belgium
64 F4 **St-Hyacinthe** Can.
30 E3 **St Ignace** U.S.A.
30 C1 **St Ignace I.** *i.* Can.
59 C6 **St Ishmael** U.K.
59 E5 **St Ives** *Eng.* U.K.
59 B7 **St Ives** *Eng.* U.K.
33 J1 **St-Jacques** Can.
30 E3 **St James** U.S.A.
20 C4 **St James, Cape** *pt* Can.
23 F4 **St-Jean, Lac** *l.* Can.
64 D4 **St-Jean-d'Angély** France
64 C3 **St-Jean-de-Monts** France
22 F4 **St-Jean-sur-Richelieu** Can.
22 F4 **St-Jérôme** Can.
24 C2 **St Joe** *r.* U.S.A.
23 G4 **St John** Can.
33 K2 **St John** *r.* Can./U.S.A.
35 F1 **St John** U.S.A.
37 M5 **St John** *i.* Virgin Is
37 M5 **St John's** Antigua
23 K4 **St John's** Can.
35 H4 **St Johns** *AZ* U.S.A.
30 E4 **St Johns** *MI* U.S.A.
29 D6 **St Johns** *r.* U.S.A.
33 H2 **St Johnsbury** U.S.A.
58 E3 **St John's Chapel** U.K.
30 D4 **St Joseph** *MI* U.S.A.
26 E4 **St Joseph** *MO* U.S.A.
30 E5 **St Joseph** *r.* U.S.A.
22 B3 **St Joseph, Lac** *l.* Can.
23 F4 **St-Joseph-de-Beauce** Can.
31 F2 **St Joseph I.** *i.* Can.
27 D7 **St Joseph I.** *i.* U.S.A.
22 F4 **St Jovité** Can.
64 E4 **St-Junien** France
59 B7 **St Just** U.K.
59 B7 **St Keverne** U.K.
56 B3 **St Kilda** *is* U.K.
16 **St Kitts and Nevis** *country* Caribbean Sea
61 B3 **St-Laureins** Belgium
St-Laurent, Golfe du *g. see* **St Lawrence, Gulf of**
43 H2 **St-Laurent-du-Maroni** Fr. Guiana
116 C4 **St Lawrence** Austr.
23 K4 **St Lawrence** Can.
23 G4 **St Lawrence** *in.* Can.
23 H4 **St Lawrence, Gulf of** *g.* Can./U.S.A.
77 V3 **St Lawrence I.** *i.* Alaska
31 K3 **St Lawrence Islands National Park** *nat. park* Can.
33 F2 **St Lawrence Seaway** *chan.* Can./U.S.A.
23 G4 **St-Léonard** Can.
23 J3 **St Lewis** Can.
23 J3 **Saint Lewis** *r.* Can.
64 D2 **St-Lô** France
100 A3 **St Louis** Senegal
30 E4 **St Louis** *MI* U.S.A.
26 F4 **St Louis** *MO* U.S.A.
30 A2 **St Louis** *r.* U.S.A.
16 **St Lucia** *country* Caribbean Sea
105 K3 **St Lucia, Lake** *l.* S. Africa
105 K4 **St Lucia Estuary** S. Africa
37 M5 **St Maarten** *i.* Neth. Ant.
57 □ **St Magnus Bay** *b.* U.K.
64 D3 **St-Maixent-l'École** France
64 C2 **St-Malo** France
64 C2 **St-Malo, Golfe de** *g.* France
105 G6 **St Marks** S. Africa
37 M5 **Saint Martin** *i.* Guadeloupe
104 B6 **St Martin, Cape** *hd* S. Africa
21 K4 **St Martin, L.** *l.* Can.
30 D3 **St Martin I.** *i.* U.S.A.
59 A8 **St Martin's** *i.* U.K.
85 H5 **St Martin's I.** *i.* Bangl.
114 C3 **St Mary Pk** *mt* Austr.
115 H8 **St Marys** Austr.
31 G4 **St Mary's** Can.
57 F2 **St Mary's** U.K.
59 A8 **St Mary's** *i.* U.K.
32 A4 **St Marys** *OH* U.S.A.
32 D4 **St Marys** *PA* U.S.A.
32 C5 **Saint Marys** U.S.A.
32 A4 **St Marys** *r.* U.S.A.
23 K4 **St Mary's, C.** *hd* Can.
77 V3 **St Matthew I.** *i.* Alaska
110 E2 **St Matthias Group** *is* P.N.G.
22 F4 **St Maurice** *r.* Can.
59 B7 **St Mawes** U.K.
64 D4 **St-Médard-en-Jalles** France
23 J3 **St Michaels Bay** *b.* Can.
62 D7 **St Moritz** Switz.
64 C3 **St-Nazaire** France
59 G5 **St Neots** U.K.
64 H2 **St-Nicolas-de-Port** France
61 C3 **St-Niklaas** Belgium
64 F1 **St-Omer** France
33 J1 **St-Pamphile** Can.
23 G4 **St Pascal** Can.
21 G4 **St Paul** Can.
13 K6 **St Paul** *i.* Indian Ocean
30 A3 **St Paul** *MN* U.S.A.
26 D3 **St Paul** *NE* U.S.A.
32 B6 **St Paul** *VA* U.S.A.
56 E7 **St Peter Port** U.K.
68 D3 **St Petersburg** Rus. Fed.
29 D7 **St Petersburg** U.S.A.
64 G5 **St-Pierre** *mt* France
23 J4 **St-Pierre** N. America
23 F4 **St-Pierre, Lake** *l.* Can.
64 D4 **St-Pierre-d'Oléron** France
64 F3 **St-Pierre-le-Moûtier** France
61 A4 **St-Pol-sur-Ternoise** France
62 G6 **St Pölten** Austria
64 F3 **St-Pourçain-sur-Sioule** France
33 H1 **Saint-Prosper** Can.
64 F2 **St-Quentin** France
64 H5 **St-Raphaël** France
33 F2 **St Regis** *r.* U.S.A.
33 F2 **St Regis Falls** U.S.A.
33 G2 **St-Rémi** Can.
33 H2 **St-Sébastien** Can.
23 G4 **St Siméon** Can.
29 D6 **St Simons I.** *i.* U.S.A.
33 K2 **St Stephen** Can.
29 E5 **St Stephen** U.S.A.
33 H2 **St-Théophile** Can.
21 L4 **St Theresa Point** Can.
31 G4 **St Thomas** Can.
64 H5 **St-Tropez** France
21 K5 **St Vincent** U.S.A.
115 F9 **St Vincent, C.** *hd* Austr.
St Vincent, Cape *c. see* **São Vicente, Cabo de**
114 B5 **St Vincent, Gulf** *b.* Austr.
16 **St Vincent and the Grenadines** *country* Caribbean Sea
61 E4 **St-Vith** Belgium
21 H4 **St Walburg** Can.
61 F5 **St Wendel** Ger.
31 G4 **St Williams** Can.
64 E4 **St-Yrieix-la-Perche** France
84 E3 **Saipal** *mt* Nepal
93 L3 **Saipan** *i.* N. Mariana Is
85 H5 **Saitlai** Myanmar
54 T3 **Saittanulkki** *h.* Fin.
42 E7 **Sajama, Nevado** *mt* Bol.
104 D5 **Sak** *watercourse* S. Africa
91 D7 **Sakai** Japan
91 C7 **Sakaide** Japan
91 C7 **Sakaiminato** Japan
81 H7 **Sakākah** Saudi Arabia
26 C2 **Sakakawea, Lake** *l.* U.S.A.
22 E3 **Sakami** Can.
22 F3 **Sakami** *r.* Can.
22 E3 **Sakami, Lac** *l.* Can.
67 M4 **Sakar** *mts* Bulg.
80 C1 **Sakarya** Turkey
80 C1 **Sakarya** *r.* Turkey
90 F5 **Sakata** Japan
95 B2 **Sa Keo** *r.* Thai.
100 C4 **Sakété** Benin
87 Q1 **Sakhalin** *i.* Rus. Fed.
77 Q4 **Sakhalinskiy Zaliv** *b.* Rus. Fed.
84 C3 **Sakhi** India
105 H3 **Sakhile** S. Africa
81 L1 **Şäki** Azer.
55 S9 **Šakiai** Lith.
84 A3 **Sakir** *mt* Pak.
87 M7 **Sakishima-shotō** *is* Japan
95 C1 **Sakon Nakhon** Thai.
95 □ **Sakra, P.** *i.* Sing.
84 B4 **Sakrand** Pak.
104 D5 **Sakrivier** S. Africa
91 B9 **Sakura-jima** *vol.* Japan
69 E6 **Saky** Ukr.
55 S6 **Säkylä** Fin.
100 □ **Sal** *i.* Cape Verde
69 G6 **Sal** *r.* Rus. Fed.
55 S8 **Sala** Latvia
55 P7 **Sala** Sweden
22 F4 **Salaberry-de-Valleyfield** Can.
55 T8 **Salacgrīva** Latvia
66 F4 **Sala Consilina** Italy
35 E5 **Salada, Laguna** *salt l.* Mex.
47 E2 **Saladillo** Arg.
47 D2 **Saladillo** *r.* Arg.
47 E1 **Salado** *r. Buenos Aires* Arg.
47 C3 **Salado** *r. Mendoza/San Luis* Arg.
47 D4 **Salado** *r. Rio Negro* Arg.
47 E2 **Salado** *r. Santa Fé* Arg.
36 E3 **Salado** *r.* Mex.
44 B3 **Salado, Quebrada de** *r.* Chile
100 B4 **Salaga** Ghana
104 F1 **Salajwe** Botswana
101 D3 **Salal** Chad
79 G6 **Şalālah** Oman
47 B1 **Salamanca** Chile
36 D4 **Salamanca** Mex.
65 D2 **Salamanca** Spain
32 D3 **Salamanca** U.S.A.
105 K3 **Salamanga** Moz.
81 L4 **Salāmatābād** Iran
45 B3 **Salamina** Col.
80 F4 **Salamīyah** Syria
30 E5 **Salamonie** *r.* U.S.A.
30 E5 **Salamonie Lake** *l.* U.S.A.
85 F5 **Salandi** *r.* India
55 R8 **Salantai** Lith.
88 D1 **Salaqi** China
65 C1 **Salas** Spain
55 T8 **Salaspils** Latvia
92 □ **Salatiga** Indon.
93 J7 **Salawati** *i.* Indon.
84 B5 **Salaya** India
93 G8 **Salayar** *i.* Indon.
15 N7 **Sala y Gómez, Isla** *i.* Chile
47 D3 **Salazar** Arg.
55 T9 **Šalčininkai** Lith.
59 D7 **Salcombe** U.K.
45 B4 **Saldaña** *r.* Col.
65 D1 **Saldaña** Spain
104 B6 **Saldanha** S. Africa
104 B6 **Saldanha Bay** *b.* S. Africa
47 E3 **Saldungaray** Arg.
55 S8 **Saldus** Latvia
115 G7 **Sale** Austr.
81 L5 **Şāleḩābād** Iran
81 M4 **Şāleḩābād** Iran
76 H3 **Salekhard** Rus. Fed.
83 E8 **Salem** India
33 H3 **Salem** *MA* U.S.A.
27 F4 **Salem** *MO* U.S.A.
28 F4 **Salem** *NJ* U.S.A.
33 G3 **Salem** *NY* U.S.A.
32 C4 **Salem** *OH* U.S.A.
24 B2 **Salem** *OR* U.S.A.
28 D4 **Salem** *VA* U.S.A.
57 C4 **Salen** U.K.
57 C4 **Salen** 187351
66 F4 **Salerno** Italy
66 F4 **Salerno, Golfo di** *g.* Italy
59 E4 **Salford** U.K.
43 L5 **Salgado** *r.* Brazil
63 J6 **Salgótarján** Hungary
43 L5 **Salgueiro** Brazil
94 C6 **Salibabu** *i.* Indon.
64 D5 **Salies-de-Béarn** France
80 B2 **Salihli** Turkey
68 C4 **Salihorsk** Belarus
103 D5 **Salima** Malawi
103 D5 **Salimo** Moz.
26 D4 **Salina** *KS* U.S.A.
35 G2 **Salina** *UT* U.S.A.
66 F5 **Salina, Isola** *i.* Italy
36 E5 **Salina Cruz** Mex.
46 D2 **Salinas** Brazil
42 B4 **Salinas** Ecuador
34 B3 **Salinas** U.S.A.
34 B3 **Salinas** *r.* U.S.A.
25 F5 **Salinas Peak** *summit* U.S.A.
27 E5 **Saline** *r. AR* U.S.A.
26 C4 **Saline** *r. KS* U.S.A.
34 D3 **Saline Valley** *v.* U.S.A.
43 J4 **Salinópolis** Brazil
42 C6 **Salinosó Lachay, Pta** *pt* Peru
59 F6 **Salisbury** U.K.
33 F5 **Salisbury** *MD* U.S.A.
29 D5 **Salisbury** *NC* U.S.A.
59 E6 **Salisbury Plain** *plain* U.K.
43 K6 **Salitre** *r.* Brazil
80 F5 **Şalkhad** Syria
85 F5 **Salki** *r.* India
54 V3 **Salla** Fin.
47 D3 **Salliqueló** Arg.
27 E5 **Sallisaw** U.S.A.
85 E3 **Sallyana** Nepal
81 K2 **Salmās** Iran
68 D2 **Salmi** Rus. Fed.
20 F5 **Salmo** Can.
24 D2 **Salmon** U.S.A.
24 D2 **Salmon** *r.* U.S.A.
20 F4 **Salmon Arm** Can.
33 F3 **Salmon Reservoir** *resr* U.S.A.
24 D2 **Salmon River Mountains** *mts* U.S.A.
55 S6 **Salo** Fin.
85 E4 **Salon** India
64 G5 **Salon-de-Provence** France
102 C4 **Salonga Sud, Parc National de la** *nat. park* Dem. Rep. Congo
63 K7 **Salonta** Romania
47 D1 **Salsacate** Arg.
69 G6 **Sal'sk** Rus. Fed.
66 C2 **Salsomaggiore Terme** Italy
104 E5 **Salt** *watercourse* S. Africa
35 G5 **Salt** *r. AZ* U.S.A.
30 B6 **Salt** *r. MO* U.S.A.
44 C2 **Salta** Arg.
59 C7 **Saltash** U.K.
57 D5 **Saltcoats** U.K.
32 B5 **Salt Creek** *r.* U.S.A.
60 E5 **Saltee Islands** *is* Rep. of Ireland
54 O3 **Saltfjellet Svartisen Nasjonalpark** *nat. park* Norway
27 B6 **Salt Flat** U.S.A.
32 C4 **Salt Fork Lake** *l.* U.S.A.
36 D3 **Saltillo** Mex.
24 E3 **Salt Lake City** U.S.A.
47 E2 **Salto** Arg.
46 C3 **Salto** Brazil
47 F1 **Salto** Uru.
46 E2 **Salto da Divisa** Brazil
44 E4 **Salto Grande, Embalse de** *resr* Uru.
35 E5 **Salton Sea** *salt l.* U.S.A.
84 C2 **Salt Ra.** *h.* Pak.
21 G2 **Salt River** Can.
32 B5 **Salt Rock** U.S.A.
29 D5 **Saluda** *SC* U.S.A.
32 E6 **Saluda** *VA* U.S.A.
84 C4 **Salumbar** India
66 B2 **Saluzzo** Italy
47 D1 **Salvador** Arg.
46 E1 **Salvador** Brazil
27 F6 **Salvador, L.** *l.* U.S.A.
35 G2 **Salvation Creek** *r.* U.S.A.
Salween *r. see* **Nu Jiang**
95 A1 **Salween** *r.* Myanmar
81 M2 **Salyan** Azer.
32 B6 **Salyersville** U.S.A.
104 B2 **Salzbrunn** Namibia
62 F7 **Salzburg** Austria
62 E4 **Salzgitter** Ger.
84 B4 **Sam** India
89 B7 **Sam, Nam** *r.* Laos/Vietnam
95 B2 **Samae San, Laem** *pt* Thai.
94 C5 **Samal** *i.* Phil.
25 F6 **Samalayuca** Mex.
94 B5 **Samales Group** *is* Phil.
80 C3 **Samandağı** Turkey
90 H3 **Samani** Japan
80 C6 **Samannûd** Egypt
94 C4 **Samar** *i.* Phil.
76 G4 **Samara** Rus. Fed.
113 K2 **Samarai** P.N.G.
45 D3 **Samariapo** Venez.
92 F7 **Samarinda** Indon.
90 D2 **Samarka** Rus. Fed.
79 K2 **Samarkand** Uzbek.
81 J4 **Sāmarrā'** Iraq
94 C4 **Samar Sea** *g.* Phil.
68 J4 **Samarskaya Oblast'** *div.* Rus. Fed.
81 M1 **Şamaxı** Azer.
102 C4 **Samba** Dem. Rep. Congo
93 F6 **Sambaliung** *mts* Indon.
85 F5 **Sambalpur** India
92 E7 **Sambar, Tanjung** *pt* Indon.
92 D6 **Sambas** Indon.
103 F5 **Sambava** Madag.
85 G4 **Sambha** India
84 D3 **Sambhal** India
84 C4 **Sambhar L.** *l.* India
69 B5 **Sambir** Ukr.
43 K5 **Sambito** *r.* Brazil
47 F2 **Samborombón, Bahía** *b.* Arg.
61 B4 **Sambre** *r.* Belgium/France
45 A2 **Sambú** *r.* Panama
91 A6 **Samch'ŏk** S. Korea
81 K3 **Samdi Dag** *mt* Turkey
102 D4 **Same** Tanz.
90 A4 **Samjiyŏn** N. Korea
81 L1 **Şämkir** Azer.
91 A7 **Samnangjin** S. Korea
106 **Samoa** *country* Pac. Oc.
66 F2 **Samobor** Croatia
68 G2 **Samoded** Rus. Fed.
67 K3 **Samokov** Bulg.
62 H6 **Šamorín** Slovakia
67 M6 **Samos** *i.* Greece
95 A5 **Samosir** *i.* Indon.
67 L4 **Samothraki** Greece
67 L4 **Samothraki** *i.* Greece
94 B3 **Sampaloc Point** *pt* Phil.
92 E7 **Sampit** Indon.
103 C4 **Sampwe** Dem. Rep. Congo
27 E6 **Sam Rayburn Res.** *resr* U.S.A.
85 E3 **Samsang** China
89 B6 **Sam Sao, Phou** *mts* Laos/Vietnam
95 C1 **Sâm Sơn** Vietnam
80 F1 **Samsun** Turkey
69 G7 **Samtredia** Georgia
95 B3 **Samui, Ko** *i.* Thai.
69 J7 **Samur** *r.* Azer./Rus. Fed.
95 B2 **Samut Prakan** Thai.
95 B2 **Samut Sakhon** Thai.
95 B2 **Samut Songkhram** Thai.
85 G3 **Samyai** China
100 B3 **San** Mali
95 C2 **San, T.** *r.* Cambodia
78 E6 **Şan'ā'** Yemen
119 C3 **Sanae** *S. Africa Base* Antarctica
101 D4 **Sanaga** *r.* Cameroon
45 A4 **San Agustín** Col.
94 C5 **San Agustin, Cape** *c.* Phil.
81 L4 **Sanandaj** Iran
34 B2 **San Andreas** U.S.A.
94 C3 **San Andres** Phil.
42 B1 **San Andrés, Isla de** *i.* Col.
25 F5 **San Andres Mts** *mts* U.S.A.
36 E5 **San Andrés Tuxtla** Mex.
27 C6 **San Angelo** U.S.A.
47 B2 **San Antonio** Chile
94 B3 **San Antonio** Phil.
27 D6 **San Antonio** U.S.A.
34 B3 **San Antonio** *r.* U.S.A.
37 H4 **San Antonio, C.** *pt* Cuba
47 F3 **San Antonio, Cabo** *pt* Arg.
34 D4 **San Antonio, Mt** *mt* U.S.A.
65 G3 **San Antonio Abad** Spain
44 C2 **San Antonio de los Cobres** Arg.
45 D2 **San Antonio de Tamanaco** Venez.
47 D4 **San Antonio Oeste** Arg.
34 B4 **San Antonio Reservoir** *resr* U.S.A.
34 B3 **San Ardo** U.S.A.
47 E3 **San Augustín** Arg.
47 C1 **San Augustín de Valle Fértil** Arg.
84 D5 **Sanawad** India
66 E3 **San Benedetto del Tronto** Italy
36 B5 **San Benedicto, I.** *i.* Mex.
27 D7 **San Benito** U.S.A.
34 B3 **San Benito** *r.* U.S.A.
34 B3 **San Benito Mt** *mt* U.S.A.
34 D4 **San Bernardino** U.S.A.
25 C5 **San Bernardino Mts** *mts* U.S.A.
47 B2 **San Bernardo** Chile
27 B7 **San Bernardo** Mex.
91 C7 **Sanbe-san** *vol.* Japan
29 C6 **San Blas, C.** *c.* U.S.A.
42 E6 **San Borja** Bol.
33 H3 **Sanbornville** U.S.A.
27 C7 **San Buenaventura** Mex.
47 C2 **San Carlos** Arg.
47 B3 **San Carlos** Chile
27 C6 **San Carlos** Mex.
94 B3 **San Carlos** *Luzon* Phil.
94 B4 **San Carlos** *Negros* Phil.
47 F2 **San Carlos** Uru.
35 G5 **San Carlos** U.S.A.
45 D4 **San Carlos** *Amazonas* Venez.
45 C2 **San Carlos** *Cojedes* Venez.
25 D6 **San Carlos, Mesa de** *h.* Mex.
47 E1 **San Carlos Centro** Arg.

54 T3 Sinettä Fin.
100 B4 Sinfra Côte d'Ivoire
101 F3 Singa Sudan
84 E3 Singahi India
84 D2 Singa Pass pass India
70 Singapore country Asia
95 B5 Singapore Sing.
95 B5 Singapore, Strait of chan. Indon./Sing.
92 □ Singaraja Indon.
95 B2 Sing Buri Thai.
31 G3 Singhampton Can.
102 D4 Singida Tanz.
93 G7 Singkang Indon.
92 D6 Singkawang Indon.
95 A5 Singkil Indon.
115 J4 Singleton Austr.
Singora see Songkhla
66 C4 Siniscola Italy
66 G3 Sinj Croatia
93 G8 Sinjai Indon.
81 H3 Sinjār Iraq
81 H3 Sinjār, Jabal mt Iraq
81 K3 Sīnji Iran
101 F3 Sinkat Sudan
Sinkiang Uighur Aut. Region div. see Xinjiang Uygur Zizhiqu
43 H2 Sinnamary Fr. Guiana
Sinneh see Sanandaj
67 N2 Sinoie, Lacul lag. Romania
69 E7 Sinop Turkey
27 D6 Sinton U.S.A.
82 B2 Sinú r. Col.
87 M3 Sinŭiju N. Korea
94 B5 Siocon Phil.
62 J7 Siófok Hungary
62 C7 Sion Switz.
60 D3 Sion Mills U.K.
26 D3 Sioux Center U.S.A.
26 D3 Sioux City U.S.A.
26 D3 Sioux Falls U.S.A.
22 B3 Sioux Lookout Can.
94 B4 Sipalay Phil.
87 M3 Siping China
21 K3 Sipiwesk Can.
21 K3 Sipiwesk L. l. Can.
84 C5 Sipra r. India
29 C5 Sipsey r. U.S.A.
92 B7 Sipura i. Indon.
37 H6 Siquia r. Nic.
94 B4 Siquijor Phil.
94 B4 Siquijor i. Phil.
84 B5 Sir r. Pak.
83 E8 Sira India
55 K7 Sira r. Norway
95 B2 Si Racha Thai.
Siracusa see Syracuse
20 E4 Sir Alexander, Mt mt Can.
81 G1 Şiran Turkey
81 M3 Sīrdān Iran
113 G3 Sir Edward Pellew Group is Austr.
30 A3 Siren U.S.A.
95 B1 Siri Kit Dam dam Thai.
84 B3 Siritoi r. Pak.
20 D2 Sir James McBrien, Mt mt Can.
79 H4 Sīrjān Iran
114 B5 Sir Joseph Bank's Group is Austr.
84 E4 Sirmour India
81 J3 Şırnak Turkey
82 D6 Sirohi India
84 D4 Sironj India
34 C4 Sirretta Peak summit U.S.A.
84 C3 Sirsa Haryana India
85 E4 Sirsa Uttar Pradesh India
20 F4 Sir Sanford, Mt mt Can.
84 D3 Sirsi India
101 D1 Sirte Libya
101 D1 Sirte, Gulf of g. Libya
81 J2 Şirvan Turkey
55 T9 Širvintos Lith.
81 K4 Sīrwān r. Iraq
20 F4 Sir Wilfred Laurier, Mt mt Can.
66 G2 Sisak Croatia
95 C2 Sisaket Thai.
104 E3 Sishen S. Africa
81 L2 Sisian Armenia
30 C2 Siskiwit Bay b. U.S.A.
95 B2 Sisŏphŏn Cambodia
34 B4 Sisquoc r. U.S.A.
26 D2 Sisseton U.S.A.
33 K1 Sisson Branch Reservoir resr Can.
79 J3 Sīstan, Daryācheh-ye marsh Afgh.
115 F8 Sisters Beach Austr.
84 C5 Sitamau India
94 A5 Sitangkai Phil.
84 E4 Sitapur India
67 M7 Siteia Greece
105 J3 Siteki Swaziland
67 K4 Sithonia pen. Greece
46 C1 Sítio da Abadia Brazil
46 D1 Sítio do Mato Brazil
20 B3 Sitka U.S.A.
84 B3 Sitpur Pak.
61 D4 Sittard Neth.
85 H4 Sittaung Myanmar
59 H6 Sittingbourne U.K.
83 H6 Sittwe Myanmar
89 □ Siu A Chau i. China
85 F5 Siuri India
80 F2 Sivas Turkey
80 B2 Sivaslı Turkey
81 G3 Siverek Turkey
81 G2 Sivrice Turkey
80 C2 Sivrihisar Turkey
61 C4 Sivry Belgium
105 H3 Sivukile S. Africa
78 B4 Sīwah Egypt
84 D3 Siwalik Range mts India/Nepal
85 F4 Siwān India
84 C4 Siwana India
64 G5 Six-Fours-les-Plages France
88 E3 Sixian China
30 E4 Six Lakes U.S.A.
60 D3 Sixmilecross U.K.
105 H2 Siyabuswa S. Africa
88 F3 Siyang China
81 M1 Siyäzän Azer.
88 C1 Siyitang China
Siziwang Qi see Ulan Hua
Sjælland i. see Zealand
67 J3 Sjenica Serb. and Mont.
55 N9 Sjöbo Sweden
54 P2 Sjøvegan Norway
45 E2 S. Juan r. Venez.
69 E6 Skadovs'k Ukr.
54 E4 Skaftafell nat. park Iceland
54 E5 Skaftárós est. Iceland
54 D3 Skagafjörður in. Iceland
55 M8 Skagen Denmark
55 L8 Skagerrak str. Denmark/Norway
24 B1 Skagit r. Can./U.S.A.
20 B3 Skagway U.S.A.
54 T1 Skaidi Norway
54 P2 Skaland Norway
54 O4 Skalmodal Sweden
55 L8 Skanderborg Denmark
33 E3 Skaneateles Lake l. U.S.A.
30 C2 Skanee U.S.A.
67 L5 Skantzoura i. Greece
55 N7 Skara Sweden
79 M2 Skardu Jammu and Kashmir
55 R7 Skärgårdshavets Nationalpark nat. park Fin.
55 M6 Skarnes Norway
63 K5 Skarżysko-Kamienna Pol.
54 R3 Skaulo Sweden
63 J6 Skawina Pol.
20 D3 Skeena r. Can.
20 D3 Skeena Mountains mts Can.
59 H4 Skegness U.K.
54 R4 Skellefteå Sweden
54 Q4 Skellefteälven r. Sweden
54 R4 Skelleftehamn Sweden
60 A6 Skellig Rocks is Rep. of Ireland
58 E4 Skelmersdale U.K.
60 E4 Skerries Rep. of Ireland
55 M7 Ski Norway
67 K5 Skiathos i. Greece
60 B6 Skibbereen Rep. of Ireland
54 R2 Skibotn Norway
58 D3 Skiddaw mt U.K.
55 L7 Skien Norway
63 K5 Skierniewice Pol.
100 C1 Skikda Alg.
58 G4 Skipsea U.K.
114 E6 Skipton Austr.
58 E4 Skipton U.K.
55 L8 Skive Denmark
54 E4 Skjálfandafljót r. Iceland
55 L9 Skjern Denmark
55 K6 Skjolden Norway
54 K5 Skodje Norway
54 T2 Skoganvarre Norway
60 F6 Skokholm Island i. Wales
30 D4 Skokie U.S.A.
59 B6 Skomer Island i. U.K.
67 K5 Skopelos i. Greece
68 F4 Skopin Rus. Fed.
67 J4 Skopje Macedonia
69 F5 Skorodnoye Rus. Fed.
55 N7 Skövde Sweden
87 M1 Skovorodino Rus. Fed.
33 J2 Skowhegan U.S.A.
55 S8 Skrunda Latvia
20 B2 Skukum, Mt mt Can.
105 J2 Skukuza S. Africa
34 D3 Skull Peak summit U.S.A.
30 B5 Skunk r. U.S.A.
55 R8 Skuodas Lith.
55 N9 Skurup Sweden
55 P6 Skutskär Sweden
69 D5 Skvyra Ukr.
57 B3 Skye i. U.K.
67 L5 Skyros Greece
67 L5 Skyros i. Greece
55 M9 Slagelse Denmark
54 Q4 Slagnäs Sweden
92 □ Slamet, Gunung vol. Indon.
60 E4 Slane Rep. of Ireland
60 E5 Slaney r. Rep. of Ireland
68 D3 Slantsy Rus. Fed.
69 G5 Slashchevskaya Rus. Fed.
116 B2 Slashers Reefs rf Austr.
30 D1 Slate Is is Can.
66 G2 Slatina Croatia
67 L2 Slatina Romania
21 G2 Slave r. Can.
100 C4 Slave Coast coastal area Africa
20 G3 Slave Lake Can.
63 O2 Slavkovichi Rus. Fed.
67 H2 Slavonija reg. Croatia
67 H2 Slavonski Brod Croatia
69 C5 Slavuta Ukr.
69 D5 Slavutych Ukr.
90 B3 Slavyanka Rus. Fed.
69 F6 Slavyansk-na-Kubani Rus. Fed.
68 D4 Slawharad Belarus
62 H3 Sławno Pol.
59 G4 Sleaford U.K.
114 A5 Sleaford B. b. Austr.
60 A5 Slea Head hd Rep. of Ireland
57 C3 Sleat pen. U.K.
57 C3 Sleat, Sound of chan. U.K.
22 E2 Sleeper Islands is Can.
30 D3 Sleeping Bear Dunes National Lakeshore res. U.S.A.
30 D3 Sleeping Bear Pt pt U.S.A.
69 H7 Sleptsovskaya Rus. Fed.
119 C3 Slessor Glacier gl. Antarctica
27 F6 Slidell U.S.A.
60 A5 Slievanea h. Rep. of Ireland
60 D3 Slieve Anierin h. Rep. of Ireland
60 D5 Slieveardagh Hills h. Rep. of Ireland
60 C4 Slieve Aughty Mts h. Rep. of Ireland
60 D3 Slieve Beagh h. Rep. of Ireland/U.K.
60 C5 Slieve Bernagh h. Rep. of Ireland
60 D4 Slieve Bloom Mts h. Rep. of Ireland
60 B5 Slievecallan h. Rep. of Ireland
60 B3 Slieve Car h. Rep. of Ireland
60 F3 Slieve Donard h. U.K.
60 B4 Slieve Elva h. Rep. of Ireland
60 C3 Slieve Gamph h. Rep. of Ireland
60 C3 Slieve League h. Rep. of Ireland
60 B5 Slieve Mish Mts h. Rep. of Ireland
60 B6 Slieve Miskish Mts h. Rep. of Ireland
60 A3 Slieve More h. Rep. of Ireland
60 D4 Slieve na Calliagh h. Rep. of Ireland
60 D5 Slievenamon h. Rep. of Ireland
60 D2 Slieve Snaght mt Rep. of Ireland
57 B3 Sligachan U.K.
60 C3 Sligo Rep. of Ireland
60 C3 Sligo Bay b. Rep. of Ireland
55 Q8 Slite Sweden
67 M3 Sliven Bulg.
68 H2 Sloboda Rus. Fed.
68 J2 Slobodchikovo Rus. Fed.
67 M2 Slobozia Romania
20 F5 Slocan Can.
68 C4 Slonim Belarus
111 F2 Slot, The chan. Solomon Is
61 D2 Slotermeer l. Neth.
59 G6 Slough U.K.
48 Slovakia country Europe
48 Slovenia country Europe
66 F1 Slovenj Gradec Slovenia
69 F5 Slov"yans'k Ukr.
62 H3 Słupsk Pol.
54 P4 Slussfors Sweden
68 C4 Slutsk Belarus
60 A4 Slyne Head hd Rep. of Ireland
86 H1 Slyudyanka Rus. Fed.
33 J3 Small Pt pt U.S.A.
23 H3 Smallwood Reservoir resr Can.
68 D4 Smalyavichy Belarus
63 N3 Smarhon' Belarus
104 E5 Smartt Syndicate Dam resr S. Africa
21 J4 Smeaton Can.
67 J2 Smederevo Serb. and Mont.
67 J2 Smederevska Palanka Serb. and Mont.
32 D4 Smethport U.S.A.
69 D5 Smila Ukr.
55 T8 Smiltene Latvia
20 G3 Smith Can.
34 C2 Smith U.S.A.
32 C6 Smith r. U.S.A.
20 D4 Smithers Can.
105 G5 Smithfield S. Africa
29 E5 Smithfield NC U.S.A.
24 E3 Smithfield UT U.S.A.
33 E5 Smith I. i. MD U.S.A.
33 F6 Smith I. i. VA U.S.A.
32 D6 Smith Mountain Lake l. U.S.A.
20 D3 Smith River Can.
31 J3 Smiths Falls Can.
115 F8 Smithton Austr.
34 C1 Smoke Creek Desert des. U.S.A.
20 F4 Smoky r. Can.
115 K3 Smoky C. hd Austr.
22 D3 Smoky Falls Can.
26 C4 Smoky Hill r. U.S.A.
26 D4 Smoky Hills h. U.S.A.
20 G4 Smoky Lake Can.
54 K5 Smøla i. Norway
68 E4 Smolensk Rus. Fed.
68 E4 Smolenskaya Oblast' div. Rus. Fed.
67 L4 Smolyan Bulg.
90 C3 Smolyoninovo Rus. Fed.
22 D4 Smooth Rock Falls Can.
22 C3 Smoothrock L. l. Can.
21 H4 Smoothstone Lake l. Can.
54 T1 Smørfjord Norway
33 F5 Smyrna DE U.S.A.
29 C5 Smyrna GA U.S.A.
32 C4 Smyrna OH U.S.A.
33 J1 Smyrna Mills U.S.A.
54 F4 Snæfell mt Iceland
58 C3 Snaefell h. U.K.
20 A2 Snag Can.
24 D3 Snake r. U.S.A.
35 E2 Snake Range mts U.S.A.
24 D3 Snake River Plain plain U.S.A.
20 G2 Snare Lake Can.
111 G6 Snares Is is N.Z.
54 N4 Snåsa Norway
61 D1 Sneek Neth.
61 D1 Sneekermeer l. Neth.
60 B6 Sneem Rep. of Ireland
104 F6 Sneeuberge mts S. Africa
23 H3 Snegamook Lake l. Can.
59 H5 Snettisham U.K.
76 K3 Snezhnogorsk Rus. Fed.
66 F2 Snežnik mt Slovenia
63 K4 Śniardwy, Jezioro l. Pol.
69 E6 Snihurivka Ukr.
57 B3 Snizort, Loch b. U.K.
24 B2 Snohomish U.S.A.
24 B2 Snoqualmie Pass pass U.S.A.
54 N3 Snøtinden mt Norway
21 J2 Snowbird Lake l. Can.
59 C4 Snowdon mt U.K.
59 D5 Snowdonia National Park U.K.
35 G4 Snowflake U.S.A.
33 F5 Snow Hill MD U.S.A.
29 E5 Snow Hill NC U.S.A.
21 J4 Snow Lake Can.
114 C4 Snowtown Austr.
24 D3 Snowville U.S.A.
115 H6 Snowy r. Austr.
115 H6 Snowy Mts mts Austr.
115 G9 Snug Austr.
23 J3 Snug Harbour Nfld and Lab. Can.
31 G3 Snug Harbour Ont. Can.
95 C2 Snuŏl Cambodia
27 D5 Snyder OK U.S.A.
27 C5 Snyder TX U.S.A.
103 E5 Soalala Madag.
103 E5 Soanierana-Ivongo Madag.
45 B3 Soata Col.
58 B3 Soay i. U.K.
101 F4 Sobat r. Sudan
93 L7 Sobger r. Indon.
91 B8 Sobo-san mt Japan
43 K6 Sobradinho, Barragem de resr Brazil
43 K4 Sobral Brazil
69 F7 Sochi Rus. Fed.
46 C3 Socorro Brazil
45 B3 Socorro Col.
25 F5 Socorro U.S.A.
36 B5 Socorro, I. i. Mex.
79 G7 Socotra i. Yemen
95 C3 Soc Trăng Vietnam
65 E3 Socuéllamos Spain
34 D4 Soda Lake l. U.S.A.
54 U3 Sodankylä Fin.
84 D2 Soda Plains plain China/Jammu and Kashmir
24 E3 Soda Springs U.S.A.
55 P6 Söderhamn Sweden
55 P7 Söderköping Sweden
55 P7 Södertälje Sweden
101 E3 Sodiri Sudan
102 D3 Sodo Eth.
55 Q6 Södra Kvarken str. Fin./Sweden
105 H1 Soekmekaar S. Africa
61 D3 Soerendonk Neth.
115 H4 Sofala Austr.
67 K3 Sofia Bulg.
Sofiya see Sofia
54 W4 Sofporog Rus. Fed.
91 G10 Sōfu-gan i. Japan
85 H3 Sog China
45 B3 Sogamoso Col.
81 G1 Soğanlı Dağları mts Turkey
55 K7 Søgne Norway
55 J6 Sognefjorden in. Norway
94 C4 Sogod Phil.
88 A1 Sogo Nur l. China
68 H2 Sogra Rus. Fed.
88 A3 Soguma China
80 C1 Söğüt Turkey
84 D5 Sohagpur India
59 H5 Soham U.K.
84 B3 Sohan r. Pak.
111 F2 Sohano P.N.G.
85 E5 Sohela India
84 D3 Sohna India
90 A4 Sŏho-ri N. Korea
61 C4 Soignes, Forêt de forest Belgium
61 C4 Soignies Belgium
54 T5 Soini Fin.
64 F2 Soissons France
84 C4 Sojat India
94 B4 Sojoton Point pt Phil.
69 C5 Sokal' Ukr.
91 A5 Sokch'o S. Korea
67 M6 Söke Turkey
69 G7 Sokhumi Georgia
100 C4 Sokodé Togo
89 □ Soko Islands is China
68 G3 Sokol Rus. Fed.
63 L4 Sokółka Pol.
100 B3 Sokolo Mali
90 C3 Sokolovka Rus. Fed.
63 L4 Sokołow Podlaski Pol.
100 C3 Sokoto Nigeria
100 C3 Sokoto r. Nigeria
69 C5 Sokyryany Ukr.
84 D3 Solan India
117 A7 Solander I. i. N.Z.
83 E7 Solāpur India
45 B2 Soledad Col.
34 B3 Soledad U.S.A.
45 E2 Soledad Venez.
69 G6 Solenoye Rus. Fed.
54 N3 Solfjellsjøen Norway
81 H2 Solhan Turkey
68 G3 Soligalich Rus. Fed.
59 F5 Solihull U.K.
76 G4 Solikamsk Rus. Fed.
76 G4 Sol'-Iletsk Rus. Fed.
61 F3 Solingen Ger.
104 A1 Solitaire Namibia
81 M1 Şollar Azer.
54 P5 Sollefteå Sweden
68 F3 Solnechnogorsk Rus. Fed.
92 C7 Solok Indon.
106 Solomon Islands country Pac. Oc.
110 F2 Solomon Sea sea P.N.G./Solomon Is
30 B2 Solon Springs U.S.A.
93 G8 Solor, Kepulauan is Indon.
62 C7 Solothurn Switz.
68 E1 Solovetskiye Ostrova is Rus. Fed.
68 H3 Solovetskoye Rus. Fed.
66 G3 Šolta i. Croatia
68 D3 Sol'tsy Rus. Fed.
33 E3 Solvay U.S.A.
55 O8 Sölvesborg Sweden
57 E6 Solway Firth est. U.K.
103 C5 Solwezi Zambia
91 G6 Sōma Japan
80 A2 Soma Turkey
96 Somalia country Africa
13 H3 Somali Basin sea feature Indian Ocean
103 C4 Sombo Angola
67 H2 Sombor Serb. and Mont.
84 C4 Somdari India
33 J2 Somerest Junction U.S.A.
55 S6 Somero Fin.
28 C4 Somerset KY U.S.A.
30 E4 Somerset MI U.S.A.
32 D5 Somerset PA U.S.A.
116 E6 Somerset, L. l. Austr.
105 F6 Somerset East S. Africa
118 B2 Somerset Island i. Can.
33 G3 Somerset Reservoir resr U.S.A.
104 C7 Somerset West S. Africa
33 H3 Somersworth U.S.A.
27 D6 Somerville Res. resr U.S.A.
81 L5 Someydeh Iran
55 O7 Sommen l. Sweden
23 G3 Sommet, Lac du l. Can.
84 B5 Somnath India
30 C5 Somonauk U.S.A.
47 C4 Somuncurá, Mesa Volcánica de plat. Arg.
85 F4 Son r. India
85 F5 Sonamukhi India
85 G5 Sonamura India
85 E5 Sonapur India
84 D4 Sonar r. India
85 H4 Sonari India
68 E2 Sondaly Rus. Fed.
55 L9 Sønderborg Denmark
62 E5 Sonderhausen Ger.
66 C1 Sondrio Italy
84 B5 Songad India
88 E4 Songbu China
95 D2 Sông Cau Vietnam
103 D5 Songea Tanz.
90 B1 Songhua Jiang r. China
88 F4 Songjiang China
89 C4 Songkan China
95 B4 Songkhla Thai.
87 M2 Songling China
88 F1 Song Ling mts China
102 B4 Songo Angola
103 D5 Songo Moz.
88 B3 Songpan China
85 G4 Songsak India
88 D3 Song Shan mt China
89 C4 Songtao China
89 F5 Songxi China
88 D3 Songxian China
87 M2 Songyuan China
89 D4 Songzi China
95 D2 Sơn Ha Vietnam
Sonid Youqi see Saihan Tal
Sonid Zuoqi see Mandalt
84 D3 Sonīpat India
54 U5 Sonkajärvi Fin.
89 B6 Sơn La Vietnam
46 D2 Sono r. Minas Gerais Brazil
43 J6 Sono r. Tocantins Brazil
35 F6 Sonoita r. Mex.
35 G6 Sonoita U.S.A.
35 E6 Sonora div. Mex.
36 B3 Sonora r. Mex.
34 B3 Sonora CA U.S.A.
27 C6 Sonora TX U.S.A.
35 F6 Sonoyta Mex.
81 L4 Sonqor Iran
45 B3 Sonsón Col.
36 G6 Sonsonate El Salvador
89 B6 Sơn Tây Vietnam
105 H5 Sonwabile S. Africa
47 F1 Sopas r. Uru.
101 E4 Sopo watercourse Sudan
67 L3 Sopot Bulg.
63 J3 Sopot Pol.
62 H7 Sopron Hungary
82 D4 Sopur Jammu and Kashmir
66 E4 Sora Italy
85 F6 Sorada India
55 P5 Söråker Sweden
22 F4 Sorel Can.
115 G9 Sorell Austr.
115 G9 Sorell L. l. Austr.
80 E2 Sorgun Turkey
65 E2 Soria Spain
76 C2 Sørkappøya i. Svalbard
54 N4 Sørli Norway
85 F5 Soro India
69 D5 Soroca Moldova
46 C3 Sorocaba Brazil
76 G4 Sorochinsk Rus. Fed.
93 L5 Sorol i. Micronesia
93 J7 Sorong Indon.
102 D3 Soroti Uganda
54 S1 Sørøya i. Norway
65 B3 Sorraia r. Port.
54 Q2 Sørreisa Norway
114 F7 Sorrento Austr.
66 F4 Sorrento Italy
103 B6 Sorris Sorris Namibia
54 P4 Sorsele Sweden
94 C3 Sorsogon Phil.
68 D2 Sortavala Rus. Fed.
54 O2 Sortland Norway
68 J2 Sortopolovskaya Rus. Fed.
68 J3 Sorvizhi Rus. Fed.
105 H2 Soshanguve S. Africa
69 F4 Sosna r. Rus. Fed.
47 C2 Sosneado mt Arg.
68 K2 Sosnogorsk Rus. Fed.
68 H2 Sosnovka Archangel. Rus. Fed.
68 G4 Sosnovka Tambov. Rus. Fed.
76 F3 Sosnovka Rus. Fed.
87 K1 Sosnovo-Ozerskoye Rus. Fed.
54 X4 Sosnovyy Rus. Fed.
55 V7 Sosnovyy Bor Rus. Fed.
63 J5 Sosnowiec Pol.
69 F6 Sosyka r. Rus. Fed.
45 A4 Sotara, Volcán vol. Col.
54 V4 Sotkamo Fin.
47 D1 Soto Arg.
36 E4 Soto la Marina Mex.
102 B3 Souanké Congo
100 B4 Soubré Côte d'Ivoire
33 F4 Souderton U.S.A.
67 M4 Soufli Greece
64 E4 Souillac France
100 C1 Souk Ahras Alg.
Sŏul see Seoul
64 D5 Soulom France
Soûr see Tyre
65 H4 Sour el Ghozlane Alg.
21 J5 Souris Man. Can.
23 H4 Souris P.E.I. Can.
21 J5 Souris r. Can./U.S.A.
43 L5 Sousa Brazil
100 D1 Sousse Tunisia
64 D5 Soustons France
96 South Africa, Republic of country Africa
31 G3 Southampton Can.
59 F7 Southampton U.K.
33 G4 Southampton U.S.A.
21 M2 Southampton Island i. Can.
92 A4 South Andaman i. Andaman and Nicobar Is
32 E6 South Anna r. U.S.A.
59 F4 South Anston U.K.
23 H2 South Aulatsivik Island i. Can.
113 F5 South Australia div. Austr.
13 N6 South Australian Basin sea feature Indian Ocean
27 F5 Southaven U.S.A.
25 F5 South Baldy mt U.S.A.
58 F3 South Bank U.K.
32 B4 South Bass I. i. U.S.A.
21 N2 South Bay b. Can.
31 F3 South Baymouth Can.
30 D5 South Bend IN U.S.A.
24 B2 South Bend WA U.S.A.
29 E7 South Bight chan. Bahamas
32 D6 South Boston U.S.A.
117 D5 Southbridge N.Z.
33 G3 Southbridge U.S.A.
South Cape c. see Ka Lae
29 D5 South Carolina div. U.S.A.
33 J2 South China U.S.A.
92 E4 South China Sea sea Pac. Oc.
26 C2 South Dakota div. U.S.A.
33 G3 South Deerfield U.S.A.
59 G7 South Downs h. U.K.
105 F2 South East div. Botswana
115 G9 South East Cape c. Austr.
15 N10 Southeast Pacific Basin sea feature Pac. Oc.
115 G7 South East Point c. Austr.
21 J3 Southend Can.
57 C5 Southend U.K.
59 H6 Southend-on-Sea U.K.
30 A5 South English U.S.A.
117 C5 Southern Alps mts N.Z.
112 C6 Southern Cross Austr.
21 K3 Southern Indian Lake l. Can.

85 H3 Tangmai China
85 F3 Tangra Yumco salt l. China
88 F2 Tangshan China
94 B4 Tangub Phil.
100 C3 Tanguieta Benin
90 A1 Tangwang r. China
89 C4 Tangyan He r. China
88 E3 Tangyin China
90 A1 Tangyuan China
54 U3 Tanhua Fin.
95 C3 Tani Cambodia
85 H3 Taniantaweng Shan mts China
93 J8 Tanimbar, Kepulauan is Indon.
94 B4 Tanjay Phil.
95 A5 Tanjungbalai Indon.
Tanjungkarang-Telukbetung see Bandar Lampung
92 D7 Tanjungpandan Indon.
92 C6 Tanjungpinang Indon.
95 A5 Tanjungpura Indon.
93 F6 Tanjungredeb Indon.
93 F6 Tanjungselor Indon.
84 B2 Tank Pak.
84 D2 Tankse Jammu and Kashmir
85 F4 Tankuhi India
111 G3 Tanna i. Vanuatu
57 F4 Tannadice U.K.
55 N5 Tännäs Sweden
116 D4 Tannum Sands Austr.
86 F1 Tannu-Ola, Khrebet mts Rus. Fed.
94 B4 Tañon Strait chan. Phil.
84 B4 Tanot India
100 C3 Tanout Niger
85 E4 Tansen Nepal
89 F5 Tanshui Taiwan
78 C3 Ṭanṭā Egypt
100 A2 Tan-Tan Morocco
114 D6 Tantanoola Austr.
36 E4 Tantoyuca Mex.
55 M7 Tanumshede Sweden
114 C5 Tanunda Austr.
91 A6 Tanyang S. Korea
96 Tanzania country Africa
95 A3 Tao, Ko i. Thai.
88 B3 Tao He r. China
89 D4 Taojiang China
88 C2 Taole China
87 M2 Taonan China
95 □ Tao Payoh Sing.
66 F6 Taormina Italy
25 F4 Taos U.S.A.
100 B2 Taoudenni Mali
100 B1 Taourirt Morocco
89 E5 Taoxi China
89 D4 Taoyuan China
89 F5 T'aoyüan Taiwan
55 T7 Tapa Estonia
94 B5 Tapaan Passage chan. Phil.
36 F6 Tapachula Mex.
43 G4 Tapajós r. Brazil
95 A5 Tapaktuan Indon.
47 E3 Tapalqué Arg.
95 A5 Tapanuli, Teluk b. Indon.
42 F5 Tapauá Brazil
42 E5 Tapauá r. Brazil
100 B4 Tapeta Liberia
84 C5 Tāpi r. India
94 B5 Tapiantana i. Phil.
30 C2 Tapiola U.S.A.
95 B4 Tapis mt Malaysia
85 F4 Taplejung Nepal
89 □ Tap Mun Chau i. China
32 E6 Tappahannock U.S.A.
32 C4 Tappan Lake l. U.S.A.
117 D4 Tapuaenuku mt N.Z.
94 B5 Tapul Phil.
94 B5 Tapul Group is Phil.
45 D5 Tapurucuara Brazil
81 K4 Ṭaqṭaq Iraq
46 B1 Taquaral, Serra do h. Brazil
46 B2 Taquari Brazil
43 G7 Taquari r. Brazil
46 A2 Taquari, Serra do h. Brazil
46 C3 Taquaritinga Brazil
46 B3 Taquaruçu r. Brazil
60 D5 Tar r. Rep. of Ireland
115 J1 Tara Austr.
60 E4 Tara, Hill of h. Rep. of Ireland
100 D4 Taraba r. Nigeria
42 E7 Tarabuco Bol.
Ṭarābulus see Tripoli
45 C4 Taracua Brazil
84 B4 Tar Ahmad Rind Pak.
84 E4 Tarahuwan India
85 G4 Tarai reg. India
93 F6 Tarakan Indon.
94 A6 Tarakan i. Indon.
80 C1 Taraklı Turkey
115 H5 Taralga Austr.
63 J3 Taran, Mys pt Rus. Fed.
115 H4 Tarana Austr.
84 D5 Tarana India
84 C3 Tārānagar India
117 E3 Taranaki, Mt vol. N.Z.
65 E2 Tarancón Spain
57 A3 Taransay i. U.K.
66 G4 Taranto Italy
66 G4 Taranto, Golfo di g. Italy
42 C5 Tarapoto Peru
117 E4 Tararua Range mts N.Z.
63 P6 Tarashcha Ukr.
42 D5 Tarauacá Brazil
42 E5 Tarauacá r. Brazil
117 F3 Tarawera N.Z.
117 F3 Tarawera, Mt mt N.Z.
82 D2 Taraz Kazak.
65 F2 Tarazona Spain
65 F3 Tarazona de la Mancha Spain
82 F1 Tarbagatay, Khrebet mts Kazak.
57 E3 Tarbat Ness pt U.K.
84 C2 Tarbela Dam dam Pak.
60 B5 Tarbert Rep. of Ireland
57 B3 Tarbert Scot. U.K.
57 C5 Tarbert Scot. U.K.
64 E5 Tarbes France
29 E5 Tarboro U.S.A.
114 A3 Tarcoola Austr.
115 G3 Tarcoon Austr.
115 G5 Tarcutta Austr.
87 P2 Tardoki-Yani, Gora mt Rus. Fed.
115 K3 Taree Austr.
114 E3 Tarella Austr.
76 L2 Tareya Rus. Fed.
24 E2 Targhee Pass pass U.S.A.
67 L2 Târgoviște Romania
67 K2 Târgu Jiu Romania
63 M7 Târgu Mureș Romania
63 N7 Târgu Neamț Romania
63 N7 Târgu Secuiesc Romania
81 L5 Tarhān Iran
93 L8 Tari P.N.G.
88 C2 Tarian Gol China
65 D4 Tarifa Spain
42 F8 Tarija Bol.
93 K7 Tariku r. Indon.
79 F6 Tarīm Yemen
Tarim Basin basin see Tarim Pendi
82 F3 Tarim Pendi basin China
93 K7 Taritatu r. Indon.
81 K4 Tarjīl Iraq
105 F6 Tarka r. S. Africa
105 G6 Tarkastad S. Africa
26 E3 Tarkio U.S.A.
76 J3 Tarko-Sale Rus. Fed.
100 B4 Tarkwa Ghana
94 B3 Tarlac Phil.
64 F4 Tarn r. France
54 O4 Tärnaby Sweden
84 A3 Tarnak r. Afgh.
63 M7 Târnăveni Romania
63 K5 Tarnobrzeg Pol.
68 G2 Tarnogskiy Gorodok Rus. Fed.
63 K5 Tarnów Pol.
85 E3 Taro Co salt l. China
116 C5 Taroom Austr.
100 B1 Taroudannt Morocco
114 D6 Tarpeena Austr.
29 E7 Tarpum Bay Bahamas
66 D3 Tarquinia Italy
65 G2 Tarragona Spain
54 Q3 Tårrajaur Sweden
115 G9 Tarraleah Austr.
115 G4 Tarran Hills h. Austr.
117 B6 Tarras N.Z.
65 G2 Tàrrega Spain
80 E3 Tarsus Turkey
44 D2 Tartagal Arg.
81 L1 Tärtär Azer.
81 L1 Tärtär r. Azer.
64 D5 Tartas France
55 U7 Tartu Estonia
80 E4 Ṭarṭūs Syria
46 E2 Tarumirim Brazil
69 H6 Tarumovka Rus. Fed.
95 A5 Tarutung Indon.
66 E1 Tarvisio Italy
22 E4 Taschereau Can.
Tashi Chho see Thimphu
81 K1 Tashir Armenia
79 G3 Tashk, Daryācheh-ye salt pan Iran
79 K1 Tashkent Uzbek.
82 D2 Tash-Kömür Kyrgyzstan
22 F2 Tasiat, Lac l. Can.
92 □ Tasikmalaya Indon.
23 G2 Tasiujaq Can.
82 F1 Taskesken Kazak.
80 E1 Taşköprü Turkey
81 J2 Taşlıçay Turkey
14 F8 Tasman Basin sea feature Pac. Oc.
117 D4 Tasman Bay b. N.Z.
115 G9 Tasman Head hd Austr.
115 F9 Tasmania div. Austr.
117 D4 Tasman Mountains mts N.Z.
115 H9 Tasman Pen. pen. Austr.
14 E9 Tasman Plateau sea feature Pac. Oc.
111 F5 Tasman Sea sea Pac. Oc.
80 F1 Taşova Turkey
34 B3 Tassajara Hot Springs U.S.A.
23 F2 Tassialujjuaq, Lac l. Can.
100 C2 Tassili du Hoggar plat. Alg.
100 C2 Tassili n'Ajjer plat. Alg.
81 K2 Tasūj Iran
77 N3 Tas-Yuryakh Rus. Fed.
93 G7 Tataba Indon.
63 J7 Tatabánya Hungary
69 D6 Tatarbunary Ukr.
76 J4 Tatarsk Rus. Fed.
87 Q1 Tatarskiy Proliv str. Rus. Fed.
68 J4 Tatarstan, Respublika div. Rus. Fed.
81 K3 Tatavi r. Iran
116 A1 Tate r. Austr.
91 F7 Tateyama Japan
91 E6 Tate-yama vol. Japan
20 F2 Tathlina Lake l. Can.
78 E5 Tathlīth, W. watercourse Saudi Arabia
115 H6 Tathra Austr.
21 K2 Tatinnai Lake l. Can.
69 H5 Tatishchevo Rus. Fed.
24 A1 Tatla Lake Can.
20 D3 Tatlatui Prov. Park res. Can.
93 H8 Tat Mailau, G. mt Indon.
115 G6 Tatong Austr.
63 J6 Tatry reg. Pol.
20 B3 Tatshenshini r. Can.
69 G5 Tatsinskiy Rus. Fed.
91 D7 Tatsuno Japan
84 A4 Tatta Pak.
46 C3 Tatuí Brazil
20 E4 Tatuk Mtn mt Can.
27 C5 Tatum U.S.A.
114 F6 Tatura Austr.
81 J2 Tatvan Turkey
55 J7 Tau Norway
43 K5 Taua Brazil
46 D3 Taubaté Brazil
104 F3 Taung S. Africa
83 J6 Taunggyi Myanmar
95 A2 Taungnyo Range mts Myanmar
84 B3 Taunsa Barrage barrage Pak.
59 D6 Taunton U.K.
33 H4 Taunton U.S.A.
117 F3 Taupo N.Z.
117 E3 Taupo, Lake l. N.Z.
55 S9 Tauragė Lith.
117 F2 Tauranga N.Z.
66 G5 Taurianova Italy
117 D1 Tauroa Pt pt N.Z.
Taurus Mountains mts see Toros Dağları
111 F2 Tauu Islands is P.N.G.
80 B3 Tavas Turkey
59 J5 Taverham U.K.
65 C4 Tavira Port.
59 C7 Tavistock U.K.
95 A2 Tavoy Myanmar
95 A2 Tavoy Pt pt Myanmar
90 B3 Tavrichanka Rus. Fed.
80 B2 Tavşanlı Turkey
59 C6 Taw r. U.K.
31 F3 Tawas Bay b. U.S.A.
31 F3 Tawas City U.S.A.
93 F6 Tawau Malaysia
59 D6 Tawe r. U.K.
84 C2 Tawi r. India
94 A5 Tawitawi i. Phil.
89 F6 Tawu Taiwan
36 E5 Taxco Mex.
82 E3 Taxkorgan China
20 C2 Tay r. Can.
57 E4 Tay r. U.K.
57 E4 Tay, Firth of est. U.K.
57 D4 Tay, Loch l. U.K.
94 B3 Tayabas Bay b. Phil.
54 X2 Taybola Rus. Fed.
57 C5 Tayinloan U.K.
20 E3 Taylor Can.
35 G4 Taylor AZ U.S.A.
31 F4 Taylor MI U.S.A.
30 B6 Taylor MO U.S.A.
26 D3 Taylor NE U.S.A.
27 D6 Taylor TX U.S.A.
33 E5 Taylors Island U.S.A.
30 C6 Taylorville U.S.A.
78 B4 Taymā' Saudi Arabia
77 L3 Taymura r. Rus. Fed.
77 M2 Taymyr, Ozero l. Rus. Fed.
77 L2 Taymyr, Poluostrov pen. Rus. Fed.
95 C3 Tây Ninh Vietnam
94 A4 Taytay Phil.
94 B3 Taytay Phil.
94 A4 Taytay Bay b. Phil.
92 □ Tayu Indon.
77 K2 Taz r. Rus. Fed.
100 B1 Taza Morocco
81 K4 Tāza Khurmātū Iraq
81 L2 Tazeh Kand Azer.
32 B6 Tazewell TN U.S.A.
32 C6 Tazewell VA U.S.A.
21 H2 Tazin r. Can.
21 H3 Tazin Lake l. Can.
101 E2 Tāzirbū Libya
65 J4 Tazmalt Alg.
76 J3 Tazovskaya Guba chan. Rus. Fed.
69 H7 T'bilisi Georgia
69 G6 Tbilisskaya Rus. Fed.
102 B4 Tchibanga Gabon
101 D2 Tchigaï, Plateau du plat. Niger
101 D4 Tcholliré Cameroon
63 J3 Tczew Pol.
117 A6 Te Anau N.Z.
117 A6 Te Anau, L. l. N.Z.
36 F5 Teapa Mex.
117 G2 Te Araroa N.Z.
117 E2 Te Aroha N.Z.
117 E3 Te Awamutu N.Z.
59 E3 Tebay U.K.
21 K2 Tebesjuak Lake l. Can.
100 C1 Tébessa Alg.
66 B7 Tébessa, Monts de mts Alg.
44 E3 Tebicuary r. Para.
92 C7 Tebingtinggi Indon.
92 B6 Tebingtinggi Indon.
66 C6 Téboursouk Tunisia
66 C6 Téboursouk Tunisia
69 H7 Tebulos Mt'a mt Georgia/Rus. Fed.
34 D5 Tecate Mex.
100 B4 Techiman Ghana
44 B6 Tecka Arg.
61 F2 Tecklenburger Land reg. Ger.
36 D5 Tecomán Mex.
34 D4 Tecopa U.S.A.
25 E6 Tecoripa Mex.
63 N7 Tecuci Romania
31 F5 Tecumseh U.S.A.
79 J2 Tedzhen Turkm.
35 H3 Teec Nos Pos U.S.A.
86 F1 Teeli Rus. Fed.
58 F3 Tees r. U.K.
58 E3 Teesdale reg. U.K.
42 E4 Tefé r. Brazil
80 B3 Tefenni Turkey
92 □ Tegal Indon.
59 D5 Tegid, Llyn l. U.K.
36 G6 Tegucigalpa Honduras
100 C3 Teguidda-n-Tessoumt Niger
34 C4 Tehachapi U.S.A.
25 C5 Tehachapi Mts mts U.S.A.
34 C4 Tehachapi Pass pass U.S.A.
21 K2 Tehek Lake l. Can.
Teheran see Tehrān
100 B4 Téhini Côte d'Ivoire
79 G2 Tehrān Iran
84 D3 Tehri India
Tehri see Tikamgarh
36 F5 Tehuantepec, Golfo de g. Mex.
36 F5 Tehuantepec, Istmo de isth. Mex.
59 C5 Teifi r. U.K.
59 D7 Teign r. U.K.
59 D7 Teignmouth U.K.
Tejo r. see Tagus
34 C4 Tejon Pass pass U.S.A.
117 D1 Te Kao N.Z.
117 C5 Tekapo, L. l. N.Z.
85 F4 Tekari India
36 G4 Tekax Mex.
102 D2 Tekezē Wenz r. Eritrea/Eth.
84 E1 Tekiliktag mt China
80 A1 Tekirdağ Turkey
81 H2 Tekman Turkey
85 H5 Teknaf Bangl.
30 E4 Tekonsha U.S.A.
117 E3 Te Kuiti N.Z.
85 E5 Tel r. India
69 H7 T'elavi Georgia
80 E5 Tel Aviv-Yafo Israel
62 G6 Telč Czech Rep.
36 G4 Telchac Puerto Mex.
20 C3 Telegraph Creek Can.
46 B4 Telêmaco Borba Brazil
47 D3 Telén Arg.
67 L2 Teleorman r. Romania
34 D3 Telescope Peak summit U.S.A.
43 G5 Teles Pires r. Brazil
59 E5 Telford U.K.
100 A3 Télimélé Guinea
20 D4 Telkwa Can.
77 V3 Teller Alaska
81 K3 Telloh Iraq
95 □ Telok Blangah Sing.
47 C4 Telsen Arg.
55 S9 Telšiai Lith.
95 B4 Teluk Anson Malaysia
31 H2 Temagami Can.
31 G2 Temagami Lake l. Can.
92 □ Temanggung Indon.
105 H2 Temba S. Africa
77 L3 Tembenchi r. Rus. Fed.
105 H3 Tembisa S. Africa
102 B4 Tembo Aluma Angola
59 E5 Teme r. U.K.
34 D5 Temecula U.S.A.
80 D2 Temelli Turkey
92 C6 Temerloh Malaysia
81 M5 Temīleh Iran
86 B1 Temirtau Kazak.
31 H2 Témiscaming Can.
31 H2 Témiscamingue, Lac l. Can.
23 G4 Témiscouata, L. l. Can.
115 F8 Temma Austr.
54 T4 Temmes Fin.
68 G4 Temnikov Rus. Fed.
115 G5 Temora Austr.
25 F6 Temósachic Mex.
35 G5 Tempe U.S.A.
66 C4 Tempio Pausania Italy
30 E3 Temple MI U.S.A.
27 D6 Temple TX U.S.A.
59 C5 Temple Bar U.K.
60 D5 Templemore Rep. of Ireland
94 A4 Templer Bank sand bank Phil.
58 E3 Temple Sowerby U.K.
69 F6 Temryuk Rus. Fed.
47 B3 Temuco Chile
117 C6 Temuka N.Z.
42 C4 Tena Ecuador
34 D1 Tenabo, Mt mt U.S.A.
83 F7 Tenali India
95 A2 Tenasserim Myanmar
95 A2 Tenasserim r. Myanmar
59 E5 Tenbury Wells U.K.
59 C6 Tenby U.K.
31 F2 Tenby Bay Can.
102 E2 Tendaho Eth.
64 H4 Tende France
83 H9 Ten Degree Channel chan. Andaman and Nicobar Is
90 G5 Tendō Japan
81 J2 Tendürek Dağı mt Turkey
100 B3 Ténenkou Mali
100 D3 Ténéré reg. Niger
100 D2 Ténéré du Tafassâsset des. Niger
100 A2 Tenerife i. Canary Is
65 G4 Ténès Alg.
93 F8 Tengah, Kepulauan is Indon.
95 □ Tengeh Res. resr Sing.
88 B2 Tengger Shamo des. China
95 B4 Tenggul i. Malaysia
89 C7 Tengqiao China
100 B3 Tengréla Côte d'Ivoire
89 D6 Tengxian China
88 E3 Tengzhou China
119 B2 Teniente Jubany Arg. Base Antarctica
119 B2 Teniente Rodolfo Marsh Chile Base Antarctica
103 C5 Tenke Dem. Rep. Congo
77 Q2 Tenkeli Rus. Fed.
100 B3 Tenkodogo Burkina
113 F3 Tennant Creek Austr.
32 B6 Tennessee div. U.S.A.
29 C5 Tennessee r. U.S.A.
25 F4 Tennessee Pass pass U.S.A.
54 P2 Tennevoll Norway
47 B2 Teno r. Chile
54 U2 Tenojoki r. Fin./Norway
36 F5 Tenosique Mex.
24 F2 Ten Sleep U.S.A.
93 G7 Tenteno Indon.
59 H6 Tenterden U.K.
115 K2 Tenterfield Austr.
29 D7 Ten Thousand Islands is U.S.A.
65 C3 Tentudia mt Spain
46 B3 Teodoro Sampaio Brazil
46 E2 Teófilo Otôni Brazil
93 H8 Tepa Indon.
25 E6 Tepache Mex.
117 D1 Te Paki N.Z.
36 D4 Tepatitlán Mex.
81 H3 Tepe Turkey
81 J3 Tepe Gawra Iraq
36 C3 Tepehuanes Mex.
67 J4 Tepelenë Albania
45 E4 Tepequem, Serra mts Brazil
36 D4 Tepic Mex.
117 C5 Te Pirita N.Z.
62 F5 Teplice Czech Rep.
68 K2 Teplogorka Rus. Fed.
68 F4 Teploye Rus. Fed.
25 D6 Tepoca, Cabo c. Mex.
117 F2 Te Puke N.Z.
65 H1 Ter r. Spain
84 D2 Teram Kangri mt China/Jammu and Kashmir
66 E3 Teramo Italy
114 E7 Terang Austr.
84 B3 Teratani r. Pak.
69 F4 Terbuny Rus. Fed.
81 H2 Tercan Turkey
63 M6 Terebovlya Ukr.
69 H7 Terek Rus. Fed.
69 H7 Terek r. Rus. Fed.
68 J4 Teren'ga Rus. Fed.
46 A3 Terenos Brazil
45 C2 Terepaima, Parque Nacional nat. park Venez.
68 H4 Tereshka r. Rus. Fed.
43 K5 Teresina Brazil
46 D3 Teresópolis Brazil
61 B5 Tergnier France
80 F1 Terme Turkey
79 K2 Termez Uzbek.
66 E6 Termini Imerese Italy
36 F5 Términos, Lag. de b. Mex.
66 F4 Termoli Italy
59 E5 Tern r. U.K.
93 H6 Ternate Indon.
61 B3 Terneuzen Neth.
90 E2 Terney Rus. Fed.
66 E3 Terni Italy
69 C5 Ternopil' Ukr.
114 C4 Terowie Austr.
87 Q2 Terpeniya, Mys c. Rus. Fed.
87 Q2 Terpeniya, Zaliv g. Rus. Fed.
20 D4 Terrace Can.
30 D1 Terrace Bay Can.
104 E2 Terra Firma S. Africa
54 N4 Terråk Norway
66 C5 Terralba Italy
23 K4 Terra Nova Nat. Pk nat. park Can.
27 F6 Terrebonne Bay b. U.S.A.
28 C4 Terre Haute U.S.A.
23 K4 Terrenceville Can.
24 F2 Terry U.S.A.
69 G5 Tersa r. Rus. Fed.
61 D1 Terschelling i. Neth.
86 C3 Terskey Ala-Too mts Kyrgyzstan
66 C5 Tertenia Italy
65 F2 Teruel Spain
95 A4 Terutao i. Thai.
54 T3 Tervola Fin.
66 G2 Tešanj Bos.-Herz.
102 D2 Teseney Eritrea
68 G4 Tesha r. Rus. Fed.
90 J3 Teshikaga Japan
90 G2 Teshio Japan
90 H3 Teshio-dake mt Japan
90 G2 Teshio-gawa r. Japan
20 C2 Teslin Can.
20 C2 Teslin r. Can.
20 C2 Teslin Lake l. Can.
46 B1 Tesouras r. Brazil
46 B2 Tesouro Brazil
100 C3 Tessaoua Niger
59 F6 Test r. U.K.
66 C6 Testour Tunisia
44 B2 Tetas, Pta pt Chile
103 D5 Tete Moz.
117 F3 Te Teko N.Z.
63 P5 Teteriv r. Ukr.
62 F4 Teterow Ger.
63 O6 Tetiyiv Ukr.
58 G4 Tetney U.K.
24 E2 Teton r. U.S.A.
24 E3 Teton Ra. mts U.S.A.
100 B1 Tétouan Morocco
67 J3 Tetovo Macedonia
84 B5 Tetpur India
68 J4 Tetyushi Rus. Fed.
44 D2 Teuco r. Arg.
104 B1 Teufelsbach Namibia
90 G2 Teuri-tō i. Japan
55 R5 Teuva Fin.
Tevere r. see Tiber
Teverya see Tiberias
57 F5 Teviot r. U.K.
57 F5 Teviotdale v. U.K.
117 A7 Te Waewae Bay b. N.Z.
105 G1 Tewane Botswana
116 E6 Tewantin Austr.
117 E4 Te Wharau N.Z.
59 E6 Tewkesbury U.K.
88 B3 Têwo China
20 E5 Texada I. i. Can.
27 E5 Texarkana U.S.A.
115 J2 Texas Austr.
27 D6 Texas div. U.S.A.
27 E6 Texas City U.S.A.
61 C1 Texel i. Neth.
27 C4 Texhoma U.S.A.
27 D5 Texoma, Lake l. U.S.A.
105 G4 Teyateyaneng Lesotho
68 G3 Teykovo Rus. Fed.
68 G3 Teza r. Rus. Fed.
85 H4 Tezpur India
85 J4 Tezu India
21 K2 Tha-anne r. Can.
105 H4 Thabana-Ntlenyana mt Lesotho
105 G4 Thaba Nchu S. Africa
105 G4 Thaba Putsoa mt Lesotho
105 H4 Thaba-Tseka Lesotho
105 G2 Thabazimbi S. Africa
95 B1 Tha Bo Laos
105 G3 Thabong S. Africa
95 A2 Thagyettaw Myanmar
89 C6 Thai Binh Vietnam
70 Thailand country Asia
95 B3 Thailand, Gulf of g. Asia
95 A3 Thai Muang Thai.
89 B6 Thai Nguyên Vietnam
84 E5 Thakurtola India
84 B2 Thal Pak.
66 C7 Thala Tunisia
95 A3 Thalang Thai.
84 B3 Thal Desert des. Pak.
95 B4 Thale Luang lag. Thai.
95 B1 Tha Li Thai.
115 H2 Thallon Austr.
105 F2 Thamaga Botswana
78 F7 Thamar, J. mt Yemen
79 G6 Thamarīt Oman
59 G5 Thame r. U.K.
117 E2 Thames N.Z.
59 H6 Thames est. U.K.
59 G6 Thames r. U.K.
31 G4 Thamesville Can.
95 A2 Thanbyuzayat Myanmar
84 C5 Thandla India
83 D7 Thāne India
84 B5 Thangadh India
95 D2 Thăng Binh Vietnam
116 D5 Thangool Austr.
95 C1 Thanh Hoa Vietnam
83 E8 Thanjavur India
95 B1 Tha Pla Thai.
95 A3 Thap Put Thai.
95 A3 Thap Sakae Thai.
84 B4 Tharad India
84 B4 Thar Desert des. India/Pak.
114 E1 Thargomindah Austr.
83 J7 Tharrawaddy Myanmar
81 J5 Tharthār, Buḥayrat ath l. Iraq
81 J4 Tharthār, Wādī ath r. Iraq
67 L4 Thasos i. Greece
35 H5 Thatcher U.S.A.
89 C6 Thât Khê Vietnam
95 A1 Thaton Myanmar
85 H4 Thaungdut Myanmar
95 A1 Thaungyin r. Myanmar/Thai.
95 C1 Tha Uthen Thai.
117 F2 The Aldermen Islands is N.Z.
35 F5 Theba U.S.A.
16 Bahamas country Caribbean Sea
29 E7 The Bluff Bahamas
58 E2 The Cheviot h. U.K.
114 C5 The Coorong in. Austr.
24 B2 The Dalles U.S.A.
26 C3 Thedford U.S.A.
57 □ The Faither pt U.K.
59 G5 The Fens reg. U.K.
96 The Gambia country Africa
78 C5 The Great Oasis oasis Egypt
79 G4 The Gulf g. Asia
61 C2 The Hague Neth.
117 C6 The Hunters Hills h. N.Z.
95 A3 Theinkun Myanmar
117 A6 The Key N.Z.
21 H2 Thekulthili Lake l. Can.
21 J2 Thelon r. Can.
21 J2 Thelon Game Sanctuary res. Can.
116 A2 The Lynd Junction Austr.

90 G4 Towada-ko *l.* Japan
117 E1 Towai N.Z.
33 E4 Towanda U.S.A.
35 H3 Towaoc U.S.A.
59 G5 Towcester U.K.
60 C6 Tower Rep. of Ireland
30 A2 Tower U.S.A.
116 A3 Towerhill Cr. *watercourse* Austr.
21 J5 Towner U.S.A.
34 D3 Townes Pass *pass* U.S.A.
24 E2 Townsend U.S.A.
115 H6 Townsend, Mt *mt* Austr.
116 D4 Townshend I. *i.* Austr.
116 B2 Townsville Austr.
93 G7 Towori, Teluk *b.* Indon.
32 E5 Towson U.S.A.
90 G3 Tōya-ko *l.* Japan
91 E6 Toyama Japan
91 E6 Toyama-wan *b.* Japan
91 E7 Toyohashi Japan
91 E7 Toyokawa Japan
91 D7 Toyonaka Japan
91 D7 Toyooka Japan
91 E7 Toyota Japan
100 C1 Tozeur Tunisia
69 G7 Tqibuli Georgia
69 G7 Tqvarch'eli Georgia
80 E4 Trâblous Lebanon
67 K4 Trabotivište Macedonia
81 G1 Trabzon Turkey
33 K2 Tracy Can.
34 B3 Tracy *CA* U.S.A.
26 E2 Tracy *MN* U.S.A.
30 A4 Traer U.S.A.
65 C4 Trafalgar, Cabo *pt* Spain
47 B3 Traiguén Chile
20 F5 Trail Can.
55 T9 Trakai Lith.
68 J2 Trakt Rus. Fed.
60 B5 Tralee Rep. of Ireland
60 B5 Tralee Bay *b.* Rep. of Ireland
45 E3 Tramán Tepui *mt* Venez.
60 D5 Tramore Rep. of Ireland
55 O7 Tranås Sweden
44 C3 Trancas Arg.
55 N8 Tranemo Sweden
57 F5 Tranent U.K.
95 A4 Trang Thai.
93 J8 Trangan *i.* Indon.
115 G4 Trangie Austr.
47 F1 Tranqueras Uru.
119 B5 Transantarctic Mountains *mts* Antarctica
21 G4 Trans Canada Highway Can.
21 K5 Transcona Can.
66 E5 Trapani Italy
115 G7 Traralgon Austr.
85 G4 Trashigang Bhutan
66 E3 Trasimeno, Lago *l.* Italy
65 E3 Trasvase, Canal de *canal* Spain
95 B2 Trat Thai.
62 F7 Traunsee *l.* Austria
62 F7 Traunstein Ger.
114 E4 Travellers L. *l.* Austr.
117 D5 Travers, Mt *mt* N.Z.
119 C1 Traversay Is *is* Atlantic Ocean
30 E3 Traverse City U.S.A.
95 C3 Tra Vinh Vietnam
27 D6 Travis, L. *l.* U.S.A.
66 G2 Travnik Bos.-Herz.
66 F1 Trbovlje Slovenia
111 F2 Treasury Is *is* Solomon Is
62 G6 Třebíč Czech Rep.
67 H3 Trebinje Bos.-Herz.
63 K6 Trebišov Slovakia
66 F2 Trebnje Slovenia
116 B2 Trebonne Austr.
30 B3 Trego U.S.A.
116 D1 Tregosse Islets and Reefs *is* Coral Sea Is Terr.
57 D4 Treig, Loch *l.* U.K.
47 F2 Treinta-y-Tres Uru.
44 C6 Trelew Arg.
55 N9 Trelleborg Sweden
59 C5 Tremadog Bay *b.* U.K.
22 F4 Tremblant, Mt *h.* Can.
66 F3 Tremiti, Isole *is* Italy
24 D3 Tremonton U.S.A.
65 G1 Tremp Spain
30 B3 Trempealeau *r.* U.S.A.
59 B7 Trenance U.K.
62 J6 Trenčín Slovakia
47 D2 Trenque Lauquén Arg.
58 G4 Trent *r.* U.K.
66 D1 Trento Italy
31 J3 Trenton Can.
26 E3 Trenton *MO* U.S.A.
33 F4 Trenton *NJ* U.S.A.
59 D6 Treorchy U.K.
23 K4 Trepassey Can.
47 F2 Tres Arboles Uru.
47 E3 Tres Arroyos Arg.
59 A8 Tresco *i.* U.K.
46 D3 Três Corações Brazil
45 B4 Tres Esquinas Col.
57 B4 Treshnish Isles *is* U.K.
46 B3 Três Lagoas Brazil
44 B7 Tres Lagos Arg.
47 D3 Tres Lomas Arg.
46 D2 Três Marias, Represa *resr* Brazil
47 B4 Tres Picos *mt* Arg.
47 E3 Tres Picos, Cerro *mt* Arg.
25 F4 Tres Piedras U.S.A.
46 D3 Três Pontas Brazil
44 C7 Tres Puntas, C. *pt* Arg.
46 D3 Três Rios Brazil
55 M6 Tretten Norway
55 L7 Treungen Norway
66 C2 Treviglio Italy
66 E2 Treviso Italy
59 B7 Trevose Head *hd* U.K.
115 G9 Triabunna Austr.
67 M6 Tria Nisia *i.* Greece
67 N6 Trianta Greece
84 B2 Tribal Areas *div.* Pak.
67 H5 Tricase Italy
83 E8 Trichur India
115 F4 Trida Austr.
62 C6 Trier Ger.
66 E2 Trieste Italy
66 E1 Triglav *mt* Slovenia
67 J5 Trikala Greece
80 D4 Trikomon Cyprus
93 K7 Trikora, Pk *mt* Indon.
60 E4 Trim Rep. of Ireland
83 F9 Trincomalee Sri Lanka
46 C2 Trindade Brazil
12 G7 Trindade, Ilha da *i.* Atlantic Ocean
42 F6 Trinidad Bol.
45 C3 Trinidad Col.
37 J4 Trinidad Cuba
42 F1 Trinidad *i.* Trinidad and Tobago
47 F2 Trinidad Uru.
25 F4 Trinidad U.S.A.
38 Trinidad and Tobago *country* Caribbean Sea
116 A1 Trinity Bay *b.* Austr.
23 K4 Trinity Bay *b.* Can.
34 C1 Trinity Range *mts* U.S.A.
29 C5 Trion U.S.A.
67 K6 Tripoli Greece
Tripoli *see* Trâblous
101 D1 Tripoli Libya
85 G5 Tripura *div.* India
84 D3 Trisul *mt* India
85 F4 Trisul Dam *dam* Nepal
83 E9 Trivandrum India
66 F4 Trivento Italy
62 H6 Trnava Slovakia
110 F2 Trobriand Islands *is* P.N.G.
54 N4 Trofors Norway
66 G3 Trogir Croatia
66 F4 Troia Italy
62 C5 Troisdorf Ger.
23 F4 Trois-Rivières Can.
69 H6 Troitskoye Rus. Fed.
55 N7 Trollhättan Sweden
43 G3 Trombetas *r.* Brazil
13 H5 Tromelin, Île *i.* Indian Ocean
47 B3 Tromen, Volcán *vol.* Arg.
105 F5 Trompsburg S. Africa
54 Q2 Tromsø Norway
34 D4 Trona U.S.A.
47 B4 Tronador, Monte *mt* Arg.
54 M5 Trondheim Norway
54 M5 Trondheimsfjorden *chan.* Norway
85 G4 Trongsa Chhu *r.* Bhutan
80 D4 Troödos Cyprus
80 D4 Troödos, Mount *mt* Cyprus
57 D5 Troon U.K.
46 D1 Tropeiros, Serra dos *h.* Brazil
35 F3 Tropic U.S.A.
60 E2 Trostan *h.* U.K.
57 F3 Troup Head *hd* U.K.
20 F2 Trout *r.* Can.
31 H3 Trout Creek Can.
35 F2 Trout Creek U.S.A.
22 B3 Trout L. *l.* Can.
20 G3 Trout Lake *Alta.* Can.
20 E2 Trout Lake *N.W.T.* Can.
20 E2 Trout Lake *l.* Can.
30 E2 Trout Lake U.S.A.
30 C2 Trout Lake *l.* U.S.A.
24 E2 Trout Peak *summit* U.S.A.
32 E4 Trout Run U.S.A.
59 E6 Trowbridge U.K.
115 F8 Trowutta Austr.
29 C6 Troy *AL* U.S.A.
24 D2 Troy *MT* U.S.A.
33 G3 Troy *NH* U.S.A.
33 G3 Troy *NY* U.S.A.
32 A4 Troy *OH* U.S.A.
32 E4 Troy *PA* U.S.A.
67 L3 Troyan Bulg.
64 G2 Troyes France
34 D4 Troy Lake *l.* U.S.A.
35 E2 Troy Peak *summit* U.S.A.
67 J3 Trstenik Serb. and Mont.
69 E4 Trubchevsk Rus. Fed.
65 C1 Truchas Spain
68 E3 Trud Rus. Fed.
90 C3 Trudovoye Rus. Fed.
37 G5 Trujillo Honduras
42 C5 Trujillo Peru
65 D3 Trujillo Spain
45 C2 Trujillo Venez.
33 G4 Trumbull U.S.A.
35 F3 Trumbull, Mt *mt* U.S.A.
95 A5 Trumon Indon.
115 G4 Trundle Austr.
95 C2 Trung Hiệp Vietnam
89 C6 Trung Khanh China
23 H4 Truro Can.
59 B7 Truro U.K.
60 C3 Truskmore *h.* Rep. of Ireland
20 E3 Trutch Can.
25 F5 Truth or Consequences U.S.A.
62 G5 Trutnov Czech Rep.
67 L7 Trypiti, Akra *pt* Greece
55 N6 Trysil Norway
62 G3 Trzebiatów Pol.
86 E2 Tsagaannuur Mongolia
69 H6 Tsagan Aman Rus. Fed.
69 H6 Tsagan-Nur Rus. Fed.
69 G7 Ts'ageri Georgia
81 K1 Tsalka Georgia
103 E5 Tsaratanana, Massif du *mts* Madag.
67 M3 Tsarevo Bulg.
104 B2 Tsaris Mts *mts* Namibia
69 H5 Tsatsa Rus. Fed.
104 A3 Tsaukaib Namibia
102 D4 Tsavo East National Park *nat. park* Kenya
69 G6 Tselina Rus. Fed.
103 B6 Tses Namibia
103 C6 Tsetseng Botswana
86 H2 Tsetserleg Mongolia
103 C6 Tshabong Botswana
103 C6 Tshane Botswana
69 F6 Tshchikskoye Vdkhr. *resr* Rus. Fed.
102 B4 Tshela Dem. Rep. Congo
102 C4 Tshibala Dem. Rep. Congo
102 C4 Tshikapa Dem. Rep. Congo
102 C4 Tshikapa *r.* Dem. Rep. Congo
105 G3 Tshing S. Africa
105 J1 Tshipise S. Africa
103 C4 Tshitanzu Dem. Rep. Congo
102 C4 Tshofa Dem. Rep. Congo
105 J2 Tshokwane S. Africa
102 C4 Tshuapa *r.* Dem. Rep. Congo
69 G6 Tsimlyansk Rus. Fed.
69 G6 Tsimlyanskoye Vdkhr. *resr* Rus. Fed.
104 E3 Tsineng S. Africa
89 □ Tsing Shan *h.* China
89 □ Tsing Shan Wan *b.* China
Tsingtao *see* Qingdao
89 □ Tsing Yi *i.* China
103 E6 Tsiombe Madag.
103 E5 Tsiroanomandidy Madag.
104 E7 Tsitsikamma Forest and Coastal National Park *nat. park* S. Africa
20 D4 Tsitsutl Pk *summit* Can.
68 H4 Tsivil'sk Rus. Fed.
69 G7 Ts'khinvali Georgia
68 G4 Tsna *r.* Rus. Fed.
84 D2 Tsokr Chumo *l.* India
105 H5 Tsolo S. Africa
105 G6 Tsomo S. Africa
84 D2 Tso Morari L. *l.* India
69 G7 Tsqaltubo Georgia
91 E7 Tsu Japan
91 G6 Tsuchiura Japan
89 □ Tsuen Wan China
90 G4 Tsugarū-kaikyō *str.* Japan
103 B5 Tsumeb Namibia
103 B6 Tsumis Park Namibia
103 C5 Tsumkwe Namibia
85 G4 Tsunthang India
91 E7 Tsuruga Japan
91 D8 Tsurugi-san *mt* Japan
90 F5 Tsuruoka Japan
91 A7 Tsushima *i.* Japan
Tsushima-kaikyō *str. see* Korea Strait
91 D7 Tsuyama Japan
104 D1 Tswaane Botswana
105 F4 Tswaraganang S. Africa
105 F3 Tswelelang S. Africa
63 M4 Tsyelyakhany Belarus
54 X2 Tsyp-Navolok Rus. Fed.
69 E6 Tsyurupyns'k Ukr.
93 J8 Tual Indon.
60 C4 Tuam Rep. of Ireland
117 D4 Tuamarina N.Z.
89 B6 Tuân Giao Vietnam
95 A5 Tuangku *i.* Indon.
69 F6 Tuapse Rus. Fed.
95 □ Tuas Sing.
117 A7 Tuatapere N.Z.
35 G3 Tuba City U.S.A.
95 □ Tuban Indon.
44 G3 Tubarão Brazil
94 A4 Tubbataha Reefs *rf* Phil.
60 C3 Tubbercurry Rep. of Ireland
62 D6 Tübingen Ger.
100 A4 Tubmanburg Liberia
94 B4 Tubod Phil.
101 E1 Tubruq Libya
25 E6 Tubutama Mex.
43 L6 Tucano Brazil
47 B3 Tucapel, Pta *pt* Chile
43 G7 Tucavaca Bol.
20 D2 Tuchitua Can.
33 F5 Tuckerton U.S.A.
35 G5 Tucson U.S.A.
35 G5 Tucson Mts *mts* U.S.A.
45 B2 Tucuco *r.* Venez.
25 G5 Tucumcari U.S.A.
45 E2 Tucupita Venez.
43 J4 Tucuruí Brazil
43 J4 Tucuruí, Represa *resr* Brazil
81 M5 Tū Dār Iran
65 F1 Tudela Spain
65 C2 Tuela *r.* Port.
89 □ Tuen Mun China
85 H4 Tuensang India
105 J4 Tugela *r.* S. Africa
94 C4 Tugnug Point *pt* Phil.
94 B2 Tuguegarao Phil.
77 P4 Tugur Rus. Fed.
87 F2 Tuhai *r.* China
95 A5 Tuhemberua Indon.
65 B1 Tui Spain
45 A2 Tuira *r.* Panama
93 G8 Tukangbesi, Kepulauan *is* Indon.
22 E2 Tukarak Island *i.* Can.
117 F3 Tukituki *r.* N.Z.
55 S8 Tukums Latvia
68 F4 Tula Rus. Fed.
85 H1 Tulagt Ar Gol *r.* China
36 E4 Tulancingo Mex.
34 C3 Tulare U.S.A.
34 C4 Tulare Lake Bed *l.* U.S.A.
25 F5 Tularosa U.S.A.
104 C6 Tulbagh S. Africa
42 C3 Tulcán Ecuador
67 N2 Tulcea Romania
69 D5 Tul'chyn Ukr.
34 C3 Tule *r.* U.S.A.
45 B1 Tulé Venez.
85 G4 Tule-la Pass *pass* Bhutan
21 J2 Tulemalu Lake *l.* Can.
27 C5 Tulia U.S.A.
20 D2 Tulit'a Can.
80 E5 Ţulkarm West Bank
60 C5 Tulla Rep. of Ireland
115 F8 Tullah Austr.
29 C5 Tullahoma U.S.A.
115 G4 Tullamore Austr.
60 D4 Tullamore Rep. of Ireland
64 E4 Tulle France
54 O5 Tulleråsen Sweden
115 G4 Tullibigeal Austr.
27 E6 Tullos U.S.A.
60 E5 Tullow Rep. of Ireland
116 B1 Tully Austr.
116 A1 Tully *r.* Austr.
60 D3 Tully U.K.
33 E3 Tully U.S.A.
116 A1 Tully Falls *waterfall* Austr.
68 D2 Tulos Rus. Fed.
27 D4 Tulsa U.S.A.
68 F4 Tul'skaya Oblast' *div.* Rus. Fed.
45 A3 Tuluá Col.
77 V3 Tuluksak Alaska
47 C1 Tulum, Valle de *v.* Arg.
77 M4 Tulun Rus. Fed.
92 □ Tulungagung Indon.
85 H4 Tulung La *pass* China
94 A4 Tuluran *i.* Phil.
45 A4 Tumaco Col.
105 G3 Tumahole S. Africa
69 J6 Tumak Rus. Fed.
55 P7 Tumba Sweden
102 B4 Tumba, Lac *l.* Dem. Rep. Congo
94 C5 Tumbao Phil.
113 J7 Tumbarumba Austr.
42 B4 Tumbes Peru
20 E3 Tumbler Ridge Can.
114 B5 Tumby Bay Austr.
54 W3 Tumcha *r.* Fin./Rus. Fed.
87 N3 Tumen China
90 A3 Tumen Jiang *r.* China/N. Korea
88 B2 Tumenzi China
42 F2 Tumereng Guyana
94 A5 Tumindao *i.* Phil.
83 E8 Tumkur India
85 G3 Tum La *pass* China
57 E4 Tummel, Loch *l.* U.K.
87 Q2 Tumnin *r.* Rus. Fed.
79 J4 Tump Pak.
95 B4 Tumpat Malaysia
100 B3 Tumu Ghana
43 G3 Tumucumaque, Serra *h.* Brazil
115 H5 Tumut Austr.
115 H5 Tumut *r.* Austr.
59 H6 Tunbridge Wells, Royal U.K.
81 G2 Tunceli Turkey
89 D7 Tunchang China
115 K4 Tuncurry Austr.
84 D4 Tundla India
103 D5 Tunduru Tanz.
67 M3 Tundzha *r.* Bulg.
85 H3 Tunga Pass *pass* China/India
94 B5 Tungawan Phil.
89 □ Tung Lung Chau *i.* China
54 D4 Tungnaá *r.* Iceland
20 D2 Tungsten Can.
68 E1 Tunguda Rus. Fed.
89 □ Tung Wan *b.* China
100 D1 Tunis Tunisia
66 D6 Tunis, Golfe de *g.* Tunisia
96 Tunisia *country* Africa
45 B3 Tunja Col.
88 D2 Tunliu China
54 N4 Tunnsjøen *l.* Norway
59 J5 Tunstall U.K.
54 V3 Tuntsa Fin.
23 H2 Tunungayualok Island *i.* Can.
47 C2 Tunuyán Arg.
47 C2 Tunuyán *r.* Arg.
88 E3 Tuo He *r.* China
88 F2 Tuoji Dao *i.* China
95 C3 Tuŏl Khpos Cambodia
34 B3 Tuolumne U.S.A.
34 C3 Tuolumne Meadows U.S.A.
89 B5 Tuoniang Jiang *r.* China
85 H2 Tuotuo He *r.* China
85 H2 Tuotuoheyan China
46 B3 Tupã Brazil
46 C2 Tupaciguara Brazil
81 L3 Tūp Āghāj Iran
44 F3 Tupanciretã Brazil
45 C3 Tuparro *r.* Col.
27 F5 Tupelo U.S.A.
42 E8 Tupiza Bol.
33 F2 Tupper Lake U.S.A.
33 F2 Tupper Lake *l.* U.S.A.
47 C2 Tupungato Arg.
47 C2 Tupungato, Cerro *mt* Arg./Chile
81 K7 Tuqayyid *w.* Iraq
45 A4 Túquerres Col.
89 C7 Tuqu Wan *b.* China
85 G4 Tura India
77 M3 Tura Rus. Fed.
78 E5 Turabah Saudi Arabia
45 D3 Turagua, Serranía *mt* Venez.
117 E4 Turakina N.Z.
87 O1 Turana, Khrebet *mts* Rus. Fed.
117 E3 Turangi N.Z.
79 H1 Turan Lowland *lowland* Asia
82 D2 Tura-Ryskulova Kazak.
80 G6 Turayf Saudi Arabia
55 T7 Turba Estonia
45 B2 Turbaco Col.
79 J4 Turbat Pak.
45 A2 Turbo Col.
63 L7 Turda Romania
81 M4 Tūreh Iran
Turfan *see* Turpan
76 H5 Turgay Kazak.
67 M3 Tŭrgovishte Bulg.
80 C2 Turgut Turkey
80 A2 Turgutlu Turkey
80 F1 Turhal Turkey
55 T7 Türi Estonia
65 F3 Turia *r.* Spain
45 D2 Turiamo Venez.
66 B2 Turin Italy
90 B2 Turiy Rog Rus. Fed.
69 C5 Turiys'k Ukr.
86 J1 Turka Rus. Fed.
102 D3 Turkana, Lake *salt l.* Eth./Kenya
67 M4 Türkeli Adası *i.* Turkey
82 C2 Turkestan Kazak.
70 Turkey *country* Asia.
30 B4 Turkey *r.* U.S.A.
69 G5 Turki Rus. Fed.
79 G2 Turkmenbashi Turkm.
80 C2 Türkmen Dağı *mt* Turkey
70 Turkmenistan *country* Asia
80 F3 Türkoğlu Turkey
37 K4 Turks and Caicos Islands *terr.* Caribbean
37 K4 Turks Islands *is* Turks and Caicos Is
55 S6 Turku Fin.
102 D3 Turkwel *watercourse* Kenya
34 B3 Turlock U.S.A.
34 B3 Turlock L. *l.* U.S.A.
117 F4 Turnagain, Cape *c.* N.Z.
57 D5 Turnberry U.K.
35 G5 Turnbull, Mt *mt* U.S.A.
36 G5 Turneffe Is *is* Belize
31 F3 Turner U.S.A.
61 C3 Turnhout Belgium
21 H3 Turnor Lake *l.* Can.
67 L3 Turnu Măgurele Romania
115 H4 Turon *r.* Austr.
68 G3 Turovets Rus. Fed.
82 G2 Turpan China
82 G2 Turpan Pendi *depression* China
57 F3 Turriff U.K.
81 K5 Tursāq Iraq
79 J1 Turtkul' Uzbek.
30 B2 Turtle Flambeau Flowage *resr* U.S.A.
21 H4 Turtleford Can.
116 D1 Turtle I. *i.* Coral Sea Is Terr.
30 A3 Turtle Lake U.S.A.
82 E2 Turugart Pass *pass* China/Kyrgyzstan
46 B2 Turvo *r. Goiás* Brazil
46 B2 Turvo *r. Goiás* Brazil
46 C3 Turvo *r. São Paulo* Brazil
35 F4 Tusayan U.S.A.
29 C5 Tuscaloosa U.S.A.
32 C4 Tuscarawas *r.* U.S.A.
32 E4 Tuscarora Mts *h.* U.S.A.
30 C6 Tuscola *IL* U.S.A.
27 D5 Tuscola *TX* U.S.A.
29 C5 Tuskegee U.S.A.
32 D4 Tussey Mts *h.* U.S.A.
81 J2 Tutak Turkey
68 F3 Tutayev Rus. Fed.
83 E9 Tuticorin India
26 D4 Tuttle Creek Res. *resr* U.S.A.
62 D7 Tuttlingen Ger.
111 J3 Tutuila *i.* Pac. Oc.
103 C6 Tutume Botswana
54 W5 Tuupovaara Fin.
54 V5 Tuusniemi Fin.
106 Tuvalu *country* Pac. Oc.
36 E4 Tuxpan Mex.
36 F5 Tuxtla Gutiérrez Mex.
45 D2 Tuy *r.* Venez.
95 C2 Tuy Dức Vietnam
89 B6 Tuyên Quang Vietnam
95 D2 Tuy Hoa Vietnam
81 M4 Tūysarkān Iran
Tuz, Lake *salt l. see* Tuz Gölü
80 D2 Tuz Gölü *salt l.* Turkey
35 F4 Tuzigoot National Monument *res.* U.S.A.
81 K4 Tuz Khurmātū Iraq
67 H2 Tuzla Bos.-Herz.
81 H2 Tuzla *r.* Turkey
69 F6 Tuzlov *r.* Rus. Fed.
55 L7 Tvedestrand Norway
68 E3 Tver' Rus. Fed.
68 E3 Tverskaya Oblast' *div.* Rus. Fed.
31 J3 Tweed Can.
57 F5 Tweed *r.* U.K.
115 K2 Tweed Heads Austr.
20 D4 Tweedsmuir Prov. Park *res.* Can.
104 C6 Tweefontein S. Africa
104 C2 Twee Rivier Namibia
61 E2 Twente *reg.* Neth.
34 D4 Twentynine Palms U.S.A.
23 K4 Twillingate Can.
24 D2 Twin Bridges U.S.A.
27 C6 Twin Buttes Res. *resr* U.S.A.
23 H3 Twin Falls Can.
24 D3 Twin Falls U.S.A.
20 F3 Twin Lakes Can.
33 H2 Twin Mountain U.S.A.
32 C6 Twin Oaks U.S.A.
34 B2 Twin Peak *summit* U.S.A.
115 H6 Twofold B. *b.* Austr.
35 G4 Two Guns U.S.A.
30 B2 Two Harbors U.S.A.
21 G4 Two Hills Can.
24 D1 Two Medicine *r.* U.S.A.
30 D3 Two Rivers U.S.A.
85 H5 Tyao *r.* India/Myanmar
54 M5 Tydal Norway
32 D5 Tygart Lake *l.* U.S.A.
32 D5 Tygart Valley *v.* U.S.A.
87 N1 Tygda Rus. Fed.
27 E5 Tyler U.S.A.
27 F6 Tylertown U.S.A.
77 O4 Tynda Rus. Fed.
20 A2 Tyndall Gl. *gl.* U.S.A.
57 F4 Tyne *r.* U.K.
58 F2 Tynemouth U.K.
55 M5 Tynset Norway
80 E5 Tyre Lebanon
21 H2 Tyrell Lake *l.* Can.
87 O1 Tyrma Rus. Fed.
54 T4 Tyrnävä Fin.
67 K5 Tyrnavos Greece
32 D4 Tyrone U.S.A.
114 E5 Tyrrell *r.* Austr.
114 E5 Tyrrell, L. *l.* Austr.
52 Tyrrhenian Sea *sea* France/Italy
77 Q3 Tyubelyakh Rus. Fed.
76 J4 Tyukalinsk Rus. Fed.
76 H4 Tyumen' Rus. Fed.
77 N3 Tyung *r.* Rus. Fed.
Tyuratam *see* Baykonur
59 C6 Tywi *r.* U.K.
59 C5 Tywyn U.K.
105 J1 Tzaneen S. Africa

U

103 C5 Uamanda Angola
45 E4 Uatatás *r.* Brazil
43 L5 Uauá Brazil
45 D5 Uaupés Brazil
45 C4 Uaupés *r.* Brazil
81 J7 U'aywij, W. *watercourse* Saudi Arabia
46 D3 Ubá Brazil
46 D2 Ubaí Brazil
46 E1 Ubaitaba Brazil
102 B4 Ubangi *r.* C.A.R./Dem. Rep. Congo
45 B3 Ubate Col.
81 J5 Ubayyiḍ, Wādī al *watercourse* Iraq/S. Arabia
91 B8 Ube Japan
65 E3 Úbeda Spain
46 C2 Uberaba Brazil
43 G7 Uberaba, Lagoa *l.* Bol./Brazil
46 C2 Uberlândia Brazil
95 □ Ubin, Pulau *i.* Sing.
95 B1 Ubolratna Res. *resr* Thai.
105 K3 Ubombo S. Africa
95 C2 Ubon Ratchathani Thai.
102 C4 Ubundu Dem. Rep. Congo
81 L1 Ucar Azer.
42 D5 Ucayali *r.* Peru
84 B3 Uch Pak.
82 F1 Ucharal Kazak.
90 G3 Uchiura-wan *b.* Japan
77 P4 Uchur *r.* Rus. Fed.
59 H7 Uckfield U.K.
20 D5 Ucluelet Can.
35 H3 Ucolo U.S.A.
24 F2 Ucross U.S.A.
77 P4 Uda *r.* Rus. Fed.
69 H6 Udachnoye Rus. Fed.
77 N3 Udachnyy Rus. Fed.
83 E8 Udagamandalam India
84 C4 Udaipur *Rajasthan* India
85 G5 Udaipur *Tripura* India
85 E5 Udanti *r.* India/Myanmar
55 M7 Uddevalla Sweden
57 D5 Uddingston U.K.
54 P4 Uddjaure *l.* Sweden
61 D3 Uden Neth.
82 E4 Udhampur Jammu and Kashmir
68 H2 Udimskiy Rus. Fed.
66 E1 Udine Italy
23 J2 Udjuktok Bay *b.* Can.
68 E3 Udomlya Rus. Fed.
95 B1 Udon Thani Thai.
77 P4 Udskaya Guba *b.* Rus. Fed.
83 D8 Udupi India
77 P4 Udyl', Ozero *l.* Rus. Fed.
62 G4 Ueckermünde Ger.
91 F6 Ueda Japan
93 G7 Uekuli Indon.
102 C3 Uele *r.* Dem. Rep. Congo
62 E4 Uelzen Ger.
102 C3 Uere *r.* Dem. Rep. Congo

83 E8 Vellore India
68 G2 Vel'sk Rus. Fed.
62 F4 Velten Ger.
61 D2 Veluwe *reg.* Neth.
61 D2 Veluwemeer *l.* Neth.
61 D2 Veluwezoom, Nationaal Park *nat. park* Neth.
21 J5 Velva U.S.A.
12 G5 Vema Fracture *sea feature* Atlantic Ocean
13 J4 Vema Trench *sea feature* Indian Ocean
57 D4 Venachar, Loch *l.* U.K.
47 E2 Venado Tuerto Arg.
66 F4 Venafro Italy
45 E3 Venamo *r.* Guyana/Venez.
45 E3 Venamo, Co *mt* Venez.
46 C3 Venceslau Bráz Brazil
64 E3 Vendôme France
68 F4 Venev Rus. Fed.
Venezia *see* Venice
38 Venezuela *country* S. America
45 C2 Venezuela, Golfo de *g.* Venez.
83 D7 Vengurla India
66 E2 Venice Italy
29 D7 Venice U.S.A.
66 E2 Venice, Gulf of *g.* Europe
64 G4 Vénissieux France
61 E3 Venlo Neth.
55 K7 Vennesla Norway
61 D3 Venray Neth.
55 R8 Venta *r.* Latvia/Lith.
55 S8 Venta Lith.
105 G4 Ventersburg S. Africa
105 G3 Ventersdorp S. Africa
105 F5 Venterstad S. Africa
59 F7 Ventnor U.K.
64 G4 Ventoux, Mont *mt* France
55 R8 Ventspils Latvia
45 D3 Ventuari *r.* Venez.
34 C4 Ventucopa U.S.A.
34 C4 Ventura U.S.A.
114 F7 Venus B. *b.* Austr.
27 C7 Venustiano Carranza Mex.
27 C7 Venustiano Carranza, Presa *l.* Mex.
44 D3 Vera Arg.
65 F4 Vera Spain
36 E5 Veracruz Mex.
84 B5 Veraval India
66 C2 Verbania Italy
66 C2 Vercelli Italy
54 M5 Verdalsøra Norway
47 D4 Verde *r.* Arg.
46 B2 Verde *r.* Goiás Brazil
46 B2 Verde *r.* Goiás Brazil
46 C2 Verde *r.* Goiás/Minas Gerais Brazil
46 B3 Verde *r.* Mato Grosso do Sul Brazil
44 E2 Verde *r.* Para.
35 G4 Verde *r.* U.S.A.
47 D3 Verde, Pen. *pen.* Arg.
46 D1 Verde Grande *r.* Brazil
94 B3 Verde Island Pass. *chan.* Phil.
62 D4 Verden (Aller) Ger.
27 E4 Verdigris *r.* U.S.A.
64 H5 Verdon *r.* France
64 G2 Verdun France
105 G3 Vereeniging S. Africa
47 G2 Vergara Uru.
33 G2 Vergennes U.S.A.
65 C2 Verín Spain
69 F6 Verkhnebakanskiy Rus. Fed.
63 Q3 Verkhnedneprovskiy Rus. Fed.
76 K3 Verkhneimbatsk Rus. Fed.
54 W2 Verkhnetulomskiy Rus. Fed.
77 O3 Verkhnevilyuysk Rus. Fed.
68 D1 Verkhneye Kuyto, Oz. *l.* Rus. Fed.
69 H5 Verkhniy Baskunchak Rus. Fed.
69 J5 Verkhniy Kushum Rus. Fed.
68 H2 Verkhnyaya Toyma Rus. Fed.
68 G2 Verkhovazh'ye Rus. Fed.
68 F4 Verkhov'ye Rus. Fed.
69 C5 Verkhovyna Ukr.
77 P3 Verkhoyansk Rus. Fed.
77 O3 Verkhoyanskiy Khrebet *mts* Rus. Fed.
46 B1 Vermelho *r.* Brazil
21 G4 Vermilion Can.
30 C5 Vermilion *r.* U.S.A.
35 F3 Vermilion Cliffs *cliff* U.S.A.
30 A2 Vermilion Lake *l.* U.S.A.
30 A2 Vermilion Range *h.* U.S.A.
26 D3 Vermillion U.S.A.
21 L5 Vermillion Bay Can.
33 G3 Vermont *div.* U.S.A.
24 E3 Vernal U.S.A.
21 G2 Verner Can.
104 D4 Verneuk Pan *salt pan* S. Africa
20 F4 Vernon Can.
35 H4 Vernon *AZ* U.S.A.
33 G4 Vernon *CT* U.S.A.
27 D5 Vernon *TX* U.S.A.
35 F1 Vernon *UT* U.S.A.
29 D7 Vero Beach U.S.A.
67 K4 Veroia Greece
66 D2 Verona Italy
47 F2 Verónica Arg.
114 B4 Verran Austr.
64 F2 Versailles France
64 D3 Vertou France
105 J4 Verulam S. Africa
61 D4 Verviers Belgium
64 F2 Vervins France
66 C3 Vescovato France
76 G4 Veselaya, G. *mt* Rus. Fed.
69 E6 Vesele Ukr.
69 G6 Veselovskoye Vdkhr. *resr* Rus. Fed.
69 G5 Veshenskaya Rus. Fed.
61 B5 Vesle *r.* France
64 H3 Vesoul France
90 D3 Vesselyy Yar Rus. Fed.
61 D3 Vessem Neth.
54 O2 Vesterålen *is* Norway
54 N2 Vesterålsfjorden *chan.* Norway
119 C3 Vestfjella *mts* Antarctica
55 L7 Vestfjorddalen *v.* Norway
54 N3 Vestfjorden *chan.* Norway
54 □ Vestmanna Faroe Is
54 C5 Vestmannaeyjar Iceland
54 C5 Vestmannaeyjar *is* Iceland
54 K5 Vestnes Norway
54 F4 Vesturhorn *hd* Iceland
Vesuvio *vol. see* Vesuvius
66 F4 Vesuvius *vol.* Italy
68 F3 Ves'yegonsk Rus. Fed.
62 H7 Veszprém Hungary
54 S5 Veteli Fin.
55 O8 Vetlanda Sweden
68 H3 Vetluga Rus. Fed.
68 H3 Vetluga *r.* Rus. Fed.
66 E3 Vettore, Monte *mt* Italy
61 A3 Veurne Belgium
62 C7 Vevey Switz.
35 F3 Veyo U.S.A.
81 M6 Veys Iran
64 E4 Vézère *r.* France
80 E1 Vezirköprü Turkey
43 K4 Viana Brazil
65 B2 Viana do Castelo Port.
Viangchan *see* Vientiane
46 C2 Vianópolis Brazil
66 D3 Viareggio Italy
55 L8 Viborg Denmark
66 G5 Vibo Valentia Italy
65 H2 Vic Spain
119 B2 Vicecomodoro Marambio *Arg. Base* Antarctica
34 C5 Vicente, Pt *pt* U.S.A.
25 C6 Vicente Guerrero Mex.
66 D2 Vicenza Italy
42 D3 Vichada *r.* Col.
45 C3 Vichada *r.* Col.
68 G3 Vichuga Rus. Fed.
47 B2 Vichuquén Chile
64 F3 Vichy France
35 F5 Vicksburg *AZ* U.S.A.
27 F5 Vicksburg *MS* U.S.A.
46 D3 Viçosa Brazil
30 A5 Victor U.S.A.
114 C5 Victor Harbor Austr.
47 E2 Victoria Arg.
114 F6 Victoria *div.* Austr.
112 F3 Victoria *r.* Austr.
20 E5 Victoria Can.
47 B3 Victoria Chile
Victoria *see* Labuan
66 F6 Victoria Malta
27 D6 Victoria U.S.A.
102 D4 Victoria, Lake *l.* Africa
114 D4 Victoria, Lake *l.* Austr.
115 G6 Victoria, Lake *l.* Austr.
85 H5 Victoria, Mt *mt* Myanmar
110 E2 Victoria, Mt *mt* P.N.G.
103 C5 Victoria Falls *waterfall* Zambia/Zimbabwe
118 B2 Victoria Island *i.* Can.
23 J4 Victoria Lake *l.* Can.
119 B5 Victoria Land *reg.* Antarctica
101 F4 Victoria Nile *r.* Sudan/Uganda
117 D5 Victoria Range *mts* N.Z.
112 F3 Victoria River Austr.
112 F3 Victoria River Downs Austr.
23 F4 Victoriaville Can.
104 E5 Victoria West S. Africa
47 D3 Victorica Arg.
34 D4 Victorville U.S.A.
47 D2 Vicuña Mackenna Arg.
35 E4 Vidal Junction U.S.A.
67 L2 Videle Romania
67 L3 Vidin Bulg.
84 D5 Vidisha India
57 □ Vidlin U.K.
68 E2 Vidlitsa Rus. Fed.
63 N3 Vidzy Belarus
68 J2 Vidz'yuyar Rus. Fed.
47 D4 Viedma Arg.
44 B7 Viedma, L. *l.* Arg.
25 D6 Viejo, Cerro *mt* Mex.
61 D4 Vielsalm Belgium
62 H6 Vienna Austria
28 B4 Vienna *IL* U.S.A.
33 F5 Vienna *MD* U.S.A.
32 C5 Vienna *WV* U.S.A.
64 G4 Vienne France
64 E3 Vienne *r.* France
95 B1 Vientiane Laos
47 B3 Viento, Cordillera del *mts* Arg.
37 L5 Vieques *i.* Puerto Rico
54 U5 Vieremä Fin.
61 E3 Viersen Ger.
62 D7 Vierwaldstätter See *l.* Switz.
64 F3 Vierzon France
27 C7 Viesca Mex.
55 T8 Viesīte Latvia
66 G4 Vieste Italy
54 Q3 Vietas Sweden
70 Vietnam *country* Asia
89 B6 Viêt Tri Vietnam
94 B2 Vigan Phil.
66 C2 Vigevano Italy
64 D5 Vignemale *mt* France
66 D2 Vignola Italy
65 B1 Vigo Spain
61 E5 Vigy France
54 T4 Vihanti Fin.
84 C3 Vihari Pak.
55 T6 Vihti Fin.
54 T5 Viitasaari Fin.
84 C3 Vijainagar India
83 F7 Vijayawada India
54 D5 Vík Iceland
54 U3 Vikajärvi Fin.
21 G4 Viking Can.
54 M4 Vikna *i.* Norway
55 K6 Vikøyri Norway
100 □ Vila da Ribeira Brava Cape Verde
100 □ Vila de Sal Rei Cape Verde
100 □ Vila do Tarrafal Cape Verde
65 B3 Vila Franca de Xira Port.
65 B1 Vilagarcía de Arousa Spain
105 K2 Vila Gomes da Costa Moz.
65 C1 Vilalba Spain
103 E5 Vilanandro, Tanjona *pt* Madag.
65 B2 Vila Nova de Gaia Port.
65 G2 Vilanova i la Geltrú Spain
100 □ Vila Nova Sintra Cape Verde
65 C2 Vila Real Port.
65 C2 Vilar Formoso Port.
46 E3 Vila Velha Brazil
42 D6 Vilcabamba, Cordillera *mts* Peru
54 P4 Vilhelmina Sweden
42 F6 Vilhena Brazil
55 T7 Viljandi Estonia
105 G3 Viljoenskroon S. Africa
55 S9 Vilkaviškis Lith.
55 S9 Vilkija Lith.
77 L2 Vil'kitskogo, Proliv *str.* Rus. Fed.
25 F6 Villa Ahumada Mex.
42 E6 Villa Bella Bol.
65 C1 Villablino Spain
47 E2 Villa Cañás Arg.
65 E3 Villacañas Spain
62 F7 Villach Austria
66 C5 Villacidro Italy
47 E2 Villa Constitución Arg.
47 D1 Villa del Rosario Arg.
47 D1 Villa del Totoral Arg.
47 D1 Villa Dolores Arg.
47 F3 Villa Gesell Arg.
47 E1 Villaguay Arg.
36 F5 Villahermosa Mex.
47 D2 Villa Huidobro Arg.
36 B3 Villa Insurgentes Mex.
47 D3 Villa Iris Arg.
65 F3 Villajoyosa Spain
27 C7 Villaldama Mex.
47 D3 Villálonga Arg.
47 D2 Villa María Arg.
47 E1 Villa María Grande Arg.
42 F8 Villa Montes Bol.
105 H1 Villa Nora S. Africa
45 B2 Villanueva Col.
65 D3 Villanueva de la Serena Spain
65 E3 Villanueva de los Infantes Spain
44 E3 Villa Ocampo Arg.
27 B7 Villa Ocampo Mex.
27 B7 Villa Orestes Pereyra Mex.
66 C5 Villaputzu Italy
47 C3 Villa Regina Arg.
47 B3 Villarrica Chile
44 E3 Villarrica Para.
47 B3 Villarrica, L. *l.* Chile
47 B3 Villarrica, Parque Nacional *nat. park* Chile
47 B3 Villarrica, Volcán *vol.* Chile
65 E3 Villarrobledo Spain
66 F5 Villa San Giovanni Italy
47 E2 Villa San José Arg.
47 C1 Villa Santa Rita de Catuna Arg.
44 C3 Villa Unión Arg.
27 C6 Villa Unión Mex.
47 D2 Villa Valeria Arg.
45 B3 Villavicencio Col.
42 E8 Villazon Bol.
64 F4 Villefranche-de-Rouergue France
64 G4 Villefranche-sur-Saône France
31 H2 Ville-Marie Can.
65 F3 Villena Spain
64 E4 Villeneuve-sur-Lot France
64 F2 Villeneuve-sur-Yonne France
27 E6 Ville Platte U.S.A.
61 B5 Villers-Cotterêts France
64 G4 Villeurbanne France
105 H3 Villiers S. Africa
62 D6 Villingen Ger.
21 G4 Vilna Can.
55 T9 Vilnius Lith.
69 E6 Vil'nyans'k Ukr.
55 T5 Vilppula Fin.
83 E8 Viluppuram India
61 C4 Vilvoorde Belgium
68 C4 Vilyeyka Belarus
77 O3 Vilyuy *r.* Rus. Fed.
77 M3 Vilyuyskoye Vdkhr. *resr* Rus. Fed.
55 O8 Vimmerby Sweden
34 A2 Vina U.S.A.
47 B2 Viña del Mar Chile
33 J2 Vinalhaven U.S.A.
65 G2 Vinaròs Spain
28 C4 Vincennes U.S.A.
54 Q4 Vindelälven *r.* Sweden
54 Q4 Vindeln Sweden
84 C5 Vindhya Range *h.* India
33 F5 Vineland U.S.A.
33 H4 Vineyard Haven U.S.A.
95 C1 Vinh Vietnam
95 C1 Vinh Linh Vietnam
95 C3 Vinh Long Vietnam
89 B6 Vinh Yên Vietnam
27 E4 Vinita U.S.A.
67 H2 Vinkovci Croatia
69 D5 Vinnytsya Ukr.
119 B3 Vinson Massif *mt* Antarctica
55 L6 Vinstra Norway
30 A4 Vinton U.S.A.
83 E7 Vinukonda India
66 D1 Vipiteno Italy
94 C3 Virac Phil.
84 C5 Viramgam India
81 G3 Viranşehir Turkey
84 B4 Virawah Pak.
21 J5 Virden Can.
64 D2 Vire France
103 B5 Virei Angola
46 D2 Virgem da Lapa Brazil
35 F3 Virgin *mts* U.S.A.
31 H1 Virginatown Can.
60 D4 Virginia Rep. of Ireland
105 G4 Virginia S. Africa
30 A2 Virginia U.S.A.
32 D6 Virginia *div.* U.S.A.
33 E6 Virginia Beach U.S.A.
34 C2 Virginia City U.S.A.
37 M5 Virgin Islands (U.K.) *terr.* Caribbean
37 M5 Virgin Islands (U.S.A.) *terr.* Caribbean
55 T6 Virkkala Fin.
95 C2 Virôchey Cambodia
30 B4 Viroqua U.S.A.
66 G2 Virovitica Croatia
55 S5 Virrat Fin.
61 D5 Virton Belgium
55 S7 Virtsu Estonia
83 E9 Virudunagar India
102 C3 Virunga, Parc National des *nat. park* Dem. Rep. Congo
66 G3 Vis *i.* Croatia
55 U9 Visaginas Lith.
34 C3 Visalia U.S.A.
84 B5 Visavadar India
94 B4 Visayan Sea *sea* Phil.
55 Q8 Visby Sweden
76 J2 Vise, O. *i.* Rus. Fed.
67 H3 Višegrad Bos.-Herz.
43 J4 Viseu Brazil
65 C2 Viseu Port.
83 F7 Vishakhapatnam India
55 U8 Višķi Latvia
84 C5 Visnagar India
66 B2 Viso, Monte *mt* Italy
67 H3 Visoko Bos.-Herz.
62 C7 Visp Switz.
34 D5 Vista U.S.A.
46 A2 Vista Alegre Brazil
67 L4 Vistonida, Limni *lag.* Greece
45 C3 Vita *r.* Col.
84 B3 Vitakri Pak.
66 E3 Viterbo Italy
66 G2 Vitez Bos.-Herz.
42 E8 Vitichi Bol.
65 C2 Vitigudino Spain
111 H3 Viti Levu *i.* Fiji
87 L1 Vitim *r.* Rus. Fed.
87 K1 Vitimskoye Ploskogor'ye *plat.* Rus. Fed.
46 E3 Vitória Brazil
Vitoria *see* Vitoria-Gasteiz
46 E1 Vitória da Conquista Brazil
65 E1 Vitoria-Gasteiz Spain
64 D2 Vitré France
64 G2 Vitry-le-François France
68 D4 Vitsyebsk Belarus
54 R3 Vittangi Sweden
66 F6 Vittoria Italy
66 E2 Vittorio Veneto Italy
14 F3 Vityaz Depth *depth* Pac. Oc.
65 C1 Viveiro Spain
105 H1 Vivo S. Africa
114 B6 Vivonne B. *b.* Austr.
25 D7 Vizcaíno, Desierto de *des.* Mex.
36 B3 Vizcaíno, Sierra *mts* Mex.
69 C7 Vize Turkey
83 F7 Vizianagaram India
68 J2 Vizinga Rus. Fed.
61 C3 Vlaardingen Neth.
63 L7 Vlădeasa, Vârful *mt* Romania
69 H7 Vladikavkaz Rus. Fed.
90 D3 Vladimir Rus. Fed.
68 G3 Vladimir Rus. Fed.
90 C3 Vladimiro-Aleksandrovskoye Rus. Fed.
68 G4 Vladimirskaya Oblast' *div.* Rus. Fed.
87 O3 Vladivostok Rus. Fed.
105 H2 Vlakte S. Africa
67 K3 Vlasotince Serb. and Mont.
104 D7 Vleesbaai *b.* S. Africa
61 C1 Vlieland *i.* Neth.
61 B3 Vlissingen Neth.
67 H4 Vlorë Albania
62 G6 Vltava *r.* Czech Rep.
62 F6 Vöcklabruck Austria
68 F2 Vodlozero, Ozero *l.* Rus. Fed.
57 □ Voe U.K.
61 D4 Voerendaal Neth.
66 C2 Voghera Italy
103 E6 Vohimena, Tanjona *c.* Madag.
55 T7 Võhma Estonia
102 D4 Voi Kenya
100 B4 Voinjama Liberia
64 G4 Voiron France
55 L9 Vojens Denmark
67 H2 Vojvodina *div.* Serb. and Mont.
68 H3 Vokhma Rus. Fed.
68 D1 Voknavolok Rus. Fed.
24 F2 Volborg U.S.A.
47 B1 Volcán, Co del *mt* Chile
Volcano Bay *b. see* Uchiura-wan
Volcano Is *is see* Kazan-rettō
55 K5 Volda Norway
69 H6 Volga *r.* Rus. Fed.
30 B4 Volga *r.* U.S.A.
69 G6 Volgodonsk Rus. Fed.
69 H5 Volgograd Rus. Fed.
69 H5 Volgogradskaya Oblast' *div.* Rus. Fed.
62 G7 Völkermarkt Austria
68 E3 Volkhov Rus. Fed.
68 D3 Volkhov *r.* Rus. Fed.
61 E5 Völklingen Ger.
105 H3 Volksrust S. Africa
90 B3 Vol'no-Nadezhdinskoye Rus. Fed.
69 F6 Volnovakha Ukr.
77 L2 Volochanka Rus. Fed.
69 C5 Volochys'k Ukr.
69 F6 Volodars'ke Ukr.
69 J6 Volodarskiy Rus. Fed.
63 O5 Volodars'k-Volyns'kyy Ukr.
63 N5 Volodymyrets' Ukr.
69 C5 Volodymyr-Volyns'kyy Ukr.
68 F3 Vologda Rus. Fed.
68 G3 Vologodskaya Oblast' *div.* Rus. Fed.
69 F5 Volokonovka Rus. Fed.
67 K5 Volos Greece
68 D3 Volosovo Rus. Fed.
63 P2 Volot Rus. Fed.
69 F4 Volovo Rus. Fed.
69 H4 Vol'sk Rus. Fed.
100 B4 Volta, Lake *resr* Ghana
46 D3 Volta Redonda Brazil
66 F4 Volturno *r.* Italy
67 K4 Volvi, L. *l.* Greece
68 J4 Volzhsk Rus. Fed.
69 H5 Volzhskiy Rus. Fed.
103 E6 Vondrozo Madag.
68 G1 Vonga Rus. Fed.
54 F4 Vopnafjörður Iceland
54 F4 Vopnafjörður *b.* Iceland
68 B2 Vörå Fin.
63 M3 Voranava Belarus
68 J3 Vorchanka Rus. Fed.
68 E2 Vorenzha Rus. Fed.
76 H3 Vorkuta Rus. Fed.
55 S7 Vormsi *i.* Estonia
69 G5 Vorona *r.* Rus. Fed.
69 F5 Voronezh Rus. Fed.
69 F5 Voronezh *r.* Rus. Fed.
69 G5 Voronezhskaya Oblast' *div.* Rus. Fed.
68 G3 Voron'ye Rus. Fed.
Voroshilovgrad *see* Luhans'k
63 Q3 Vorot'kovo Rus. Fed.
69 E5 Vorskla *r.* Rus. Fed.
55 T7 Võrtsjärv *l.* Estonia
55 U8 Võru Estonia
104 E5 Vosburg S. Africa
64 H2 Vosges *mts* France
55 K6 Voss Norway
Vostochno-Sibirskoye More *sea see* East Siberian Sea
86 G1 Vostochnyy Sayan *mts* Rus. Fed.
90 D1 Vostok Rus. Fed.
90 D2 Vostretsovo Rus. Fed.
76 G4 Votkinsk Rus. Fed.
46 C3 Votuporanga Brazil
61 C5 Vouziers France
64 E2 Voves France
68 J3 Voya *r.* Rus. Fed.
28 A1 Voyageurs Nat. Park *nat. park* U.S.A.
54 W4 Voynitsa Rus. Fed.
68 F2 Vozhe, Ozero *l.* Rus. Fed.
68 G2 Vozhega Rus. Fed.
69 D6 Voznesens'k Ukr.
90 C3 Vrangel' Rus. Fed.
77 T2 Vrangelya, O. *i.* Rus. Fed.
67 J3 Vranje Serb. and Mont.
67 M3 Vratnik *pass* Bulg.
67 K3 Vratsa Bulg.
66 G2 Vrbas *r.* Bos.-Herz.
67 H2 Vrbas Serb. and Mont.
105 H3 Vrede S. Africa
105 G3 Vredefort S. Africa
104 B6 Vredenburg S. Africa
104 C5 Vredendal S. Africa
61 C5 Vresse Belgium
83 E8 Vriddhachalam India
55 O8 Vrigstad Sweden
67 J2 Vršac Serb. and Mont.
104 F3 Vryburg S. Africa
105 J3 Vryheid S. Africa
68 D2 Vsevolozhsk Rus. Fed.
67 J3 Vučitrn Serb. and Mont.
67 H2 Vukovar Croatia
76 G3 Vuktyl' Rus. Fed.
105 H3 Vukuzakhe S. Africa
66 F5 Vulcano, Isola *i.* Italy
35 F5 Vulture Mts *mts* U.S.A.
95 C3 Vung Tau Vietnam
55 U6 Vuohijärvi Fin.
54 U4 Vuolijoki Fin.
54 R3 Vuollerim Sweden
54 U3 Vuostimo Fin.
68 H4 Vurnary Rus. Fed.
103 D4 Vwawa Tanz.
84 C5 Vyara India
68 J3 Vyatka *r.* Rus. Fed.
68 E4 Vyaz'ma Rus. Fed.
68 G3 Vyazniki Rus. Fed.
69 H5 Vyazovka Rus. Fed.
68 D2 Vyborg Rus. Fed.
68 J2 Vychegda *r.* Rus. Fed.
68 H2 Vychegodskiy Rus. Fed.
68 C4 Vyerkhnyadzvinsk Belarus
68 D4 Vyetryna Belarus
68 E2 Vygozero, Ozero *l.* Rus. Fed.
68 G4 Vyksa Rus. Fed.
69 D6 Vylkove Ukr.
63 L6 Vynohradiv Ukr.
68 E3 Vypolzovo Rus. Fed.
68 D3 Vyritsa Rus. Fed.
59 D5 Vyrnwy, Lake *l.* U.K.
69 F6 Vyselki Rus. Fed.
68 G4 Vysha Rus. Fed.
69 D5 Vyshhorod Ukr.
68 E3 Vyshnevolotskaya Gryada *ridge* Rus. Fed.
68 E3 Vyshniy-Volochek Rus. Fed.
62 H6 Vyškov Czech Rep.
69 D5 Vystupovychi Ukr.
68 F2 Vytegra Rus. Fed.

W

100 B3 Wa Ghana
61 D3 Waal *r.* Neth.
22 B3 Wabakimi L. *l.* Can.
20 G3 Wabasca *r.* Can.
20 G3 Wabasca-Desmarais Can.
30 E5 Wabash U.S.A.
30 E5 Wabash *r.* U.S.A.
30 A3 Wabasha U.S.A.
31 E1 Wabatongushi Lake *l.* Can.
102 E3 Wabē Gestro *r.* Eth.
102 E3 Wabē Shebelē Wenz *r.* Eth.
21 K4 Wabowden Can.
22 C2 Wabuk Pt *pt* Can.
23 G3 Wabush Can.
23 G3 Wabush L. *l.* Can.
34 C2 Wabuska U.S.A.
29 D6 Waccasassa Bay *b.* U.S.A.
27 D6 Waco U.S.A.
79 K4 Wad Pak.
115 H6 Wadbilliga Nat. Park *nat. park* Austr.
101 D2 Waddān Libya
61 C1 Waddeneilanden *is* Neth.
61 D1 Waddenzee *chan.* Neth.
114 B4 Waddikee Austr.
20 D4 Waddington, Mt *mt* Can.
61 C2 Waddinxveen Neth.
116 E5 Waddy Pt *pt* Austr.
59 C7 Wadebridge U.K.
21 J4 Wadena Can.
26 E2 Wadena U.S.A.
101 F2 Wadi Halfa Sudan
101 F3 Wad Medani Sudan
34 C2 Wadsworth U.S.A.
88 G2 Wafangdian China
115 G5 Wagga Wagga Austr.
112 C6 Wagin Austr.
84 C2 Wah Pak.
Wāḩāt al Bahrīyah *see* Bahariya Oasis
Wāḩāt al Dākhilah *see* Dakhila Oasis
Wāḩāt al Farāfirah *see* Farafra Oasis
Wāḩāt al Khārijah *see* The Great Oasis
34 □1 Wahiawa U.S.A.
26 D3 Wahoo U.S.A.
26 D2 Wahpeton U.S.A.
35 F2 Wah Wah Mts *mts* U.S.A.
34 □1 Waialee U.S.A.
34 □1 Waialua U.S.A.
34 □1 Waialua Bay *b.* U.S.A.
34 □1 Waianae U.S.A.
34 □1 Waianae Ra. *mts* U.S.A.
117 D5 Waiau *r.* N.Z.
62 G7 Waidhofen an der Ybbs Austria
93 J6 Waigeo *i.* Indon.
117 E2 Waiharoa N.Z.
117 E2 Waiheke Island *i.* N.Z.

117 E2 Waihi N.Z.
117 E2 Waihou r. N.Z.
93 F8 Waikabubak Indon.
117 B6 Waikaia r. N.Z.
34 □1 Waikane U.S.A.
117 D5 Waikari N.Z.
117 E2 Waikato r. N.Z.
117 F2 Waikawa Pt pt N.Z.
114 C5 Waikerie Austr.
34 □1 Waikiki Beach beach U.S.A.
117 C6 Waikouaiti N.Z.
34 □2 Wailuku U.S.A.
117 D5 Waimakariri r. N.Z.
34 □1 Waimanalo U.S.A.
117 C4 Waimangaroa N.Z.
117 F3 Waimarama N.Z.
117 C6 Waimate N.Z.
34 □1 Waimea HI U.S.A.
84 D5 Wainganga r. India
93 G8 Waingapu Indon.
59 C7 Wainhouse Corner U.K.
21 G4 Wainwright Can.
117 E3 Waiouru N.Z.
117 E3 Waipa r. N.Z.
117 B7 Waipahi N.Z.
34 □1 Waipahu U.S.A.
117 F3 Waipaoa r. N.Z.
117 B7 Waipapa Pt pt N.Z.
117 D5 Waipara N.Z.
117 F3 Waipawa N.Z.
117 F3 Waipukurau N.Z.
117 F3 Wairakei N.Z.
117 E4 Wairarapa, L. l. N.Z.
117 D4 Wairau r. N.Z.
117 F3 Wairoa N.Z.
117 F3 Wairoa r. Hawke's Bay N.Z.
117 E1 Wairoa r. Northland N.Z.
117 F3 Waitahanui N.Z.
117 B6 Waitahuna N.Z.
117 E2 Waitakaruru N.Z.
117 C6 Waitaki r. N.Z.
117 E3 Waitara N.Z.
117 E2 Waitoa N.Z.
117 E2 Waiuku N.Z.
117 B7 Waiwera South N.Z.
89 F5 Waiyang China
91 E6 Wajima Japan
102 E3 Wajir Kenya
91 D7 Wakasa-wan b. Japan
117 B6 Wakatipu, Lake l. N.Z.
21 H4 Wakaw Can.
91 D7 Wakayama Japan
26 D4 WaKeeney U.S.A.
31 K3 Wakefield Can.
117 D4 Wakefield N.Z.
58 F4 Wakefield U.K.
30 C2 Wakefield MI U.S.A.
33 H4 Wakefield RI U.S.A.
32 E6 Wakefield VA U.S.A.
90 G4 Wakinosawa Japan
90 G2 Wakkanai Japan
105 J3 Wakkerstroom S. Africa
114 F5 Wakool Austr.
114 E5 Wakool r. Austr.
23 G2 Wakuach, Lac l. Can.
62 H5 Wałbrzych Pol.
115 J3 Walcha Austr.
62 E7 Walchensee l. Ger.
62 H4 Wałcz Pol.
33 F4 Walden U.S.A.
62 F6 Waldkraiburg Ger.
59 C7 Waldon r. U.K.
32 E5 Waldorf U.S.A.
56 E5 Wales div. U.K.
115 H3 Walgett Austr.
102 C4 Walikale Dem. Rep. Congo
30 B4 Walker IA U.S.A.
26 E2 Walker MN U.S.A.
34 C2 Walker r. U.S.A.
104 C7 Walker Bay b. S. Africa
29 E7 Walker Cay i. Bahamas
34 C2 Walker Lake l. U.S.A.
34 C4 Walker Pass pass U.S.A.
31 G3 Walkerton Can.
26 C2 Wall U.S.A.
24 C2 Wallace U.S.A.
31 F4 Wallaceburg Can.
115 J2 Wallangarra Austr.
114 B4 Wallaroo Austr.
59 D4 Wallasey U.K.
115 D5 Wallaville Austr.
116 G5 Walla Walla Austr.
24 C2 Walla Walla U.S.A.
104 B5 Wallekraal S. Africa
115 H5 Wallendbeen Austr.
33 F4 Wallenpaupack, Lake l. U.S.A.
59 F6 Wallingford U.K.
33 G4 Wallingford U.S.A.
111 J3 Wallis, Îles is Pac. Oc.
111 J3 Wallis and Futuna Is terr. Pac. Oc.
115 K4 Wallis L. b. Austr.
33 F6 Wallops I. i. U.S.A.
24 C2 Wallowa Mts mts U.S.A.
57 □ Walls U.K.
116 C6 Wallumbilla Austr.
21 H2 Walmsley Lake l. Can.
58 D3 Walney, Isle of i. U.K.
30 C5 Walnut U.S.A.
35 G4 Walnut Canyon National Monument res. U.S.A.
27 F4 Walnut Ridge U.S.A.
85 J3 Walong India
112 C6 Walpole-Nornalup National Park nat. park Austr.
59 F5 Walsall U.K.
25 F4 Walsenburg U.S.A.
116 A1 Walsh r. Austr.
29 D5 Walterboro U.S.A.
29 C6 Walter F. George Res. resr U.S.A.
114 F2 Walter's Ra. h. Austr.
31 J3 Waltham Can.
28 C4 Walton KY U.S.A.
33 F3 Walton NY U.S.A.
103 B6 Walvis Bay Namibia
12 K7 Walvis Ridge sea feature Atlantic Ocean
102 C3 Wamba Dem. Rep. Congo
93 K7 Wamena Indon.
84 B2 Wana Pak.
114 F2 Wanaaring Austr.
117 B6 Wanaka N.Z.
117 B6 Wanaka, L. l. N.Z.
89 E5 Wan'an China
31 G2 Wanapitei Lake l. Can.
33 F4 Wanaque Reservoir resr U.S.A.
114 D5 Wanbi Austr.
117 C6 Wanbrow, Cape c. N.Z.
114 D2 Wancoocha, Lake salt flat Austr.
90 C2 Wanda Shan mts China
118 B4 Wandel Sea Greenland
82 J6 Wanding China
116 C6 Wandoan Austr.
95 A1 Wang, Mae Nam r. Thai.
117 E3 Wanganui N.Z.
117 E3 Wanganui r. N.Z.
115 G6 Wangaratta Austr.
114 A5 Wangary Austr.
88 C3 Wangcang China
89 D4 Wangcheng China
88 F1 Wanghai Shan h. China
89 E4 Wangjiang China
89 C5 Wangmo China
87 N3 Wangqing China
84 B5 Wankaner India
102 E3 Wanlaweyn Somalia
89 E4 Wannian China
89 D7 Wanning China
88 E1 Wanquan China
61 D3 Wanroij Neth.
89 D6 Wanshan Qundao is China
117 F4 Wanstead N.Z.
59 F6 Wantage U.K.
31 G2 Wanup Can.
89 C4 Wanxian China
89 C4 Wanxian China
88 C3 Wanyuan China
89 E4 Wanzai China
32 A4 Wapakoneta U.S.A.
30 B5 Wapello U.S.A.
22 C3 Wapikopa L. l. Can.
20 F4 Wapiti r. Can.
27 F4 Wappapello, L. resr U.S.A.
30 A5 Wapsipinicon r. U.S.A.
88 B3 Waqên China
84 A4 Warah Pak.
83 E7 Warangal India
114 F6 Waranga Reservoir resr Austr.
84 E5 Waraseoni India
115 F8 Waratah Austr.
115 F7 Waratah B. b. Austr.
112 E5 Warburton Austr.
114 B1 Warburton watercourse Austr.
21 G2 Warburton Bay l. Can.
116 B5 Ward watercourse Austr.
117 A6 Ward, Mt mt Southland N.Z.
117 B5 Ward, Mt mt West Coast N.Z.
114 B5 Wardang I. i. Austr.
105 H3 Warden S. Africa
84 D5 Wardha India
84 D6 Wardha r. India
20 D3 Ware Can.
33 G3 Ware U.S.A.
59 E7 Wareham U.K.
33 H4 Wareham U.S.A.
61 D4 Waremme Belgium
62 F4 Waren Ger.
62 C5 Warendorf Ger.
115 J2 Warialda Austr.
95 C2 Warin Chamrap Thai.
117 E2 Warkworth N.Z.
58 F2 Warkworth U.K.
21 H4 Warman Can.
104 C4 Warmbad Namibia
105 H2 Warmbad S. Africa
59 E6 Warminster U.K.
33 F4 Warminster U.S.A.
61 C2 Warmond Neth.
34 D2 Warm Springs NV U.S.A.
32 D5 Warm Springs VA U.S.A.
104 D6 Warmwaterberg mts S. Africa
33 H3 Warner U.S.A.
24 B3 Warner Mts mts U.S.A.
29 D5 Warner Robins U.S.A.
42 F7 Warnes Bol.
115 K2 Warning, Mt mt Austr.
84 D5 Warora India
115 J1 Warra Austr.
114 E6 Warracknabeal Austr.
115 J5 Warragamba Reservoir resr Austr.
115 F7 Warragul Austr.
114 C2 Warrakalanna, Lake salt flat Austr.
114 A4 Warramboo Austr.
115 G2 Warrambool r. Austr.
112 D4 Warrawagine Austr.
113 J5 Warrego r. Austr.
116 A5 Warrego Ra. h. Austr.
115 G3 Warren Austr.
31 G2 Warren Can.
27 E5 Warren AR U.S.A.
31 F4 Warren MI U.S.A.
26 D1 Warren MN U.S.A.
32 C4 Warren OH U.S.A.
32 D4 Warren PA U.S.A.
32 C4 Warrendale U.S.A.
60 E3 Warrenpoint U.K.
26 E4 Warrensburg MO U.S.A.
33 G3 Warrensburg NY U.S.A.
104 F4 Warrenton S. Africa
32 E5 Warrenton U.S.A.
100 C4 Warri Nigeria
117 C6 Warrington N.Z.
59 E4 Warrington U.K.
29 C6 Warrington U.S.A.
114 C3 Warriota watercourse Austr.
114 E7 Warrnambool Austr.
26 E1 Warroad U.S.A.
114 A5 Warrow Austr.
115 H3 Warrumbungle Ra. mts Austr.
114 D2 Warry Warry watercourse Austr.
84 B2 Warsak Dam dam Pak.
63 K4 Warsaw Pol.
30 E5 Warsaw IN U.S.A.
26 E4 Warsaw MO U.S.A.
32 D3 Warsaw NY U.S.A.
32 E6 Warsaw VA U.S.A.
Warszawa see Warsaw
62 G4 Warta r. Pol.
115 K2 Warwick Austr.
59 F5 Warwick U.K.
33 F4 Warwick NY U.S.A.
33 H4 Warwick RI U.S.A.
25 E4 Wasatch Range mts U.S.A.
105 J4 Wasbank S. Africa
34 C4 Wasco U.S.A.
26 E2 Waseca U.S.A.
30 C5 Washburn IL U.S.A.
33 J1 Washburn ME U.S.A.
26 C2 Washburn ND U.S.A.
30 B2 Washburn WV U.S.A.
84 D5 Wāshīm India
32 E5 Washington DC U.S.A.
29 D5 Washington GA U.S.A.
30 B5 Washington IA U.S.A.
30 C5 Washington IL U.S.A.
28 C4 Washington IN U.S.A.
26 F4 Washington MO U.S.A.
29 E5 Washington NC U.S.A.
33 F4 Washington NJ U.S.A.
32 C4 Washington PA U.S.A.
35 F3 Washington UT U.S.A.
24 B2 Washington div. U.S.A.
119 B5 Washington, C. c. Antarctica
33 H2 Washington, Mt mt U.S.A.
32 B5 Washington Court House U.S.A.
30 D3 Washington Island i. U.S.A.
27 D5 Washita r. U.S.A.
81 L5 Wasit Iraq
22 E3 Waskaganish Can.
21 K3 Waskaiowaka Lake l. Can.
104 C3 Wasser Namibia
34 C2 Wassuk Range mts U.S.A.
22 E4 Waswanipi, Lac l. Can.
93 G7 Watampone Indon.
33 G4 Waterbury CT U.S.A.
33 G2 Waterbury VT U.S.A.
21 H3 Waterbury Lake l. Can.
60 D5 Waterford Rep. of Ireland
32 D4 Waterford U.S.A.
60 E5 Waterford Harbour harbour Rep. of Ireland
60 C5 Watergrasshill Rep. of Ireland
21 H4 Waterhen r. Can.
31 G4 Waterloo Can.
30 A4 Waterloo IA U.S.A.
33 H3 Waterloo ME U.S.A.
32 E3 Waterloo NY U.S.A.
30 C4 Waterloo WV U.S.A.
59 F7 Waterlooville U.K.
105 H1 Waterpoort S. Africa
30 C2 Watersmeet U.S.A.
20 G5 Waterton Lakes Nat. Park nat. park Can.
33 E3 Watertown NY U.S.A.
26 D2 Watertown SD U.S.A.
30 C4 Watertown WV U.S.A.
105 J2 Waterval-Boven S. Africa
114 C4 Watervale Austr.
33 J2 Waterville U.S.A.
21 G3 Waterways Can.
31 G4 Watford Can.
59 G6 Watford U.K.
26 C2 Watford City U.S.A.
21 J3 Wathaman r. Can.
32 E3 Watkins Glen U.S.A.
Watling i. see San Salvador
27 D5 Watonga U.S.A.
21 H4 Watrous Can.
102 C3 Watsa Dem. Rep. Congo
30 D5 Watseka U.S.A.
102 C4 Watsi Kengo Dem. Rep. Congo
21 J4 Watson Can.
20 D2 Watson Lake Can.
34 B3 Watsonville U.S.A.
20 F3 Watt, Mt h. Can.
57 E2 Watten U.K.
57 E2 Watten, Loch l. U.K.
21 J2 Watterson Lake l. Can.
114 A2 Wattiwarriganna watercourse Austr.
59 H5 Watton U.K.
30 C2 Watton U.S.A.
93 J7 Watubela, Kepulauan is Indon.
110 E2 Wau P.N.G.
101 E4 Wau Sudan
30 D3 Waucedah U.S.A.
115 K3 Wauchope Austr.
29 D7 Wauchula U.S.A.
30 D4 Waukegan U.S.A.
30 C4 Waukesha U.S.A.
30 B4 Waukon U.S.A.
30 C3 Waupaca U.S.A.
30 C4 Waupun U.S.A.
27 D5 Waurika U.S.A.
30 C3 Wausau U.S.A.
32 A4 Wauseon U.S.A.
30 C3 Wautoma U.S.A.
30 C4 Wauwatosa U.S.A.
59 J5 Waveney r. U.K.
30 A4 Waverly IA U.S.A.
32 B5 Waverly OH U.S.A.
29 C4 Waverly TN U.S.A.
32 E6 Waverly VA U.S.A.
30 E1 Wawa Can.
100 C4 Wawa Nigeria
30 E5 Wawasee, Lake l. U.S.A.
93 L8 Wawoi r. P.N.G.
34 C3 Wawona U.S.A.
27 D5 Waxahachie U.S.A.
29 D6 Waycross U.S.A.
32 B6 Wayland KY U.S.A.
30 B5 Wayland MO U.S.A.
26 D3 Wayne U.S.A.
29 D5 Waynesboro GA U.S.A.
27 F6 Waynesboro MS U.S.A.
32 E5 Waynesboro PA U.S.A.
32 D5 Waynesboro VA U.S.A.
32 C5 Waynesburg U.S.A.
27 E4 Waynesville U.S.A.
27 D4 Waynoka U.S.A.
101 D3 Waza, Parc National de nat. park Cameroon
84 C2 Wazirabad Pak.
100 C3 W du Niger, Parcs Nationaux du nat. park Niger
22 B3 Weagamow L. l. Can.
58 E3 Wear r. U.K.
113 J3 Weary B. b. Austr.
27 D5 Weatherford U.S.A.
24 B3 Weaverville U.S.A.
31 G2 Webbwood Can.
22 C3 Webequie Can.
20 D3 Weber, Mt mt Can.
102 E3 Webi Shabeelle r. Somalia
33 H3 Webster MA U.S.A.
26 D2 Webster SD U.S.A.
30 A3 Webster WV U.S.A.
26 E3 Webster City U.S.A.
32 C5 Webster Springs U.S.A.
44 D8 Weddell I. i. Falkland Is
119 B2 Weddell Sea sea Antarctica
114 E6 Wedderburn Austr.
24 B3 Weed U.S.A.
32 D4 Weedville U.S.A.
115 H2 Weemelah Austr.
105 J4 Weenen S. Africa
61 F1 Weener Ger.
61 D3 Weert Neth.
115 G4 Weethalle Austr.
115 H3 Wee Waa Austr.
63 K3 Węgorzewo Pol.
88 B2 Wei r. Henan China
88 D3 Wei r. Shaanxi China
88 E1 Weichang China
88 F2 Weifang China
88 G2 Weihai China
88 E3 Weihui China
115 G2 Weilmoringle Austr.
62 E5 Weimar Ger.
88 C3 Weinan China
89 B5 Weining China
113 H2 Weipa Austr.
115 H2 Weir r. Austr.
21 L3 Weir River Can.
32 C4 Weirton U.S.A.
24 C2 Weiser U.S.A.
88 E3 Weishan China
88 E3 Weishan Hu l. China
88 E3 Weishi China
62 E6 Weißenburg in Bayern Ger.
29 C5 Weiss L. l. U.S.A.
104 C2 Weissrand Mts mts Namibia
89 B5 Weixin China
88 B3 Weiyuan Gansu China
89 B4 Weiyuan Sichuan China
62 G7 Weiz Austria
89 C6 Weizhou Dao i. China
62 J3 Wejherowo Pol.
21 K4 Wekusko Can.
21 K4 Wekusko Lake l. Can.
32 C6 Welch U.S.A.
33 H2 Weld U.S.A.
102 D2 Weldiya Eth.
34 C4 Weldon U.S.A.
102 D3 Welk'ītē Eth.
105 G3 Welkom S. Africa
31 H4 Welland Can.
59 G5 Welland r. U.K.
31 H4 Welland Canal canal Can.
31 G4 Wellesley Can.
113 G3 Wellesley Is is Austr.
20 B2 Wellesley Lake l. Can.
33 H4 Wellfleet U.S.A.
59 G5 Wellingborough U.K.
115 H4 Wellington N.S.W. Austr.
114 C5 Wellington S.A. Austr.
117 E4 Wellington N.Z.
104 C6 Wellington S. Africa
59 E5 Wellington Eng. U.K.
59 D7 Wellington Eng. U.K.
24 F3 Wellington CO U.S.A.
27 D4 Wellington KS U.S.A.
34 C2 Wellington NV U.S.A.
32 B4 Wellington OH U.S.A.
27 C5 Wellington TX U.S.A.
35 G2 Wellington UT U.S.A.
44 A7 Wellington, I. i. Chile
115 G7 Wellington, L. l. Austr.
30 B5 Wellman U.S.A.
20 E4 Wells Can.
59 E6 Wells U.K.
24 D3 Wells NV U.S.A.
33 F3 Wells NY U.S.A.
112 D5 Wells, L. salt flat Austr.
32 E4 Wellsboro U.S.A.
117 E2 Wellsford N.Z.
20 E4 Wells Gray Prov. Park res. Can.
59 H5 Wells-next-the-Sea U.K.
32 B5 Wellston U.S.A.
32 E3 Wellsville U.S.A.
35 E5 Wellton U.S.A.
62 G6 Wels Austria
33 K2 Welshpool Can.
59 D5 Welshpool U.K.
59 G6 Welwyn Garden City U.K.
59 E5 Wem U.K.
105 H4 Wembesi S. Africa
20 F3 Wembley Can.
22 E3 Wemindji Can.
29 E7 Wemyss Bight Bahamas
88 F3 Wen r. China
24 B2 Wenatchee U.S.A.
89 D7 Wenchang China
89 F5 Wencheng China
100 B4 Wenchi Ghana
88 B4 Wenchuan China
35 F5 Wenden U.S.A.
88 G2 Wendeng China
102 D3 Wendo Eth.
24 D3 Wendover U.S.A.
31 F2 Wenebegon Lake l. Can.
89 C5 Weng'an China
89 E5 Wengyuan China
88 B4 Wenjiang China
89 F4 Wenling China
42 □ Wenman, Isla i. Ecuador
30 C5 Wenona U.S.A.
89 B6 Wenshan China
59 H5 Wensum r. U.K.
114 D5 Wentworth Austr.
33 H3 Wentworth U.S.A.
88 B3 Wenxian China
89 F5 Wenzhou China
105 G4 Wepener S. Africa
104 E2 Werda Botswana
62 F4 Werder Ger.
20 C2 Wernecke Mountains mts Can.
114 D5 Werrimull Austr.
115 J3 Werris Creek Austr.
62 D6 Wertheim Ger.
62 C5 Wesel Ger.
62 D4 Weser r. Ger.
26 C4 Weskan U.S.A.
31 J3 Weslemkoon Lake l. Can.
33 K2 Wesley U.S.A.
23 K4 Wesleyville Can.
113 G2 Wessel, C. c. Austr.
113 G2 Wessel Is is Austr.
105 H3 Wesselton S. Africa
26 D2 Wessington Springs U.S.A.
30 C4 West Allis U.S.A.
119 A4 West Antarctica reg. Antarctica
13 L5 West Australian Basin sea feature Indian Ocean
13 L6 West Australian Ridge sea feature Indian Ocean
84 B5 West Banas r. India
80 E5 West Bank terr. Asia
23 J3 West Bay Can.
27 F6 West Bay b. U.S.A.
30 C4 West Bend U.S.A.
85 F5 West Bengal div. India
31 E3 West Branch U.S.A.
59 F5 West Bromwich U.K.
33 H3 Westbrook U.S.A.
115 G8 Westbury Austr.
59 E6 Westbury U.K.
115 G5 Westby Austr.
30 B4 Westby U.S.A.
33 F5 West Chester U.S.A.
33 G2 West Danville U.S.A.
31 F3 West Duck Island i. Can.
29 E7 West End Bahamas
34 D4 Westend U.S.A.
29 E7 West End Pt pt Bahamas
62 D3 Westerland Ger.
33 H4 Westerly U.S.A.
21 H1 Western r. Can.
112 D4 Western Australia div. Austr.
104 D6 Western Cape div. S. Africa
78 B4 Western Desert des. Egypt
83 D8 Western Ghats mts India
114 F7 Western Port b. Austr.
96 Western Sahara terr. Africa
61 B3 Westerschelde est. Neth.
44 D8 West Falkland i. Falkland Is
26 D2 West Fargo U.S.A.
30 D5 Westfield IN U.S.A.
33 G3 Westfield MA U.S.A.
33 K1 Westfield ME U.S.A.
32 D3 Westfield NY U.S.A.
61 E1 Westgat chan. Neth.
116 B6 Westgate Austr.
33 K2 West Grand Lake l. U.S.A.
57 F3 Westhill U.K.
26 C1 Westhope U.S.A.
119 D5 West Ice Shelf ice feature Antarctica
32 B5 West Lancaster U.S.A.
117 B5 Westland National Park nat. park N.Z.
59 J5 Westleton U.K.
34 B3 Westley U.S.A.
32 B6 West Liberty KY U.S.A.
32 B4 West Liberty OH U.S.A.
57 E5 West Linton U.K.
57 B2 West Loch Roag b. U.K.
20 G4 Westlock Can.
31 G4 West Lorne Can.
27 F5 West Memphis U.S.A.
32 E5 Westminster MD U.S.A.
29 D5 Westminster SC U.S.A.
32 C5 Weston U.S.A.
59 E6 Weston-super-Mare U.K.
33 F5 Westover U.S.A.
29 D7 West Palm Beach U.S.A.
27 F4 West Plains U.S.A.
114 A5 West Point pt S.A. Austr.
115 F8 West Point pt Tas. Austr.
27 F5 West Point MS U.S.A.
33 F4 West Point NY U.S.A.
31 J3 Westport Can.
117 C4 Westport N.Z.
60 B4 Westport Rep. of Ireland
34 A2 Westport U.S.A.
21 J4 Westray Can.
57 E1 Westray i. U.K.
31 G2 Westree Can.
61 F5 Westrich reg. Ger.
20 E4 West Road r. Can.
115 G7 West Sister I. i. Austr.
33 H2 West Stewartstown U.S.A.
61 D1 West-Terschelling Neth.
33 H4 West Tisbury U.S.A.
33 G2 West Topsham U.S.A.
33 G3 West Townshend U.S.A.
30 B4 West Union IA U.S.A.
32 B5 West Union OH U.S.A.
32 C5 West Union WV U.S.A.
30 D5 Westville U.S.A.
32 C5 West Virginia div. U.S.A.
34 C2 West Walker r. U.S.A.
116 D4 Westwood Austr.
34 B1 Westwood U.S.A.
115 G4 West Wyalong Austr.
24 E2 West Yellowstone U.S.A.
61 C2 Westzaan Neth.
93 H8 Wetar i. Indon.
20 G4 Wetaskiwin Can.
30 D2 Wetmore U.S.A.
62 D5 Wetzlar Ger.
110 E2 Wewak P.N.G.
60 E5 Wexford Rep. of Ireland
21 H4 Weyakwin Can.
30 C3 Weyauwega U.S.A.
59 G6 Weybridge U.K.
21 J5 Weyburn Can.
59 E7 Weymouth U.K.
33 H3 Weymouth U.S.A.
117 F2 Whakatane N.Z.
117 F3 Whakatane r. N.Z.
95 A3 Whale B. b. Myanmar
20 B3 Whale B. b. U.S.A.
29 E7 Whale Cay i. Bahamas
21 L2 Whale Cove Can.
56 F1 Whalsay i. U.K.
57 □ Whalsay i. U.K.
117 E2 Whangamata N.Z.
117 E3 Whangamomona N.Z.
117 E1 Whangarei N.Z.
22 E2 Whapmagoostui Can.
58 F4 Wharfe r. U.K.
31 F2 Wharncliffe Can.
21 J2 Wharton Lake l. Can.
30 A5 What Cheer U.S.A.
20 F2 Wha Ti Can.
24 F3 Wheatland U.S.A.
30 C5 Wheaton U.S.A.
25 F4 Wheeler Peak summit NM U.S.A.
35 E2 Wheeler Peak summit NV U.S.A.
32 C4 Wheeling U.S.A.
47 E2 Wheelwright Arg.
58 E3 Whernside h. U.K.
114 A5 Whidbey, Point pt Austr.
24 B3 Whiskeytown-Shasta-Trinity Nat. Recreation Area res. U.S.A.
57 E5 Whitburn U.K.
31 H4 Whitby Can.
58 G3 Whitby U.K.
59 E5 Whitchurch U.K.
20 A2 White r. Can./U.S.A.
27 E4 White r. AR U.S.A.
35 G5 White r. AZ U.S.A.
24 E3 White r. CO U.S.A.
28 C4 White r. IN U.S.A.
30 D4 White r. MI U.S.A.
35 E2 White r. NV U.S.A.
26 C3 White r. SD U.S.A.
30 B2 White r. WV U.S.A.
112 E4 White, L. salt flat Austr.
23 J3 White Bay b. Can.
26 C2 White Butte mt U.S.A.
114 E3 White Cliffs Austr.
30 E4 White Cloud U.S.A.
20 F4 Whitecourt Can.
30 A2 Whiteface Lake l. U.S.A.
33 H2 Whitefield U.S.A.
31 G2 Whitefish Can.
24 D1 Whitefish U.S.A.
30 D3 Whitefish r. U.S.A.
21 H2 Whitefish Lake l. Can.

30 E2 Whitefish Pt *pt* U.S.A.
60 D5 Whitehall Rep. of Ireland
57 F1 Whitehall U.K.
33 G3 Whitehall *NY* U.S.A.
30 B3 Whitehall *WV* U.S.A.
58 D3 Whitehaven U.K.
60 F3 Whitehead U.K.
59 G6 Whitehill U.K.
20 B2 Whitehorse Can.
59 F6 White Horse, Vale of *v.* U.K.
35 E1 White Horse Pass *pass* U.S.A.
117 F2 White I. *i.* N.Z.
27 E6 White L. *l.* *LA* U.S.A.
30 D4 White L. *l.* *MI* U.S.A.
115 H7 Whitemark Austr.
113 J8 Whitemark Austr.
33 H2 White Mountains *mts* U.S.A.
34 C3 White Mt Peak *summit* U.S.A.
78 C7 White Nile *r.* Sudan/Uganda
104 C1 White Nossob *watercourse* Namibia
35 E2 White Pine Range *mts* U.S.A.
33 G4 White Plains U.S.A.
22 C4 White River Can.
35 H5 Whiteriver U.S.A.
33 G3 White River Junction U.S.A.
35 E2 White River Valley *v.* U.S.A.
116 A1 White Rock Austr.
35 E2 White Rock Peak *summit* U.S.A.
25 F5 White Sands Nat. Mon. *res.* U.S.A.
32 B6 Whitesburg U.S.A.
76 E3 White Sea *g.* Rus. Fed.
21 K4 Whiteshell Prov. Park *res.* Can.
24 E2 White Sulphur Springs *MT* U.S.A.
32 C6 White Sulphur Springs *WV* U.S.A.
29 E5 Whiteville U.S.A.
100 B4 White Volta *r.* Ghana
30 C4 Whitewater U.S.A.
35 H5 Whitewater Baldy *mt* U.S.A.
22 C3 Whitewater L. *l.* Can.
21 J4 Whitewood Can.
115 G6 Whitfield Austr.
59 J6 Whitfield U.K.
57 D6 Whithorn U.K.
117 E2 Whitianga N.Z.
33 K2 Whiting U.S.A.
59 C6 Whitland U.K.
58 F2 Whitley Bay U.K.
29 D5 Whitmire U.S.A.
31 H3 Whitney Can.
34 C3 Whitney, Mt *mt* U.S.A.
33 K2 Whitneyville U.S.A.
59 J6 Whitstable U.K.
116 C3 Whitsunday Group *is* Austr.
116 C3 Whitsunday I. *i.* Austr.
116 C3 Whitsunday Pass. *chan.* Austr.
114 F6 Whittlesea Austr.
59 G5 Whittlesey U.K.
115 G5 Whitton Austr.
21 H2 Wholdaia Lake *l.* Can.
35 F5 Why U.S.A.
114 B4 Whyalla Austr.
95 A1 Wiang Phran Thai.
95 B1 Wiang Sa Thai.
31 G3 Wiarton Can.
61 B3 Wichelen Belgium
27 D4 Wichita U.S.A.
27 D5 Wichita Falls U.S.A.
27 D5 Wichita Mts *mts* U.S.A.
57 E2 Wick U.K.
35 F5 Wickenburg U.S.A.
59 H6 Wickford U.K.
115 E7 Wickham, C. *pt* Austr.
60 E5 Wicklow Rep. of Ireland
60 F5 Wicklow Head *hd* Rep. of Ireland
60 E5 Wicklow Mountains *mts* Rep. of Ireland
60 E4 Wicklow Mountains National Park *nat. park* Rep. of Ireland
116 E5 Wide B. *b.* Austr.
115 G2 Widgeegoara *watercourse* Austr.
59 E4 Widnes U.K.
61 F4 Wiehl Ger.
63 J5 Wieluń Pol.
Wien *see* Vienna
62 H7 Wiener Neustadt Austria
61 C2 Wieringermeer Polder *reclaimed land* Neth.
62 D5 Wiesbaden Ger.
62 J3 Wieżyca *h.* Pol.
58 E4 Wigan U.K.
27 F6 Wiggins U.S.A.
59 F7 Wight, Isle of *i.* U.K.
21 H2 Wignes Lake *l.* Can.
59 F5 Wigston U.K.
58 D3 Wigton U.K.
57 D6 Wigtown U.K.
57 D6 Wigtown Bay *b.* U.K.
61 D3 Wijchen Neth.
61 C3 Wijnegem Belgium
35 F4 Wikieup U.S.A.
31 G3 Wikwemikong Can.
24 C2 Wilbur U.S.A.
114 E3 Wilcannia Austr.
21 J4 Wildcat Hill Wilderness Park *res.* Can.
34 D2 Wildcat Peak *summit* U.S.A.
105 H5 Wild Coast *coastal area* S. Africa
30 C1 Wild Goose Can.
20 F4 Wildhay *r.* Can.
20 A2 Wild Rice Lake *l.* U.S.A.
62 E7 Wildspitze *mt* Austria
29 D6 Wildwood *FL* U.S.A.
33 F5 Wildwood *NJ* U.S.A.
105 H3 Wilge *r.* *Free State* S. Africa
105 H2 Wilge *r.* *Gauteng/Mpumalanga* S. Africa
114 A3 Wilgena Austr.
32 C4 Wilhelm, Lake *l.* U.S.A.
110 E2 Wilhelm, Mt *mt* P.N.G.
62 D4 Wilhelmshaven Ger.
33 F4 Wilkes-Barre U.S.A.
119 B6 Wilkes Land *reg.* Antarctica
21 H4 Wilkie Can.
119 B2 Wilkins Ice Shelf *ice feature* Antarctica
20 D3 Will, Mt *mt* Can.
24 B2 Willamette *r.* U.S.A.
59 D7 Willand U.K.
114 F4 Willandra Billabong *watercourse* Austr.
24 B1 Willapa B. *b.* U.S.A.
32 B4 Willard U.S.A.
33 F5 Willards U.S.A.
35 H5 Willcox U.S.A.
61 C3 Willebroek Belgium
37 L6 Willemstad Neth. Ant.
21 H3 William *r.* Can.
114 E6 William, Mt *mt* Austr.
114 B2 William Cr. Austr.
35 F4 Williams *AZ* U.S.A.
34 A2 Williams *CA* U.S.A.
30 A5 Williamsburg *IA* U.S.A.
32 A6 Williamsburg *KY* U.S.A.
30 E3 Williamsburg *MI* U.S.A.
32 E6 Williamsburg *VA* U.S.A.
29 E7 Williams I. *i.* Bahamas
20 E4 Williams Lake Can.
23 H1 William Smith, Cap *c.* Can.
32 E3 Williamson *NY* U.S.A.
32 B6 Williamson *WV* U.S.A.
30 D5 Williamsport *IN* U.S.A.
32 E4 Williamsport *PA* U.S.A.
29 E5 Williamston U.S.A.
33 G3 Williamstown *MA* U.S.A.
33 F3 Williamstown *NY* U.S.A.
32 C5 Williamstown *WV* U.S.A.
33 G4 Willimantic U.S.A.
116 D1 Willis Group *atolls* Coral Sea Is Terr.
104 D5 Williston S. Africa
29 D6 Williston *FL* U.S.A.
26 C1 Williston *ND* U.S.A.
20 E3 Williston Lake *l.* Can.
59 D6 Williton U.K.
34 A2 Willits U.S.A.
26 E2 Willmar U.S.A.
20 F4 Willmore Wilderness Prov. Park *res.* Can.
114 B3 Willochra *watercourse* Austr.
20 E4 Willow *r.* Can.
21 H5 Willow Bunch Can.
35 F4 Willow Hill U.S.A.
20 F2 Willow Lake *l.* Can.
104 E6 Willowmore S. Africa
30 C3 Willow Reservoir *resr* U.S.A.
34 A2 Willows U.S.A.
27 F4 Willow Springs U.S.A.
115 J3 Willow Tree Austr.
105 H6 Willowvale S. Africa
112 E4 Wills, L. *salt flat* Austr.
33 G2 Willsboro U.S.A.
114 C5 Willunga Austr.
114 C4 Wilmington Austr.
33 F5 Wilmington *DE* U.S.A.
29 E5 Wilmington *NC* U.S.A.
32 B5 Wilmington *OH* U.S.A.
33 G3 Wilmington *VT* U.S.A.
59 E4 Wilmslow U.K.
114 C3 Wilpena *watercourse* Austr.
26 D4 Wilson *KS* U.S.A.
29 E5 Wilson *NC* U.S.A.
25 F4 Wilson, Mt *mt CO* U.S.A.
35 E2 Wilson, Mt *mt NV* U.S.A.
26 D4 Wilson Res. *resr* U.S.A.
33 H2 Wilsons Mills U.S.A.
115 G7 Wilson's Promontory *pen.* Austr.
115 G7 Wilson's Promontory Nat. Park *nat. park* Austr.
30 B5 Wilton *IA* U.S.A.
33 H2 Wilton *ME* U.S.A.
61 D5 Wiltz Lux.
112 D5 Wiluna Austr.
59 J7 Wimereux France
114 E6 Wimmera *r.* Austr.
30 D5 Winamac U.S.A.
116 A6 Winbin *watercourse* Austr.
105 G4 Winburg S. Africa
59 E6 Wincanton U.K.
33 G3 Winchendon U.S.A.
22 E4 Winchester Can.
59 F6 Winchester U.K.
30 B6 Winchester *IL* U.S.A.
35 C5 Winchester *IN* U.S.A.
32 A6 Winchester *KY* U.S.A.
33 G3 Winchester *NH* U.S.A.
29 C5 Winchester *TN* U.S.A.
32 D5 Winchester *VA* U.S.A.
24 E3 Wind *r.* U.S.A.
114 B3 Windabout, L. *salt flat* Austr.
26 C3 Wind Cave Nat. Park *nat. park* U.S.A.
58 E3 Windermere U.K.
58 E3 Windermere *l.* U.K.
103 B6 Windhoek Namibia
26 E3 Windom U.S.A.
113 H5 Windorah Austr.
35 H4 Window Rock U.S.A.
30 D4 Wind Pt *pt* U.S.A.
24 E3 Wind River Range *mts* U.S.A.
59 F6 Windrush *r.* U.K.
115 J4 Windsor Austr.
23 J4 Windsor *Nfld and Lab.* Can.
23 H5 Windsor *N.S.* Can.
31 F4 Windsor *Ont.* Can.
23 F4 Windsor *Que.* Can.
59 G6 Windsor U.K.
33 G4 Windsor *CT* U.S.A.
29 E5 Windsor *NC* U.S.A.
33 F3 Windsor *NY* U.S.A.
32 E6 Windsor *VA* U.S.A.
33 G3 Windsor *VT* U.S.A.
33 G4 Windsor Locks U.S.A.
37 M5 Windward Islands *is* Caribbean Sea
37 K5 Windward Passage *chan.* Cuba/Haiti
29 C5 Winfield *AL* U.S.A.
30 B5 Winfield *IA* U.S.A.
27 D4 Winfield *KS* U.S.A.
58 F3 Wingate U.K.
115 J3 Wingen Austr.
115 K3 Wingham Austr.
31 G4 Wingham Can.
22 C2 Winisk Can.
22 C2 Winisk *r.* Can.
22 C3 Winisk L. *l.* Can.
22 C3 Winisk River Provincial Park *res.* Can.
95 A2 Winkana Myanmar
21 K5 Winkler Can.
33 J2 Winn U.S.A.
100 B4 Winneba Ghana
30 C3 Winnebago, Lake *l.* U.S.A.
30 C3 Winneconne U.S.A.
24 C3 Winnemucca U.S.A.
34 C1 Winnemucca Lake *l.* U.S.A.
26 D3 Winner U.S.A.
27 E6 Winnfield U.S.A.
26 E2 Winnibigoshish L. *l.* U.S.A.
21 K5 Winnipeg Can.
21 K4 Winnipeg *r.* Can.
21 K4 Winnipeg, Lake *l.* Can.
21 J4 Winnipegosis Can.
21 J4 Winnipegosis, Lake *l.* Can.
33 H3 Winnipesaukee, L. *l.* U.S.A.
27 F5 Winnsboro U.S.A.
35 G4 Winona *AZ* U.S.A.
30 C2 Winona *MI* U.S.A.
30 B3 Winona *MN* U.S.A.
27 F5 Winona *MS* U.S.A.
33 G2 Winooski U.S.A.
33 G2 Winooski *r.* U.S.A.
61 F1 Winschoten Neth.
59 E4 Winsford U.K.
35 G4 Winslow U.S.A.
33 G4 Winsted U.S.A.
29 D4 Winston-Salem U.S.A.
29 D6 Winter Haven U.S.A.
33 J2 Winterport U.S.A.
34 B2 Winters U.S.A.
61 E3 Winterswijk Neth.
62 D7 Winterthur Switz.
105 H4 Winterton S. Africa
33 J1 Winterville U.S.A.
33 J2 Winthrop U.S.A.
113 H4 Winton Austr.
117 B7 Winton N.Z.
59 G5 Winwick U.K.
114 C4 Wirrabara Austr.
59 D4 Wirral *pen.* U.K.
114 B3 Wirraminna Austr.
114 D6 Wirrega Austr.
114 A4 Wirrulla Austr.
59 H5 Wisbech U.K.
33 J2 Wiscasset U.S.A.
30 C3 Wisconsin *div.* U.S.A.
30 B4 Wisconsin *r.* U.S.A.
30 C4 Wisconsin, Lake *l.* U.S.A.
30 C4 Wisconsin Dells U.S.A.
30 C3 Wisconsin Rapids U.S.A.
32 B6 Wise U.S.A.
57 E5 Wishaw U.K.
63 J4 Wisła *r.* Pol.
62 E4 Wismar Ger.
59 J7 Wissant France
30 B3 Wissota L. *l.* U.S.A.
20 D4 Wistaria Can.
105 H2 Witbank S. Africa
104 C2 Witbooisvlei Namibia
59 H6 Witham U.K.
59 G4 Witham *r.* U.K.
33 G2 Witherbee U.S.A.
58 H4 Withernsea U.K.
113 G5 Witjira National Park *nat. park* Austr.
59 F6 Witney U.K.
105 J2 Witrivier S. Africa
105 G5 Witteberg *mts* S. Africa
30 C3 Wittenberg U.S.A.
62 E4 Wittenberge Ger.
62 E4 Wittenburg Ger.
64 H3 Wittenheim France
62 C6 Wittlich Ger.
61 F1 Wittmund Ger.
62 F4 Wittstock Ger.
110 E2 Witu Is *is* P.N.G.
103 B6 Witvlei Namibia
115 K1 Wivenhoe, Lake *l.* Austr.
62 J3 Władysławowo Pol.
63 J4 Włocławek Pol.
33 H2 Woburn Can.
115 G6 Wodonga Austr.
61 D5 Wœvre, Forêt de *forest* France
93 J8 Wokam *i.* Indon.
90 B1 Woken *r.* China
85 H4 Wokha India
59 G6 Woking U.K.
59 G6 Wokingham U.K.
30 D5 Wolcott *IN* U.S.A.
32 E3 Wolcott *NY* U.S.A.
20 C2 Wolf *r.* Can.
30 C3 Wolf *r.* U.S.A.
42 □ Wolf, Volcán *vol.* Ecuador
24 D2 Wolf Creek U.S.A.
25 F4 Wolf Creek Pass *pass* U.S.A.
33 H3 Wolfeboro U.S.A.
31 J3 Wolfe I. *i.* Can.
62 E4 Wolfenbüttel Ger.
20 C2 Wolf Lake *l.* Can.
24 F1 Wolf Point U.S.A.
62 G7 Wolfsberg Austria
62 E4 Wolfsburg Ger.
23 H4 Wolfville Can.
62 F3 Wolgast Ger.
62 G4 Wolin Pol.
44 C9 Wollaston, Islas *is* Chile
21 J3 Wollaston Lake Can.
21 J3 Wollaston Lake *l.* Can.
115 J5 Wollongong Austr.
105 F3 Wolmaransstad S. Africa
114 D6 Wolseley Austr.
104 C6 Wolseley S. Africa
58 F3 Wolsingham U.K.
61 E2 Wolvega Neth.
59 E5 Wolverhampton U.K.
30 E3 Wolverine U.S.A.
61 F5 Womrather Höhe *h.* Ger.
116 D6 Wondai Austr.
114 F3 Wongalarroo Lake *salt l.* Austr.
115 H4 Wongarbon Austr.
85 G4 Wong Chhu *r.* Bhutan
89 □ Wong Chuk Hang China
89 □ Wong Leng *h.* China
89 □ Wong Wan Chau *i.* China
87 N4 Wŏnju S. Korea
113 J7 Wonnangatta Moroka National Park *nat. park* Austr.
114 E3 Wonominta *watercourse* Austr.
87 N4 Wŏnsan N. Korea
114 F7 Wonthaggi Austr.
114 B3 Woocalla Austr.
113 G2 Woodah, Isle *i.* Austr.
59 J5 Woodbridge U.K.
32 E5 Woodbridge U.S.A.
20 G3 Wood Buffalo National Park *nat. park* Can.
115 K2 Woodburn Austr.
24 B2 Woodburn U.S.A.
30 E4 Woodbury *MI* U.S.A.
33 F5 Woodbury *NJ* U.S.A.
32 A6 Wood Creek Lake *l.* U.S.A.
34 C2 Woodfords U.S.A.
33 C3 Woodlake U.S.A.
34 B2 Woodland U.S.A.
25 F4 Woodland Park U.S.A.
95 □ Woodlands Sing.
111 F2 Woodlark I. *i.* P.N.G.
112 F5 Woodroffe, Mt *mt* Austr.
24 E3 Woodruff U.S.A.
113 F3 Woods, L. *salt flat* Austr.
21 L5 Woods, Lake of the *l.* Can./U.S.A.
32 C5 Woodsfield U.S.A.
115 G7 Woodside Austr.
115 G6 Woods Pt Austr.
116 B2 Woodstock Austr.
23 G4 Woodstock *N.B.* Can.
31 G4 Woodstock *Ont.* Can.
30 C4 Woodstock *IL* U.S.A.
32 D5 Woodstock *VA* U.S.A.
33 F5 Woodstown U.S.A.
33 G2 Woodsville U.S.A.
117 E4 Woodville N.Z.
32 E3 Woodville *NY* U.S.A.
27 E6 Woodville *TX* U.S.A.
27 D4 Woodward U.S.A.
58 E2 Wooler U.K.
115 K3 Woolgoolga Austr.
115 K2 Wooli Austr.
114 C3 Wooltana Austr.
114 B3 Woomera Austr.
114 A3 Woomera Prohibited Area *res.* Austr.
33 H4 Woonsocket U.S.A.
116 C5 Woorabinda Austr.
32 C4 Wooster U.S.A.
104 C6 Worcester S. Africa
59 E5 Worcester U.K.
33 H3 Worcester U.S.A.
62 F7 Wörgl Austria
58 D3 Workington U.K.
59 F4 Worksop U.K.
24 F2 Worland U.S.A.
61 C2 Wormerveer Neth.
59 C6 Worms Head *hd* U.K.
104 B1 Wortel Namibia
59 G7 Worthing U.K.
26 E3 Worthington U.S.A.
93 G7 Wotu Indon.
61 C3 Woudrichem Neth.
26 C3 Wounded Knee U.S.A.
116 D4 Wowan Austr.
93 G7 Wowoni *i.* Indon.
Wrangel I. *i. see* Vrangelya, O.
20 C3 Wrangell U.S.A.
20 C3 Wrangell I. *i.* U.S.A.
57 C2 Wrath, Cape *c.* U.K.
26 C3 Wray U.S.A.
59 F5 Wreake *r.* U.K.
104 B4 Wreck Point *pt* S. Africa
59 E4 Wrexham U.K.
94 C4 Wright Phil.
24 F3 Wright U.S.A.
27 E5 Wright Patman L. *l.* U.S.A.
35 G6 Wrightson, Mt *mt* U.S.A.
20 E2 Wrigley Can.
62 H5 Wrocław Pol.
62 H4 Września Pol.
88 E2 Wu'an China
88 D2 Wubu China
89 E4 Wuchang China
89 D6 Wuchuan *Guangdong* China
89 C4 Wuchuan *Guizhou* China
88 D1 Wuchuan *Nei Monggol Zizhiqu* China
88 C2 Wuda China
88 F1 Wudan China
88 D3 Wudang Shan *mt* China
88 C3 Wudang Shan *mts* China
85 H2 Wudaoliang China
88 E2 Wudi China
89 B5 Wuding China
88 D2 Wuding *r.* China
114 A4 Wudinna Austr.
88 B3 Wudu China
89 D4 Wufeng China
89 D5 Wugang China
88 C3 Wugong China
88 C2 Wuhai China
89 E4 Wuhan China
88 E3 Wuhe China
88 F4 Wuhu China
89 E6 Wuhua China
84 D2 Wüjang China
89 C6 Wujia China
89 C4 Wu Jiang *r.* China
100 C4 Wukari Nigeria
85 H3 Wulang China
84 C2 Wular L. *l.* India
88 F2 Wuleidao Wan *l.* China
88 F3 Wulian China
89 B4 Wulian Feng *mts* China
82 K6 Wuliang Shan *mts* China
93 J8 Wuliaru *i.* Indon.
89 C4 Wuling Shan *mts* China
89 C4 Wulong China
89 B5 Wumeng Shan *mts* China
89 C6 Wuming China
88 A4 Wungda China
89 E4 Wuning China
83 J6 Wuntho Myanmar
35 G4 Wupatki National Monument *res.* U.S.A.
89 E5 Wuping China
62 C5 Wuppertal Ger.
104 C6 Wuppertal S. Africa
88 C2 Wuqi China
88 E2 Wuqiao China
88 E2 Wuqing China
62 D6 Würzburg Ger.
88 B3 Wushan *Gansu* China
88 C4 Wushan *Sichuan* China
88 D4 Wu Shan *mts* China
89 C4 Wusheng China
89 C6 Wushi China
Wusuli Jiang *r. see* Ussuri
88 D2 Wutai China
88 D2 Wutai Shan *mt* China
110 E2 Wuvulu I. *i.* P.N.G.
88 E4 Wuwei *Anhui* China
88 B2 Wuwei *Gansu* China
88 F4 Wuxi *Jiangsu* China
88 C4 Wuxi *Sichuan* China
Wuxing *see* Huzhou
89 C6 Wuxu China
89 C6 Wuxuan China
89 E4 Wuxue China
88 D3 Wuyang China
89 F4 Wuyi China
87 N2 Wuyiling China
89 F5 Wuyishan China
89 E5 Wuyi Shan *mts* China
89 E4 Wuyuan *Jiangxi* China
88 C1 Wuyuan *Nei Monggol Zizhiqu* China
88 D2 Wuzhai China
88 D4 Wuzhen China
88 C2 Wuzhong China
89 D6 Wuzhou China
30 B5 Wyaconda *r.* U.S.A.
115 G4 Wyalong Austr.
31 F4 Wyandotte U.S.A.
116 A6 Wyandra Austr.
30 C5 Wyanet U.S.A.
115 H4 Wyangala Reservoir *resr* Austr.
114 F2 Wyara, Lake *salt flat* Austr.
114 E6 Wycheproof Austr.
59 E6 Wye *r.* U.K.
59 F6 Wylye *r.* U.K.
59 J5 Wymondham U.K.
112 E3 Wyndham Austr.
114 F6 Wyndham-Werribee Austr.
27 F5 Wynne U.S.A.
115 F8 Wynyard Austr.
21 J4 Wynyard Can.
30 C5 Wyoming *IL* U.S.A.
30 E4 Wyoming *MI* U.S.A.
24 E3 Wyoming *div.* U.S.A.
24 E3 Wyoming Peak *summit* U.S.A.
115 J4 Wyong Austr.
114 D5 Wyperfeld Nat. Park *nat. park* Austr.
58 E4 Wyre *r.* U.K.
33 E4 Wysox U.S.A.
63 K4 Wyszków Pol.
59 F5 Wythall U.K.
32 C6 Wytheville U.S.A.
33 J2 Wytopitlock U.S.A.

X

102 F2 Xaafuun Somalia
81 M1 Xaçmaz Azer.
104 E1 Xade Botswana
85 H3 Xagquka China
84 D1 Xaidulla China
85 G3 Xainza China
103 D6 Xai-Xai Moz.
88 C1 Xamba China
92 C2 Xam Hua Laos
95 B1 Xan *r.* Laos
95 C2 Xan, Xé *r.* Vietnam
103 C6 Xanagas Botswana
88 B1 Xangd China
88 D1 Xangdin Hural China
103 B5 Xangongo Angola
81 L2 Xankändi Azer.
67 L4 Xanthi Greece
42 E6 Xapuri Brazil
81 M2 Xaraba Şähär Sayı *i.* Azer.
81 M2 Xärä Zirä Adası *is* Azer.
85 F3 Xarba La *pass* China
88 F1 Xar Moron *r.* *Nei Monggol Zizhiqu* China
88 D1 Xar Moron *r.* *Nei Monggol Zizhiqu* China
65 F3 Xàtiva Spain
103 C6 Xau, Lake *l.* Botswana
43 J6 Xavantes, Serra dos *h.* Brazil
95 C3 Xa Vo Đat Vietnam
32 B5 Xenia U.S.A.
88 F1 Xi *r.* China
90 B2 Xiachengzi China
89 D6 Xiachuan Dao *i.* China
88 B3 Xiahe China
89 E5 Xiajiang China
88 E2 Xiajin China
89 F5 Xiamen China
88 C3 Xi'an China
88 E3 Xiancheng China
88 C2 Xianchengbu China
89 C4 Xianfeng China
88 D3 Xiangcheng China
88 D3 Xiangfan China
Xianghuang Qi *see* Xin Bulag
95 B1 Xiangkhoang Laos
84 D3 Xiangquan He *r.* China
89 F4 Xiangshan China
89 D5 Xiangtan China
Xianguan *see* Dali
89 D5 Xiangxiang China
89 D4 Xiangyin China
89 F4 Xianju China
89 E4 Xianning China
89 D4 Xiantao China
89 E5 Xianxia Ling *mts* China
88 E2 Xianxian China
88 C3 Xianyang China
89 F5 Xianyou China
89 F4 Xianyuan China
88 D4 Xiaochang China
89 C6 Xiaodong China
89 D4 Xiaogan China
87 N2 Xiao Hinggan Ling *mts* China
88 B4 Xiaojin China
88 B3 Xiaonan China
85 H2 Xiaonanchuan China
89 F4 Xiaoshan China
89 E5 Xiaotao China
88 E2 Xiaowutai Shan *mt* China
88 E3 Xiaoxian China
89 B4 Xiaoxiang Ling *mts* China
88 D2 Xiaoyi China
89 F5 Xiapu China
88 D3 Xiayukou China
89 B5 Xichang China
88 B4 Xichong China
89 B6 Xichou China
88 D3 Xichuan China
89 B4 Xide China
45 D4 Xié *r.* Brazil
89 C6 Xieyang Dao *i.* China
88 E3 Xifei He *r.* China
89 C5 Xifeng China
88 C3 Xifeng China
82 G5 Xigazê China
88 C3 Xihan Shui *r.* China
88 B3 Xihe China
88 A1 Xi He *watercourse* China
88 B3 Xiji China
89 D6 Xi Jiang *r.* China
85 G2 Xijir China
85 G2 Xijir Ulan Hu *salt l.* China
88 B2 Xijishui China
88 D1 Xil China
88 G1 Xiliao *r.* China
89 B5 Xilin China
88 E1 Xilinhot China
88 A1 Ximiao China
88 C2 Xin China

89 F4 Xin'anjiang China
89 F4 Xin'anjiang Sk. resr China
105 K2 Xinavane Moz.
88 D1 Xin Bulag China
88 E3 Xincai China
89 F4 Xinchang China
88 A2 Xincheng Gansu China
89 C5 Xincheng Guangxi China
88 C2 Xincheng Ningxia China
88 C2 Xinchengbu China
89 D6 Xindu Guangxi China
88 B4 Xindu Sichuan China
89 E5 Xinfeng Guangdong China
89 E5 Xinfeng Jiangxi China
89 E6 Xinfengjiang Sk. resr China
89 D5 Xing'an China
89 E5 Xingan China
88 F1 Xingcheng China
89 E5 Xingguo China
82 J3 Xinghai China
88 D1 Xinghe China
88 F3 Xinghua China
89 F5 Xinghua Wan b. China
90 C2 Xingkai China
Xingkai Hu l. see Khanka, Lake
89 E5 Xingning China
89 D4 Xingou China
88 C3 Xingping China
89 B5 Xingren China
88 A3 Xingsagoinba China
88 D4 Xingshan China
88 E2 Xingtai China
43 H4 Xingu r. Brazil
43 H6 Xingu, Parque Indígena do nat. park Brazil
89 B4 Xingwen China
88 D2 Xingxian China
88 D3 Xingyang China
89 B5 Xingyi China
89 E4 Xingzi China
88 E1 Xin Hot China
89 D5 Xinhua China
88 B2 Xinhuacun China
89 C5 Xinhuang China
89 F1 Xinhui China
89 D6 Xinhui China
88 A2 Xining China
88 E2 Xinji China
89 E4 Xinjian China
88 D3 Xinjiang China
85 D1 Xinjiang Uygur Zizhiqu div. China
86 D3 Xinjiang Uygur Zizhiqu div. China
88 C2 Xinjie China
89 B4 Xinjin China
88 G1 Xinkai r. China
88 G1 Xinmin China
89 E5 Xinning China
89 A5 Xinping China
89 E5 Xinquan China
89 D5 Xinshao China
88 E3 Xintai China
89 D5 Xintian China
88 E4 Xinxian China
88 D3 Xinxiang China
89 D6 Xinxing China
88 E3 Xinyang Henan China
88 E3 Xinyang Henan China
88 D3 Xinye China
88 F3 Xinye r. China
89 D6 Xinyi Guangdong China
88 F3 Xinyi Jiangsu China
89 C7 Xinying China
89 E5 Xinyu China
82 F2 Xinyuan China
88 D2 Xinzhou Shanxi China
88 D2 Xinzhou China
65 C1 Xinzo de Limia Spain
88 D3 Xiping Henan China
88 E3 Xiping Henan China
88 A3 Xiqing Shan mts China
43 K6 Xique Xique Brazil
88 C1 Xishanzui China
89 C4 Xishui Guizhou China
89 E4 Xishui Hubei China
Xi Ujimqin Qi see Bayan Ul Hot
89 F4 Xiuning China
89 C4 Xiushan China
89 E4 Xiushui China
89 E4 Xiu Shui r. China
89 C5 Xiuwen China
88 D3 Xiuwu China
88 G1 Xiuyan China
89 D6 Xiuying China
85 F3 Xixabangma Feng mt China
88 D3 Xixia China
88 E3 Xixian Henan China
88 D2 Xixian Shanxi China
88 C3 Xixiang China
89 F5 Xiyang Dao i. China
89 B5 Xiyang Jiang r. China
86 D5 Xizang Zizhiqu div. China
88 F2 Xizhong Dao i. China
85 H3 Xoka China
95 C3 Xom An Lôc Vietnam
95 C3 Xom Duc Hanh Vietnam
89 C4 Xuan'en China
88 C4 Xuanhan China
88 B2 Xuanhepu China
88 E1 Xuanhua China
95 C3 Xuân Lôc Vietnam
89 B5 Xuanwei China
88 F4 Xuanzhou China
88 D3 Xuchang Henan China
87 K5 Xuchang Henan China
81 M1 Xudat Azer.
102 E3 Xuddur Somalia
89 C5 Xuefeng Shan mts China
85 H2 Xugui China
85 E2 Xungba China
85 F3 Xungru China
88 C3 Xun He r. China
89 D6 Xun Jiang r. China
89 E5 Xunwu China
88 E3 Xunxian China
88 C3 Xunyang China
88 C3 Xunyi China
89 D5 Xupu China
85 F3 Xuru Co salt l. China
88 E2 Xushui China
89 D6 Xuwen China
88 F3 Xuyi China
89 B4 Xuyong China
88 E3 Xuzhou China

Y

116 D4 Yaamba Austr.
89 B4 Ya'an China
114 E5 Yaapeet Austr.
100 C4 Yabassi Cameroon
102 D3 Yabēlo Eth.
87 K1 Yablonovyy Khrebet mts Rus. Fed.
88 B2 Yabrai Shan mts China
88 B2 Yabrai Yanchang China
80 F5 Yabrūd Syria
90 A2 Yabuli China
45 C2 Yacambu, Parque Nacional nat. park Venez.
89 C7 Yacheng China
89 C5 Yachi He r. China
42 E6 Yacuma r. Bol.
82 G5 Yadong China
68 H4 Yadrin Rus. Fed.
90 G2 Yagishiri-tō i. Japan
101 D3 Yagoua Cameroon
85 E3 Yagra China
85 H2 Yagradagzê Shan mt China
47 F2 Yaguari r. Uru.
Yaguarón r. see Jaguarão
95 B4 Yaha Thai.
80 D2 Yahşihan Turkey
80 E2 Yahyalı Turkey
84 B3 Yahya Wana Afgh.
91 F6 Yaita Japan
91 F7 Yaizu Japan
89 A4 Yajiang China
80 F3 Yakacık Turkey
24 B2 Yakima U.S.A.
24 B2 Yakima r. U.S.A.
100 B3 Yako Burkina
20 B3 Yakobi I. i. U.S.A.
90 C2 Yakovlevka Rus. Fed.
90 G3 Yakumo Japan
91 B9 Yaku-shima i. Japan
20 B3 Yakutat U.S.A.
20 B3 Yakutat Bay b. U.S.A.
77 O3 Yakutsk Rus. Fed.
69 E6 Yakymivka Ukr.
95 B4 Yala Thai.
31 F4 Yale U.S.A.
116 A5 Yalleroi Austr.
115 G7 Yallourn Austr.
89 A5 Yalong Jiang r. China
80 B1 Yalova Turkey
69 F6 Yalta Donets'k Ukr.
69 E6 Yalta Krym Ukr.
80 C2 Yalvaç Turkey
90 G5 Yamada Japan
90 G5 Yamagata Japan
91 B9 Yamagawa Japan
91 B7 Yamaguchi Japan
76 H2 Yamal, Poluostrov pen. Rus. Fed.
115 K2 Yamba Austr.
115 E7 Yambacoona Austr.
21 G2 Yamba Lake l. Can.
45 C4 Yambi, Mesa de h. Col.
101 E4 Yambio Sudan
67 M3 Yambol Bulg.
76 J3 Yamburg Rus. Fed.
88 A2 Yamenzhuang China
83 J6 Yamethin Myanmar
91 G6 Yamizo-san mt Japan
55 V7 Yamm Rus. Fed.
100 B4 Yamoussoukro Côte d'Ivoire
24 E3 Yampa r. U.S.A.
69 D5 Yampil' Ukr.
84 E4 Yamuna r. India
84 D3 Yamunanagar India
85 G3 Yamzho Yumco l. China
88 D2 Yan r. China
77 P3 Yana r. Rus. Fed.
114 D6 Yanac Austr.
86 D8 Yanam India
88 C2 Yan'an China
42 D6 Yanaoca Peru
89 A5 Yanbian China
78 D5 Yanbu' al Baḩr Saudi Arabia
88 F3 Yancheng China
112 C6 Yanchep Austr.
88 C2 Yanchi China
88 D2 Yanchuan China
115 G5 Yanco Austr.
114 D3 Yanco Glen Austr.
115 F3 Yanda watercourse Austr.
114 D3 Yandama Cr. watercourse Austr.
116 E6 Yandina Austr.
100 B3 Yanfolila Mali
88 E1 Yang r. China
85 H3 Ya'ngamdo China
85 G3 Yangbajain China
88 D3 Yangcheng China
89 D6 Yangchun China
88 D1 Yanggao China
88 E2 Yanggu China
79 K1 Yangiyul' Uzbek.
89 D6 Yangjiang China
83 J7 Yangôn Myanmar
88 D4 Yangping China
88 D2 Yangquan China
89 D5 Yangshan China
89 D5 Yangshuo China
Yangtze r. see Tongtian He
89 E4 Yangtze r. China
88 F4 Yangtze, Mouth of the est. China
102 E2 Yangudi Rassa National Park nat. park Eth.
89 D6 Yangxi China
88 C3 Yangxian China
91 A6 Yangyang S. Korea
88 E1 Yangyuan China
88 F3 Yangzhou China
89 C4 Yanhe China
85 E2 Yanhuqu China
114 A4 Yaninee, Lake salt flat Austr.
87 N3 Yanji China
89 B4 Yanjin China
100 C4 Yankara National Park nat. park Nigeria
26 D3 Yankton U.S.A.
89 D5 Yanling China
77 P2 Yano-Indigirskaya Nizmennost' lowland Rus. Fed.
82 G2 Yanqi China
88 E1 Yanqing China
88 E2 Yanshan Hebei China
89 E4 Yanshan Jiangxi China
89 B6 Yanshan Yunnan China
88 E1 Yan Shan mts China
85 H2 Yanshiping China
90 A2 Yanshou China
77 P2 Yanskiy Zaliv g. Rus. Fed.
115 F2 Yantabulla Austr.
88 F2 Yantai China
114 E2 Yantara Lake salt flat Austr.
63 J3 Yantarnyy Rus. Fed.
89 A5 Yanyuan China
88 E3 Yanzhou China
100 D4 Yaoundé Cameroon
88 C3 Yaoxian China
95 A3 Yao Yai, Ko i. Thai.
93 K5 Yap i. Micronesia
45 D4 Yapacana, Co mt Venez.
93 K7 Yapen i. Indon.
93 K7 Yapen, Selat chan. Indon.
14 E5 Yap Tr. sea feature Pac. Oc.
36 C3 Yaqui r. Mex.
45 C2 Yaracuy r. Venez.
113 H4 Yaraka Austr.
68 H3 Yaransk Rus. Fed.
114 A4 Yardea Austr.
80 C3 Yardımcı Burnu pt Turkey
81 M2 Yardımlı Azer.
59 J5 Yare r. U.K.
68 K2 Yarega Rus. Fed.
111 G2 Yaren Nauru
68 J2 Yarensk Rus. Fed.
45 B5 Yari r. Col.
91 E6 Yariga-take mt Japan
45 C2 Yaritagua Venez.
31 J3 Yarker Can.
84 C1 Yarkhun r. Pak.
Yarlung Zangbo r. see Brahmaputra
23 G5 Yarmouth Can.
59 F7 Yarmouth U.K.
33 H4 Yarmouth Port U.S.A.
35 F4 Yarnell U.S.A.
68 F3 Yaroslavl' Rus. Fed.
68 F3 Yaroslavskaya Oblast' div. Rus. Fed.
90 C2 Yaroslavskiy Rus. Fed.
114 F6 Yarra r. Austr.
115 G7 Yarram Austr.
115 J1 Yarraman Austr.
116 A6 Yarronvale Austr.
116 A3 Yarrowmere Austr.
85 H3 Yartö Tra La pass China
76 K3 Yartsevo Rus. Fed.
68 E4 Yartsevo Rus. Fed.
45 B3 Yarumal Col.
85 F5 Yasai r. India
111 H3 Yasawa Group is Fiji
69 F6 Yasenskaya Rus. Fed.
69 G6 Yashalta Rus. Fed.
69 H6 Yashkul' Rus. Fed.
69 E2 Yasnaya Polyana Rus. Fed.
95 C2 Yasothon Thai.
115 H5 Yass Austr.
115 H5 Yass r. Austr.
80 B3 Yatağan Turkey
111 G4 Yaté New Caledonia
27 E4 Yates Center U.S.A.
21 K2 Yathkyed Lake l. Can.
91 F7 Yatsuga-take vol. Japan
91 B8 Yatsushiro Japan
59 E6 Yatton U.K.
42 D5 Yavari r. Brazil/Peru
84 D5 Yavatmāl India
81 H2 Yavi Turkey
45 D3 Yaví, Co mt Venez.
69 B5 Yavoriv Ukr.
91 C8 Yawatahama Japan
85 E1 Yawatongguz He r. China
85 H5 Yaw Ch. r. Myanmar
79 G3 Yazd Iran
80 G2 Yazıhan Turkey
27 F5 Yazoo r. U.S.A.
27 F5 Yazoo City U.S.A.
55 L9 Yding Skovhøj h. Denmark
67 K6 Ydra i. Greece
95 A2 Ye Myanmar
114 F6 Yea Austr.
59 D7 Yealmpton U.K.
82 E3 Yecheng China
25 E6 Yécora Mex.
29 D7 Yeehaw Junction U.S.A.
114 A5 Yeelanna Austr.
68 F4 Yefremov Rus. Fed.
81 K2 Yeghegnadzor Armenia
69 G6 Yegorlyk r. Rus. Fed.
69 G6 Yegorlykskaya Rus. Fed.
90 E2 Yegorova, Mys pt Rus. Fed.
68 F4 Yegor'yevsk Rus. Fed.
101 F4 Yei Sudan
88 E4 Yeji China
76 H4 Yekaterinburg Rus. Fed.
69 G5 Yelan' Rus. Fed.
69 G5 Yelan' r. Rus. Fed.
115 J2 Yelarbon Austr.
69 F4 Yelets Rus. Fed.
100 A3 Yélimané Mali
57 □ Yell i. U.K.
30 B3 Yellow r. U.S.A.
32 D4 Yellow Creek U.S.A.
115 G4 Yellow Mt h. Austr.
Yellow River r. see Huang He
87 N4 Yellow Sea sea Pac. Oc.
24 F2 Yellowstone r. U.S.A.
24 E2 Yellowstone L. l. U.S.A.
24 E2 Yellowstone Nat. Park nat. park U.S.A.
24 E2 Yellowtail Res. resr U.S.A.
57 □ Yell Sound chan. U.K.
69 D5 Yel'sk Belarus
70 Yemen country Asia
68 G2 Yemetsk Rus. Fed.
68 G2 Yemtsa Rus. Fed.
68 J2 Yemva Rus. Fed.
54 W3 Yena Rus. Fed.
69 F5 Yenakiyeve Ukr.
85 H5 Yenangyat Myanmar
85 H5 Yenangyaung Myanmar
85 H6 Yenanma Myanmar
89 B6 Yên Bai Vietnam
115 G5 Yenda Austr.
100 B4 Yendi Ghana
102 B4 Yénéganou Congo
81 L3 Yengejeh Iran
80 D1 Yeniçağa Turkey
67 M5 Yenice Turkey
80 E3 Yenice Turkey
80 D2 Yeniceoba Turkey
80 B1 Yenişehir Turkey
76 L4 Yenisey r. Rus. Fed.
76 L4 Yeniseysk Rus. Fed.
76 L4 Yeniseyskiy Kryazh ridge Rus. Fed.
76 J2 Yeniseyskiy Zaliv in. Rus. Fed.
89 B6 Yên Minh Vietnam
69 H6 Yenotayevka Rus. Fed.
84 C5 Yeola India
Yeotmal see Yavatmāl
115 H4 Yeoval Austr.
59 E7 Yeovil U.K.
Yeo Yeo r. see Bland
25 E6 Yepachi Mex.
116 D4 Yeppoon Austr.
77 M3 Yerbogachen Rus. Fed.
81 K1 Yerevan Armenia
76 J4 Yereymentau Kazak.
69 H6 Yergeni h. Rus. Fed.
34 C2 Yerington U.S.A.
80 E2 Yerköy Turkey
27 B7 Yermo Mex.
34 D4 Yermo U.S.A.
87 M1 Yerofey Pavlovich Rus. Fed.
69 J5 Yershov Rus. Fed.
68 G2 Yertsevo Rus. Fed.
Yerushalayim see Jerusalem
69 H5 Yeruslan r. Rus. Fed.
76 H4 Yesil' Kazak.
80 E2 Yeşilhisar Turkey
80 F1 Yeşilırmak r. Turkey
80 B3 Yeşilova Turkey
69 G6 Yessentuki Rus. Fed.
77 M3 Yessey Rus. Fed.
59 C7 Yes Tor h. U.K.
115 J2 Yetman Austr.
83 J6 Yeu Myanmar
64 C3 Yeu, Île d' i. France
81 L1 Yevlax Azer.
69 E6 Yevpatoriya Ukr.
88 D3 Yexian China
85 E1 Yeyik China
69 F6 Yeysk Rus. Fed.
68 H1 Yezhuga r. Rus. Fed.
68 D4 Yezyaryshcha Belarus
88 D3 Yi r. Henan China
88 D3 Yi r. Shandong China
47 F2 Yí r. Uru.
89 B4 Yibin China
85 F2 Yibug Caka salt l. China
89 D4 Yichang Hubei China
89 D4 Yichang Hubei China
88 D4 Yicheng Hubei China
88 D3 Yicheng Shanxi China
88 D3 Yichuan China
87 N2 Yichun Heilongjiang China
89 E5 Yichun Jiangxi China
89 E4 Yifeng China
89 E5 Yihuang China
88 C3 Yijun China
90 A1 Yilan China
67 M4 Yıldız Dağları mts Turkey
80 F2 Yıldızeli Turkey
89 B5 Yiliang Yunnan China
89 B5 Yiliang Yunnan China
88 C4 Yilong China
89 B6 Yilong Hu l. China
89 B5 Yimen China
90 A2 Yimianpo China
88 F3 Yinan China
88 C2 Yinchuan China
89 D5 Yingde China
89 C7 Yinggehai China
88 E3 Ying He r. China
88 G1 Yingkou China
88 B2 Yingpanshui China
89 E4 Yingshan Hubei China
88 C4 Yingshan Sichuan China
88 E3 Yingshang China
89 E4 Yingtan China
88 D2 Yingxian China
82 F2 Yining China
89 C5 Yinjiang China
85 H5 Yinmabin Myanmar
88 C1 Yin Shan mts China
85 H3 Yi'ong Zangbo r. China
89 A5 Yipinglang China
102 D3 Yirga Alem Eth.
88 F2 Yi Shan mt China
88 F3 Yishui China
95 □ Yishun Sing.
82 H2 Yiwu China
89 E4 Yixian Anhui China
88 F1 Yixian Liaoning China
88 F4 Yixing China
89 D4 Yiyang Hunan China
89 E4 Yiyang Jiangxi China
89 D5 Yizhang China
89 C5 Yizhou China
55 S6 Yläne Fin.
54 S5 Ylihärmä Fin.
54 T4 Yli-Ii Fin.
54 T4 Yli-Kärppä Fin.
54 U4 Ylikiiminki Fin.
54 V3 Yli-Kitka l. Fin.
54 S5 Ylistaro Fin.
54 S3 Ylitornio Fin.
54 T4 Ylivieska Fin.
55 S6 Ylöjärvi Fin.
27 D6 Yoakum U.S.A.
90 G3 Yobetsu-dake vol. Japan
92 □ Yogyakarta Indon.
92 □ Yogyakarta div. Indon.
20 F4 Yoho Nat. Park nat. park Can.
101 D4 Yokadouma Cameroon
91 E7 Yokkaichi Japan
101 D4 Yoko Cameroon
91 F7 Yokohama Japan
91 F7 Yokosuka Japan
90 G5 Yokote Japan
90 G4 Yokotsu-dake mt Japan
101 D4 Yola Nigeria
95 B2 Yom, Mae Nam r. Thai.
100 B4 Yomou Guinea
91 G6 Yonezawa Japan
114 C4 Yongala Austr.
89 E5 Yong'an China
88 A2 Yongchang China
88 E3 Yongcheng China
91 A7 Yŏngch'ŏn S. Korea
89 F5 Yongchun China
88 B2 Yongdeng China
89 E5 Yongding China
88 E2 Yongding r. China
91 A6 Yŏngdŏk S. Korea
89 C5 Yongfu China
85 H3 Yonggyap pass India
89 F4 Yongjia China
88 B3 Yongjing China
91 A6 Yŏngju S. Korea
89 F4 Yongkang China
88 E2 Yongnian China
89 C6 Yongning China
89 A5 Yongren China
89 C4 Yongshun China
89 F5 Yongtai China
91 A6 Yŏngwol S. Korea
89 E5 Yongxing China
89 D5 Yongxing China
89 E4 Yongxiu China
89 D5 Yongzhou China
33 G4 Yonkers U.S.A.
64 F2 Yonne r. France
45 B3 Yopal Col.
112 C6 York Austr.
58 F4 York U.K.
26 D3 York NE U.S.A.
32 E5 York PA U.S.A.
29 D5 York SC U.S.A.
113 H2 York, C. c. Austr.
58 F3 York, Vale of v. U.K.
114 B5 Yorke Peninsula pen. Austr.
114 B5 Yorketown Austr.
58 E3 Yorkshire Dales National Park nat. park U.K.
58 G4 Yorkshire Wolds reg. U.K.
21 J4 Yorkton Can.
32 E6 Yorktown U.S.A.
100 B3 Yorosso Mali
34 C3 Yosemite National Park nat. park U.S.A.
34 C3 Yosemite Village U.S.A.
91 C8 Yoshino-gawa r. Japan
91 D7 Yoshino-Kumano National Park Japan
68 H3 Yoshkar-Ola Rus. Fed.
80 E7 Yotvata Israel
60 D6 Youghal Rep. of Ireland
32 D5 Youghiogheny River Lake l. U.S.A.
89 C6 You Jiang r. China
115 H5 Young Austr.
47 F2 Young Uru.
114 B3 Younghusband, L. salt flat Austr.
114 C5 Younghusband Pen. pen. Austr.
119 A6 Young I. i. Antarctica
32 C4 Youngstown U.S.A.
89 D4 You Shui r. China
100 B3 Youvarou Mali
89 F5 Youxi China
89 D5 Youxian China
89 C4 Youyang China
90 B1 Youyi China
88 D2 Youyu China
115 F1 Yowah watercourse Austr.
80 E2 Yozgat Turkey
46 A3 Ypané r. Para.
46 A3 Ypé-Jhú Para.
24 B3 Yreka U.S.A.
Yr Wyddfa mt see Snowdon
55 N9 Ystad Sweden
59 D5 Ystwyth r. U.K.
Ysyk-Köl see Balykchy
82 E2 Ysyk-Köl salt l. Kyrgyzstan
57 F3 Ythan r. U.K.
77 P3 Ytyk-Kyuyel' Rus. Fed.
95 A1 Yuam, Mae r. Myanmar/Thai.
88 D4 Yuan'an China
89 C5 Yuanbao Shan mt China
89 D4 Yuanjiang Hunan China
89 A6 Yuanjiang Yunnan China
89 D4 Yuan Jiang r. Hunan China
89 B6 Yuan Jiang r. Yunnan China
89 F5 Yüanli Taiwan
89 D4 Yuanling China
89 A5 Yuanmou China
88 D2 Yuanping China
88 D3 Yuanqu China
89 B6 Yuanyang China
34 B2 Yuba r. U.S.A.
34 B2 Yuba City U.S.A.
90 G3 Yūbari Japan
89 C4 Yubei China
36 F5 Yucatán pen. Mex.
36 G4 Yucatan Channel str. Cuba/Mex.
35 E4 Yucca U.S.A.
34 D3 Yucca L. l. U.S.A.
34 D4 Yucca Valley U.S.A.
88 E2 Yucheng China
88 D2 Yuci China
77 P4 Yudoma r. Rus. Fed.
89 E5 Yudu China
89 C4 Yuechi China
112 F4 Yuendumu Austr.
89 □ Yuen Long China
89 F4 Yueqing China
89 E4 Yuexi Anhui China
89 B4 Yuexi Sichuan China
89 D4 Yueyang China
89 E4 Yugan China
76 H3 Yugorsk Rus. Fed.
Yugoslavia see Serbia and Montenegro
77 R3 Yugo-Tala Rus. Fed.
68 K2 Yugydtydor Rus. Fed.
89 F4 Yuhuan China
88 E2 Yuhuang Ding mt China
89 E4 Yujiang China
89 D6 Yu Jiang r. China
77 R3 Yukagirskoye Ploskogor'ye plat. Rus. Fed.
80 E2 Yukarısarıkaya Turkey
102 B4 Yuki Dem. Rep. Congo
18 Yukon r. Can./U.S.A.
20 B2 Yukon Territory div. Can.
81 K3 Yüksekova Turkey
112 F5 Yulara Austr.
116 C6 Yuleba Austr.
29 D6 Yulee U.S.A.
89 F6 Yüli Taiwan
89 D6 Yulin Guangxi China
89 C7 Yulin Hainan China
88 C2 Yulin Shaanxi China
35 E5 Yuma U.S.A.
35 E5 Yuma Desert des. U.S.A.
45 A4 Yumbo Col.
86 G4 Yumen China
80 E3 Yumurtalık Turkey
80 C2 Yunak Turkey
89 D6 Yunan China
88 E3 Yuncheng Shandong China
88 D3 Yuncheng Shanxi China
89 D6 Yunfu China
89 B5 Yun Gui Gaoyuan plat. China
89 F4 Yunhe China
89 D6 Yunkai Dashan mts China
88 D4 Yunmeng China
89 A5 Yunnan div. China
88 D4 Yun Shui r. China
114 C4 Yunta Austr.
89 D6 Yunwu Shan mts China
88 D3 Yunxi China
88 D3 Yunxian China
89 E6 Yunxiao China
88 D3 Yunyang Henan China
88 C4 Yunyang Sichuan China
89 C5 Yuping China
88 E1 Yuqiao Sk. resr China
89 C5 Yuqing China
76 K4 Yurga Rus. Fed.
42 C5 Yurimaguas Peru
45 E3 Yuruán r. Venez.
45 E3 Yuruari r. Venez.
45 C2 Yurubi, Parque Nacional nat. park Venez.
84 E1 Yurungkax He r. China
68 J3 Yur'ya Rus. Fed.
68 G3 Yur'yevets Rus. Fed.

SYMBOLS

RELIEF

METRES		FEET
6000		19686
5000		16404
4000		13124
3000		9843
2000		6562
1000		3281
500		1640
200		656
SEA		LEVEL
200		656
2000		6562
4000		13124
6000		19686

Additional bathymetric contour layers are shown at scales greater than 1:2 million. These are labelled on an individual basis.

213
△ Summit
height in metres

BOUNDARIES

International

International disputed

Ceasefire line

Main administrative (U.K.)

Main administrative

Main administrative through water

STYLES OF LETTERING

Country name	**FRANCE**	Island	*Gran Canaria*
	BARBADOS	Lake	*LAKE ERIE*
Main administrative name	HESSEN	Mountain	*ANDES*
Area name	*ARTOIS*	River	*Zambeze*

COMMUNICATIONS

Motorway

Motorway tunnel

Motorways are classified separately at scales greater than 1:5 million. At smaller scales motorways are classified with main roads.

Main road

Main road under construction

Main road tunnel

Other road

Other road under construction

Other road tunnel

Track

Main railway

Main railway under construction

Main railway tunnel

Other railway

Other railway under construction

Other railway tunnel

⊕ Main airport

✈ Other airport

PHYSICAL FEATURES

Freshwater lake

Seasonal freshwater lake

Saltwater lake *or* Lagoon

Seasonal saltwater lake

Dry salt lake *or* Salt pan

Marsh

River

Waterfall

Dam *or* Barrage

Seasonal river *or* Wadi

Canal

Flood dyke

Reef

Volcano

Lava field

Sandy desert

Rocky desert

Oasis

Escarpment

923 Mountain pass *height in metres*

Ice cap *or* Glacier

OTHER FEATURES

National park

Reserve

Ancient wall

∴ Historic or Tourist site

SETTLEMENTS

POPULATION	NATIONAL CAPITAL	ADMINISTRATIVE CAPITAL	CITY OR TOWN
Over 5 million	▣ **Beijing**	⊚ **Tianjin**	⊙ **New York**
1 to 5 million	▣ **Seoul**	⊚ **Lagos**	⊙ **Barranquilla**
500000 to 1 million	▣ **Bangui**	⊚ **Douala**	⊙ **Memphis**
100000 to 500000	☐ Wellington	○ Mansa	○ Mara
50000 to 100000	☐ Port of Spain	○ Lubango	○ Tuzla
10000 to 50000	▫ Malabo	○ Chinhoyi	○ El Tigre
Less than 10000	▫ Roseau	○ Ati	○ Soledad

Urban area